HENRYK SIENKIEWICZ AND JEREMIAH CURTIN, WARSAW, 1900.

THE

# KNIGHTS OF THE CROSS.

BY

HENRYK SIENKIEWICZ,

AUTHOR OF "QUO VADIS," "WITH FIRE AND SWORD,"
"CHILDREN OF THE SOIL," ETC.

*AUTHORIZED AND UNABRIDGED TRANSLATION FROM
THE POLISH BY*

JEREMIAH CURTIN.

FIRST HALF.

BOSTON:
LITTLE, BROWN, AND COMPANY.
1901.

TO COUNTESS ANNA BRANITSKI OF VILLANOV.

MADAM, — You know the language of this translation as accurately as you know Polish; you reverence what is true and beautiful in literature as well as in life; to you therefore I leg to dedicate these volumes.

JEREMIAH CUR TIN.
WARSAW, May 1, 1900.

INTRODUCTION

THE period embraced in " The Knights of the Cross " is one of the most dramatic and fruitful of results in European annals, — a period remarkable for work and endeavor, especially in the Slav world.

Among Western Slavs the great events were the Hussite wars and the union of Lithuania and Poland. The Hussite wars were caused by ideas of race and religion which were born in Bohemia. These ideas produced results which, beyond doubt, were among the most striking in European experience. The period of Bohemian activity began in 1403 and ended in 1434, the year of the battle of Lipan, which closed the Bohemian epoch.

The marriage in 1386 of Queen Yadviga to Yagello, Grand Prince of Lithuania, brought Poland into intimate relations with all the regions owing allegiance to the Lithuanian dynasty, and made it possible to crush at Tannenberg the Knights of the Cross, whose object was the subjection of Poland and Lithuania, and a boundless extension of German influence in eastern Europe.

Bohemian struggles made the religious movement of the next century possible in Germany. The Polish victory at Tannenburg called forth that same movement. Had the Knights of the Cross been victorious at Tannenburg and found the East open to conquest and their apostolic labor, it is not conceivable that the German princes would have taken action against Rome, for such action would not have been what we call practical politics, and the German princes were pre-eminently

practical. But when the road to the East was barred by Polish victory there was no way for Germany to meet Rome but with obedience or a new religion; hence the German Reformation. Luther himself declared that he could not have succeeded had Huss not lived before him. Huss gave the intellectual experience needed by the Germans while Polish victory threw them back upon Germany and thus forced the issue between Roman and German tendencies.

The history ending at Tannenberg is of profound interest, whether we consider the objects sought for on each side, or the details involved in the policy and the acts, diplomatic and military, of the two opposing forces.

The struggle between German and Slav began long before the Knights of the Cross were in existence. Originating in earlier ages in what undoubtedly was mere race opposition, it grew envenomed at the beginning of the ninth century, after the restoration, or more correctly, perhaps, after the creation of the Western Empire in 800, in the person of Charlemagne. This new Roman Empire was German; there was little of Roman in it save the claim to universal dominion. This pretension to empire was reinforced greatly by association with the Church, whose unbending resolve it was to bring all men to the doctrine of Christ, that is, to bring them within its own fold and jurisdiction.

The position of peoples outside the Empire and the Church, that is, people independent and not Christian, who refused the rule of the Empire and the teachings of the Church, was that of rebels against Imperial authority, and'dupes of Satan.

The position was aggravated intensely by the fact that those peoples were forced to accept political subjection and the new religion together. Political subjection meant that the subordinated race went into contempt and inferiority, was thrust down to a servile condition;

the race lost land, freedom, language, race institutions, primitive ideas, and that aboriginal philosophy which all races have without exception, no matter what be their color or what territory they occupy.

North Germany from the Elbe eastward is Germanized Slav territory; the struggle to conquer the region between the Elbe and the Oder lasted till the end of the twelfth century, the process of Germanizing lasted during centuries afterward. Those of the Slav leaders in this region who were of use in managing the people and were willing to associate themselves with the invaders retained their positions and became German. The present ducal houses of Mecklenburg-Strelitz and Mecklenburg-Schwerin are of this kind, Slav in origin.

After the fall of those Slavs between the Elbe and the Oder the German (Roman) Empire and Poland stood face to face.

Omitting details for which there is no space here it suffices to state that the early leaders of the Poles saw at once the supreme need in their own case of separating religion from other questions. The first historic ruler of Poland, Miezko I., 963-992, married a Bohemian princess and introduced Christianity himself. He forestalled the Germans and deprived them of the apostolic part of their aggressive movement, and one great excuse for conquest.

Being Christianized the Poles maintained themselves against the Germans, but as they were Christian they felt obliged to extend Christianity to places embraced within their territory or connected with it.

Along the Baltic from the Vistula to the Niemen lived the Prussians, a division of the Lithuanian stock. The Lithuanians are not exactly Slavs, but they are much nearer to the Slavs than to any other people, and are among the most interesting members of the great Aryan race. In their language are preserved verbal

forms which are more primitive than those retained in Sanscrit, and with the single exception of the Gaelic of Ireland and Scotland it has preserved in actual use the most primitive forms of Aryan speech, though its grammatical methods are not so primitive as some used in the Gaelic.

The Prussians had a great love for their own primitive racial religion and for their independence; this religion and this independence they considered as inseparable. They inhabited a portion, or what was considered a portion, of the territory of Konrad, Prince of Mazovia, who tried to convert them; but instead of succeeding in his attempt he met with failure, and the Prussians took revenge by invading that part of his territory which was purely Polish and Christian, and which was known as Mazovia, immediately south of and bordering on Prussia, which, as stated already, touched on the Baltic and extended from the Vistula to the Niemen. The chief town of Mazovia was Warsaw, which became afterward the capital of Poland.

Among measures taken by Konrad to convert Prussia was the formation of a military order called the Brothers of Dobryn. These Brothers the Prussians defeated terribly in 1224.

In 1226 Konrad called in the Knights of the Cross to aid in converting the stubborn

Prussians, and endowed them with land outside of Prussia, reserving sovereign rights to himself, at least implicitly. The Knights, however, intended from the very first to take the territory from Konrad and erect a great German State in the east of Europe on Slav and Lithuanian ruins. They had no intention of performing apostolic labor without enjoying the highest earthly reward for it, that is, sovereign authority.

Before he had received the grant from Konrad, the Grand Master of the Order obtained a privilege from

the Emperor Frederick II., who in virtue of his pretended universal dominion bestowed the land which Konrad might give for the use of the Knights, and in addition all territory which the Order could win by conquest.

The work of conquest and conversion began. A crusade against Prussia was announced throughout Europe. From Poland alone went twenty thousand men to assist in the labor.

Soon, however, Konrad wished to define his sovereign rights more explicitly. The Order insisted on complete independence. In 1234 a false 1 document was prepared and presented by the Grand Master to Pope Gregory IX. as the deed of donation from Konrad. The Pope accepted the gift, gave the territory in fief to the Order, informed Konrad, August, 1234, of the position of the Knights, and enjoined on him to aid them with all means in his power.

Konrad of Mazovia was in an awkward position. He had brought in of his own will a foreign power which had all western Europe and the Holy See to support it, which had, moreover, unbounded means of discrediting the Poles; and these means the Order never failed in using to the utmost.

In half a century after their coming the Knights, aided by volunteers and strengthened by contributions from the rest of Europe had subjugated and converted Prussia, and considered Lithuania and Poland as sure conquests, to be made at their own leisure and in great part at the expense of Western Christendom.

This was the power which fell at Tannenberg.

The German military Order of The Teutonic Knights, or Knights of the Cross, was founded in Palestine in 1190 to succeed an Order of Knight Hospitallers, also German, which was founded about 1128.

Pzieje Narodu Polskiego Dr. A. Lewicki, p. 82, Warsaw, 1899,

From 1190 to 1210 there were three Grand Masters of this Order. In 1210 was elected the fourth, Hermann von Salza, who transferred the order to Europe, established it first in Hungary and later in Prussia, where he laid the foundations of its power and settled the conditions according to which it rose and fell.

The policy of the Order in Prussia was to carry on apostolic labor through military conquest, found a State, and later pull down other States to strengthen the one it had founded. When broken on the field of battle it had no principle through which it might rise again to its previous significance.

The further fate of this Order is described briefly in my introduction to " The Deluge," pages ix and x.

The Order of Knights of the Sword was founded in 1205 to spread Christianity in Livonia, east of Prussia. After a career of thirty-three years it was united with the Order of Knights of the Cross during the time of the Grand Master Hermann von Salza.

JEREMIAH CURTIN. WARSAW, May 1, 1900.

# THE

# KNIGHTS OF THE CROSS.

CHAPTER I.

IN Tynets, at the Savage Bull, an inn which belonged to the monastery, were sitting a number of persons, listening to the tales of a veteran warrior, who had come from distant parts, and was relating adventures through which he had passed in war and on the road.

He was a bearded man, in the vigor of life, broad shouldered, almost immense, but spare of flesh; his hair was caught up in a net ornamented with beads; he wore a leathern coat with impressions made on it by armor; his belt was formed entirely of bronze squares; under this belt was a knife in a horn sheath; at his side hung a short travelling-sword.

Eight there near him, behind the table, sat a youth with long hair and a gladsome expression of eye, evidently the man's comrade, or perhaps his armor-bearer, for he was also in travelling-apparel, and wore a similar coat, on which were impressions of armor. The rest of the society was composed of two country people from the neighborhood of Cracow and three citizens in red folding caps, the sharp-pointed tops of which hung down on one side a whole yard.

The innkeeper, a German wearing a yellow cowl and collar with indented edge, was pouring to them from a pitcher into earthen tankards substantial beer, and listening with interest to the narrative of warlike adventures.

But with still greater interest did the citizens listen. In those days the hatred which, during the time of Lokietek, distinguished citizens from knightly landowners, had decreased notably; citizens held their heads higher than in later centuries. They were still called at that time " des aller durchluchtigsten Kuuiges und Herren" l and their readi-

1 See note at the end of Volume II. VOL. i. — 1

ness " ad concessionem pecuniarum " (to pay money) was esteemed; hence it happened frequently that merchants were seen drinking in inns on the footing of lord brother with nobles. Nobles were even glad to see them, for merchants, as persons who possessed ready coin, paid usually for men with escutcheons.

So this time they sat and conversed, winking from moment to moment at the innkeeper to replenish the tankards.

"Then, noble knights," said one of the merchants, "ye have examined a piece of the world ? "

" Not many of those now assembling in Cracow from all parts have seen as much," answered the knight.

"And not a few will assemble," continued the citizen. " Great feasts, and great happiness for the kingdom! They say, too, and it is certain, that the king has ordered for the queen a brocade bed embroidered with pearls, and above it a canopy. There will be festivals and tournaments within barriers, such as the world has not seen to this day."

" Interrupt not the knight, Gossip Gamroth," said a second merchant.

" I am not interrupting him, Gossip Eyertreter, but I think that he himself will be glad to know what people are saying, for surely he is going to Cracow. As it is, we shall not return to the city to-day, for the gates would be closed before us; and at night insects, hatched among chips, do not let people sleep, so we have time for everything."

" But you answer one word with twenty. You are growing old, Gamroth."

" Still I can carry a piece of damp cloth under my arm."

" Oh, indeed ! but such cloth that light passes through it, as through a sieve."

Further conversation was interrupted by the warrior.

" It is sure," said he, " that I shall stop in Cracow, for 1 have heard of the tournaments, and shall be glad to try my strength in the lists, — and this nephew of mine here also, who, though young and beardless, has seen more than one coat of mail on the ground."

The guests looked at the youth, who smiled joyously, and, when he had put his long hair behind his ears with both hands, raised the tankard of beer to his lips.

" Even if we wished to return," added the old knight, " we have no place to which we could go."

" How is that ? " asked one of the nobles. "Whence are ye, and what are your names?"

" I am called Matsko of Bogdanets, and this stripling is the son of my brother; his name is Zbyshko. Our shield is the Blunted Horseshoe, with watchword Hail! "

" Where is your Bogdanets? "

"Oh, better ask me, lord brother, where it was, for it exists no longer. Even during the wars of the Grymaliti and Nalentchi our Bogdanets was burned to its foundations, and what we had there people took from us; our serving-men fled. The place was left naked, for neighboring land-tillers went farther into the wilderness. I with my brother, the father of this stripling, built up our castle anew, but the next year water swept it away from us. After that my brother died, and then I was alone with his orphan. ' I shall not stay here,' thought I. At that time people were talking of war, and of this, that Yasko of Olesnitsa, whom King Vladislav sent to Vilno to succeed Mikolai of Moskorzov, was seeking knights diligently throughout Poland. As I knew Yanko, the worthy abbot of Tulcha, I pledged my laud to him, and with borrowed money bought arms and horses. I found for myself the outfit usual in war, this lad, who was twelve then, I seated on a pony, and away to Yasko of Olesnitsa."

"With this stripling?"

" My dear, he was not even a stripling at that time, but he was a sturdy little fellow. At twelve he could put his crossbow on the ground, press with his stomach, and so turn the bow crank that no Englishman whom we saw at Vilno could do better."

" Was he so strong? "

" He carried my helmet at twelve, and when thirteen winters old he carried my shield."

" Then there was no lack of wars there? "

" Thanks to Vitold, there was not. The prince was always urging the Knights of the Cross, and every year they sent expeditions to Lithuania against Vilno. Various nations went with them : English, who are the first of bowmen, French, Germans, Bohemians, Swiss, and Burgundians. They felled forests, built fortresses on the way, and at last harried Lithuania savagely with fire and sword, so that all the people who dwelt in that land wished to leave it, and search out another, even at the end of the world,— even among sons of Belial, if only far from Germans."

" It was reported here that all Lithuanians wished to go away with their children and wives; we did not believe that"

"But I saw it. Hei! had it not been for Mikolai of Moskorzov, and Yasko of Olesnitsa, and without boasting, had it not been for us, Vilno would not now be existing."

" "We know. Ye would not surrender the castle."

" And we did not. Listen, then, attentively to what I tell you; for I am a man who has served, I am a warrior of experience. People of the old time said in their day, ' Lithuania is venomous,' and they spoke truly. The Lithuanians fight well single-handed, but in the open field they cannot measure with the knighthood. When the horses of the Germans sink in swamps, or when they are in a dense forest, it is different."

" The Germans are good knights! " exclaimed the citizens.

"They stand like a wall, man to man, in iron armor, so covered that hardly is the eye of a dog brother of them to be seen through his vizor. And they go in line. It used to happen that the Lithuanians would strike them and be scattered like sand, and if they were not scattered the Germans put them down like a pavement and trampled them. But the Germans are not alone, for all nations in the world serve with the Knights of the Cross. Ah, those strangers are gallant! More than once a foreign knight would bend forward, lower his lauce, and even before battle strike all alone into a whole army, like a falcon into a flock."

"Christ! " called out Gamroth. " Who is the best among the foreigners?"

" It depends on the weapon. At the crossbow the English are best; they pierce armor through and through with a shaft, and hit a dove a hundred steps distant. The Chehs cut terribly with axes. At the two-handed sword no one surpasses the German. The Swiss delight in breaking thick helmets with iron flails. But the greatest knights are those who come from the French land. They will fight with thee on foot or on horseback, and hurl terribly valiant words at thee; words which thou wilt not at all understand, for their speech is as if one were to rattle a tin plate, though these people are God-fearing. They have accused us, through German interpreters, of defending Pagans and Saracens against Knights of the Cross, and have bound themselves to prove it by a knightly duel. There is to be a judgment of God between four of their knights and four of ours; the meeting is appointed at the court of Vatslav, the Roman Emperor and King of Bohemia."

Here greater curiosity seized the country people and the
merchants, so that they stretched their necks over the tankards toward Matsko of Bogdanets and inquired,— • " And of ours who will meet the French? Tell quickly! "

Matsko raised his beer to his lips, drank, and answered:

" Ei! have no fear for our men. They are Yan of Vlosh-chova, castellan of Dobryn; Mikolai of Vashmuntov; Yasko of Dakov; and Yarosh of Chehov. All are knights to be proud of, deadly fellows. Whether they do battle with lance, sword, or axe — it is nothing new to them! Men's eyes will have something to look at, and their ears something to hear. I have said, put foot on the throat of a Frenchman and he will send knightly words at thee. So help me God and the Holy Cross! as the French talk, so do ours slay."

" There will be glory, if God bless us," said one of the nobles.

" And Saint Stanislav! " added another. Then, turning to Matsko, he continued: "Well, now go on! You have glorified the Germans and other knights, saying that they are brave and that they broke Lithuanians easily. But against you was it not more difficult? Did they go against you with the same willingness? How did God favor? Give praise to our side! "

Evidently Matsko was no braggart, hence he answered modestly, —

" Whoso- is fresh from distant lands strikes us willingly, but after he has tried us once and a second time he has not the same courage, for our people are stubborn. We have been reproached often with this stubbornness. ' Ye despise death,' say our enemies, ' but ye help the Saracens, and for this ye will be damned!' But in us stubbornness increases, for what they say is untrue. The double kingdom baptized Lithuania, and all people there confess Christ the Lord, though not every one does so with knowledge. We know that when a devil was cast out of the cathedral in Plotsk, our gracious lord gave command to set up a candle to him, and priests had to tell the king that it was improper to do that. Well, how must it be in the case of a common man? More than one says to himself: 'The prince has given command to be christened, he has given command to bow down to Christ, so I bow down; but why should I spare a pot of curds on the ancient pagan devils, why not throw them a toasted turnip, or pour to them beer foam? Unless I do so my horses will drop dead, or my cows will be

sick, or their milk will grow bloody, or there will be harm to the harvest.' Many act in this way, and fall under suspicion. But they act thus through ignorance and through fear of devils. Formerly those devils had pleasant lives. They had their groves, their houses, horses to ride on, and they received tithes. But now the groves are cut down, they have nothing to eat; bells are rung in the towns, so this vileness is confined in the deepest forests and howls there in anguish. If a Lithuanian goes to the forest among pines, one devil or another pulls him by the coat, and says 4 Give!' Some give, but there are bold fellows who give nothing, and even catch the devils. One man poured roasted peas into an ox bladder, and thirteen devils crawled in right away. He shut them in with a service-wood plug and took them for sale to the Franciscan monks in Vilno, who gave him twenty groshes with gladness, so as to destroy the enemies of Christ's name. I myself saw that bladder, and a disgusting odor entered a man's nostrils at a distance from it; by such odors do foul spirits express their terror of holy water."

But who counted the thirteen devils ? " asked the merchant Gamroth, cleverly.

"A Lithuanian who saw them crawl in counted. It was evident that they were there, for that was shown by the stench, but no one would take out the plug."

" Those are wonders, wonders! " cried one of the nobles.

" I have looked my fill at great wonders not a few. "We cannot say that those Lithuanian people are pleasant, everything about them is strange. They are shaggy, and hardly a prince among them curls his hair; they eat roasted turnips, preferring them to all other food, for they say that turnips increase bravery. They live in the same house with their cattle and their serpents, they know no moderation in eating and drinking. They hold married women in no esteem, but maidens they reverence highly and recognize great power in them; so if any maiden rubs a man's stomach with dried sycamore, gripes leave him that moment."

"Well, one would not be sorry to have the gripes if the maiden were shapely," called out Eyertreter.

" Ask Zbyshko," replied Matsko of Bogdanets.

Zbyshko laughed till the bench shook beneath him. "There are wonderful maidens among them!" said he. "Was not Ryngalla wonderful?"

" What Ryngalla ? Some gay one? Tell us immediately."

" Have ye not heard of Ryngalla? " inquired Matsko.

" Not a word."

" Well, she is Prince Vitold's sister, and was the wife of Henryk, Prince of Mazovia."

"How is that? What Prince Henryk? There was only one Mazovian prince of that name, the bishop elect of Plotsk, but he died."

" The same man. A dispensation was to come from Rome to him, but death gave him the first dispensation; evidently he did not delight the Lord over much with his conduct. I was sent in that time with a letter from Yasko of Olesnitsa, to Prince Vitold, when Prince Henryk came from King Vladislav to Ritterswerder, as the bishop elect of Plotsk. The war had already become disagreeable to Vitold for this reason specially, that he could not take Vilno, and to our king his own brothers and their loose conduct had become disagreeable. The king, seeing then greater skill and more wisdom in Vitold than in his own brothers, sent the bishop to him with proposals to leave the Knights of the Cross and incline to obedience, for which the government of Lithuania would be given him. Vitold, always eager for change, listened to the pleasant message. There were feasts and tournaments. The bishop mounted a horse with delight, and exhibited his knightly prowess in the lists, though other bishops did not approve of this conduct. By nature all princes of Mazovia are strong, and it is notorious that even maidens of that stock break horseshoes easily. So one day the prince bishop swept three knights of ours from their saddles, another day five, and me among them, while the horse under Zbyshko he put on his haunches. He received all rewards from the hands of the marvellous Ryngalla, before whom he knelt in full armor. And they so fell in love that at feasts attendant clerics drew him away by the sleeves from her, and Vitold restrained the princess his sister. Then the prince bishop said : ' I give a dispensation to myself, and the pope will confirm it, if not the pope in Rome, he of Avignon, and we will have the marriage straightway, or I shall be consumed.' It was a great offence against God, but Vitold did not wish to offend the king's envoy. Then the young couple went to Suraj, and later to Slutsk, to the great grief of this Zbyshko here, who, in German fashion, had chosen Princess Ryngalla as the lady of his heart, and vowed fealty till death to her."

" Indeed, this is true! " broke in Zbyshko. " But after-
ward people said that Princess Ryngalla, understanding that it was not proper for her to be married to the bishop elect (for though married, he had no wish to abandon his spiritual dignity), and because such a marriage could not be blessed by the Lord, poisoned her husband. Hearing of this, I prayed a holy hermit near Lublin to free me from my vow."

" He was a hermit indeed," answered Matsko, with a smile, " but I am not sure that he was holy, for we came upon him one Friday in the forest, where he was cracking bear-bones with an axe, and sucking out the marrow till there was gurgling in his throat."

" But he said that marrow was not flesh, and besides that he had a dispensation to eat it, for he had miraculous visions in sleep after eating marrow, and could prophesy on the morrow till mid-day."

" Well, well," replied Matsko. "But the wonderful Ryngalla is a widow, and she may summon thee to service."

" She would summon me in vain, for I shall choose another lady to serve till death, and besides I shall find a wife."

" First find the belt of a knight."

" Of course! but will there not be tournaments after the queen's delivery? Before that, or after it, the king will belt more than one man. I shall challenge every one. The prince would not have unseated me had my horse not sat on his haunches."

" There will be better men there than thou."

Then a nobleman from near Cracow exclaimed, —

"By the dear God! in presence of the queen will appear, not such men as thou, but the most renowned knights on earth: Zavisha of Garbov, and Farurey and Dobko of Olesnitsa, and Povala of Tachev, and Pashko Zlodye of Bis-kupitsi, and Yasko Nashan, and Abdank of Gora, and Andrei of Brohotsitsi, and Krystin of Ostrov, and Yakov of Kobylani! How couldst thou cope with these, with whom no man can cope either here or at the court of Bohemia or Hungary. What sayest thou, art thou better than they ? How old art thou ? "

"Eighteen," replied Zbyshko.

" Then each man of them could bend thee between his fingers."

"We shall see."

"I have heard," said Matsko, "that the king rewards

bountifully knights returning from the Lithuanian war. Say ye who come from the capital if that be true ? "

"True as God lives!" said one of the nobles. "The bountifulness of the king is known throughout the world, but now it will not be easy to squeeze up to him, for in Cracow it is just swarming with guests who are assembling to be there during the delivery of the queen and the christening, wishing thus to show honor and fealty to our king. The King of Hungary is to be there, and they say the Roman P^mperor too, and various princes, counts, and knights as numerous as poppy seed, because each man hopes that he will not go away empty-handed. They have said, even, that Pope Boniface himself will come; he also needs the aid and favor of our lord against his enemy in Avignon. In such a throng it will not be easy to gain audience, but if it be gained, and our lord's feet embraced, he will care for a man of merit bountifully, be assured."

"Then I will embrace his feet, for I have rendered service, and if there be war I will go again. I have gained booty, and received something from Prince Vitold as reward. I feel no need, but my evening years are coming, and in old age, when strength leaves his bones, a man is glad to have a quiet corner."

"The king was rejoiced to see those who returned from Lithuania under Yasko of Olesuitsa, and they are all eating fatly at present."

" Well ! I did not return at that time, I warred on; for ye should know that that peace between the king and Prince Vitold was ground out upon the Germans. The prince recovered his hostages cunningly, and then attacked the Order. He stormed and burnt castles, slew knights, cut down a multitude of people. The Germans wished to take revenge in company with Swidrygello, who fled to them. There was a great expedition again. Conrad himself, the Grand Master, went with it, leading immense forces. They besieged Vilno, strove to storm castles from great towers, tried to take them by treason, but had no success in anything! And in their retreat so many fell that not one half escaped. We took the field once more against the brother of the Grand Master, Ulrich of Jungingen, burgomaster of Sambia. But Ulrich was afraid of the prince and fled with weeping. Since that flight there is peace, and they are building up Vilno anew. A certain holy monk, who could walk on red-hot iron barefoot, prophesied that thenceforth while the world was

the world Vilno would not see near its walls an armed German. But if that be true, whose hands did the work? "

Matsko of Bogdanets stretched forth his hands, which were broad and strong beyond measure ; others began to nod and add,

" Yes, yes! he is right in what he says."

But further conversation was interrupted by a noise coming through the windows, from which the panes had been taken because the night was bright and warm. From afar was heard a clinking, the voices of people, the snorting of horses, and songs. Those present were astonished, for the hour was late and the moon had risen high iu the heavens. The innkeeper, a German, ran out to the court of the inn, but before the guests could drain the last tankard he returned still more hurriedly.

" Some court is coming! " exclaimed he.

A moment later at the door appeared a youth in a blue kaftan, and on his head a red folding cap. He stopped, looked at the company, and seeing the host said, —

" Wipe the tables there and trim the lights; Princess Anna Danuta will halt here to rest."

Then he turned away. In the inn there was a movement, the host called to his servants and the guests looked at one another with astonishment.

" Princess Anna Danuta! " said one of the citizens; " that is the daughter of Keistut; she is wife of Yanush of Mazovia. She has passed two weeks already in Cracow, but went out to Zator, to Prince Vatslav on a visit, and now is returning of course."

" Gossip Gamroth," said the second citizen, " let us go to the hay in the barn ; this company is too high for us."

"I do not wonder that they travel at night," remarked Matsko, " for it is hot in the day-time; but why come to an inn when there is a cloister near by ? "

Here he turned to Zbyshko.

"A sister, a full sister of the wonderful Ryngalla. Dost mclerstand?"

" But there must be many Mazovian damsels with her, hei! " said Zbyshko.

CHAPTER II.

MEANWHILE the princess passed in. She was a smiling-faced, middle-aged lady, dressed in a red mantle and a green, closely fitting robe; at her hips was a golden girdle, which dropped downward in front and was fastened low with a great clasp. Behind the lady walked damsels of her court, some older, others not full-grown yet; most of them had gar-lauds of roses and lilies on their heads, and lutes in their hands. Some carried whole bunches of fresh flowers, evidently plucked along the road. The room was filled, for after the damsels came a number of courtiers and young boys. All entered briskly, with gladness in their faces, conversing loudly, or singing, as if intoxicated with the beautiful evening and bright moonlight. Among the courtiers were two choristers, one with a lute, the other with a guitar at his girdle. One of the damsels, quite young yet, perhaps twelve years of age, carried behind the princess a lute adorned with brass nails.

" May Jesus Christ be praised ! " said the princess, halting in the middle of the room.

"For the ages of ages. Amen! " answered those present, making low bows as they spoke.

" But where is the host? "

The German, hearing the summons, pushed forward and knelt in German fashion.

" We shall stop here for rest and refreshment," said the lady. " But move about briskly, for we are hungry."

The citizens had departed already, but now the two city nobles, and Matsko of Bogdanets with young Zbyshko, unwilling to disturb the court, bowed a second time with the intention of leaving the room; but the princess detained them.

" Ye are nobles, ye will not interrupt! Make the acquaintance of our courtiers. Whence is God conducting you?"

At once they announced their names, their escutcheons, their service, and the villages by which they entitled themselves. It was only when the lady heard from Matsko whence he was returning that she clapped her hands, and said, —

12 THE KNIGHTS OF THE CROSS.

" See, here is luck! Tell us of Vilno; tell of my brother and sister. Will Prince Vitold come to the delivery of the queen and to the christening?"

" He would like to come, but not knowing whether he will be able, he has sent a silver cradle in advance by priests and boyars, as a gift to the queen. I and my nephew have come to guard this cradle on the road."

kfc Then is the cradle here? I should like to see it. Is it all silver?"

All silver, but it is not here. They have taken it to Cracow."

" But what are ye doing in Tynets? "

"We have turned back to visit the procurator of the cloister, our relative, and confide to the care of the worthy mouks what war has given us, and what the Prince has bestowed."

"Then God has shown favor? Was the booty considerable ? But tell us why my brother was uncertain of coming."

" Because he is preparing an expedition against the Tartars."

"I know that, but it troubles me, since the queen has prophesied an unhappy end to it, and what she prophesies always comes true."

Matsko smiled.

"Our lady is saintly, there is no den3 T ing that," said he, " but a host of our knighthood will go with Prince Vitold, splendid men; to meet them will not be easy for any force."

" And ye will not go?"

"No, for I was sent with others to take the cradle; besides I have not taken armor from my body for five years," said Matsko, pointing to the impressions of the armor on his elkskin coat. "Only let me rest, then I will go; and if I should not go I will give Zbyshko, this nephew of mine, to Pan Spytek of Melshtyn, under whose lead all our knights will enroll themselves."

Princess Anna looked at the stately figure of Zbyshko, but further conversation was interrupted by the arrival of a monk from the cloister, who, when he had greeted the princess, began humbly to reproach her for not having sent a courier with the announcement of her coming, and for not halting at the monastery instead of a common inn, which was unworthy of her dignity. There was no lack in the monastery of houses and edifices in which even an ordinary person could find entertainment, and what would be done in case of

majesty, especially that of the spouse of a prince from whose ancestors and relatives the abbey had received so many benefactions ?

" We have stopped only to rest our limbs," said the princess, good-humoredly; "in the morning we must go to Cracow. We have slept enough in the day, and are travelling at night, because it is cool; and as it was past cock-crow I did not wish to rouse the pious monks, especially with a company which has singing and dancing more in mind than rest."

But when the monk continued to insist, she added, —

" No. We will remain here. A good hour will pass in listening to worldly songs; we shall be at the church for morning mass, to begin the day with God."

" There will be a mass for the prosperity of the gracious prince and princess," said the monk.

"The prince, my consort, will come only after four or five days."

" The Lord God has power to send fortune from afar; but meanwhile let it be permitted us poor people to bring even wine from the cloister."

" We shall thank you for it gladly," said the princess.

"Hei! Danusia, Dauusia!" called she, when the monk had gone; ' ' come out on the bench and rejoice our heart with that same song which thou gavest us in Zator."

Thereupon the courtiers placed a bench quickly in the mid die of the room. The choristers sat, one at each end of it, between them stood that young girl who had borne behind the princess the lute adorned with brass nails. On her head was a garland, her hair was flowing over her shoulders; her robe was blue, her shoes red, with long tips. Standing on the bench she seemed a child, but at the same time a wonderful child, — a church statue, as it were, or a marionette. It was evident also that this was not the first time that she stood up and sang to the princess, for not the slightest confusion was evident in her.

" Go on, Danusia, go on! " cried the damsels.

She held the lute in front of her, raised her head like a bird about to sing, and closing her eyes, began in her silvery voice, —

" Oh had I wings as a wild goose, I would fly after Yasek, I would fly after him to Silesia! "

The choristers accompanied her promptly, one on a guitar, the other on a large lute; the princess, who loved worldly songs beyond everything, swayed her head from side to side, and the little maiden sang on in a thin, childlike, fresh voice. It was like the singing of birds in a forest in springtime.

" I would sit on a fence in Silesia, Look at rue, Yasek dear, Look at the poor little orphan."

And again the choristers accompanied.

Young Zbyshko of Bogdanets, accustomed from childhood to war and its stern images, had never seen anything like that in his life. He nudged in the shoulder a Mazovian standing near by, and inquired, —

" Who is she ? "

" She is a maiden of Princess Anna's suite. There is no lack of choristers with us who amuse the court; but she is the dearest little chorister of all, and the princess listens to no person's songs with such eagerness as to hers."

" That is no wonder to me. I thought her a real angel, and I cannot gaze at her sufficiently. What is her name ? "

" But have j-ou not heard ? — Danusia. Her father is. Yurand of Spyhov, a wealthy and valiant count, who is of those in advance of the banner."

" Hei! human eyes have not seen the like of her."

" All love her, for her singing, and her beauty."

" But who is her knight?"

" She is a child yet."

Conversation was interrupted a second time by Danusia's singing.

From one side Zbyshko gazed at her, — at her bright hair, her raised head, her half-closed eyes, and at her whole figure, illuminated both by the light of the wax candles and the li<_ r ht of the moon-rays coming in through the open window ; and he was more and more astonished. It seemed to him that he had seen her sometime, but he could not remember where, — in a dream, or at Cracow, in a church window. Then he pushed the courtier, and asked in a low voice, —

" Is she of your court, then? "

" Her mother came from Lithuania with Princess Anna Danuta, who gave her in marriage to Yurand of Spyhov. She was beautiful and of a great family, beloved of the princess beyond other damsels, and loving the princess herself. For this reason she named her daughter Anna Danuta. Five

years ago, when the Germans fell upon our court at Zlotoria, she died of fright. Princess Anna took the little girl at that time, and is rearing her. Her father comes often to the court, and is glad when he sees his child in good health and beloved of the princess. But, as often as he looks at her, he sheds tears thinking of his dead one; and then he turns against the Germans, to seek vengeance for the terrible wrong which they wrought on him. No man loved his own wife more than he up to that time in all Mazovia, and he has slain a host of Germans already in revenge for her."

Zbyshko's eyes gleamed in one moment, and the veins thickened on his forehead.

" Then did the Germans kill her mother? " asked he.

" They killed her, and they did not kill her. She died of fright. Five years ago there was peace; no one was thinking of war, and each man went about with no feeling of danger. The prince went to build a castle in Zlotoria, without troops, but with his court, as is usual in peace time. Just then the German traitors attacked us without declaration of war, without cause. Forgetting the fear of God, and all the benefactions which they had received from his ancestors, they lashed the prince to a horse, bore him away, and slew his people. The prince sat long in captivity among them, and only when King Vladislav threatened war did they set him free, out of fear; but during that attack Danusia's mother died, for her heart rose in her throat, and it choked her."

"And you were present? What is your name? I have forgotten."

" I am Mikolai of Dlugolyas; my surname is Obuh. I was present at the attack. I saw a German, with peacock-plumes on his helmet, strap Danusia's mother to his saddle, and saw her grow white before his eyes. They cut me down with a halberd, the mark of which I bear yet."

Then he showed a deep scar which extended from beneath his hair to his brow.

A moment of silence followed. Zbyshko fell to gazing at Danusia again, and inquired, —

" And you say that she has no knight? "

But he did not await the answer, for at that moment the singing ceased. One of the choristers, a large, weighty man, stood up on a sudden; by this the bench tipped at one end; Danusia tottered, spread out her arms; but before she could fall, or jump off, Zbyshko sprang forward with the speed of a wildcat, and caught her in his arms. The princess, who at

16 THE KNIGHTS OF THE CROSS.

the first moment screamed out from fear, began at once to laugh, and said, —

"Here is Danusia's knight! Come hither, young knight, and give us our dear little songstress! "

"He caught her gallantly!" cried voices among the courtiers.

Zbyshko went toward the princess, holding Dauusia at his breast; she, clinging to his neck with one arm, raised the lute high with the other, fearing lest she might break it. Her face was smiling and gladdened, though she was somewhat frightened.

Meanwhile the youth, on reaching the princess, placed Danusia before her; then kneeling and raising his head, he said, with a boldness marvellous at his age, —

" Let it be according to your words, gracious lady! It is time for this charming maiden to have her knight; and it is time, too, for me to have my lady, whose beauty and virtue I shall recognize; so with your leave I will make vows to this one, and be faithful to her unto death in all trials."

Astonishment shot over the face of the princess, not because of Zbyshko's words, but because all had happened so suddenly. The custom of knightly vows was not Polish, it is true; but Mazovia, being on the German boundary, and seeing knights frequently from even distant lands, was acquainted with that custom better than other provinces, and accepted it rather early. The princess had heard of it also still earlier, at the court of her renowned father, where all Western customs were looked on as law, and as models for the noblest warriors. For these reasons she did not find in Zbyshko's wish anything to offend her or Danusia. On the contrary, she was glad that this little girl, who was dear to her, should begin to attract the hearts and eyes of knights. So with delighted face she turned to the little maid.

" Danusia, Danusia ! dost wish to have thy knight?"

The blond-haired Danusia sprang up three times in her red shoes, and then, seizing the princess by the neck, began to cry, with as much delight as if they had offered her a plaything permitted only to older persons for amusement:

"I do, I do, I do!"

The princess laughed till her eyes were filled with tears, but at last the lady, freeing herself from Danusia's arms, said to Zbyshko,—

" Well! make the vow! make the vow! What dost thou vow to her ? "

Zbyshko, who amidst the laughter had preserved an unshaken dignity, spoke up with equal seriousness, without rising from his knee,—

" I vow to her that when I reach Cracow I will hang my shield in front of an inn, and on it a declaration, which a cleric learned in letters will write for me : that Panna Danusia, daughter of Yurand, is the most beautiful and virtuous among the damsels who inhabit all kingdoms. And should any man deny this I will do battle with him till I perish or he perishes, unless he should prefer to go into slavery."

"Well done! It is clear that thou knowest knightly customs. And what more ?"

" And, since I have learned from Pan Mikolai that Panna Danusia's mother yielded her last breath through the act of a German with peacock-plumes on his helmet, I vow to gird my body with a hempen cord, and, though it should eat me to the bone, I will not remove the cord till I have slain three German knights, torn three such plumes from their helmets, and placed them at the feet of my lady."

At this the princess grew serious and inquired,—

" Art thou not making this vow to raise laughter? "

" So help me God and the Holy Cross," answered Zbyshko, " I will repeat this vow in the church before priests."

" It is praiseworthy to give battle to the fierce enemy of our race, but I grieve for thee, since thou art young and mayst perish easily."

Then pushed forward Matsko of Bogdanets. Till that moment, like a man of past times he had merely shrugged his shoulders; now he thought fit to speak.

"As to that be not troubled, gracious lady. Death in battle may meet any man, and to a noble, whether old or young, this is even praiseworthy. But war is no wonder to this lad, for though years are lacking him, it has happened him more than once to fight on horseback and on foot with lance or axe, with a long or a short sword, with a shield or without one. For a knight to make vows to a damsel whom he looks on with gladness is a novel custom, but as Zbyshko has promised his three peacock-plumes I make no reproach. He has harried the Germans, let him harry them again; and if from that harrying a pair of German heads should burst, he will have only the more glory."

"I see that the affair is not with some common youth," said the princess, and she turned to Danusia. " Sit thou in

my place, as the first person at present, but do not laugh, for it is not becoming."

Danusia took Princess Anna's place and wished to feign seriousness, but her blue eyes laughed at the kneeling Zbyshko, and she was unable to restrain herself from moving her feet through delight.

" Give him thy gloves," said the princess.

Danusia drew off her gloves which she gave to Zbyshko, who took them with great respect.

" I will fasten these to my helmet," said he, pressing them to his lips, " and whoso tries to get them, woe to him." Then he kissed Danusia's hands, and after the hands her feet, and rose. But that moment his former seriousness deserted him, and great joy filled his heart because thenceforth he would pass as a mature man before all that court; so, shaking Danusia's gloves, he cried, half in joy, half in anger,—

"Come on, dog brothers with your peacock-plumes! Come on !"

But at that moment the same monk entered the inn who had been there before; and with him two others, older than he. Behind them monastery servants bore wicker baskets, and in them vessels of wine, and various dainties collected quickly. Those two fell to greeting the princess and reproaching her for not having gone to the monastery; but she explained a second time that, since she had slept and the whole court had slept in the daytime, they were travelling at night, hence needed no sleep; and not wishing to rouse the distinguished abbot, or the worthy monks, she preferred to halt at the inn and rest their limbs there.

After many courteous phrases they decided finally on this : that after matins and early mass the princess and her court would accept a meal and rest in the monastery. Besides the Mazovians, the hospitable monks invited the landowners of Cracow, and Matsko of Bogdanets, who intended in every case to go to the monastery and leave there the property which he had won in war, or had received as gifts from the bountiful Vitold, and which was intended to free Bogdanets from pledge. Young Zbyshko had not heard the invitations, for he had run to his own and his uncle's wagons, which were under guard of their attendants, so as to dress and stand in more befitting costume before Danusia and the princess. Taking his boxes from the wagon, he commanded to bear them to the servants' room, and he dressed there. First he

arranged his hair hurriedly and thrust it into a silk net, in which were interwoven amber beads with real pearls in front. Then he put on a " jacket" of white silk embroidered with gold griffins, and at the bottom with ornamented border; above this he girded himself with a double gilded girdle, from which depended a small sword in a scabbard inlaid with silver and ivory. All this was new, gleaming, and not stained with any blood, though taken as booty from a young Frisian knight, serving with the Knights of the Cross. Next, Zbyshko put on very beautiful trousers, one leg of which was striped red and green, the other yellow and violet: both ended above in many-colored squares. When he had put on purple shoes with long, pointed toes, splendid and fresh, he betook himself to the general room.

When he stood on the threshold the sight of him made indeed a strong impression on all. The^princess, when she saw what a beautiful knight had made vows to Danusia, was delighted still more, and Danusia at the first moment sprang toward him like a deer. But, whether she was restrained by the beauty of the youth, or the voices of admiration from the courtiers, she stopped before she had run to him; so that, halting a step distant from Zbyshko, she dropped her eyes suddenly, and clasping her hands began, blushing and confused, to twist her fingers.

But after her came up others: the princess herself, the courtiers, the damsels, the choristers and the monks; for all wished to look at him more closely. The Mazovian maidens gazed at Zbyshko as at a rainbow, each regretting that he had not chosen her. The elder ones admired the costliness of the dress; and round him was formed a circle of the curious; Zbyshko stood in the centre with a boastful smile on his face, turning somewhat on the spot where he stood, so that they might look at him better.

"Who is that?" asked one of the monks.

"That is a young knight, the nephew of this lord here," replied the princess, pointing to

Matsko; " he has just now made a vow to Danusia."

The monks showed no astonishment, since such vows bound to nothing. Vows were made frequently to married ladies, and in notable families, among whom Western customs were known, almost every lady had her knight. If a knight made vows to a damsel, he did not become her betrothed thereby: on the contrary, she took another for husband most frequently; but he, in so far as he possessed

the virtue of constancy, did not cease in fealty to her, but he married another.

Danusia's youth astonished the monks somewhat more, but not over much, for in that age youths of sixteen became castellans. The great queen Yadviga herself was only fifteen when she came from Hungary, and girls of thirteen were given in marriage. Besides, they were looking more in that moment at Zbyshko than Danusia, and were listening to Matsko, who, proud of his nephew, had begun to relate how the young man had come to possess such famous apparel.

" A year and nine weeks ago," said he, " we were invited to feasts by Saxon knights; and with them as guest was a certain knight from the distant nation of the Frisians, who dwell far away at the edge of the ocean, and he had with him his son, three years older than Zbyshko. Once at a feast that son told Zbyshko .unbecomingly that he had neither beard nor moustache. Zbyshko, being quick-tempered, would not listen to this calmly, but seizing him at once by the lips plucked out all the hair from them, for which afterward we fought for death or servitude."

"How is that? Did you fight?" asked Mikolai.

"I did, for the father took his son's part, and I Zbysh-ko's; so we fought, four of us, in presence of the guests, on a space of trampled earth. We made an agreement of this sort, that whoso conquered should take the wagons and horses and servants of the conquered. And God favored us. We slew those Frisians, though with no little toil, for they lacked neither courage nor strength; and we took Damons booty. There were four wagons, for each wagon a pair of draught-horses four immense stallions, nine servants, and two excellent suits of armor, such as one might find rarely with our people. The head-pieces we broke, it is true, in the battle, but the Lord Jesus consoled us with other things, for in a box bound famously with iron were suits of costly apparel, and that suit in which Zbyshko has now arrayed himself was with them."

At this the two nobles from Cracow, and all the Mazovians looked with greater respect on the uncle and nephew, and Mikolai, surnamed Obuh, said, —

" Ye are, I see, unyielding, stern men."

"We believe now that this young man will get the three peacock-plumes."

Matsko smiled, wherewith in his stern face there was something quite predatory.

Meanwhile the monastery servants had drawn forth from the wicker baskets wine and tidbits, and from the servants' quarters girls had begun to bring plates full of smoking fried eggs flanked with sausages from which went forth a pronounced and savory odor of wild-boar flesh. At sight of this a desire to eat seized all, and they moved toward the tables.

No one, however, took a place earlier than the princess. When she had sat down at the middle of the table she commanded Danusia and Zbyshko to sit side by side, and then said to Zbyshko, —

"It is proper that thou eat from one dish with Danusia, but act not as other knights do with their ladies, bring not thy foot to hers under the table, touch not her knees, for she is too young."

"I will not, gracious lady," replied he, " unless after two or three years, when the Lord Jesus will permit me to perform my vow, and when this berry will ripen; and as to treading on her feet, I could not do that if I wished, for they are hanging in the air."

"True!" answered the princess, "and it is pleasant to see that thou hast decent manners."

Then followed silence, for all had begun to eat. Zbyshko cut the fattest bits of sausage and gave them to Danusia, or put them directly into her mouth, and she, glad that so stately a knight was serving her, ate with full cheeks, blinking and smiling,, now at him, now at the princess.

After the plates had been cleared the monastery servants poured out sweet, fragrant wine, to men in abundance, to women sparingly; but Zbyshko's knightlinesa appeared specially when they brought in full measures of nuts from the monastery; native wild nuts, and, rare in that time, Italian nuts brought from afar, which the company seized very eagerly, so that after a while throughout the whole room nothing was heard save the noise of nutshells cracked between jaws. It would be vain to suppose that Zbyshko thought only of himself, for he preferred to show the princess and Danusia his knightly strength and abstinence rather than lower himself in their eyes through greed for dainties. Taking from moment to moment a handful of nuts, whether Italian or native, he did not put them between his teeth as did others, but squeezed them with his iron fingers, cracked the shells, and gave clean kernels to Danusia. He invented even an amusement for her. After he had

removed the kernels he put his hand to his lips and blew the shells suddenly with his mighty breath to the ceiling. Danusia laughed so much that the princess, fearing lest the girl might choke herself, commanded him to abandon the amusement. Seeing, however, Danusia's delight, she asked, —

Well, Danusia, is it nice to have thy knight ? "

Oi, nice! " answered the maiden. And putting forth a rosy finger she touched Zbyshko's white silk jacket, withdrew the finger suddenly, and asked, —

" And will he be mine to-morrow ? "

" To-morrow, in a week, and till death," answered Zbyshko.

The supper came to an end when, after the nuts, sweet pancakes full of berries were brought to them. Some of the courtiers wished to dance, others preferred to hear the singing of the choristers, or of Danusia; but toward the end of the supper Danusia's eyelids began to grow heavy; her head dropped first to one side, then to the other ; once and a second time she looked at the princess, then at Zbyshko; again she rubbed her eyes with her fists and immediately rested with great confidence against the knight's shoulder, and fell asleep.

" Is she asleep?" asked the princess. " Now thou hast thy ' lady.'"

" She is dearer to me sleeping than another in a dance," answered Zbyshko, sitting erect and motionless so as not to rouse the maiden.

But not even the playing and singing of the choristers roused her. Some kept time to the music with their feet, others accompanied by beating the dishes, but the greater the noise the better she slept, with her mouth open, like a little fish. She woke only when, at cock-crow and the sound of church bells, all moved from the table crying, —

" To matins ! to matins! "

" We will go on foot to praise God," said the princess.

And taking the awakened Danusia by her hand, she went forth first from the inn, and after her the whole court. The night had grown pale. On the eastern sky a slight brightness was visible, green at the top, rosy below that, and under all a narrow golden ribbon as it were, which widened as one looked at it. On the west the moon seemed to withdraw before that brightness. The dawn became rosier and clearer each instant. The world awoke wet from abundant dew, refreshed and joyful.

THE KNIGHTS OF THE CROSS. 23

" God has given fine weather, but the heat will be violent," said the courtiers.

"That is no harm," answered Pan Mikolai, quieting them, " we shall take a sleep at the cloister and reach Cracow about evening."

" For another feast, surely."

" There are feasts every day now in Cracow, and after the tournaments there will be greater ones."

" We shall see how Danusia's knight will exhibit himself."

" Ei! They are in some sort men of oak! Have ye heard what they said of that battle of four ? "

" Perhaps they will join our court, for they are counselling together about something."

And really they were counselling, for Matsko was not greatly rejoiced over what had happened; moving, therefore, in the rear of the retinue, and lingering purposely, so as to speak more at freedom, he said, —

" In truth there is no profit for thee in this. I shall push up to the king somehow, even with this court, and mayhap I shall gain something. I should like wonderfully to get some little castle or town. Well, we shall see. In good time we shall redeem Bogdanets from pledge, for what thy fathers possessed we must possess also. But whence are we to get men? Those whom the abbot settled he will take back again; land without men has no value, so mark what I say: Make vows to whom it may please thee, or make them not, but go with Pan Melshtyn to Prince Vitold against the Tartars. Should the expedition be summoned before the queen's deliver\'7d 7 , wait not for delivery or tournaments, but go, for there may be profit. Thou knowest how bountiful Prince Vitold is, and he knows thee already; acquit thyself manfully, he will reward thee well. And above all, if God favor, thou mayst get captives beyond number. The Tartars are like ants in the world. In case of victory there will be sixty for each warrior."

Here Matsko, who was greedy for land and labor, began to imagine, —

" God give me a blessing to drive in about fifty men and settle them in Bogdanets. We should open a strip of wilderness and increase, both of us. And knowest thou, that nowhere wilt thou collect so many men as thou mayst collect there."

But Zbyshko shook his head.

24 THE KNIGHTS OF THE CROSS.

" Oh, I should find horse boys who live on horse carrion, people unused to land work ! What good would they be in Bogdanets? Besides, I have vowed to get three German peacock-plumes. Where should I find them among Tartars ? "

"Thou hast vowed, for thou art stupid, and so are the vows."

"But my noble and knightly honor, how with that?"

" How was it with Ryngalla? "

" Ryngalla poisoned the prince, and the hermit absolved me."

" The abbot in Tynets will absolve thee. An abbot is better than a hermit ; that man looked more like a robber than a monk."

" I want no absolution."

Matsko stopped, and asked with evident anger, —

"Well, how will it be?"

" Go yourself to Vitold, for I will not go."

" Thou knecht! But who will bow down before the king? And art thou not sorry for my bones ? "

"A tree might fall on your bones and not break them. But even were I sorry for you I am unwilling to go to Vitold."

"What wilt thou do? "Wilt thou be a falconer, or a chorister at the Mazovian court?"

" Is a falconer something evil? Since it is your wish to grumble rather than listen, then grumble."

" W T here wilt thou go? Is Bogdanets nothing to thee? Wilt thou plow in it with thy nails, without men? "

" Not true ! you have argued bravely with your Tartars. Have you heard what the people of Rus say, — ' Thou wilt find as many Tartars as there are corpses of them on the field, but no man will seize a captive, for no man can overtake a Tartar in the steppe.' On what could I overtake one ! On those heavy stallions which we took from the Frisians ? And what booty could I find? Mangy sheepskin coats, nothing else! And only when I return rich to Bogdanets will they call me comes (count)."

Matsko was silent, for there was much justice in Zbyshko's words, and only after a while did he say, —

" But Prince Vitold would reward thee."

" Oh yes! you know; he rewards one man too much and gives another nothing."

"Then tell me, whither art thou going?"

"To Yurand, of Spyhov."

Matsko twisted the belt of his skin kaftan with anger, and said, —

" God daze thy eyes! "

"Listen," answered Zbyshko, calmly. "I have talked with Pan Mikolai, and he says that Yurand is seeking vengeance on the Germans for his wife. I will go and assist him. You have said, first of all, that it is nothing wonderful for me to fight with Germans, for I know them, and I know methods against them. Secondly, I shall find the peacock-plumes there at the boundary more quickly, and third, you know that no common man wears a peacock-plume above his head, so that if the Lord Jesus will grant the crests, he will grant booty at the same time. Finally, a captive taken there is not a Tartar. To settle such a one in the forest is not the same as — Pity me, O God! "

" What! hast lost thy reason, boy ? There is no war now, and God knows when there will be."

" Oh, simplicity! The bears have made peace with the bee-keepers; bears injure no bee-nests now, they eat no honey. Ha ! ha ! But is it news to you that, though great armies are not warring, and though the king and the Grand Master have put their seals to parchment, there is always a terrible uproar on the boundary? If some one takes cattle, a number of villages will be burnt for each cow, and castles will be attacked. But what as to seizing boys and maidens and merchants on the highways ? Do you remember earlier times, of which you yourself haye told me ? Was it hard for that Nalench who seized forty men who were going to the Knights of the Cross? He put them under the ground and would not let them out till the Grand Master sent him a wagon full of coin. Yurand of Spyhov does nothing else but seize Germans, and near the boundary there is work at hand always."

For a while they walked on in silence; meanwhile the daylight came, and bright sun-rays lighted the cliffs on which the monastery was built.

" God can give luck everywhere," said Matsko at last, with a satisfied voice. " Pray that He give it thee."

It is sure that His favor is everything ! "

"And think of Bogdanets, for thou wilt not persuade me that thou hast the wish to go to

Bogdanets, and not to Yurand of Spyhov, for that chatterer."

" Speak not in that way, or I shall be angry. I look on her with gladness and do not deny it; that is a different vow

from the one to Ryngalla. Hast thou met a more beautiful maiden ? "

"What is her beauty to me? Take her when she grows up, if she is the daughter of a great comes."

Zbyshko's face grew bright with a kindly smile.

"That may happen too. No other lady, no other wife. When your bones grow weak you will nurse my grandchildren and hers."

Then Matsko smiled in turn, and he said, entirely pacified:

"Hail! Hail! Storms of them, and let them be like hail! Joy for old age, and salvation after death. Give that to us, O Jesus."

## CHAPTER III.

PRINCESS Anna Danuta, Matsko, and Zbysbko, had been in Tynets before, but in the retinue were courtiers who saw it for the first time, and these, when they raised their eyes, looked with astonishment on the magnificent abbey, on the indented walls running along cliffs above precipices, on edifices standing now on the slopes of the mountain, now within battlements piled up, lofty, and shining in gold from the rising sun. By these noble walls, edifices, houses, and buildings destined for various uses, and the gardens lying at the foot of the mountain, and carefully cultivated fields which the eye took in from above, it was possible at the first glance to recognize ancient inexhaustible wealth, to which people from poor Mazovia were not accustomed, and at which they must unavoidably be astonished. There existed, it is true, old and wealthy Benedictine monasteries in other parts of the kingdom, as, for example, in Lubush on the Odra, in Plotsk, in Great Poland, in Mogilno, and other places, but none could compare with Tynets, whose possessions exceeded not only dependent principalities, but whose incomes might rouse envy even in kings at that period.

Among the courtiers, therefore, astonishment increased, and some of them were almost unwilling to believe their own eyes. Meanwhile the princess, wishing to shorten the road for herself, and rouse the curiosity of her attendant damsels, fell to begging one of the monks to relate the old and terrible tale of Valger the Charming, which had been told her in Cracow, though not with much detail.

Hearing this, the damsels gathered in a close flock around the lady and walked up the mountain-side slowly in the early rays of the sun, looking like a troop of moving flowers.

" Let the tale of Valger be told by Brother Hidulf, to whom he appeared on a certain night," said one monk, looking at another, a man of gray years already, who with a body somewhat bent walked at the side of Pan Mikolai.

" Have you seen him with your own eyes, pious father?" asked the princess.

"I have seen him," replied the monk, gloomily; "for times are granted when God's will permits him to leave his hellish underground dwelling and show himself in the light."

" When does this happen? "

The monk glanced at the other two and was silent, for there was a tradition that Valger's ghost was to appear when the morals of the Knights of the Cross should become lax and the monks think more than was proper of worldly pleasures and wealth. No one wished to confess aloud that it was said also that the ghost foretold war or other misfortunes; so Brother Hidulf, after a moment's silence, said, —

" His ghost heralds nothing good."

" I should not like to see him," said the princess, making the sign of the cross on herself ; ' ' but why is he in hell ? — since, as I hear, he only avenged too severely a personal wrong."

"Though during his whole life he had been virtuous," answered the monk, sternly, "he would have been damned in every case, for he lived during pagan times, and was not cleansed by holy baptism."

At these words the brows of the princess contracted with pain, for she remembered that her mighty father, whom she had loved with her whole soul, had died also in pagan error, and must burn through all eternity.

"We are listening," said she after a moment of silence.

Brother Hidulf began his narrative, —

"There lived in pagan times a wealthy count, who because of great beauty was called Valger the Charming. This country, as far as the eye sees, belonged to him, and on expeditions, besides footmen he led forth a hundred spearmen, for all nobles on the west to Opole and on the east to Sandomir were his vassals. No man could count his cattle, and in Tynets he had a fortress filled with coin, just as the Knights of the Cross have in Malborg at present."

" I know they have ! " interrupted Princess Anna.

" And he was like a giant," continued the monk, — " he tore up oak trees by the roots; and in beauty, in playing on the lute, and in singing, no man on earth could compare with him. But once, when he was at the court of the King of France, the king's daughter, Helgunda, fell in love with him. Her father had wished to give her to a convent for the glory of God, but she fled with Valger to Tynets, where

THE KNIGHTS OF THE CROSS. 29

they lived in vileness, for no priest would give them Christian marriage. In Vislitsa lived Vislav the Beautiful, of the race of King Popiel. Once this Vislav, during the absence of Valger, fell to ravaging the lands of Tynets. Valger conquered him and brought him to Tynets, not remembering that every woman who looked on Vislav was ready straightway to desert father, mother, and husband, so be it that she could satisfy her desire. And so it happened with Helgunda. She invented such bonds for Valger that though he was a giant, though he tore up oak trees, he was not able to break the bonds, and she delivered him to Vislav, who took him to Vislitsa. But Vislav had a sister named Rynga. When she heard Valger singing in an underground dungeon she fell in love with him straightway, and freed him from under the earth. When he had slain Helgunda and Vislav with a sword, Valger left their bodies to the crows and returned to Tynets with Rynga."

" Did not he do what was right? " inquired the princess.

"If he had received baptism, and given Tynets to the Benedictines," answered Hidulf, " perhaps God would have remitted his sins, but since he did not do that the earth swallowed him."

"Were the Benedictines in this kingdom at that time? "

" The Benedictines were not in this kingdom, for pagans alone lived here then."

"In such case how could he receive baptism, or give away Tynets ? "

" He could not, and for that very reason he is condemned to endless torments in hell," replied the monk, with dignity.

" Surely he speaks the truth! " said a number of voices.

They were now approaching the main gate of the monastery, in which the abbot at the head of a numerous retinue of monks and nobles was waiting for the princess. There Avere always many laymen, " messengers, advocates, procurators," and monastery officials there. Many landholders, even great nobles, held countless cloister lands by feudal tenure, rather exceptional in Poland, and these, as vassals, were glad to appear at the court of the " suzerain," where near the high altar it was easy to receive a grant, an abatement, and every kind of benefaction, — dependent frequently on some small service, clever word, or a moment of good-humor in the mighty abbot. While preparing for solemnities in the capital many also of such vassals assembled from distant places; those of them for whom it was difficult, be-

cause of the throng, to find an inn in Cracow, found lodgings in Tynets. For these reasons the Abbas centum vittarum (abbot of a hundred villas) might greet the princess with a retinue still more numerous than common.

He was a man of lofty stature, with an austere and wise face, with a head shaven on the crown, but lower down, above the ears, encircled by a garland of hair growing gray. On his forehead was a scar from a wound received evidently during years of young knighthood; eyes penetrating, haughty, looked out from beneath dark brows. He was dressed in a habit like other monks, but over it was a black mantle lined with purple, and on his neck a gold chain from the end of which depended a cross, also gold and inlaid with precious stones, the emblem of his dignity as abbot. His whole bearing indicated a man haughty, accustomed to command, and self-confident. But he greeted the princess cordially, and even with humility, for he remembered that her husband came of that stock of Mazovian princes from which King Vladislav and Kazimir the Great were descended on the female side, and at present the reigning queen was the mistress of one of the broadest realms on earth. He passed the threshold of the gate, therefore, inclined his head low, and, when he had made the sign of the cross over Anna Uanuta and the whole court, with a golden tube which he held in the fingers of his right hand, he said, —

"Be greeted, gracious lady, at the poor threshold of monks. May Saint Benedict of Murcia, Saint Maurice, Saint Boniface, and Saint Benedict of Anagni, and also Saint John of Ptolomeus, our patrons who dwell in eternal light, endow thee with health and with happiness; may they bless thee seven times daily through every period of thy life."

" They would have to be deaf not to hear the words of so groat an abbot," said the princess, courteously; "all the more since we have come here to mass, during which we shall place ourselves under their protection."

Then she extended her hand to him, which he, kneeling with courtliness on one knee, kissed in knightly fashion; after that they passed in through the gateway without delay. Those inside were waiting evidently for mass to begin, for at that moment the bells great and small were rung, trumpeters sounded shrill trumpets at the church door, in honor of the princess, while others beat enormous kettle-drums made of ruddy copper and covered with rawhide; these gave forth

a roaring sound. On the princess, who was not born in a Christian country, every church had thus far produced a deep impression, but that church of Tynets produced it all the more, since in respect of grandeur there were few others to compare with it. Gloom filled the depth of the sanctuary. Only at the high altar were trembling rows of various lights mingled with the glitter of candles, illuminating the gilding and the carving. A monk in full vestments came out with the chalice, bowed to the princess, and began mass. Directly rose the smoke of abundant incense, which, hiding the priest and the altar, went upward in quiet clusters, increasing the mysterious solemnity of the church.

Anna Danuta bent her head backward, and spreading her hands at the height of her face began to pray earnestly. But when the organ — organs were rare in churches at that time —

shook the whole nave with majestic thunder, filled it with angels' voices, scattering as it were the song of the nightingale, the eyes of the princess were uplifted, on her face besides devotion and awe was depicted delight beyond limit, and it might seem to one looking at her that she was some blessed one, gazing at heaven opened in miraculous vision.

Thus prayed the daughter of Keistut, born in paganism. Though in daily life, like all people of that period, she mentioned the name of God in a friendly and intimate manner, in the house of the Lord she raised her eyes in childlike dread, and in subjection to a mysterious and infinite power.

In a like pious manner, though with less awe, did the whole court pray. Zbyshko knelt outside the stalls among the Mazovians, for only the princess and her damsels were inside, and he committed himself to the guardianship of God, and at moments looked at Danusia, who sat with closed eyes near the princess; and he thought that in truth there was worth in becoming the knight of such a maiden, Hit also that he had promised her uo common thing. Under the " jacket" which he had won, he had girded on uie hempen rope, but that was only one part of the vow, after which he had to accomplish the other, which was incomparably more difficult. So now, when the wine and beer which he had drunk in the inn had gone from his head, he was troubled in no slight degree as to the manner in which he should accomplish it. There was no war. In the disturbance on the boundary it was indeed easy for him to meet an armed German, break his skull, or lay down his own head. This he

had told Matsko also. "But," thought he, "not every German wears peacock or ostrich plumes on his helmet:" of guests of the Knights of the Cross only certain counts, am? of the Knights of the Cross themselves only comturs, and then not every one. If there should be no war, years might pass before he could find his three plumes. This too came to his head, that not being belted, he could only challenge unbelted men to combat in battle. He hoped, it is true, to receive the belt of a knight from the king in time of the tournaments which were promised after the christening, for he had earned it long before — but what next? He would go to Yurand of Spyhov, and assist him; he would crush warriors as far as possible, and that would be the end. But common warriors were not knights with peacock-plumes on their helmets.

In this suffering and uncertainty, seeing that without the special favor of God he would not do much, he began to pray: "Grant, O Jesus, war with the Knights of the Cross, and the Germans who are the enemies of this kingdom and of us all; and rub out those men who are more ready to serve the chieftain of hell than they are to serve Thee, bearing in their hearts hatred against us, most angry of all that our king and queen, having baptized Lithuania, prevent them from cutting down Thy servants with the sword. For which anger chastise them.

"And I, sinful Zbyshko, am penitent before Thee and implore aid from Thy five wounds to send me, at the earliest, three noted Germans with peacock-plumes on their helmets, and permit me in Thy mercy to slay them, because I have vowed those plumes to Panna Danusia, the daughter of Yurand; she is Thy servant, and I have sworn on my knightly honor. And of what is found on the slain I will bestow the tenth part on Thy church faithfully, so that Thou, sweet Jesus, may receive profit and honor from me; and know Thou that I promise with a sincere heart, and not idly. And as this is true, so help me. Amen."

But as he prayed, his heart melted more and more from devotion, and he added a new promise, that after freeing Bogdanets from pledge he would give to the church all the wax which the bees should make during a whole year. He hoped that his uncle Matsko would not oppose this, and .the Lord Jesus especially would be rejoiced at having wax for candles, and from wishing to receive it at the earliest would help him the sooner. This thought seemed so just that

de-

THE KNIGHTS OF THE CROSS. 33

light filled Zbyshko's soul thoroughly. He was almost certain now that he would be heard, that war would come soon, and even should it not come he would get his own in every case. He felt in his hands and feet a strength so great that he would at that moment have attacked a whole company. He thought, even, that when he had made the promises to God he might have added two more Germans to Danusia. The young man's impulsiveness urged him to this, but prudence gained the victory, for he feared to weary God's patience by excessive demand.

His confidence, however, increased when, after mass and a long repose, to which the whole court gave itself, he heard a conversation which the abbot held with Anna Danuta at breakfast.

The wives of princes and kings in that age, through devotion, and because of lordly gifts, which the Order did not spare on them, showed the Knights of the Cross great friendship. Even the saintly Yadviga restrained, while her life lasted, the hand of her powerful husband raised above them. Anna Danuta alone, having experienced the Order's cruel injustice in her family, hated the Knights from her whole soul. So when the abbot inquired about Mazovia and its affairs she fell to accusing the Knights of the Cross bitterly.

" What is to be done in a principality which has such neighbors ? There is peace, as it were; embassies and messages pass, but still we cannot be sure of the day or the hour. The man at the border who lies down to sleep in the evening never knows but he may wake up in bonds, or with a sword-edge at his throat, or a burning roof above his head. Oaths, seals, and parchments give no security against betrayal. It was not otherwise at Zlotoria, when in time of profound peace the prince was snatched away into captivity. The Knights of the Cross declared that his castle might become a threat to them. But castles are made for defence, not attack; and what prince is there who has not the right to build castles on his own land, or repair them? Neither weak nor strong are respected by the Knights of the Cross; the weak they despise, and they strive to bring the strong down to ruin. To him who does them good they return evil. Is there in the world an Order which has received in other kingdoms such benefactions as they have received from Polish princes ? And how have they paid for them ? "With hatred, with ravaging of lands, with war and betrayal. As to complaint, it is useless. It is useless to complain to the Apos-

VOL. I. — 3

tol'ic See itself, for living in pride and malice they disobey the Pope of Rome even. They have sent now, as it were, an embassy on the occasion of the queen's delivery, and for the coming christening, but only because they wish to turn away the wrath of the powerful king, which has been roused by their deeds in Lithuania. In their hearts, however, they are always meditating the ruin of this kingdom and the whole Polish race."

The abbot listened attentively and agreed, but said afterward, —

" I know that the comtur, Lichtenstein, has come to Cracow at the head of an embassy; he is a brother highly esteemed in the Order for his distinguished family, his bravery, and his wisdom. Perhaps you will see him here soon, gracious lady, for he sent me notice yesterday that, wishing to pray before our relics, he would come on a visit to Tynets."

When she heard this the princess began to raise new complaints.

" People declare, and God grant with truth, that a great war will come soon, — a war in which there will be on one side the Polish kingdom and all peoples whose speech resembles ours, and on the other all Germans and the Knights of the Cioss. Very likely there is a prophecy of some saint touching this."

" Of Saint Bridget," interrupted the learned abbot; " eight years ago she was reckoned among the saints. The pious Peter of Alvaster, and Mathew of Linkoping wrote down her visions, in which a great war is really predicted."

Zbj'shko quivered with delight at these words, and unable to restrain himself asked, — And is it to come soon? "

The abbot, occupied with the princess, did not hear, or perhaps feigned not to hear, this question.

Young knights among us," continued the princess, 44 are delighted with this war, but those who are older and more sober of judgment speak thus: 4 Not the Germans do we fear, though great is their pride and strength; not swords and lances, but the relics which the Knights have do we fear, for against them the strength of man is as nothing.' "

Here Princess Anna looked with fear at the abbot and added in a low voice: " Likely they have the true wood of the Holy Cross; how, then, is it possible to war with them?"

The King of the French sent it to them," answered the abbot.

THE KNIGHTS OF THE CROSS. 35

A moment of silence followed, after which was heard the voice of Mikolai, surnamed Obuh, a man of experience and training.

u I was in captivity among the Knights," said he, " and I saw processions at which that great sacred relic was carried. But besides, there is in the cloister at Oliva a number of others most important, without which the Order would not have risen to such power."

At this the Benedictines stretched their necks toward the speaker, and asked with great curiosity, —

" Will you tell us what they are ? "

" There is a border from the robe of the Most Holy Virgin, there is a back tooth of Mary Magdalen, and branches from the fiery bush in which God the Father appeared to Moses; there is a hand of Saint Liberius; and as to bones of other saints, a man could not count them on his toes and fingers."

"How war with them?" repeated the princess, with a sigh.

The abbot wrinkled his lofty forehead, stopped for a moment, then said, —

"It is difficult to war with them, if only for the reason that they are monks and bear the cross on their mantles; but if they have exceeded the measure in sin, residence among them may become hateful to those relics, and in that hour not only will the relics not add, but they will detract from them, so as to fall into more pious hands. May God spare Christian blood, but should a great war come there are relics also in our kingdom which will act on our side. The voice in the vision of Saint Bridget said : ' I have placed them as bees of usefulness and fixed them on the border of Christian lands. But behold they have risen against me, they care not for souls and spare not the bodies of people who, out of error, turned to the Catholic faith, and to me. They have made slaves of these people and fail to teach them God's commands ; depriving them of the holy sacraments, they condemn them to greater torments of hell than if they had remained in paganism. And they make war to satisfy theii greed.' Therefore have confidence in God, gracious lady, for their days are numbered rather than yours; but meanwhile receive with thankful heart this tube here, in which is a toe of Saint Ptolomeus, one of our patrons."

The princess stretched forth her hand trembling from delight, and on her knees received the tube, which she pressed to her lips immediately. The delight of the lady was shared by the courtiers and the damsels, for no one doubted that blessing and prosperity would be diffused over all, and perhaps over the whole principality from such a gift. Zbyshko also felt happy, for it seemed to him that war ought to follow straightway after the Cracow festivities.

CHAPTER IV.

IT was well on in the afternoon when the princess with her retinue moved out of hospitable Tynets for Craeow. Knights of that period, before entering the larger cities or castles to visit notable personages, arrayed themselves frequently in full battle armor. It was the custom, it is true, to remove this immediately after passing the gates. At castles the host himself invited them with the time-honored words, " Remove your armor, noble lords, for ye have come to friends ; " none the less, however, the "war" entrance was considered the most showy, and enhanced the significance of the knight. In accordance with this showiness, Matsko and Zbyshko arrayed themselves in their excellent mail and shoulder-pieces which they had won from the Frisian knights, — bright, gleaming, and adorned on the edges with an inlaid thread of gold. Pan Mikolai, who had seen much of the world and many knights in his life, and who was no common judge of military matters, saw at once that that mail was forged by armorers of Milan, the most famous in the world, — mail of such quality that only the richest knights could afford it; a suit was equal in value to a good estate. He inferred from this that those Frisians must have been famous knights in their nation, and he looked with increased respect at Matsko and Zbyshko. Their helmets, though also not of the poorest, were less rich; but their gigantic stallions, beautifully caparisoned, roused admiration and envy among the courtiers. Matsko and Zbyshko, sitting on immensely high saddles, looked down on the whole court. Each held a long lance in his hand; each had a sword at his side, and an axe at his saddle. They had sent their shields, it is true, for convenience, to the wagons; but even without them, they looked as if marching to battle, not to the city.

Both rode near the carriage, in which, on the rear seat, was the princess with Danusia. In front, the stately lady Ofka, the widow of Krystin of Yarzambek, and old Pan Mikolai. Danusia looked with great interest at the iron knights; and the princess, taking from her bosom repeatedly the tube with the relic of St. Ptolomeus, raised it to her lips.

" I am terribly curious to know what bones are inside," said she at last; " but I will not open it myself, through fear of offending the saint. Let the bishop open it in Cracow."

" Oh, better not let it out of your hands," said the cautious Pan Mikolai; " it is too desirable."

" Mayhap you speak justly," said the princess, after a moment's hesitation; then she added: "No one has given me such consolation for a long time as that worthy abbot, — first with this gift, and second because he allayed my fear of the Knights of the Cross."

"He speaks wisely and justly," said Matsko. "The Germans had at Vilno various relics, especially because they wished to convince their guests that the war was against pagans. Well, and what came of this? Our people saw that if they spat on their hands and struck out with the axe straight from the ear, a helmet and a head fell. The saints give aid ; it would be a sin to say otherwise ; but they aid only the honest who go in a right cause to do battle in God's name. So I think, gracious lady, that when it comes to a great war, though all other Germans were to help the Knights, we shall beat them to the earth, since our people are more numerous; and the Lord Jesus has put greater strength in our bones. And as to relics, have we not in the monastery of the Holy Cross the wood of the Holy Cross ?"

"True, as God is dear to me!" answered the princess. " But it will remain in the monastery, and they will take theirs to the field with them."

" It is all one! Nothing is far from God's power."

" Is that true? Will 3*011 tell how it is?" asked the princess, turning to the wise Mikolai.

"Every bishop will bear witness to this," answered he. " It is far to Rome, but the pope governs the world, — what must it be in the case of God! "

These words calmed the princess completely; so she turned the conversation to Tynets and its magnificence. In general the Mazovians were astonished, not only by the wealth of the cloister, but by the wealth and also the beauty of the whole country through which they were passing. Round about were large and wealthy villages; at the sides of these, gardens full of fruit trees, linden groves, with storks' nests on the lindens, and on the ground beehives with straw covers. Along the road on one side and the other extended grain fields of all sorts. At moments the wind bent a sea of wheat ears still partly green; among these, thick as stars in the sky, twinkled heads

of the blue-star thistle and the bright red poppy. Here and there, far beyond the fields, darkened a pine wood; here and there, bathed in sunlight, oak and alder groves rejoiced the eye; here and there were damp, grassy meadows, and wet places above which mews were circling; next were hills occupied by cottages, and then fields. Clearly, that country was inhabited by a numerous and industrious people enamoured of land; and as far as the eye saw, the region seemed to be not only flowing with milk and honey, but happy and peaceful.

" This is the royal management of Kazimir," said the princess ; " one would like to live here, and never die."

" The Lord Jesus smiles on this land," said Mikolai; " and the blessing of God is upon it. How could it be otherwise, since here, when they begin to ring bells, there is no corner to which the sound does not penetrate? It is known, indeed, that evil spirits, unable to endure this, must flee to the Hungarian boundary, into deep fir woods."

"Then it is a wonder to me," said Pani Ofka, "that Valger the Charming, of whom the monks have been telling us, can appear in Tynets, for they ring the bells there seven times daily."

This remark troubled Mikolai for a moment, and he answered only after some meditation, —

"First, the decisions of God are inscrutable ; and second, consider for yourselves that Valger receives a special permission each time."

" Be that as it may, I am glad that we shall not pass a night in the cloister. I should die of terror if such a hellish giant appeared to me."

" Ei ! that is not known, for they say that he is wonderfully charming."

" Though he were the most beautiful, I would not have a kiss from one whose mouth is breathing sulphur."

" Ah, even when devils are mentioned, kissing is in your head."

At these words the princess, and with her Pan Mikolai and the two nobles from Bogdanets, fell to laughing. Dauusia, following the example of others, laughed without knowing why; for this reason Ofka turned an angry face to Mikolai, and said, —

" 1 would prefer him to you."

"Ei! do not call the wolf from the forest," answered the Mazovian, joyfully, " for a hellish fury drags along the road frequently between Cracow and Tynets; and especially toward evening he may hear you, and appear the next moment in the form of the giant."

" The charm on a dog! " answered Ofka.

But at that moment Matsko, who, sitting on his lofty stallion, could see farther than those in the carriage, reined in his steed, and said, —

" Oh, as God is dear to me! What is that? "

"What?"

" Some giant is rising from behind the hill before us."

" The word has become flesh! " cried the princess. " Do not say anything!"

But Zbyshko rose in his stirrups, and said: " As I am alive, the giant Valger, no one else! "

From terror the driver stopped the horses, and, without letting the reins out of his hands, fell to making the sign of the cross; for now he too saw from his seat the gigantic figure of a horseman on the opposite eminence.

The princess stood up, but sat down immediately with a face changed by fear. Danusia hid her head in the folds of the princess's robe. The courtiers, the damsels, and the choristers, who rode behind, when they heard the ominous name, began to gather closely around the carriage. The men feigned laughter yet, but alarm was in their eyes; the damsels grew pale; but Mikolai, who had eaten bread from more than one oven, preserved a calm countenance; and, wishing to pacify the princess, he said, —

" Fear not, gracious lady. The sun has not set, and even were it night Saint Ptolomeus could hold his own against Valger."

Meanwhile the unknown horseman, having ascended the prolonged summit of the hill, reined in his horse and stood motionless. He was perfectly visible in the rays of the setting sun, and really his form seemed to exceed the usual dimensions of men. The distance between him and the princess's retinue was not more than three hundred yards.

" Why has he stopped? " asked one of the choristers.

"Because we too have stopped," answered Matsko.

" He is looking toward us, as if to take his choice," remarked the second chorister. " If I knew that he was a man, and not the evil one, I would go and strike him on the head with my lute."

The women, now thoroughly terrified, began to pray aloud, but Zbyshko, wishing to exhibit his courage before the princess and Danusia, said, —

" I will go anyhow. What is Valger to me? "

At this Danusia began to call, half in tears: " Zbyshko! Zbyshko!" but he had ridden forward and was advancing more quickly, confident that, even should he find the real Valger, he would pierce him with his lance.

" He seems a giant," said Matsko, who had a quick eye, "because he stands on the hilltop. He is large indeed, but an ordinary man —nothing more. I will go, and not let a quarrel spring up between him and Zbyshko."

Zbyshko, advancing at a trot, was thinking whether to lower his lance at once, or only see, when near by, how that man on the eminence looked. He decided to see first, and soon convinced himself that that thought was better, for as he approached the unknown lost his uncommon proportions. The man rode a gigantic steed, larger than Zbyshko's stallion, and was immense himself, but he did not surpass human measure. Besides, he was without armor; he wore a velvet, bell-shaped cap and a white linen mantle, which kept away dust; from under the mantle peeped forth green apparel. Standing on the hilltop the knight's head was raised and he was praying. Evidently he had halted to finish his evening prayer.

'' Ei, what kind of a Valger is he ? '' thought the young man.

He had ridden up so near that he could reach the unknown with a lance. The stranger, seeing before him a splendidly armed knight, smiled kindly, and said, —

"Praised be Jesus Christ."

"For the ages of ages."

" Is not that the court of the Princess of Mazovia down there?"

" It is."

" Then ye are coming from Tynets ? "

But there was no answer to that question, for Zbyshko was so astonished that he did not even hear it. He stood for a moment as if turned to stone, not believing his own eyes. About twenty-five rods beyond the unknown man he saw between ten and twenty mounted warriors, at the head of whom, but considerably in advance, rode a knight in complete shining armor and a white mantle, on which was a black cross ; on his head was a steel helmet with a splendid peacock-plume on the crest of it.

" A Knight of the Cross! " muttered Zbyshko.

And he thought that his prayer had been heard; that

God in His mercy had sent him such a German as he had prayed for in Tynets; that he ought to take advantage of God's favor. Hence, without hesitating an instant, before all this had flashed through his head, before he had time to recover from his astonishment, he bent in the saddle, lowered his lance half the distance to his horse's ear, and giving his family watchword " Hail! hail! " rushed against the Knight of the Cross as fast as his horse could spring.

The knight was astonished also; he reined in his steed and without lowering the lance which was standing in his stirrup, looked forward, uncertain whether the attack was on him.

" Lower your lance! " shouted Zbyshko, striking the iron points of his stirrups into the flanks of his stallion. " Hail! hail! "

The distance between them was decreasing. The Knight, seeing that the attack was really against him, reined in his steed, presented his weapon, and Zbysbko's lance was just about to strike his breast when that instant some mighty hand broke it right near the part which Zbyshko held, as if it had been a dried reed; then that same hand pulled back the reins of the young man's stallion with such force that the beast buried his forefeet in the earth and stood as if fixed there.

" Madman, what art thou doing? " called a deep, threatening voice. " Thou art attacking an envoy, insulting the king! "

Zbyshko looked and recognized that same gigantic man who, mistaken for Valger, had frightened a while before Princess Anna's court ladies.

" Let me go against the German! Who art thou? " cried he, grasping at the handle of his axe.

" Away with the axe! —by the dear God! Away with the axe, I say, or I will whirl thee from the horse! " cried the unknown, still more threateningly. " Thou hast insulted the majesty of the king, thou wilt be tried."

Then he turned to the people who were following the knight and shouted, —

lk Come hither! "

Meanwhile Matsko had ridden up with an alarmed and ominous face. He understood clearly that Zbyshko had acted like a madman, and that deadly results might come of the affair; still, he was ready for battle. The entire retinue of the unknown knight and of the Knight of the Cross were barely tifteeu persons, armed some with darts and some with

crossbows. Two men in complete armor might meet them, and not without hope of victory. Matsko thought, therefore, that if judgment were awaiting them in the sequel it might be better to avoid it, break through those people, and hide somewhere till the storm had passed. So his face contracted at once, like the snout of a wolf which is ready to bite, and thrusting his horse in between Zbyshko and the unknown, he inquired, grasping his sword at the same time, —

" Who are you? Whence is your right?"

"My right is from this," answered the unknown, "that the king has commanded me to guard the peace of the region about here; people call me Povala of Tachev."

At these words Matsko and Zbyshko looked at the knight, sheathed their weapons, already half drawn, and dropped their heads. It was not that fear flew around them, but they inclined their foreheads before a loudly mentioned and widely known name; for Povala of Tachev was a noble of renowned stock and a wealthy lord, possessing many lands around Radorn; he was also one of the most famous knights of the kingdom. Choristers celebrated him in songs, as a pattern of honor and bravery, exalting his name equally with that of Zavisha of Garbov, and Farurey, and Skarbek of Gora, and Dobko of Olesnitsa, and Yasko Nanshan, and Mikolai of Moskorzov, and Zyndram of Mashkovitse. At that moment he represented the person of the king ; hence for a man to attack him was the same as to put his head under the axe of an executioner.

So Matsko, when he had recovered, said, in a voice full of respect, —

" Honor and obeisance to you, O lord, to your glory and bravery."

"Obeisance to you also, O lord, though I should prefer not to make acquaintance with you on such an unpleasant occasion," replied Povala.

" How is that? " inquired Matsko.

But Povala turned to Zbyshko: " What is the best that thou hast done, young lad? On the public highway thou hast attacked an envoy near the king! Kuowest thou what awaits thee for that?"

" He attacked an ei^voy because he is young and foolish; for that reason it is easier for him to act than consider," said Matsko. "But judge him not severely, for I will tell the whole story."

"It is not I who will judge him. My part is merely to put bonds on him."

" How is that? " asked Matsko casting a gloomy glance at the whole assembly of people.

" According to the king's command."

At these words silence came on them.

" He is a noble," said Matsko at length.

"Then let him swear on his knightly honor that he will appear before any court."

I will swear on my honor! " cried Zbyshko.

" That is well. What is thy name ? "

Matsko mentioned his name and escutcheon.

"If of the court of the princess, pray her to intercede for thee before the king."

"We are not of the court. We are journeying from Lithuania, from Prince Vitold. Would to God that we had not met any court! From the meeting misfortune has come to this youth."

Here Matsko began to relate what had happened in the inn; hence he spoke of the meeting with the court of the princess, and Zbyshko's vow, but at last he was seized by sudden anger against Zbyshko, through whose thoughtlessness they had fallen into such a grievous position, and turning to him he cried, —

" Would to God that thou hadst fallen at Vilno! What wert thou thinking of, young wild boar?"

u Oh," said Zbyshko, "after the vow, I prayed to the Lord Jesus to grant me Germans, and I promised Him gifts; so when I saw peacock-plumes, and under them a mantle with a black cross, straightway some voice in me cried: ' Strike the German, for this is a miracle!' Well, I rushed forward — who would not have rushed forward?"

" Hear me," interrupted Povala, " I do not wish you evil, for I see clearly that this youth has offended more through giddiness peculiar to his age than through malice. I should be glad to take no note of his act, and go on as if nothing had happened. But I can do so only in case this comtur should promise not to complain to the king. Pray him on that point; mayhap he will take compassion on the youth."

" I should rather go to judgment than bow before a Knight of the Cross; it does not become my honor as a noble."

Povala looked at him severely and said: "Thou art acting ill. Thy ciders know better than thou what is proper, and.

what is not proper, for the honor of a knight. People have heard of me also, and I will say this to thee, that had I done a deed like thine I should not be ashamed to beg forgiveness for it."

Zbyshko blushed, but casting his eyes around, he said: " The ground is even here, if it were a little trampled. Rather than pray the German, I should prefer to meet him on horseback or on foot to the death, or to slavery."

" Thou art stupid ! " said Matsko. " How couldst thou do battle with an envoy ? It is not for thee to do battle with him, or him with thee, a beardless youth."

" Forgive, noble lord," said he, turning to Povala. " The boy has become insolent because of the war. Better not let him talk to the German, for he would offend him a second time. I will beg, and if after his mission is ended that comtur wishes to fight in an inclosure, man against man, I will meet him."

" He is a knight of great family, who will not meet everyone," answered Povala.

"Is he ? But do I not wear a belt and spurs ? A prince might meet me."

"That is true, but speak not to him of battle unless he mentions it himself; I fear lest he might grow malignant against you. Well, may God aid you! "

" I will go to take thy trouble on myself," said Matsko to his nephew, " but wait here."

Then he approached the Knight of the Cross, who, having halted some yards distant, was sitting motionless on his horse, which was as large as a camel. The man himself looked like a cast-iron statue, and listened with supreme indifference to the above conversation. Matsko, during long years of war, had learned German; so now he began to explain to the comtur in that language what had happened. He laid blame on the youth and impulsive character of the young man to whom it had seemed that God himself had sent a knight with a peacock-plume, and finally began to beg forgiveness for Zbyshko.

But the comtur's face did not quiver. Stiff and erect, with raised head, he looked with his steel eyes at the speaking Matsko with as much indifference and at the same time with as much unconcern as if he were not looking at the knight or even at a man, but at a stake or a fence. Matsko noted this, and though his words did not cease to be polite, the soul in him began evidently to storm; he spoke with

increasing constraint, and on his sunburnt cheeks a flush appeared. It was evident that in presence of that cool insolence he struggled not to grit his teeth and burst out in awful anger.

Povala saw this, and, having a good heart, resolved to give aid. He too, during the years of his youth, had sought various knightly adventures at the Hungarian, Austrian, Burgundian, and Bohemian courts, — adventures which made his name widely famous; he had learned German, so now he spoke to Matsko in that language, in a voice conciliatory and purposely facetious, —

" You see, gentlemen, that the noble comtur considers the whole affair as not worth one word. Not only in our kingdom, but everywhere, striplings are without perfect reason; such a knight as he will not war against children, either with the sword or the law."

Lichtenstein, in answer, pouted with his yellow moustaches, and without saying a word urged his horse forward, passing Matsko and Zbyshko; but wild anger began to raise the hair under their helmets, and their hands quivered toward their swords.

1 ' Wait, son of the Order! " said the elder master of Bog-danets through his set teeth, " I make the vow now, and will find thee when thou hast ceased to be an envoy."

" That will come later," said Povala, whose heart had begun also to be filled with blood. " Let the princess speak for you now, otherwise woe to the young man."

Then he rode after Lichtenstein, stopped him, and for some time they conversed with animation. Matsko and Zbyshko noticed that the German did not look on Povala with such a haughty face as on them, and this brought them to still greater anger. After a time Povala turned toward the two men, and waiting a while till the Knight of the Cross had gone forward, he said, —

" have spoken on your behalf, but that is an unrelenting man. He says that he will refrain from making complaint only in case you do what he wishes."

" What does he wish ? "

"'I will stop to greet the princess of Mazovia,' said he; ' let them ride up to where we are, come down from their horses, take off their helmets, and on the ground, with bare heads, beg of me.'" Here Povala looked quickly at Zbyshko, and added: " This is difficult for men of noble birth— I understand, but I must forewarn thee that if thou wilt not do this it is unknown what awaits thee, perhaps the sword of the executioner."

The faces of Matsko and Zbyshko became as of stone. Silence followed a second time.

" Well, and what?" asked Povala.

" Only this," answered Zbyshko, calmly, and with such dignity as if in one moment twenty years had been added to his age: "The power of God is above people."

" What does that mean?"

"This, that even had I two heads, and were the executioner to cut off both, I have one honor, which I am not free to disgrace."

At this Povala grew serious, and turning to Matsko inquired, —

"What do you say?"

" I say," answered Matsko, gloomily, " that I have reared this lad from infancy; besides, our whole family is in him, for I am old; but he cannot do that, even if he had to die."

Here his stern face quivered, and all at once love for his nephew burst forth in him with such strength that he seized the youth in his iron inclosed arms and cried, —

"Zbyshko! Zbyshko!"

The young knight was astonished, and said, yielding to the embrace of his uncle, —

" Oh, I did not think that you loved me so!"

" I see that you are true knights," said Povala, with emotion, " and since the young man has sworn on his honor to appear, I will not bind him; such people as you may be trusted. Be of good cheer. The German will stay a day in Tynets ; so I shall see the king first, and will so explain the affair as to offend him least. It is fortunate that I was able to break the lance — very fortunate! "

" If I must give my head," said Zbyshko, " I ought at least to have had the pleasure of breaking the bones of that German."

" Thou wishest to defend thy honor, but this thou dost not understand, that thou wouldst have disgraced our whole nation," answered Povala, impatiently.

" I understand that, and therefore I am sorry."

"Do you know," continued Povala, turning to Matsko, "that if this stripling escapes in any way you will have to hood him as falcons are hooded; otherwise he will not die his own death."

" He might escape if you gentlemen would conceal from the king what has happened."

" But what shall we do with the German? I cannot tie his tongue in a knot, of course."

"True! true!"

Thus speaking they advanced toward the retinue of the princess. Povala's attendants, who before mixed with Liechtenstein's people, now rode behind them. From afar were visible among Mazovian caps the waving peacock-plumes of the Knight of the Cross, and his bright helmet gleaming in the sun.

" The Knights of the Cross have a wonderful nature," said Povala of Tachev, as if roused from meditation. "When a Knight of the Cross is in trouble he is as reasonable as a Franciscan, as mild as a lamb, and as sweet as honey, so that a better man thou wilt not find in the world; but let him once feel strength behind him, none is more swollen with pride, with none wilt thou find less mercy. It is evident that the Lord Jesus gave them flint instead of hearts. I have observed very many nations, and more than once have I seen a true knight spare the weaker, saying to himself, ' My honor will not be increased if I trample on the prostrate.' But just when the weaker is down the Knight of the Cross is most unbending. Hold him by the head and he will not be proud; if thou act otherwise woe to thee. Take this envoy; he required right away, not merely your prayer for pardon, but your disgrace. I am glad that that will not happen."

" There is no waiting for it! " called out Zbyshko.

After these words they rode up to the retinue and joined the court of the princess.

The envoy of the Knights of the Cross, when he saw them, assumed immediately an expression of pride and contempt. But they feigned not to see him. Zbyshko halted at Danu-sia's side and told her joyfully that Cracow was clearly visible from the hill. Matsico began to tell a chorister of the uncommon strength of Povala, the lord of Tachev, who broke a spear in Zbj'shko's hand as if it had been a dry reed.

But why did he break it? " asked the chorister.

"Because the young man had levelled it at the German, but only in jest."

The chorister, who was a noble and a man of experience, did uot think such a jest very becoming, but seeing that

Matsko spoke of it lightly he did not look on the matter with seriousness. Meanwhile such bearing began to annoy the German. He looked once and a second time at Zbyshko, then at Matsko; at last he understood that they would not dismount, and paid no attention to him purposely. Then something, as it were steel, glittered in his eyes, and straightway he took leave. At the moment when he started Povala could not restrain himself, and said to him at parting, —

" Advance without fear, brave knight. This country is in peace and no one will attack you, unless some boy in a jest."

"Though manners are strange in this country, I have sought not your protection, but your society," answered Lichtenstein; " indeed I think that we shall meet again, both at this court and elsewhere."

In the last words sounded a hidden threat; therefore Povala answered seriously, —

" God grant." Then he inclined and turned away; afterward he shrugged his shoulders and said in an undertone, but still loud enough to be heard by those nearest him, —

" Dry bones! I could sweep thee from the saddle with the point of my lance, and hold thee in the air during three ' Our Fathers.' ' :

Then he began to converse with the princess, whom he knew well. Anna Danuta asked what he was doing on the highway, and he informed her that he was riding at command of the king to maintain order in the neighborhood, where, because of the great number of guests coming from all parts to Cracow, a dispute might arise very easily. And as a proof he related that of which he had been himself a witness a little while earlier. Thinking, however, that there would be time enough to beg the intercession of the princess for Zbyshko when the need came, he did not attach too much significance to the event, not wishing to interrupt gladsome-ness. In fact, the princess even laughed at Zbyshko for his haste to get peacock-plumes. Others, learning of the broken lance, admired the lord of Tachev because he had broken it so easily with one hand.

Povala, being a little boastful, was pleased in his heart that they were glorifying him, and at last began to tell of the deeds which had made him famous, especially in Burgundy at the court of Philip the Bold. Once in time of a tournament, after he had broken the spear of a knight of the Ardennes, he caught him by the waist, drew him from his saddle and hurled him up a spear's length in the air, though the

man of Ardennes was clad from head to foot in iron armor. Philip the Bold presented him with a gold chain for the deed, and the princess gave him a velvet slipper, which he wore on his helmet thenceforward.

On hearing this narrative all were greatly astonished, except Pan Mikolai, who said, —

" There are no such men in these effeminate days as during my youth, or men like those of whom my father told me. If a noble at present succeeds in tearing open a breastplate, or stretching a crossbow without a crank, or twisting an iron cutlass between sticks he is called a man of might and exalts himself above others. But formerly young girls used to do those things."

"I will not deny that formerly people were stronger," answered Povala, " but even to-day strong men may be found. The Lord Jesus was not sparing of strength in my bones, still I will not say that I am the strongest in the kingdom. Have you ever seen Zavisha of Garbov? He could overcome me."

"I have seen him. He has shoulders as broad as«the bell of Cracow."

And Dobko of Olesnitsa? Once he was at a tournament which the Knights of the Cross held in Torun ; he stretched out twelve knights with great glory to himself and our nation."

"But our Mazovian, Stashko Tsolek was stronger than you, or Zavisha, or Dobko. It was said that he took a green stick in his hand and squeezed sap from it." will squeeze sap from one too ! " exclaimed Zbyshko.

And before any one could ask him for a trial, he sprang to the roadside, broke off a good twig from a tree, and there, before the eyes of the princess and Danusia, he pressed it near one end with such force that the sap began really to fall in drops on the road.

" Ei! " cried Pani Of ka at sight of this, " do not go to war; it would be a pity for such a man to die before marriage."

It would be a pity," repeated Matsko, growing gloomy on a sudden.

But Pan Mikolai began to laugh, and the princess joined him. Others, however, praised Zbyshko's strength aloud, and since in those times an iron hand was esteemed above all other qualities, the damsels cried to Danusia: 44 Be glad!" And she was glad, though she did not understand well what she could gain from that morsel of squeezed wood. Zbyshko,

THE KNIGHTS OF THE CROSS. 51

forgetting the Knight of the Cross altogether, had such a lofty look that Mikolai, wishing to bring him to moderation, said, —

" It is useless to plume thyself with strength, for there are stronger than thou. I have not seen what thou hast done, but my father was witness of something better which happened at the court of Carolus, the Roman Emperor. King Kazimir went on a visit to him with many courtiers, among whom was this Stashko Tsolek, famous for strength and son of the voevoda Andrei. The emperor boasted that among his men he had a certain Cheh who could grasp a bear around the body and smother him immediately. Then they had a spectacle and the Cheh smothered two bears, one after the other. Our king was greatly mortified, and not to go away shamefaced he said : ' But my Tsolek will not let himself be put to shame.' They appointed a wrestling match to come three days later. Knights and ladies assembled, and after three days the Cheh grappled with Tsolek in the courtyard of the castle; but the struggle did not last long, for barely had they embraced when Tsolek broke the Cheh's back, crushed in all his ribs and only let him out of his arms when dead, to the great glory of our king. Tsolek, surnamed Bonebreaker from that day, once carried up into a tower a great bell which twenty townspeople could not stir from the earth."

" But how many years old was he? " inquired Zbyshko.

" He was young."

Meanwhile Povala, riding at the right near the princess, bent at last toward her ear and told her the whole truth concerning the seriousness of what had happened, and at the same time begged her to support him, for he would take the part of Zbyshko, who might have to answer grievously for his act. The princess, whom Zbyshko pleased, received the intelligence with sadness, and was greatly alarmed.

" The bishop of Cracow has a liking for me," said Povala. " I can iinplore him, anJ the queen too, for the more intercessors there are, the better for the young man."

" Should the queen take his part a hair will not fall from his head," said Anna Dauuta ; " the king honors her greatly for her saintliness and her dower, especially now when the reproach of sterility is taken from her. But in Cracow is also the beloved sister of the king, Princess Alexandra; go to her. I too will do what I can, but she is his sister while I am a cousin."

" The king loves you also, gracious lady."

" Ei, not as her," replied the princess, with a certain sadness; " for me one link of a chain, for her a whole chain; for me a fox skin, for her a sable. The king loves none of his relatives as he does Alexandra. There is no day when she goes away empty-handed."

Tims conversing they approached Cracow. The road, crowded beginning with Tynets, was still more crowded. They met landholders going to the city at the head of their men; some were in armor, others in summer garments and straw hats; some on horseback, others in wagons with their wives and daughters, who wished to see the long promised tournaments. In places the entire road was crowded with the wagons of merchants, who were not permitted to pass Cracow, and thus deprive the city of numerous toll dues. In those wagons were carried salt, wax, wheat, fish, oxhides, hemp, wood. Others leaving the city were laden with cloth, kegs of beer, and the most various merchandise of the city. Cracow was now quite visible; the gardens of the king, of lords and of townspeople surrounded the city on all sides; beyond them were the walls and the church towers. The nearer they came, the greater the movement, and at the gates it was difficult to pass amid the universal activity.

" This is the city! there is not in the world another such," said Matsko.

"It is always like a fair," said one of the choristers. " Is it long since you were here? "

" Long. And I wonder at Cracow as if I were looking at it for the first time, as we come now from wild countries.""They say that Cracow has grown immensely through King Yagello."

That is true. From the time that the Grand Prince of Lithuania ascended the throne, the vast regions of Lithuania and Rus have become open to the traffic of Cracow; because of this the city has increased day by day in population, in wealth, and in buildings; it has become one of the most important in the world."

"ki jhe cies of the Knights of the Cross are respectable too," said the weighty chorister again.

"If we could only get at them!" said Matsko. "There would be a respectable booty ! "

But Povala was thinking of something else, namely, that young Zbyshko, who had offended only through stupid impulsiveness, was going into the jaws of the wolf as it were.

The lord of Tachev, stern and stubborn in time of war, had a real dovelike heart in his mighty breast; since he knew better than others what was waiting for the offender, pity for the youth seized the knight.

" I am meditating and meditating," said he to the princess, " whether to tell the king what has happened, or not tell him. If the German knight does not complain, there will be no case, but it he is to complain it would be better to tell earlier, so that our lord should not flame up in sudden anger."

" If the Knight of the Cross can ruin any man, he will ruin him," said the princess. " But I first of all will tell the young man to join our court. Perhaps the king will not punish a courtier of ours so severely."

Then she called Zbyshko, who, learning what the question was, sprang from his horse, seized her feet, and with the utmost delight agreed to be her attendant, not only because of greater safety, but because he could in that way remain near Danusia.

" Where are you to lodge ? " asked Povala of Matsko.

" In an inn."

" There is no room in the inns this long time."

"Then I will go to a merchant, an acquaintance, Amyley. Perhaps he will shelter us for the night."

" But I say to you, come as guests to me. Your nephew might lodge in the castle with the courtiers of the princess, but it will be better for him not to be under the hand of the king. What the king would do in his first anger, he would not do in his second. It is certain also that you will divide your property, wagons, and servants, and to do that, time is needed. With me, as it is known to you, you will be safe and comfortable."

Matsko, though troubled a little that Povala was thinking so much of their safety, thanked him with gratitude, and they entered the city. But there he and Zbyshko forgot again for a time their troubles at sight of the wonders surrounding them. In Lithuania and on the boundary they had seen only single castles, and of more considerable towns only Vilno. — badly built, and burnt, all in ashes and ruins. In Cracow the stone houses of merchants were often more splendid than the castle of the Grand Prince in Lithuania. Many houses were of wood, it is true, but many of those astonished the beholder by the loftiness of the walls and the roofs, with windows of glass, the panes fitted into lead sashes, panes which so reflected the rays of the setting sun

54 THE KNIGHTS OF THE CROSS.

that one might suppose the house burning. But along streets near the market were large houses of red brick, or entirely of stone, lofty, ornamented with plates and the cross charm on the walls. They stood one at the side of the other, like soldiers in line, some wide, others narrow, as narrow as nine ells, but erect, with arched ceiling — often with the picture of the Passion, or with the image of the Most Holy Virgin over the gate. On some streets were two rows of houses, above them a strip of sky, below a street entirely paved with stones, and on both sides as far as the eye could see, shops and shops, rich, full of the most excellent, ofttimes wonderful or wholly unknown goods, on which Matsko, accustomed to continual war and taking of booty, looked with an eye somewhat greedy. But the public buildings brought both to still greater astonishment; the church of the Virgin Mary in the square, then other churches, the cloth market, the city hall with an enormous " cellar " in which they sold Schweidnitz beer, cloth shops, the immense mercatorium intended for foreign merchants, also a building in which the city weights were kept, barber-shops, baths, places for smelting copper, wax, gold, and silver, breweries, whole mountains of kegs around the so-called Schrotamt, — in a word, plenty and wealth, which a man unacquainted with the city, even though the wealthy owner of a " town," could not imagine to himself.

Povala conducted Matsko and Zbyshko to his house on Saint Ann Street, commanded to give them a spacious room, intrusted them to attendants, and went himself to the castle; from which he returned for supper rather late in the evening with a number of his friends. They used meat and wine in abundance and supped joyously; but the host himself was somehow anxious, and when at last the guests went away he said to Matsko, —

"I have spoken to a canon skilled in writing and in /aw; he tells me that insult to an envoy is a capital offence. Pray to God, therefore, that Lichtenstein make no complaint."

When they heard this both knights, though at supper they had in some degree passed the measure, went to rest with hearts that were not so joyous. Matsko could not sleep, and some time after they had lain down he called to his nephew, —

"Zbyshko!"

"But what?"

THE KNIGHTS OF THE CROSS. 55

" "Well, taking everything into account, I think that they will cut off thy head."

" Do you think so ? " asked Zbyshko, with a drowsy voice. And turning to the wall he fell asleep sweetly, for he was wearied by the road.

Next day the two owners of Bogdanets together with Povala went to early mass in the Cathedral, through piety and to see the guests who had assembled at the castle. Indeed Povala had met a multitude of acquaintances on the road, and among them many knights famous at home and abroad; on these young Zbyshko looked with admiration, promising himself in spirit that if the affair with Lichtenstein should leave him unharmed, he would strive to equal them in bravery and every virtue. One of those knights, Topor-chyk, a relative of the castellan of Cracow told him about the return from Rome of Voitseh Yastrernbets, a scholastic, who had gone with a letter from the king to Pope Boniface IX., inviting him to Cracow. Boniface accepted the invitation, and though he expressed doubt as to whether he could come in person, he empowered his ambassador to hold in his name the infant at the font, and begged at the same time, as a proof of his love for both kingdoms, to name the child Bonifacius or Bonifacia.

They spoke also of the approaching arrival of Sigismond of Hungary, and expected it surely; for Sigismond, whether invited or not, went always to places where there was a chance of feasts, visits, and tournaments, in which he took part with delight, desiring to be renowned universally as a ruler, a singer, and one of the first of knights. Povala, Zavisha of Garbov, Dobko of Olesnitsa, Nashan, and other men of similar measure remembered with a smile how, during former visits of Sigismond, King Vladislav had begged them in secret not to push too hard in the tournament, and to spare the "Hungarian guest," whose vanity, known throughout the world, was so great that in case of failure it brought tears from his eyes. But the greatest attention among the knighthood was roused by the affair of Vitold. Wonders were related of the splendor of that cradle of pure silver, which princes and boyars of Lithuania had brought from Vitold and his wife Anna. Before divine service groups of people were formed as is usual; these related news to each other. In one of those groups Matsko, when he heard of the cradle, described the richness of the gift, but still more Vitold's intended immense expedition against the Tar-

tars; he was covered with questions about it. The expedition was nearly ready, for great armies had moved to Eastern Rus, and in case of success it would extend the supremacy of King Yagello over almost half the earth, to the unknown depths of Asia, — to the boundaries of Persia, and the banks of the Aral. Matsko, who formerly had been near the person of Vitold, and who was able to know his plans therefore, knew how to tell them in detail, and even so eloquently that before the bell had sounded for mass a crowd of the curious had formed around him in front of the cathedral. " It was a question,"he said, "of an expedition in favor of the Cross. Vitold himself, though called Grand Prince, rules Lithuania by appointment of Yagello, and is merely viceroy. His merit, therefore, will fall on the king. And what glory for newly baptized Lithuania, and for Polish power, if their united armies shall carry the Cross to regions in which if the name of the Saviour has ever been mentioned, it was only to be blasphemed, regions in which the foot of a Pole or Lithuanian has never stood up to this time! The expelled Tohtamysh, if Polish and Lithuanian troops seat him again on the last Kipchak throne, will call himself ' son' of King Vladislav and, as he has promised, will bow down to the Cross together with the whole Golden Horde."

They listened to these words with attention, but many did not know well what the question was, — whom was Vitold to assist? against whom was he to war? Hence some said:

" Tell us clearly, with whom is the war?"

" With Timur the Lame," answered Matsko.

A moment of silence followed. The ears of Western knighthood had been struck more than once, it is true, by the names of the Golden, Blue, and Azoff Hordes, as well as various others, but Tartar questions and domestic wars between individual Hordes were not clearly known to them. On the other hand, one could not find a single man in Europe of that day who had not heard of the awful Timur the Lame, or Tamerlane, whose name was repeated with not less dread than the name of Attila aforetime. Was he not "lord of the world" and "lord of times," ruler of twenty-seven conquered kingdoms, ruler of Muscovite Rus, ruler of Siberia, China to India, Bagdad, Ispahan, Aleppo, Damascus,—a man whose shadow fell across the sands of Arabia onto Egypt, and across the Bosphorus onto the Byzantine Empire, destroyer of the human race, monstrous builder of pyramids made of human skulls, victor

in all battles, defeated in none, " master of souls and bodies " ?

Tohtamysh had been seated by Tamerlane on the throne of the Blue and the Golden Hordes, and recognized as " son." But when Tohtamysh's lordship extended from the Aral to the Crimea, over more lands than there were in all remaining Europe, the " son '" wished to be independent ; therefore, deprived of his throne by " one finger " of the terrible father, he fled to the Lithuanian prince imploring aid. It was this man precisely whom Vitold intended to conduct back to his kingdom, but to do so he would have first to measure strength with the world-ruling Limper. For this reason his name produced a powerful impression on the listeners, and after a time of silence one of the oldest knights, Kazko of Yaglov, said, —

" It is not a dispute with some trifling man."

" But it is about some trifling thing," said Pan Mikolai, prudently. " What profit to us if far off there beyond the tenth land a Tohtamysh, instead of a Kutluk, rules the sons of Belial?"

" Tohtamysh would receive the Christian faith," answered Matsko.

"He would receive it, but he has not received it. Is it possible to believe dog brothers, who do not confess Christ?"

" But it is a worthy deed to lay down one's life for the name of Christ," replied Povala.

"And for the honor of knighthood," added Toporchykj " among us are men who will go. Pan Spytko of Melshtyn has a young and beloved wife, but he has gone to Prince Vitold for the expedition."

" And no wonder," put in Yasko Nashan ; " though a man had the foulest sin on his soul, he would receive sure forgiveness for his part in such a war, and certain salvation."

" And glory for the ages of ages," said Povala. " If there is to be a war, let it be a war, and that it is not with some common person is all the better. Timur conquered the world and has twenty-seven kingdoms under him. What a glory for our people to rub him out."

" Why should we not ? " answered Toporchyk, " even if he possessed a hundred kingdoms, let others fear him, not we! Ye speak worthily ! Only call together ten thousand good lancers — we will ride through the world."

So spoke the knights, and Zbyshko wondered why the desire had not come to him earlier of going into the wild steppes with Vitold. During his stay in Vilno he had wished to see Cracow, the court, take part in knightly tournaments, but now he thought that here he might find condemnation and infamy, while there, at the worst, he would find a death full of glory. But Kazko of Yaglov, a hundred years old, whose neck was trembling from age, and who had a mind answering to his age, cast cold water on the willingness of the knighthood.

"Ye are foolish," said he. "Has no one of you heard that the image of Christ has spoken to the queen ? And if the Saviour himself admits her to such confidence, why should the Holy Ghost, the third person of the Trinity, be less gracious. For this reason she sees future things, as if they were happening in her presence, and she said this — "

Here he stopped, shook his head for a moment, and then continued, —

" I have forgotten what she did say, but I will recall it directly."

And he began to think; they waited with attention, for the opinion was universal that the queen saw future events.

" Aha! I have it! " said he at last " The queen said that if all the knighthood of this country should go with Prince Vitold against the Limper, pagan power might be crushed. But that cannot be, because of the dishonesty of Christians. It is necessary to guard our boundaries against Chehs, and Hungarians, and against the Knights of the Cross, for it is not possible to trust any one. And if only a handful of Poles go with Vitold, Tiinur will finish them, or his voevodas will, for they command countless legions."

"• But there is peace at present," said Toporchyk, " and the Order itself will give some aid, perhaps, to Vitold. The Knights of the Cross cannot act otherwise, even for .shame's sake ; they must show the holy father that they are ready to fight against pagans. People say at court that KUDO Lichtenstein is here not only for the christening, but also to counsel with the king."

" Ah. here he is! " exclaimed Matsko, with astonishment.

" True I " said Povala, looking around. " As God lives, it is he! He stayed a short time with the abbot; he must have left Tynets before daybreak."

"lie was in haste for some reason," said Matsko, gloomily.

Meanwhile Kuno Lichtensteiu passed near them. Matsko

recognized him by the cross embroidered on his mantle, but the envoy knew neither him nor Zbyshko, because the first time he had seen them they were in helmets, and in a helmet, even with raised vizor, it was possible to see only a small part of the face. While passing he nodded toward Povala and Toporchyk, then, with his attendants, he ascended the steps of the cathedral, with an important and majestic tread.

Just at that moment the bells sounded, announcing that mass would begin soon, and frightening a flock of daws and doves gathered in the towers. Matsko and Zbyshko, some-what disturbed by the quick return of Lichtenstein, entered the church with others. But the old man was now the more disturbed, for the king's court took all the young knight's attention. Never in his life had Zbyshko seen anything so imposing as that church and that assembly. On the right and on the left he was surrounded by the most famous men of the kingdom, renowned in counsel, or in war. Many of those whose wisdom had effected the marriage of the Grand Prince of Lithuania with the marvellous young Queen of Poland had died, but some were still living, and on them people looked with uncommon respect. The youthful knight could not gaze enough at the noble figure of Yasko of Tenchyn, the castellan of Cracow, in which severity and dignity were blended with uprightness; he admired the wise and dignified faces of other counsellors, and the strong visages of knights with hair cut straight above their brows and falling in long locks at the sides of their heads and behind. Some wore nets, others only ribbons holding the hair in order. Foreign guests, envoys of the King of Rome, Bohemians, Hungarians, Austrians, with their attendants, astonished with the great elegance of their dresses; the princes and boyars of Lithuania, standing near the side of the king, in spite of the summer and the burning days, for show's sake wore shubas lined with costly fur; the Russian princes, in stiff and broad garments, looked, on the background of the walls and the gilding of the church, like Byzantine pictures.

But Zbyshko waited with the greatest curiosity for the entrance of the king and queen, and forced his way up as much as possible toward the stalls, beyond which, near the altar, were two velvet cushions, — for the royal couple always heard mass on their knees. Indeed, people did not wait long; the king entered first, by the door of the sacristy,

and before he had come in front of the altar it was possible to observe him well. He had black hair, dishevelled and growing somewhat thin above his forehead; at the sides it was put back over his ears; his face was dark, entirely shaven, nose aquiline and rather pointed; around his mouth there were wrinkles; his eyes were black, small, and glittering. He looked on every side, as if he wished before reaching the front of the altar to make estimate of all people in the church. His countenance had a kindly expression, but also the watchful one of a man who, elevated by fortune beyond his own hopes, has to think continually whether his acts correspond to his office, and who fears malicious blame. But for this reason specially there was in his face and his movements a certain impatience. It was easy to divine that his anger must be sudden, and that he was always that same prince who, roused by the wiles of the Knights of the Cross, had cried to their envoys: "Thou strikest at me with a parchment, but I at thee with a dart! "

Now, however, a great and sincere piety restrained his native quick temper. Not only the newly converted princes of Lithuania, but also Polish magnates, pious from the example of grandfather and great-grandfather, were edified at sight of the king in the church. Often he put the cushion aside, and knelt, for greater mortification, on the bare stones; often he raised his hands, and held them raised till they fell of themselves from fatigue. He heard at least three masses daily, and heard them almost with eagerness. The exposure of the chalice and the sound of the bell at the Elevation always filled his soul with ecstasy, enthusiasm, and awe. At the end of mass he went forth from the church as if he had been roused from sleep, calmed and mild;

soon courtiers discovered that that was the best time to beg him for gifts or forgiveness.

Yadviga entered by the sacristy door. Knights nearest the stalls, when they saw her, though mass had not begun, knelt at once, yielding involuntary honor to her, as to a saint. Zbyshko did the same, for in all that congregation no one doubted that he had really before him a saint, whose image would in time adorn the altars of churches. More especially during recent years the severe penitential life of Yadviga had caused tin's, that besides the honor due a queen, they rendered her honor well-nigh religious. From mouth to mouth among lords and people passed reports of miracles wrought by her. It was said that the touch of her hand cured the sick; that people deprived of strength in their members recovered it by putting on old robes of the queen. Trustworthy witnesses affirmed that with their own ears they had heard Christ speaking to her from the altar. Foreign monarchs gave her honor on their knees ; even the insolent Knights of the Cross respected her, and feared to offend her. Pope Boniface IX. called her a saint and the chosen daughter of the Church. The world considered her acts, and remembered that that was a child of the house of Anjou and of the Polish Piasts; that she was a daughter of the powerful Ludvik ; that she was reared at the most brilliant of courts; that she was the most beautiful of maidens in the kingdom; that she had renounced happiness, renounced a maiden's first love, and married as queen the " wild" prince of Lithuania, so as to bend with him to the foot of the Cross the last pagan people in Europe. What the power of all the Germans, the power of the Knights of the Cross, their crusading expeditions, and a sea of blood had not effected, her single word had effected. Never had apostolic labor been joined with such devotion; never had woman's beauty been illuminated by such angelic goodness and such quiet sorrow.

Therefore minstrels in all the courts of Europe celebrated her; knights from the most remote lands came to Cracow to see that " Polish Queen ; " her own people, whose strength and glory she had increased by her alliance with Yagello, loved her as the sight of their eyes. Only one great grief had weighed upon her and the nation, — God through long years had refused posterity to this His chosen one.

But when at last that misfortune had passed, the news of the implored blessing spread like lightning from the Baltic to the Black Sea, to the Carpathians, and filled all people of the immense commonwealth with delight. It was received joyfully even at foreign courts, but not at the capital of the Knights of the Cross. In Rome they sang a "Te Deum." In Poland the final conviction was reached that whatever the " holy lady" might ask of God would be given beyond doubt.

So people came to implore her to ask health for them ; deputations came from provinces and districts, begging that in proportion as the need might be she would pray for rain, for good weather, for crops, for a favorable harvest, a good yield of honey, for abundance of fish in the lakes, and beasts in the forests. Terrible knights from border castles and towns, who, according to customs received from the Germans, toiled at robbery or war among themselves, at one reminder

from her sheathed their swords; freed prisoners without ransom ; returned stolen herds; and gave hands to one another in concord. Every misfortune, every poverty hurried to the gates of the castle of Cracow. Her pure spirit penetrated the hearts of men, softened the lot of subjects, the pride of lords, the harshness of judges, and soared like the light of happiness, like an angel of justice and peace above the whole country.

All were waiting then with beating hearts for the day of blessing.

The knights looked diligently at the form of the queen, so as to infer how long they would have to wait for the coming heir or heiress to the throne. Vysh, the bishop of Cracow, who was besides the most skilful physician in the country, and even celebrated abroad, did not predict yet a quick delivery. If they were making preparations, it was because it was the custom of the age to begin every solemnity at the earliest, and continue it whole weeks. In fact, the lady's form, though somewhat more pronounced, preserved so far its usual outlines. She wore robes that were even too simple. Reared in a brilliant court, and being the most beautiful of contemporary princesses, she had been enamoured of costly materials, — chains, pearls, gold bracelets and rings; but at this time, and even for some years, not only did she wear the robes of a nun, but she covered her face, lest the thought of her beauty might rouse worldly pride in her. In vain did

Yagello, when he learned of her changed condition, recom mend, in the ecstasy of his delight, to adorn the bedchamber with cloth of gold, brocade, and precious stones. She answered that, having renounced show long before, she remembered that the time of birth was often the time of death; and hence it was not amidst jewels, but with silent humility, that she ought to receive the favor with which God was visiting her.

The gold and precious stones went meanwhile to the Academy or to the work of sending newly baptized Lithuanian youths to foreign universities.

The queen agreed to change her religious appearance only in this, that from the time when the hope of motherhood had become perfect certainty she would not hide her face, considering justly that the dress of a penitent did not befit her from that moment forward.

And in fact all eyes rested now in love on that wonderful face, to which neither gold nor precious stones could add

ornament. The queen walked slowly from the sacristy to the altar with her eyes uplifted, in one hand a book, in the other a rosary. Zbyshko saw the lily-colored face, the blue eyes, the features simply angelic, full of peace, goodness, mercy, and his heart began to beat like a hammer. He knew that by command of God he ought to love his king and his queen, and he had loved them in his own way, but now his heart seethed up in him on a sudden with great love, which comes not of command, but which bursts forth of itself, like a flame, and is at once both the greatest honor and humility, and a wish for sacrifice. Zbyshko was young and impulsive ; hence a desire seized him to show that love and faithfulness of a subject knight, to do something for her, to fly somewhere, to slay some one, to capture something, and lay down his head at the same time. " I will go even with Prince Vitold," said he to himself, " for how else can I serve the saintly lady, if there is no war near at hand? " It did not even come to his head that he could serve otherwise than with a sword, or a javelin, or an axe, but to make up for that he was ready to go alone against the whole power of Timur the Lame. He wanted to mount his horse immediately after mass and begin — what? He himself did not know. He knew only that he could not restrain himself, that his hands were burning, that his whole soul within him was burning.

So again he forgot altogether the danger which was threatening him. He forgot even Dauusia for a while, and when she came to his mind because of the childlike singing which was heard all at once in the church, he had a feeling that that was "something else." To Danusia he had promised faithfulness, he had promised three Germans, and he would keep that promise; but the queen was above all women, and when he thought how many he would like to kill for the queen he saw in front of him whole legions of breastplates, helmets, ostrich and peacock plumes, and felt that according to his wish that was still too little.

Meanwhile he did not take his eyes from her, asking in his swollen heart, " With what prayer can I honor her? " for he judged that it was not possible to pray for the queen in common fashion. He knew how to say, " Pater noster, qui es in coelis, sanctificetur nomen Tuum," for a certain Franciscan in Vilno had taught him those words; perhaps the monk himself did not know more, perhaps Zbyshko had forgotten the rest; it is enough that he was unable to say the whole Pater uoster (Our Father), so he began to repeat in succes-

sion those few words which in his soul meant, " Give our beloved lady health, and life, and happiness — and think more of her than of all others." And since this was said by a man over whose head judgment and punishment were hang-incr, there was not in that whole church a more sincere prayer.

At the end of mass Zbyshko thought that if it were permitted him to stand before the queen, fall on his face and embrace her feet, then even let the end of the world come. But the first mass was followed by a second, and then a third; after that the lady went to her apartments, for usually she fasted till mid-day, and took no part in joyful breakfasts at which, for the amusement of the king and guests, jesters and jugglers appeared. But old Pan Mikolai came and summoned him to the princess.

"At the table thou wilt serve me and Danusia, as my attendant," said the princess ; " and may it be granted thee to please the king with some amusing word or act, by which thou wilt win his heart to thyself. If the German knight recognizes thee, perhaps he will not make a complaint, seeing that at the king's table thou art sen-ing me."

Zbyshko kissed the princess's hand, then turned to Danusia, and though he was more used to war and battles than to courtly customs, he _knew evidently what a knight ought to do on seeing the lady of his thoughts in the morning, for he stepped back and assuming an expression of surprise exclaimed, while making the sign of the cross, —

" In the name of the Father, Son, and Holy Ghost!"

" But why does Zbyshko make the sign of the cross?" inquired Danusia, raising her blue eyes to him.

"Because, lovely damsel, so much beauty has been added to thee that I wonder."

But Pan Mikolai, as an old man, did not like new foreign knightly customs, hence he shrugged his shoulders, and said, —

" Why wilt thou lose time for nothing and talk about her beauty? That is a chit which has hardly risen above the earth."

Zbyshko looked at him immediately with indignation.

"You are mad to call her that," said he, growing pale from anger. " Know this, that if your years were less I would command at once to trample earth behind the castle, and let my death or yours come! "

" Be quiet, stripling! I could manage thee even to-day! "

" Be quiet! " repeated the princess. " Instead of thinking of thy own head, thou art looking for other quarrels! I ought to have found a more sedate knight for Danusia. But I tell thee this, if thou hast a wish to quarrel move hence to whatever place may please thee, for here such men are not needed."

Zbyshko, put to shame by the words of the princess, began to beg her pardon, thinking, meanwhile, that if Pan Mikolai had a grown-up son he would challenge him to a combat sometime, on foot or on horseback, unless the word were forgiven. He determined, however, to deport himself like a dove in the king's chambers, and not to challenge any one unless knightly honor commanded it absolutely.

The sound of trumpets announced that the meal was ready; so Princess Anna, taking Danusia by the hand, withdrew to the king's apartments, before which lay dignitaries and knights stood awaiting her arrival. The Princess Alexandra had entered first, for as sister of the king she occupied a higher place at the table. Straightway the room was filled with foreign guests, invited local dignitaries, and knights. The king sat at the head of the table, having at his side the bishop of Cracow and Voitseh Yastrembets, who, though lower in dignity than mitred persons, sat as ambassador of the pope, at the right hand of the king. The two princesses occupied the succeeding places. Beyond Anna Danuta in a broad arm-chair, Yan, the former archbishop of Gnesen, had disposed himself comfortably. He was a prince descended from the Piasts of Silesia, a son of Bolko III., Prince of Opole. Zbyshko had heard of him at the court of Vitold, and now, standing behind the princess and Danusia, he recognized the man at once by his immensely abundant hair, twisted in rolls like a holy-water sprinkler. At the courts of Polish princes they called him Kropidlo, and even the Knights of the Cross gave him the name " Grapidla." 1 He was famed for joyfulness and frivolity. Having received the pallium for the archbishopric of Gnesen against the will of the king he wished to occupy it with armed hand; expelled from the office for this and exiled, he connected himself with the Knights of the Cross, who gave him the poor bishopric of Kamen. Understanding at last that it was better to be in accord with a powerful king, he implored Yagello's forgiveness, returned to the country, and was wait-

1 This is a German mispronunciation of Kropidlo, a sprinkler. Kropidlo is derived from kropic, to sprinkle. VOL. i. — 5

ing till a see should be vacant, hoping to receive it from the hands of his kindly lord. In fact he was not deceived; meanwhile he was endeavoring to win the king's heart with pleasant jests. But the former inclination towards the Knights of the Cross had remained with him, and even then, at the court of Yagello, though not looked upon too favorably by knights and dignitaries, he sought the society of Lichtenstein, and was glad to sit next him at table.

Zbyshko, standing behind Princess Anna's chair, found himself so near the Knight of the Cross that he could touch him with his hand. In fact his hands began to itch immediately and to move; but that was involuntary, for he restrained his impulsiveness, and did not permit himself any erratic thought. Still he could not refrain from casting occasional glances that were somewhat greedy at Lichtenstein's flax-colored head, which was growing bald behind, at his neck, his shoulders, and his arms, wishing to estimate at once whether he would have much work were he to meet him either in battle or in single combat. It seemed to him that he would not have overmuch, for, though the shoulder-blades of the knight were rather powerful in outline, under his closely fitting garment of thin gray cloth, he was still a skeleton in comparison with Povala, or Pashko Zlodye, or the two renowned Sulimchiks, or Kron of Koziglove, and many other knights sitting at the king's table.

On them indeed Zbyshko looked with admiration and envy, but his main attention was turned toward the king, who, casting glances on all sides, gathered in, from moment io moment, his hair behind his ears, as if made impatient by this, that the meal had not begun yet. His glance rested for the twinkle of an eye on Zbyshko also, and then the young knight experienced the feeling of a certain fear; and at the thought that surely he would have to stand before the angry face of the king a terrible alarm mastered him. At first he thought, it is true, of the responsibility and the punishment which might fall on him, for up to that moment all this had seemed to him distant, indefinite, hence not worthy of thought.

But the German did not divine that the knight who had attacked him insolently on the road was so near. The meal began. They brought in caudle, so strongly seasoned with eggs, cinnamon, cloves, ginger, and saffron, that the odor went through the entire hall. At the same time the jester,

Tsarushek, sitting in the doorway on a stool, began to imitate the singing of a nightingale, which evidently delighted the king. After him another jester passed around the table with the servants who were carrying food; he stood behind the chairs without being noticed, and imitated the buzzing of a bee so accurately that this man and that laid down his spoon and defended his head with his hand. At sight of this, others burst into laughter.

Zbyshko served the princess and Danusia diligently, but when Lichtenstein in his turn began to slap his head, which was growing bald, he forgot his danger again and laughed till the tears came. A young Lithuanian prince, son of the viceroy of Smolensk, helped him in this so sincerely that he dropped food from the tray.

The Knight of the Cross, noting his error at last, reached to his hanging pocket, and turning to bishop Kropidlo, said something to him in German which the bishop repeated immediately in Polish.

" The noble lord declares," said he, turning to the jester, " that thou wilt receive two coins; but buzz not too near, for bees are driven out and drones are killed."

The jester pocketed the two coins which the knight had given him, and using the freedom accorded to jesters at all courts, he answered, —

"There is much honey in the land of Dobryn; that is why the drones have settled on it. Kill them, O King Vladislav! "

" Ha! here is a coin from me too, for thou hast answered well," said Kropidlo; "but remember that when a ladder falls the bee-keeper breaks his neck. Those Malborg drones which have settled on Dobryn have stings, and it is dangerous to climb to their nests."

" Oh! " cried Zyndram of Mashkov, the sword-bearer of Cracow, "we can smoke them out."

"With what?"

" With powder."

" Or cut their nests with an axe!" said the gigantic Pashko Zlodye.

Zbyshko's heart rose, for he thought that such words heralded war. But Kuno Lichtenstein understood the words too, for having lived long in Torun and in Helmno he had learned Polish speech, and he failed to use it only through pride. But now, roused by Zyndram's words, he fixed his gray eyes on him and answered, —

"We shall see."

"Our fathers saw at Plovtsi, and we have seen at Vilno," answered Zyndram.

" Pax vobiscum! Pax, pax!" exclaimed Kropidlo. " Only let the reverend Mikolai of Kurov leave the bishopric of Kuyav, and the gracious king appoint me in his place, I will give you such a beautiful sermon on love among nations, that I will crush you completely, for what is hatred if not ignis (fire), and besides ignis infemails (hell fire), — a fire so terrible that water has no effect on it, and it can be quenched only with wine. With wine, then! We will go to the ops! as the late bishop Zbisha said."

" And from the ops to hell, as the devil said," added the jester.

"May he take thee!"

" It will be more interesting when he takes you; the devil has not been seen yet with a Kropidlo (holy-water sprinkler), but I think that all will have that pleasure."

" I will sprinkle thee first," said Kropidlo. " Give us wine, and long life to love among Christians! "

"Among real Christians!" repeated Lichtenstein, with emphasis.

" How is that?" asked the bishop of Cracow, raising his head. " Are you not in an old-time Christian kingdom? Are not the churches older here than in Malborg? "

" I know not," answered the Knight of the Cross.

The king was especially sensitive on the question of Christianity. It seemed to him that perhaps the Knight of the Cross wished to reproach him; so his prominent cheeks were covered at once with red spots, and his eyes began to flash.

" What," asked he in a loud voice. " Am I not a Chris* tian king? "

"The kingdom calls itself Christian," answered Lichtenstein coldly, " but the customs in it are pagan."

At this, terrible knights rose from their seats, — Martsin Vrotsimovitse, Floryan of

Korytnitsa, Bartosh of Vodzinek, Domarat of Kobylany, Povala of Tachev, Pashko Zlodye, Zyndram of Mashkovitee, Yasha of Targovisko, Kron of Koziglove, Zygmunt of Bobova, and Stashko of Harbimo-vitse,powerful, renowned, victors in many battles and in many tournaments; at one instant they were flushing with anger, at another pale, at another gritting their teeth they exclaimed, one interrupting another, —

Woe to us! for he is a guest and cannot be challenged ! "

But Zavisha Charny, the most renowned among the renowned, the " model of knights," turned his frowning brows to Liechtenstein, and said, —

"Kuno, I do not recognize thee. How canst thou, a knight, shame a noble people among whom thou, being an envoy, art threatened by no punishment?"

But Kuno endured calmly his terrible \ooks and answered slowly and emphatically, —

" Our Order before coming to Prussia warred in Palestine, but there even Saracens respected envoys. Ye alone do not respect them, and for this reason I have called your customs pagan."

At this the uproar became still greater. Around, the table were heard again the cries of "Woe! woe!"

They grew silent, however, when the king, on whose face anger was boiling, clapped his hands a number of times in Lithuanian fashion,, Then old Yasko Toporof Tenchyn, the castellan of Cracow, rose, — he was gray, dignified, rousing fear by the truthfulness of his rule, — and said, —

" Noble knight of Lichtenstein, if any insult has met you as an envoy, speak, there will be satisfaction and stern justice quickly."

"This would not have happened to me in any other Christian land," answered Kuno. "Yesterday, on the road to Tynets, one of your knights fell upon me, and though from the cross on my mantle it was easy to see who I was, he attempted my life."

Zbyshko, when he heard these words grew deathly pale and looked involuntarily at the king whose face was simply terrible. Yasko of Tenchyn was astounded, and said, —

"Can that be?"

" Ask the lord of Tachev, who was a witness of the deed."

All eyes turned to Povala who stood for a while gloomy, with drooping eyelids, and then said, —

" It is true! "

"When the knights heard this they called out: "Shame! shame ! The ground should open under such a one." And from shame some struck their thighs and their breasts with their hands, others twisted the pewter plates on the table between their fingers, not knowing where to cast their eyes.

" Why did'st thou not kill him? " thundered the king.

" I did not because his head belongs to judgment," replied Povala.

" Did you imprison him?" asked the Castellan of Cracow.

" No. He is a noble, who swore on his knightly honor that he would appear."

" And he will not appear! " said Liechtenstein, with a sneer and raising his head.

With that a plaintive youthful voice called out not far from the shoulders of the Knight of the Cross, —

"May God never grant that I should prefer shame to death. *It was I who did that, I, Zbyshko of Bogdanets."

At these words the knights sprang toward the hapless Zbyshko, but they were stopped by a threatening beck of the king, who rose with flashing eyes, and called in a voice panting from anger, a voice which was like the sound of a wagon jolting over stones, —

"Cut off his head! cut off his head! Let the Knight of the Cross send his head to the Grand Master at Malborg!"

Then he cried to the young Lithuanian prince, son of the viceroy of Smolensk, —

" Hold him, Yamont!"

Terrified by the king's anger, Yamont laid his trembling hand on the shoulder of Zbyshko, who, turning a pallid face toward him, said, —

"I will not flee."

But the white-bearded castellan of Cracow raised his hand in sign that he wished to speak, and when there was silence, he said,

" Gracious king! Let that comtur be convinced that not thy auger, but our laws punish with death an attack on the person of an envoy. Otherwise he might think the more justly that there are no Christian laws in this kingdom. I will hold judgment on the accused to-morrow! "

He pronounced the last words in a high key, and evidently not admitting even the thought that that voice would be disobeyed, he beckoned to Yamont, and said, —

" Confine him in the tower. And you, lord of Tachev, will give witness."

" I will tell the whole fault of that stripling, which no mature man among us would have ever committed," said Povala, looking gloomily at Lichtenstein.

" He speaks justly," said others at once; " he is a lad yet; why should we all be put to shame through him ? "

Then came a moment of silence and of unfriendly glances at the Knight of the Cross; meanwhile Yamont led away Zbyshko, to give him into the hands of the bowmen standing in the courtyard of the castle. In his young heart he felt

pity Tor the prisoner; this pity was increased by his innate hatred for the Germans. But as a Lithuanian he was accustomed to accomplish blindly the will of the grand prince; and, terrified by the anger of the king, he whispered to Zbyshko in friendly persuasion, —

" Knowst what I will say to thee? hang thyself! The best is to hang thyself right away. The king is angry, — and they will cut off thy head. Why not make him glad? Hang thyself, friend! with us it is the custom."

Zbyshko, half unconscious from shame and fear, seemed at first not to understand the words of the little prince; but at last he understood, and stood still from astonishment.

" What dost thou say?"

" Hang thyself! Why should they judge thee? Thou wilt gladden the king! " repeated Yamont.

"Hang thyself, if thou wish!" cried Zbyshko. "They baptized thee in form, but the skin on thee has remained pagan; and thou dost not even understand that it is a sin for a Christian to do such a thing."

" But it would not be of free will," answered the prince, shrugging his shoulders. "If thou dost not do this, they will cut off thy head."

It shot through Zbyshko's mind that for such words it would be proper to challenge the young boyarin at once to a conflict on foot or on horseback, with swords or with axes; but he stifled that idea, remembering that there would be no time for such action. So, dropping his head gloomily and in silence, he let himsjelf be delivered into the hands of the leader of the palace bowmen.

Meanwhile, in the dining-hall universal attention was turned in another direction.

Danusia, seeing what was taking place, was so frightened at first that the breath was stopped in her breast. Her face became as pale as linen; her eyes grew round from terror, and, as motionless as a wax figure in a church, she gazed at the king. But when at last she heard that they were to cut off her Zbyshko's head, when they seized him and led him forth from the hall, measureless sorrow took possession of her; her lips and brows began to quiver; nothing was of effect, — neither fear of the king nor biting her lips with her teeth; and on a sudden she burst into weeping so pitiful and shrill that all faces turned to her, and the king himself asked, —

"What is this?"

"Gracious king! " exclaimed Princess Anna, " this is the daughter of Yurand of Spyhov, to whom this ill-fated young knight made a vow. He vowed to obtain for her three peacock-plumes from helmets; and seeing such a plume on the helmet of this comtur, he thought that God himself had sent it to him. Not through malice did he do this, lord, but through folly; for this reason be merciful, and do not punish him; for this we beg thee on bended knees."

Then she rose, and taking Danusia by the hand, hurried with her to the king, who, seeing them, began to draw back. But they knelt before him, and Danusia, embracing the king's feet with her little hands, cried, —

" Forgive Zbyshko, O king; forgive Zbyshko! "

And, carried away at the same time by fear, she hid her bright head in the folds of the gray mantle of the king, kissing his knees, and quivering like a leaf. Princess Anna knelt on the other side, and, putting her palms together, looked imploringly at Yagello, on whose face was expressed great perplexity. He drew back, it is true, with his chair, but he did not repulse Danusia with force; he merely pushed the air with both hands, as if defending himself from flies.

" Give me peace! " said he; " he is at fault, he has shamed the whole kingdom! let them cut off his head! "

But the little hands squeezed the more tightly around his knees, and the childlike voice called still more pitifully, —

" Forgive Zbyshko, O king; forgive Zbyshko! "

Then the voices of knights were heard.

" Yurand of Spyhov is a renowned knight, a terror to Germans."

"And that stripling has done much service at Vilno," added Povala.

The king, however, continued to defend himself, though he was moved at sight of Danusia.

"Leave me in peace! He has not offended me, and I cannot forgive him. Let the envoy of the Order forgive him, then I will pardon; if he will not forgive, let them cut off his head."

" Forgive him, Kuno," said Zavisha Charny; "the Grand Master himself will not blame thee."

" Forgive him, lord! " exclaimed the two princesses.

"Forgive him, forgive him ! " repeated voices of knights.

Kuno closed his eyes, and sat with forehead erect, as if delighted that the two princesses and such renowned knights were imploring him. All at once, in the twinkle of an eye, he changed; he dropped his head, and crossed his arms on his breast; from being insolent, he became humble, and said, in a low, mild voice, —

"Christ, our Saviour, forgave the thief on the cross, and also his own enemies."

" A true knight utters that!" exclaimed the bishop of Cracow.

" A true knight, a true knight! "

"Why should I not forgive him," continued Kuno, — "I, who am not only a Christian, but a monk ? Hence, as a servant of Christ, and a monk, I forgive him from the soul of my heart."

" Glory to him! " thundered Povala of Tachev.

" Glory to him ! " repeated others.

" But," added the Knight of the Cross, " I am here among you as an envoy, and I bear in my person the majesty of the whole Order, which is Christ's Order. Whoso offends me as an envoy, offends the Order; and whoso offends the Order offends Christ himself; such a wrong I before God and man cannot pardon. If, therefore, your law pardons it, let all the rulers of Christendom know of the matter."

These words were followed by a dead silence. But after a while were heard here and there the gritting of teeth, the deep breathing of restrained rage, and the sobbing of Danusia.

Before evening all hearts were turned to Zbyshko. The same knights who in the morning would have been ready at one beck of the king to bear Zbyshko apart on their swords were exerting their wits then to see how to aid him. The princesses resolved to go with a prayer to the queen, asking her to persuade Liehtenstein to drop his complaint altogether, or in case of need to write to the Grand Master of the Order, begging that he command Kuno to drop the affair. The way seemed sure, for such uncommon honor surrounded Yadviga that the Grand Master would bring on himself the anger of the pope and the blame of all Christian princes if he refused her such a request. It was not likely that he would, and for this reason, that Conrad Von Jungin-gen was a calm man, and far milder than his predecessors. Unfortunately the bishop of Cracow, who was also chief physician of the queen, forbade most strictly to mention even one word to her touching the matter. " She is never pleased to hear of death sentences," said he, " and though the question be one of a simple robber, she takes it to heart at once; and what would it be now, when the life of a young man is at stake, — a young man who might justly expect her

mercy. Any excitement may easily bring her to grievous illness; her health means more for the whole kingdom than the lives of ten knights." He declared, finally, that if any one dared to disturb the lady in spite of his words, he would bring down on that person the terrible wrath of the king, and lay also the curse of the Church on aim or her.

Both princesses feared this declaration, and resolved to be silent before the queen, but to implore the king until he showed some favor. The whole court and all the knights were on the side of Zbyshko. Povala asserted that he would confess the whole truth, but would give testimony favorable to the young man, and would represent the entire affair as the impulsiveness of a boy. Still, every one foresaw, and the castellan of Cracow declared openly, that, if the German insisted, stern justice must have its own.

The hearts of knights rose with growing indignation against Lichtenstein, and more than one thought, or even said openly: " He is an envoy and cannot be summoned to the barriers, but when he returns to Malborg, may God not grant him to die his own death." And those were no idle threats, for it was not permitted belted knights to drop a vain word; whoso said a thing must show its truth or perish. The terrible Povala proved the most stubborn, for he had in Tachev a beloved little daughter of Dauusia's age; there fore Danusia's tears crushed the heart in him utterly.

In fact, he visited Zbyshko that very day in the dungeon, commanded him to be of good cheer, told him of the prayers of botli princesses and the tears of Danusia. Zbyshko, when lie heard that the girl had thrown herself at the feet of the king, was moved to tears, and not knowing how to express his gratitude and his longing, said, wiping his eyelids with the back of his hand, —

"Oh, may God bless her, and grant me a struggle on foot or on horseback for her sake as soon as possible. I promised her too few Germans, — for to such a one was due a number equal to her years. If the Lord Jesus will rescue me from these straits I will not be stingy with her;" and he raised his eyes full of gratitude.

"First vow something to a church," said the lord of Tachev, "for if thy vow be pleasing to God thou wilt be free of a certainty. And second, listen: Thy uncle has gone to Lichtenstein, and I will go too. There would be no shame for thee to ask forgiveness, for thou art at fault; and thou wouldst beg, not Lichtenstein, but an envoy. Art thou willing ? "

" Since such a knight as your Grace says that it is proper, I will do so, but if he wishes me to beg him as he wanted on the road to Tynets, then let them cut my head off. My uncle will remain, and my uncle will pay him when his mission is ended."

" We shall see what he will answer to Matsko," replied Povala.

Matsko had really visited the German, but went from his presence as gloomy as night, and betook himself directly to the king, to whom the castellan himself conducted him. The king, who had become perfectly calm, received him kindly. When Matsko knelt, Yagello commanded him at once to rise, and inquired what he wanted.

" Gracious lord," said Matsko, " there has been offence, there must be punishment; otherwise law would cease in the world; but the offence is mine, for not only did I not restrain the natural passionateness of this stripling, but I praised it. I reared him in that way, and from childhood war reared him. It is my offence, gracious king, for more than once did I say to him: ' Strike first, and see afterward whom thou hast struck.' That was well in war, but ill at court. Still, the lad is like pure gold; he is the last of our race, and I grieve for him dreadfully."

"He has disgraced me, he has disgraced the kingdom," said the king. "Am I to rub honey on him for such deeds ?"

Matsko was silent, for at remembrance of Zbyshko sorrow pressed his throat suddenly, and only after a long time did he speak again, with a moved voice, —

" I knew not that I loved him so much, and only now is it shown, after misfortune has come. I am old, and he is the last of our family. When he is gone — we shall be gone. Gracious king and lord, take pity on us!'

Here Matsko knelt again, and stretching forth hands that were wearied from war, he said, with tears, —

"We defended Vilno. God gave booty; to whom shall I leave it? The German wants punishment; let there be punishment, but let me yield my head. What is life to me without Zbyshko ? He is young; let him free his land and beget posterity as God commands men to do. The Knight of the Cross will not even inquire whose head has fallen, if pnly one falls. Neither will any disgrace come on the family for that. It is hard for a man to meet death, but, when we look at the matter more carefully, it is better that one man should die than that a family should be extinguished."

Thus speaking be embraced the feet of the king. Yagello blinked, which with him was a sign of emotion, and finally he said, —

"I shall never command to behead a belted knight! — never, never! "

" And there would be no justice in doing so," added the castellan. " Law punishes the guilty, but it is not a dragon which sees not whose blood it is gulping. Consider what disgrace would fall on your family; for were your nephew to consent to what you propose all would hold him and his descendants disgraced."

" He would not consent. But if it were done without his knowledge he would avenge me afterward, as I should avenge him."

" Bring the German to abandon his complaint," said the castellan.

I have been with him already."

"And what," inquired the king, stretching his neck, " what did he say?"

" He spoke thus: * Ye should have prayed for pardon on the Tynets road; ye had no wish then, I have no wish now.'"

" And why did ye not wish?"

" For he commanded us to come down from our horses and beg him for pardon on foot."

The king put his hair behind his ears and wished to say something, when an attendant came in with the announcement that the knight of Lichtenstein begged for an audience.

Yagello looked at the castellan, then at Matsko, but commanded them to remain, perhaps in the hope that on this occasion he would soften the affair by his kindly office

Meanwhile the Knight of the Cross entered,°bowed to the king, and said, —

"Gracious lord, here is a written complaint touching the insult which met me in your kingdom."

"Complain to him," answered the king, pointing to the castellan.

"I know neither your laws nor your courts, but I know
the envoy of the Order can make complaint only
to the king himself," said the kuight, looking straight into

Yagello's small eyes glittered with impatience; but he stretched forth his hand, took the complaint, and gave it to the castellan. The castellan unrolled it and began to read, but as he read his face grew more vexed and gloomy.

"Lord," said he at length, "you insist on taking the life of that youth, as if he were a terror to the whole Order. Do you Knights of the Cross fear children ? "

" We Knights of the Cross fear no one," replied the comtur, haughtily.

" Especially God," added the old castellan, in a low voice.

Next day Povala of Tachev did all that was in his power before the court to dimmish Zbyshko's guilt. But in vain did he ascribe the deed to youth and inexperience, in vain did he say that even if some one who was older had made a vow to give three peacock-plumes, and had prayed to have them sent to him, and afterward had seen such a plume before him on a sudden, he too might have thought that to be a dispensation of God.

The honorable knight did not deny that had it not been for him Zbyshko's lance would have struck the German's breast. Kuno on his part had caused to be brought into court the armor worn by him that day, and it was found to be of thin plate, worn only on ceremonial visits, and so frail that, considering Zbyshko's uncommon strength, the point of the lance would have passed through the envoy's body and deprived him of life. Then they asked Zbyshko if he had intended to kill the knight.

Zbyshko would not deny. " I called to him from a distance," said he, " to lower his lance; of course he would not have let the helmet be torn from his head while alive, but if he had called from a distance that he was an envoy I should have left him in peace."

These words pleased the knights, who through good-will for the youth had assembled numerously at the court, and straightway many voices were raised. " True ! why did he not cry out?" But the castellan's face remained stern and gloomy. Enjoining silence on those present he was silent himself for a while, then he fastened an inquiring eye on Zbyshko, and asked, —

" Canst thou swear, on the Passion of the Lord, that thou didst not see the mantle and the cross ? "

"I cannot!" answered Zbyshko; "if I had not seen the cross I should have thought him one of our knights, and I should not have aimed at one of our men."

" But how could a Knight of the Cross be near Cracow unless as an envoy, or in the retinue of an envoy ? "

To this Zbyshko made no answer, for he had nothing to say. It was too clear to all that, had it not been for the lord of Tachev, not the armor of the envoy would be before the court then, but the envoy himself with breast pierced, to the eternal shame of the Polish people; hence even those who from their whole souls were friendly to Zbyshko understood that the decision could not be favorable. In fact, after a time the castellan said, —

" In thy excitement thou didst not think whom thou wert striking, and didst act without malice. Our Saviour will reckon that in thy favor and forgive thee; but commend thyself, hapless man, to the Most Holy Virgin, for the law can not pardon thee."

Though he had expected such words, Zbyshko grew somewhat pale when he heard them, but soon he shook back his long hair, made the sign of the cross on himself, and said:

"The will of God! Still, it is difficult."

Then he turned to Matsko and indicated Lichteustein with his eyes, as if leaving the German to his uncle's memory; and Matsko motioned with his head in sign that he understood and would remember. Lichtenstein too understood that look and that motion, and though there beat in his breast both a brave and stubborn heart, a quiver ran through him at that moment, so terrible and ill-omened was the face of the old warrior. The Knight of the Cross saw that between him and that knight there would be thenceforth a struggle for life and death ; that even if he wanted to hide from him he could not, and when he ceased to be an envoy they must meet, even at Malborg.

The castellan withdrew to the adjoining chamber to dictate the sentence against Zbyshko to his secretary skilled in writing. This one and that of the knighthood approached the envoy during this interval, saying, —

"God grant thee to be judged with more mercy at the last judgment! Thou art glad of blood! "

But Lichtenstein valued only the opinion of Zavisha, for he, because of his deeds in battle, his knowledge of the rules of knighthood, and his uncommon strictness in observing them, was widely known throughout the world. In the most complicated questions in which the point was of knightly honor, men came to him frequently from a very great distance, ami no oue ever dared to oppose, not only because

rtingle combat with him was impossible, but also because men esteemed him as the "mirror of honor." One word of praise or of blame from his lips passed quickly among the knighthood of Poland, Hungary, Bohemia, Germany, and sufficed to establish the good or evil fame of a knight.

Lichtenstein therefore approached him and said, as if wishing to justify his stubbornness, —

" Only the Grand Master himself with the Chapter could grant him grace — I cannot."

"Your Grand Master has nothing to do with our laws' not he, but our king has power to show grace here."

"I, as an envoy, must demand punishment."

"Thou wert a knight, Lichtenstein, before becoming an envoy."

" Dost thou think that I have failed in honor? "

" Thou knowest our books of knighthood, and thou know-est that a knight is commanded to imitate two beasts, the lion and the lamb. Which hast thou imitated in this affair? "

" Thou art not my judge."

" Thou hast asked if thou hast failed in honor, and I have answered as I think."

" Thou hast answered badly, for I cannot swallow this."

" Thou wilt choke with thy own anger, not mine."

" Christ will account it to me that I have thought more of the majesty of the Order than of thy praise."

" He too will judge us all."

Further conversation was interrupted by the entrance of the castellan and the secretary. Those present knew that the sentence would be unfavorable, still a dead silence set in. The castellan took his place at the table and grasping a crucifix in his hand, commanded Zbyshko to kneel.

The secretary read the sentence in Latin. Neither Zbyshko nor the knights present understood it, still all divined that that was a death sentence. Zbyshko, when the reading was finished, struck his breast with his closed hand a number of times, repeating: "O God, be merciful to me a sinner!" Then he rose and cast himself into the arms of Matsko, who in silence kissed his head and his eyes.

On the evening of that day, the herald proclaimed, with sound of trumpets, to knights, guests, and citizens, at the four corners of the square, that the noble Zbyshko of Bog-danets was condemned by the sentence of the castellan to be beheaded with a sword.

But Matsko prayed that the execution should not take

80 THE KNIGHTS OF THE CROSS.

place immediately. This prayer was granted the more easily since people of that age, fond of minute disposition of their property, were given time generally for negotiations with their families, and also to make peace with God. Lichteustein himself did not care to insist on the speedy execution of the sentence, since satisfaction had been given the majesty of the Order; moreover, it was not proper to offend a powerful monarch to whom he had been sent, not only to take part in the solemnities of the christening, but also for negotiations touching the land of Dobryn. But the most important consideration was the health of the queen. The bishop of Cracow would not hear of an execution before her delivery, thinking rightly that it would be impossible to hide such an event from the lady, that should she hear of it she would fall into a "distress" which might injure her grievously. In this way a few weeks of life, and perhaps more, remained to Zbyshko, before the last arrangement and parting with his acquaintances.

Matsko visited him daily and comforted him as best he could. They spoke sadly of Zbyshko's unavoidable death, and still more sadly of this, that the family would disappear.

"It cannot be but you must marry," said Zbyshko once.

" I should prefer to adopt some relative, even if distant," replied Matsko, with emotion. " How can I think of marrying when they are going to cut off thy head. And even should it come to this that I must take a wife, I could not do so till I had sent Lichtenstein the challenge of a knight, till I had exacted my vengeance. I shall do that, have no fear!"

"God reward you! Let me have even that consolation! But I knew that you would not forgive him. How will you do it?"

" When his office of envoy is at an end, there will be either war or peace — dost understand ? If war comes I will send him a challenge to meet me in single combat before battle."

" On trampled earth?"

"On trampled earth, on horseback or on foot, but to the death, not to slavery. If there be peace, I will go to Malborg, strike the castle gate with my lance and command a trumpeter to announce that I challenge him to the death. He will not hide, be assured."

" Of course he will not hide. And you will handle him in a way that I should like to see."

"Shall I handle him? I could not handle Zavisha, or Pashko, or Povala; but without boasting, 1 can handle two like him. His mother, the Order, will witness that! "Was not the Frisian knight stronger ? And when I cut from above through his helmet, where did my axe stop ? It stopped in his teeth, did it not ?"

Zbyshko drew breath at this with great consolation, and said, —

" He will die more easily than the Frisian."

The two men sighed; then the old noble said with emotion, —

"Be not troubled. Thy bones will not be seeking one another at the day of resurrection. I will have an oaken coffin made for thee of such kind that the canouesses of the church of the Virgin Mary have not a better. Thou wilt not die like a peasant, or like a nobleman created by patent. Nay! I will not even permit that thou be beheaded on the same cloth on which they behead citizens. I have agreed already with Amyley for entirely new stuff, from which a king's coat might be made. And I shall not spare masses on thee — never fear! "

Zbyshko's heart was delighted by this, so grasping his uncle's hand he repeated, —

" God reward you! "

But at times, despite every consolation, dreadful yearning seized him; hence another day, when Matsko had come on a visit, and they had scarcely exchanged greetings, he asked while looking through the grating in the wall, —

"But what is there outside?"

" Weather like gold," replied the warrior, "and warmth of the sun makes the whole world lovely."

Then Zbyshko put both hands on his uncle's shoulders and bending back his head, said, —

"O mighty God! To have a horse under one and ride over fields, over broad fields. It is sad for a young man to die — awfully sad!"

"People die even on horseback," said Matsko.

" Yes. But how many do they kill before dying! "

And he began to inquire about the knights whom he had seen at the court of the king: about Zavisha, Farurey, Povala, Lis, and all the others, — what were they doing, how did they amuse themselves, in what honorable exercises did their time pass? And he listened eagerly to the narrative of Matsko, who said that in the morning they jumped in full

VOL. I. —6

armor over a horse, that they pulled ropes, fought with swords and leaden-edged axes, and finally that they feasted, and sang songs. Zbyshko desired with his whole heart and soul to fly to them, and when he learned that immediately after the christening Zavisha would go far away somewhere to Lower Hungary against the Turks, he could not restrain himself from weeping.

"They might let me go with him! and let me lay down my life against pagans."

But that could not be. Meanwhile something else took place: The two Mazovian princesses continued to think of Zbyshko, who interested them with his youth and beauty; finally Princess Alexandra resolved to send a letter to the Grand Master. The Master could not, it is true, change the sentence pronounced by the castellan, but he could intercede for Zbyshko before the king. It was not proper for Yagello to grant pardon, since the question was of an attack on an envoy; it seemed, however, undoubted that he would be glad to grant it at the intercession of the Grand Master. Hence hope entered the hearts of both ladies anew. Princess Alexandra herself, having a weakness for the polished Knights of the Cross, was uncommonly esteemed by them. More than once rich gifts went to her from Malborg, and letters in which the Master declared her venerated, saintly, a benefactress, and special patroness of the Order. Her words might effect much, and it was very likely that they would not meet a refusal. The only question was to find a courier who would show all diligence in delivering the letter at the earliest, and in returning with an answer. When he heard of this, old Matsko undertook the task without hesitation.

The castellan, on being petitioned, appointed a time up to which he promised to restrain the execution of the sentence. Matsko, full of consolation, busied himself that very day with his departure; later he went to Zbyshko to announce the happy tidings.

At the first moment Zbyshko burst out in great delight, as if the doors of the prison were open before him already; later, however, he grew thoughtful, and soon he became sad and gloomy.

" Who can receive any good from Germans? Lich-tenstein might have asked the king for pardon, — and he would have done well, for he would have guarded himself from revenge, — but he would not do anything."

" He grew stubborn because we would not beg him on the Tynets road. Of Conrad, the Master, people do not speak ill. Besides, as to losing, thou wilt not lose anything."

"True," said Zbyshko, "but do not bow down low to him."

"How bow down? I carry a letter from Princess Alexandra — nothing more."

" Then if you are so good, may the Lord God assist you." All at once he looked quickly at his uncle, and said: "If the king forgives me, Lichtenstein will be mine, not yours. Remember."

" Thy head is not sure; make no promises. Thou hast had enough of those stupid vows," said the old man, in auger.

Then they threw themselves into each other's arms — and Zbyshko remained alone. Hope and uncertainty in turn shook his soul, but when night came, and with it a storm in the sky, when the barred windows were illuminated with the ominous blaze of lightning, and the walls quivered from thunder, when at last the whirlwind struck the tower with its whistle, and the dim candle went out at his bedside, Zbyshko, sunk in darkness, lost every hope again, and the whole night he could not close his eyes for a moment.

"I shall not escape death," thought he, "and nothing will help me in any way."

But next morning the worthy Princess Anna came to visit him, and with her Danusia, having a lute at her girdle. Zbyshko fell at the feet of one and then the other; though he was suffering after the sleepless night, in misfortune and uncertainty, he did not so far forget the duty of a knight as not to show Danusia his astonishment at her beauty. But the princess raised to him eyes full of sadness.

" Do not admire her," said she, " for if Matsko brings back no good answer, or if he does not return at all, poor fellow, thou wilt soon admire something better in heaven."

Then she shed tears, thinking of the uncertain lot of the young knight, and Danusia accompanied her forthwith. Zbyshko bent again to their feet, for his heart grew as soft as heated wax at those tears. He did not love Danusia as a man loves a woman, but he felt that he loved her with all his soul, and at sight of her something took place in his breast, as if there were in it another man, less harsh, less impulsive, breathing war less, and at the same time thirsting for sweet love. Finally, immense sorrow seized him because he would

have to leave her and not be able to keep the promise which he had made.

"Now, poor girl, I shall not place the peacock-plumes at thy feet," said he. " But if I stand before the face of God, I will say: ' Pardon my sins, O God, but whatever there is of good in all the world, give it to no one else but Danusia, daughter of Yurand of Spyhov V

" Ye became acquainted not long ago," said the princess. " May God grant that it was not in vain."

Zbyshko remembered all that had taken place at the inn of Tynets, and was filled with emotion. At last he begged Danusia to sing for him that same song which she sang when he had seized her from the bench and borne her to the princess.

Danusia, though she had no mind for singing, raised her head at once toward the arch, and closing her eyes like a bird, she began,—

" Oh, had I wings like a wild goose 1 would fly after Yasek, I would fly after him to Silesia! I would sit on a fence in Silesia. Look at me Yasek dear — "

But on a sudden from beneath her closed eyelids abundant tears flowed forth; she could sing no longer. Then Zbyshko seized her in his arms in the same way that he had at the inn in Tynets, and began to carry her through the room, repeating in ecstasy,—

" No, but I would seek thee. Let God rescue me, grow up thou, let thy father permit, then I will take thee, O maiden ! Hei!"

Danusia, encircling his neck, hid her face wet with tears on his shoulder, and in him sorrow rose more and more, sorrow which, flowing from the depth of the sylvan Slav nature, changed in that simple soul almost into the pastoral song:

" Thee would I take, maiden 1 Thee would I take! "

Meanwhile came an event in view of which other affairs lost all significance in people's eyes. Toward the evening of June 21, news went around the castle of a sudden weakness of the queen. The physicians who were summoned, together with the bishop of Cracow, remained in her chamber all night,

and it was learned soon from servants that premature labor threatened the lady. The castellan of Cracow sent couriers that same night to the absent king. Early next morning the news thundered throughout the city and the country. Hence all the churches were filled with people, on whom the priests enjoined prayers for the recovery of the queen. All doubt ceased after services. Knightly guests, who had assembled for the approaching solemnity, nobles, deputations of merchants repaired to the castle; guilds and brotherhoods appeared with their banners. Beginning with mid-day the castle of Vavel was surrounded by numberless swarms of people, among whom the king's bowmen maintained order, enforcing peace and quiet. The city was almost depopulated, but from time to time there passed through the deserted streets peasants of the neighborhood, who also had heard of the illness of the idolized lady, and were hastening toward the castle.

Finally, in the main gate appeared the bishop and the castellan, accompanied by the canons of the cathedral, the counsellors of the king, and also knights. They went along the walls, among the people, and, with faces announcing news, began with a stern command to refrain from all outcries, for shouts might injure the sick lady. Then they declared to all in general that the queen had given birth to a daughter.

The news filled the hearts of all with delight, especially since it was known at the time that, though the birth was premature, there was no evident danger for the child or the mother. The crowds began to separate, as it was not permitted to shout near the castle, and each one wished to give way to his delight. Indeed, when the streets leading to the square were filled, songs were heard and joyful shouts. People were not even grieved that a daughter had come to the world. " Was it bad," said they, " that King Louis had no sons, and that the kingdom came to Yadviga? Through her marriage with Yagello the power of the kingdom has been doubled. So will it be this time. Where can such an heiress be found as our king's daughter, since neither the Roman Caesar, nor any king is master of such a great State, such broad lands, such a numerous knighthood! The most powerful monarchs of the earth will strive for her hand, they will bow down to the king and the queen, they will visit Cracow, and from this, profit will come to us merchants; besides, some new kingdom, the Bohemian or the Hungarian, will be joined to ours." Thus spoke the merchants among themselves,

86 THE KNIGHTS OF THE CROSS.

and joy increased every moment. People feasted in private houses and in inns. The market square was full of lanterns and torches. In the suburbs country people from the regions around Cracow (more of these drew near the city continually) camped by their wagons. The Jews held council in their synagogue near the Kazimir. The square was crowded till late at night, almost till daybreak, especially near the City Hall and the weighing-house, as in time of great fairs. People gave news to one and another; they sent to the castle and crowded around those who returned with news.

The worst information was that the bishop had christened the child the night of its birth, from which people inferred that it must be very weak. Experienced citizens, however, quoted examples showing that children born half dead received power of life just after baptism. So they were strengthened with hope, which was increased even by the name given the infant. It was said that no Bonifacius or Bonifacia could die immediately after birth, for it was predestined them to do something good, and in the first years, and all the more in the first months of life, a child could do neither good nor evil.

On the morrow, however, came news unfavorable for child and mother; this roused the city. All day there was a throng in the churches as in time of indulgence. There were numberless votive offerings for the health of the queen and the infant. People saw with emotion poor villagers offering, one a measure of wheat, another a lamb, a third a hen, a fourth a string of dried mushrooms, or a basket of nuts. Considerable offerings came from knights, merchants, and handicraftsmen. Couriers were sent to miracle-working places. Astrologers questioned the stars. In Cracow itself solemn processions were ordered. All the guilds and brotherhoods appeared. There was a procession also of children, for people thought that innocent creatures would obtain God's favor more easily. Through the gates of the city entered new crowds from the surrounding country.

And thus day followed day amid the continual tolling of bells, the noise in the churches, the processions, and the masses. But when a week had passed and the child and the patient were alive yet, consolation began to enter hearts. It seemed to people an improbable thing that God would take prematurely the ruler of a realm who having done so much for Him would have to leave an immense work unfinished, and the apostolic woman whose sacrifice of her own happiness had brought to Christianity the last pagan people in Europe. The learned called to mind how much she had done for the Academy; the clergy, how much for the glory of God; statesmen, how much she had done for peace among Christian monarchs ; Jurists, how much for justice; the poor, how much for their poverty; and it could not find place in the heads of any that a life so needful to the kingdom and the whole world might be cut down untimely.

Meanwhile on the 13th of July the bells announced sadly the death of the child. The city seethed up again, and alarm seized people; crowds besieged Vavel a second time, inquiring for the health of the queen.

But this time no one came out with good news. On the contrary, the faces of lords entering the castle or going out through the gates were gloomy, and every day more gloomy. It was said that the priest, Stanislav of Skarbimir, a master of liberal sciences in Cracow, did not leave the queen, who received communion daily. It was said also that immediately after each communion her room was filled with a heavenly light, — some even saw it through the window; this sight, however, rather terrified hearts devoted to the lady, as a sign that, for her, life beyond the earth had begun already.

Some did not believe that a thing so dreadful could happen, and those strengthened themselves with the thought that the just heavens would stop with one sacrifice. But on Friday morning, July 17th, it was thundered among people that the queen was dying. Every person living hastened to the castle. The city was deserted to the degree that only cripples remained in it, for even mothers with infants hurried to the gates. Cellars were closed, no food was prepared. All affairs stopped, and under the castle of Vavel there was one dark sea of people — disquieted, terrified, but silent.

About one o'clock in the afternoon a bell sounded on the tower of the cathedral. People knew not at once what that meant, but fear raised the hair on their heads. All faces, all eyes were turned to the tower, to the bell moving with increasing swing, — the bell, the complaining groan of which others in the city began to accompany; bells were tolled in the church of the Franciscans, the Holy Trinity, and the Virgin Mary, and throughout the length and the breadth of the city.

The city understood at last what those groans meant; the souls of men were filled with terror and with such pain as if

88 THE KNIGHTS OF THE CROSS.

the bronze hearts of those bells were striking directly into the hearts of all present.

Suddenly there appeared on the tower a black flag with a great skull in the middle, under which in white were two human shank-bones placed crosswise. Every doubt vanished that moment. The queen had given her soul to God.

Roars burst forth at the foot of the castle, the wails of a hundred thousand persons, and they mingled with the dismal sound of the bells. Some threw themselves on the ground; others rent the clothing on their bodies, or tore their faces; others looked at the walls in dumb bewilderment; some groaned with deep and dull sound; some, stretching their hands to the church and the chamber of the queen, called for a miracle and the mercy of God. There were heard also angry voices which in frenzy and despair went to blasphemy. "Why was our beloved one taken from us? To what profit were our processions, our prayers, and our imploring ? The gold and the silver offerings were dear, but is there nothing in return for them? To take, they were taken ; but as to giving, nothing was given back! " Others, .however, repeated, with floods of tears and with groaning, "Jesus! Jesus! Jesus!"

Throngs wished to enter the castle, to look once again on the beloved face of the lady. They were not admitted, but the promise was given that the body would be exposed in the church; then every one would be able to look at it, and to pray near it.

Later, toward evening, gloomy crowds began to return to the city, telling one another of the last moments of the queen, and of the coming burial, as well as of the miracles which would be performed near her body and around her tomb; of the miracles, all were perfectly convinced. It was said also that the queen would be canonized immediately after her death; when some doubted whether this could be done, others grew impatient and threatened with Avignon.

Gloomy sadness fell on the city and on the whole country; it seemed, not merely to common people, but to all, that with the queen the lucky star of the kingdom was quenched.

Even among the lords of Cracow there were some who saw the future in darkness. They began to ask themselves and others: "What will corne now? Will Yagello, after the death of the queen, have the right to reign in the kingdom; or will he return to his own Lithuania, and be satisfied there with the throne of Grand Prince? " Some foresaw, and not

without reason, that he would desire to withdraw, and that in such case broad lands would fall away from the crown; attacks would begin again from the side of Lithuania, and bloody reprisals from the stubborn citizens of the kingdom ; the Knights of the Cross would grow more powerful, the Roman Cassar would increase, and also Hungary; while the Polish kingdom, yesterday one of the strongest on earth, would come to fall and to shame.

Merchants, for whom the extensive regions of Lithuania and Rus had been opened, foreseeing losses, made pious offerings to the end that Yagello might remain in the kingdom, but in such a case again they predicted a sudden war with the Order. It was known that only the queen restrained Yagello. People remembered how once, when indignant at the greed and rapacity of the Knights of the Cross, she said to them in prophetic vision: " While I live, I shall restrain the hand and just wrath of my husband, but remember that after my death punishment will fall on you for your sins."

They in their pride and blindness had no fear of war, it is true, considering that after the death of the queen the charm of her holiness would not stop the influx of volunteers from Western kingdoms. Thousands of warriors from Germany, Burgundy, France, and yet more remote countries, would come to aid them. Still, the death of Yadviga was such a far-reaching event that the envoy Lichtenstein, without waiting for the return of the absent king, hurried away with all speed to Malborg, to lay before the Grand Master and the Chapter the important, and, in some sense, terrible news.

The Hungarian, Austrian, Roman, and Bohemian envoys departed a little later, or sent couriers to their monarchs. Yagello came to Cracow in grievous despair. At the first moment he declared that he had no wish to reign without the queen, and that he would go to his inheritance in Lithuania. Then from grief he fell into torpor ; he would not decide any affair nor answer any question; at times he grew terribly angry at himself because he had gone from Cracow, because he had not been present at the death of Yadviga, because he had not taken farewell of her, because he had not heard her last words and advice.

In vain did Stanislav of Skarbimir and the bishop of Cracow explain to him that the queen's illness had happened unexpectedly, that according to human reckoning he had had time to return had the birth taken place in its own proper

season. This brought no relief to him, and mildened no sorrow.

" I am not a king without her," said he to the bishop, *' but a penitent sinner who will never know solace." Then he fixed his eyes on the floor, and no one could win another word from him.

Meanwhile all thoughts were occupied with the funeral of the queen. From every part of the country new crowds of lords, nobles, and people began to assemble; especially came the indigent, who hoped for abundant profit from alms at the funeral, which was to last a whole month. The queen's body was placed in the cathedral on an elevation, and placed in such manner that the wider part of the coffin, in which rested the head of the deceased, was considerably higher than the narrower part. This was done purposely, so that people might see the queen's face.

In the cathedral masses were celebrated continually; at the catafalque thousands of wax candles were burning, and amid those gleams and amid flowers she lay calm, smiling, like a white mystic rose, with her hands crossed on laurel cloth. The people saw in her a saint; they brought to her people who were possessed, cripples, sick children; and time after time, in the middle of the church was heard the cry, now of some mother who noted on the face of her sick child a flush, the herald of health, now of some paralytic who on a sudden recovered strength in his helpless limbs. Then a quiver seized the hearts of people, news of the miracle flew through church, castle, and city, then ever increasing crowds of human wretchedness appeared, wretchedness which could hope for help only through a miracle.

Meanwhile Zbyshko was entirely forgotten, for who, in face of such a gigantic misfortune, could think of an ordinary noble youth and his imprisonment in a bastion of the castle!

Zbyshko, however, knew from the prison guards of the queen's death, he had heard the uproar of the people around the castle, and when he heard their weeping and the tolling of bells he cast himself on his knees, and calling to mind his own lot, mourned with his whole soul the death of the idolized lady. It seemed to him that with her something that was his had been quenched also, and that in view of such a death it was not worth while for any one to live in the world.

The echo of the funeral, the church bells, the singing of processions, and the movement of crowds, reached him for

whole weeks. During this time he grew gloomy, he lost desire for food, for sleep, and walked up and down in his dungeon like a wild beast in a cage. Loneliness weighed on him, for there were days when even the prison guard did not bring him fresh food and water, so far were ah 1 people occupied by the funeral of the queen. From the time of her death no one had visited him, neither the princess nor Danusia, nor Povala, they who a little while before showed him so much good will, nor Matsko's acquaintance, the merchant Amyley. Zbyshko thought with bitterness that were Matsko to die all would forget him. At moments it came to his head that perhaps justice too would forget him, and that he would rot to death in that prison; he prayed then to die.

At last, when a month had passed after the queen's funeral and a second month had begun, he fell to despairing of his uncle's return; for Matsko had promised to come quickly and not spare his horse. Malborg was not at the end of the earth. It was possible to go and return in twelve weeks, especially if one were in a hurry. "But mayhap he is not in a liurr\'7d 7 ," thought Zbyshko with grief. " Mayhap he has found a wife on the road for himself, and will take her with gladness to Bogdanets, and wait for posterity himself, while I shall stay here forever, expecting God's mercy."

At last he lost reckoning of time, he ceased to speak with the guard, and only from the cobwebs which covered abundantly the iron grating in the window did he note that autumn was in the world. He sat for whole hours on the bed, with his elbows on his knees and his fingers in his hair, which reached now far below his shoulders, and half in sleep, half in torpor, he did not even raise his head when the guard, bringing food, spoke to him. But on a certain day the hinges squeaked, and a known voice called from the threshold, —

" Zbyshko! "

"Uncle dear!" cried Zbyshko, springing from his plank bed.

Matsko seized him by the shoulders, then embraced his bright head with his hands, and began to kiss it. Grief, bitterness, and longing, so rose in the heart of the young man that he cried on his uncle's breast like a little child.

"I thought that you would never return," said he, sobbing.

"Well, I came near that," answered Matsko.

Only then did Zbyshko raise his head and looking at him cry,—

" But what has happened you?" And he gazed with astonishment at the emaciated face of the old warrior, which had fallen in and was as pale as linen; he looked on his bent figure and on his iron gray hair.

" What has happened? " repeated he.

Matsko seated himself on the plank bed, and for a while breathed heavily.

" What has happened!" said he at last. " Barely had I passed the boundary when Germans shot me in a forest, from a crossbow. Robber knights! knowest thou ? It is hard yet for me to breathe. God sent me aid, or thou wouldst not see me here."

" Who saved you ? "

" Yurand of Spyhov," answered Matsko.

A moment of silence followed; then Matsko said, —

" They attacked me, and half a day later he attacked them. Hardly one half of them escaped. He took me to his castle, and there in Spyhov I wrestled three weeks with death. God did not let me die, and though suffering yet, I am here."

"Then you have not been at Malborg?"

"What had I to take there? The Germans stripped me naked, and with other things seized the letter. I returned to implore Princess Alexandra for a second one, but missed her on the road; whether I can overtake her, I know not, for I must also make ready for the other world."

Then he spat on his hand, which he stretched out toward Zbyshko and showed unmixed blood on it.

" Dost see? Clearly the will of God," added he, after a while.

Under the weight of gloomy thoughts both were silent some time, then Zbyshko inquired, —

" Do you spit blood all the time?"

" Why not, with an arrow-head fastened half a span deep between my ribs? Thou wouldst spit also — never fear! But I grew better in Yurand's castle, though now I suffer terribly, for the road was long and I travelled fast."

" Oh ! why did you hurry? "

" I wished to find Princess Alexandra here and get another letter. ' Go,' said Yurand to me, ' and bring back a letter. I shall have Germans here under the floor; I will let out one on his knightly word, and he will take the letter to the Grand Master.' Yurand keeps a number of Germans there always, and listens gladly when they groan in the night-time and rattle their chains, for he is a stern man. Dost understand?"

" I understand. But this astonishes me, that you lost the first letter, for as Yurand caught the men who attacked you they must have had the letter."

" He did not catch all; something like five escaped. Such is our luck! "

Matsko coughed, spat blood again, and groaned some from pain in his breast.

" They wounded you badly," said Zbyshko. " How was it ? From an ambush ? "

"From a thicket so dense that a yard away nothing was visible. I was travelling without armor, since merchants had said that the road was safe — and the weather was hot."

" Who commanded the robbers? A Knight of the Cross? "

" Not a monk, but a man fromHelmno who lives in Lentz, a German notorious for robbing and plundering."

" What happened to him? "

"Yurand has him in chains. But he has also two nobles of Mazovia in his dungeon; these he wishes to exchange for thee."

Again there was silence.

" Dear Jesus! " said Zbyshko, at length. "Lichtenstein will live, and he of Lentz also, while we must die unavenged. They will cut off my head, and you will not live through the winter."

"More than that, I shall not live until winter. If only I could save thee in some way! "

" Have you seen any one?"

" I have been with the castellan of Cracow; for when I heard that Lichtenstein had gone I thought that the castellan would favor thee."

"Has Lichtenstein gone?"

" He went to Malborg immediately after the queen's death. I was with the castellan, and he said: ' Your nephew's head will be cut off, not to please Lichtenstein, but because of the sentence; and whether Lichtenstein be present or absent, it is all one. Even were he to die, that would change nothing; for,' said he, ' law is according to justice, — not like a coat which may be turned inside out. The king,' said he, 4 may pardon, but no one else.'"

" And where is the king? "

" After the funeral he went to Rue."

" Then there is no escape ? "

"None. The castellan added: 'I am sorry for him; Princess Anna too entreats in his favor, but since I can do nothing, I am powerless.'"

" Then is Princess Anna here yet? "

"May God reward her! She is a kindly lady. She is here yet, for Yurand's daughter is ill, and the princess loves her as if she were her own child."

" Oh, for God's sake! And sickness has fallen on Danusia! What is the matter with her? "

" Do I know? The princess says that some one has bewitched her."

" Surely Lichtenstein! no one else except Lichtenstein — a dog is his mother! "

"Perhaps it was he. But what canst thou do to him? Nothing!"

" Since Danusia is sick all here have forgotten me — "

Zbyshko walked M'ith great strides through the room, then he grasped Matsko's hand and said, after kissing it, —

" God reward you for everything! You will die for my sake; but since you have gone to Prussia, before you lose the rest of your strength do one other thing. Go to the castellan; beg him to let me out, on the word of a knight, for twelve weeks even. I will return then and let them cut off my head. But it cannot be that we should die unavenged. You know — I will go to Malborg and straightway challenge Lichtenstein. It cannot be otherwise. His death, or mine! "

Matsko fell to rubbing his forehead.

" As to going, I will go; but will the castellan grant permission ?"

" I will give the word of a knight. Twelve weeks — I need no more."

"It is easy to say twelve weeks. But if thou art wounded and cannot return, what will they say of thee?"

" I will return even on my hands and feet. Have no fear! Besides, the king may come back from Rus by that time; it will be possible then to bow down to him for pardon."

"True!" answered Matsko; but after a while he added: "The castellan told me this also: ' We forgot your nephew because the queen died, but now let the affair be finished.'"

"Ei! he will permit," said Zbyshko, with consolation. " He knows well that a noble will keep his word, and whether they cut off my head now or after Saint Michael's, it is all one to the castellan."

"I will go this day."

" Go to Amyley's house to-day and lie down a little. Let them put some cure on your wound; to-morrow you will go to the castellan."

" Well, then, with God!"

They embraced and Matsko turned to the door; but he stopped on the threshold and wrinkled his brow as if thinking of something on a sudden.

"Well, but thou dost not wear a knight's belt yet. Lich-tensteinwill answer that he cannot fight with an unbelted man, and what wilt thou do?"

Zbyshko was perplexed for a while, and then asked, —

"But how is it in war? Must belted men choose only belted men as opponents?"

" War is war, but a duel is different."

"True — but — wait— There is need to arrange this. Yes, you see, — there is a way! Prince Yanush of Mazovia will give me a belt. When the princess and Danusia beg him, he will gird me. And on the road I will fight right away with the sou of Mikolai of Dlugolyas."

"What for?"

" Because Pan Mikolai — he who is with the princess and whom they call Obuh — said that Danusia was a chit."

Matsko looked at him with astonishment. Zbyshko, wishing evidently to explain better what the question was, continued, —

" I cannot forgive him that, you know ; but with Mikolai I will not fight, for he is about eighty years old."

" Listen, boy! " said Matsko. " I am sorry for thy head, but not for thy sense; thou art as stupid as a hornless he-goat."

" But what are you angry about? "

Matsko said nothing, and wanted to go; but Zbyshko sprang up once more to him.

"And how is Danusia? Is she well? Be not angry for a trifle. Besides, you were absent so long."

And he bent again to the old man's hand. Matsko shrugged his shoulders and said, "Yurand's daughter is in good health, but they do not let her out of the room. Farewell."

Zbyshko was left alone, but reborn, as it were, in soul and body. It was pleasant for him to think that he would have three months more of life, that he would go to distant lands, seek out Lichteustein, and fight a mortal battle with him. At the very thought of this, delight filled his breast.

It was pleasant to feel that even for twelve weeks he would have a horse under him, ride through the broad world, fight, and not die unavenged. And then, let happen what might. Besides, that was an immense stretch of time; the king might return from Rus and pardon his offence; perhaps the war would break out which all had been predicting a long time; perhaps the castellan himself, when after three months he would see him victorious over the haughty

Lichtenstein, would say, " Go now to the forests! " Zbyshko felt clearly that no one cherished hatred against him save the Knight of the Cross, and that only through constraint had the stern castellan condemned him.

So hope entered his breast more and more, because he doubted not that those three months would be granted. Nay, he thought that they would give him even more; for that a noble who had sworn on the honor of a knight should not keep his word would not even come to the head of the old castellan. Therefore, when Matsko came to the prison next day about nightfall, Zbyshko, who could hardly remain sitting, sprang to him at the threshold and asked, —

" Has he permitted ? "

Matsko sat on the plank bed; he could not stand because of weakness ; he breathed awhile heavily, and said at last:

" The castellan answered in this way: ' If you need to divide land or property, I will let out your nephew, on the word of a knight, for one or two weeks, but not longer.'"

Zbyshko was so astonished that for some time he could not utter a word.

"For two weeks?" asked he, at length. "But in one week I could not even go to the boundary! What is that? Did you tell the castellan my reason for going to Malborg? "

" Not only did I beg for thee, but Princess Anna begged also — "

"Well, and what?"

" The old man told her that he did not want your head, and that he himself grieves for you. ' If I could find some law on his side,' said the castellan, ' nay, some pretext, I would let him out altogether; but as I cannot find it, I cannot free the man. It will not be well,' said he, * in this kingdom, when people close their eyes to law and show favor through friendship; this I will not do, even were it a question of my relative, Toporchyk, or even of iny brother.' So stern is the man ! And he added besides: ' We need not consider the Knights of the Cross too much,

but we are not permitted to disgrace ourselves before them. What -would they think, and their guests, who assemble from the whole world, if I should let out a noble condemned to death because he wants to go to them for a duel? Would they believe that punishment would touch him, or that there is justice in our kingdom? I would rather cut off one head than yield the king and the kingdom to death." To this the princess replied that justice which did not allow a relative of the king to get pardon for a man seemed to her strange justice. ' Mercy serves the king, but lack of justice serves him not,' said the castellan. At last they fell to disputing, for the princess was borne away by her anger. ' Then do not let him rot in prison !' said she. ' To-morrow I will give the order to make a scaffold on the square,' replied the castellan. With that they parted. Poor boy, the Lord Jesus alone can save thee ! "

A long silence followed.

"How?" asked Zbyshko, in a low voice. "Then it will be right away?"

" In two or three days. When there is no help, there is no help; I have done all I could. I fell at the castellan's feet, I begged for pardon, but he held to his position : ' Find a law or a pretext.' But what could I find? I went to Father Stauislav of Skarbimir to bring the Lord God to thee. Let even that glory be thine, that the man confessed thee who confessed the queen. But I did not find him at home; he was with Princess Anna."

"Perhaps with Danusia? "

" Oh, pray to the Lord for thyself. That girl is better and better. I will go to the priest before da\'7d 7 break tomorrow. They say that after confessing to him, salvation is as sure to thee as if thou hadst it tied up in a bag."

Zbyshko sat down, rested his elbows on his knees, and bent his head so that the hair covered his face altogether. The old man looked at him a long time, and said at last in a low voice, —

"Zbyshko! Zbyshko!"

The youth raised his face, which was angry and filled with cold stubbornness rather than pain.

" Well, what is it? "

" Listen carefully, for I may have found something." He pushed up nearer and spoke almost in a whisper: "Thou hast heard of Prince Vitold, how formerly he was imprisoned in Krev by Yagello, our present king; he escaped from con-

VOL. I. — 7

fmement in the dress of a woman. No woman will stay here in thy place, but take thou my coat, take my cowl, and go forth. Dost understand? They will not notice thee, be sure. That is certain. Beyond the doors it is dark. They will not look into thy eyes. They saw me yesterday as I went out; no one looked at me. Be quiet, and listen. They will find me to-morrow— Well, what? Will they cut off my head? That would be a pleasure to them, when as it is my death is appointed for a time two or three weeks distant. But as soon as thou art out, mount thy horse and ride straight to Vitold. Name thyself, bow down to him; he will receive thee, and with him thou wilt be as with the Lord God behind a stove. Here people say that the armies of the prince have been swept away by the Tartar. It is unknown if that be true; it may be, for the late queen prophesied that the expedition would end thus. If it be true, the prince will need knights all the more, and will be glad to see thee. But do thou adhere to him, for there is not in the world a better sen-ice than his. If another king loses a war, it is all over with him; but in Prince Vitold there is such deftness that after defeat he is stronger than ever. He is bountiful, and he loves us immensely. Tell him everything as it happened. Tell him that it was thy wish to go with him against the Tartar, but that thou wert confined in the tower. God grant that he will present thee with land and men, make a belted knight of thee, and take thy part before the king. He is a good advocate."

Zbyshko listened in silence, and Matsko, as if urged by his own words, continued, —

"It is not for thee to die in youth, but to return to Bogdanets. When there, take a wife at once, so that our race may not perish. Only when thou hast children wilt thou be free to challenge Lichtenstein to mortal combat; but before that see that thou keep from revenge, for they would shoot thee somewhere in Prussia, as they did me, — then there would be no help for thee. Take the coat, take the cowl, and move in God's name."

Matsko rose and began to undress, but Zbyshko rose also, seized his hand, and cried, —

" What do you wish of me? I will not do that! so help me God and the Holy Cross! "

"Why?" asked Matsko, with astonishment.

"Because I will not."

Matsko grew pale from emotion and anger.

" "Would to God thou hadst not been born! "

" You have told the castellan that you would give your head for mine."

" Whence knowest thou? "

" Povala of Tachev told me."

"Well, what of that?"

" The castellan told you that disgrace would fall on me, and on our whole race. Would it not be a still greater disgrace were I to flee hence and leave you to the law's vengeance ? "

" What vengeance? What can the law do to me when I shall die anyhow ? For God's sake, have reason."

" But have it you all the more. May God punish me if I desert you, a man sick and old. Pfu! shame! "

Silence followed; nothing was to be heard but the heavy, rattling breath of Matsko, and the call of the bowmen standing on guard at the gate. It was dark night now outside.

" Hear me," said Matsko at last, in a broken voice. " It was no shame for Prince Vitold to flee in disguise, it will be no shame for thee — "

" Hei!" answered Zbyshko, with a certain sadness. " Vitold is a great prince. He has a crown from the king's hands; he has wealth and dominion; but I, a poor noble, have nothing — save honor."

After a while he cried, as if in a sudden outburst of anger, —

" But can you not understand this, that I so love you that I will not give your head for mine ? "

Matsko rose on trembling feet, stretched forth his hand, and, though the nature of people in that age was as firm as if forged out of iron, he bellowed on a sudden in a heartrending voice, —

"Zbyshko!"

On the following day court servants began to draw beams to the square for a scaffold which was to be erected before the main gate of the city hall.

Still Princess Anna continued to take counsel with Yastrem-bets, and Father Stanislav of Skarbimir, and other learned canons skilled equally in written and customary law. She was encouraged to these efforts by the words of the castellan, who declared that, should they find "law, or pretext," he would not be slow in releasing Zbyshko. They counselled long and earnestly as to whether it was possible to find something; and

though Father Stanislav prepared Zbyshko for death, and gave the last sacraments to him, he went straight from the dungeon to a consultation which lasted almost till daybreak.

Meanwhile the day of execution had come. From early morning crowds had been gathering on the square, for the head of a noble roused more curiosity than that of a common man, and besides this the weather was wonderful. Among women the news had spread also of the youthful years and uncommon beauty of Zbyshko; hence the whole road leading from the castle was blooming as with flowers from whole myriads of comely women of the citizen class. In the windows on the square, and in outbulging balconies were to be seen also caps, gold and velvet head-dresses, or the bare heads of maidens ornamented only with garlands of lilies and roses. The city counsellors, though the affair did not pertain to them really, had all come to lend themselves importance, and had taken their places just behind the knights, who, wishing to show sympathy with the young man, had appeared next the scaffold in a body. Behind the counsellors stood a many-colored crowd, composed of the smaller merchants and handicraftsmen, in the colors of their guilds. Students and children, who had been pushed back, circled about like dissatisfied flies in the midst of the multitude, crowding in wherever there appeared even a little free space. Above that dense mass of human heads was seen the scaffold covered with new cloth, on which were three persons: one the executioner, broad-shouldered and terrible, a German in a red coat and a cowl of the same stuff, with a heavy double-edged sword in his hand, — with him two assistants, their arms bared, and ropes around their loins. At their feet was a block, and a cotlin, covered also with cloth; on the towers of the church of the Virgin Mary bells were tolling, filling the place with metallic sound, and frightening flocks of daws and doves.

People looked now at the road leading from the castle, now at the scaffold and the executioner standing upon it with his sword gleaming in the sunlight; then, finally, at the knights, on whom citizens looked always with respect and eagerness. This time there was something to look at, for the most famous were standing in a square near the scaffold. So they admired the breadth of shoulders and the dignity of Zavisha Charny, his raven hair falling to his shoulders. They admired the square stalwart form and the column-like legs of Zyndram of Mashkovitse, and the gigantic, almost preterhu-

man stature of Pashko Zloclye, the stern face of Voitseh of Vodzinka, and the beauty of Dobko of Olesnitsa, who in the tournament at Torun had finished twelve German knights, and Zygmunt of Bobova, who made himself famous in like manner in Hungary at Koshytse, and Kron of Koziglove, and Lis of Targovisko, terrible in hand-to-hand combat, and Stashko of Harbimovitse, who could overtake a horse at full speed. General attention was roused also by Matsko of Bogdanets with his pallid face; he was supported by Floryan of Korytnitse, and Martsin of Vrotsimovitse. It was supposed generally that he was the father of the condemned.

But the greatest curiosity was roused by Povala of Tachev, vrho, standing in the first rank, held on his powerful arm Danusia, dressed in white altogether, with a garland of rue around her bright hair. People did not understand what that meant, and why that maiden dressed in white was to witness the execution. Some said that she was Zbyshko's sister, others divined in her the lady of his thoughts; but even those could not explain to themselves her dress, or her presence at the scaffold. But in all hearts her face, like a blushing apple, though it was covered with tears, roused emotion and sympathy. In the dense throng of people they began to murmur at the unbendingness of the castellan, and the sternness of the law; these murmurs passed gradually into a roar which was simply terrible. At last here and there voices rose, saying that if the scaffold were torn away the execution would be deferred of necessity.

The crowd became animated and swayed. From mouth to mouth the statement was sent that, were the king present, beyond doubt he would pardon the youth, who, as men affirmed, was not guilty of any crime.

But all became silent, for distant shouts announced the approach of the bowmen and the king's halberdiers, in the midst of whom marched the condemned. Indeed the retinue appeared soon on the square. The procession was opened by the funeral brotherhood dressed in black robes which reached the ground, and with face coverings of similar material with openings for their eyes. People feared those gloomy figures, and at sight of them became silent. Behind those marched a detachment of crossbowmen formed of select Lithuanians, wearing coats of elkskin untanned. That was a detachment of the royal guard. Behind this were seen the halberds of another detachment; in the centre of this, between the court secretary, who had read the sentence, and Father Stanislav of Skarbimir, who bore a crucifix, walked Zbyshko.

All eyes were turned to him; from every window and balcony female forms bent forward. Zbyshko advanced dressed in the white jacket which he had won; it was embroidered with gold griffins and adorned at the bottom with a beautiful gold fringe. In this brilliant attire he seemed to the eyes of the audience a prince, or a youth of some lofty house. From his stature, his shoulders, evident under the closely fitting dress, from his strong limbs and broad breast, he seemed a man quite mature, but above that stature of a man rose a head almost childlike, and a youthful face, with the first down on its lips, which was at the same time the face of a royal page, with golden hair cut evenly above his brows and let down long on his shoulders.

Zln'shko advanced with even and springy tread, but with a pallid face. At moments he looked at the throng, as if at something in a dream; at moments he raised his eyes to the towers of the churches, to the flocks of doves, and to the swinging bells, which were sounding out his last hour to him; at moments also there was reflected on his face, as it were, wonderment that those sounds and the sobs of women, and all that solemnity were intended for him. Finally he saw on the square from afar the scaffold, and on it the red outline of the executioner. He quivered and made the sign of the cross on himself; at that moment the priest gave him the crucifix to kiss. A few steps farther on a bunch of star thistles, thrown by a young maiden, fell at his feet. Zbyshko bent down, raised it, and smiled at the maiden, who burst into loud weeping. But he thought evidently that in presence of those crowds, and in presence of women waving handkerchiefs from the windows, he ought to die bravely, and leave behind the memory of a "valiant youth " at the least. So he exerted all his courage and will; with a sudden movement he threw back his hair, raised his head higher, and advanced haughtily, almost like a victor in knightly tournaments which he had finished, a victor whom men were conducting to receive his reward.

The advance was slow, for in front the throng became denser and denser, and gave way unwillingly. In vain did the Lithuanian crossbowinen, who moved in the first rank, cry continually: "Eyk shalin! Eyk shalin!" (Out of the road!). People had no wish to know what those words meant — and crowded the more. Though the citizens of

Cracow at that time were two-thirds of them German, still round about were heard dreadful curses against the Knights of the Cross. "Shame! shame! May the German wolves perish if children must die to please them. It is a shame for the king and the kingdom! " The Lithuanians, seeing this resistance, took their bows, already drawn, from their shoulders, and looked frowningly at the people ; they dared not, however, shoot into the crowd without orders. But the captain sent halberdiers in advance, for it was easier to open the road with halberds. In that way they reached the knights standing in the square around the scaffold.

These opened without resistance. First the halberdiers entered, after them came Zbyshko with the priest and the secretary, after that something took place which no one had expected.

Suddenly from among the knights stepped forth Povala, with Danusia on his arm, and cried "Stop!" with such a thundering voice that the whole retinue halted as if fastened to the earth. Neither the captain nor any of the soldiers dared oppose a lord and a belted knight whom they saw daily in the castle, and often talking with the king confidentially. Finally others, also renowned, cried with commanding voices: "Stop! stop!" Povala approached Zbyshko and gave him Danusia dressed in white.

Zbyshko, thinking that that was the farewell, seized her, embraced her, and pressed her to his bosom; but Danusia, instead of nestling up to him and throwing her arms around his neck, pulled as quickly as possible from her bright hair and from under the garland of rue a white veil and covered Zbyshko's head with it entirely, crying at the same time, —

" He is mine! he is mine! "

" He is hers! " repeated the powerful voices of the knights. "To the castellan!"

" To the castellan! To the castellan! " answered a shout from the people which was like thunder.

The priest raised his eyes, the court secretary was confused, the captain and the halberdiers dropped their weapons, for all understood what had happened.

It was an old Polish and Slav custom, as valid as law, known in Podhale, in Cracow, and even farther, that when an innocent maiden threw her veil over a man on the way to execution, as a sign that she wanted to marry him, she saved the man from death and punishment by that act. The knights knew this custom, yeomen knew it, the Polish people

of the city knew it, and Germans inhabiting from remote times Polish cities and towns knew its force. Old Matsko grew weak from emotion at that sight, the knights, pushing back the crossbowmen promptly, surrounded Zbyshko and Danusia; the people were moved, and in their delight cried with still louder voices: " To the castellan! to the castellan! " The crowd rose suddenly like gigantic waves of the sea. The executioner and his assistants fled with all haste from the scaffold. There was a disturbance, for it had become clear to everyone that if the castellan wished to oppose the sacred custom a terrible uproar would rise in the city. In fact a column of people rushed at the scaffold. In the twinkle of an eye they dragged off the cloth and tore it to pieces, then the planks and beams, pulled away with strong hands, or cut with axes, bent, cracked, broke — and a few Our Fathers later there was no trace of the scaffold on that square.

Zbyshko, holding Danusia in his arms, returned to the castle, but this time as a real conquering triumphator; for around him, with joyful faces, advanced the first knights of the kingdom, at the sides, in front, and behind, crowded thousands of men, women, and children, crying in heaven-piercing voices, singing, stretching out their hands to Danusia and glorifying the courage and the beauty of both. From the windows the white hands of ladies clapped applause to them; everywhere were visible eyes filled with tears of rapture. A shower of garlands of roses and lilies, a shower of ribbons, and even of gold belts and knots fell at the feet of the happy youth, and he, radiant as the sun, his heart filled with gratitude, raised aloft his white little lady from moment to moment; sometimes he kissed her knees with delight, and that sight melted young maidens to the degree that some threw themselves into the arms of their lovers, declaring that should these lovers incur death they would be freed in like manner.

Zbyshko and Danusia had become, as it were, the beloved children of knights, of citizens, and of the great multitude. Old Matsko, whom Floryan and Martsin supported on either side, almost went out of his mind from delight, —and from astonishment also, that such a means of saving his nephew had not even occurred to him.

In the general uproar Povala of Tachev told the knights in his powerful voice how Yastrembets and Stanislav of Skarbimir, skilled in written and customary law, had invented, or rather remembered, this method while advising with the princess. The knights wondered at its simplicity, saying among themselves that except those two, no one else had remembered the custom, which, in a city occupied by Germans, had not been practised for a long period.

But everything depended still on the castellan. The knights and people went to the castle where the castellan lived during the king's absence, and straightway the court secretary, Father Stanislav, Zavisha, Farurey, Zyndram, and Povala of Tachev went to him to represent the validity of the custom, and remind him how he himself had said that if "law or pretext" were found by them, he would free Zbyshko. What law could surpass ancient custom, which had never been broken? The castellan answered, it is true, that that custom referred more to common people and robbers than to nobles; but he was too well versed in every law not to recognize the force of it. Meanwhile he covered his silver beard with his hand and smiled under his fingers, for he was glad evidently. At last he went out on a low porch; at his side stood Princess Anna Danuta, with some of the clergy and knighthood.

Zbyshko, seeing him, raised up Danusia again; the castellan placed his aged hand on her golden hair, held it a while there, and then nodded his gray head with kindness and dignity.

All understood that sign, and the very walls of the castle quivered from shouts. "God aid thee! Live long, just lord! live and judge us! " shouted people from all sides. New shouts were raised then for Danusia and Zbyshko. A moment later both ascended the porch and fell at the feet of the kind princess, Anna Dauuta, to whom Zbyshko owed his life; for with the learned men it was she who had discovered the law and taught Danusia what to do.

" Long live the young couple ! " cried Povala, at sight of them on their knees.

" Long life to them! " repeated others.

But the old castellan turned to the princess and said, —

" Well, gracious lady, the betrothal must take place at once, for custom demands that."

" The betrothal I will have at once," answered the good lady, with radiant face; " but I will not permit marriage without consent of her father, Yurand of Spyhov."

Matsko and Zbyshko consulted with the merchant Amyley as to what they should do. The old knight looked for his own

speedy death, and because the Franciscan father, Tsybek, skilled in wounds, had foretold it, he wished to go to Bogdauets and be buried with his fathers in the graveyard of Ostrov.

But not all of his "fathers" were lying there, for once the family had been numerous. In time of war they were summoned with the watchword, " Grady " (" Hail ") ; they had on their shield the Blunt Horseshoe, considering themselves better than other possessors of land, who had not always the right of an escutcheon. In the year 1331, at the battle of Plovtsi, seventy-four warriors from Bogdanets were killed in a swamp by German crossbowmen; only one survived,— Voitek, surnamed Tur (Wild Bull), to whom King Vladislav Lokietek, after crushing the Germans, confirmed in special privilege his shield and the lauds of Bogdanets. The bones of the seventy-four relatives lay bleaching thenceforth on the field of Plovtsi; Voitek returned to his domestic hearth, but only to see the utter ruin of his family. For, while the men of Bogdanets were dying beneath the arrows of the Germans, robber knights from adjoining Silesia had attacked their nest, burnt the buildings to the ground, slain the people, or led them captive to be sold in remote German Provinces.

Voitek was all alone as the heir of broad but unoccupied lands, which had belonged once to a whole ruling family. Five years later he married and begat two sons, Yasko and Matsko, and while hunting in the forest was killed by a wild bull.

The sons grew up under care of their mother, Kasia of Spalenitsa, who in two expeditions took vengeance on the Silesian Germans for their former injustice. In the third expedition she fell; but already she had built Bogdanets castle with the hands of captives, through which Yasko and Matsko, though from former times they were always called possessors, became considerable people. Yasko, coming to maturity, took in marriage Yagenka of Motsarzev, who gave birth to Zbyshko; but Mntsko, remaining unmarried, took care of his nephew's property in so far as military expeditious permitted.

But when, in time of civil war between the Grymaliti and the Nalenchi, the castle in Bogdanets was burned a second time, and the people scattered, the lonely Matsko strove in vain to rebuild it. After he had struggled not a few years, he left the land at last to the abbot of Tulcha, his relative, and went himself with Zbyshko, yet a boy, to Lithuania the Germans.

But he had never lost sight of Bogclanets. To Lithuania he went with the hope that after he had grown rich from booty he would return in time to redeem the land, settle it with captives, rebuild the castle, and fix in it Zbyshko. Now, after the happy escape of the youth, he was thinking of this and counselling with him concerning it at the house of the merchant, Amyley.

They had something with which to redeem the land. From booty, and ransoms which knights taken captive by them had paid, and from the gifts of Vitold, they had collected supplies which were rather considerable. Especially large was the profit which that battle to the death against the two Frisian knights had brought them. The armor alone which they had taken formed a real fortune in that period; besides armor they took wagons, horses, servants, clothing, money, and a whole rich military outfit. The merchant Amyley purchased much of that booty, and among other things two pieces of wonderful Frisian cloth which the provident and wealthy knights had brought with them in the wagons.

Matsko had sold also the costly armor, thinking that in view of near death it would be of no use to him. The armorer who bought it sold it the next day to Martsin of Vrotsimovitse with considerable profit, since armor of Milan was esteemed above all other armor on earth at that period. Zbyshko regretted the armor with his whole soul.

" If God return health to you," said he to his uncle, "where will you find another such?"

"Where I found that, — on a German," answered Matsko. " But I shall not escape death. The iron broke in my ribs, and the fragment remained in me. By plucking at it, and trying to drag it out with my nails. I pushed it in the more deeply; and now there is no cure for me."

" If you would drink a pot or two of bear's fat! "

" Yes. Father Tsybek also says that that would be well, for perhaps the fragment might slip out in some way. But how can I get it here? In Bogdanets we should only need to take an axe and watch one night under a bee-hive."

" Then we must go to Bogdanets. Only, you must not die on the road."

Old Matsko looked with a certain tenderness on his nephew.

" I know where thou wishest to go, — to the court of Prince Yanush, or to Yuraiid of Spyhov, to attack Germans of Helmno."

" I do not deny that. I should go gladly to Warsaw with the court of the princess, or to Tsehanov, so as to be as long as possible with Danusia. I cannot live now without her in any way; she is not only my lady, but my love. I am so glad when I see her that when I think of her a shiver takes hold of me. I would go with her even to the end of the earth, but you are at present my first law. You did not leave me, and I will not desert you. If to Bogdanets, then to Bogdanets! "

" Thou art a good boy! "

" God would punish me were I not good to you. See, they are packing the wagons already, and one I have filled with hay for you. Amyley has presented besides a feather bed, but I know not whether you will be able to stay on it from heat. We will drive slowly with the princess and the court, so that care may not fail you. Afterward they will go to Mazovia, and we to our place. God aid us! "

" Only let me live long enough to rebuild the castle," said Matsko ; " for I know that after my death thou wilt not think often of Bogdanets."

"Why should I not think?"

" For in thy head will be love and battles."

"But was there not war in your own head? I have marked out exactly what I am to do; the first thing is to build a castle of strong oak — and we shall have a moat dug around it in order."

"Is that thy way of thinking?" inquired Matsko, with roused curiosity. " But when will the castle be built? Tell that!"

"The castle will be built before my visit to Princess Anna's court in Warsaw or Tsehanov."

"After my death? "

" If you die soon, it will be after your death. If you die I will bury you worthily first of all; and if the Lord Jesus give you health you will stay in Bogdanets. The princess has promised that I shall receive a knight's belt from the prince. Without that, Lichtenstein would not fight with me."

" After that wilt thou go to Malborg? "

" To Malborg, or to the end of the earth, if I can only find Lichtenstein."

"I will not blame thee in that. Thy death or his! "

"Ah! I will bring his glove and his belt to Bogdanets. have no fear."

" But guard against treason. With them treason is ready."

"I will bow down before Prince Yanush to send to the Grand Master for a safe-conduct. There is peace now. I will go with the safe-conduct to Malborg; at Malborg there is always a throng of foreign knights. Do you know? First, Lichtenstein; and then I will see who have peacock-plumes on their helmets; in turn I will challenge them. May God aid me ! Should the Lord Jesus give victory I will perform my vow at once."

Thus speaking Zbyshko smiled at his own thoughts; thereupon his face was like that of a boy who is telling what knightly deeds he will do when he grows up to manhood.

" Hei," said Matsko, nodding his head, " shouldst thou finish three knights of famous stock, not only would thy vow be accomplished, but thou wouldst take some good gear at the same time. O thou dear God! "

"What are three?" cried Zbyshko. "When I was in prison I said to myself that I would not be niggardly with Danusia. As many knights as she has fingers on her hands, — not three! "

Matsko shrugged his shoulders.

"You wonder, but do not believe," said Zbyshko. "I will go from Malborg to Yurand of Spyhov. Why should I not bow down to him, since he is Danusia's father? With him I will go against the Germans of Helmno. You said yourself that he is the greatest wolf-man in Mazovia against Germans."

" But if he will not give thee Danusia? "

" He has no reason not to give her! He is seeking his own revenge, I mine. Whom better can he find? Besides, since the princess has permitted the betrothal, he will not oppose."

" I note one thing," said Matsko, " that thou wilt take all the people from Bogdanets, so as to have a retinue proper for a knight, though the place be left without hands. While T am alive I will not permit this, but when I am dead I see that thou wilt take them."

"The Lord will provide an escort; besides, our relative, the abbot of Tulcha, will not be stingy."

At that moment the doors opened, and, as if in proof that the Lord God was providing an escort for Zbyshko, in walked two men, dark, strong, dressed in yellow kaftans, like Jews. They wore also red skullcaps, and immense, broad trousers. Standing in the door they fell to putting their fingers to their foreheads, their lips, and their breasts, and then to making obeisances down to the floor.

"What sort of renegades are ye?" inquired Matsko. "Who are ye?"

" Your captives," answered the newly arrived, in broken Polish.

" But how is that ? Whence are ye ? Who sent you here ? "

" Pan Zavisha sent us as a present to the young knight, to be his captives."

" Oh, for God's sake, two men more!" cried Matsko, with delight. " And of what people? "

"We are Turks."

" Are ye Turks?" inquired Zbyshko. "I shall have two Turks in my retinue. Uncle, have you ever seen Turks? "

And jumping up to the captives he began to turn the men around and look at them, as he might at strange creatures from beyond the sea.

" As to seeing, I have not seen, but I have heard that the lord of Garbov has Turks in his service, whom he captured when fighting on the Danube with the Roman Caesar, Sigis-inond. How is that? Are ye pagans, ye dog brothers?"

"Our lord gave command to christen us," said one of them.

"And ye had not the means to ransom yourselves?"

"We are from afar, from the Asiatic shore; we are from Brussa."

Zbyshko, who listened eagerly to every narrative of war, especially when it concerned deeds of the renowned Zavisha, asked them how they had fallen into captivity. But in the narrative of the captives there was nothing uncommon: Zavisha had attacked some tens of them three years before in a ravine; some he cut down, others he captured; of these he gave away afterward many as gifts. The hearts of Zbyshko and Matsko were filled with delight at sight of such a notable present, especially as it was difficult to get men in that time, and the possession of them was genuine property.

After a while Zavisha himself came, in company with Povala and Pashko. Since all had striven to save Zbyshko and were glad that they had succeeded, each man made him some present in farewell and remembrance. The bountiful lord of Tachev gave him a caparison for his horse, wide, rich, embroidered on the breast with golden fringe; and Pashko, a Hungarian sword worth ten gryvens. Later came Lis, Farurey, Krou, Martsin, and, last of all, Zyndram, each with full hands.

Zbyshko greeted them with overflowing heart, made happy both by the gifts, and by this, that the most renowned knights in the kingdom had shown him friendship. They inquired of him touching his departure, and the health of Matsko, recommending, like experienced people, though young, various ointments and remedies which cured wounds wonderfully.

But Matsko merely recommended Zbyshko to them; as for himself, he was preparing for the other world. It was difficult to live with a piece of iron sticking under the ribs. He complained that he spat blood continually, and had no appetite. A quart of shelled nuts, two spans of sausage, a plate of fried eggs, — that was his whole daily sustenance. Father Tsybek bled him a number of times, thinking to draw the fever from under his heart and restore desire for food; that gave no relief either.

But he was so delighted with gifts for his nephew that he felt better that moment; and when the merchant Amyley commanded to bring a small keg of wine to entertain guests so notable, he sat down to the cup with them. They fell to talking of the rescue of Zbyshko, and of his betrothal. The knights had no thought that Yurand would oppose the will of the princess, especially if Zbyshko would avenge the memory of Danusia's mother and win the peacock-plumes.

" But as to Lichtenstein," said Zavisha, " I am not sure that he will meet thee ; he is a monk, and an elder in the Order besides. Nay! the people in his retinue declare that if he waits he will in time be Grand Master."

" Should he refuse combat he will lose his honor," said Lis.

"No," answered Zyndram; "he is not a lay member, hence he is not free to meet in single combat."

" But it happens often that they do."

"Yes, for laws in the Order are corrupted; they make various vows, and are famed for breaking them time after time, — to the scandal of all Christendom. But in a conflict to the death a Knight of the Cross, and especially a comtur, may refuse to appear."

" Ha! then you will meet him only in war."

" They tell us there will be no war, since at present the Knights of the Cross fear our people."

" This peace will not endure long," answered Zyndram. " Agreement with a wolf is impossible, for he must live on others."

" Meanwhile we may have to take Timur the Lame by the shoulders," said Povala. " Prince Vitold has suffered defeat from Edyge'i, —that is undoubted."

" And Spytko, the voevoda, has not returned," added Pashko.

" And a multitude of Lithuanian princes remained on the field."

" The late queen foretold this end," said Povala.

" Then we may have to march against Timur."

Here conversation turned to the Lithuanian campaign against the Tartars. There was no longer any doubt that Vitold, a leader more impulsive than skilful, had suffered on the Vorskla a great defeat, in which a multitude of Lithuanian and Russian boyars had fallen, and with them a handful of Polish auxiliaries, and even Knights of the Cross. Those assembled at Amyley's house mourned above all the fate of young Spytko of Melshtyn, the greatest lord in the kingdom; he had gone as a volunteer, and after the battle had disappeared without tidings. They exalted to the sky his real knightly act, which was this: that having received a cap of safety from the leader of the enemy, he would not wear it during battle, preferring a glorious death to life at the favor of a pagan ruler. It was uncertain yet whether he had perished or had been taken captive. From captivity he had, of course, means to ransom himself; because his wealth surpassed reckoning, and besides, King Vladislav had given him all Podolia in vassal possession.

The defeat of the Lithuanians might be terrible for the entire realm of Yagello also; for no one knew well whether the Tartars, encouraged by victory over Vitold, would not hurl themselves on the lands and cities of the Grand Principality. In such case the kingdom too would be involved in the struggle. Many knights, then, who like Zavisha, Farurey, Dobko, and even Povala, were accustomed to seek adventures and battles at foreign courts, remained in Cracow designedly, not knowing what the near future might bring. If Tamerlane, the lord of twenty-seven kingdoms, were to move the whole Mongol world, the danger might become terrible. There were men who thought they foresaw this.

"If the need come, we must measure with the Limper himself. He will not find it so easy to meet our people as all those whom he conquered and destroyed. Besides, other Christian princes will come to assist us."

To this, Zyndram, who was flaming with special hatred against the Order, said with bitterness, —

"As to princes, I know not; but the Knights of the Cross are ready to make friends with the Tartars and strike us on the opposite flank."

"There will be war!" exclaimed Zbyshko. "I will go against the Knights of the Cross! "

But other knights contradicted. " The Knights of the Cross know no fear of God, and seek only profit; still, they will not assist pagans agairist Christian people. Moreover, Timur is warring somewhere far off in Asia; and the Tartar sovereign, Edygei, has lost so many warriors in the battle that likely he is terrified at his own victory. Prince Vitold is a man of resources, and surely has supplied his fortresses well; though success has not come to the Lithuanians this time, it is no new thing for them to overcome Tartars."

" Not with Tartars, but with Germans must we fight for life and death," said Zyndram; "from Germans will our ruin come, unless we destroy them. And Mazovia will perish first of all," said he, turning to Zbyshko. "Thou wilt always find work there, have no fear! "

" Ei ! if uncle were well, I would go there immediately."

" God strengthen thee! " said Povala, raising his goblet. " To thy health and Danusia's! "

" Destruction to the Germans! " added Zyndram.

And they began to take farewell of him. Meanwhile a courtier from the princess entered with a falcon on his hand, and, bending to the knights present, turned with a certain strange smile to Zbyshko.

" My lady, the princess, commanded me to tell you," said he, " that she will pass this night in Cracow, and take the road to-morrow morning."

" That is well, but why is this? Has any one fallen ill? *

" No. The princess has a guest from Mazovia."

" Has the prince himself come? "

"Not the prince, but Yurand of Spyhov," answered the courtier.

When Zbyshko heard this he was terribly confused, and his heart began to beat as it did when they read the death sentence to him.

VOL. I. 8

CHAPTEE V.

PRINCESS Anna did not wonder overmuch at the arrival of Yuraud, for it happened often that in the midst of continual pursuits, attacks, and battles with neighboring German knights, he was overcome by a sudden longing to see Dauusia. He appeared then unexpectedly either in Warsaw, Tsehanov, or wherever the court of Prince Yanush was living. At sight of the child dreadful grief burst forth in him always; for in the course of years Danusia had grown so much like her mother that when he saw her it seemed to him that he was looking at his dead one, such as he had known her on a time with Princess Anna in Warsaw. More than once people thought that from such grief his heart would break, — that heart given only to vengeance. The princess implored him often to leave his bloody Spyhov and remain at the court near Danusia. Prince Yanush, esteeming Yurand's bravery and value, and wishing also to avoid those vexations to which the continual happenings at the boundary exposed him, offered his favorite the dignity of swordbearer. Always in vain. It was just the sight of Danusia that opened the old wounds in Yurand. After some days he lost desire for food, conversation, and sleep. His heart began evidently to be indignant and to bleed; at last he vanished from the court and returned to the swamps of Spyhov, to drown his grief and anger in bloodshed.

"Woe to the Germans!" said the people then. "They are no sheep, except for Yurand; to the Germans Yurand is a wolf." In fact, after a certain time it was reported that foreign volunteers were seized while passing along the boundary road to the Knights of the Cross; then news came of burnt castles, of captured servants, or of life and death combats, in which the terrible Yurand was always victorious.

With the predatory disposition of the Mazovians and the German knights who by the authority of the Order rented lands and castles in the adjoining Mazovia, even in time of profound peace between the princes of Mazovia and the Order the uproar of battle never ceased on the boundary.

Even while cutting fuel in the forest, or during harvest, citizens went out with spears or crossbows. People lived in uncertainty of the morrow, in continual military preparation, in hardness of heart. No one was satisfied with simple defence, but returned robbery for robbery, fire for fire, attack for attack. And it happened that when Germans were stealing along silently through forest boundaries to surprise some castle, carry off people, or drive away herds, Mazovians at the same time were intent on a similar action. , More than once they met and fought to the death, but frequently only the leaders were challenged to a mortal struggle, after which the victor took the retinue of his vanquished opponent. So that when complaints against Yurand were brought to the court in Warsaw, the prince answered with complaints of attacks made by German knights elsewhere. In this way when both sides demanded redress neither side had the wish or the power to give it; all robberies, burnings, attacks went entirely unpunished.

In his swampy Spyhov, which was overgrown with reeds, Yurand, burning with an unappeasable desire of vengeance, became so oppressive to his neighbors beyond the border that at last the fear of him became greater than their stubbornness. The fields adjoining Spyhov lay fallow, the forests were filled with wild hops and hazelnuts, the meadows with weeds. More than one German knight accustomed to fist law in his fatherland tried to settle near Spyhov, but each, after a certain time chose to flee from land, flocks, and servants, rather than live at the side of an implacable enemy. Frequently also knights combined to make a common attack upon Spyhov, but each of these found an end in defeat. They tried various methods. Once they brought in, to challenge Yurand to trampled earth, a knight from the Mien, famed for strength and sternness, a man who in all struggles had won victory. But when they stood within barriers the heart in the German knight fell as if by magic at sight of the terrible Mazovian, and he turned his horse to flee. Yurand, unarmored, shot after the man and pierced him through the back, thus depriving him of the light of day and of honor. Thenceforth the greater alarm seized his neighbors, and if any German, even from afar, saw the smoke of Spyhov he made the sign of the cross on himself and began a prayer to his patron in heaven, for the belief became established that Yurand had sold his soul to unclean powers for the sake of vengeance.

Besides, terrible things were related of Spyhov. It was said that through sticky swamps in the midst of deep quagmires overgrown with duck plant and water snake-weed, a road led to it which was so narrow that two horsemen could not ride abreast there; that on both sides of this road were lying German bones; that in the night-time the heads of drowned people walked along on spider legs, groaning, howling, and dragging down to the depths passers-by with their horses.

It was repeated that at the castle itself stood a picket fence adorned with human skulls. In all this the only truth was that in barred cellars, dug under the house in Spyhov, groaned always some prisoners, or some tens of them, and that the name of Yurand was more terrible than the inventions about skeletons, and ghosts of drowned people.

Zbyshko, when he learned of Yurand's coming, hastened straightway to meet him, but as he was going to Danusia's father there was in his heart a certain fear. He had chosen Danusia as the lady of his thoughts and made a vow to her; no one could forbid that, but later the princess had caused the betrothal. What would Yurand say of that act? Would he consent, or would he not? What would happen were he, as Danusia's father, to shout and say that he would never permit such a thing? These questions pierced Zbyshko's soul with dread, since he cared more for Danusia than for all else on earth. This thought alone gave him solace, that Yurand would consider his attack on Lichtenstein a service, not a drawback, for he had made it to take revenge for Danusia's mother, and had thereby lacked little of losing his own head.

Meanwhile he fell to inquiring of the courtier who had come to Amyley's for him.

" And whither are you taking me? To the castle?"

"To the castle. Yurand has stopped with the court of the princess."

"Tell me, what kind of man is he? — that I may know how to talk with him."

" What shall I tell you? He is a man entirely different from others. They say that once he was gladsome, till the blood boiled in his liver."

" Is he wise?"

"He is cunning, for he plunders others, and does not give himself up. Hei! lie has one eye, — the Germans shot out the other with a crossbow, — but with that one he looks right

through you. No man can insist on his own with him. But the princess, our lady, he loves, for he took her damsel as wife, and now his daughter is reared with us."

Zbyshko drew a breath of relief.

" Then you say that he does not oppose the will of the princess ? "

" I know what you would like to learn, and what I have heard I will tell. The princess spoke with him about your betrothal, for it would not be well to conceal it, but it is unknown what he answered."

Thus conversing they reached the gate. The captain of the royal bowmen, the same who had conducted Zbyshko to death, nodded to him now in a friendly manner; so, passing the guards, they found themselves in the court, and then entered on the right to the part occupied by the princess. The courtier, meeting a page before the door inquired, —

" Where is Yurand of Spyhov ? "

"In the Winding Room with his daughter."

" It is over there," said the courtier, indicating the door.

Zbyshko made the sign of the cross on himself, and, raising a curtain in the opened door, entered with beating heart. But he did not see Yurand and Danusia, for the room was not merely " winding," but dark. Only after a while did he see the bright head of the maiden; she was sitting on her father's knees; they did not hear when he entered, so he halted at the curtain, coughed and said at last, —

" May He be praised! "

" For the ages of ages! " answered Yurand, rising.

At that moment Danusia sprang to the young knight, and seizing him by the hand, exclaimed, —

" Zbyshko! Papa has come! "

Zbyshko kissed her hand, and with her approached Yurand.

" I have come to bow down to you," said Zbyshko. " Do you know who I am?"

Then he inclined slightly and made a motion with his hands as if wishing to seize Yurand's feet. But Yurand took his hand, turned him toward the light and examined him silently.

Zbyshko had recovered somewhat, so he raised his eyes full of curiosity to Yurand, and saw before him a man of immense stature, with blond hair and light moustaches, a face pitted with small-pox, and having only one eye, which was of an iron color. It seemed to Zbyshko as if that eye

would bore him through and through; hence confusion again seized him. Not knowing at last what to say, but wishing desperately to break the vexatious silence with some speech, he asked,—

"Are you Yurand of Spyhov, the father of Danusia?"

But the other indicated to him an oaken seat, on which he himself sat, and without uttering a word he looked at him longer.

Zbyshko was impatient at last.

" You know," said he, " that it is awkward for me to sit here as if under judgment."

Only then did Yurand say: " Hadst thou the wish to fight with Lichtenstein ? "

I had," answered Zbyshko.

In the C3 T e of the lord of Spyhov flashed a kind of wonderful light, and his terrible countenance brightened somewhat. After a while he looked at Danusia and inquired again, —

" And was it for her? "

" For whom should it be ? Uncle must have told you how I vowed to her to strip peacock-plumes from German heads! Not three of them, but as many as there are fingers on both her hands. Therefore I will help you to take revenge; it is for Danusia's mother."

" Woe to them! " said Yurand.

Again silence followed.

Zbyshko noticed that by showing his hatred against the Germans he was touching Yurand's heart.

" I will not forgive them my own wrongs," said he; " for they came near cutting my head off." Here he turned to Danusia and added, " She saved me."

u I know," replied Yurand.

" And you are not angry because of that?"

"Since thou hast promised her, serve her; for such is knightly custom."

Zbyshko hesitated somewhat, but after a while he began again with evident alarm, —

"Think of this: she covered my head with a veil; the whole knighthood heard her say, 4 He is mine;' the Franciscan, also, who was at my side with the cross, heard her. And certain it is that I shall belong to no other till death; so may God help me ! "

Then he knelt again, and wishing to show that he knew knightly customs, he kissed with great respect the shoes of

Danusia, who was sitting on the arm of the seat; then he turned to Yurand and asked, —

" Have you ever seen another like her ? "

Yurand placed his terrible man-killing hands on his own head suddenly, and closing his eyes, said in a deep voice:

" I have, but the Germans killed her."

"Then listen," said Zbyshko, with enthusiasm; "one wrong has met both of us, and one vengeance belongs to us. They, the dog brothers, slew with crossbows a multitude of my relatives from Bogdanets when their horses sank in a quagmire. You will find no one better than me for your labor. It is nothing new to me! Ask uncle. The lance or the axe, the long or the short sword, are all one to me! My uncle has told you of those Frisians ? I will slaughter Germans like sheep for you; and as to the maiden, I swear on my knees to fight for her, as God lives, with the very elder of hell; and I will not yield her either for land or for flocks, or for any gear; and though a castle with glass windows were offered me without her, I would reject the castle and wander off to the edge of the world for her."

Yurand sat some time with his head on his hands; but at last he recovered as if from sleep, and said with pity and sadness, —

" Thou hast pleased me, boy; but I will not give her to thee, for she is not fated to thee, poor fellow."

When he heard this, Zbyshko grew dumb and looked at Yurand with round eyes, unable to utter a word. But Danusia hastened to aid him. Zbyshko was very dear to her, and it was pleasant for her to pass, not for a " chit," but a "grown-up young lady." The betrothal pleased her, and the sweet things which the young knight brought in daily; so now, when she understood that they wished to take all this away from her, she dropped as quickly as possible from the arm of the seat, and hiding her face on her father's knee, began to repeat, —

" Tatulo, tatulo (papa dear), I will cry! "

Evidently he loved her above everything, for he placed his hand on her head mildly. His face expressed neither hatred nor anger, only sadness.

Meanwile Zbyshko recovered and asked: "How is that? Then you wish to oppose the will of God ?"

"If it be the will of God, you will get her; but I cannot incline my own will. I would" be glad to incline it, but that is not possible."

He raised Danusia then, and taking her on his arm, he turned toward the door; when Zbyshko wished to bar the way, he halted for a moment and said, —

" I shall not be angry with thee about knightly service, but ask me not for more; I cannot say another word to thee."

And he passed out

CHAPTER VI.

THE next day Yurand did not avoid Zbyshko in the least, or hinder him from showing Danusia on the way various services which as a knight it was his duty to show her. On the contrary, Zbyshko, though greatly mortified, noticed that the gloomy lord of Spyhov looked at him in a friendly manner, and, as it were, with sorrow because he had been forced to give such a cruel answer. The young man tried more than once, therefore, to approach him and begin conversation. About an hour's journey from Cracow it was not difficult to find an opportunity, for both accompanied the princess on horseback. Yurand, though usually silent, spoke willingly enough; but when Zbyshko wished to learn something of the secret hindrances separating him from Danusia, conversation stopped on a sudden. Yurand's face became cloudy; he looked unquietly at Zbyshko, as if fearing to betray himself in something. Zbyshko thought that the princess knew facts; so, selecting a favorable moment, he tried to obtain information from her; but neither could she explain much to him.

" There is a secret," said she. " Yurand himself told me this; but he begged me at the same time not to ask him, for he is not only unwilling but unable to tell it. Doubtless he is bound by some oath, as happens among people. God grant, however, that in time all this will explain itself."

" Without Danusia I should be in this world like a dog on a leash, or a bear in a pit. No delight of any kind, no pleasure. Nothing beyond disappointment and sighing. I would go now with Prince Vitold to Tavan, and let the Tartars there kill me. But I must take my uncle home to begin with, and then snatch those peacock-plumes from the heads of the Germans, as I have sworn. Maj r hap they will kill me while doing so; I should rather die than see another man taking Danusia."

The princess raised her kindly blue eyes on him, and inquired, with a certain astonishment, —

"And thou wouldst not permit that? "

"That will not be, while there is breath in my nostrils! Unless.my hand were to wither, and be without power to hold an axe! "

"Well, thou wilt see."

" But how could I take her in spite of her father? "

To this the princess answered, as if to herself, —

" Mighty God! surely that will not be! Is God's will not stronger than the will of a father?" Then she said to Zbyshko: " And what did Yurand himself say? ' If it be the will of God, he will get her.'"

" He said that to me," replied Zbyshko. ' If it be the will of God,' said he, ' thou wilt get her.'"

"Well, seest thou?"

" Yes, in thy favor, gracious lady, is my only solace."

"Thou hast my favor, and Danusia will adhere to thee. Only yesterday 1 said to her, ' Dauusia, but wilt thou hold to Zbyshko ?' and she answered: ' I shall be Zbyshko's, or no one's.' That is a green berry yet, but whatever she says she will hold to, for she is a noble's child, not some wanderer. And her mother was of the same kind."

" May God grant!" replied Zbyshko.

"But remember that thou hold to her; for more than one man is giddy; he promises to love faithfully, and directly he rushes to another, so that thou couldst not hold him on a rope! I tell the truth! And you meet a man sometimes who at every girl he sees neighs like a horse fat on oats."

" May the Lord Jesus punish me first! " cried Zbyshko with energy.

"Well, remember that. And when thou hast taken thy uncle home come to our court. Thou wilt have a chance there to win spurs, and by that time we shall see what God gives. Danusia will have ripened and will feel the will of God, for now she loves thee indeed greatly, — I cannot express it otherwise, — but not yet as mature maidens love. Perhaps too Yurand will incline to thee later, for, as I notice, he would be glad to incline. Thou wilt go to Spyhov too, and with Yurand against the Germans; it may happen that thou wilt serve him in some way and win him completely."

" Gracious lady, I intended to act in just that way, but with permission it will be easier."

This conversation added much courage to Zbyshko. Meanwhile at the first halt old Matsko grew so ill that there was need to stop and wait till he could regain even a little strength for the farther journey. The kind princess, Anna Danuta, left him medicines and remedies from all that she had brought, but she was forced herself to travel on, and the owners of Bogdauets had to part with the Mazovian court.

Zbyshko fell his whole length at the feet of the princess, then once more he vowed true knightly service to Danusia, promised to go soon to Tsehanov, or Warsaw; finally he seized her in his strong arms, and raising her said with a voice of emotion, —

"Think of me, dearest flower; remember me, my golden fish!"

And Danusia, embracing him with her arms, just as a younger sister embraces a dear brother, put her little upturned nose to his cheek and cried, with tears each as big as a pea, —

"I will not go to Tsehanov without Zbyshko! I will not go to Tsehanov !"

Yurand saw this, but he did not burst out in anger; on the coutrarj 7 , he took farewell of the youth very kindly, and when he had mounted his horse he turned once again to him, and added,—

"Be with God, and cherish no feeling of offence toward me."

"How should I have a feeling of offence against you, Danusia's father?" said Zbyshko, sincerely. And he inclined before him to the stirrup. Yurand pressed his hand firmly, and said, —

"God give thee luck in all undertakings. Dost understand?"

And he rode away. Zbyshko understood the great goodwill in those final words, and turning to the wagon in which Matsko was lying, he said, —

" Do you know, he too would be glad, but something prevents him. You were in Spyhov, and you have quick reason ; try to understand what this means."

But Matsko was too ill. The fever which he had in the morning increased toward evening to the degree that he began to lose consciousness; hence, instead of answering Zbyshko, he looked at him as if in astonishment, and asked, —

"But where are the bells ringing here?"

Zbyshko was frightened, for it occurred to him that if the sick man heard bells it was evident that death was approaching. He thought too that the old man might die without a priest, without confession, and thus put himself, if not entirely in hell, at least for long ages in purgatory — hence he resolved to take him farther, so as to bring him to some parish where he might receive the last sacraments.

With this object they moved on during the whole night. Zbyshko sat in the wagon on the hay where the sick man was lying, and watched him till daybreak. From time to time he gave him wine, which the merchant Amyley had furnished for the road, and which the thirsty Matsko drank eagerly, for it brought him evident relief. When he had drunk a second quart he even recovered consciousness; after the third quart he fell asleep, so deeply that Zbyshko bent over him at moments to be sure that he was not dead.

At thought of this, great sorrow seized Zbyshko. Till the time of his imprisonment in Cracow he had not understood how he loved that "uncle," who in life had been to him father and mother. But now he knew well, and also he felt that after the death of that "uncle "he would be terribly alone in the world — without blood relations; save only the abbot who had Bogdanets in pledge, he would be without friends, without aid. At the same time it occurred to him that if Matsko died his death would come through Germans, through whom he himself had lacked little of losing his life, through whom all his family had perished, and Danusia's mother, and many, many blameless people whom he had known, or of whom he had heard from acquaintances; and at last wonder seized hold of him. "Is there," said he to himself, " in this whole kingdom a man who has not suffered injustice from Germans, and who is not thirsting for vengeance?" Here he remembered those with whom he had fought at Vilno, and he thought: " Even Tartars are surely not more cruel in war than the Germans, and of a certainty there is not another such nation on earth."

The dawn interrupted his meditation. The day rose clear, but cool. Matsko was evidently better, for he breathed evenly and quietly. He woke only when the sun had warmed the world well; he opened his eyes and said, —

" I feel better. Where are we? "

"We are entering Olkush. You know — the place where they dig silver, and pay taxes to the treasury."

"Oh, to have what there is in the ground! Then we might build up Bogdanets."

" It is evident tliat you are better," said Zbyshko, smiling. "Hei! it would be enough to build a walled castle. But let us go to the priest's house, for there they will give us entertainment, and you will be able to confess. All is in God's hands, but it is better to have the conscience in order."

"I am a sinful man; I am glad to be penitent," said Matsko. "I dreamed in the night that devils were pulling the boots from my feet, and were gabbling to one another in German. God was gracious, relief came. Butthou didst sleep like a log ? "

" How sleep when I was watching you? "

" Then lie down a little. When we arrive I will wake thee."

" What time have I to sleep?"

" But what hinders thee ? "

What unless love ? " said Zbyshko, looking at his uncle with the eyes of a child. " Pains have collected in my breast from sighing, but I will sit on horseback a little, and that will relieve me."

He crawled out of the wagon and mounted a horse, which one of the Turks given by Zavisha held carefully. Matsko meanwhile held his side because of pain, but clearly he had something else besides his own sickness in mind, for he shook his head, smacked his lips, and said at last, —

" I wonder, and I cannot stop wondering, how thou hast become so eager for that love, for neither thy father nor I were of that kind."

Zbyshko, instead of answering, straightened himself quickly in the saddle, put his hand on his hips, threw up his head, and thundered with all the power in his breast: —

" I wept all the night, I wept in the morning. Where hast thou gone, dearest maiden ? Nothing avails me, though I weep my eyes out, For I never shall see thee, 0 maiden.

Hei!"

And that " Hei!" rushed through the forest, struck the trees by the roadside, was heard at last in a distant echo, and grew still in the thickets.

But Matsko put his hand again on his side where the German arrow-point had stuck, and said, groaning slightly, —

" Formerly people were wiser — dost understand?" But after a while he grew thoughtful, as if remembering some of the old times, and added: "Though even in old times an odd man was foolish."

Meanwhile they issued from the forest, after which they beheld sheds for miners, and farther on the indented walls of Olkush, reared by-King Kazimir, and the tower of the church built by Vladislav Lokietek.

CHAPTER VIL

THE canon of the church heard Matsko's confession, and kept the two men all night hospitably, so that they set out again only next moruing early. Beyond Olkush they turned towards Silesia, along the boundary of which they were to pass till they reached Great Poland. The road lay for the greater part through a wilderness, in which were heard frequently about suuset the bellowing of wild bulls and bisons, which sounded like underground thunder, in hazelnut thickets at night glittered wolves' eyes. The greatest danger, however, threatening travellers on this road was from Germans or Germanized knights of Silesia, whose castles rose here and there on the border. It is true that, because of war with Opolchyk the naderspan, who was assisted against King Vladislav by his Silesian nephews, Polish hands had destroyed the greater part of these castles, but it was needful at all times to guard one's self, and not let weapons out of one's hands, especially after sunset.

But they advanced slowly, so that the road annoyed Zbyshko, and only when they were one day's wheel-travelling distant from Bogdanets did he on a certain night hear behind them the trampling and snorting of horses.

" Some people are following us," said Zbyshko.

Matsko, who was not sleeping, looked at the stars, and answered, like a man of experience, —

" Dawn is not distant. Robbers would not attack at the end of night, for they must be at home before daylight."

Zbyshko, however, stopped the wagon, arranged his men across the road, faced those who were approaching, pushed forward himself, and waited.

Indeed, after a certain time, he saw in the darkness between ten and twenty horsemen. One rode in front a few yards in advance of the others; evidently he had no intention of hiding, for he was singing. Zbyshko could not hear his words, but to his ears came the joyous : " Hots ! hots I " with which the unknown finished each verse of the song.

" Onr people! " said he.

But after a while he called, —

"Stop!"

*' And do thou sit still! " answered a jesting voice.

" What ones are ye? "

" What others are ye? "

" But why ride onto us? "

" Why do ye stop the road? "

"Answer, for our crossbows are drawn."

" But our bowstrings are stretched — shoot."

" Answer in human fashion, or there will be trouble."

A joyful song answered Zbyshko: —

" One misery with another is dancing, Is dancing at the crossroad —

Hots ! hots! hots !» What good is the dance to them ? The dance is good, but the miseries

—

Hots ! hots ! hots ! "

Zbyshko was astonished at hearing such an answer; but the song stopped, and the same voice inquired,—

" How is old Matsko? Is he breathing yet? "

Matsko rose up in the wagon, and said, —

" As God lives, that is one of our people!"

Zbyshko moved forward with his horse.

" Who is inquiring about Matsko? "

" A neighbor, Zyh of Zgorzelitse. I am riding a whole week after you, and inquiring of people along the road."

" Oh save us! Uncle ! Zyh of Zgorzelitse is here!" cried Zbyshko.

They fell to greeting each other joyfully, for Zyh was their neighbor, and besides a kind man, loved everywhere for his immense joyousness.

"But how are you?" asked he, shaking Matsko's hand. 41 Is it hots yet, or is it not hots? "

"Hei, no longer hots," said Matsko. "But I am glad to see you. Dear God ! this is as if I were already in Bogdanets."

"But how is it with you? I have heard that the Germans shot you."

"They shot me, the dog brothers. The arrow-point remained between my ribs."

" Fear God ! Well, what have you done ? Have you tried drinking bear's-fat?"

" You see," said Zbyshko, " every bear is full of fat. If

1 The o in hots is long, like o in note.

we reach Bogdanets I will go at once in the night with an axe to a bee's-nest."

" Maybe Yagenka has bear's fat; if not, I will send elsewhere to look for it."

" What Yagenka ? But was not yours Malgosia ? " inquired Matsko.

" Oo! what Malgosia? On Saint Michael's it will be the third autumn that Malgosia is lying in the priest's field. She was a grand housekeeper — the Lord light her soul! But Yageuka is like her, only she is young.

" Beyond the valleys shine the mountains; As the mother, so the daughter — Hots! hotsl"

But to Malgosia I used to say, * Do not climb pine trees when tliou art fifty years old.' She would not obey me, she climbed. A limb broke under her, and flop! she dug a hole in the ground I tell you; but in three days she gave out her last breath."

"The Lord light her! " said Matsko. "I remember, I remember — when she put her hands on her hips and looked threateningly the boys hid in the hay. But as to housekeeping she was accurate ! And to think that she fell from a pine tree ! Do you see people! "

"She flew down like a pine cone in winter. Oi, but there was grief! Do you know ? after the funeral I got so drunk from sorrow that they could not wake me for three days. They thought that I too had turned my toes upward. And how I cried! — you could not have carried out my tears in a pail! But as to management, Yagenka is accurate. All is on her head now."

" I hardly remember her. When I went away she was not taller than an axe-handle. She could walk under a horse without touching its belly. But that is long ago, and she must have grown up."

" On Saint Agnes day she finished her fifteenth year; but I have not seen her either for nearly a twelvemonth."

" What were you doing? Whence are you coming?"

" From the war. It is captivity for me to sit at home when I have Yagenka."

Matsko. though sick, pricked up his ears eagerly at mention of war, and asked,—

" Were you. perhaps, with Prince Vitold at the Vorskla?"

" I was," said Zyh, joyously. " Well, the Lord God re

fused luck. We suffered a dreadful defeat from Edyge'i. First they killed our horses. The Tartar will not strike hand to hand, like a Christian, but shoots from a distance with bows. If thou press him he will flee, and shoot again. Do thy best, he will have his way. See you, in our army the knights boasted without bounds, and talked thus : ' We will not even level a lance, nor draw swords; we will just dash that vermin apart with our horse-hoofs.' So they boasted till shafts groaned around them, till the air was dark with arrows; and after the battle, what ? Barely one out of ten was alive. Will you believe? More than half the army, with seventy Lithuanian and Russian princes, remained on the field; and as to boyars and various courtiers, or whatever they are called, youths, you could not count them in less than a fortnight — "

"I have heard," interrupted Matsko. "And of our auxiliary knights a great many fell also."

"Yes, even nine Knights of the Cross, for these too had to serve Vitold. And of our people a crowd, for, as you know, others may look behind, but our people never. The Grand Prince had most confidence in Polish knights, and would have no guard but them near his person in battle. Hi! hi! They lay like a pavement around him, and nothing touched Vitold! Pan Spytko of Melshtyn fell, and Bernat, the swordbearer, and Mikolai, the cupbearer, and Prokop, and Pretslav, and Dobrogost, Yasko of Lazevitse, Pilik Mazur, Varsh of Mihov, Soha the voevoda, Yasko of Dom-brova, Pietrko of Miloslavie, Schepetski, and Oderski, and Tomko Lagoda. Who could count them all? And I have seen some so filled with arrows that they looked like dead hedgehogs, till laughter seized me at sight of them."

Then he laughed outright, as if telling the most amusing thing possible, and began to sing at once,—

" Oi, thou wilt learn what the Tartar is, When he has rubbed thy skin well! "

"Well, afterward what?" asked Zbyshko.

" Afterward the Grand Prince fled; but straightway he took courage as he does always. The more thou bend him, the better he springs, like a hazel twig. We rushed then to defend the Tavan ford. A handful of new knights came from Poland. All quiet! Very well! Edge'i came next day with a Tartar host, but did nothing. Oh, it was pleasant! Wherever he tried to pass the ford we gave it in the

VOL. I. — 9

snout to him. He could not pass anywhere. "We beat them and seized not a few. I caught five myself, and am taking them home. You will see in the daylight their dog snouts."

" In Cracow people said that war may come to our kingdom."

" But is Edyge'i a simpleton? He knows well what a knighthood we have ; and this too, that the greatest knights stayed at home, for the queen was displeased when Vitold began the war single-handed. Ei, he is cunning — old Edygei! He noticed immediately at Tavan that the prince grew in strength, and he went back far away beyond the ninth land!"

" But you returned?"

"I returned. There is nothing there to do now. In Cracow I learned that you started a little before me."

How did you know that we were the persons ? "

" I knew because I inquired at halting-places everywhere." Here he turned to Zbyshko. " Ei, my God, I saw thee a little fellow the last time, but now even in the dark I see thee as big as a wild bull. And thou art ready at once to draw the crossbow! It is clear that thou hast been in war."

" War reared me from childhood. Let uncle tell if I lack experience."

" Your uncle has no need to say anything. In Cracow I saw Povala of Tachev — he told me about thee. Likely that Mazovian does not wish to give thee his daughter, but I would not be so stubborn, for thou pleasest me. Thou wilt forget her, only look at my Yagenka. She is a turnip!"

" Not true! I will not forget though I saw ten like your Yagenka."

"Mochydoly, where the mill is, will go with her; when I went away there were twelve good mares in the meadows with their colts. More than one man will bow down to me for Yagenka — never fear! "

Zbyshko wanted to answer, "But not I!" when Zyh began to sing again, —

"I will bow down to your knees, And for that give me Yagna. God grant you! — "

" Gladness and singing are in your head always," re' marked Matsko.

"Yes, but what are blessed souls doing in heaven?"

" Singing."

"Well, see then! And the damned weep. I would rather go to the singing than the weeping ones. Saint Peter will say too: ' We must admit him to paradise or the rascal will sing in hell, and that would not be proper.' See, it is dawning already."

And indeed day was coming. After a while they rode out onto a broad plain, where everything was visible. On a lake occupying the greater part of the plain some people were fishing, but at sight of armed men they threw their nets aside, rushed from the water, seized their spears and poles as quickly as might be, and stood in a threatening attitude, ready for battle.

" They have taken us for robbers," said Zbyshko, laughing. "Hei, fishermen! whose are ye?"

They stood some time in silence looking with distrust, but at last the oldest among them recognized the knights, and answered,—

" We belong to the reverend abbot of Tulcha."

" Our relative," said Matsko, "who holds Bogdanets in pledge. This must be his forest, though bought not long since."

" God help you, he buy! He fought for it with Vilk of Brozova, and evidently he won it. A year ago they were to meet on horseback with lances and long swords for all this side of the country here, but I know not how it ended, for I was gone at the time."

" Well, we are relatives, he will not fight with us; he may also remit some of the pledge money."

" He may. If only it accords with his will, he may add something of his own. He is a knightly abbot, for whom it is no novelty to cover his head with a helmet. And he is pious besides, and celebrates mass beautifully. But you must remember — when he thunders out during mass, the swallows under the roofs fly out of their nests. Well, and the glory of God increases."

" Why should I not remember? Why, with his breath he quenches a candle on the altar ten steps away. Has he looked in even once at Bogdanets ? "

"Of course he has. He has settled five new men, with their wives, on cleared land. He has been with us too, for, as you know, he baptized for me Yagenka; he has always liked her very much, and he calls her his daughter."

" God grant him to leave me the men," said Matsko.

" Oh, of course! What are five men to such a rich person as he is? Besides, if Yagenka asks him, he will leave them."

Here the conversation ceased for a moment, since above the dark pine -wood, and above the ruddy dawn the bright sun rose and lighted up the country. The knights greeted it with the usual " May He be praised! " and then, making the sign of the cross on themselves, they began morning prayers. Zyh finished first and striking his breast repeatedly, said to his companions, —

"Now I will look at you carefully. Hei, you have both changed ! You, Matsko, must return to health, the first thing. Yagenka will nurse you, as there is no woman's care in your house. Yes, it is clear that a fragment is sticking between your ribs — and that is not very good." Here he turned to Zbyshko. " Do thou show thyself too — Oh, God of might! I remember thee as a little fellow, how thou wouldst climb over a colt's tail to his back; now, by all the — What a young knight! He has the clean lip of a stripling, but what shoulders! Such a man might close with a bear."

" What is a bear to him? " said Matsko, in answer. " He was younger than he is to-day when that Frisian called him a naked lip, and he, as that name did not please him, plucked out the Frisian's moustache right there."

"I know," said Zyh. " You fought afterward and took their retinue. Povala told me all.

" ' The German went out with great splendor, But naked his snout when they buried him, Hots ! hots !' "

And he looked at Zbyshko with amusement in his eyes. Zbyshko, too, looked with great curiosity on Zyh's figure as tall as a pole, at his thin face with immense nose, and his round eyes full of laughter.

"Oh," said he, "with such a neighbor, if God would return health to uncle, there would not be any sadness."

" With a joyous neighbor there can be no quarrels," said Zyh. "But listen now to what I will say, in good, Christian fashion. You have not been at home for a long time; you will find there no order. I will not say in the land management, for the abbot has done well — he has cleared a strip of forest and settled new men on it. But, as he has visited Bogdanets only occasionally, the storehouses will be

empty; yes, and in the house itself there is hardly a bench, or a narrow straw-tick to lie down on. A sick man needs comfort. So, do you know what ? Come with me. Stay at my house a short month or two; that will be to my heart, and during that time Yagenka will think of Bogdanets. Only depend on her, and let not your head ache about anything. Zbyshko will go to look after the management; I will bring to you the reverend abbot and you can reckon at once with him. The girl will take as much care of you, Matsko, as if you were her own father, and in sickness a woman's care is better than any other. Well, my friends, will you do as I beg you ?"

" It is a known fact that you are a kind man, and have always been such," said Matsko, with emotion; "but, see you, if I am to die by this ugly iron in my ribs I prefer to die in my own house. Besides, at home, though a man be sick, he inquires about more than one thing, and arranges more things than one. Should God command me to that world — there is no help for it. Whether the care be greater or less, I shall not twist out. To hardships we are accustomed in war. An armful of pea-straw is pleasant to him who has slept for years on bare earth. But I thank you much for your kindliness, and if I shall not thank you sufficiently, God grant that Zbyshko will."

Zyh, really famous for kindness, and obliging in character, began again to insist and beg, but Matsko had grown stubborn. If he had to die he would die in his own house! He had suffered whole years through his absence from Bogdanets; so now, when the boundary was not distant, he would not renounce it for anything, even were it to be his last camping-place. God had been kind hitherto in even permitting " the old man " to drag himself that far.

Here he pushed away with his fists the tears which had risen under his eyelids, and looked around.

" If these pine woods belong to Vilk of Brozova," said he, " we shall arrive just after mid-day."

" Not Vilk owns them now, but the abbot," said Zyh.

The sick Matsko laughed at this and after a while added,—

" If they are the abbot's they may be ours sometime."

" Oh," cried Zyh, joyously, " a little while since you were talking of death, but now you would like to outlive the abbot."

" Not I would outlive him, but Zbyshko."

Further conversation was interrupted by sounds of horns

in the forest, which were heard far in advance of them. Zyh reined his horse in at once, and listened.

" Some one is hunting, it would seem," said he. " Wait a while ! It may be the abbot — it would be well if you were to meet him just now. But be quiet! "

Here he turned to the retinue.

"Halt!"

They halted. The horns sounded nearer, and a little while later the barking of dogs was heard.

" Halt!" repeated Zyh. "They are coming toward us."

Zbyshko sprang from his horse, and cried, —

" Give me the crossbow ! Mayhap a beast will run out of the forest. Quick! quick! "

And seizing the crossbow from the hands of an attendant, he pushed it against the ground, pressed it with his stomach, bent, stretched his back into the form of a bow, and grasping the string in both hands pulled it up in the twinkle of an eye to an iron notch, then he put in an arrow and sprang forward into the pine wood.

" He stretched the string without a crank ! " whispered Zyh, astonished at the sight of strength so uncommon.

"Ho! he is a deadly fellow! " whispered Matsko, with pride.

Meanwhile the horns and the barking of dogs were heard still nearer, till, all at once, on the right side of the forest was heard a heavy trampling, the crack of breaking twigs and branches, and onto the road rushed, like lightning, an old bearded bison, with gigantic head held low, with bloody eyes, and tongue hanging out. He was panting terribly. Coming out at a hole by the roadside he crossed it with a bound, fell on his forefeet, but rose quickly and was ready to vanish on the opposite side of the road in a thicket, when the ominous string of the crossbow whizzed on a sudden, the whistle of the shaft was heard, the beast reared, squirmed, bellowed dreadfully, and tumbled to the earth as if struck by a lightning flash.

Zbyshko stepped out from behind a tree, drew the string of the crossbow a second time, and, ready to shoot, approached the prostrate beast, which was still digging the earth with its hind feet. But after he had looked a while he turned calmly to the retinue, and cried from a distance, —

"lie has so got it that he is dying ! "

" But just think," said Zyh, approaching, " from one arrow! "

" Oh, it was a close shot, and he was running tremendously. Look! not only the point, but the shaft is hidden entirely just behind his foreleg."

"The hunters must be near; surely they will take him."

" I will not give him ! " answered Zbyshko; "he was killed on the road, and no one owns the road."

" But if the abbot is hunting? "

" If it is the abbot, let him take the beast."

Meanwhile some tens of dogs rushed from the woods. When they saw the bison they sprang at him with a terrible uproar, fastened to his body in a crowd, and began soon to fight among themselves.

" The hunters will come immediately," said Zyh. " Look, there they are already 1 but they have come out some distance in front of us and do not see the beast yet. Hop! hop! come this way, come this way! It is lying here! lying here!"

But all at once he was silent, and shaded his eyes with his hand.

" For God's sake, what is this? " called he, after a while. " Am I blind, or am I deceived
— "

" There is one in front on a black horse," said Zbyshko.
But Zyh exclaimed quickly,—
" Dear Jesus! As I live, that is Yagenka! "
And he began to shout,—
" Yagna ! Yagna ! "
Then he rushed forward, but before he could urge his steed to a gallop, Zbyshko saw the
most wonderful sight in the world: On a swift pied horse hastened toward them, sitting man
fashion, a young girl with a crossbow in her hand and a spear at her shoulder. To her hair, which
had dropped down somewhat from the speed of riding, had clung wild hops, her face was as
ruddy as the dawn, on her breast was an open shirt, above the shirt a coat with the wool inside.
When she had ridden up she reined in her horse suddenly. For a moment incredulity,
astonishment, and delight were depicted on her features; but at last, unable to gainsay the
testimony of her ears and eyes, she began to cry with a thin voice, which was still somewhat
childlike,—
"Tatulo! tatulo!"
In one twinkle she slipped from her horse, and when Zyh had sprung down from his beast
to greet her on the ground, she flung herself on his neck. For a long time Zbyshko heard
only the sound of kisses and the two words: "Tatulo! (Papadear!) Yagula! (Aggiedear!)"
"Tatulo! Yagula!" repeated with delight.
Both escorts came up; Matsko came also in his wagon, and they were still repeating,
"Tatulo! Yagula!" and still had their arms around each other's necks. When at last they had had
sufficient exclamations and greetings, Yagenka inquired,—
"Then are you coming from the war? Are you well?"
" From the war. Why should I not be well? And thou? And the younger people ? I think
they are well — are they not? Otherwise thou wouldst not be flying through the forest. But what
is the best that thou art doing here, girl? "
"Thou seest that I am hunting," replied Yagenka, laughing.
" In other people's forests?"
" The abbot gave permission. Besides, he sent me trained men and dogs." *
Here she turned to her servants.
" Take off the dogs for me; they will tear the beast's hide!"
Then she addressed Zyh, —
u Oh, but I am glad, glad to be looking at you ! All is well at home."
"But am I not glad?" replied Zyh. "Give thy face again, girl!"
And again they began to kiss, and when they had finished Yagenka said,—
" There is a long piece of road from here to the house — so far did we chase after that
beast. As many as ten miles, so that the horses are tired. But he is a strong bison — have you
seen ? He has three of my arrows in him ; he must have fallen from the last one."
" He fell from the last one, but not from thine; this young knight here shot him."
Yagenka gathered back her hair, which had dropped to her eyes, and looked quickly at
Zbyshko, though not with excess of good-will.
" Dost thou know who he is? " inquired Zyh.
" I do not."
"No wonder that thou dost not know him, for he has grown. But perhaps thou knowest

old Matsko of Bog-dauets? "

" For God's sake! is that Matsko of Bogdanets?" cried Yagenka.

And approaching the wagon she kissed Matsko's hand.

"Is this you?"

" It is I. But in a wagon, for the Germans shot me."

" What Germans? The war surely was with Tartars! I know that, for I begged papa not a little to take me with him."

" There was war with the Tartars, but we were not at that war, for earlier we were fighting in Lithuania, I and Zbyshko."

" But where is Zbyshko? "

"Dost thou not know that this is Zbyshko?" asked Matsko, with a smile.

" Is that Zbyshko? " cried the girl, looking again at the young knight.

" Of course it is! "

"Give him thy lips for acquaintance!" cried Zyh, joyously.

Yagenka turned briskly toward Zbyshko, but drew back on a sudden, and covering her eyes with her hands said,—

" If I am ashamed ? "

" But we are acquainted from childhood," said Zbyshko.

" Ah, we know each other well. I remember, I remember! About eight years ago you and Matsko came to us, and my dead mother brought us nuts and honey. But you, as soon as the older ones went from the room, put a. fist to my nose, and ate the nuts yourself."

"He would not do that now," said Matsko. "He has been with Prince Vitolcl, and in Cracow at the castle, and knows courtly customs."

But something else came to Yagenka's head, for turning to Zbyshko, she asked,—

" Then it was you who killed the bison? "

" I."

" Let us see where the arrow is."

" You will not see, for it is hidden entirely behind the fore leg."

" Never mind, do not examine," said Zyh. " We all saw how he shot him, and we saw something better yet, for he drew the crossbow in a second without a crank."

Yagenka looked a third time at Zbyshko, but now with astonishment.

4 'Did you draw the crossbow without a crank?" asked she.

Zbyshko felt, as it were, a certain incredulity in her voice,

so he put on the earth the end of the crossbow from which he had shot before, drew it in a twinkle till the iron hoop squeaked, then, wishing to show that he knew court customs, he knelt on one knee and gave it to Yagenka.

The girl, instead of taking it from his hands, blushed suddenly without herself knowing why, and drew up around her neck the coarse linen shirt which had opened from swift riding through the forest.

CHAPTER VIII.

THE day after their arrival at Bogdanets Matsko and Zbyshko began to look around at their old seat, and soon saw that Zyh spoke correctly when he said that privations not a few would annoy them at first.

In the land management matters moved after a fashion. A few acres were worked by old-time men, or those settled in recently by the abbot. Formerly there had been far more cultivated land in Bogdanets, but from the period when the race of " the Grady " perished to the second last man in the battle of Plovtsi there was a lack of working-hands, and after the attack of the Silesian Germans and the war of the Grymaliti with the Nalenchi, the fields of Bogdanets, formerly fruitful, had grown over for the greater part with forests. Matsko could do nothing unaided. In vain had he tried some years before to attract free cultivators from Kresnia and give them land beyond the meadows, but these preferred to sit on their own " small plots " to working large fields owned by other men. He enticed in, however, some homeless people, and in various wars seized a few prisoners, whom he had married and then settled in cottages ; in this way the village began to increase anew.

But Matsko met difficulty in management; hence, when a chance to pledge the place offered itself, he mortgaged all Bogdanets quickly, thinking first, that it would be easier for the rich abbot to manage the land, and second, that war would help Zbyshko and him to men and to money.

The abbot had worked indeed actively. He had increased the laboring force in Bogdanets by five families; he had increased the herds of horses and cattle; besides, he had built a granary, a brush cow-house, and also a stable of similar material. But, as he was not living in Bogdanets permanently, he had not thought of a house, and Matsko, who had supposed sometimes that when he came back he would find a castle surrounded by a moat and a palisade, found all as he had left it, — with this difference only, that the corners of the house had grown a little crooked and the walls appeared lower, for they had settled and sunk in the earth somewhat.

The house was composed of an enormous front room, two

spacious inner apartments, with chambers and a kitchen. In the inner rooms were windows with panes of membrane. In the middle of each room, on a floor made of clay, was a fireplace from which smoke issued through holes in the ceiling. This ceiling was blackened completely. In better times it had served also as a smoking place, for on hooks fixed in the beams hung in those days hams of pigs, wild boars, bears, and elks, hind legs of deer, backs of oxen, and whole strings of sausage. In Bogdanets the hooks were now empty, as well as shelves along the walls, on which in other " courts " were placed earthen and tin plates. But the walls under the shelves did not seem now too naked, for Zbyshko had commanded his people to hang on them breastplates, helmets, short and long swords, and farther on, spears, forks, crossbows, and horse-trappings. The armor grew black from being hung in the smoke thus, and there was need to clean it frequently; but, to compensate, everything was at hand; and besides, worms did not gnaw the wood of lances, crossbows, and axehandles. Matsko had commanded to carry carefully to his own sleeping room all valuable clothing.

In the front chambers, near the windows, were tables of pine plank, and benches of like material on which the masters sat down to eat with the servants. For men unaccustomed during long years of war to comforts, not much was needed. But in Bogdanets, bread, flour, and various other supplies were lacking, and especially utensils. The peasants had brought in what they could. Matsko had counted mainly on this, that, as happens in such cases, neighbors would aid him ; and indeed he was not mistaken, at least not in Zyh.

The second day after his arrival Matsko, wishing to enjoy the serene autumn weather, was seated on a log before the house, when Yagenka rode into the yard on the same horse which she had ridden at the hunt. The servant, who was cutting wood near the fence, wished to help her dismount, but she sprang down in one instant, panting a little from swift riding, and ruddy as an apple she approached Matsko.

" May He be praised ! I have come to bow down to you from papa, and to ask about your health."

" It is not worse than on the road," answered Matsko; " a man has slept in his own house at least."

"But you must feel much discomfort, and a sick man needs care."

u We are firm fellows. There are no comforts yet, of course, but there is no hunger either. I have commanded to kill an ox and two sheep; there is meat enough. The women have brought in too some flour and eggs, but that is not much with us, the greatest lack is utensils."

" Well, 1 have had two wagons filled. In one of them are two beds, and cooking utensils ; in the other, food of various kinds. There are cakes and flour, salt meat, dried mushrooms, a small keg of beer, another of mead; there is a little of everything that we have in the house."

Matsko, always pleased with every addition, stretched out his hand and stroked Yagenka's head.

" God repay thee, and thy father. When we begin to manage we will return this."

" God prosper you! But are we Germans, to take back what we give ? "

" Well, then God will pay thee and thy father still more. Thy father told what a housekeeper thou art. Thou hast managed all thy father's place for a twelvemonth."

" Yes ! And when you want something more send a man, but one who knows what is needed, for at times a dull servant comes who knows not what he was sent for."

Here Yagenka began to look around somewhat. Matsko, noting this, smiled, and asked,

—

" For whom art thou looking ? "

" I am not looking for any one ! "

" I will send Zbyshko; let him thank thee and Zyh for me. Has Zbyshko pleased thee ? "

" But I have not looked at him."

" Then look at him now, for he is just coming."

Indeed Zbyshko was coming from watering animals, and seeing Yagenka he hastened his step. He wore an elkskin coat and a round felt cap such as was used under helmets, his hair was without a net, cut evenly above his brows, and at the sides it fell in golden waves to his shoulders. He approached quickly, large, comely, exactly like an armor-bearer of a great house.

Yagenka turned entirely to Matsko to show that she had come only to him, but Zbyshko greeted her joyously, and taking her hand raised it to his lips in spite of the girl's resistance.

11 Why kiss me on the hand?" inquired she. "Am I a priest? "

" Resist not! Such is the custom! "

"And should thou kiss her on the other hand for what she has brought," put in Matsko, " it would not be too much."

" What has she brought ? " inquired Zbyshko, looking around in the yard, not seeing anything save the horse tied to a post.

" The wagons have not come yet, but they will come," answered Yageuka.

Matsko began to name what she had brought, not omitting anything. When he mentioned the two beds Zbyshko said:

" I am glad to lie down on an oxskin, but I thank you for having thought of me also."

"It was not I, but papa," said the girl, blushing. "If you prefer a skin you are free to prefer it."

"I prefer what comes to hand. On the field more than once after battle we slept with a dead Knight of the Cross for a pillow."

" But have you ever killed a Knight of the Cross ? Surely not!"

Zbyshko, instead of answering, began to laugh.

" Fear God, girl! " cried Matsko; "thou dost not know him! He has done nothing else but kill Germans till it thundered. He is ready for lances, for axes, for everything; and when he sees a German from afar, even hold him on a rope, he will pull to him. In Cracow he wanted to slay Lichtenstein, the envoy, for which they lacked little of cutting his head off. That is the kind of man he is! And I will tell thee of the two Frisians from whom we took their retinue, and a booty so valuable that with one half of it one might buy Bogdanets."

Here Matsko told of the duel with the Frisians, and then of other adventures which had met them, and deeds which they had accomplished. They had fought behind walls, and in the open field with the greatest knights from foreign lands. They had fought with Germans, French, English, and Burgundians. . They had been in raging whirls of battle, when horses, men, arms, Germans, and feathers formed one mass, as it were. And what had they not seen besides! They had seen castles of red brick belonging to Knights of the Cross, Lithuanian wooden fortresses, and churches such as there are not near Bogdanets, and towns, and savage wildernesses, in which Lithuanian divinities, driven out of their sanctuaries, whine in the night-time; and various marvels. And in all places where it came to battle Zbyshko

was in front, so that the greatest knights wondered at him.

Yagenka, who had sat down on the log near Matsko, listened with parted lips to that narrative, turning her head, as if on a pivot, now toward Matsko, now toward Zbyshko, and looking at the young knight with ever increasing wonder. At last, when Matsko had finished, she sighed, and said :

" Would to God that I had been born a man ! "

Zbyshko, who during the narrative was looking at her with equal attention, was thinking at that moment of something else evidently, for he said on a sudden, —

" But you are a beautiful maiden! "

" You are more beautiful than I, you see that," said Yagenka, half unwillingly, half in sadness.

Zbyshko might without untruth have replied that he had not seen many maidens like her, for Yagenka was simply radiant with a splendor of health, youth, and strength. It was not without reason that the old abbot declared that she looked half a raspberry, half a pine tree. Everything about her was beautiful, her lithe form, her broad shoulders, her breast as if chiselled from stone, red lips, and blue eyes quickly glancing. She was dressed more carefully than before at the hunt in the forest. She had red beads around her neck, she wore a sheepskin coat open in front and covered with green cloth, a petticoat of strong striped stuff, and new boots. Even old Matsko noted the handsome dress while looking at her, and when he had looked at her a while he inquired, —

" But why art thou arrayed as if for a festival? "

Instead of answering she called out, —

" The wagons are coming! the wagons are coming! "

As they came in she sprang toward them, and after her followed Zbyshko. The unloading continued till sunset, to the great satisfaction of Matsko, who examined every article separately, and praised Yagenka for each one. Twilight had come when the girl was preparing for home. When ready to mount Zbyshko seized her around the waist suddenly, and before she could utter one word he had raised her to the saddle and fixed her there. She blushed like the dawn and turned her face toward him.

" You are a strong lad," said she, in a voice suppressed somewhat.

Zbyshko who because of the darkness took no note of her confusion and blushes, laughed, and inquired, —

" But have you no fear of beasts? Night will come straightway."

"There is a spear in the wagon — give it to me."

Zbyshko went to the wagon, took out a spear, and handed it to her.

"Be well!"

"Be well!"

"God repay you! I will go to-morrow, or the next day to your father's house to bow down to him, and to you for your neighborly kindness."

" Come ! We shall be glad! "

And urging forward her horse she vanished in a moment among the thickets by the roadside. Zbyshko turned to his uncle.

" It is time for you to go in."

But Matsko answered without moving from the log, —

"Hei! what a girl! The yard was just bright from her."

"Surely!"

A moment of silence came next. Matsko appeared to be thinking of something while looking at the stars which were coming out; then he continued, as if to himself, —

" And active, and a housekeeper, though not more than fifteen years of age."

" Yes," said Zbyshko, " and old Zyh loves her as the eye in his head."

" They say that Mochydoly will go with her, and there in the meadows is a herd of mares with their colts."

" But in the Mochydoly forests there are terrible swamps, very likely."

" There are beaver dams in them also."

Again followed silence. Matsko looked aslant some time at Zbyshko, and asked at last,
—

" What art thou thinking of ? Thou art meditating on some subject."

" Yes, for, see you, Yagenka so reminded me of Danusia that something pained me in the heart."

" Let us go to the house," said the old man. " It is late." And rising with difficulty he leaned on Zbyshko, who conducted him to his room.

Next morning Zbyshko went directly to Zyh's house, for Mfttsko hurried the visit greatly. He insisted also that for show's sake his nephew should have two attendants, and array himself in his best, so as to show honor in that way

and exhibit due gratitude. Zbyshko yielded and went arrayed as if for a wedding, in that same gold-embroidered, golden-clasped, white-satin jacket won by them. Zyh received him with open arms, with delight and with songs. Yagenka, on reaching the threshold of the main room, stopped as if fixed to the spot, and came near dropping the pitcher of wine when she saw Zbyshko, for she thought that some king's son had come to them. She lost her boldness immediately and sat in silence, merely rubbing her eyes from time to time, as if trying to rouse herself from slumber.

Zbyshko, who lacked experience, thought that for reasons which he knew not, she was not glad to see him; so he talked only to Zyh, praising his bounty as a neighbor and admiring his court, which really resembled Bogdanets in nothing.

Abundance and wealth were there visible on all sides. In the rooms were windows with panes of horn scraped so smooth and thin that they were almost as transparent as glass. There were no fires in the middle of rooms, but great chimneys with niches in the corners. The floor was of larch plank well washed, on the walls were arms and a multitude of plates, shining like the sun, a beautifully cutout spoon-rack with rows of spoons, two of which were silver. In one place and another hung carpets plundered in wars, or obtained from travelling merchants. Under the tables lay gigantic tawny skins of wild bulls, also skins of wild boars and bisons.

Zyh showed his wealth with willingness, saying from moment to moment that that was Yagenka's housekeeping. He conducted Zbyshko also to a room, odorous of pitch and mint, from the ceiling of which hung wolf, fox, beaver, and marten skins in whole bundles. He showed him the cheese house, he showed stores of wax and honey, barrels of flour and rusks, hemp, and dried mushrooms. Then he took him to the granaries, the cowhouses, the stables and pens, to sheds in which were wagons, implements for hunting, with nets for fishing, and so dazzled his eyes with abundance that when the young man came back to supper he could not refrain from expressions of wonder.

"One should live here and never die," said Zbyshko.

"In Mochydoly there is almost the same order," said Zyh. " Thou dost remember Mochydoly? That is toward Bogdanets. Formerly our fathers quarrelled about the boundary, and sent challenges to each other to fight, but I will not quarrel."

Here he touched his tankard of mead with Zbyshko's, and asked,—

" But, perhaps, thou hast the wish to sing something ? "

" No," replied Zbyshko, " I listen to you with curiosity."

" The young bears, seest thou, will get this place. If only they do not fight about it some time!"

" How, the young bears ? "

" Yes, the boys, Yagenka's brothers."

' l Hei! the\'7d 7 will not need to suck their paws in winter."

" Oh no. But neither will Yagenka's mouth in Mochydoly lack a bit of cheese."

" Surely not! "

" But why not eat and drink ? Yagenka, pour out to him and to me ! "

" I am eating and drinking as much as I am able."

"If thou art not able to eat more, ungirdle— That is a beautiful belt! Ye must have taken brave booty in Lithuania?"

" We make no complaint," answered Zbyshko, who used the occasion to show that the heirs of Bogdanets were not poor little possessors. "We sold a part of the booty in Cracow and received forty gryvens of silver — "

" Fear God! One might buy a village for that much."

" Yes, for there was one suit of Milan armor which uncle sold when expecting to die, and that, you know— "

"I know! That is worth going to Lithuania for. In my time I wanted to go, but I was afraid."

'• Of what? The Knights of the Cross? Ei, who is afraid of the Germans? Why fear till they attack? — and when they attack there is no time for fear. I was afraid of those pagan gods or devils. In the forest there are as many of them as of ants, very likely."

" But where are they to live, since their temples are burnt? In old times they had plenty, but now they live only on ants and mushrooms."

" But hast thou seen them? "

" I have not seen them myself, but I have heard that people do see them. One of those devils will thrust out his hairy paw from behind a tree, and shake it, asking to give him something."

" Matsko said the same thing," remarked Yagenka.

" Yes, on the road he said the same thing to me," added Zyh. "Well, it is no wonder! For that matter, with us here, though the country is Christian this long time, some-thing laughs in the swamps, and even in houses; though the priests scold, it is better always to put out a plate of food for the imps, or they will scrape on the wall so that thou wilt not close an eye — Yagenka! put out a plate on the threshold, daughter."

Yagenka took an earthen plate full of paste with cheese and put it on the threshold. •

"The priests blame and punish!" said Zyh. "But the glory of the Lord Jesus will not be decreased by some paste ; and when satisfied and well-wishing, the imps will guard a man from fire, and from evil-doers."

" Thou mightst ungirdle and sing something," said he, turning to Zbyshko.

" Sing you, for I see that you have the wish this long time; but perhaps Panna Yagenka would sing?"

" We will sing in turn," cried Zyh, rejoiced. " There is a lad in the house too who plays on a wooden flute and accompanies us. Call him! "

They called the lad, who took his seat on a block, put the flute to his mouth, spread his fingers over it, and looked at those present, waiting to see whom he was to accompany.

They began to dispute then, for none wished to be first. Finally Zyh commanded Yagenka to set an example; Yagenka, though greatly abashed before Zbyshko, rose from the bench, put her hands under her apron, and began, —

"Oh, had I wings like a wild goose, I wortld fly after Yasek, 1 would fly after him to Silesia 1"

Zbyshko opened his eyes widely to begin with, then sprang to his feet and cried in a loud voice, —

" Whence do you know that?"

Yagenka looked at him with astonishment.

" But all sing it here. What wonder to you? "

Zyh, who thought that Zbyshko had drunk a little too much, turned to him with delighted face, and said, —

"Ungirdle thyself! It will be easier right away."

Zbyshko stood for a while with changing face, then mastering his emotion he said to Yagenka, —

"Pardon me. I remembered something unexpectedly. Sing on."

" Maybe it makes you sad to listen?"

" Ei,*why? " asked he, with a quivering voice. " I could listen all night to that song."

Then he sat down, covered his brows with his hand, and was sileut, not wishing to lose a word. Yagenka sang the second verse, but when she had finished it she saw a great tear passing over Zbyshko's fingers; then she pushed up to him quickly, and touching him with her elbow inquired, —

" Well, what is the matter? I do not wish you to weep. Tell what the matter is."

"Nothing! nothing!" replied Zbyshko, with a sigh. "It would take long to tell. What happened has passed. I ana more cheerful now."

" Perhaps you might drink some sweet wine."

"Honest girl!" cried Zyh. "Why say 'you' to each other? Say ' Zbyshko' to him, and say thou ' Yagenka' to her. Ye knew each other from childhood." Then he turned to his daughter. " That he beat thee in the old time is nothing ! He will not do so now."

" I will not," said Zbyshko, joyously. " Let her beat me if she chooses."

At this Yagenka, wishing to amuse him perfectly, closed her hand, and while laughing pretended to beat him.

" Here is for my broken nose! and here! and here! "

" Wine! " cried the jollified Zyh.

Yagenka ran to the cellar and soon brought out a stone jug full of wine, two beautiful tankards ornamented with silver flowers, wrought by silversmiths of Vrotslav, and two cakes of cheese, odorous from afar.

This sight made Zyh, who had something in his head, altogether tender; so gathering the stone jug to himself he pressed it to his bosom, feigning to think it Yagenka, and repeated,—

" Oi, my dear daughter! Oi, poor orphan! What shall I, lone unfortunate, do here when thou art taken from me? What shall I do?"

" You will have to give her away before long!" cried out Zbyshko.

In the twinkle of an eye Zyh passed from tenderness to laughter.

"Hi! hi! The girl is fifteen years of age, but she is drawn toward those two boys already! When she sees one from afar her knees smite each other."

"Papa, I will go away! " said Yagenka.

" Go not! It is pleasant in thy company."

Then he blinked mysteriously at Zbyshko.

"The two will come here: one, young Vilk, son of old Vilk of Brozova; the other, Stan of Rogov. If they should find thee here they would grit their teeth at thee as they do at each other."

" Oh! " exclaimed Zbyshko.

Then he turned to Yagenka, and saying "thou" to her according to Zyh's command, he inquired,—

" Which one dost thou prefer? "

"Neither."

" But Vilk is strong! " remarked Zyh.

"Let him howl in some other direction!" retorted Yagenka.

"And Stan?"

Yagenka laughed.

" Stan," said she, turning to Zbyshko, " has as much hair on his face as a goat, his eyes are covered; and there is as much fat on him as on a bear."

Zbyshko struck his head as if remembering something on a suclden, and said, —

" But if ye would be so kind I should beg of you; have ye not bear's fat in the house ? My uncle needs it for medicine, and in our house I have not been able to find any."

" We had some," said Yagenka, " but the men took it to rub on their bows, and the dogs ate what was left."

" Was none left?"

" They licked it up clean."

" There is no way but to look for fat in the woods."

" Call a hunt; there is no lack of bears, and shouldst thou need hunter's gear we will give it."

" How can I wait? I will go for a night to the bee nests."

" Take about five assistants. There are good fellows among them."

" I will not go with a crowd; they would frighten the beast away."

" How then ? Wilt thou go with a crossbow ? "

" What should I do with a crossbow in the dark in a forest. Besides, the moon does not shine at present. I will take a barbed fork, with a good axe, and go alone tomorrow."

Yagenka was silent for a while, then alarm was evident on her face.

"Last year," said she, " Bezduh, a hunter, went from here, and a bear tore him to pieces. It is always most dangerous, for when the bear sees a lone man in the night,

and moreover at bee nests, he stands on his hind legs immediately."

" Should he run away, thou wouldst never get him," answered Zbyshko.

Zyh, who had been dozing, woke up on a sudden, and began to sing,—

" But thou, Kuba, art coming from labor, And I, Matsek, am coming from sport! Go early with plow to the clear land, But I 'd rather visit with Kasia the wheat,

Hots! hots!"

Then he said to Zbyshko, —

" Thou knowest there are two of them: Vilk of Brozova, and Stan of Rogov — and thou — "

But Yagenka, fearing lest Zyh might say too much, approached Zbyshko quickly, and inquired,—

" And when wilt thou go? To-morrow?"

" To-morrow after sunset."

" To what bee nests? "

" To ours in Bogdanets, not far from your hillocks, at the side of the Radzikov swamp. People tell me that there bears are found easily."

CHAPTER IX.

ZBYSHKO set out as he had said, for Matsko felt worse, considerably. In the beginning delight and the first occupations at home enlivened him, but his fever returned on the third day, and the pain in his side made itself felt so acutely that he was forced to lie down. Zbyshko made a first visit to the forest in the daytime, examined the bee nests, and saw that near them was an immense trail to the swamp. He spoke with the bee keeper, Vavrek, who slept near by at night in a hut, with a couple of fierce shepherd dogs of Podhale; but Vavrek was just about moving to the village because of severe autumn frosts.

The two men pulled the hut apart, took the dogs in hand, and smeared a little honey here and there on the trees to lure the bear on by its odor. Zbyshko went home then and prepared for the trial. For warmth's sake he put on a sleeveless short coat of elkskin, and also an iron helmet with wire cape, lest the bear might tear his scalp off; he took then a well-tempered fork with two barbed tines, and a broad steel axe on an oak handle, which was not so short as those used by carpenters. In his place at the time of evening milking, he selected a convenient spot, made the sign of the cross on himself, sat down, and waited.

The rays of the setting sun shone among the evergreen branches. Crows had assembled on the pine tops, cawing and clapping their wings; here and there hares were springing swiftly toward the water, making a rustle among berry bushes which were growing yellow, and among fallen leaves ; at times the swift marten sped past. In the thickets was heard yet the twittering of birds, which ceased gradually.

At the moment of sunset there was no rest in the forest. A herd of wild boars, with great uproar and grunting, soon passed by near Zbyshko, then elks in a long row, each holding its head near the tail of another. The dry branches cracked beneath their hoofs, and the forest resounded, shining red in the sunrays; they were hastening to the swamp, where at night they felt safe and happy. At last the evening light shone in the sky; from this the tops of the pines seemed as if in fire, burning, and gradually all became quiet

The forest went to sleep. Gloom rose from the earth and lifted itself toward the bright light of evening, which at last began to fail, to grow sombre, to be black, and to perish. " Now it will be silent till the wolves begin," thought Zbyshko.

He regretted, however, that he had not taken a crossbow, for he could have brought down an elk or a wild boar with ease. Meanwhile from the side of the swamp came for some time yet stifled voices, like painful groaning and whistling.

Zbyshko looked toward that swamp with a certain timidity, for the man Radzik, who on a time had lived in a mud hut there, had vanished with his family, as if he had dropped through the earth. Some said that robbers had borne them away, but there were persons who saw later along the side of the hut certain strange tracks, neither human nor animal, and they racked their heads over this greatly; they were even thinking whether or not to bring the priest from Kresnia to bless that place. It did not come to this, it is true, for no man was found willing to live there, and the hut, or rather the clay on the brush walls of it, dropped down during rain, but thenceforth the place enjoyed no good repute. Vavrek, the bee man, did not indeed care for that; he spent his nights there in summer, but there were various reports about Vavrek also.

Zbyshko, having a fork and an axe, had no fear of wild beasts, but he thought of unclean powers with a certain alarm, and was glad when these noises ceased finally.

The last gleams of light had vanished, and perfect night had come. The wind ceased; there was not even the usual sigh in the tops of the pine trees. Now and then here and there a pine cone fell, giving out on the background of the general stillness a far-reaching, sharp sound ; except this, the silence was such that Zbyshko heard his own breathing.

He sat a long time in this manner, thinking first of the bear that might come, and then of Danusia, who was moving with the Mazovian court into distant regions. He remembered how he had caught her in his arms at the moment of parting with the princess, how her tears had flowed down his cheeks ; he remembered her bright face, her blond head, her garland of star thistles, her singing, her red shoes with long tips, which he had kissed at the moment of parting, — finally, everything that had happened since they had become acquainted; and such sorrow seized him because she was

not near, and such longing for her, that he was sunk in it thoroughly; he forgot that he was in the forest, that he was hunting a wild beast, and he said in his soul,—

" I will go to thee, for I cannot live without thee."

And he felt that this was true, that he must go to Mazovia; if not, he would perish in Bogdanets. Yurand came to his mind, and his wonderful resistance; hence he thought it all the more needful to go, and to learn what the secret was, what the obstacles were, and if some challenge to a mortal struggle might not remove them. Finally it seemed to him that Danusia was stretching her hands to him, and crying: "Come, Zbyshko, come!" How was he to avoid going to her?

He did not sleep — he saw her as clearly as in a vision or a dream. Behold, Danusia was riding near the princess, thrumming on her lute and singing. She was thinking to see him soon, and perhaps she was looking around to see if he were not galloping up behind them; meanwhile he was in the dark forest.

Here Zbyshko came to himself — and he came to himself, not merely because he saw the dark forest, but for the reason that from afar behind him was heard a certain rustling. He grasped the fork in his hands more firmly, held his ear forward, and listened.

The rustling approached and after a time became perfectly clear. Dry limbs crackled under cautious footsteps, the fallen leaves and the berry bushes gave out their sounds. Something was advancing.

At times the rustling ceased, as if the beast halted at trees, and then such silence set in that there was noise in Zbyshko's ears; then again were heard slow and careful footsteps. In general there was something so cautious in that approach that amazement seized Zbyshko.

" It must be that the ' Old Fellow ' fears the dogs which have been at the hut here," said he to himself; " but perhaps a wolf sniffs me."

Meanwhile the steps ceased. Zbyshko heard clearly that something had halted, perhaps twenty or thirty steps behind him, and had sat down, as it seemed. He looked around once and a second time, but, though the trees were outlined clearly enough in the darkness, he could not see anything. There was no other way but to wait.

And he waited so long that astonishment seized him a second time.

" A bear would not come here to sleep under the bee nest, and a wolf would have smelt me and would not wait here till morning."

Suddenly shivers passed from head to foot through him.

" Had something ' foul' crawled from the swamps and come up from behind toward him? Would the slippery arms of some drowned one grasp hold of him unexpectedly, or the green eyes of a vampire leer into his face, or something laugh dreadfully there at his back, or some blue head on spider legs creep out from beyond a pine tree ? "

And he felt that the hair was rising under his iron helmet.

But after a while rustling was heard in front, this time more distinctly than ever. Zbyshko drew a breath of relief. He admitted, it is true, that the same " wonder" had gone around him, and was approaching now from the front; but he preferred this. He grasped the fork well, rose in silence, and waited.

At that moment he heard the sound of the pine trees above his head, on his face he felt a strong breeze from the swamp, and the same instant there flew to his nostrils the odor of a bear.

There was not the least doubt now, the bear was approaching!

In a moment Zb3"shko ceased to fear, and, inclining his head, he exerted his sight and his hearing. The steps came up, heavy, distinct, the odor grew sharper; soon panting and growling were heard.

" If only two are not coming! " thought Zbyshko.

But at that moment he saw before him the great and dark form of a beast which advancing with the wind could not smell him till the last moment, especially as the beast was occupied with the odor of honey rubbed on the tree trunks.

"Come on, grandfather!" cried Zbyshko, pushing out from behind the pine.

The bear gave a short roar, as if frightened by the unexpected vision, but was too near to save itself by flight, so in one instant it rose on its hind legs, opening its forelegs, as if to embrace. This was just what Zbyshko was waiting for; so, collecting himself, he sprang like lightning, and with all the power of his strong arms, together with his own weight, drove the fork into the bosom of the beast.

The whole forest trembled then from a penetrating roar. The bear seized the fork with his paws wishing to tear it away, but the barbs at the points held it in; so, feeling

pain, he thundered all the more terribly. Trying to reach Zbyshko he pressed onto the fork and drove it into himself the more effectually. Zbyshko, not knowing whether the points had sunk deeply enough, did not let go the handle. The man and the beast pulled and struggled. The pine wood trembled unceasingly from the roar, in which rage and despair were united.

Zbyshko could not use the axe till he had first planted the other sharp end of the fork in the earth, and the bear, grasping the handle with his paws, shook both it and Zbyshko, as if understanding what the struggle meant, and, despite the pain caused by every movement of the deeply buried barbs, he did not let himself be " planted." In this way the terrible struggle continued, and Zbyshko understood that his strength would be worn out at last. He might fall, too, and in that case be lost; so he collected himself, stretched his arms, planted his feet apart, bent forward, like a bow, so as not to be thrown on his back, and in his excitement repeated through set teeth, —

"My death, or thine! "

Finally such rage possessed him, and such resolution, that really he would have preferred at the moment to die, rather than let that bear go. At last his foot struck a root of the pine ; he tottered and would have fallen had it not been that a dark figure stood by him; another fork " propped " the beast, and a voice right at his ear cried, —

"With the axe! "

Zbyshko in the ardor of battle did not stop for the twinkle of an eye to learn whence the unexpected aid had come, but grasped his axe and struck terribly. The fork handle cracked, then broke from the weight and the last convulsions of the bear, which, as if struck by a lightning flash tumbled to the earth, and groaned there. But the groaning stopped immediately. Silence followed, broken only by the loud panting of Zbyshko, who leaned against the tree, for the legs were tottering under him. He raised his head only after a while, looked at the figure standing by his side, and was frightened, thinking that, perhaps, it was not a person.

" Who art thou? " asked he, in alarm.

" Yagenka! " answered a thin female voice.

Zbyshko was dumb from amazement, not believing his own ears.

But his doubt did not last long, for Yagenka's voice was heard again.

" I will strike a fire," said she.

At once the steel sounded against the flint, sparks flew, and with their twinkling light Zbyshko saw the white forehead and dark brows of the maiden, her lips pushed forward in blowing the lighted puuk. Only then did he think that she had come to that forest to help him, that without her fork it might have gone ill with him, and he felt such immense gratitude that, without thinking long, he grasped her by the waist and kissed both her cheeks.

Her punk and steel fell to the ground.

"Let me go! What is this?" said she, in a smothered voice; still she did not push his face away; on the contrary, her lips even touched his, as if by accident.

He let her go, and said, —

"God reward! I know not what might have happened without thee."

Yagenka, feeling around in the darkness to find the punk and steel, began to explain, —

" I feared that something might harm thee. Bezduh went out also with a fork and an axe, but the bear tore him. God guard from that! Matsko would suffer; as it is, he is barely breathing. "Well, I took the fork and came."

" So that was thou behind the pines there? "

"I."

" And I thought it was the ' evil one.'"

" No small fear seized me too, for here around the Rad-zikov swamp it is not well in the night without fire."

" Why didst thou not call? "

"I was afraid that thou mightst drive me away."

Then she struck fire again, and placed dry hemp-stalks on the punk; these shot up a bright flame immediately.

" J have two handfuls, but do thou collect dry limbs in a hurry; there will be a fire."

After a time a really cheerful fire burst forth, the flames of which shone on the enormous ruddy carcass of the bear, which was lying in a pool of blood.

"Ei! a savage creature!" said Zbyshko, with a certain boastfulness.

" But the head is almost cut in two! O Jesus!"

When she said this she bent down and buried her hand in the bear's fur to learn if he had much fat; then she raised it with a gladsome face.

" There will be fat for a couple of years!"

" But the fork is broken. Look ! "

" That is a pity; what can I say at home ? "

" What dost thou need to say? "

" Something, for papa would not have let me come to the forest, so I had to wait till all were in bed."

After a while she added, —

" Say not that I was here, so that they may not wonder at me."

" But I will conduct thee home, for the wolves might attack thee, and thou hast no fork."

"Well, do so!"

And they conversed thus for some time by the cheerful light of the fire, near the body of the bear, both like some young creatures of the forest.

Zbyshko looked at Yagenka's charming face, lighted by the gleam of the flame, and said in involuntary astonishment:

" Another girl like thee there is not in the whole world, I think. Thou shouldst go to the war! "

She looked into his eyes for a moment, then answered almost sadly, —

" I know — but do not laugh at me."

CHAPTER X.

YAGENKA herself melted out a large pot of bear's fat, the first quart of which Matsko drank with pleasure, for it was fresh, not burnt, and had the odor of angelica, which the girl, skilled in plants, had added to the pot in measure. Matsko was strengthened in spirit at once, and received hope of recovery.

" That was needed," said he. " When everything inside is oiled properly, that dog mother of an arrow-point may slip out of me somewhere."

The succeeding quarts did not taste so well to him as the first, but he drank because of good sense. Yagenka comforted him too, saying,—

" You will recover. Zbilud of Ostrog had a link of armor driven deeply into his shoulder, and it came out from bear's fat. But when the wound opens one must stop it with beaver fat."

"Hast thou that fat?"

" We have. If fresh fat is needed we can go with Zbyshko to the beaver dam. It is not hard to get beavers. But it would be no harm either, if you would make a vow to some saint who is a patron of the wounded."

" That came to my head also, but I know not well to what saint. Saint George is the patron of knights. He guards a warrior from accidents, and in need gives him valor; they say that often in his own person he stands on the just side and helps to conquer those who are hateful to God. But a saint who fights gladly is rarely willing to cure, and there is perhaps another with whom he would interfere if he did so. Every saint has his own work in heaven, his own management— that we understand. One of them never meddles with another, for disagreements might spring up, and in heaven it would not befit saints to dispute or to quarrel. There are Cosmo and Damian, great saints too; to these doctors pray, so that disease may not vanish from the earth ; if it did doctors would have no subsistence. There is also Saint Appolonia for teeth, and Saint Laborious for the gravel — but all this is not to the point! The abbot will come and tell me to whom I should turn, for not every common priest knows all God's secrets, and not every one knows such things though he have a shaven head."

" But might you not make a vow to the Lord Jesus himself?"

" Certainly, because He is above all. But that would be as if, for example, thy father killed a peasant of mine and I should go with a complaint to the king at Cracow. What would the king say ? He would say this to me: ' I am master over the whole kingdom, and thou comest to me with thy peasant! Are there not officials ? Canst thou not go to the town, to my castellan, and my intermediary?' The Lord Jesus is master over the whole world — dost understand ? but for small affairs He has saints."

"Then I will tell you what," said Zbyshko, who came in at the end of the conversation, " make a vow to our late queen that, if she acts for you, you will make a pilgrimage to her tomb in Cracow ; are the miracles few that were performed in our presence there? Why seek foreign saints when we have our own lady, who is better than others ? "

" True! If I knew that she was for wounds."

" And if she is not for wounds ! No common saint will dare refuse her, and should he refuse she will get what she asks from the Lord God, for she is no ordinary weaver woman, but the Queen of Poland."

" Who brought the last pagan land to the Christian faith. Thou hast spoken wisely," said Matsko. " She must stand high in God's counsels, and it is certain that no common person will contradict her. So, to gain health, I will do as thou sayest."

This advice pleased also Yagenka, who could not refrain from admiring Zbyshko's good sense; and Matsko made a solemn vow that same evening, and thenceforth drank bear's fat with still greater confidence, waiting from day to day for unfailing recovery. But in a week he began to lose hope. He said that the fat was " storming," in his stomach, and on his skin near the last rib something was rising which looked like a knob. After ten days he was still worse ; the lump increased and grew red; Matsko was very weak, and when a fever came he began to prepare again for death. On a certain night he roused Zbyshko on a sudden.

"Light the torch quickly," said he, "for something is happening me, — whether good or bad, I know not."

Zbyshko sprang to his feet, and, without striking a flint, blew a fire in the next room, lighted a pine torch and returned.

"What is the matter?"

"What is the matter with me? Something has pricked through the knob! Surely an arrow-head! I hold it! I cannot pull it out, but I feel it clink and move."

" The point! nothing else. Catch it firmly and pull."

Matsko squirmed and hissed from pain, but he thrust his fingers deeper and deeper till he held the hard object firmly; then he dragged and pulled.

"O Jesus! "

" You have it? " asked Zbyshko.

" I have. Cold sweat has come out on me. But here it is! Look!"

He showed Zbyshko a long, sharp splinter which had broken from the badly bound arrow and had stuck for some months in his body.

" Glory to God and Queen Yadviga! You will get well now."

" Perhaps; I am relieved, but I feel terrible pain," answered Matsko, squeezing the sore, from which blood mixed with matter flowed abundantly. " The less of this vileness there is in a man, the more must sickness leave him. Yagenka said that now we must apply beaver's fat."

" We will go for a beaver to-morrow."

Next day Matsko grew notably better. He slept till late, and on waking called for food. He could not look at bear's fat, but they broke up twenty eggs to be fried for him, as through caution Yagenka would not permit more. He ate these with relish, together with half a loaf of bread, and drank a pot of beer. He asked to bring Zyh then, for he felt joyous.

Zbyshko sent one of his Turks for Zyh, who mounted a horse and came before mid-day, just when the young people were preparing to go to Odstayani Lake for a beaver. At first there was laughing, joking, and singing over mead beyond measure, but later the old men talked of the children, and each praised his own.

"What a man that Zbyshko is," said Matsko; " in the world there is not another such. He is brave, he is as nimble as a wild cat, and skilful. And, do you know, when they were leading him to death in Cracow the girls in the windows were squealing as if some one behind were sticking awls into them; and what girls ! — the daughters of knights and castellans, not to mention various wonderful daughters of citizens."

" Let them be daughters of castellans, and wonderful, but they are not better than my Yagenka," said Zyh.

" Do I tell you that they are better? A nicer girl to people than Yagenka could not be found, I think."

" Neither do I say anything against Zbyshko; he can draw a crossbow without a crank."

" And will prop up a bear himself alone. Have you seen how he cut him ? Split off his head and one paw."

" He knocked off his head, but he did not prop him alone. Yagenka helped him."

" Did she help him? He did not tell me that."

" For he promised her — because the girl was ashamed to go at night to the forest. She told me right away how it was. Others would be glad to invent, but she will not hide the truth. Speaking sincerely I was not pleased, for who knows — I wanted to shout at her, but she said: ' If I cannot guard myself, you, papa, will not guard me;' but never fear, Zbyshko knows also what knightly honor is."

" That is true."

" They have gone alone to-day."

"But they will come back in the evening. The devil is worse at night; girls need not be ashamed then, for it is dark."

Matsko thought a while, then said, as if to himself, —

" But in every case they are glad to see each other."

" Oh, if he had not made a vow to that other one! "

"That, as you know, is a knightly custom. Whoso among young men has not his lady is looked on by others as a simpleton. He has vowed peacock-plumes, and he must get them, for he has sworn on his knightly honor; he must also get Lichtenstein, but the abbot may free him from other vows."

" The abbot will come any day."

" Do you think so ? " inquired Matsko. " But what is such a vow when Yurand told him directly that he would not give the girl. Whether he had promised her to another, or devoted her to the service of God, I know not, but he said directly that he would not give her."

"I have told you," said Zyh, "that the abbot loves Yagenka as if she were his own. The last time he spoke thus to her: ' I have relatives only by the distaff, 1 but by that distaff there will be more threads for thee than for them.'"

At this Matsko looked with alarm, and even suspiciously, at Zyh, and answered only after a while, —

1 This means on the female side of the family. VOL. i. —11

" Still you wish no injustice to us."

" Mochydoly will go with Yagenka," said Zyh, evasively.

"Right away?"

" Right away. I would not give it to another, but I will to her."

" As things stand, half Bogdanets is Zbyshko's, and if God grant health I will work for him, as is proper. Do you like Zbyshko?"

At this Zyh began to blink, and said, —

" The worst is that, when Zbyshko is mentioned, Yagenka turns to the wall that moment."

" And when you mention others?"

" When I mention another she just flies up, and says: 'What?"

" Well now, do you see? God grant that with such a girl Zbyshko will forget the other. I am old, and I too would forget. Will you drink some mead? "

" I will drink some."

" Well, the abbot — there is a wise man for you! Among abbots there are, as you know, laymen; but this abbot, though he does not live among monks, is a priest, and a priest always gives better counsel than a common man, for he understands reading, and he is near the Holy Ghost. But you will give the girl Mochydoly immediately — that is right. And I, if the Lord Jesus give me health, will entice his people away from Vilk of Brozova as far as I am able. I will give good land by lot to each man, for in Bogdanets there is no lack of land. Let them bow down to Vilk on Christmas and then come to me. Are they not free to do so? In time I will build a castle, a nice castle, oak with a moat around it. Let Zbyshko and Yagenka go hunting together now — I think that we shall not wait long for snow. Let them grow accustomed to each other, and the boy will forget that first one. Let them go together. Why talk long over this? Would you give him Yagenka, or would you not?"

" I would give her. Besides, we have long ago arranged that one was for the other, and that Mochydoly and Bogdanets would be for our grandchildren."

" Hail! " cried Matsko, with delight. " God grant them to come like hail! The abbot will christen them."

" If he would come! " cried Zyh, joyously. "But it IB long since I have seen you so delighted."

" I am pleased at heart. The splinter has come out; but

as to Zbyshko, have no fear of him. Yesterday, when Ya-genka was mounting her horse

—you know — the wind was blowing. I asked Zbyshko then, 'Didst thou see?' and right away a shiver took him. And I noted too that at first they talked little, but now whenever they walk together they are always turning their heads toward each other, and talking and talking. Drink some more."

"I will drink."

" To the health of Zbyshko and Yagenka! "

CHAPTER XL

THE old man was not mistaken when he said that Zbyshko and Yagenka were glad to be together, and even that they yearned for each other. Yagenka, under pretext of visiting the sick Matsko, came frequently to Bogdanets, with her father or alone. Zbyshko, through simple gratitude, looked in from time to time at Zyh's, so that soon in the course of days close intimacy and friendship grew up between them. They began to like each other and to consult together willingly, which meant " to talk" about everything which could concern them. There was also a little mutual admiration in this friendship. For the young, stately Zbyshko, who had distinguished himself in war, taken part in tournaments, and been in kings' chambers, seemed to the girl a real courtly knight, almost a king's son in comparison with Stan or Vilk ; and he at times was astonished at the beauty of Yagenka. He remembered his Danusia faithfully, but more than once when he looked at Yagenka on a sudden, whether in the house or the forest, he said to himself involuntarily, "Ei! that's a deer! " but when he caught her by the waist, placed her on horseback, and felt under his hands her body firm as if cut from stone, disquiet took hold of him, and as Matsko said, ' ' shivers " seized the youth, and something passed through his bones and deadened him like a dream.

Yagenka, haughty by nature, quick to laugh, and even to attack, grew more obedient to him gradually, altogether like a servant who only looks into the eyes to learn how to serve and to please. He understood this great inclination of hers, he was grateful, and it was more and more agreeable for him to be with her. At last, especially since Matsko had begun to drink bear's fat, they saw each other almost daily, and after the arrow splinter came out they went together for a beaver to get fresh fat, greatly needed to heal the wound.

They took crossbows, mounted their horses, and rode on, first to Mochydoly, which was to be Yagenka's dower, then toward the forest, where they left the horses with a servant, and went farther on foot, since it was difficult to ride through swamps and thickets. On the road Yagenka pointed

out broad meadows covered with weeds, as well as a blue line of forests.

" Those forests belong to Stan of Rogov," said she.

"To him who would be glad to take thee."

" He would take if I would only give myself," said she, laughing.

" Thou canst defend thyself easily, having Vilk as assistant, who, as I hear, grits his teeth at the other. It is a wonder to me that a challenge to the death has not passed between them already."

" It has not because papa, when he was going to the war, said: ' If ye fight I shall not set eyes on either of you.' What were they to do? When at our house they fume at each other, but drink at the inn afterward in Kresnia together till the\'7d 7 fall under the table."

" Stupid fellows! "

"Why?"

" Because when Zyh was not at home, one or the other ought to have made an attack and taken thee forcibly. What could Zyh have done, if on his return he had found thee with a child in thy arms ? "

Yageuka's blue eyes flashed at once.

" Dost thou think that I would have yielded? — or that we have not people, or that I cannot handle a spear, or a crossbow ? If they had tried ! I should have hunted each man of them home ; besides, I should myself have attacked Brozova or Rogov. Papa knows that he can go to the war very safely."

Thus speaking she wrinkled her beautiful brows, and shook the crossbows so threateningly that Zbyshko laughed and said, —

" Well, thou shouldst be a knight, not a maiden."

But she grew calm and said, —

" Stan guarded me from Vilk, and Vilk from Stan. I was under the care of the abbot, moreover, and it is better for every man not to dispute with the abbot."

" Oh, indeed ! " answered Zbyshko; " every one here fears the abbot. But I, so help me Saint George as I speak the truth, should have feared neither the abbot nor Zyh, nor the hunters at thy father's house, nor thee, but I would have taken thee —

At this Yagenka stopped on the spot, and raising her eyes to Zbyshko, inquired with a certain strange, mild, halting voice, —

" Wouldst thou have taken me? "

Then her lips parted, and she waited for the answer, blushing like the dawn. But clearly he was thinking only of what he would have done in the place of Vilk or Stan, for after a while he shook his golden head, and said, —

" Why should a maiden fight with men, when she has to marry? If a third one does not come, thou must choose one of them, for how — "

" Do not say that to me," answered she, sadly.

" Why not? I have not been here long, hence I know not whether there is any one near by who would please thee more."

" Ah! " exclaimed Yagenka. " Give me peace ! "

They went on in silence, pushing forward through the thicket, which was all the denser because the brush and trees were covered with wild hops. Zbyshko went ahead, tearing apart the green ropes, breaking branches here and there. Yagenka pushed after him, with crossbow on her shoulders, resembling some hunting goddess.

" Beyond this thicket," said she, " is a deep stream, but I know a ford."

" I have leggings to the knees, we shall pass over dry," answered Zbyshko.

After a time they reached the water. Yagenka, knowing the Mochydoly forest well, found the ford easily. It turned out, however, that the little stream had risen from rain somewhat, and was rather deep. Then Zbyshko, without a question, caught the girl up in his arms.

ki I could go on foot," said Yagenka.

" Hold to my neck! " said Zbyshko.

He went through the swollen water slowly, trying with his foot at every step whether there was not a deep place, she nestled up to him according to command; at last, when they were not far from the other shore, she said, —

" Zbyshko!"

"Well?"

" I will not have either Stan or Vilk."

Meanwhile he carried her over, put her down carefully on the gravel, and said with some agitation, ——

"May God give thee the best one! He will not suffer."

It was not far to the lake now. Yagenka, going in advance this time, turned at moments and, putting her finger to her lips, enjoined silence on Zbyshko. They advanced through a clump of gray weeping-willows, over wet and low ground. From the right hand the uproar of birds flew to them.

Zbyshko wondered at this; for at that season birds had already departed.

"This is a swamp that never freezes," said Yagenka-, " ducks winter here, but even in the lake water freezes only at the shore in time of great frost. .See how it steams! "

Zbyshko looked through the willows and saw before him, as it were, a cloud of mist; that was Odstayani Lake.

Yagenka put her finger to her lips again, and after a while they arrived. First the girl climbed in silence a large old weeping-willow bent over the water completely. Zbyshko climbed another, and for a long time they lay in silence without seeing anything in front of them because of the mist, hearing only the complaining call of mews above their heads. At last the wind shook the willows with their yellow leaves, and disclosed the sunken surface of the lake, wrinkled somewhat by the breeze, and unoccupied.

" Is there nothing to be seen? " whispered Zbyshko.

"Nothing to be seen. Be quiet! "

After a while the breeze fell and perfect silence followed. On the surface of the water appeared a dark head, then a second; but at last, and much nearer, a bulky beaver let himself down from the bank to the water, with a freshly cut limb in his mouth, and began to swim through the duckweed and cane, keeping his jaws in the air, and pushing the limb before him. Zbyshko, lying on a tree somewhat lower than Yagenka, saw all at once how her elbow moved silently, and how her head bent forward; evidently she was aiming at the animal, which suspected no danger, and was swimming not farther than half a shot distant, toward the open surface of the lake.

At last the string of the crossbow groaned, and at the same moment Yagenka cried, ——

"Struck! struck!"

Zbyshko climbed higher in a twinkle of an eye, and looked through the branches at the water. The beaver was diving, and coming to the surface, plunging, and showing at moments his belly more than his back.

" He has got it well! He will be quiet soon! " said Yagenka.

She had told the truth, for the movements of the animal grew fainter and fainter, and at the end of one Hail Mary he came to the surface belly upward.

" I will go to bring him," said Zbyshko.

" Go not. Here at this shore is an ooze as deep as the height of many men. Whoever does not know how to manage will be drowned surely."

" But how shall we get him? "

"He will be in Bogdanets this evening. Let not thy head ache over that; but for us it is time to go."

" But thou hast shot him well! "

" Oh, he is not my first beaver."

" Other girls are afraid to look at a crossbow, but with such as thou one might hunt through the forests for a lifetime."

Yagenka, on hearing this praise, smiled with pleasure, but said nothing, and they returned by the same road through the willows. Zbyshko inquired about the beaver dam, and she told him how many beavers there were in Mochydoly, how many in Zgorzelitse, and how they waded along the paths and mounds.

On a sudden she struck her hip with her hand.

"Oh," cried she, "I have forgotten my arrows on the willow! Wait here."

And before he could answer that he would go himself for them, she had sprung away like a deer, and vanished from his sight in a moment.

Zbyshko waited and waited; at last he began to wonder why she was gone so long.

" She must have lost her arrows, and is looking for them," said he to himself; " I will go to see if anything has happened."

He had gone barely a few steps when the girl stood before him with the crossbow in her hand, the beaver on her shoulder, her face ruddy and smiling.

" For God's sake ! " cried Zbyshko, " but how didst thou get him?"

" How? I went into the water! It is not the first time for me; I would not let you go, for if a man does not know how to swim there the ooze will swallow him."

"But I have been waiting here, like an idiot! Thou art a cunning girl! "

"Well, and what? Was I to undress before thee, or how?"

" So thou hadst not forgotten the arrows? "

" No, I only wanted to lead thee away from the water."

"Well! but if I had followed thee, I should have seen a wonder. There would have been something to wonder at J Would there not?"

" Be quiet! "

" As God is dear to me, I should have gone! "

"Stop!"

After a while, wishing evidently to change the conversation, she said, —

" Squeeze out ray hair, for it wets my shoulders."

Zbyshko grasped her tresses near her head with one hand, with the other he twisted them, saying, —

" Better unbraid them, the wind will dry thy hair immediately."

But she would not because of the thicket through which she had to push. Zbyshko took the beaver on his shoulder.

" Matsko will recover now quickly," said Yagenka, walking ahead; ' ' there is no better remedy than bear's fat to drink, and beaver's fat to rub outside. He will be on horseback in a fortnight."

"God grant ! " said Zbyshko. " I await that as salvation, for I cannot in any way leave him sick, but for me it is a punishment to stay here."

" Punishment for thee to stay here?" inquired Yagenka. "How so?"

" Has Zyh told thee nothing of Danusia? "

"He told me something — I know—that she covered thee with a veil — I know — he told me- also that every knight makes some vow, that he will serve his lady — But he said that such a service was nothing — for some men, though married, serve a lady; and that Danusia — Zbyshko, what is she? Tell me? Who is Danusia?"

And, pushing up nearer, she raised her eyes and began to look with great alarm at his face. Without paying the least heed to her voice of alarm and her gaze, he said, —

" She is my lady, but also my dearest love. I do not say that to any one, but I will say it to thee as my beloved sister, for we know each other from the time that we were little. I would follow her beyond the ninth river, and beyond the ninth sea, to the Germans, and to the Tartars, for in the whole world there is not such another. Let uncle stay here in Bogdanets, but I will go straight to Danusia. For what is Bogdanets to me without her, what are utensils and herds, and the wealth of the abbot! I will mount a horse and go against the Germans, so help me God ! What I have vowed to her I will accomplish, unless I fall first."

"I did not know this," said Yagenka, in a dull voice.

Zbyshko then told how he had become acquainted with Danusia in Tynets, how he had made a vow to her immediately, and all that had happened afterward, hence his imprisonment, and how Danusia had rescued him, Yurand's refusal, their farewell, his longing, and finally his delight that after Matsko's recovery he would be able to go to the beloved maiden, and do what he had promised. The narrative was only interrupted at sight of the man waiting with horses at the edge of the forest.

Yageuka mounted her horse at once, and began to take leave of Zbyshko.

" Let the man take the beaver with thee, but I will go home."

" But wilt thou not go to Bogdanets? Zyh is there."

" No, papa was to return, and he told me to go home."

" Well, God reward thee for the beaver."

"With God!"

And after a while Yagenka was alone. While riding homeward through the heather, she looked some time after Zbyshko, and when at last he had vanished behind the trees, she covered her eyes with one hand, as if guarding them from sunrays. But soon from beneath her hand great tears flowed along her cheeks and fell one after the other, like peas, on the mane of the horse and the saddle.

CHAPTER XII.

AFTER the conversation with Zbyshko, Yagenka did not show herself for three days in Bogdanets. Only on the third day did she drop in with the news that the abbot had come to her father's.

Matsko received the news with a certain emotion. He had, it is true, something with which to pay the amount of the mortgage, and even had calculated that enough would remain to increase the number of settlers, and introduce herds and other things needful in management; still in the whole affair much depended on the good-will of the wealthy relative who could, for example, take away the men settled by him in the clearings, or leave them, and by that act decrease or heighten the value of the property.

Matsko, therefore, made very minute inquiries of Yagenka touching the abbot. In what mood had he come? Was he gladsome, or gloomy? What had he said of them, and when would he visit Bogdanets ?

Yagenka answered his questions wisely, trying to strengthen and calm him on every point. She said that the abbot had arrived in good health and spirits, with a considerable retinue, in which, besides armed attendants, were some wandering clerics and choristers ; that he was singing with Zyh, and was glad to lend his ear not only to hymns, but to worldly melodies. She remarked also, that he had inquired with great attention about Matsko, and had listened eagerly to Zyh's narratives of Zbyshko's adventures in Cracow.

"Ye yourselves know better what to do," said the shrewd girl, at last; " but I think that it would be well for Zbyshko to go at once and greet the elder relative, without waiting for him to come first to Bogdanets."

This advice struck Matsko, and convinced him; hence he commanded to call Zbyshko, and said, —

"Array thyself nicely, and go to embrace the feet of the abbot, show him honor, so that he also may be gracious to thee."

Then he turned to Yagenka : " Even wert thou simple, I ,should not wonder, for thou art a woman, but because thou

hast wit I admire thee. Tell me how to entertain the abbot best, and how to please him when he comes hither."

"As to eating, he will tell himself what he relishes. He likes to eat well, but if there is plenty of saffron it will not hurt ! "

When he heai'd this Matsko seized his head.

" Where shall I find saffron for him ? "

" I have brought some," said Yagenka.

"God grant that such girls be born on stones!" cried Matsko, delighted. " And to the eye they are dear, and good housekeepers, and wise, and pleasant to people. Oh, if I were young, I would take thee this minute! "

Yagenka glanced now an instant at Zbyshko, and, sighing in silence, said, —

" I have brought also dice and a cup and a cloth, for after every meal he likes to amuse himself with dice."

" He had this custom before, but therewith he was very qu ick-tempered."

"He is quick-tempered now; often he throws the cup to the ground, and rushes out through the door to the field. But afterward he comes back smiling, and is the first to blame his own anger — besides you know him; only do not oppose, and there is no better man in the world."

"But who would oppose him, since he has more mind than others ? "

They were conversing in this way while Zbyshko was dressing in his room. He came out at last so fine-looking that Yagenka was dazzled, just as she had been when first he ca^ie in his "white jacket" to her father's house. But now deep sorrow possessed her at the thought that that beauty of his was not for her, and that he loved another.

Matsko was glad, for he believed that the abbot would be pleased with Zbyshko, and would raise no difficulty in bargaining. He was even pleased so much at this thought that he decided to go himself.

" Command to get the wagon ready," said he to Zbyshko. " I was able to ride hither from Cracow with iron between my ribs, I can go now without iron to Zyh's house."

" Unless you faint on the road," said Yagenka.

"Ei, nothing will happen me, for I feel strength in myself. And even if I should faint a little, the abbot will know how I hurried to him, and will show himself the more bountiful."

" Your health is dearer to me than his bounty," said Zbyshko.

But Matsko was determined and insisted on his own way. He groaned on the road somewhat, but did not cease to tell Zbyshko how he must bear himself ; especially did he enjoin on him obedience and humility in presence of the rich relative, who never endured the least opposition.

On reaching Zyh's "court" they found him and the abbot on the porch looking out at God's serene universe and drinking wine. Behind, on a bench near the wall, sat six attendants in a row, among them two choristers and one pilgrim, whom it was easy to distinguish by his curved staff, by the bag at his girdle, and by the shells worked on his dark mantle. The others looked like clerics, for they had shaven crowns, but they wore the dress of laymen, they were girded with oxhide, and had swords at their sides.

At sight of Matsko in the wagon, Zyh went out quickly; but the abbot, mindful as it seemed of his spiritual dignity, remained in his seat, only he began to speak to his clerics, some more of whom came out through the open door of the front room. Zbyshko and Zyh brought in the feeble Matsko r holding him by the arms.

"I am a little weak yet," said Matsko, kissing the abbot's hand ; " but I have come to bow down to you, my benefactor, to thank you for your management, and beg your blessing, which is needed most of all by a sinful man."

" I have heard that you are better," said the abbot, pressing his head, " and that you have made a vow to the tomb of our late queen."

" Not knowing to which saint I should turn, I betook myself to her."

" You have done well!" cried the abbot, passionately; " she is better than others, and let any one dare to envy her! "

And anger came to his face in one moment, his cheeks filled with blood, his eyes began to flash.

Those present knew his irritability, so Zyh laughed, and cried, —

" Strike, whoso believes in God! "

The abbot panted loudly, turned his eyes on all present, then laughed as suddenly as he had burst out before, and looking at Zbyshko inquired, —

" This is your nephew, and my relative ? "

Zbyshko inclined, and kissed his hand.

" I saw him when he was little; I should not have known him now. But show thyself! "

He examined Zbyshko from head to foot, with quick eyes.

" Too good-looking! A maiden, not a knight! " said he, at last.

" The Germans took that maiden to dance," said Matsko; •" but whoever took her fell, not to rise again,"

" And he bent a bow without a crank! " cried Yagenka, suddenly.

" But what art thou doing here ? " asked the abbot, turning to her.

She blushed till her neck and ears were rosy, and said in great confusion, —

" I saw him."

" Have a care that he should not shoot thee perchance; thou wouldst need three-quarters to recover."

At this the choristers, the pilgrim, and the " wandering clerics " burst into one immense laugh, from which Yagenka lost herself completely, so that the abbot took compassion on her, and, raising his arm, showed her the enormous sleeve of his robe.

" Hide here, girl," said he, " for the blood will spurt from thy cheeks."

Meanwhile Zyh seated Matsko on the bench, and commanded to bring wine, for which Yagenka hurried. The abbot turned his eyes to Zbyshko.

" Enough of joking! " said he, "I compared thee to a girl, not to blame thee, but from pleasure at thy good looks, which more than one maiden might envy. I know that thou art a splendid fellow! I have heard of thy deeds at Vilno; I have heard of the Frisians, and of Cracow. Zyh has told me everything — dost understand! "

Here he looked sharply into Zbyshko's eyes, and after a while said again, —

" If thou hast vowed three peacock-plumes, find them, it is praiseworthy and pleasing to God to hunt down the enemies of our race; but if thou hast vowed something else in addition, know that while thou art waiting here I can absolve thee from those vows, for I have the power."

" When a man has promised something in his soul to the Lord Jesus, what power can absolve him?" said Zbyshko.

On hearing this, Matsko looked with a certain dread at the abbot; but evidently the abbot was in excellent humor, for,

instead of bursting into anger, he threatened Zbyshko joyously with his finger, and said, —

" Ah, thou art a witling! See that that does not happen thee which happened the German, Beyhard."

" And what happened him? " inquired Zyh.

" They burned him at the stake."

"Why?"

'' Because he said that a layman is just as well able to understand the secrets of God as a spiritual person."

" They punished him severely! "

"But justly ! " thundered the abbot, " for he blasphemed against the Holy Ghost. What do ye think? Can a layman make any decisions as to God's secrets?"

" He cannot in any way! " called the wandering clerics, in an agreeing chorus.

" But ye ' playmen ' sit quietly," said the abbot; " for ye are no clerics, though ye have shaven crowns."

" We are not thy playmen nor indigents, but the attendants of your grace," answered one of them, looking that moment at a great pitcher from which at a distance came the odor of hops and malt.

"See! he talks as if from a barrel! " cried the abbot. " Hei, thou bearded! Why look at the pitcher? Thou wilt not find Latin at the bottom of it."

" I am not looking for Latin, but beer which I cannot find."

The abbot turned then to Zbyshko, who was gazing at those attendants with wonder, and said, —

" All these are ' clerici scholares,' though each one would prefer to fling his book away, seize a lute and wander through the world with it. I have taken them all in and feed them, for what can I do ? They are good-for-nothings, inveterate vagrants; but they know how to sing, and have picked up the divine liturgy a little, so in the church 1 find use for them, and defence in them when need comes, for some are resolute fellows. This pilgrim here says that he has been in the holy land; but it would be vain to ask him about any sea or land, for he does not know the name of the Greek emperor, or in what city he has his residence."

" I knew," said the pilgrim, in a hoarse voice, " but when the fever shook me on the Danube, it shook everything out of me."

" I wonder most at their swords," said Zbyshko; " for I have never seen such at any time with wandering clerics."

" They are free to carry swords," replied the abbot; " for they are not consecrated, and that I bear a sword too at my side is no wonder. A year ago I challenged Vilk to trampled earth, for those forests through which you passed before reaching Bogdanets. He did not appear."

"How was he to meet a spiritual person?"interrupted Zyh.

At this the abbot grew excited, and, striking the table with his fist, he cried, —

" When in armor I am not a priest, but a noble! And he did not appear, because he preferred to attack me at night with his attendants in Tulcha. That is why I carry a sword at my side! Otnnes leges, omniaque iura vim vi repellere cunctis-que sese defensare permittunt. (All laws, all rights, permit us all to defend ourselves with force against force.) That is why I have given them swords."

When they heard the Latin, Zyh and Matsko and Zbyshko grew silent and bent their heads before the wisdom of the abbot, for not a man understood one word of it; he looked around a while longer with angry eyes, and said at last,—

" Who knows that he will not attack me here?"

" Oh, just let him come! "said the wandering clerics, grasping their sword hilts.

"Let him attack! It is dreary for me too without a battle."

"He will not attack," said Zyh; "he will come with obeisance and peace rather. He has renounced the forest; he is thinking now of his son — you understand. But there is no use in his waiting."

Meanwhile the abbot was pacified, and said,—

" I saw young Vilk drinking with Stan in the inn at Kres-nia. They did not know us at first, for it was dark; besides they were talking of Yagenka." Here he turned to Zbyshko, " And of thee."

" What did they want of me?"

" They did not want anything; but it was not to their liking to find a third man in the neighborhood. This is how Stan spoke to Vilk: ' When I tan his skin he will not be pretty;' and Stan said: ' Maybe he will fear us; if not, I will break his bones in a twinkle!' Then both declared that thou wouldst be afraid."

When Matsko heard this, he looked at Zyh, Zyh at him, and their faces took on a cunning and delighted expression.

Neither felt sure as to whether the abbot had really heard such conversation, or had invented it only to prick Zbyshko. Both understood, but especially Matsko, who knew Zbyshko well, that there was no better way in the world to push him to Yagenka.

" And indeed they are deadly fellows! " added the abbot, as i'f purposely.

Zbyshko did not betray anything on his face, but he asked Zyh, with a kind of strange voice, —

" Will to-morrow be Sunday? "

" Sunday."

" Shall you go to holy mass? "

"Yes."

" Whither —to Kresnia? "

u Yes, for it is nearer. Where should we go? "

" Very well, we shall go! "

VOL. I. — 12

CHAPTER XIII.

ZBYSHKO, when he had overtaken Zyh and Yagenka, who were riding in company with the abbot and his clerics, joined them, and they rode together to the churci.; for with him the question was to show the abbot that he had no fear of Vilk or Stan, and did not think of hiding before them. From the first moment he was astonished again at the beauty of Yagenka, for though he had seen her more than once at her father's house, and in Bogdanets dressed beautifully to appear among guests, he had never seen her arrayed for church as at present. She wore a robe of red cloth, lined with ermine, red gloves, and a gold-trimmed ermine hood, from under which two braids of hair dropped on her shoulders. She was not sitting on the horse man-fashion, but on a lofty saddle with a handle, and with a bench beneath her feet, which were barely visible under the long petticoat plated in even folds. For Zyh, who permitted the girl to wear at home a skin coat and boots of cowhide, was anxious that in front of the church every one should know that not the daughter of some gray-coated landowner, or patented noble had come, but a young lady of a rich, knightly house. With this object, her horse was led by two youths whose lower garments were close-fitting, and the upper ones wide, as was usual with pages. Four house attendants rode behind, and near them the abbot's clerics, with swords and lutes at their girdles.

Zbyshko admired the whole company greatly, above all Yagenka, who looked like an image, and the abbot, who, in red and with immense sleeves to his robe, seemed to him like some prince on a journey. Attired most plainly of all was Zyh, who desired ostentation in others, but for himself only gladness and singing.

When Zbyshko came up, they rode on in a line, the abbot, Yagenka, Zbyshko, and Zyh. The abbot at first commanded his " playmen" to sing pious hymns, only later, when he had listened sufficiently, did he begin to talk with Zbyshko, who looked with a smile at his mighty sword, which was not smaller than the two-handed blades of the Germans.

" I see," said he, with seriousness, " that thou art wondering at my svord. Know then that the synods permit swords to the clergy and even balistas and catapults, on a journey, and we are on a journey. Moreover, when the Holy Father forbade swords and red garments to priests, he surely had men of low station in mind. God created the noble for arms, and whoso should wish to disarm him, would resist God's eternal decrees." »

" I have seen Henryk, Prince of Mazovia, who took part in tournaments," answered Zbyshko.

" He is not to be blamed because he took part in tournaments," replied the abbot, raising his finger; " bat because he married, and moreover unhappily, for he married a for-nicariam et bibulam mulierem, who from youth, as they say, worshipped Bacchus and was moreover adulteram, from whom nothing good could come."

Here he stopped his horse and exhorted with still greater seriousness, —

" Whoso wishes to choose a wife, and to marry, must see that she is God-fearing, of good habits, a housekeeper, and neat, — all of which is enjoined not only through the fathers of the church, but through a certain pagan sage by name Seneca. And how wilt thou know that thou hast hit well if thou know not the nest from which thy comrade for a lifetime is chosen ? For another sage of the Lord says, Pomus nam cadit absque arbore (The apple falls from its tree). As the ox, so the skin, as the mother, so the daughter, — from which take this lesson, sinful man, seek a wife not in the distance, but near by; for if thou find a malicious and gallant one, thou wilt weep for her more than once, as wept that philosopher whose quarrelsome mate used to throw out always on his head in her anger aquam sordidam (dirty water)."

" In secula secidorum (For the ages of ages), amen!" thundered in unison the wandering clerics, who, 'always answering the abbot in that way, were not very careful whether they answered according to meaning.

All listened to the abbot's words with deep attention, wondering at his eloquence and skill in the Scriptures. He did not direct this conversation straight at Zbyshko, but rather turned to Zyh and Yagenka, as if to edify them in particular. Yagenka understood evidently what the point was, for she looked carefully from beneath her long eyelashes at the youth, who wrinkled his brows and dropped his head, as if in deep meditation over what he had heard.

After a time the company moved on, but in silence; only when Kresuia was in sight did the abbot feel at his girdle and turn the side toward the front so that he might seize his swordhilt easily.

"Old Vilk of Brozova will come, and surely with a large retinue," said he.

" Surely," confirmed Zyh, " but the servants said something about his being sick."

" One of my clerics heard that he was to attack us before the inn after mass."

" He would not do that without announcement, and especially after holy mass."

44 May God send him thoughtfulness; I seek war with no man, and endure injustice patiently."

Here he looked around on his "playmen," and said,—

" Do not draw your swords, and remember that ye are clerical servants; but if the others draw theirs first, go at them ! "

Zbyshko, riding at Yagenka's side, inquired of her touching that which concerned him principally -

" We shall find young Vilk and Stan in Kresnia, surely. Show the men to me at a distance, so that I may know them."

" Very well, Zbyshko," answered Yagenka.

" Before church and after church they meet thee, of course. What do they do then ?"

" They serve me as the\'7d 7 know how."

" They will not serve thee to-day, dost understand ?"

She answered again, almost with humility, " Very well, Zbyshko."

Further conversation was interrupted by the sound of wooden knockers, because there were no bells then in Kresnia. After a while they arrived. From the crowds, waiting for mass before the church, came forth at once young Vilk and £tan; but Zbyshko was quicker, he sprang from his horse before they could come, seizing Yagenka by the side he helped her from the saddle, took her arm, looked at them challengingly, and led her to the church.

At the entrance a new disappointment was awaiting them. Both hastened to the holy water font, and dipping their hands in it, extended them to the maiden. But Zbyshko did the same; she touched his fingers, made the sign of the cross on herself, and entered the church with him. Not only young Vilk, but Stan of Rogov, though he had a small mind,

divined that all was done purposely; and such savage anger seized both that the hair rose beneath their head nets. They preserved presence of mind enough to refrain in their anger from entering the church, through fear of God's punishment. Vilk rushed out and flew like a mad man among trees through the graveyard, not knowing himself the direction in which he was going. Stan flew behind him, not knowing with what intent he was acting.

They stopped in the corner of the fence where large stones lay prepared for the foundation of a bell tower to be built in Kresnia. Then Vilk, to get rid of the anger which was raging in his breast to the throat, seized a stone and began to shake it with all his strength; seeing this, Stan grasped it also, and after a while both rolled it with rage through the graveyard as far as the church gate.

People looked at them with wonder, thinking that they were performing some vow, and that they wished in this way to aid in building the bell tower. But the effort relieved them considerably, so that both regained composure, only they had become pale from exertion, and panted, looking at each other with uncertain glance. Stan was the first to break silence.

" Well, and what ? " asked he.

" But what ? " answered Vilk.

" Shall we attack him right off ? "

u How ! attack him in the church ? "

" Not in the church, but after mass."

" He is with Zyh — and with the abbot. Dost remember what Zyh said : ' Let there be a fight, and I will drive both from Zgorzelitse.' Had it not been for that I should have broken thy ribs for thee long since."

" Or I thine for thee! " replied Stan, as he clinched his strong fists.

And their eyes began to flash ominously; but both soon moderated, for they had greater need of concord than ever. More than once had they fought, but they had always grown reconciled afterward, for though love for Yagenka divided them, they could not live without each other, and yearned for each other always. At present they had a common enemy, and both felt him to be terribly dangerous. So after a time Stan inquired, —

" What is to be done ? Send a declaration to Bogdanets."

Vilk was wiser, but he did not know what to do at the moment. Fortunately the knockers came to their aid,

and sounded a second time, in sign that mass was about to begin.

"What shall we do?" repeated Vilk. "Go to mass; what God gives will come."

Stan was pleased with this wise answer.

" Maybe the Lord Jesus will inspire us," said he.

"And bless us," added Vilk.

" According to justice."

They went to the church, and after they had heard mass piously they received consolation. They did not lose their heads even when Yagenka, after mass, took holy water again from Zbyshko's hand at the entrance. In the graveyard at the gate they fell at the feet of Zyh and Yagenka, though the abbot was old Vilk's enemy, they fell also at his feet. They looked at Zbyshko with a frown, it is true ; but neither one grumbled, though the hearts in their breasts were whining from anger, from pain, and from jealousy, for never had Yagenka seemed to them so queenlike, so wonderful. Only when the brilliant company moved homeward, and when from afar the gladsome song of the wandering clerics came to them, did Stan wipe the sweat from his face with young beard on it, and snort as a horse might. But Vilk gnashed his teeth and said, —

" To the inn ! to the inn ! Woe to me ! "

Remembering then what had eased them before, they seized the stone a second time, and rolled it to its former place, passionately.

Zbyshko rode at Yagenka's side listening to the songs of the abbot's playmen ; but when they had gone about the third of a mile, he reined in his horse suddenly, —

" Oh, I was to have a mass said for my uncle's health," cried he; " but forgot it, I am going back."

"Do not go!" said Yagenka, "we can send from Zgorzelitse."

" I will return ; do not wait for me. Farewell ! "

" Farewell ! " said the abbot. " Go back! "

And his face became gladsome. When Zbyshko had vanished from their sight, he punched Zyh in the side slightly, and added, —

" Dost understand? "

" What am I to understand? "

" He will fight Vilk and Stan in Kresnia, as sure as there is amen in Our Father; that is what I wanted, and that is what I have brought about."

"They are deadly fellows! They will wound him; but what of that?"

"How, what of that? If he fights for Yagenka, how can he think of Yurand's daughter ? Yagenka will be his lady — not that one; this is what I want, for he is my relative, and pleases me."

"But the vow?"

"While he is waiting, I will absolve him. Have you not heard me promise already ? "

" Your head is equal to anything," answered Zyh.

The abbot was pleased with the praise ; he pushed up to Yagenka, and inquired, —

" Why art thou so serious? "

She bent in the saddle, and, seizing the abbot's hand, raised it to her lips. " Godfather, but maybe you would send a couple of ' playmen' to Kresnia ? "

" What for? They would get drunk in the inn, nothing more."

" But they might prevent some quarrel."

The abbot looked her quickly in the eyes, and said, with some harshness, —

" Even should they kill him! "

" Then let them kill me," cried Yagenka.

And the bitterness which had collected with sorrow in her breast from the time of talking with Zbyshko flowed down now in a sudden flood of tears. Seeing this, the abbot embraced the girl with one arm, so that he covered her almost with his immense sleeve.

"Fear not, my daughter," said he. "A quarrel may happen; but still those two are nobles, they will not attack him together, but will challenge him to the field according to knightly custom; and there he will help himself, even had he to fight with both at one time. And as to Yuraud's daughter of whom thou hast heard, there are no trees growing in any forest for that bed."

" Since she is dearer to him, I do not care for him," answered Yagenka, through her tears.

4 ' Then why art thou sniffling ? "

"I am afraid that some one will harm him."

" There is woman's wit!" said the abbot, laughing. Then, bending down to Yagenka's ear, he said, —

" Moderate thyself, girl, though he should marry thee, it will happen him to fight more than once; a noble is for that work." Here he bent still lower, and added, —

" But he will marry thee, and that before long, as God is in heaven ! "

" Well, we shall see! " answered Yagenka.

And at the same time she began to laugh through her tears, and look at the abbot as if wishing to ask how he knew that.

Meanwhile Zbyshko returned to Kresnia, and went straight to the priest, for he wished a mass said for his uncle's recovery; then he went directly to the inn in which he expected to find young Vilk and Stan of Rogov.

In fact he found both, and also a crowd of people, — nobles by birth and patent, landworkers, and some jugglers showing various German tricks.

At the first moment he could not distinguish any one, for the inn windows, with oxbladder panes, let in little light; and only when a boy of the place threw pine sticks on the fire did he see in one corner Stan's hairy snout, and Vilk's angry, passionate visage behind tankards of beer.

Then he went toward them slowly, pushing people aside on the way; and at last coming up, he struck the table with his fist till he made everything thunder through the inn.

They rose at once, and pulled up their leather girdles before grasping their sword hilts. Zbyshko threw his glove on the table, and, speaking through his nose as was the custom of knights when they challenged, he uttered the following unexpected words, —

" If either of you two, or other knightly men in this room deny that the most wonderful and most virtuous maiden in the world is Panna Danusia, the daughter of Yurand of Spyhov, I challenge him to a combat on foot, or on horseback, to his first kneeling, or his last breath."

Stan and Vilk were astonished, as the abbot would have been had he heard anything similar; and for a time they could utter no word. What lady is that? Moreover for them the question was of Yagenka, not of her, and if that wildcat did not care about Yagenka, what did he want of them? Why had he made them angry before the church? Why had he come there? Why was he seeking a quarrel? From these queries such confusion rose in their heads that their mouths opened widely. Stan stared as if he had before him, not a man, but some kind of German wonder.

Vilk, being quicker-witted, knew something of knightly customs, and knew that knights often vow service to some Tomen and marry others; he thought that in this case it

might be so, and that if there was such a chance of taking Yagenka's part, he ought to seize it on the wing. So he pushed from behind the table, and approached Zbyshko with a hostile face.

" How is that, dog brother ?" asked he. " Is not Yagenka, the daughter of Zyh, the most wonderful? "

After him came Stan, and people began to crowd around them; for it was known to all present that this would not end in anything common.

186 THE KNIGHTS OF THE CROSS-
CHAPTER XIV.

ON reaching home Yagenka sent a servant straightway to Kresuia to learn if a fight had taken place at the inn, or if any man had challenged another. But he, receiving coin on the road, began to drink with the priest's men, and had no thought of returning. Another, sent to Bogdanets to inform Matsko of a visit from the abbot, returned after he had done his errand, and declared that he had seen Zbyshko playing dice with his uncle.

This calmed Yagenka somewhat, for, knowing Zbyshko's skill and experience, she had not such fear of a challenge as of some harsh, severe accident in the inn. She desired to go with the abbot to Bogdanets, but he opposed, for he wished to talk with Matsko about the mortgage, and about another affair, of still greater importance, in which he did not wish to have Yagenka as witness.

Moreover he was preparing to spend the night there. When he heard of Zbyshko's happy return, he fell into excellent humor, and commanded his wandering clerics to sing and to shout till the pine woods should quiver, so in Bogdanets itself all the cottagers looked out of their cottages to see if there were not a fire, or if some foe were not attacking. But the pilgrim with curved staff rode ahead and quieted them, declaring that a spiritual person of high dignity was travelling. So they bowed down, and some even made the sign of the cross on their breasts; the abbot, seeing how they respected him, rode on in joyous pride, delighted with the world and full of good-will to men.

Matsko and Zbyshko, on hearing the shouts and songs, went to the gate to give greeting. Some of the clerics had been with the abbot in Bogdanets earlier, but some had joined the company recently, and saw the place for the first time. The hearts of these fell at sight of the poor house, which could not be compared with the broad court in which Zyh lived. They were strengthened, however, at sight of smoke making its way through the straw thatch of the roof, and were comforted perfectly when on entering the first room they caught the odor of saffron and various meats, and saw also two tables full of pewter dishes, empty as yet, it

is true, but so large that all eyes must be gladdened at sight of them. On the smaller table shone a plate of pure silver, prepared for the abbot, and also a tankard carved wonderfully; both of these had been won with other wealth from the Frisians.

Matsko and Zbyshko invited at once to the table; but the abbot, who had eaten heartily before leaving Zyh's house, refused, all the more since something else held him occupied. From the first moment of his coming, he had looked carefully and also uuquietly at Zbyshko, as if wishing to find on him traces of fighting; seeing the calm face of the young man, he was evidently impatient, till at last he could restrain his curiosity no longer.

" Let us go to the small room," said he, " and talk of the mortgage. Resist not, or I shall be angry! " . Then he turned to the clerics and thundered, —

" But sit ye here quietly, and let me have no listening at the doorway! " Then he opened the door to the room, in which he could hardly find place, and after him entered Matsko and Zbyshko. There, when they had seated themselves on boxes, the abbot turned to his youthful relative, •—

" Didst thou go back to Kresnia?"

"I did."

" Well, and what ? "

" I gave money to celebrate mass for my uncle's recovery, and returned."

The abbot moved impatiently on the box. " Ha!" thought he, "he did not meet Stan or Vilk; maybe they were not there, maybe he did not look for them. I was mistaken! "

But he was angry because he thought that he had been mistaken, and because his calculation had failed, so his face grew red at once, and he panted, —

" Let us talk of the mortgage," said he, after a while. " Have ye money ? — if ye have not, the land is mine."

At this Matsko, who knew how to act with him, rose in silence, opened the box on which he was sitting, took out a bag of gryvens already prepared, as it seemed, and said:

" We are poor people, but we have money, and we will pay what is proper, as it stands on the ' paper' and as I have promised with the sign of the Holy Cross. If you wish increased pay for the management and the cattle, we will not oppose, we will pay your demand, and embrace your feet, benefactor."

188 THE KNIGHTS OF THE CROSS.

Saying this he bowed down to the abbot's knees, and after him Zbyshko did the same. The abbot, who expected disputes and bargaining, was greatly astonished by such action, and even was not at all glad, for in bargaining he wanted to bring forward various conditions, meanwhile the opportunity had vanished. So in delivering the " paper," on which Matsko had drawn the sign of the cross, he said, —

" What is this about paying in addition ?"

" We do not wish to take for nothing," answered Matsko, cunningly, knowing that the more he opposed in this case the more he should win.

In fact the abbot grew red in the twinkle of an eye.

"Look at them! " said he. "They will not take anything for nothing from a relative ! Bread troubles people! I did not receive wildernesses, and I do not return them. If it please rne to throw this bag away I will throw it!"

" You will not do that! " cried out Matsko.

" I will not do it? Here is your mortgage! And here is your money! I gave the money because of good-will; and if I wish I will leave it on the road, that is no concern of yours. This is what I will do ! "

So saying, he caught the bag by the mouth, and hurled it to the floor, so that coin rolled out through the torn linen.

" God reward you! God reward you, father and benefactor !" cried Matsko, who was only waiting for that moment. " From another I would not take it, but I will from a priest and a relative."

The abbot looked threateningly for some time, first at Matsko, then at Zbyshko, at last he said, —

" I know what I am doing, though I am angry, so keep what you have; for I tell you this, you will not see another grosh from me."

" We did not expect the present gift."

" But know ye that Yagenka will have what remains after me."

" And the land too? " inquired Matsko, innocently.

" The land too! " roared the abbot.

At this Matsko's face lengthened, but he mastered himself, and said, —

" Ei! to think of death! May the Lord Jesus give you a hundred years, or more, but before that a good bishopric."

"And even if He should! Am I worse than others?" asked the abbot.

" Not worse, but better."

These words acted soothingly on the abbot, for in general his anger was short lived.

"Yes," said he, "ye are my relatives, while she is only a goddaughter, but I like her and Zyh these many years. A better man than Zyh there is not on earth, nor a better girl than Yagenka. Who will say aught against them?"

And he looked around with challenging glance; but Matsko not only made no contradiction, he asserted quickly that it would be useless to search the whole kingdom to find a better neighbor.

" And as to the girl," said he, " I could not love my own daughter more. She was the cause of my recovery, and till death I shall never forget it."

" Ye will be damned both the one and the other, if ye forget her," said the abbot; " and I shall be the first man to curse you. I wish you no harm, for ye are my blood relatives, hence I have thought out a method by which everything left by me will be yours and Yagenka's. Do ye understand ? "

" God grant that to happen! " said Matsko. " Dear Jesus ! I would walk from the queen's grave in Cracow to Bald Mountain to bow down before the wood of the Holy Cross."

The abbot was delighted at the sincerity with which Matsko spoke, so he laughed and continued, —

" The girl has the right to be choice; she is beautiful, she has a good dowry, she is of good stock. What is Stan or Vilk to her when a voevoda's son would not be too much? But if I, without alluding to any one, propose a bridegroom, she will marry him; for she loves me, and knows that I would not give bad advice to her."

" It will be well for the man whom you find for Yagenka," said Matsko.

"And what sayst thou?" asked the abbot, turning to Zbyshko.

" I think as uncle does."

The honest face of the abbot grew still brighter; he struck Zbyshko with his hand on the shoulder, so that the sound filled the room, and asked, —

" Why didst thou not let Stan or Vilk come near Yagenka at church ? Why ? "

" Lest they might think that I feared them, and lest you also might think so."

" But thou gavest her holy water."

" I did."

The abbot struck him a second time.

"Then — take her! "

"Take her! " exclaimed Matsko, like an echo.

At this Zbyshko gathered his hair under the net, and answered calmly, —

" How am I to take her when I made a vow in Tynets before the altar to Danusia, the daughter of Yurand? "

" Thou didst promise peacock-plumes, find them, but take Y"agenka now."

" No," answered Zbyshko, "when she threw a veil over me I promised to marry her."

The abbot's face was filling with blood, his ears became blue, and his eyes were swelling out; he approached Zbyshko, and said in a voice choking with anger, —

" Thy vows are chaff, and I am wind, dost understand? Here ! "

And he blew at his head with such force that his hair net flew off, and the hair was scattered in disorder over his arms and shoulders. Then Zbyshko wrinkled his brows, and, looking straight into the abbot's eyes, answered, —

"In my vow is my honor, and I am guardian myself of that honor."

When he heard this the abbot, unaccustomed to resistance, lost breath to the degree that speech was taken for a time from him. Next came an ominous silence, which Matsko broke finally, —

" Zbyshko! " cried he, "remember thyself. What is the matter with thee ? "

The abbot now raised his arm, and, pointing at the young man, he shouted, —

" What is the matter with him? I know what the matter is. The soul in him is not knightly, and not noble, it is the soul of a hare ! This is the matter with him, he is afraid of Vilk and Stan."

But Zbyshko, who had not lost his cool blood for an instant, shrugged his shoulders, and said, —

" Oh, pshaw! I smashed their heads in Kresnia."

" Fear God ! " cried Matsko.

The abbot looked at Zbyshko for some time with staring eyes, anger struggled in him with admiration; and at the same time his native quick wit began to remind him that from that beating of Vilk and Stan he might gain for his plans sonic advantage. So, recovering somewhat, he shouted at Zbyshko, —

" Why didst thou not mention that?"

" I was ashamed. I thought that they would challenge me, as became knights, to battle on foot, or on horseback; but they are robbers, not knights. First, Vilk took a plank from the table, Stan took another, and at me ! What was I to do ? I caught up a bench, well — you know what! "

'' But didst thou leave them alive ? " asked Matsko.

" Alive, though the\'7d 7 fainted. But they regained breath before I left the inn."

The abbot listened, rubbed his forehead, then sprang up suddenly from the box on which he had been sitting for befr ter thought, and cried, —

*' Wait ! I will tell thee something now."

" And what will you tell? " inquired Zbyshko.

" I will tell thee this, that if thou hast fought for Yagenka, and broken men's heads for her, thou art her knight, not the knight of another, and thou must take her."

Saying this, he put his hands on his sides, and looked triumphantly at Zbyshko.

But Zbyshko only smiled and said, "Hei, I knew well why you wished to set me at them; but it has failed you completely."

" How failed me ? — Tell ! "

" I told them to acknowledge that the most beautiful and most virtuous maiden in the world was Danusia, the daughter of Yuraud ; and they took the part of Yagenka exactly, and that was the cause of the battle."

When he heard this, the abbot stood in one place for a while, as if petrified, and only by the blinking of his eyes was it possible to know that he was alive yet. All at once he turned in his place, pushed the door open with his foot, rushed into the front room, seized the hooked staff from the hands of the pilgrim, and began to belabor his " playmen," bellowing meanwhile like a wounded bison, —

"To horse, ye buffoons! to horse, dog-faiths! A foot of mine will never be in this house again. To horse, whoso believes in God ! to horse! — "

And opening another door he went out, the terrified, wondering clerics followed after. So moving with an uproar to the sheds, they fell to saddling the horses in haste. Matsko ran out after the abbot in vain, in vain did he beg him, implore him, declare in God's name that no fault attached to him — nothing availed! The abbot cursed the house, the people, the fields; and when they gave him his horse, he

sprang on without putting his foot in the stirrup, and went at a gallop from the place, and with his great sleeves blown apart by the wind he looked like a red giant bird. The clerics flew after him in fear, like a herd hastening after its leader.

Matsko looked at the party till it vanished in the pine wood ; then he turned slowly to the house, and, nodding his head gloomily, said to Zbyshko, —

' ' Thou hast done a fine thing ! "

" This would not have happened had I gone away earlier; I did not go because of you."

" How, because of me? "

" Yes ; for I would not go leaving you in sickness."

" But now how will it be? "

"Now I will go."

"Whither?"

" To Mazovia, to Danusia, — and to seek peacock-plumes among the Germans."

Matsko was silent a while, then he said, —

" He has given back the ' paper,' but the pledge is recorded in the court book. The abbot will not forgive us a grosh now."

"Let him not forgive. You have money, and I need none for the road. People will receive me everywhere, and give food to my horses ; while I have armor on my back, and a sword in my grasp, I have no care for anything."

Matsko fell to thinking, and began to weigh everything that had happened. Nothing had gone according to his wish, or his heart. He had desired Yagenka for Zbyshko with all his soul; but he understood that there could be no bread from that flour, and that, considering the abbot's anger, considering Zyh and Yagenka, considering finally the battle with Vilk and Stan, it was better that Zbyshko should go than be the cause of more disputes and quarrels.

"Ah!" said he, at last, " thou must seek heads of the Knights of the Cross anyhow; so go, since there is no other way out. Let it happen according to the will of the Lord Jesus; but I must go to Zgorzelitse at once, mayhap I can talk over Zyh and the abbot — I am sorry, especially for Zyh."

Here he looked into Zbyshko's eyes, and asked quickly:

"But art thou not sorry for Yagenka? "

" May God give her health, and all that is best! " replied Zbvshko.

CHAPTER XV.

MATSKO waited a number of days patiently. Would some news come from Zyh's house? Would the abbot be pacified? At last he was wearied from waiting in uncertainty, and resolved to visit Zyh. Everything that had happened had happened without fault of his, but he wished to know whether Zyh felt offended; as to the abbot, Matsko was convinced that his anger would continue to weigh on him and his nephew.

He wished, however, to do all in his power to soften that anger; hence, on the road he was thinking and fixing in his mind what to say to diminish the feeling of offence and maintain old neighborly friendship. Somehow the thoughts in his head did not cleave to one another; hence, he was glad to find Yagenka alone. She received him in former fashion, with an obeisance, a kissing of the hand,—in a word, with friendliness, though with some sadness.

" Is your father at home ? " inquired Matsko.

" At home, but he has gone to hunt with the abbot — short waiting till they come."

She conducted him to the chief room, where, when they had sat down, both were silent for some time.

"Is it dull for you alone in Bogdanets?" asked she, breaking the silence.

u Dull," answered Matsko. " Dost thou know that Zbyshko is gone ? "

" I know," answered Yagenka, sighing silently. " I knew the same day, and thought that he would come here to say even a kind word; but he came not."

" How was he to come ? The abbot would have torn him; and thy father would not have been glad to see him."

" Ei ! I would not have let any one harm him," said Yagenka, shaking her head.

At this Matsko, though he had a tempered heart, was moved; he drew the girl toward him, and said, —

" God reward thee, girl! For thee there is sadness ; but for me also. I will only tell thee that neither the abbot nor thy own father loves thee more than I. Better I had died

VOL. 1. — 13

from this wound of which thou hast cured me, if he had only taken thee, and not another."

Hereupon came to Yagenka one of those moments of grief and sorrow in which one can make no concealment.

" I shall never see him again, or if I see him it will be with Yurand's daughter, and I would rather cry my eyes out than see them," said she, raising a corner of her apron, and covering her tearful eyes with it.

"Be quiet!" said Matsko. "He has gone; but with God's favor he will not bring Yurand's daughter back with him."

"Why should he not?" asked Yagenka, from under her apron.

" Because Yurand will not give her to him."

Yagenka uncovered her face suddenly, and, turning to Matsko, inquired with vivacity, —

" He told me that, but is it true?"

" True, as God is in heaven."

"But why?"

" Who knows. Some vow, and for a vow there is no remedy! Zbyshko pleased him in so far as he promised to aid him in seeking revenge, but even that did not help. The intercession of Princess Anna was useless. Yurand would not listen to prayer, persuasion, or command. He said that he could not. Well, it is clear that the cause is such that he cannot; and he is a firm man, who does not change what he says. Do not lose courage, girl, and be strong. In truth, the boy had to go, for he swore in the church to get peacock-plumes; the girl, too, covered him with a veil, in sign that she wanted him for husband, without which they would have cut off his head, — for this he is indebted to her; there is nothing to be said on that point. She will not be his, God grant, but according to law he is hers. Zyh is angry with him; the abbot will be sure to take revenge on him till his skin smarts; I am sorry for this affair, too: still, when we look over everything, what was Zbyshko to do? Since he was indebted to that girl, he had to go to her. Besides, he is a noble. I will tell thee this though, that unless the Germans in those parts maim him, he will return as he went, — and will return not only to me, old man, not only to Bogdanets,but to thee, for he is wonderfully glad to see thee."

" Glad to see me? " Then she pushed up to Matsko, and touching him with her elbow, asked, —

" How do you know? How? Surely it is not true."

"How do I know? I saw how pained he was to go. And besides, when it was decided that he must, I asked him: 'Art thou not sorry for Yagenka?' and he answered: 4 May God give her health, and all that is best.' He began to sigh then, as if he had the bellows of a blacksmith in his breast."

"Surely not true!" repeated Yagenka, in a low voice; "but tell on."

"As God is dear to me it is true! That other one will not be so pleasant to him after thee, for thou knowest thyself that a firmer and a fairer maiden than thou is not to be found in all the world. He felt the will of God for thee, never fear— perhaps more than thou for him."

" Fear God ! " cried Yagenka.

And noting that she had said something impulsively, she covered her face, which was as ruddy again as an apple. Matsko smiled, drew his hand along his moustaches, and said, —

" Ei, if I were young ! But be patient, for I see how it will end. He will go, he will get his spurs at the Mazovian court; the boundary is near, and it is easy to find Knights of the Cross. I know that among Germans there are strong men, and that iron does not rebound from his skin, but I think that no common man will be able to meet him, for in battle the rogue is tremendously skilful. See how he knocked down Vilk and Stan in one flash, though people call them strong as bears, and grand fellows. He will bring his plumes, but he will not bring them to Yurand's daughter ; for I too have talked with Yurand, and I know how matters are. Well, and what will be afterward? Afterward he will come hither, for whither should he go? "

" When will he come ? "

" Well, if thou wait not there will be no feeling against thee. But now repeat to Zyh and the abbot what I tell thee. Let them soften their anger against Zbyshko even a little."

"How am I to explain? Papa is vexed rather than angry, but it is dangerous to speak of Zbyshko in presence of the abbot. He gave it to me, and to papa, because of the man whom I sent to Zbyshko."

Whatman?"

" We had a Cheh here, you know, whom papa captured at Boleslavets, a good man and faithful. His name is Hlava.

Papa gave him to me as attendant, for the man said that he was a noble in his own country. I gave Hlava good armor, and sent him to attend Zbyshko, to guard him in danger, and, which God forefend ! — to inform us (should anything happen). I gave him a purse for the road, and he swore to me by his soul's salvation that till his death he would serve Zbyshko faithfully."

" Oh, thou my girl! May God reward thee ! But did Zyh not oppose ? "

" Of course he opposed. At first he would not permit this for anything; only when I seized his feet was the victory on my side. There is no trouble with papa, but when the abbot heard of the matter from his buffoons he cursed the whole room-full in one moment, and there was such a day of judgment that papa ran out to the barns. Only in the evening did the abbot take pity on my tears, and give me besides a rosary. But I was willing to suffer, if only Zbyshko had. a larger retinue."

" As God is dear to me, I know not which one I love more, Zbyshko or thee, but in every case he had a good retinue — and I gave him money too, though he did not wish to take it. Moreover, Mazovia is not beyond the sea."

Further conversation was interrupted by the barking of dogs, shouts, and the sound of brass trumpets in front of the house. When they heard these Yagenka said, —

" Papa and the abbot are coming from the hunt. Let us go to the porch, for it is better that the abbot should see you first from a distance, and not in the house on a sudden."

Then she conducted Matsko to the porch, from which they saw on the snow in the yard a crowd of men, horses, dogs; also elks and wolves pierced with spears, or with bolts shot from crossbows. The abbot, seeing Matsko before dismounting, hurled a spear toward him, — not to strike, it is true, but to show in that way more definitely his resentment against the people of Bogdanets. But Matsko bowed to him from afar, cap in hand, as if he had noticed nothing. Yagenka had not observed this, for she was astonished first of all at the presence of her two suitors in the retinue.

"Stan and Vilk are there ! " cried she, "they must have met papa in the forest."

And with Matsko it went so far that something seemed to prick his old wound at sight of them. It passed through his head in a flash that one of the two might get Yagenka, and with her Mochydoly, the lauds of the abbot, his forests

and his money. Sorrow and rage seized his heart, especially a moment later when he saw something new. Vilk, though the abbot had wished not long before to fight with his father, sprang to the abbot's stirrup to assist him from the horse, and he in dismounting leaned in a friendly manner on the young noble's shoulder.

" The abbot will be reconciled with old Vilk in this way," thought Matsko, " that he will give the forests and the land with the girl." But these bitter thoughts of his were interrupted by Yagenka, who said at that moment, —

" The beating they got from Zbyshko is healed, but though they were to come here every day, nothing will be waiting for them ! "

Matsko looked; the girl's face was as ruddy from anger as it was cold, and her blue eyes flashed with rage, though she knew well that Vilk and Stan had stood up for her in the inn, and were beaten because of her.

" But you will do what the abbot commands," said Matsko.

"The abbot will do what I want," said she from where she stood.

" Dear God," thought Matsko, "and that foolish Zbyshko ran away from such a girl!"

CHAPTER XVI.

THE "foolish Zbyshko" bad ridden out of Bogdanets with a heavy heart, really. First, he felt strange somehow and awkward without his uncle, from whom during jpany years he had not parted, and to whom he was so accustomed that he did not know well how to live without him either on the road or in war. Second, he regretted Yagenka; for, though he said to himself that he was going to Danusia, whom he loved with all his soul, it had been so pleasant for him near Yagenka that he felt now for the first time what delight there had been in her company, and what sadness there might be without her. And he wondered at his regret, and was even disturbed by it. Had he been longing for Yagenka as a brother for a sister it would be nothing; but he saw that he wanted to grasp her by the waist and seat her on the horse, or take her from the saddle, to carry her through streams, squeeze water from her hair, go with her through the forests, look at her, and take " counsel " with her. So accustomed had he grown to this, and so pleasant was it to him that now, when he began to think of it, he forgot straightway and entirely that he was journeying on a long road to Mazovia, and immediately that moment was present to his eyes when Yagenka gave him aid in the forest while he was struggling with the bear. And it seemed to him that that was yesterday, as also it was yesterday when they were going to find the beaver in Odstayani Lake. He had not seen her when she swam in after the beaver, but now it seemed to him that he saw her, and at once those same shivers seized him which had seized him a couple of weeks earlier, when the wind played too freely with Yagenka's clothing. Then he remembered how she had gone to church in Kresnia dressed splendidly, and he had wondered that a simple maiden seemed to him like some lady of high lineage on a journey with her court.

All this was the cause that around his heart something began to make a disturbance, at once sweet and sad and full of desire, and if he thought besides that he might have done what he wished with her, that she was drawn to him also, if he remembered how she gazed into his eyes, how she nestled

up to him, he was hardly able to sit on his horse. " If I had met her somewhere and said farewell and embraced her on the road," said he to himself, " she might have let me; " then he felt that that was untrue, and that she would not have let him, for at the very thought of such a parting sparks passed along his body, though there was frost in the world at that moment.

At last he was frightened at those recollections, too much resembling desires, and he shook them from his soul as he would dry snow from an overcoat.

" I am going to Danusia, to my dearest," said he to himself. And he remarked at once that that was another love, as it were, — more pious, and passing less through the bones. Gradually, too, in proportion as his feet became chilled in the stirrups, and the cold wind cooled his blood, all his thoughts flew to Danusia. To her in truth he owed them. Had it not been for her, his head would have fallen long before on the square of Cracow. For when she said, in presence of knights and citizens, "He is mine," she took him by those words from the hands of the executioner, and thenceforth he belonged to her as much as a slave to his master. It was not he who had taken her, it was she who had taken him; no opposition from Yurand could avail against that fact. She alone could release him, as a lady might release a servant, though he in that case would not go far, for he was bound by his vow. But he thought that she would not release, that she would rather go with him even from the Mazovian court to the end of the world; and thinking thus he began in his soul to praise her to the prejudice of Yagenka, as if it were Yagenka's fault exclusively that temptations had attacked him, and that his heart had been divided. It did not occur to him now that Yagenka had cured old Matsko, and besides, without her aid, perhaps the bear that night would have taken the skin from his head ; and he was deliberately indignant at Yagenka, thinking that he was serving Danusia in that way, and justifying himself in his own eyes.

But now appeared the Cheh, Hlava, who had been sent by Yagenka, and who brought with him a pack-horse.

'' Let Him be praised ! " said he, bowing low.

Zbyshko had seen the man once or twice at Zyh's house, but did not recognize him ; so he said, —

" Praised for the ages of ages! But who art thou? "

" Your attendant, renowned lord."

" How my attendant? Here are my attendants," said he, pointing to the two Turks given him by Zavisha, and two sturdy youths who sitting on two stumpy horses were leading the knight's stallions. "These are mine — but who gent thee ? "

" Panna Yagenka."

" Panna Yagenka? "

Zbyshko, who had been full of indignation, and whose heart was full yet of ill-will, said,—

" Go home and thank Panna Yagenka for her kindness. I do not need thee."

The Cheh shook his head.

" I will not go, lord. I have been given to you; and besides, I have sworn to serve you till death."

" If thou hast been given me, then thou art my servant."

" Yours, lord."

" Then I command thee to return."

" I have sworn, and though I am a prisoner and a poor man, I am a noble."

Zbyshko was angry.

" Be off! How is this? Wilt thou serve me against my will, or what ? Be off, or I shall command to draw a crossbow on thee."

Hlava unstrapped quietly a cloth mantle lined with wolfskin, and gave it to Zbyshko, saying, —

" Panna Yagenka sent you this, lord."

"Dost wish that I should break thy bones?" inquired Zbyshko, taking a spear from the hands of an attendant.

" And here is a purse at your command."

Zbyshko aimed the spear, but remembering that the man, though a prisoner, was a noble by blood, who had remained with Zyh only because he had not the means to redeem himself, lowered the spear point. The Cheh bowed to his stri-rup, and said,—

" Be not angry, lord. If you do not command me to go with you, I will go behind you one or two furlongs; but I will go, for I have sworn on my soul's salvation to do so."

" But if I give command to kill, or to bind thee? "

" If you command to kill me it will not be my sin ; if you command to bind me I will remain bound till good people unbind me, or till wolves devour me."

Zbyshko did not answer, he merely urged his horse forward, and his people moved after him. Illava, with a cross-

bow at his shoulder and an axe in his hand, dragged on behind, taking shelter in the shaggy skin of a bison; for a sharp wind began to blow, bringing snow-flakes.

The storm increased with every moment. The Turks, though in skin coats, were stiff from cold. Zbyshko's attendants began to swing their arms, to beat themselves with their hands, and he also, not clothed sufficiently, cast his eyes once and a second time on the wolf-skin mantle brought by Hlava, and after a while told one of the Turks to bring it to him.

Wrapping himself closely in the mantle he soon felt warmth passing over his whole body; especially convenient was the hood, which sheltered his eyes and a considerable part of his face, so that the storm almost ceased to annoy him. Then he thought, in spite of himself, that Yagenka was an honest maiden to the bones, and he reined in his horse somewhat, for the desire seized him to ask Hlava about her, and everything that had happened at Zyh's house. So beckoning to the man he asked, —

" Does old Zyh know that Panna Yagenka sent thee to me?"

"He knows."

" And he did not oppose?"

" He opposed."

" Tell how it was."

" Pan Zyh was walking through the room, and Panna Yagenka after him. He screamed, but she not a word; when he turned toward her she dropped to her knees. And not a word. Pan Zyh said at last: ' Art thou deaf, that thou sayst nothing in answer to me? Speak, for at last I shall permit, and when I permit the abbot will take off my head.' Then the young lady saw that she would get what she wanted, and began to thank him with tears. The old man reproached her for tormenting him, and complained that everything had to be as she wished, but at last he said: ' Promise me that thou wilt not run out in secret to take farewell of him; if thou promise I will permit, otherwise I will not.' Panna Yagenka was vexed, but she promised; and he was glad, for he and the abbot were terribly afraid that the wish might come to her to see your grace. But that was not the end, for later the lady wished that there should be two horses, and he refused; she wanted a wolf-skin and a purse; he refused. But what value in those refusals ? If she had thought to burn down the house

her father would have consented. For this reason you have the second horse, the wolf-skin, and the purse."

"An honest girl!" thought Zbyshko in his soul. After a time he asked,—

" But was there no trouble with the abbot? "

Hlava laughed like a shrewd man, who takes note of everything passing around him, and answered, —

They both kept secrets from the abbot, and I know not what would have happened if he had known this, for I went away earlier. The abbot, as an abbot, thunders sometimes at the young lady, but then he casts his eyes at her, and looks to see if he has not done her too much injustice. I have seen myself how he scolded her once, and then hurried to a casket and brought a chain such that a better could not be found in Cracow, and he said, ' Here.' She cau get on with the abbot too, for her own father does not love her more than he does."

" That is true certainly."

" As God is in heaven."

Here they were silent, and went on farther through the wind and the snow-flakes; but suddenly Zbyshko reined in his horse, for from one side of the forest was heard a certain complaining voice, half smothered by the sound of the trees.

" Christian, save a servant of God from misfortune! "

At the same moment a person dressed half like a cleric, half like a laj'man, ran out to the road, where he stood before Zbyshko and said, —

" Whoever thou be, O lord, give aid to a man and a neigl> bor in dire distress! "

"What has happened, and who art thou?"asked the young knight.

" I am a servant of God, though without ordination, and it has happened this morning that my horse broke away, having on his back a casket with sacred objects. I was left alone, without arms; evening is coming, and it is short waiting till savage beasts will be heard in the forest. I shall perish unless you save me."

" If thou perish because of me must I answer for thy sins? How am I to know that thou speakest truth, and that thou art not a cutpurse, or a vagabond, many of whom are dragging along the roads these days?"

You will know by my caskets. More than one man would give a purse filled with ducats to possess what is iu

them, but I will share their contents with you if you take me and them."

" Thou callest thyself God's servant and knowest not that a man is to be rescued for heavenly, not for earthly rewards. But how hast thou kept the caskets, since the horse ran away ?"

" Before I found the horse the wolves had devoured him in an opening of the forest, and the caskets were left. I brought them to the road so as to wait for the favor and help of good people."

Thus speaking, and wishing to show that he had told truth, he pointed at two bark caskets lying under a pine tree. Zbyshko looked at the man rather suspiciously, for to him this stranger did not seem over honest; and besides, his speech, though pure, betrayed an origin in distant regions. Zbyshko, however, was loath to refuse assistance, and permitted the man to sit, with his caskets, which proved to be very light, on that detached horse led by Hlava.

" May God increase your victory, valiant knight! " said the unknown. Then, seeing the youthful face of Zbyshko, he added in an undertone, "and also the hairs in your beard."

A moment later he was riding by the side of the Cheh. For some time they could not talk, as a strong wind was blowing and the noise of the forest was tremendous, but when it had calmed somewhat Zbyshko heard the following conversation behind,—

" I do not deny thy visit to Rome, but thou hast the look of a beer guzzler."

" Guard thyself against eternal damnation," answered the unknown, " for thou art talking with a man who last Easter ate hard-boiled eggs with the Holy Father. Talk not on such a cold day to me of beer, even though it we're heated; but if thou hast on thy person a flask of wine, give me two or three gulps of it, and I will give a month's indulgence from purgatory."

" Thou art not ordained, for I heard thee say so thyself; how couldst thou, then, give me indulgence for a month of purgatory ? "

" I am not ordained, but I have a shaven head, for which I received a dispensation ; besides, I bear with me indulgences and relics."

"In those caskets?"

i" In these caskets. And if thou wert to see what I have,

thou wouldst fall on thy face, — not only thou, but all the pines in the forests, and all the wild beasts."

The Cheh, who was clever and experienced, looked suspiciously at the dealer in indulgences, and added, —

" But the wolves ate thy horse."

"They did, for they are the devil's relatives; but they burst. I saw one of them burst with my own eyes. If thou hast wine give it, for though the wind has stopped, I am chilled from sitting at the roadside."

Hlava did not give the wine, and again they rode on in silence, till the dealer in relics inquired,—

" AVhither are ye going?"

" Far. But at present to Sieradz. Wilt thou go with us ? "

" I must. I will sleep in the stable, and to-morrow mayhap that pious knight will give me a horse, and I shall go farther."

" Whence comest thou? "

" From the land of the Prussian lords, from near Malborg."

Hearing this, Zbyshko turned his head, and beckoned the unknown to him.

"Thou art from near Malborg? Whence comest thou now?"

" From near Malborg."

" But thou art not a German, thou speakest our language so well. What is thy name? "

"I am a German, and they caU me Sanderus; I know your language, for I was born in Torun, where all people speak it. Later I lived in Malborg, but it is the same there. Nay! even brothers of the Order understand your language."

"And art thou long from Malborg? "

" I have been in the Holy Land, in Constantinople, and in Rome, whence I returned through France to Malborg; from Malborg I went to Mazovia, carrying holy relics, which pious Christians buy gladly to save their souls."

" Wert thou in Plotsk, and also in Warsaw? "

"I was in both places. May God give health to both princesses! Not without cause do the Prussian lords themselves love Princess Alexandra; she is a saintly lady, though Princess Anna, the wife of Prince Yanush, is not inferior."

" Hast thou seen the court in Warsaw?"

" I have not met it in Warsaw, but in Tsehanov, where the prince and the princess received me hospitably as a servant of God, and gave me rich gifts for the road. But I left relies which must bring them God's blessing."

Zbyshko wished to inquire about Danusia, but at once a certain indecision possessed him, and a certain shame; for he understood that that would be the same as to confess his love to an unknown man of low origin, who, besides, had a suspicious look, and might be some common deceiver. So after a moment's silence, he asked, —

" AVhat relics art thou bearing through the world ? " "I bear indulgences and relics; the indulgences are various. 1 have plenary indulgences, indulgences for five hundred years, for three hundred, for two hundred years, and less, cheaper, so that even poor people acquire them, and thus shorten the torments of purgatory for themselves. I have indulgences for past sins, and for future; but do not think, lord, that I put away the money which people pay for them. A morsel of black bread and a gulp of water suffices me; the rest of what I collect I take to Rome, so that iu time I may make a new journey. There are many money grabbers who go through the world, it is true, but have only false things, indulgences, relics, testimonials, and seals; such persons as these the Holy Father pursues justly with his letters, but on me the prior of Sieradz has wrought injustice and wrong, for my seals are genuine. Look, lord, at the wax and you will know yourself." " But what did the prior of Sieradz do?" " Oh, as God lives, I thought unjustly that he was tainted with the heretical teaching of Wyclif. And if, as your attendant has told me, you are going to Sieradz, I prefer not to show myself to him, so as not to bring him to sin and blaspheme against holy things."

' l That means, without saying much, that he took thee for a cheat and a cutpurse."

" May I forgive him, lord, through love for my neighbor, as indeed I have done already; but he has blasphemed against my sacred wares, for which I fear greatly that he will be damned beyond rescue." "What sacred wares hast thou?"

" Such that it is not proper to speak of them with covered head; but since I have indulgences with me, I give you, O lord, permission not to take off your cowl, since the wind is now blowing afresh. Buy of me, therefore, a little indulgence to have in supply, and the sin will not be accounted to you. What is it that I have not? I have a hoof of the ass on which the flight to Egypt took place ; it was found near the pyramids. The King of Aragoii offered me indeed fifty

ducats for it. I have a feather from a wing of the Archangel Gabriel, who dropped it during the Annunciation; 1 have two heads of quails sent to the Israelites in the wilderness; I have oil in which pagans wished to boil Saint John, and a round from the ladder which Jacob saw in his vision. I have tears dropped by Mary of Egypt, and some rust from the keys of Saint Peter. I cannot mention all, because I am chilled, and your attendant, O lord, would not give me wine; and moreover I could not name them all between this time and evening."

" Those relics are great if they are genuine," said Zbyshko.

" If they are genuine? Take the lance from the hand of that attendant and plant it before you, for the devil is near who gives you such ideas. Keep him, O lord, at the length of the lance.

And if you will not bring misfortune on yourself buy of me an indulgence for that sin; unless you do, the one whom you love most on earth will die in three weeks."

Zbyshko was terrified at the threat, for Danusia came to his mind, and he said, —

"It is not I who doubt, but the prior of Dominicans in Sieradz."

" Look yourself at the wax of the seals; as to the prior, God knows if he is alive yet, for Divine justice is swift."

But when they arrived at Sieradz it appeared that the prior was alive. Zbyshko even betook himself to him to give for two masses, one of which was to be offered for the benefit of Matsko, the other on account of those peacock-plumes for which Zbyshko was going. The prior, like many in Poland at that time, was a foreigner, from Tsylia by origin, but during fourteen years' residence in Sieradz he had learned Polish well, and was a great enemy of the Knights of the Cross. When he heard, therefore, of Zbyshko's undertaking, he said: " A greater punishment of the Lord will meet them yet, but I will not dissuade thee from what thou hast intended; first, because thou hast taken an oath, and, second, because a Polish hand can never squeeze them sufficiently for what they did here in Sieradz."

"What did they do?" inquired Zbyshko, who was glad to hear of every injustice committed by the Knights of the Cross.

Here the old prior spread apart his hands and began to repeat audibly " Eternal rest; " then he sat on a bench, and kept his eyes closed for a while, as if to summon old memories.

" Vincent of Shamotur brought them here," said he at last. " I was twenty years old then, and had just come from Tsylia, whence my uncle, Petzoldt, the custodian, brought me. The Kuights of the Cross attacked this town in the night, and burned it immediately. From the walls we saw them put men, women, and children to the sword on the market square, and hurl infants into the fire; I saw them kill even priests, for in their rage they spared no man. And it happened that the prior Mikolai, from Elblang by origin, knew Hermann, the comtur, the leader of the Germans. The prior went out with the older monks to that savage knight, and Kneeling down, implored him in German to spare Christian blood. ' I understand not,' replied Hermann the comtur, and gave command to go on with the slaughter. Then they slew the monks, and with them my uncle, Petzoldt; next they bound Mikolai the prior to the tail of a horse. Toward morning there was not a living man in the town, save the Knights of the Cross, — and save me; I was hidden on a beam in the belfry. God punished them for that at Plovtsi, but they are rising up continually to the destruction of this Christian kingdom, and they wUl rise up till the arm of God crushes them utterly."

" At Plovtsi too," answered Zbyshko, " nearly all the men of my family perished; but I feel no regret for them, since God gave King Lokietek such a victory, and destroyed twenty thousand Germans."

" Thou wilt see a still greater war, and greater victories," said the prior.

' ' Amen! " replied Zbyshko. And they spoke then of something else.

The young knight asked a little about the dealer in relics whom he had found on the road, and learned that many such cheats were wandering about on the highways, deceiving the credulous. The prior told him also that there were papal bulls commanding bishops to punish such dealers, and, in case a man had not genuine letters and seals, to condemn him immediately. Since the testimonies of this wanderer had seemed suspicious to the prior, he wished to send him at once to the jurisdiction of the bishop. If it appeared that he was a genuine bearer of indulgences no wrong would be done him. But this man preferred flight. Perhaps he feared delay on his journey, but through this flight he subjected himself to still greater suspicion.

Toward the end of Zbyshko's visit the prior invited the young man to rest and pass the night in the cloister; but he could not accept, since he wished to hang up a card before the inn with a challenge to battle " on foot or on horseback" to all knights who should deny that Panna Danusia was the most beautiful and virtuous maiden in the kingdom. It was not proper in any way to attach such a challenge to the gate of the cloister. Neither the prior nor other priests would even write a card for him. In consequence of this the young knight grew greatly vexed and knew not at all how to help himself. It occurred to him only on his return to the inn to ask aid of the dealer in indulgences.

" The prior does not know whether thou art a rascal or not, for he says: 'If he has genuine testimony why did he fear the bishop's court?"

"I fear not the bishop, but monks who have no knowledge of seals. I wished to go to Cracow, but as I have no horse I must wait till some man gives me one. Meanwhile I will send a letter, to which I shall put my own seal."

" I too thought to myself that if thou wouldst show that thou knowest letters it would be a sign that thou art not a simple fellow. But how wilt thou send the letter? "

" Through some pilgrim or wandering monk. Are the people few in number who go to the queen's grave in Cracow? "

" But couldst thou write a letter for me? "

"I will write anything that you command, smoothly and to the point, even on a board."

" Better on a board," said Zbyshko, delighted, "for it will not. drop off, and will be good for another time."

So when Zbyshko's attendants had found and brought in a new board, Sanderus sat down to write. Zbyshko could not read what he wrote, but he commanded straightway to fasten the challenge on the gate, and to hang beneath it his shield, which the Turks guarded one after the other. Whoso should strike the challenge with his spear would indicate that he accepted it. But in Sieradz there was evidently a lack of volunteers for such matters, for neither on that day nor the day following till noon did the shield resound from a blow; at noon the young man, somewhat vexed, continued his journey. But first Sanderus came to him and said, —

" If you had hung up your shield in the land of the Prussian lords surely your attendant would have to strap on your armor." -

" How is that? Knights of the Cross, being monks, cannot have ladies whom they love, for it is not permitted them."

"I know not whether it is permitted, but I know that they have them. It is true that a Knight of the Cross cannot engage without sin in single combat, for he takes an oath that he will fight with others only for the faith, but there is a multitude of lay knights from distant lands who come to aid the Order. These men are looking only to find some one with whom to fight, especially the French knights."

" Oh, indeed! I have seen them at Vilno, and God grant me to see them also at Malborg. I need peacock-plumes from helmets, for I have vowed to get them — dost understand ? "

" Buy, O lord, two or three drops of the sweat which fell from Saint George when he fought the dragon. No relic is of more service to a knight. Give for them that horse on which you commanded me to sit. I will give besides an indulgence for the Christian blood which you will shed in the struggle."

" Say no more, or I shall be angry. I will not take thy wares till I know that they are genuine."

" You are going, lord, as you said, to the Mazovian court, to Prince Yanush. Inquire there how many relics they took of me, — the princess herself and knights and damsels at weddings where I was present."

" What weddings? "

" As usual before Advent. The knights marry one with more haste than another, because people say that there will be war between the King of Poland and the Prussian knights for the land of Dobryn. A man says to himself: ' God knows whether I shall return alive ;' and he wishes, before the war comes, to experience happiness with a woman."

The news of the war occupied Zbyshko greatly, but still more that which Sanderus had said about weddings; so he inquired, —

" What damsels were married? "

" Oh, Princess Anna's damsels. I know not whether one remained, for I heard her say that she would have to seek new ladies-in-waiting."

When he heard this Zbyshko was silent for a time; after that he asked with a somewhat changed voice, —

" But Panna Danuta, the daughter of Yurand, whose name stands on the board, — was she married also? "

Sanderus hesitated in answering, first, because he knew nothing clearly, and second, because he thought that by keeping the knight in suspense he would win a preponder-

TOL. I. — 14

ance over him and be able to exploit him the better. He had considered already in his mind that he ought to hold fast to that knight, who had a good retinue and sufficient supplies. Sauderus knew men and things. Zbyshko's great youth permitted him to suppose that the knight would be bountiful and not provident, casting around money easily. He had observed also that costly Milan armor, and the immense stallions for battle, which not every man could own; so he said to himself that with a young lord like him he would find secure hospitality at courts, and more than one chance to sell indulgences with profit; he would have safety on the road, and, finally, abundance of food and drink, which for him was supremely important. So when he heard Zbyshko's question he wrinkled his forehead, raised his eyes as if straining his memory, and answered, —

" Panna Danuta, —but whence is she?"

" Danuta, the daughter of Yurand of Spyhov."

" I saw them all, but what their names were I do not remember clearly."

" She is young yet, plays on the lute, and rejoices the princess with singing."

" Ah! — young — plays on the lute — young maidens also got married. Is she not dark as an agate? "

Zbyshko was relieved.

"That is not she ! She is white as snow, but there is a blush on her cheeks, she is blond."

" One as black as an agate," said Sanderus, " remained with the princess, almost all the others got married."

" Thou sayst ' almost all;' that means not to the last one. By the dear God! if thou wish of me anything then bring it to mind."

"In three or four days I could recall everything; but most precious to me would be a horse on which 1 could carry my sacred objects."

" If thou tell truth, thou wilt get one."

" The truth will be known at the Mazovian court," said Illava, who had been listening to the conversation from the first and was laughing in his fist.

Sanderus looked at him awhile and asked; "Dost thou think that I fear the Mazovian court?"

" I do not say that thou hast fear of the Mazovian court, but if it shall appear that thou hast lied thou wilt not go away on thy own legs, for his grace will give command to break both."

" As true as life! " said Zbyshko.

In view of such an announcement Sanderus thought it better to be cautious, and answered, —

"If I had wished to lie I should have answered at once that she was married, or was not married, but I said that I did not remember. If thou hadst wit thou wouldst have noted my virtue at once by this answer."

" My wit is not a brother to thy virtue, for thy .virtue may be a dog's sister."

" My virtue does not bark like thy wit, and whoso barks during life may easily howl after death."

" And in truth thy virtue will not howl after death, but gnash, unless during life it loses its teeth in the service of Satan."

And they began a war of words, for the Cheh had a nimble tongue, and for every word from the German he found two. Meanwhile Zbyshko gave command to start, and they pushed on, having inquired first carefully of experienced people about the road to Lenchytsa. A little beyond Sieradz they entered deep pine forests with which the greater part of the country was covered. But through them in parts was a road, ditched at the sides, in low places even paved with round stones, a remnant of King Kazimir's management. It is true that after his death, amid disorders of the war roused by the Nalen-chi and the Grymaliti, roads had been neglected somewhat, but during Yadviga's time, after the pacification of the kingdom, spades appeared again in the hands of dexterous people along swamps and in forests appeared axes. Toward the end of her life the merchant might conduct his laden wagons between the most important towns without fear of seeing them broken in ruts or stuck fast in mud holes. Wild beasts or robbers might meet one on the road, but against beasts there were torches at night, and crossbows during daylight; as to robbers and rascals, there were fewer of them than in neighboring countries. Moreover, the man who went with an escort and armed might advance without fear.

So Zbyshko feared neither robbers nor armed knights ; he did not even think of them, for great alarm had fallen on him, and his whole soul was at the Mazovian court. Would he find his Danusia a damsel of the princess, or the wife of some knight of Mazovia? He knew not himself, and from daylight till darkness he wrestled with his thoughts on this question. Sometimes it seemed to him impossible that she should forget him, but at other times it came to his head that perhaps

Yurand had come to the court from Spyhov and given her in marriage to some friend or neighbor. He had told him while in Cracow that Danusia was not fated for him, Zbyshko, and that he could not give her; so, evidently, he had promised her to another; evidently he was bound by an oath, and now he was keeping it. It seemed certain to Zbyshko that he would not see her again as a maiden. Then he called Sanderus and inquired a second time, but he merely made the affair still more doubtful. More than once he recollected the damsel, the daughter of Yurand, and her wedding, and then suddenly he put his finger to his lips, thought a moment, and answered, " It must be that it was not that one." In wine, which was to create clearness in his head, the German did not regain memory, and he kept the young knight continually between hope and mortal fear.

So Zbyshko travelled on in anxiety, suffering, and uncertainty. On the way he had no thought of his own or of Zyh's house, he was thinking only of what it behooved him to do. First of all was the need to go and learn the truth at the Mazovian court; hence he rode on hurriedly, halting only for short night rests at courts, inns, and towns, so as not to wear out his horses. In Lenchytsa he commanded to hang up his board again with the challenge before the gate, understanding in his soul that, whether Danusia remained in a maiden condition or was married, she was always the lady of his heart, and he was obliged to do battle for her. But in Lenchytsa there were not many who knew how to read the challenge; those of the knights to whom clerics skilled in letters explained it, shrugged their shoulders, not knowing foreign customs, and said: "Some fool is travelling ; how can any man agree with him, or contradict him. unless he has seen the girl with his own eyes?"

And Zbyshko went on with increasing vexation and increasing haste. Never had he ceased to love his Danusia; when at home and while " advising" almost daily with Yagenka, and looking at her beauty, he had not thought so often of the other, but now she did not leave his eyes, his memory, or his thoughts day or night. In sleep even he saw her before him, blond-haired, with a lute in her hand, with red shoes, and with a garland on her head. She stretched forth her hands to him, but Yurand drew her away. In the morning, when dreams fled, greater longing than ever came straightway in place of them, and never had Zbvshko loved that maiden when in Bogdanets as he loved

her then, when he was not sure but they had taken her away from him.

It came also to his head that surely she had been married in spite of her; hence at heart, he did not blame Danusia, especially since, being a child, she could not have her own will yet. But in soul he was angry at Yurand and Princess Anna, and when he thought of Danusia's husband his heart rose to his throat, and he looked around threateningly on his attendants who carried his armor under a covering. He settled too, with himself, that he would not cease to serve her, and that though he might find her the wife of another he would lay the peacock-plumes down at her feet. But there was more grief in that thought than solace, for he knew not what he could begin to do afterward. Nothing consoled him save the thought of a great war. Though he had no wish to live without Danusia, he did not promise to perish surely, but he felt that somehow his spirit and his memory would be so diverted during war that he would be free of all other cares and vexations. And a great war was hanging in the air, as it were. It was unknown whence news of it had come, for peace reigned between the king and the Order; still in all places whithersoever Zbyshko went, men spoke on no other subject. People had, as it were, a foreboding that it must come, and some men said openly: ' ' "Why did we unite with Lithuania, unless against those wolves, the Knights of the Cross? We must finish with them once and forever, so that they may be rending our entrails no longer." But others said: "Mad monks! Plovtse did not suffice them ! death is hanging over them, and still they seized Dobryn, which they must vomit up with their blood." And throughout all territories of the kingdom people without boasting prepared seriously, as is usual in a life-and-death struggle, with the deep determination of strong men who had endured injustice too long and were making ready at last to mete out dreadful punishment. In all houses Zbyshko met men who were convinced that the need might come any day to sit on horseback ; and he was astonished, for though thinking, as well as others, that war must come, he had not heard that it would begin so soon. It had not occurred to him that the desire of people had anticipated events that time. He believed others, not himself, and was rejoiced in heart at sight of that hurry preceding conflict which he met everywhere. In all places all other anxieties gave way to anxiety about a horse and armor; everywhere men were testing with great care lances, swords, axes, spears, helmets, mail, straps for breastplates, horse trappings. Smiths were beating night and day on iron plates with their hammers, forging rude heavy armor which elegant knights of the West could hardly move, but which the sturdy " heirs "of Great and Little Poland carried easily. Old men drew forth from caskets in their closets faded bags with coin in them, to procure military outfits for their sons. Once Zbyshko passed the night with a rich noble, Bartosh of Belav, who having twenty-two stalwart sons mortgaged broad lands to the cloister in Lovich so as to buy twenty-two suits of armor, as many helmets, and other arms for the conflict. So Zbyshko, though he had not heard of this in Bogdanets, thought, also, that he would have to go to Prussia directly, and thanked God that he was equipped for the expedition so splendidly.

Indeed his armor roused admiration everywhere. People esteemed him the son of a voevoda, but when he said that he was only the son of a simple noble, and that such armor might be bought among the Germans if one would pay with an axe properly, hearts gained warlike desire. But more than one man unable to stifle greed at sight of this armor caught up with Zbyshko on the road, and asked, "Well, wilt thou fight for it ?" But being in a hurry he would not fight; besides, the Cheh drew his crossbow. Zbyshko ceased even to hang out the board with the challenge at inns, for he noticed that the farther he advanced from the boundary the less 'people understood it, and the more they considered him foolish.

In Mazovia men spoke less of the war. They believed even there that it was coming, but they knew not the time. In Warsaw there was peace, the more since the court was at Tsehanov, which Prince Yanush had built over after the old attack of the Lithuanians, or rather he had built it entirely new, for of the earlier place there remained only the castle. In the town of Warsaw Yasko Soha, the starosta of the castle, son of the voevoda Abraham, who fell at the Vorskla, received Zbyshko. Yasko knew the young knight, for he had been with Princess Anna in Cracow; hence he was glad to entertain him. But before sitting down to food and drink Zbyshko inquired about Danusia. "Had she not been given in marriage at the same time with other damsels?"

Yasko could not answer that question. The prince and princess had lived in the castle of Tsehanov since early

autumn. In "Warsaw only he and a handful of bowmen had remained as a guard. He heard that in Tsehanov there had been various amusements and weddings, as happens usually before Advent, but who of the damsels had married and who had remained single he, as a married man, had not inquired.

" I think, however," said he, " that Yurand's daughter is not married. How could the marriage take place without Yurand? and I have not heard of his arrival. Two brothers of the Order are visiting at the court, —one is from Yansbork, the other from Schytno, — and with them are some foreign guests, it is likely ; at such times Yurand never comes, for the sight of a white mantle rouses him to madness. Unless Yurand was there, there was no wedding. But if it is thy wish I will send a messenger to inquire, and will order him to return quickly, though, as I live, I think that thou wilt find Yurand's daughter yet in the maiden state."

" I shall go myself to-morrow, but God reward thee for the comfort. Only let my horses rest, and I shall go, for I cannot rest till I know the truth. But God repay thee; thou hast relieved me at once."

Soha did not stop here; he inquired of one and another among the nobles, who were stopping by chance in the castle, and the soldiers, if any had heard of the marriage of Yurand's daughter. No one had heard, though there were men who had been in Tsehanov, and had even been at weddings. " Unless some one had taken her during recent weeks or recent days." It might have happened, indeed, for in those days people did not lose time in reflection. But Zbyshko went to sleep greatly strengthened. While therein bed he thought whether or not to dismiss Sanderus on the morrow; but he considered that the man might be useful, because of his knowledge of German, when the time came to go against Lichtensteiii. He thought, too, that Sanderus had not deceived him; and though at inns he was very expensive, since he ate and drank as much as four persons, still he was serviceable, and showed his new lord a certain attachment. Besides, he had the art of writing, thus surpassing the Cheh and Zbyshko himself.

All these considerations caused the young knight to let Sanderus go to Tsehanov; at which the man rejoiced, not only because of the food, but because he thought that in honorable company he would rouse more confidence and find purchasers more easily for his relics. After another night

spent at Naselsk, and travelling neither too briskly nor too slowly, they saw toward evening of the next day the walls of Tsehanov Castle. Zbyshko halted at the inn to put on his armor and enter the castle, according to knightly custom, in a helmet, and lance in hand. So he mounted his gigantic stallion and advanced, after he had made a sign of the cross in the air.

But he had not gone ten steps when the Cheh riding, behind caught up with him, and said,—

" Your grace, certain knights are riding up after us,— Knights of the Cross, I think."

Zbyshko turned his horse and saw a showy retinue not farther than fifty rods distant; at the head of it on strong Pomeranian horses rode two knights, both in full armor, each in a white mantle with a black cross, and in a helmet with lofty peacock-plumes.

" Knights of the Cross, by the dear God! " said Zbyshko.

And involuntarily he inclined in the saddle, and placed his lance half-way down to the horse's ears; seeing which, the Cheh spat on his palm so that the axe might not slip from it.

Zbyshko's attendants, men of experience, knowing the custom of war, stood ready also, — not for battle, it is true, for in knightly conflicts servants took no part, but to measure out a space for the struggle on horseback, or to trample the snowy earth for a combat on foot.

Being a noble, the Cheh was to take part; but he too hoped that Zbyshko would speak before he struck, and in his soul he was wonderfully astonished even that the young lord lowered his lance before challenging.

But Zbyshko recollected himself in season. He recalled that mad act of his near Cracow when he wished without foresight to do battle with Lichtenstein, and remembered all the misfortunes which had come of it; so he raised his lance, which he gave to the Cheh, and without drawing his sword moved on horseback toward the Knights of the Cross. When he had ridden up he saw that besides them there was still a third knight, also with plumes upon his helmet, and a fourth, long haired, without armor; to him this last man seemed a-Mazoviau. When he saw them he said to himself, —

" I vowed in prison to my lady, not three plumes, but as many as she has fingers on her hands; but three, if they are not envoys, might be found at once." He thought, however, that they must surely be envoys to the Prince of Mazovia; so he called aloud, —

" Praised be Jesus Christ."

" For the ages of ages," answered the long-haired, un-armored horseman.

' ' God give you fortune !"

" And to you, lord."

" Glory to Saint George ! "

" He is our patron. Lord, be greeted on the road."

Here they bowed to each other; and then Zbyshko announced his name, his escutcheon, his watchword, and the place whence he was going to the court of Mazovia. The long-haired knight declared that he was Yendrek of Kropiv-nitse, and that he was conducting guests of the prince, Brother Gottfried and Brother Rotgier, with Foulk de Lorche of Lorraine, who, while visiting the Knights of the Cross, wished to see with his own eyes the Prince of Mazovia, and especially the princess, daughter of the famous "Kynstut." l

While their names were in course of mention, the foreign knights, sitting erect on their horses, bent their heads covered with iron helmets, and bowed repeatedly; for they thought, judging from Zbyshko's brilliant armor, that the prince had sent out some distinguished person, perhaps a son or relative, to meet them.

" The comtur," continued Yendrek, "or, as you would say in our language, the starosta, of Yansbork is stopping as a guest with the prince, to whom he mentioned these three knights. ' They have a lively desire to come,' said he, ' but do not dare, especially the Knight of Lorraine, because, journeying from afar, he thinks that immediately beyond the boundary of the Order dwell Saracens, with whom war never ceases.' The prince, as a hospitable lord, sent me at once to the boundary to conduct them in safety among the castles."

" Could they not have passed without your aid? "

" Our people are terribly enraged at the Knights of the Cross, and not so much for their attacks, since we look in at them also, as for their great treachery. If a Knight of the Cross embrace thee to thy face and kiss thee, he is ready to plunge a knife into thy back at that very moment, — a custom quite swinish and hateful to us Mazovians. Yes! that is it! Every one will receive a German under his roof and do no harm to his guest, but on the road he is glad to attack him. And there are some who do nothing else

1 Keistut.

through revenge, or for the glory which may God grant to every one."

" Who is the most famous among you? "

" There is one, and it would be better for a German to look at death than see him; they call him Yurand of Spyhov."

The young knight's heart quivered when he heard this name; he determined at once to draw Yendrek by the tongue.

" I know," said he; "I have heard of him; he is the man whose daughter Dauusia was Princess Anna's damsel till she was married."

As he said this he looked carefully at the eyes of the Mazovian, stopping the breath in his breast almost; but the other answered with great astonishment: "Who told you that? She is a damsel. True it happens that damsels marry, but Yurand's daughter is not married. Six days ago, when I rode away from Tsehanov, I saw her with the princess. How could she marry in Advent?"

Zbyshko, while hearing this, used all his strength of will to avoid seizing the Mazovian by the neck and shouting, u God reward thee for the news!" but he restrained himself, and said, —

" I heard that Yuraud gave her to some one."

" The princess, not Yurand, wanted to give her in marriage, but she could not go against Yurand's will. She wanted to give her to a knight in.Cracow, who made a vow to the girl, and who is loved by her."

" Is he? " cried Zbyshko.

At this Yendrek looked at him quickly, smiled, and said, —

" Do you know, somehow you are terribly curious about that girl?"

u I am curious about acquaintances to whom I am going."

Little of Zbyshko's face could be seen under the helmet, — barely his eyes, his nose, and a small part of his cheeks, — but his nose and his cheeks were so red that the crafty Mazovian, who was given to jesting, said, —

" It is sure that your face has grown as red from cold as an Easter egg."

The young man was still more confused and answered, " Sure."

They moved on, and rode some time in silence; only the horses snorted, throwing out columns of steam from their nostrils, and the foreign knights began to jabber among themselves. After a while, however, Yendrek asked, —

What is your name, for I did not hear well?"

" Zbyshko of Bogdanets."

"Oh, indeed! he who made the vow to Yurand's daughter had the same name."

" Do you think that I shall contradict? " answered Zbyshko, quickly and with pride.

" No, for there is no reason. Dear God, then you are that Zbyshko whose head the girl covered with a veil! After the return from Cracow the damsels talked of no one but you, and, while listening, tears flowed down the cheeks of more than one of them. So this is you! Hei! there will be joy at the court, for the princess also is fond of you."

" God bless her, and bless you for the good news— for when people told me that she was married I suffered."

' l What, marry! A girl like that is a dainty bit, for all of Spyhov stands behind her; but though there are many shapely fellows at the court, no one has looked into her eyes, for each respects her deed and your vow. Neither would the princess permit such conduct. Hei! there will be joy. It is true that sometimes the damsels jested with her; one would say, ' Your knight will not come,' then she would stamp with her feet and cry, ' He will! he will!' Though more than once, when some one told her that you had taken another, it came to tears,"

These words touched Zbyshko, but anger at peoples' talk seized him straightway; so he said, —

" I will challenge any one who barked such things of me!"

" Women said them," answered Yendrek, beginning to laugh. " Will you challenge women? What can you do with a sword against a distaff?"

Zbyshko, glad that God had sent him so kind and cheerful a companion, fell to inquiring about Danusia, then about the habits of the Mazoviau court, and again about Danusia; then about Prince Yanush and the princess, and again about Danusia. But at last, remembering his vows, he told Yendrek what he had heard on the way about war, how people were preparing, how they were waiting day by day for it, and at last he inquired if they had the same thoughts in Mazovia.

Yendrek did not think war so near. People said that it must be near, but he had heard the prince say to Pan Mikolai once that the knights had drawn in their horns, and, since they feared the power of King Yagello, were he to insist, they would withdraw from the lauds of Dobryn which they

had seized, or at least they would put off the war till they were well prepared.

" Moreover," said he, " the prince went to Malborg, where, during the absence of the Master, the Grand Marshal entertained him and had tournaments for him, and at present comturs are visiting the prince, and now fresh guests are on the way to him."

Here he stopped and added after a while, —

" People say that the knights are visiting us, and Prince Ziemovit in Plotsk. They would like, of course, that in case of war our princes should help them and not the King of Poland; and if they are unable to bring the princes to act thus to induce them to remain aside quietly — But this will not happen."

" God grant that it will not! How could you stay at home? Your princes are connected with the Polish kingdom. They would not sit quietly, I think."

"They would not."

Zbyshko looked again at the foreign knights and at their peacock-plumes.

"Then are these going for that purpose?" asked he.

"The brothers of the Order, perhaps, for that purpose. Who knows?"

" And that third man?"

" The third is going because he is curious."

" He must be some considerable person."

" Yes! three wagons follow him with rich utensils, and he has nine attendants. God grant to close with such a man! It brings water to one's mouth."

" But can you not do it? "

"How! The prince commanded me to guard him. A hair will not fall from his head till he reaches Tsehanov."

" But if I should challenge them? They might like to do battle with me."

" You would have to do battle with me first, for while I live nothing of that sort will happen."

When Zbyshko heard this he looked in a friendly manner at the young noble, and said, —

" You understand what knightly honoris. I will not fight with you, for I am your friend; but in Tsehanov I shall find a cause against the Germans, God grant."

" In Tsehanov do what may please you. It will not pass there without tournaments; then it may go to the sharp edge, should the prince and the comturs give permission,"

" I have a board on which is a challenge to every man who will not admit that Panna Danusia, the daughter of Yurand, is the most beautiful and virtuous maiden on earth. But, do you know, people everywhere shrugged their shoulders, and laughed — "

" Yes, for that is a foreign custom, and, to tell the truth, stupid, which people among us do not know unless somewhere on the borders. So this man of Lorraine too attacked a noble on the road, commanding him to glorify some lady of his above others. But nobody understood him, and I would not let them do battle."

" How is that? He commanded to glorify his lady? Fear God! It must be that he has no shame in his eyes."

Here he glanced at the foreign knight, as if he wished to be sure how a man looked who had no shame in his eyes; but in his soul he had to confess that Foulk de Lorche did not seem at all like a common rascal. On the contrary, from beneath his raised visor gazed mild eyes; his face was youthful, but full of a certain pensiveness. Zbyshko saw with astonishment, also, that the knight's neck was thrice surrounded by a rope of hair which passed along his armor to one ankle, and ended by being wound around it three times.

""What kind of rope is he wearing?" inquired Zbyshko.

" I could not learn accurately myself, for they do not understand our language, except Brother Rotgier, who is able to say a couple of words, but not very well. I think, however, that that young knight has made a vow not to remove the rope till he has performed some great knightly deed. In the day he wears it over his armor, in the night on his bare body."

" Sanderus! " called Zbyshko, suddenly.

" At your service! " answered the German, approaching.

" Ask that knight who is the most virtuous and most wonderful maiden in the world."

" Who is the most wonderful and most virtuous maiden in the world ? " asked Sauderus.

" Ulrica de Elner! " answered De Lorche. And raising his eyes he sighed repeatedly.

Indignation stopped the breath in Zbyshko's breast when he heard blasphemy like that; great anger seized him and he reined in his stallion on the spot; but before he was able to speak Yendrek interposed his own horse between him and the foreigner, and said, —

" You will not quarrel here!"

Zbyshko turned again to the dealer in relics, and commanded, —

" Tell him from me that he loves an owl."

" My lord declares, noble knight, that you love an owl," repeated Sanderus, as an echo.

At this De Lorche dropped his reins, and with his right hand began to straighten and then to draw off his iron glove; next he threw it in the snow before Zbyshko, who beckoned to his Cheh to raise it with the point of his lance.

Hereupon Yendrek turned to Zbyshko with a face now threatening, and said, —

" You will not meet, I say, while my guard lasts. I will not permit you or him."

"But I did not challenge him, he challenged me."

Yes, but for the owl. This is enough for me, but if any one opposes — hei! I know how to twist a girdle."

" I do not wish to do battle with you."

li But you will have to meet me, for I have sworn to defend this man."

" How will it be? " asked the stubborn Zbyshko.

" It is not far to Tsehanov."

" But what will the German think? "

" Let your man tell him that there cannot be a meeting here, and that first there must be permission from the prince for 3*ou, and from the comturs for him."

" But if they will not give permission? "

" Then manage as you like. Enough has been said."

Zbyshko, seeing that there was no way out, and understanding that Yendrek could not permit a battle, called Sanderus again to explain to the Knight of Lorraine that they would give battle only when in the place for i£ De Lorche, on hearing the German's words, nodded in sign that he understood, and then extending his hand held Zbyshko's palm for a moment, and pressed it three times firmly, which, according to knightly custom, signified that they would do battle with each other wherever and whenever they could find opportunity. They moved then in apparent concord toward Tsehanov Castle, whose broad-topped towers were now visible on the background of the ruddy sky.

They entered during daylight; but before they had announced themselves at the castle gate and the bridge had been lowered, deep night had come.

They were received and entertained by Zbyshko's acquaintance, Pan Mikolai, who commanded the garrison made up of a handful of knights and three hundred unerring Kurpie bowmen.

Immediately after entering Zbyshko learned to his great vexation that the court was not present. The prince, wishing to entertain the comturs of Schytno and Yansbork, had arranged a great hunt in the Kurpie wilderness, to which the princess also and the ladies of her court had gone so as to lend greater brilliancy to the spectacle. Of ladies whom he knew Zbyshko found only Pani Ofka, the widow of Kryh of Yarzambek, who was housekeeper in the castle. She was very glad to see him, for from the time of their return from Cracow she had told every one who was willing or unwilling to listen, of his love for Danusia and his adventure with Lichtenstein. These narrations had won for her high esteem among the younger courtiers, and the damsels; hence she was grateful to Zbyshko, and tried now to console the young man in the sadness with which the absence of Danusia filled him.

"Thou wilt not know her," said she. "The maiden's years advance, the seams of her robe are splitting at the neck, for everything in her is growing. She is not a chit as before, and she loves thee differently now from what she did the first time. Let any one cry ' Zbyshko!' in her ear, it is as if some one pricked her with an awl. Such is the lot of us women, against which no help avails. Since it is at God's command— But thy uncle, thou say'st, is well? Why did he not come? — That is our fate. It is dreary for a woman alone in the world. It is a mercy from God that the girl has not broken her legs, for she climbs the tower daily and looks down the road. Every woman of us needs friendship — "

" I will only feed my horses, and go to her, even if I go in the night," answered Zbyshko.

" Do so, but take a guide from the castle, or thou wilt go astray in the wilderness."

Indeed at the supper, which Mikolai made ready for the guests, Zbyshko declared that he would follow the prince straightway, and begged for a guide. The road-weary brothers of the Order pushed up, after the feast, to the immense fireplaces in which whole logs of pine wood were burning, and decided to go only on the morrow, after they had rested. But De Lorche, when lie had inquired what the

question was, declared his wish to go with Zbyshko, saying that otherwise they might be late for the hunt, which he wished to see absolutely.

Then he approached Zbyshko, and extending his hand to him pressed his palm thrice again.

THE KNIGHTS OF THE CROSS. 225

CHAPTEE XVII.

BUT it was not to come this time either to a battle, for Pan Mikolai, learning from Yendrek of the question between them, took his word from each that he would not do battle without knowledge of the prince and the comturs; in case of opposition he threatened to close the gates. Zbyshko desired to see Danusia at the earliest, hence he dared not oppose; and De Lorche, who fought willingly when there was need, was not bloodthirsty, and took an oath readily on his knightly honor, that he would wait for permission from the prince, all the more that acting otherwise he might fear to offend him. The Knight of Lorraine, who had heard many songs about tournaments, liked brilliant assemblies and showy solemnities; he wished to combat in presence of court dignitaries and ladies, for he thought that his victory would thus obtain greater fame, and that thus he would win golden spurs the more easily. Moreover, the country and the people roused his curiosity; hence delay pleased him, especially as Mikolai, who had passed whole years in captivity among Germans and was able to talk easily with foreigners, told wonders of the prince's hunts, and of various beasts unknown in western regions. So De Lorche started with Zbyshko about midnight for Prasnysh, having his own numerous retinue and people, with torches as a defence against wolves, which during winter collected in countless numbers, and might show themselves terrible, even for more than ten horsemen, though armed in the best manner possible. At the south side of Tsehanov there was no lack of forests, either, which not far beyond Prasnysh were lost in the giant Kurpie wilderness, which joined on the east with the impenetrable forests of Podlasie and Farther Lithuania. Somewhat previous to that time the wild Lithuanians, avoiding, however, the terrible Kurpie, came out by those forests, usually to Mazovia. In 1337 they came to Tsehanov and destroyed it. De Lorche listened with the utmost curiosity to narratives of this event told by the old guide, Matsko of Turoboy, for he was burning in soul with desire to measure himself with Lithuanians, whom he, like other knights of the West, considered Saracens. He had come to those

VOL. I.— 15

regions for an expedition with the Knights of the Cross, wishing to win glory, and also salvation for his soul. While on the road he thought that war, even with the Mazovians, as a people half pagan, would secure him a plenary indulgence. He hardly believed his eyes, therefore, when on his arrival in Mazovia he saw churches in the towns, crosses on the towers, priests, knights with sacred emblems on their armor, and a people turbulent, it is true, passionate, ready for quarrel and battle, but Christian, and in no way more given to robbery than the Germans through whose country the young knight had passed. When they told him, therefore, that those people had confessed Christ for generations, he knew not what to think of the Knights of the Cross; when he learned that Lithuania too had been baptized by the late queen, his astonishment, and at the same time his sorrow, had no bounds.

He asked Matsko then if in those forests to which they were going there were not dragons to which people were forced to offer maidens, and with which it was possible to fight. But Matsko's reply in this regard too caused complete disappointment.

" In the forests live various good beasts, such as wolves, bisons, wild bulls, and bears; against these there is plenty oi work," answered the Mazovian. " It may be too that foul spirits dwell in the swamps, but I have not heard of dragons; even if there were some, surely we should not give them maidens, but should go in a crowd against them. And even had there been dragons here long ago, the Kurpie would be wearing girdles of their skin now."

" What kind of people are the Kurpie, and cannot one fight with them ? "

" Yes, that is possible, but it is not healthy," answered Matsko; " and finally it does not become a knight, since the Kurpie are peasants."

"The Swiss also are peasants. Do they recognize Christ?"

" There are none in Mazovia who do not, and they are our people, subject to the prince. But you have seen the bowmen at the castle. Those are Kurpie; there are no better bowmen on earth."

" The English and Scotch whom I saw at the Burgundian court — "

" I saw them also in Malborg," interrupted the Mazovian. '• Sturdy fellows, but may God never let them stand against

the Kurpie! Among the Kurpie a boy of seven years gets nothing to eat till he shoots down his food from the top of a pine-tree."

" Of what are ye talking? " asked on a sudden Zbyshko, whose ears had been struck frequently by the word "Kurpie."

" We are talking of the Kurpie and the English bowmen. This knight says that the English, and therefore the Scotch, surpass all."

" I, too, saw them at Vilno. Oh, pshaw! I heard their arrows around my ears. There, too, from all countries were knights who declared that they would eat us without salt; but when they had tried us once and a second time they lost desire for the food."

Matsko laughed, and repeated Zbyshko's words to De Lorche.

" That was mentioned at various courts," replied the Knight of Lorraine; " the bravery of your knights was praised, but they were blamed because they defend pagans against the cross."

" We defended against invasion and injustice a people who wanted baptism. The

Germans wished to hide them behind paganism, so as to have an excuse for war."

" God will judge them," said De Lorche.

" And He may judge them soon," replied Matsko.

But the Knight of Lorraine, hearing that Zbyshko had fought at Vilno made inquiries of Matsko, because tidings of knightly battles and duels fought there had gone about the world widely. The imagination of Western warriors was roused, especially by that duel in which four French and four Polish knights had engaged. So De Lorche began now to look with more esteem on Zbyshko as a man who had taken part in such famous battles; and he rejoiced in heart that he would have to meet no common person.

They went on in apparent concord, showing politeness to each other at halting-places and entertaining each other with wine, of which De Lorche had considerable supplies in his wagons. When, from conversation between him and Matsko, it turned out that Ulrica de Elner was not a maiden, but a matron forty years old, with six children, Zbyshko's pride was the more indignant that that strange foreigner not only dared to compare an " old woman " to Danusia, but to exact superiority. He thought, however, that perhaps the man was not in full mind, that he was one for whom a dark chamber and whips would be better than a journey through the world,

and this thought restrained in him an outburst of immediate anger.

" Think you not," said he to Matsko, " that the evil spirit has disturbed his reason? The devil may be sitting in his head, like a worm in a nut kernel, and may be ready in the night to jump out of him and into one of us. We ought to be careful."

Matsko opposed this, it is true, but still began to look with a certain dread at the Knight of Lorraine.

" Sometimes it happens," said he at last, " that a hundred and more of them are sitting in a possessed man, and if crowded they are glad to seek residence in another. The worst devil also is one sent in by a woman." Then he turned to the knight on a sudden. "Praised be Jesus Christ!" said he.

" I, too, praise Him," answered De Lorche, with astonishment.

Matsko was set at rest perfectly.

"Well, you see," said he, "if the evil one had been in him he would have foamed at the mouth- right away, or the devil would have thrown him to the earth, for I broke out to him on a sudden. We may travel on."

So they moved forward without fear. From Tsehanov to Prasnysh was not very far; in summer a courier on a good horse might in two hours pass over the road between the two places. But they went much more slowly because of the night, the halts, and the snowdrifts in the forest; and since they had set out considerably after midnight, they arrived about daybreak at the prince's hunting house, which was beyond Prasnysh, on the brink of the forest. The house stood almost resting on the wilderness, strong, low, built of wood, but having glass panes in its windows. Before the house were two sheds for horses, and a well-sweep; around the house was a crowd of huts, made hastily from pine branches, and tents formed of skins. In the gray of dawn fires glittered brightly; in front of the tents, and around them, were huntsmen in sheepskin coats, the wool outside, in fox, wolf, and bear skin mantles. To De Lorche it seemed as if he were looking at savage beasts on two legs before the fire, for the greater number of those people wore caps made of skins from the heads of wild animals. Some were leaning on spears, others on crossbows; some were occupied in making enormous rope nets, others were turning over the coals immense quarters of bisons and elks, intended evidently for

the morning meal. The glitter of the flame fell on the snow, lighting up also those wild forms, veiled somewhat by the smoke of the fires, the cloud of breaths, and the steam which rose from roasting meat. Beyond them were visible the ruddy-colored trunks of giant pines, and new crowds of people, the number of which astonished the Knight of Lorraine, unaccustomed to the sight of such hunting multitudes.

" Your princes go to a hunt as to a war," said he.

" As you see," answered Matsko of Turoboy, " they lack neither hunting gear nor people. These are the prince's beaters, but there are others also who come from the depth of the wilderness to trade."

" What shall we do?" interrupted Zbyshko; "they are asleep in the house yet."

" Wait till they wake," answered Matsko. " We will not strike the doors and wake our lord the prince."

So saying, he conducted them to a fire near which the Kurpie threw down bisou and bear skins, and then began promptly to entertain them with steaming meat. Hearing foreign speech, they crowded to look at the German. Soon it was spread about by Zbyshko's retinue that the stranger was a knight "from beyond the sea," and then they so crowded about that Matsko had to use his authority to save the foreigner from overmuch curiosity. In the crowd De Lorche noticed women dressed in skins also, but ruddy as apples and uncommonly good-looking ; so he inquired if they took part in hunts also.

Matsko explained that they did not belong to the hunts, but that they came with the beatei'S through female curiosity, or as to a fair to buy local products and sell the wealth of the forest. Such was the case in reality. That house of the prince was a centre around which, even during his absence, two elements met, — those of the town and the forest. The Kurpie did not like to go forth from their wilderness, for they felt strange without the sound of trees above their heads; so the people of Prasnysh took to that edge of the forest their renowned beer; flour ground in local windmills or in watermills on the Vengerka; salt, rare in the forest and sought for with eagerness; iron implements, straps, and similar products of industry. In return they received skins, costly furs, dried mushrooms, nuts, healing herbs, or pieces of amber found without too much trouble among the Kurpie. So a continual market was active around the house of Prince Yanush. The activity was intensified

230 THE KNIGHTS OF THE CROSS.

during the prince's hunts, when duty and curiosity brought out people who dwelt in the depths of the forests.

De Lorche listened to Matsko's narrations, looking with interest at the forms of the beaters, who, living in wholesome air and nourished mainly on flesh, as were most peasants for that matter in those days, astonished foreign travellers more than once by their strength and great stature. But Zbyshko, sitting near the fire, looked unceasingly at the doors and windows of the house, barely able to stay in one place. One window was lighted, evidently that of the kitchen, for smoke came out through cracks between panes not sufficiently fastened. Other windows were dark, gleaming only from daylight, which grew whiter every instant, and silvered with growing intensity the snowy wilderness behind the hunting-house. In small doors, cut in the side walls of the building, appeared in time servants in the prince's colors, who with pails or pots on their shoulders ran to the wells for water. When inquiry was made of these servants if all were sleeping yet, they answered that the court, wearied by yesterday's hunt, was still resting, but that food for the early meal to be eaten before they started was cooking.

In fact, through the kitchen windows the odor of meat and saffron began to issue and spread far about among the fires. At last the main door squeaked and opened, discovering the interior of a hall brightly lighted, and out to the porch came a man in whom at first glance Zbyshko recognized a chorister whom he had seen among Princess Anna's servants in Cracow. At that sight, without waiting for De Lorche or Matsko, he sprang toward the house with such impetus that the Knight of Lorraine was astounded.

" What has happened to that youthful knight? "inquired he.

" Nothing," answered Matsko ; " but he loves a damsel of the princess and would like to see her at the earliest."

" Ah! " answered De Lorche, putting both hands to his heart. And raising his eyes he sighed time after time, so sadly that Matsko shrugged his shoulders and said inwardly, —

" Is lie sighing in that way to his old woman? Is he not really unsound in mind?"

Meanwhile he conducted him to the house, and both found themselves in a spacious hall adorned with great horns of bisons, elks, wild bulls and deer, and illuminated by dry logs blazing on an immense fireplace. In the centre stood a table covered with matting and plates ready for food.

Barely a few courtiers were present, with whom Zbyshko was talking. Matsko made them acquainted immediately with De Lorche, but as they had no knowledge of German, he had himself to entertain the knight further. But every moment new courtiers came, — for the greater part splendid fellows, untrained yet, but large, broad-shouldered, yellow-haired, dressed as if for the wilderness.

Those who were acquainted with Zbyshko and knew of his Cracow adventure greeted him as an old friend, and it was evident that he enjoyed consideration among them. Some looked on him with that wonder with which people look on a man over whose neck the axe of the executioner has been lifted. Round about were heard voices: " Yes, the princess is here! Yurand's daughter is here, thou wilt see her at once, my clear fellow." " And thou wilt go to the hunt with us?" AVith that entered two guests, Knights of the Cross, — Brother Hugo von Danveld, starosta in Ortelsburg, or in Schytno, whose relative had in his time been Marshal; and Siegfried von Lowe, whose family had rendered service in the Order,—he was bailiff of Yansbork. The first was rather young yet, but fat, — he had the face of a crafty beer-guzzler, with moist and thick lips; the other was tall, with stern though noble features.

It seemed to Zbyshko that he had seen Danveld somewhere with Prince Yitold, — that Henry, Bishop of Plotsk, had unhorsed him in a tournament; but this recollection was disturbed by the entrance of Prince Yanush, to whom courtiers and Knights of the Cross made obeisance. De Lorche and the comturs and Zbyshko approached him; he greeted them affably, but with dignity on his beardless, rustic face, surrounded with hair cut evenly on the forehead, but hanging to the shoulders on both sides.

Soon trumpets thundered outside in sign that the prince was ready to take his seat at the table: they thundered once, twice, thrice. The third time the heavy door on the right of the dining-hall opened, and in it appeared Princess Anna, having at her side a marvellous golden-haired maiden with a lute hanging from her shoulder.

Seeing her, Zbyshko pushed forward, and putting his joined hands to his lips, dropped on both knees in a posture full of respect and homage.

At this sight a murmur rose in the hall, for Zbyshko's act had astonished the Mazovians, and some of them were even offended.

" By my faith," said some of the older men, " he has learned that custom surely from knights beyond the sea, and perhaps from real pagans, for it does not exist even among Germans." "That is not strange," thought the younger ones, " for he owes his life to the maiden."

The princess and Dauusia did not recognize Zbyshko immediately, for he had knelt with his back toward the fire and his face was shaded. Princess Anna thought at the first moment that he was a courtier who had failed in duty to the prince and was begging her intercession ; but Dauusia, who had a quicker glance, pushed forth a step, and inclining her bright head, cried suddenly in a voice thin and piercing, —

" Zbyshko!"

Then, without thinking that the whole court and the foreign guests were looking at her, she sprang like a deer toward the j'oung knight, and seizing him with her arms fell to kissing his eyes, his lips, his cheeks, nestling up to him and piping meanwhile with great delight, till the Mazovians thundered forth in one great burst of laughter, and the princess drew her to herself by the collar. Danusia looked then at the people, and, confused terribly, hid behind the princess with equal swiftness, covering herself with the folds of her robe so that barely the tip of her head remained visible.

Zbyshko embraced Princess Anna's feet; she raised him, greeted him, and at the same time inquired about Matsko, — was he dead, or was he alive yet ; if alive, had he come to Mazovia? Zbyshko answered those questions with no very great presence of mind, for, bending to one side and the other, he tried to see behind the princess Danusia, who thrust her head out from that lady's robe and then dived into its folds again. The Mazovians seized their sides at sight of this, even the prince himself laughed, till at last the hot dishes were brought and the delighted lady turned to Zbyshko with these words, —

4 ' Serve us, dear attendant, and God grant not only at this table, but forever."

Then she said, — ·

" But thoti, tortured fly, crawl out from behind my robe, or thou wilt tear it to pieces."

Danusia came out flushed, confused, raising from moment to moment on Zbyshko eyes that were frightened, put to shame, and curious, and so marvellous that the heart was not onlv melting in him but in other men. Hugo von Danveld

put his hand to his thick moist lips repeatedly; De Lorche was astonished, raised both hands, and inquired, —

" By Saint lago of Compostello, who is that maiden? "

To this Dauveld, who with his fatness was of low stature, rose a finger's length, and said in the ear of the Knight of Lorraine, —

" The devil's daughter."

De Lorche looked at him, blinked, then frowned, and said with nasal accent, —

" He is not a true knight who calumniates beauty."

" I wear golden spurs, and I am a monk," replied Hugo, with haughtiness.

So great was the respect for belted knights that De Lorche dropped his head ; but after a while he replied, —

" I am a blood relative of the princes of Brabant."

"Pax! Pax! (Peace! Peace!)," said the Knight of the Cross. " Honor to the powerful princes and friends of the Order, from whose hands you will receive golden spurs shortly. I do not deny beauty to that maiden, but hear who her father is."

He was not able, however, to tell, for at that moment Prince Yanush took his seat, and learning previously from the Starosta of Yansbork of the great connections of De Lorche, he gave a sign to him to sit near. Opposite Prince Yanush sat the princess with Danusia. Zbyshko took his place, as in Cracow, behind their chairs, at their service. Danusia held her head over the dish as low as possible, for she felt shame in the presence of people, but a little to one side, so that Zbyshko might see her face. He looked eagerly and with rapture at her small bright head, at her rosy cheeks, at her shoulders dressed in a closely fitting garment, — shoulders which had ceased to be those of a child, — and he felt rising in him, as it were, a river of new love which would inundate his whole being. He felt also on his eyes, on his lips, on his face her recent kisses. She had given them before as a sister to a brother, and he had received them as from a dear child. Now at the fresh remembrance of them this happened which happened when he was with Yagenka, — shivers seized him, and a faintness possessed him beneath which was hidden a warmth, like a fire covered with ashes. Danusia seemed to him an entirely grown lady, for she had bloomed in reality and matured. Besides, so much had been said in her presence of love, and so frequently, that as a bunch of flowers warmed with sun rays grows

beautiful and opens more and more, so her eyes were opened to love, and in consequence there was something in her then which had not been there previously, — a certain beauty no longer a child's beauty, a certain mighty attraction, intoxicating, issuing from her as heat from a flame or as odor from a rose.

Zbyshko felt this, but did not give himself account of it, for he forgot himself. He forgot even that he had to serve at the table. He did not see that the courtiers were looking at him, nudging each other with their elbows, showing Danusia and him to one another, and laughing; neither did he notice De Lorche's face, as it were petrified by amazement, nor the staring eyes of Danveld, which were fixed on Danusia, and reflecting the flame of the chimney seemed as red and as flashing as the eyes of a wolf. He recovered only when the trumpet sounded again in sign that it was time for the wilderness, and when Princess Anna turned to him and said, —

" Thou wilt go with us, so as to be able to have pleasure, and speak to the maiden of love; to this I shall be glad to listen."

She left the table then with Danusia, so as to be ready to mount. Zbyshko sprang to the yard where men were holding horses covered with hoar frost, and snorting. These were for the prince and princess, guests, and courtiers. In the yard there were not so many people as before, for the beaters had gone out in advance with snares, and had vanished in the wilderness. The fires had died down ; day had appeared, bright, frosty, the snow squeaked under foot; and the trees, moved by a light breeze, scattered dry, glittering frost flakes.

The prince came out promptly and mounted ; he was followed by an attendant with a crossbow, and a spear so heavy and long that few men could wield it. Prince Yauush Avielded it, however, with ease, for he, like other Mazovian Piasts, possessed uncommon strength. There were even women of that stock, who in marrying foreign princes wound around on their fingers at the wedding feast broad plates of iron. Near the prince were two other attendants ready to aid in emergency ; these were chosen from all heirs in the lands of Tsehanov and Warsaw, and they were tremendous to look at, with shoulders like forest trees. De Lorche, who had come from afar, looked on these men with amazement.

Now the princess and Danusia came out, both wearing hoods of white weasel-skin. The undegenerate daughter of Keistut knew better how to " sew" with an arrow than a needle. So behind her was borne a crossbow a little lighter than others, and adorned. Zbyshko, kneeling on the snow, held out his hand, on which the lady rested her foot when mounting; Danusia he raised to the saddle as he had Yagenka in Bogdauets; and they rode on.

The retinue stretched out like a long snake, turned to the right from the house, varied and shining on the border of the wilderness, like a colored selvage on the edge of black cloth, and then began to sink into it slowly.

They were rather deep in the forest when the princess said, turning to Zbyshko, —

" Why dost thou not talk? Now talk to her."

Zbyshko, though thus encouraged, was silent awhile yet, since a certain irresolution had mastered him; and only after the length of one or two Hail Marys did he say, —

" Danusia! "

"What, Zbyshko?"

" I love thee so."

Here he stopped to seek words which were difficult to find, for though he had knelt like a foreign knight before Danusia, though he showed her honor in every way, and strove to avoid common expressions, he strove in vain for courtliness, since his soul being full he could only speak simply. Hence he said, after a while, —

" I love thee so that my breath stops! "

She raised on him from beneath her weasel hood blue eyes, and a face which the cold forest breeze had made rosy.

"And I, Zbyshko!" said she, as if in haste. And she covered her eyes with their lids, for she knew then what love was.

" Hei, thou my little one! hei, thou my maiden! " said Zbyshko.

And again he was silent from emotion and happiness; but the kind and also curious princess came to aid him a second time.

" Tell her," said she, " how dreary it was for thee without her, and when there is a thicket, thou mightst even kiss her on the lips. I shall not be angry, for that is the best way to give witness of thy love."

So he began to tell her how dreary his life had been without her in Bogdanets while he was caring for Matsko, and while

236 THE KNIGHTS OF THE CROSS.

be was among the " neighbors." Of Yagenka the cunning a voider uttered no word. As to the rest he spoke truly, for at that moment he so loved the fair Danusia that he would have seized her, taken her over on to his horse, kept her before him, and held her at his breast.

He did not dare to do this; but when the next thicket separated them from the courtiers and the guests riding behind, he bent toward her, put his arm around her waist, and hid his face in the weasel-skin hood, testifying to his love by that act.

But as in winter there are no leaves on hazel nut bushes, Danveld and De Lorche saw him; courtiers saw him also, and began to talk among themselves.

44 He kissed her in presence of the princess! I believe that the lady will soon have the wedding."

44 He is a gallant fellow, but Yurand's blood is sulphurous."

44 Flint and steel, though the girl seems like a dove. Sparks will fly from them, never fear! He has fastened a claw to the quick in her."

So they conversed, laughing; but Hugo turned to De Lorche his goatish, malignant, lustful face.

44 Could you wish that some Merlin would change you by magic into that young knight?" asked he.

' 4 And you ? " inquired De Lorche.

At this the Knight of the Cross, in whom evidently envy and desire were now boiling, jerked his horse with impatient hand, and answered, —

" On my soul! — "

In that moment, however, he recollected himself, and inclining added —

" I am a monk who has vowed chastity."

And he looked quickly at De Lorche, fearing lest he might see a smile on his face; for the Order had an evil fame in the world on that point, and Danveld among monks had the worst. Some j*ears before, when assistant starosta in Sam-bria, complaints had become so loud against him that in spite of every condescension with which such things were regarded in Malborg they had to transfer him to the post of commander in Schytno. Having arrived some days before with a secret commission to the court of Prince Yanush, and seeing the charming daughter of Yurand, he was inflamed with desire for her, against which Danusia's age was no curb, for in those days girls younger than she were given in marriage. But since at the same time Hugo knew of what stock

she was, and since in his mind the name of Yurand connected her with dreadful reminiscences, his desire rose on the basis of savage hatred.

De Lorche fell to inquiring about those events.

" You have called this beautiful maiden ' devil's daughter ; ' why have you called her thus ? "

Hugo narrated then the history of Zlotoria, — how at the building of the castle they had seized the prince and his court, how in that affair the girl's mother had perished, and how Yuraud had avenged her since that time on all Knights of the Cross in a fearful manner. During the narrative Hugo's hatred burst forth like a flame, since for this feeling he had personal reasons also. He had met Yurand two years before, but at sight of the terrible "Wild boar of Spyhov " the heart fell in him, for the first time in life, so contemptibly that he deserted two relatives, deserted his attendants, left his plunder, and fled a whole day like a madman, till he reached Schytno, where he was sick a long time from fright. When he returned to health the Grand Marshal of the Order brought him to trial. The sentence of the knightly court released him, it is true, for Hugo swore, on the cross and his honor, that an enraged horse had borne him away from the field of battle; but it closed his path to higher dignities in the Order. In presence of De Lorche the Knight of the Cross was silent about these events; but he made so many complaints against the cruelty of Yurand and the insolence of the whole Polish nation, that what he said could hardly find place in the head of the Knight of Lorraine.

" But," said De Lorche, after a while, " we are with Mazo-vians, not Poles."

" The principality is separate, but the people are the same," answered Hugo; "their vileness and hatred of the Order are equal. God grant the German sword to destroy the whole race ! "

"You speak truly, lord; for, just think, this prince, apparently honorable, dared to build a hostile castle on your land; I have never heard of such lawlessness, even among pagans."

" The castle was hostile, but Zlotoria is on his land, not ours."

" Then, glory to Christ who gave you the victory. How did that war end ? "

" There was no war at the time."

" And did you gain a victory at Zlotoria? "

" Just in this did God bless us, that the prince was without an army; he had only a court and women."

How was that?" asked De Lorche, looking at the knight with astonishment. " Then you fell upon women in time of peace, and upon the prince who was building a castle on his own land?"

" When the glory of the Order and Christianity are in question no deeds are dishonorable."

"And that terrible knight is only avenging his young wife killed in time of peace by you?"

"Whoso raises a hand against a Knight of the Cross is a son of darkness."

De Lorche was amazed when he heard this, but he had no time to answer Danveld, for they had ridden out onto a broad, snowy, weed-covered plain, on which the prince had alighted from his horse, and after him others began to dismount.

Skilled foresters under the lead of the chief huntsman disposed guests and the court in a long row at the edge of the plain, so that being in concealment themselves they had in front of them an empty space which facilitated shooting from crossbows and bows. The two shorter sides of the plain were beset with snares, behind which were woodmen, whose duty it was to turn a beast toward the hunters, or if it would not be frightened it became entangled in the snares and they killed it with spears.

Innumerable crowds of Kurpie, disposed skilfully in a so-called circle, were to drive out every living creature to the plain from the depth of the forest.

Beyond the hunters was a net, so that any beast which succeeded in passing the line might be caught in its meshes, and killed.

The prince stood in the centre of the line, in a slight depression which passed through the whole width of the plain. The chief huntsman, Mrokota of Motsarzev, chose this position for him, knowing that just there the largest beasts would seek escape from the circle. The prince had a crossbow in his hand, near his side stood against a tree a heavy spear, and a little behind him were two " defenders " with axes on their shoulders, immense fellows, as bulky as trees of the forest, who besides axes had drawn crossbows, to be given to the prince should he need them.

The princess and Danusia did not dismount; the prince never permitted that, because of danger from wild bulls and

bisons, before whose rage it was harder in case of attack to escape on foot than on horseback. De Lorche, though invited by the prince to take a place at his right, begged permission to remain on horseback to defend the ladies, and took his position at some distance from the princess, looking like a long bar with a knight's spear, at which the Mazovians smiled jeeringly in silence, as at a weapon of small value in hunting.

Zbyshko planted his spear in the snow, put his crossbow on his shoulder, and standing near Danusia's horse, raised his head and whispered to her; at moments he embraced her feet and kissed her knees, for he did not hide his love now at all from people. He ceased only when Mrokota, who in the wilderness made bold to reprimand the prince even, enjoined silence severely.

Meanwhile far, far away in the depth of the wilderness, were heard the horns of the Kurpie, which were answered briefly from the plain by the shrill sound of winding trumpets ; then followed perfect silence. Only, at long intervals, did a grossbeak cry in the top of a pine tree. Sometimes men in the circle croaked like ravens. The hunters strained their eyes over the empty space, on which a breeze moved the frost-covered weeds and the leafless clumps of brush, — each waiting with impatience to see what beast would be first to appear on the snow. In general a rich and splendid hunt was predicted, for the wilderness was swarming with bisons, wild bulls, and wild boars.

The Kurpie had smoked out from their dens a certain number of bears, which thus roused went through the thickets, mad, alert, and hungry, feeling that they would soon have to struggle, not for a quiet winter's sleep, but for life.

There was still a long time of waiting, since the men who were urging the beasts to the clasps of the circle, and to the plain, occupied an enormous extent of forest, and were coming from such a distance that the ears of hunters were not touched even by the barking of dogs, which immediately after the sounding of trumpets were freed from their leashes. One of these dogs, freed evidently too early, or wandering apart after men, appeared on the plain, and having run over all of it with his nose to the ground, passed between the hunters. Again the place was empty and silent; only the woodmen cawed continually like ravens, announcing in this way that work would begin soon.

In fact, after an interval long enough to repeat a few Our

Fathers, at the edge appeared wolves, which, as the most wary, tried first to escape from the circle. Of these there were few. After they had come out on the plain and caught the odor of people, they plunged into the forest anew, seeking evidently another escape. Wild boars sprang out next and ran in a long black chain over the snowy expanse, seeming in the distance like a drove of tame pigs, which at the call of a woman hurry homeward with shaking ears. But that chain halted, listened, scented, turned and listened again, bore to one side toward the snares, sniffed the woodmen, moved again toward the hunters, grunting, approaching more and more cautiously, but still nearer, till at last the sound of iron was heard on the crossbows, then the whiz of arrows, and the first blood stained the white, snowy surface.

A piercing squeal was heard and the drove scattered, as if struck by lightning; some went at random straightforward, some rushed toward the snares, some ran either singly or in small groups, mixing among other beasts with which the plain was now swarming. At this time was heard clearly the sound of horns, the barking of dogs, and the distant noise of men advancing along the main line from the depth of the forest. The beasts of the wilderness, driven from both sides by the extended wings of the circle, filled the forest plain more and more densely. No sight like that could be seen in foreign parts, or even in other Polish lands, where there were no such wild forests as in Mazovia. The Knights of the Cross, though they had been in Lithuania, where at times bisons by striking an army produced confusion in it, wondered not a little at the immense number of beasts, but especially did De Lorche wonder. Standing near the princess and the damsels, like a stork on the watch, and unable to speak with any one, he had begun to be annoyed, while freezing in his armor, and thinking that the hunt was a failure. At last he saw before him whole herds of fleet-footed deer, yellow stags, and elks with weighty-horned heads, mingled together, storming over the plain, blinded with fear and seeking in vain for an exit.

The princess, in whom at sight of this the blood of her father Keistut began to play, sent shaft after shaft into that many-colored throng, and screamed with delight when a stricken deer or an elk rose in its career, then fell heavily and dug the snow with its feet. Damsels bent their faces often toward the crossbows, for the ardor of hunting had seized every person.

Zbysbko alone had no thought for hunting, but leaning his elbow on Danusia's knees, and his head on his palm, he gazed into her eyes; and she, half smiling, half abashed, tried to close his eyelids with her fingers, as if unable to endure such a glance.

De Lorche's attention was occupied by a bear, enormous, with gray legs and shoulders, which had come out of the weeds unexpectedly near the hunters. The prince sent a bolt from his crossbow, and then attacked the beast with a spear. When the bear, roaring awfully, rose on his hind legs the prince pierced him before the eyes of the whole court, so quickly and surely that neither of the two " defenders " had need of an axe.

The young Knight of Lorraine thought then that there were not many lords in the castles at which he had stopped on his journey who would have had courage for amusement like that, and that with such princes and such people the Order might have a difficult adventure, and pass through grievous hours sometime. But farther on he saw pierced in that same way by other men terrible, immense, white-tusked boars, far larger and more savage than any in Lower Lorraine or the forests of Germany. Never had he seen such trained hunters, nor any so confident in the strength of their hands, nor such spear-thrusts. As a man of experience, he concluded that all those people living in boundless forests were accustomed from years of childhood to the crossbow and spear, hence they attained greater skill in the use of them than others.

At last the plain was strewn thickly with bodies of all kinds of beasts, but it was far to the end of the hunt yet. The most interesting and also the most dangerous moment was coming, for the circle had just pressed to the open space a number of tens of wild bulls and bisons. Though in the forest these lived apart usually, they went now mixed together, but not at all headlong from fear; they were rather threatening than terrified. They advanced not very quickly, as if confident, in the feeling of immense power, that they would break every obstacle and pass; the earth resounded beneath the weight of them. Bearded bulls, going in crowds with their heads close to the ground, halted at moments as if considering in what direction to strike. From their monstrous lungs went forth deep roars which were like underground thunder. From their nostrils issued steam, and digging the snow with their fore feet they seemed

VOL. I. 16

to be looking with bloody eyes from beneath their shaggy manes for a hidden enemy.

Meanwhile the woodmen raised a mighty shout, to which answer was given from the main line and from the wings of the circle by hundreds of loud voices; horns and whistles made an uproar; the wilderness quivered to its remotest depths, and at the same moment the dogs of the Kurpie rushed out to the plain with a fearful tumult, and chased along on the trail. The sight of them roused rage in the twinkle of an eye among female beasts which had their young with them. The herd of animals, going hitherto slowly, scattered over the whole plain in mad haste. A wild bull, tawny, gigantic, almost monstrous, surpassing bisons in size, rushed with great springs toward the line of hunters; he turned toward the right side of the plain, then, seeing horses some tens of yards distant, among the trees, he halted, and roaring, began to plough the earth with his horns, as if rousing himself to spring forward and fight.

At this sight the woodmen raised a still greater shout. In the line of hunters were heard piercing voices, —

" The princess ! the princess! Save the princess! "

Zbyshko grasped his spear planted in the snow and sprang to the edge of the forest; after him went a number of Lithuanians ready to die in defence of the daughter of Keistut; meanwhile a crossbow sounded in the hands of the lady, a shaft whistled, and, flying over the inclined head of the bull, it fastened in his neck.

" He has got it!" cried the princess; "he will come no nearer! "

But a roar so dreadful that horses rose on their haunches drowned further words of hers. The bull hurled himself like a storm straight against the princess. But suddenly, and with no less impetus, the manful De Lorche rushed forth from among the trees; bent forward on his horse, with lance lowered as in a knightly tournament, he bore straight on the animal. In one twinkle of an eye those present saw buried in the neck of the bull a lance which bent like a reed and broke into small splinters, then the immense horned head disappeared altogether under the belly of De Lorche's horse, and before any one present could utter a cry, the steed and the rider flew through the air as if sent from a sling.

The horse, falling on his side, began in mortal agony to struggle with his feet, entangling them in his own intestines,

which had dropped from the body. De Lorche lay near by motionless, looking like an iron wedge on the snow. The wild bull seemed for an instant to hesitate whether to pass them and strike other horses; but having his first victims there before him, he turned again and began to gloat over the hapless steed, crushing him with his head, and tearing in rage the open belly with his horns.

People rushed out from the forest, however, to save the foreign knight. Zbyshko, concerned for the safety of the princess and Danusia, came first, and thrust in his sharp spear behind the foreleg of the beast. But he struck with such force that the handle, when the bull turned suddenly, broke in his hand, and he himself fell face forward on the snow.

"He is lost! he is lost!" cried Mazovians, rushing to aid him.

Meanwhile the bull's head had covered Zbyshko and was pressing him to the earth. From the prince's side two powerful "defenders" rushed up; but help would have been late had not Hlava, the man given by Yagenka, preceded them luckily. He ran ahead, and raising a broad-axe with both hands cut the bent neck of the bull right behind his horns.

The blow was so terrible that the beast dropped as if struck by lightning, his backbone was severed and his head half chopped away ; but in falling he pressed Zbyshko. Both "defenders" pulled off the monstrous body in a twinkle, but meanwhile the princess and Danusia sprang from their horses, and dumb with fright, ran to Zbysbko. Pale, covered with his own blood and the blood of the bull, he raised himself somewhat, tried to stand, but staggered, fell on his knees, and leaning on his hand could utter only one word:

" Danusia! "

Then he threw out blood through his mouth, and darkness embraced his head. Danusia, standing at his back, seized his arms, but unable to hold him, cried for assistance. People surrounded him from all sides, rubbed him with snow, poured wine into his mouth ; finally the chief hunter, Mrokota, gave command to put him on a cloak, and stay the blood-flow with soft pine punk.

" He will live if only a rib and not his spine is broken," said he, turning to the princess.

Meanwhile other damsels, assisted by hunters, were saving De Lorche. They turned him on every side, seeking on

his armor for dints or holes made by the horns of thft bull; but beyond traces of snow, packed in between joints of the armor, they could find nothing. The bull had taken revenge mainly on the horse, now dead, with all his entrails out under him ; De Lorche had not been struck. He had only fainted from the fall, and, as appeared later, his right arm was disjointed. When they removed his helmet and poured wine into his mouth, he opened his eyes straightway and regained consciousness. Seeing the anxious faces of young and comely damsels bent over him, he said in German, —

" Surely I am in paradise, and angels are above me."

The damsels did not understand what he said, it is true, but glad that he had recovered and spoken, they smiled at him, and, with the help of hunters, raised him from the snow. Feeling pain in his right arm he groaned; with his left he leaned on the arm of one of the " angels; " for a while he stood motionless, fearing to move a step, for he did not feel firm on his feet. Then he cast a glance, which was dull yet, over the field of struggle. He saw the yellow carcass of the bull, which near by seemed enormous. He saw Danusia wringing her hands over Zbyshko, and Zbyshko himself on a cloak.

" Did that knight come to aid me?" inquired he. u Is he alive ? "

" He is hurt seriously," answered one of the courtiers, who knew German.

" From this day forth I shall fight not against him, but for him," said the man of Lorraine.

At that moment Prince Yanush, who had been standing over Zbyshko, approached De Lorche and praised him, saying that by his daring deed he had guarded the princess and other ladies from great peril, and had even saved their lives, perhaps, for which, in addition to knightly rewards, he would be surrounded by fame among people then living, and among their descendants.

" In these effeminate times," said he, " fewer and fewer real knights pass through the world; be my guest, therefore, as long as is possible, or stay in Mazovia altogether, for you have won my favor, and you will win as easily the favor of people by your worthy deeds."

De Lorche's heart, eager for glory, was melted by these words; for when he considered that he had accomplished such a preponderant deed of knighthood, and won such praise in those distant Polish lands of which in the West such marvellous things were related, his delight was such that he hardly felt any pain in his disjointed arm. He understood that a knight who at the court of Brabant or Burgundy could say that he had saved at a hunt the life of Princess Anna of Mazovia, would walk in glory as. in sunlight. Under the influence of these thoughts, he wanted even to go directly to the princess and vow, on his knees, faithful service to her; but the lady herself and Danusia were busied with Zbyshko.

Zbyshko had regained consciousness again for a moment; but he only smiled at Danusia, raised his hand to his forehead, now covered with cold sweat, and fainted a second time. Experienced hunters, seeing his closed hands and open mouth, said that he would not recover; but the still more experienced Kurpie, many of whom carried on their persons marks of bears' claws, wild boars' tusks, or wild bulls' horns, gave better hope, asserting that the bull's horn had slipped along the knight's ribs ; that one or two ribs might be broken, but that his spine was safe; otherwise he could not have raised himself up for a moment. They showed also a snowdrift on the place where Zbyshko had fallen, that had saved him; for the beast, pressing him between his horns, was unable to crush either his breast or his back.

Unfortunately Father Vyshonek, Princess Anna's doctor, though usually at hunts, was not present; he was occupied at the house in baking wafers. The Cheh, learning this, hurried after him, but meanwhile the Kurpie carried Zbyshko on a cloak to the prince's house. Danusia wished to go on foot with him, but Princess Anna opposed, for the road was long, and in the forest depths was much snow; haste, therefore, was needed.

Danveld helped the girl to mount, and then riding near her, just behind the men who were carrying Zbyshko, spoke in Polish, in a suppressed voice, so that he could be heard by her only: —

"I have in Schytno a wonderful healing balsam, which I got from a hermit in the Hercynian forest, and which I could bring in three days."

"God will reward you," answered Danusia.

" God rewards every deed of mercy, but can I hope for pay from you also ? "

" What could I pay you? "

The Knight of the Cross pushed up near her with his horse;

evidently he wished to tell something, but hesitated, and only after a while did he say, —

" In the Order, besides brothers, there are sisters; one of them will bring the healing balsam, and then I will mention pay."

CHAPTEE XVIII.

FATHER VYSHONEK dressed Zbyshko's wound. He found only one rib broken, but the first day he could not answer for recovery, since he could not tell "whether the heart in the sick man was wrenched, or his liver torn." Toward evening so great a faintness seized De Lorche that he had to lie down. On the following day he could move neither hand nor foot without great pain in all his bones.

The princess and Danusia, with other damsels, attended the sick men, and prepared for them, according to directions of the priest, various ointments and herbs. Zbyshko was seriously wounded, and from time to time vomited blood, which alarmed the priest greatly. Still, he was conscious, and the next day, though very much weakened, when he learned from Danusia who it was to whom he was indebted for life, he called his Cheh, to thank and reward him. But he had to remember that Hlava had come from Yagenka, and that had it not been for her well-wishing heart he would have perished. This thought was to him even burdensome, for he felt that he never could repay the honest girl with good for good, and that he would be for her only the cause of suffering and terrible sadness. He said to himself, it is true, immediately after, "I cannot indeed hew myself in two," but at the bottom of his soul there remained, as it were, a reproach of conscience. The Cheh inflamed still more this internal disquiet.

" I swore to my lady," said he, " on my honor as a noble, to guard you, and I will do so without any reward. Not to me, but to her, are you indebted for rescue."

Zbyshko gave no answer, but began to breathe heavily. Hlava was silent for a while, then he said, —

" If you command me to hurry to Bogdanets, I will hurry. You might wish to see the old lord, for God knows what will happen you."

" What does the priest say ?" inquired Zbyshko.

" The priest says that he will know at the new moon, and there are four days to the new moon."

" Ei! there is no need to go to Bogdanets. Either I shall die before my uncle could come, or I shall recover."

"You might send even a letter to Bogdanets. Sanderns will write it all clearly. They would know about you, at least, and perhaps have a mass said."

" Leave me at present, for I am weak. If I die, thou wilt return to Zyh's house, and tell how it was; they will give money then for a mass there. And people will bury me here, or in Tsehanov."

" In Tsehanov, or in Prasnysh, for only Kurpie are buried in the forest, where wolves howl over them. I have heard from the servants, also, that the prince will go with the court in two days to Tsehanov, and thence to Warsaw."

"They will not desert me here," said Zbyshko.

In fact he had divined rightly, for the princess had gone that very day to the prince with the request to let her stay in the forest house with Danusia, the damsels, and the priest, who was opposed to the early removal of Zbyshko to Prasnysh.

De Lorche was considerably better in two days, and was 011 his feet. But learning that the "ladies" would remain, he remained also to accompany them on their return, and in case of a " Saracen" attack, to defend them from evil accident. Whence these " Saracens" were to come was a question which the gallant knight of Lorraine had not given himself. In the distant west, it is true, Lithuanians were called thus; from them, however, no danger could threaten the daughter of Keistut; she was the full sister of Vitold, and the cousin of Yagello, the " mighty king at Cracow."

But in spite of what he had heard in Mazovia of the christening of Lithuania, and the union of two crowns on the head of one sovereign, De Lorche had lived too long among Knights of the Cross not to believe that every evil might be expected from Lithuanians at all times. The

Knights of the Cross had told him this, and he had not entirely lost faith in the Order.

Meanwhile an event happened which fell as a shadow between the Knights of the Cross and Prince Yanush. On the day before the departure of the court, brothers Gottfried and Rotgier arrived; they had been in Tsehanov before; and with them came a certain De Fourcy as the herald of news unfavorable for Knights of the Cross. Behold, it had happened that foreign guests visiting with the starosta of Lubov, namely, he, De Fourcy, De Bregov, and Meinegger, all from families of previous merit in the Order, when they had heard of Yurand of Spyhov, not only were they not frightened, but they decided to entice the renowned warrior to the field and

convince themselves whether he was really as terrible as people declared him.

The starosta, it is true, opposed, referring to the peace between the Order and the princes of Mazovia; but at last, in the hope, perhaps, of freeing himself from a terrible neighbor, he determined not only to look at the affair through his fingers, but to let men at arms go also.

The knights sent a challenge to Yurand, who accepted it eagerly on condition that they would send away their men, and they three fight with him and two comrades on the very boundary of Prussia and Spyhov. When they were unwilling to dismiss their men at arms and withdraw from the lands of Spyhov, he fell upon them, slew their men at arms, thrust a spear through Meinegger, took Bregov prisoner and threw him into the dungeon of Spyhov. De Fourcy alone was unhurt, and after wandering three days through Mazo-vian forests, he learned from a tar-boiler that Knights of the Cross were tarrying in Tsehanov ; he made his way to these knights so as to complain with them to the majesty of the prince, pray for punishment, and a command to free Bregov.

These tidings obscured at once the good relations between Prince Yauush and the guests, for not only did the two brothers who arrived then, but also Danveld and Siegfried von Lowe demand of the prince insistently to do justice to the Order, free the boundary of a robber, and mete out punishment with usury for all his offences. Danveld, especially, having with Yurand his own old accounts, the remembrance of which burnt him with pain and with shame, demanded vengeance almost threateningly.

" A complaint will go to the Grand Master," said he, " and if we obtain no justice from your Princely Grace, he will be able to find it, even should all Mazovia take the part of that murderer."

The prince, though mild by nature, grew angry, and said:

" What justice are ye asking for? If Yurand had been the first to attack you, if he had burnt villages, driven away herds, and killed people, I should summon him to judgment, and measure out punishment. But it was ye who attacked him. Your starosta let armed men go on the expedition; but what did Yurand do? He accepted your challenge, and only asked you to send off your serving men. How am I to punish him for that, or to summon him to judgment? Ye attacked a dreadful man, feared by all, and of your own choice brought down on your own heads disaster. What do

ye want, then? Am I to command him not to defend himself whenever ye are pleased to attack him? "

" It was not the Order who attacked him, but guests, foreign knights," replied Danveld.

" The Order answers for guests, and besides, with them were men at arms from the Lubov garrison."

" Was the starosta to yield up guests, as for slaughter? "

At this the prince turned to Siegfried, and said, —

"See what justice becomes in your mouths, and see if your evasions are not offensive to

God."

"De Bregov must be freed from captivity," answered the stern Siegfried; "for men of his family were chiefs in the Order, and have rendered great service to the Cross."

"And the death of Meinegger must be avenged," added Hugo.

The prince gathered the hair on both sides of his head, and rising from his seat, approached the Germans with an ominous face; but after a moment he remembered evidently that they were his guests; so he restrained himself once more, placed his hand on Siegfried's arm, and said, —

"Listen, starosta, you wear the cross on your mantle, so answer on that cross according to conscience. Was Yurand right or not?"

"De Bregov must be freed from captivity," answered Siegfried.

"God grant me patience," said the prince, after a moment of silence.

"The injustice which has met us in the persons of our guests is merely an additional cause of complaint," continued Siegfried, in a voice as sharp as a sword-edge. "Since the Order is an order, never in Palestine, or in Transylvania, or in pagan Lithuania up to this time, has one common man done us so much evil as that bandit of Spyhov. Your Princely Grace, we desire redress and punishment, not for one injustice, but a thousand; not for one battle, but for five hundred; not for one blood spilling, but for whole years of deeds for the like of which the fire of heaven should burn that godless nest of cruelty and wickedness. Whose groans are calling to God there for vengeance? Ours! Whose tears? Ours! In vain have we brought complaints, in vain have we called for judgment. Never has satisfaction been rendered us."

When he heard this Prince Yanush nodded his head. '•Iu former years," said he, "Knights of the Cross were

guests often in Spyhov, and Yurand was not your enemy till his beloved wife died in your bonds. How many times have you attacked him yourselves, as now, because he challenged and conquered your knights? How many times have you set murderers on him, or sent bolts at him from crossbows in the pine woods ? He has attacked you, it is true, for vengeance was burning him ; but have not you, or knights living on your lands, attacked peaceful people in Mazovia? Have you not driven away herds, burnt villages, slaughtered men, women, and children ? And when I made complaint to your Master he answered from Malborg: ' An ordinary brawl on the boundary!' Give me peace! It does not become you to complain, you who seized me when I was unarmed, in time of peace, on my own land; and had it not been for terror before the anger of the king at Cracow, I might have been groaning to this hour in your underground dungeons. That is how you paid me, who came from the family of your benefactors. Leave me in peace; it is not for you to speak of justice! "

When they heard this the Knights of the Cross looked at one another with impatience, for it was bitter to them and a shame that the prince mentioned that event in Zlotoria in presence of De Fourcy; so Danveld, wishing to put an end to further conversation on that subject, said, —

"In the case of your Princely Grace there was a mistake, which we corrected, not out of fear of the king at Cracow, but for the sake of justice. As to brawls on the boundary, our Master cannot answer for them, since in all kingdoms of the world everywhere there are turbulent spirits on the boundaries."

"Thou sayst that, but art calling for justice against Yurand. What do ye wish ? "

" Justice and punishment."

The prince balled his bony fists and repeated, —

" God give me patience! "

" Let your Princely Grace remember this, too," continued Danveld, " that our turbulent men harm only lay persons not of the German race; but yours raise their hands against the German Order, by which they offend the Saviour himself. And what tortures and punishments can suffice those who offend the Cross?"

" Hear me! " said the prince. " Do not carry on war by means of God, for Him thou wilt not deceive ! " And placing his hands on the shoulders of the Knight of the Cross, he

shook him violently. The German was alarmed at once, and began in a milder voice, —

4 ' If it be true that the guests attacked Yurand first, and they did not dismiss their men at arms, I do not applaud them. But did Yurand really accept the challenge? "

Then he looked at De Fourcy, blinking stealthily the while, as if to inform him that he was to deny; but De Fourcy, unable, or unwilling to do so, replied,—

" He wished in company with two other men to do battle against us, after we had sent away the men at arms."

' 4 Are you certain ? "

" On my honor! De Bregov and I agreed, but Meinegger would not join us."

4 4 Starosta of Schytno!" interrupted the prince, ' 4 you know better than other men that Yuraud does not avoid a challenge." Here he turned to all, and said: 44 Whoever of you would like to challenge Yurand to a battle on foot or on horseback, to him I give permission. Should Yurand be killed, or taken captive, Bregov will be freed without ransom. Ask no more of me, for you will not receive it."

After these words deep silence followed. Danveld and Siegfried, and Brother Rotgier, and Brother Gottfried, though brave, were too well acquainted with the terrible heir of Spy-hov for any man of them to undertake a life-and-death battle against him; only a stranger might do that, — a man from distant parts, like De Lorche, or De Fourcy; but De Lorche was not present at the conversation, and De Fourcy was still too much influenced by heartfelt fear.

" I have seen him once," muttered he, 44 and have no wish to look at him a second time."

44 A monk is not permitted to engage in single combat," said Siegfried, " unless with special permission of the Master and the Grand Marshal; but we do not demand permission for battle, only that De Bregov be liberated from captivity, and Yurand put to death."

44 You are not the law in this land."

44 We have endured patiently, so far, a grievous neighborhood. But our Master will be able to measure out justice."

4 'Therefore there will be justice to the Master and to you from Mazovia ! "

44 Behind the Master are the Germans and the Roman emperor."

44 And behind me is the Polish king, to whom more lands and nations are subject."

" Does your Princely Grace wish war with the Order?"

" If I wished war, I should not wait for you in Mazovia, I should go to you; but do not threaten me, for I am not afraid."

" What am I to report to the Master? "

" Your Master has made no inquiry of me. Report what you like to him."

" Then we will measure out punishment and revenge ourselves."

The prince stretched out his arms and began to move his finger threateningly in the very face of the Knight of the Cross.

"Have a care ! " said he, in a voice of suppressed anger. " Have a care; I have permitted you to challenge Yuraud, but if you break into my country with troops of the Order, I will strike you — and you will sit here, not as a guest, but a captive."

Evidently his patience was exhausted, for he threw his cap against the table with all "his strength, went out of the room, and slammed the door behind him. The Knights of the Cross were pale from rage, and De Fourcy looked at them as if bewildered.

" What will happen now? " inquired Brother Rotgier.

But Danveld sprang almost with closed fists at De Fourcy.

" Why didst thou say that ye attacked Yurand first? "

"Because it is true! "

" There was need of a lie."

"I came here to fight, not to lie."

"Thou hast fought fiercely—there is no word on that score! "

" And hast thou not run away before Yurand to Schytno? "

" Pax, pax ! " exclaimed Siegfried. " This knight is a guest of the Order."

" It is all one what he said," put in Brother Gottfried. " They would not have punished Yurand without trial, and at a trial the affair would have been explained."

" What will happen now? " repeated Brother Rotgier.

A moment of silence followed.

"We must finish finally with that bloody cur!" said Siegfried, in a stern and resolute voice. " De Bregov must be freed from confinement. Let us assemble the garrisons from Schytno, Insburg, and Lubov. Let us summon the nobles of Helmno, and attack Yurand. It is time to put an end to him! "

But the adroit Danveld, who knew how to weigh everything on both sides, put his hands on his head, frowned, and said, after thinking, —

"Impossible, without permission of the Master."

" If it succeeds, the 'Master will praise," said Gottfried.

"But if not? If the prince moves his spearmen, and falls on us ? "

' ' There is peace between him and the Order; he will not strike."

" Yes, there is peace, but we shall be the first to break it. Our garrisons are not enough against the Mazovians."

"Then the Master will take our side, and there will be war."

Danveld frowned again, and was thoughtful.

"No, no," said he, after a while. "If it succeeds, the Master will be glad at heart. Envoys will go to the prince, there will be discussions, and we shall get off without punishment. But in case of defeat, the Order will not take our part, and will not declare war against the prince. For that another Master would be needed. Behind Prince Yanush stands the Polish king, and the Grand Master will not quarrel with him."

" Still, we took the land of Dobryn; it is evident that Cracow is not a terror to us."

" There were pretexts, — Opolchyk. We took, as it were, a mortgage, and even that — " Here he looked around, and added in a low voice, " I have heard in Malborg that if we were threatened with war, we should give up the mortgage, if the money were returned."

"Ach!" said Rotgier, "if Markward of Salzbach were among us, or if Schaumberg, who smothered Vitold's whelps, — they would manage Yurand. Who is Vitold? Yagello's viceroy ! — Grand Prince ; still Schaumberg cared nothing, — he smothered Yitold's children — made nothing of it. Indeed, there is a lack among us of men who can find means to do anything."

Hearing this, Hugo von Danveld put his elbows on the table and his head on his hands, and sank for a long time in thought. Suddenly his eyes grew bright, he wiped his thick moist lips with the back of his hand as his wont was, and said, —

"Blessed be the moment in which you recalled, pious brother, the name of the valiant Schaumberg."

" Why so ? Have you thought of something ? " inquired Siegfried.

" Speak quickly! " cried Rotgier and Gottfried.

"Listen: Yurand has a daughter here, his only child, whom he loves as the sight of his eye."

" He has; I know her. Princess Anna Danuta loves her also."

"She does. Now listen: If you were to carry off that maiden, Yurand would give for her not only Bregov, but all the prisoners, with himself and Spyhov in addition."

" By the blood of Saiut Boniface shed in Dohum! " cried Brother Gottfried, "it would be as you say."

Then they were silent, as if frightened by the boldness and the difficulties of the undertaking. Only after a while did Brother Rotgier turn to Siegfried.

"Your wit and experience," said he, "are equal to your valor; what do you think of this ? "

"I think it a question which deserves consideration."

" For," continued Rotgier, " the maiden is a companion of the princess; more, she is almost a beloved daughter. Think, pious brothers, what an uproar would rise."

"You have said yourself," said Hugo, laughing, "that Schaumberg smothered Vitold's whelps, — and what was done to him for doing so ? They will raise an outcry for any cause; but if we should send Yurand in chains to the Master, reward would await us more certainly than punishment."

"True," said Siegfried, "there is a chance for attack. The prince will go away, Anna Danuta will remain here with only her damsels. But an attack on the prince's court in time of peace is no common matter. The prince's court is not Spyhov. Then it will be again as in Zlotoria. Again complaints will be sent to all kingdoms, and to the Pope, against the violence of the Order; again the cursed Yagello will be heard with a threat, and the Master — you know him, moreover — he is glad to take what he can, but he does not want war with Yagello. Yes ! a shout would rise in all the lands of Mazovia and Poland."

"Meanwhile Yurand's bones would be bleaching on a hook," said Danveld. "Besides who tells you to snatch her away here from the court, from the side of the princess ? "

" Not from Tsehanov, I hope, where in addition to nobles there are three hundred bowmen."

"No. But may not Yurand get sick, and send people for his daughter? The princess would not forbid her to go in that case, and should the girl be lost on the road, who will say to you or to me, ' Thou didst snatch her away ?' "

"Pshaw!" said Siegfried, impatiently; "then make Yu-rand get sick and send for the maiden."

At this Hugo smiled in triumph, and answered, —

" I have a goldsmith at home, who was driven out of Mal-borg for crime, and who settled in Schytno. This man can imitate any seal; I have men too, who, though our subjects, are descended from Mazovians. Dost not understand me yet?"

" I understand ! " exclaimed Gottfried excitedly.

Brother Rotgier raised his hands aloft, and said, —

" God give thee happiness, pious brother, for neither Markward of Salzbach, nor Schaumberg would have found a better method."

Then he blinked as if trying to see something in the distance. "I see," said he, "Yurand standing with a rope around his neck at the Dantzig Gate in Malborg, and our men at arms kicking him."

" And his daughter will be a servant of the Order," added Hugo.

Hearing this, Siegfried turned severe eyes at Danveld, who drew the back of his hand ° '•oss his lips again, and said, —

"But now to Schytno as quickly as possible."

CHAPTEE XIX.

BUT before starting for Schytno, the four brethren and De Fourcy had to take farewell of the prince and the princess. That was a farewell not over friendly, but the prince, in accord with ancient Polish custom, unwilling to let guests depart empty handed, gave each man a fine bundle of fur, and a gryven of silver; they received these with delight giving assurance that, as brethren of the Cross, who had vowed poverty, they never kept money, but gave it to the poor, whom they recommended at the same time to pray for the health, glory, and future salvation of Prince Yanush.

The Mazovians smiled under their moustaches at these statements, for the greed of the Order was well known to them, and still better known were the lies of the Knights of the Order. In Mazovia the saying was, " A Knight of the Cross lies as a skunk gives out odor." The prince waved his hand and said after they had gone that a man might go to heaven on their prayers, perhaps crab fashion.

But still earlier, at parting with the princess, when Siegfried kissed her hand, Danveld approached Danusia, placed his hand on her head, and while stroking it said, —

"It is commanded us to return good for evil, and love even our enemies ; so a sister of the Order will bring to you, young lady, the healing balsam."

" How am I to thank you? " answered Danusia.

" Be a friend of the Order, and the Knights of the Cross."

De Fourcy had noted this conversation, and because the beauty of the maiden had struck him, he asked after they had moved toward Schytno, —

"What beautiful damsel is that with whom you were talking?"

" She is the daughter of Yurand."

"The one whom you are going to seize?" asked De Fourcy, in wonder.

" The same. And if we have her, Yurand is ours."

" It is clear that not everything coming from Yurand is evil. It is worth while to be the keeper of such a prisoner."

"Do you think that it would be easier to war with her, than with Yuraud ? " TOL. i. —17

"That means that I think the same as you do. Her father is an enemy of the Order, but with the daughter you have spoken words rubbed with honey, and have promised her a balsam, besides."

Apparently Hugo von Danveld felt the need of justifying himself in some words before Siegfried, who, though not better than others, still observed strict rules of morality, and therefore had criticised certain brothers more than once.

"I have promised her a balsam," said he, "for that young knight who was crushed by the bull, and to whom she is betrothed, as you know. Should there be an outcry after we have seized the girl, we shall say that not only have we wished no harm, but we have sent them a cure according to Christian charity."

"Very well," replied Siegfried. "But we must send some safe person."

" I will send a pious woman completely devoted to the Order. I will command her to observe, and to listen. When our people go, as if sent by Yurand, they will find everything ready."

" It will be difficult to bring such people together."

" No. We have men who speak the same language that they do. We have them even among servants and the garrison, — men who are outlawed from Mazovia, fugitives, murderers, criminals, it is true, but fearless, and ready for anything. I shall promise them every reward if they do the work ; if they fail, the halter."

" Very well! But in case of treason? "

"There will be no treason, for every man of them has earned impalement on the stake, and upon each one a sentence is hanging. We only need to give them proper clothing and they will pass for real servants of Yurand, but the main thing is a letter with Yurand's seal."

"We must foresee everything," said Rotgier. "After the last battle Yurand will wish to see the prince, perhaps, so as to complain of us, and justify himself. Being in Tsehanov he will go to his daughter in the forest. It may happen that our men appearing on Yurand's business will meet Yurand himself."

" The men whom I shall select are cunning ruffians. They know that if they strike Yurand they will go to the hook. Their lives will depend on not meeting him."

" Still, should it happen them to be captured?"

"We shall get rid of them, and the message. Who will say that we sent them? Finally if the girl is not carried away, there will be no outcry, and if a few gallows'-birds of Mazovia are quartered, no harm will happen from that to the Order."

" I understand neither your politeness nor your fear lest it be known that the girl was carried away by our command," said Brother Gottfried, the youngest among the Knights. " Having her once in hand we must, of course, send some person to Yurand to say to him: ' Thy daughter is with us; dost thou wish that she should receive freedom, give for her Bregov and thyself.' How else is it to be? But then it will be known that we seized the girl."

"True," said De Fourcy, whom the whole affair did not please overmuch. "Why hide that which must be discovered?"

But Danvetd laughed, and turning to Brother Gottfried asked,—

" How long do you wear the white mantle ? "

"The sixth year will be finished the first week after Trinity Sunday."

" When you have worn it another six years you will understand the Order more intimately. Yurand knows us better than you do at present. This will be told him: 'Brother Schaumberg has charge of thy daughter, and if thou squeak a word, remember the children of Vitold.'"

"But later?"

" Later Bregov will be free, and the Order will be rid of Yurand."

"Well!" exclaimed Brother Eotgier, "everything is so wisely thought out that God must bless our undertaking."

" God will bless all undertakings that have for object the good of the Order," replied the gloomy Siegfried.

They went on in silence, and before them, two or three arrow-shots distant, went their escort to clear the road, which was drifted, for abundant snow had fallen in the night. On the trees was deposited much frost; the day was cloudy, but warm, so that steam rose from the horses. From the forest, toward human dwellings, flew flocks of crows, filling the air with foreboding caws.

De Fourcy fell back behind the knights a little, and rode on in deep thought. He had been for some years a guest of the Order; he had taken part in expeditions to Lithuania, where he had shown great valor and had been received every-

where as only Knights of the Cross knew how to receive guests from distant regions. He had grown strangely attached to them, and, not having a fortune, intended to enter their ranks. Meanwhile he had lived in Malborg; he had visited known localities, seeking in journeys amusement and adventures. Having come shortly before to Lubov with the wealthy Bregov, and hearing of Yurand, he had become excited with the desire to measure himself with a man who roused universal terror. The arrival of Meinegger, who had come out victorious from every encounter, hastened the adventure. The comtur of Lubov had given them mea, but had told the three knights not only of the fierceness, but the stratagems and perfidy of Yurand, so that when the latter had asked them to send away their men they would not agree, fearing that should they do so he would surround and destroy them, or throw them into the dungeons of Spyhov. Yurand, thinking that they had in mind not only a knightly struggle, but robbery, attacked them offensively and inflicted a dreadful defeat.

De Fourcy saw Bregov overturned with his horse, he saw Meinegger with a broken lance in his bowels, he saw men simply begging for pity. He had been barely able himself to break away, and had wandered for days over roads and through forests where he might have died of hunger, or fallen a prey to wild beasts had he not come by chance to Tseha-nov, where he found Gottfried and Rotgier. From the whole expedition he brought away a feeling of humiliation and hatred together with sorrow for Bregov, who was a near friend of his. He joined, therefore, heartily in the complaint of the Knights of the Cross when they demanded punishment for Yurand and liberation for their unfortunate comrade, and when that complaint found no attention, he was ready at the first moment to use every means of vengeance against Yurand. But now sudden scruples were roused in him. More than once while listening to conversations of the knights, and especially to Hugo's words, he could not avoid astonishment. Having become acquainted more intimately in the course of years with the Knights of the Cross, he saw really that they were not what in Germany and in the West they claimed to be. In Malborg he had known a few just and strict knights, those same who had often made charges against the corruption of the Brotherhood, against their profligacy and want of discipline, and De Fourcy felt that these charges were true; but being himself profligate

and undisciplined, he did not take those faults into account too much, especially as Knights of the Cross atoned for them with valor. He had seen them at Vilno, meeting breast to breast with Polish knights, at the taking of castles defended with superhuman resolve by Polish garrisons ; he had seen them dying under blows of swords and axes, in general storms or in single combat. They were unsparing and cruel to Lithuania, but they were lion-like, and walked in glory as in sunlight. Now, however, it seemed to De Fourcy that Hugo von Danveld was saying things and proposing methods which ought to shock the soul in every knight ; and the other brothers not only did not rise against him, but confirmed every word of his. Hence astonishment possessed him more and more, and at last he began to think deeply as to whether he could put his hands to such deeds.

Had it been simply a question of snatching a girl away, or exchanging her for Bregov later on, perhaps he might consent, though the beauty of Danusia had touched him and captivated his heart. If it had come to him to be her guardian he might perhaps have had nothing against the task, or even would not have been sure that she would go from his hands in the same state in which she had come to them. But with the Knights of the Cross the question was clearly something else. Through her they wished to get, with Bregov, also Yurand himself, by promising him that they would release her if he would give himself for her; then they would kill him, and with him, to conceal the deceit and the crime beyond any doubt, kill the girl herself also. In every case the same fate threatened her that came on the children of Vitold in case Yurand dared to complain. " They will not observe anything; they will deceive both and kill both," thought De Fourcy; "still they carry the cross and ought to hold honor higher than others."

And the soul stormed up in him more and more mightily every moment because of such shamelessness; but he determined to satisfy himself as to how far his suspicions were just, so he rode up to Hugo again and inquired,—

"If Yurand gives himself to you, will you liberate the girl?"

" If we should liberate her the whole world would know at once that we took both of them."

" But what will you do with her? "

Hugo inclined toward the speaker, and exhibiting by his smile Ihe decayed teeth under his thick lips, asked, —

" Of what are you inquiring? Of what we shall do with her before or after ? "

De Fourcy, knowing now what he wanted, was silent; for a while he seemed to struggle with himself, then rising in his stirrups somewhat, he said so loudly that all four Knights of the Cross heard him, —

"The pious Brother Ulrich of Jungingen, a model and ornament of chivalry, said once to me: ' Among the old men in Malborg thou wilt still find worthy brothers of the Cross; but those in the boundary districts bring naught save reproach to the Order.' "

"We are all sinners; but we serve the Saviour," said Danveld.

"Where is your knightly honor? The Saviour is not served by infamous actions. Know, then, that not only will I take no part in this action, but I will not permit you to do so."

" Why will you not permit? "

"To permit deceitful attack, treason, infamy?"

" But how are you going to prevent? In the battle with Yurand you lost your escort and your wagons. You must live by the favor of the Order; you would die of hunger should we be unwilling to throw a piece of bread to you. Besides, are we not four here while you are one? How will you prevent?"

" How will I prevent?" repeated De Fourcy. " I can return to the house and forewarn the prince ; I can announce your intention before the whole world."

At this the Knights of the Cross looked at one another, and their faces changed in the twinkle of an eye. Especially did Dauveld look for a time with an inquiring glance into the eyes of Siegfried ; then he turned to De Fourcy.

" Your ancestors," said he, " served in the Order, and you wish to enter it; but we will not receive traitors."

" In answer to that I say that I will not serve traitors."

"Ho! you will not carry out your threat. Understand this, that the Order knows how to punish not merely brothers of the Cross."

De Fourcy, roused by these words, drew his sword ; he seized its edge with his left hand, his right hand he placed on the hilt, and said, —

" On this hilt, which has the form of a cross, on the head of Saint Dionysius, my patron, and on my knightly honor, I shall warn the Prince of Mazovia and the Grand Master."

Danveld looked again with an inquiring glance at Siegfried, and the latter closed his eyes, as if in sign that he agreed to something. Then Danveld spoke with a strangely changed and dull voice, —

' ' Saint Dionysius might have carried his severed head under his arm," said he, " but if yours once falls — "

"Are you threatening me?" interrupted De Fourcy.

" No, but I shall kill you! " answered Danveld.

And he plunged a knife into his side with such force that the blade was hidden to the handle. De Fourcy shrieked with a terrible voice; for a moment he tried to seize with his right hand the sword which before he had held in his left, but he dropped it to the ground; that same moment the other three brothers fell to stabbing him without mercy in the breast and the bowels, till he dropped from the horse.

Then came silence. De Fourcy, bleeding terribly from a number of wounds, quivered on the snow, and tore it with fingers twisted by convulsions. From beneath a leaden sky came only the croaking of crows as they flew from empty deserts to human habitations.

And then a hurried conversation began among the murderers.

" The attendants have seen nothing! " said Danveld, in a panting voice.

" Nothing. The attendants are in advance, they are out of sight," answered Siegfried.

" Listen : there will be occasion for a new complaint. We shall spread the report that Mazovian knights attacked us, and killed our comrade. We will make a noise, — until Mal-borg hears that the prince sets murderers on guests even. Do you hear? We must say that the prince not only was unwilling to listen to our complaints against Yurand, but that he gave command to kill the man who made the complaint."

De Fourcy meanwhile turned on his back during his last convulsion, and lay motionless with bloody foam on his lips, and terror in his eyes now opened widely. Brother Rotgier looked at him, and said, —

" Consider, pious brothers, how God punishes even the intention of treason."

"What we have done has been done for the good of the Order," said Gottfried. "Praise to him who did the deed — "

But he stopped, for in that instant from behind them, at the turn of the snowy road, appeared a horseman who raced with the speed of his horse. Seeing him, Hugo called quickly, —

" Whoever that man be, he must die."

"I recognize him," said Siegfried, who, though the oldest among the brothers, had an uncommonly quick eye. " He is the attendant who killed the wild bull with an axe. True, that is he! "

" Hide your knives, lest he be frightened," said Danveld. " I will strike first again; you support me."

Meanwhile the Cheh rode up, and about ten or eight steps away checked his horse in the snow. He saw a corpse in a pool of blood, a horse without a rider, and astonishment was depicted on his face; it remained, however, but the twinkle of an eye. Next moment he turned to the brethren as though he had seen nothing, and said, —

" I salute you, brave knights! "

" We recognized thee," answered Hugo, approaching him slowly. " Hast thou any question with us? "

" The knight Zbyshko of Bogdanets, whose spear I carry, has sent me, — he who was wounded by the wild bull at the hunt; he was not able himself to come."

" What does your master want of us? "

" Because you complained of Yurand of Spyhov unjustly, to the detriment of his knightly honor, my master gives command to declare to you that you have not acted as true knights, but that you have barked as dogs; and that he summons the man who used the words to a combat on foot or on horseback to the last breath, in which struggle he will meet you when you indicate the place, and when, with God's favor and mercy, his present sickness permits him."

" Tell your master that Knights of the Cross endure insults patiently, for the sake of the Saviour; as to a struggle without personal permission from the Master or the Grand Marshal, they cannot answer, but for this permission, however, we will write to Malborg."

Again the Cheh looked at the body of De Fourcy, for it was to him that he had been sent specialty. Zbyshko knew that the Knights of the Cross did not accept challenges; but hearing that among the five was a lay knight, he wished to challenge that one, thinking thus to influence and win Yurand. Now the man was lying there slaughtered like an ox in the presence of four Knights of the Cross.

Hlava, it is true, did not know what had happened ; but, inured from childhood to danger of all kinds, he sniffed peril of some sort. He was astonished also that Danveld, while talking, drew up more and more to him, and the others began to surround him from the sides, as if wishing to encircle him without being noticed. For these reasons he began to have a care of himself, especially since he had no weapons on his person; for in his haste he had not succeeded in taking them.

Meanwhile Danveld was there before him, and continued:

" I have promised thy master a healing balsam, so then he repays kindness with evil. Among Poles this is common; but since he is grievously wounded, and may soon appear before God, tell him — "'

Here he placed his left palm on the Cheh's shoulder.

" Tell him then that just this is what I answer."

That moment a knife gleamed near Hlava's throat; but before Danveld could stab, the Cheh, who had noted his movements, seized with his two iron hands the right arm, which he twisted till joints and bones cracked in it, and only when he heard a terrified roar of pain did he put spurs to his horse and shoot off like an arrow, before the others were able to stop huii.

Brothers Rotgier and Gottfried started to chase, but returned soon, frightened by the terrible cry of Danveld. Siegfried held him by the shoulder; but he, with pale and blue face, cried so that the attendants, who had advanced with the wagons considerably, stopped their horses.

" What is the matter ? " inquired the brothers.

But Siegfried ordered them to ride on with all speed-and bring a wagon, for evidently Danveld could not hold himself in the saddle. After a while cold sweat covered his forehead, and he fainted.

When the wagon was brought he was placed on straw, and they moved toward the boundary. Siegfried hurried, for he understood, after what had happened, that they had no time to lose, even in nursing Danveld. Sitting with him on the wagon, he rubbed his face with snow from time to time, but was unable to bring him to consciousness. Only when near the boundary did Danveld open his eyes and look around, as if in astonishment.

" How is it with you? " asked Siegfried.

" I feel no pain, but neither do I feel my hand."

u It is benumbed, so feeling has vanished. In a warm room pain will return to you. Meanwhile thank God, even for a moment of relief."

Then Rotgier and Gottfried approached the wagon.

"An accident has happened," said the first; "what are we to do now?"

"We will say," answered Danveld, with a weak voice, "that the attendant killed De Fourcy."

" Their new crime, and the author of it, is known !" added Rotgier.

CHAPTER XX.

MEANWHILE the Cheh flew with all speed straightway to the hunting-house, and finding the prince there, told him first of all what had happened. Fortunately there were courtiers who had seen that the Cheh had ridden out with out weapons. One of them had even called on the road to him, half jestingly, to take some kind of iron, or the Germans would beat him. He, fearing lest the Germans might pass the boundary, had sprung to his horse in his jacket, and rushed after them. These testimonies scattered all doubts of the prince as to who could have murdered De Fourcy; but it filled him with alarm and such anger that in the first moment he wished to send pursuit after the Germans, so as to convey them in chains to the Grand Master for punishment. After a while, however, he saw himself that pursuit could not reach the knights before the boundary, and he said, —

" Still, I will send a letter to the Master and inform him what they are doing here. Evil has begun in the Order; formerly obedience was absolute, now any comtur does what he pleases. God grant that after offence will come punishment."

He thought a while and then said to the courtiers, —

" I cannot understand why they killed a guest, and were it not that the young man went without weapons, I should suspect him."

" You might," said the priest; " but what wish could he have to kill a man whom he had never seen before, and then, if he had weapons, how was he, one man, to attack five, and their armed escort in addition?"

"You speak truth," said the prince. "It must be that that guest opposed them in something, or that he would not lie as they wished; even here I noticed that they winked at him to say that Yurand was the first to begin."

" The Cneh is a gallant fellow," said Mrokota, " if he has crushed the paw of that dog of a Danveld."

He says that he heard the bones break in the German," answered the prince; "and noticing how he fought in the forest that may well be. It is clear that both servant and master are doughty fellows. Had it not been for Zbyshko the wild bull would have hurled himself at the princess' horse. Both he and the Knight of Lorraine did much to save her."

" Indeed he is a resolute man," said Father Vyshonek; " even now when barely breathing he takes Yurand's part and has challenged those Germans. The master of Spyhov needs just such a son-in-law."

" Yurand talked rather differently in Cracow ? — but he will not object now, I think," said Prince Yanush.

" The Lord Jesus will bring it about," said the princess, who entering that moment heard the last words of the conversation. " Yurand cannot refuse now, if God return health to Zbyshko. But there must be a reward from us also."

" The best reward for him is Danusia, and I think that he will get her, for this reason, that when women undertake something even a Yuraud is helpless."

" But have I not undertaken a good work?" inquired the princess. "That Zbyshko is impulsive I will not deny; but there is not a truer man on earth than he. And the girl is as true as he is. She does not go one step from him, she thinks of him only, and he smiles at her in his pain so that tears fall from my eyes at moments. I tell thee the truth. Love like that is worth helping, for God's own mother delights in seeing human happiness."

" If only the will of God be there," said the prince, " happiness will come. But to tell the truth, they came near cutting his head off because of that maiden, and now the wild bull has crushed him."

" Do not say because of her! " exclaimed the princess; " no other but Danusia saved him in Cracow."

" That is true; but had it not been for her he would never have struck against Lichteustein to wrest the plume from his helmet, and he would not have exposed himself for the man of Lorraine with such readiness. As to the reward, I have said that that belongs to both, and in Tsehanov I will provide it."

" Nothing would Zbyshko like to see so well as the belt of a knight and golden spurs."

The prince smiled good-naturedly, and added, —

" Let the girl take them to him, and when his wound is. healed we shall see that all is finished in proper fashion. And let her take them quickly, for sudden pleasure is best."

The princess, hearing this, embraced her husband in presence of the courtiers; then she kissed his hands repeatedly. He smiled meanwhile, and said, —

" Well, you see, a good affair is settled! The Holy Ghost has not withheld wit even from women! Call the girl in."

4 ' Danusia! Danusia! " cried the princess.

After a while, in the doorway of the side chamber appeared Danusia, her eyes red from watching, in her hands a two-handled basin, full of steaming kasha with which Father Vyshonek was to poultice Zbyshko's bruised bones, and which an old court lady had just given her.

"Come, little orphan," said the prince. "Put down the vessel and come hither."

She approached him somewhat timidly, for the "Pan" roused a certain dread in her; he drew her toward him kindly, and stroked her face, saying, —

" Well, child, grief has come to thee, has it not?"

"It has indeed!" replied Danusia. And having sorrow in her heart, and tears ready, she burst into weeping at once, but quietly, so as not to offend Prince Yanush.

'_' Why art thou crying ? " inquired he.

"Because Zbyshko is sick," replied she, putting her fists in her eyes.

Have no fear; nothing will harm him. Is not that true, Father Vyshonek? "

" By God's will he is nearer marriage than death," said the kind priest.

"Wait," said the prince; will give a medicine that will help, or cure him altogether."

"The balsam which the Knights of the Cross sent?" cried Danusia, vivaciously, taking her hands from her eyes.

" Better nib a dog with what the Knights of the Cross sent than thy dear young knight whom thou lovest. I will give thee something else." Then he turned to the courtiers and called: "Will some one go to the store chamber for spurs and a belt ? "

When they were brought, he said to Danusia: " Take these to Zbyshko, and say that henceforth he is belted. If he dies he will stand before God a belted warrior; if he lives I will finish the rest in Tsehauov or Warsaw."

When Danusia heard this she embraced the prince's feet; then she grasped with one hand the insignia of knighthood, with the other the basin, and sprang to the room in which

Zbyshko was lying. The princess followed, not wishing to lose sight of their pleasure.

Zbyshko was very sick, but seeing Danusia, he turned to her with face pale from pain, and asked, —

" But the Cheh, my berry, has he returned?"

" What matter about him ? I bring better news. Our lord has belted thee as a knight, and here are the things which he has sent by me," said she, placing the belt and golden spurs at his side.

Zbyshko's pale cheeks flushed with delight and astonishment ; he looked at Danusia, next at the insignia; then he closed his eyes, and asked, —

"How could he belt me as a knight? "

But when at that moment the princess came in, he raised himself on his arms somewhat and thanked her, asking pardon of the gracious lady because he could not fall at her feet, for he divined at once that through her intercession it was that such fortune had befallen him. She commanded quiet, however, and with her own hands helped Danusia to lower his head to the pillow.

Meanwhile the prince entered, and with him Father Vys-honek, Mrokota, and a number of others. From a distance Prince Yanush gave a sign with his hand that Zbyshko was not to move, and then, sitting down by the bedside, spoke as follows: —

" It is no wonder to people, as you know, that there is reward for noble and valiant deeds;

were there not, honor would go unconsidered, and injustice would move through the world without punishment. Since thou hast not spared thy life, and with loss of health hast defended us from terrible sorrow, we permit thee to gird thyself with the belt of a knight, and to be henceforth in renown and in honor."

" Gracious lord," answered Zbyshko, " I should not grieve for ten lives — "

He was unable to continue, both from emotion and because the princess placed her hand on his lips, when Father Vys-houek forbade him to speak. But the prince continued, —

"I think that thou knowest the duties of a knight, and wilt wear these ornaments worthily. Thou art to serve our Redeemer, as is befitting, and war against the elder of Hell. Thou art to be loyal to the Lord's anointed on earth, avoid unjust wars, defend oppressed innocence, in which may God and His Holy Passion assist thee ! "

«Amen! " responded the priest.

Then the prince rose, took farewell of Zbyshko, and in going away, added, —

"When thou art well, come directly to Tsehanov; whither I will bring Yurand alsol"

CHAPTEK XXL

THREE days later came the promised woman with the Hercynian balsam, and with her a captain of bowmen from Schytno bearing a letter signed by the brothers, and furnished with Danveld's seal. In this letter the Knights of the Cross called heaven and earth to witness the wrongs which had met them in Mazovia; and under threat of God's vengeance demanded punishment for the murder of their "guest and dear comrade." Danveld had added to the letter a complaint of his own, demanding, in words both humble and menacing, payment for the grievous maiming of himself, and a sentence of death against Hlava.

The prince tore the letter before the eyes of the captain, threw it under his feet, and said, —

"The Master sent them, oh, their crusading mothers, to gain my good-will, but they have brought me to anger. Tell them from me that they slew the guest themselves, and tried to slay the Cheh; of this I shall write to the Master, and I shall add also that he is to choose other envoys if he wishes me to be neutral when war comes between the Order and the king at Cracow."

"Gracious lord," replied the captain, "is that the only answer that I am to take to the pious and mighty brotherhood ? "

"If that is not enough, say that I look on them as dog brothers, and not as real knights."

This ended the audience. The captain rode away, for the prince went that day to Tsehanov. But the "sister" remained with the balsam, which the suspicious Father Vysho-nek would not use, especially as the sick man had slept soundly the night before, and woke in the morning weakened greatly, it is true, but without fever. After the prince's departure the sister sent back one of her servants immediately, as if for a new remedy, a "basilisk's egg," which, as she declared, had power to restore strength even to the dying. She went herself along the court submissively, and without the use of one hand, in a lay dress, — but one resembling that of a religious,—with a rosary, and a small pilgrim gourd at her girdle. Speaking Polish well, she inquired

of the servants with great care about Zbyshko and Danusia; when the occasion offered, she made Danusia a present of a rose of Jericho; and the following day, when the maiden was sitting in the dining-hall, she pushed up to her and said, —

" God bless you, young lady. Last night, after prayer, I dreamed that two knights came through the snow to you; one arrived first, and wound you in a white mantle, but the other said, '

I see only snow, she is not here;' and he went back again."

Danusia, who wished to sleep, opened her blue eyes at once, and inquired, —

" But what does that signify? "

" This, that the one who loves you most will get you."

"That is Zbyshko!"

" I cannot tell, for I saw not his face; I saw only a white mantle, and I woke then immediately, for every night the Lord Jesus sends me pain in my feet; and one arm He has taken from me altogether."

" But has the balsam not helped you? "

" Even the balsam will not help me, young lady, because of my sin, which is too great; if you wish to know what it is, I will tell you."

Danusia nodded, in token that she was willing to know; so the sister continued, —

"There are in the Order women also who serve, though they make no vows, for they can marry, still, with respect to the Order they are bound to serve the Brotherhood; and whoever of them is met by such a favor and honor receives a pious kiss from a brother knight in sign that henceforth in deed and speech she is to serve the Order. Oh, young lady, such a great favor was to visit me; but I, in my sinful stubbornness, instead of receiving it gratefully, committed much sin, and drew down on myself punishment."

"What did you do?"

"Brother Danveld came and gave me the kiss of the Order. I thought it given through frivolousness, and raised my godless hand on him."

Then she beat her breast, and repeated a number of times,—

" O God, be merciful to me a sinner! "

" And what happened ? " inquired Danusia.

" My hand was taken at once from me, and from that hour I have been maimed. I was young and foolish; I was ignorant! Still, I was punished. For though it might

VOL. I. — 18

seem to a woman that a brother of the Order wished to do something evil, she must leave judgment to God; she is not to oppose, for should she oppose a Knight of the Cross, or a Brother, God's anger would blast her."

Danusia listened to those words with disgust and with fear; the sister, however, sighed, and continued, —

" I am not old even to-day, barely thirty ; but God, when He took the use of my hand from me, took my youth also and beauty."

"If your hand had not been taken," said Danusia, " you might live without complaint."

After that, followed silence. Then the sister, as if calling something to mind, said, —

"But I dreamt that some knight wrapped you in a white mantle on the snow; he was a Knight of the Cross, perhaps, they wear white mantles."

" I want neither the Knights of the Cross nor their mantles," answered the maiden.

Further conversation was stopped by the priest, who entered the hall, nodded at Danusia, and said, —

"Praise God, and go to Zbyshko. He is awake, and wishes to eat. He is much better."

Such was the case in reality. Zbyshko's health had improved, and Father Vyshonek felt almost certain that he would recover, when all at once an unexpected event disturbed all combinations and hopes. Messengers from Yurand came to the princess with a letter which contained the worst and most terrible tidings. A part of Yurand's castle in Spyhov had caught fire. He himself, while trying to save the building, had been crushed by a burning beam. Father Kaleb, who had written the letter in Yurand's name, declared, it is true, that Yurand might recover, but that the sparks and coals had so burnt his sound eye, that not much sight was left in it, and inevitable blindness threatened him.

For this reason Yurand summoned his daughter to come quickly to Spyhov; he wished to see her once more before blindness seized him. He said, too, that she would remain thenceforth with him; for if even blind men who go out to beg bread have each of them a child to lead him and show the way, why should he be deprived of this last consolation, and die among strangers? The letter contained also profound thanks to the princess, who had reared the girl as if she had been her mother, and at the end Yurand promised

that, though blind, he would visit Warsaw again to fall at the feet of the lady, and implore her favor for Danusia in the future.

When Father Vyshonek read this letter to her, the princess was hardly able to utter a word for some time. She had hoped that when Yurand, who visited his child five or six times every year, came at the approaching holidays, she would, by her authority and that of Prince Yanush, win him over to Zbyshko, and gain his consent to an early wedding. This letter not only destroyed all her plans, but deprived her of Danusia, whom she loved as if she had been her own daughter. It occurred to her also that Yurand might give the girl immediately to one of his neighbors, so as to pass the rest of his days among his own kindred. A visit by Zbyshko to Spyhov was out of the question, for his ribs had only just begun to knit, and besides, who could tell how Yurand would receive him ? The princess knew that Yurand had refused him outright, and told her that for mysterious reasons he would never permit the marriage. In her grievous vexation, Princess Anna gave command to summon the elder among the messengers so as to inquire of him touching the misfortune at Spyhov, and learn something of Yurand's plans also.

She was astonished when a man entirely unknown answered her summons, not old Tolima, Yurand's shield-bearer, who came with him usually. The stranger explained that Tolima had been terribly wounded in the last battle with the Germans; that he was wrestling with death in Spyhov; that Yurand, brought down with great pain, begged for the speedy return of his daughter, for he saw less and less, and in a couple of days might be blind altogether. The messenger begged, therefore, earnestly for permission to take the girl the moment his horses had rested, but as it was evening the princess opposed decisively. She would not break the hearts of Zbyshko and Danusia and herself utterly by such a sudden parting.

Zbyshko knew of everything already, and was lying in his room as if struck on the head with the poll of a hatchet; and when the princess entered, wringing her hands and saying at the threshold, "There is no help, for this is a father," he repeated after her, like an echo, " There is no help," and closed his eyes like a man who thinks that death will come to him straightway.

But death did not come, though increasing grief rose in

his breast, and through his head darker and darker thoughts flew, like clouds which, driven by a storm one after another, hide the light of day and extinguish all earthly pleasure. Zbyshko understood, as well as the princess, that if Danusia went to Spyhov she would be the same as lost to him. " Here," thought he, " all wish me well; there Yurand may not even receive me, or listen to me, especially if a vow or some unknown reason binds him. Besides, how can I go to Spyhov when I am sick and barely able to move on this bed." A few days before, by the favor of the prince, golden spurs with the belt of a knight had been given him. He thought on receiving them that joy would overcome sickness, and he prayed with his whole soul to rise quickly and measure himself with the Knights of the Order, but now he lost every hope, for he felt that if Danusia were absent from his bedside, desire to live would be absent and the strength to struggle with death would be absent also. To-morrow would come, and the day after, and the eves of festivals, and the festivals themselves; his bones would pain him in just the same way, and in just the same way would faintness seize him, and that brightness would not be near him, which spread through the whole room from Danusia, nor would that delight for the eyes which looked at her. What a consolation, what a solace to ask a number of times every day, "Am I dear to thee?" and to see her as, laughing and confused, she covered her eyes with her hands, or bent down and answered, " Who could be dear if not Zbyshko? " Sickness will stay behind, and pain and grief, happiness will go, and not return to him.

Tears gleamed in Zbyshko's eyes and flowed over his cheeks slowly; then he turned to the princess and said, —

" Gracious lady, I think that I shall never see Danusia in this life again."

" Wert thou to die from grief it would not be a wonder," answered the princess, herself full of sorrow. " But the Lord Jesus is merciful."

After a while, wishing to strengthen him even a little, she added,—

" Though if Yurand were to die before thee, without giving this as an example, guardianship would come to the prince and to me, and we should give thee the maiden immediately."

" If he d'ics! " answered Zbyshko. ,

But ali at once some new thought flashed through his head,

for he raised himself, sat up in the bed, and said in changed accents, —

*' Gracious lady — "

At that point he was interrupted by Danusia, who ran in weeping and began to call from the threshold, —

"Thou knowest already, Zbyshko! Oi, I am sorry for papa, but I am sorry for thee, poor boy! "

Zbyshko, when she came near him, gathered in with his sound arm his darling, and said, —

" How am I to live without thee? It was not to lose thee that I made vows and served thee. It was not to lose thee that I have ridden hither through forests and rivers. Hei! grief will not relieve me, tears will not relieve me, death itself will not relieve ; for though the green grass were to grow over me, my soul would not forget thee even in the court of the Lord Jesus, and in the chambers of God the Father Himself. I say there is no help, but help must be found; without help there is no escape anyhow! I feel torture in my bones and great pain, but do thou, Danusia, fall at the feet of our lady, for I am not able to do so, and do thou beg a favor for both of us."

When Danusia heard this she sprang to the feet of the princess, and embracing them hid her bright face in the folds of her heavy robe ; the lady turned her eyes, which were filled with pity but also with astonishment, at Zbyshko.

"How can I show favor? If I do not let the child go to her father I shall bring down the anger of God on my head."

Zbyshko, who had raised himself previously, dropped again to the pillow, and for a time made no answer because breath was lacking him. But gradually he moved one hand up to the other on his breast till at last he joined both as if in prayer.

" Rest," said the princess, "then tell what thy wish is, but do thou, Dauusia, rise from my knees."

" Do not rise, but join in my prayer," said Zbyshko. Then he began in a weak and broken voice, —

" Gracious lady—Yurand was opposed to me in Cracow — he will be opposed to me now, but if Father Vyshonek marries me to Danusia— she may go to Spyhov, for then no human power can take her from me."

These words were so unexpected for Princess Anna that she sprang up from the bench, then sat down again, and said, as if not understanding well what the question was, —

" God's wounds! — Father Vyshonek? "

" Gracious lady! gracious lady! " begged Zbyshko.

" Gracious lady! " repeated Danusia after him, embracing the knees of the princess a second time.

" How could that be without parental permission? "

" The law of God is superior," answered Zbyshko.

"But fear God!"

""Who is a father, if not the prince? who a mother, if not you, gracious lady?"

" Gracious beloved mother! " said Danusia.

" True! I have been, and am a mother to her," said the princess, " and besides it was from my hand that Yurand received his wife. True! The moment the marriage takes place all is finished. Yurand may be angry, still he is bound to the priuce, as his lord. Moreover we need not tell him immediately unless he wants to give her to another, or make her a nuu. —And if he has taken some vow it will not be his fault (that she is married). Against the will of God no man can do anything. — By the living God! maybe this is Heaven's will."

" It must be! " cried Zbyshko.

""Wait," said the princess, filled with emotion, "let me think a little ! If the prince were here I should go to him now and ask, ' Are we to give Danusia, or not?' But without him I am afraid to act. — My breath just stops, and there is no time for waiting in this case, since the girl must go in the morning. — O dear Jesus! let her go married, if only there is peace. But I cannot come to my mind, and somehow I am afraid. Art thou not afraid, Danusia? Speak!"

" If this is not done I shall die! " exclaimed Zbyshko.

Danusia rose from the knees of the princess, and because she was really admitted by the kind lady not only to intimacy, but to fondling, she seized her around the neck, and pressed her with all her strength.

" "Without Father Vyshonek I will say nothing to thee," answered the princess. " Run for him as quickly as possible."

Danusia ran for Father Vyshonek; Zbyshko turned his pallid face to the princess, and said, —

" "What the Lord Jesus has predestined will happen, but for this comfort may God reward you, gracious lady."

"Do not bless me yet," said the princess, " for it is unknown what will happen. And thou must swear to me on

thy honor that if the marriage takes place thou wilt not prevent Danusia from going at once to her father, so as not to draw his curse on thyself and on her; against that may God guard thee."

" I swear on my honor," answered Zbyshko.

" Well, remember thy oath. But there is no need for the girl to say anything to Yurand at present. Better keep back the news lest it burn him like fire. We will send for him from

Tsehanov, to come with Danusia, and then I will tell him myself; I will beg the prince even to do so. When he sees that there is no help for it he will consent. For that matter, Yurand has not disliked thee."

"No, he has not disliked me, so he may even be glad in soul that Danusia will be mine. For if he has made a vow he will not be in fault if I get her."

The coming of Father Vyshonek and Danusia interrupted further conversation. The princess called him to counsel that instant, and told him with great excitement of Zbyshko's wish, but he, after barely hearing what the question was, made the sign of the cross on himself, and said, —

"In the name of the Father, Son, and Holy Ghost! — how can I do this ? Why, it is Advent! "

" As God lives, that is true ! " cried the princess.

Silence followed. The anxious faces showed what a blow Father Vyshonek's words were to all of them.

After a while he added, —

"Were there a dispensation I would not oppose, since I sympathize with you. I should not ask absolutely for Yu-rand's permission ; if you permit, gracious lad\'7d r , and guarantee the consent of the prince, our lord, of course he and you are father and mother of all Mazovia. But without a dispensation from the bishop — I cannot. If Bishop Yakob of Kurdvanov were among us, perhaps he would not refuse a dispensation, though severe, — not like his predecessor, Bishop Mamphiolus, who answered every question with ' Bene! bene!'" (Granted ! granted !)

" Bishop Yakob loves the prince and me greatly," put in the lady.

" Then I say that he would not refuse a dispensation, .if there are reasons for it.— The girl must go, and this young man is sick, and will die, perhaps — Hm! in articulo mortis. But without a dispensation it is impossible."

" I could get a dispensation of Bishop Yakob later, — and though I know how severe he is, he will not refuse me this favor. — Oh, I guarantee that he will not refuse."

To this Father Vyshonek, who was a good and mild man, replied, —

"The word of an anointed of God like you is great. I am afraid of the bishop, but your word has power. The young man too might promise something to the cathedral in Plotsk — I know not. — Seest thou this is always a sin till dispensation comes, and the sin of no one but me? — Hml the Lord Jesus is indeed merciful; if any man sins not to his own profit, but out of compassion for the suffering of others He forgives the more readily. — But this is a sin, and should the bishop be stubborn, who would absolve me ? "

" The bishop will not be stubborn!" cried Princess Anna.

" That Sanderus, who came with me has indulgences for everything," said Zbyshko.

Father Vyshonek did not believe altogether, perhaps, in Sanderus's indulgences, but he was glad to seize at a pretext even, if only it favored Zbyshko and Dauusia, for he had great love for the maiden, whom he had known from her childhood. At last he considered that church penance was the worst that might befall him, so he turned to the princess and said, —

" I am a priest, it is true, but also I am the prince's servant. What do you command, gracious lady ? "

" I do not command, I request," replied she. "But if that Sanderus has indulgences — "

" He has. But it is a question of the bishop. He deals strictly with rules there in Plotsk."

" Have no fear of the bishop. He has forbidden to priests bows and swords, as I hear, as well as various acts of license, but he has not forbidden good deeds."

" Then let it be according to your will," said Father Vyshonek, raising his eyes and his hands.

At these words delight possessed their hearts. Zbyshko dropped again to his pillow, but the princess, Danusia, and Father Vyshonek sat around the bed and " counselled " how the affair was to be accomplished. They determined to preserve the secret, so that not a living soul in the house should know of it ; they determined also that neither ought Yurand to know till the princess herself should inform him in Tsehanov of everything. The priest was to write a letter immediately from the princess to Yurand, asking him to come at once to Tsehanov, where they could find better cures for his wounds, and he would not be so troubled by

loneliness. Finally it was arranged that Zbyshko and Danusia should prepare for confession. The marriage would take place in the night, when all had lain down to sleep.

For a moment Zbyshko had thought to take the Cheh as a witness of the marriage, but he rejected the plan when he remembered that Hlava had come from Yagenka. For a while Yagenka stood before him in memory, as if living. She stood in such a way that it seemed to him that he was looking at her ruddy face, and her eyes that had been weeping, and he heard her imploring voice, which said: ' ' Do not do that! do not pay me with evil for good, with misfortune for love! " All at once great compassion for her seized him, because he felt that grievous pain would be inflicted on her, after which she would not find solace either under her father's roof or in the depth of the forest, or in the field, or in the gifts of the abbot, or in the love-making of Stan and Vilk. So he said to her in spirit: " God grant thee, O maiden, everything that is best, but, though I should be glad to bend down the heavens for thee, I cannot." And, in fact, the conviction that that was not in his power brought i-elief at once and restored peace to him, so that he thought then only of Danusia and the marriage.

But he could not dispense with the aid of the Cheh, so, though he had determined to say nothing in his presence of what was to happen, he asked to have him called.

" I am going to confession," said he to Hlava, " and to the Table of the Lord; so array me in the best manner possible, as if I were going to royal chambers."

The Cheh was alarmed somewhat, and looked at his face. Zbyshko understood what this meant, and said,—

' ; Have no fear; people confess before other events as well as death; but this time'is all the more fitting since the holidays are near, when the princess and Father Vyshonek are going to Tsehanov, and there will be no priest nearer than Prasnysh."

" But will your Grace not go? " asked the attendant.

"I shall go if I recover; but my recovery is in God's hands."

Hlava was pacified, and hurrying to the box brought that white, gold-embroidered jacket in which the knight arrayed himself for great solemnities, and also a beautiful rug to cover his feet in the bed. Then, when he had raised Zbyshko, with the aid of the two Turks, he washed him, combed his long hair, around which he put a scarlet head-band. Finally he

propped him, thus arrayed, against red pillows, and, pleased with his own work, he added, —

" If your Grace were able to dance now, you might go to a wedding."

" They would have to do without our dancing," answered Zbyshko, with a smile.

Meanwhile, the princess in her chamber was thinking how to array Danusia, since for her womanly nature it was a question of great importance, and she was unwilling that the dear maiden reared by her should stand up to be married in an every-day garment. The maidens to whom information was given that Danusia had arrayed herself in the color of innocence for confession, found white robes easily in the boxes. For the dressing of her head there was trouble. At the thought of this wonderful sadness possessed the princess, so that she fell to complaining, —

" O thou my orphan, where shall I find a garland of rue for thee ? In this forest there is no little flower of any sort, nor a leaf, unless mosses flourish under the snow."

Dauusia, standing there with flowing hair, was troubled also, for she, too, wished a garland; but after awhile she pointed to strings of immortelles hanging on the walls of the chamber, and said, —

" Use those, for I shall find nothing else, and Zbyshko will take me even in such a garland."

The princess would not consent at first, fearing a bad omen, but since there were no flowers in that house, to which they came only for hunting, they settled on what they had. Father Vyshonek, who had heard Zbyshko's confession, came, and took Dauusia now to confess; after that dark night appeared. When supper was over, the servants went to bed at command of the princess. Yurand's messengers lay down, some in the servants' rooms, others with the horses in the stables. Fires in the servants' rooms were covered with ashes and went down, till at last it was perfectly silent in the hunting-lodge, save that from time to time dogs barked toward the forest at wolves.

But in the chambers of the princess, of Father Vyshonek, and of Zbyshko the windows did not cease to give light; they cast ruddy gleams on the snow which covered the courtyard. In these chambers they were watching in silence, listening to the beating of their own hearts, disquieted and filled with the solemnity of that moment which was to come very soon. After midnight the princess took Danusia's

hand and conducted her to Zbyshko's chamber, where Father Vyshonek was waiting for them with the Lord God (the Holy Sacrament).

In that chamber a great fire was burning in the chimney, and by its abundant but uneven light, Zbyshko beheld Danusia, somewhat pale from lack of sleep, in white, with a garland of immortelles on her temples, dressed in a stiff robe which reached the floor. Her eyelids were closed from emotion, her arms were dropped at her sides, and she looked like a painting on window-panes. There was something church-like about her, so that Zbyshko wondered at the sight; for it seemed to him that that was not an earthly maiden, but some heavenly soul which he was to take in marriage. And he thought so still more when she knelt with folded hands for communion, and with head thrown back closed her eyes altogether. She seemed to him as if dead, so that terror even seized his heart. But this did not last long, for hearing the voice of the priest saying, Ecce Agnus Dei, 1 he became collected in spirit, and his thoughts flew toward God straightway. In the chamber no noise was heard now save the solemn voice of the priest: Domine, non sum dignus^ and the crackling of the sparks in the fire, and the crickets singing persistently, and, as it were, with sadness in a cranny of the chimney. Outside the house the wind rose and sounded through the snow-covered forest, but it fell again.

Zbyshko and Danusia remained some time in silence. Father Vyshonek took the chalice to the chapel, and returned soon, not alone, however, but with De Lorche, and, noticing astonishment on the faces of those present, he put his finger on his lips as if to prevent an exclamation.

" I understood," said he, " that it would be better to have two witnesses of the marriage; hence, I have just instructed this knight, who has sworn to me on his honor and on relics that he will keep the secret as long as may be needed."

De Lorche knelt first before the princess then before Danusia. After that he rose and stood in silence, arrayed in ceremonial armor, along the joints of which bright reflections shone from the fire. Tall, motionless, sunk as it were in ecstasy; for to him also that white maiden with a garland of immortelles on her head seemed an angel on the window-panes of a Gothic cathedral.

1 Behold the Lamb of God. 2 Lord, I am not worthy.

The priest brought her to Zbyshko'e bedside, and, putting his stole over their arms, began the usual ceremony. Tears one after another flowed down the honest face of the princess, but in her soul there was no fear at that moment; for she felt that she was doing good by uniting those two wonderful and innocent children.

De Lorche knelt a second time, and, leaning with both hands on the hilt of his sword, he looked exactly like a knight who has a vision.

The couple repeated the words of the priest in turn : "I
— take thee — to myself — " and in accompaniment to these low and pleasant words the crickets chirped again in the crevices of the chimney, and the fire crackled in the billets of hornbeam.

"Vhen the ceremony was over, Danusia fell at the feet of the princess, who blessed both, and who said as she gave them into the guardianship of the heavenly powers, —

Rejoice now, for she is thine, and thou art hers."

Then Zbyshko stretched out his sound arm to Danusia, and she encircled his neck with her arms, and for a while the others heard how they repeated to each other, —

" Thou art mine, Danusia! "

" Thou art mine, Zbyshko! "

But immediately after Zbyshko grew weak, for the emotion was too great for his strength, and dropping on the pillow he breathed heavily. He did not faint, however, and did not cease to smile at Danusia, who wiped his face, bedewed with cold sweat, and he did not cease to repeat even yet, "Thou art mine, Danusia!" at which she bent her blond head each time toward him. This spectacle moved to the utmost De Lorche, who declared that in no land had it happened him to see such tender hearts, wherewith he made a solemn vow to meet on foot or on horseback any knight, magician, or dragon who might dare to stand in the way of their happiness. And, in fact, he took that vow immediately on the cross-formed hilt of a misericordia, or small sword, which served knights in despatching the wounded. The princess and Father Vyshonek were called as witnesses of that vow.

The princess, not understanding a marriage without some rejoicement, brought wine, and they drank of it. The hours passed one after another. Zbyshko, overcoming his weakness, drew Danusia toward him a second time, and said, —

" Since the Lord Jesus has given thee to me, no one will take thee from me now, dearest berry."

"Papa and I will come to Tsehanov," answered Danusia.

" If only sickness or something else does not attack thee. God guard thee from evil event. Thou must go to Spyhov, I know. Hei! thanks to the highest God, and the gracious lady that thou art mine, for the power of man cannot unmake a marriage."

But since that marriage had taken place in the night and mysteriously, and since immediately afterward a separation was to follow, a certain strange melancholy seized at moments, not only Zbyshko, but all. Conversation was interrupted. From time to time the fire ceased to blaze in the chimney, and peoples' heads sank in obscurity. Father Vyshonek threw new sticks on the coals then, and when a stick crackled with a plaintive sound, as it does sometimes when the wood is fresh, he said, —

" What dost thou wish for, O soul doing penance ? "

The crickets answered him, and the increasing flame, which brought out from the shadow watching faces, was reflected in the armor of De Lorche, illuminating at the same time Danusia's white robe and the garland on her head.

The dogs in the yard barked again toward the forest as if at wolves.

And as the night passed silence fell more and more on them, till at last the princess said, —

"Dear Jesus! is it to be thus after a marriage? Better go to sleep; but since we must wait till morning, play to us on the lute, little flower, play, for the last time before thy going, to me and to Zbyshko."

Danusia, who was weary and drowsy, was glad to rouse herself with anything ; so she sprang for the lute, and returning after a while with it sat by Zbyshko's bed.

" What am I to play ? " asked she.

"What shouldst thou play," asked the princess, "if not that song which thou didst sing in Tynets, when Zbyshko saw thee the first time?"

"Hei! I remember — and till death I shall not forget," said Zbyshko. "After that always the tears came to my eyes when I heard it."

" I will sing it in that case," said Danusia.

And straightway she began to finger the lute; then throwing her head back as usual she began: —

" Oh, had I wings like a wild goose, I would fly after Yasek ;

I would fly after him to Silesia I I would sit on a fence in Silesia. Look at me, Yasek dear, Look at the poor little orphan."

But all at once her voice broke, her lips quivered, and from beneath her closed lids tears came out on her cheeks in spite of her. For a time she tried not to let them come, but she had not power to restrain them, and at last she wept heartily, just as she had when, the time before, she sang that same song to Zbyshko in the prison at Cracow.

"Dauusia! What is thy grief, Danusia?" asked Zbyshko.

"Why art thou weeping? What kind of wedding is this?" cried the princess. "Why dost thou weep?"

"I know not," answered Danusia, sobbing. "I feel so much sadness. I grieve so for Zbyshko and the lady."

Therefore all were sad, and fell to comforting her, explaining that her absence would not be lasting; that surely she would go with her father at Christmas to Tsehauov. Zbyshko embraced her again with his arm, drew her to his bosom, and kissed the tears from her eyes; but the weight remained on all hearts, and under this weight the remaining hours of the night passed.

At last a noise was heard in the yard, so sudden and sharp that all quivered. The princess, springing up from her seat, cried, —

" Oh, as God lives ! The well-sweeps! They are watering the horses !"

Father Vyshonek looked through the window, in which the glass panes were taking on a gray color, and said, —

" Night is growing pale, and day is coming. Ave Maria, yratias plena !" (Hail, Mary, full of grace !)

Then he went out of the chamber, and returning after a while, said, —

" Day is dawning, though the day will be gloomy. Yurand's people are watering the horses. It is time for thee to take the road."

At these words the princess and Danusia broke into loud weeping, and they and Zbyshko lamented, as do simple people when they part; that is, in their lament there was something ceremonial, a complaint, half spoken, half chanted, which comes forth from full souls as naturally as tears from the eyes, —

" Hei, weeping will help us no longer.

We give thee farewell, dearest love; Weeping will help us no longer, We give thee farewell. God aid thee, we give thee farewell! "

Zbyshko drew Danusia to his bosom for the last time, and held her there long, as long as his breath lasted, and until the princess tore her away from him to dress her for the road.

Day had dawned now completely. All in the house were awake and moving.

Hlava came to Zbyshko to learn about his health and ask for orders.

" Draw the bed to the window," said the knight.

The Cheh drew the bed easily to the window, but he wondered when Zbyshko commanded him to open it; but he obeyed, covering, however, the lord with his own fur, for it was cold out of doors, though cloudy, and abundant soft snow was falling.

Zbyshko looked through the snow-flakes flying from the clouds. In the yard a sleigh was visible; around it, on steaming horses which had hoar frost on them, were Yurand's people. All were armed, and over their sheepskins some wore armor, on which the pale and uncertain light of day was reflected. The forest was covered entirely with snow; the fences and the gate were hardly visible.

Dauusia rushed into Zbyshko's room once more, wrapped now in her shuba and fur cloak; once more she put her arms around his neck, and once more she said to him in parting:

" Though I go, I am thine."

He kissed her hands, her cheeks, and her eyes, which he could hardly see under the foxskin hood, and said,—

" God guard thee ! God go with thee! Thou art mine, mine till death! "

And when they drew her away from him again, he raised himself as much as he was able, rested his head against the window, and looked. Through the snow-flakes, as through a kind of veil, he saw Danusia take her place in the sleigh; he saw the princess hold her long in her embrace, and the court damsels kiss her, and Father Vyshonek make the sign of the cross on her for the road. She turned toward him once more at the very parting, and stretched out her arms.

" Be with God, Zbyshko 1"

" God grant me to see thee in Tsehanov — " But the snow fell as thickly as if it wished to benumb and cover everything, hence those last words were so dulled when they reached them that it seemed to both as if they were calling from afar to each other.

THE KNIGHTS OF THE CROSS. 289

CHAPTER XXII.

AFTER abundant snow, followed severe frosts, with bright, dry weather. In the daytime the frosts sparkled in the rays of the sun, ice bound the rivers and stiffened the swamps. Clear nights came, during which frost increased so much that trees in the forest burst with explosions; birds approached houses; the roads became dangerous because of wolves, which collected in great numbers and attacked, not only single people, but even villages. Men, however, rejoiced in their smoky cottages at their firesides, predicting a fruitful season after the frosty winter, and awaited the near holidays joyfully. The princess, with her court and Father Vyshonek, had left the hunting-lodge and gone to Tsehanov.

Zbyshko, notably stronger, but not strong enough yet to travel on horseback, had remained with his men, Sanderus and the Cheh, with the servants of the place, over whom a steady woman exercised the authority of housekeeper.

But the soul in the knight was rushing to his young wife. The idea that now Danusia was his, and that no human power could take her away, was to him an immense solace, indeed, but, on the other hand, that very same idea intensified his yearning. For whole days he had sighed for the moment in which he could leave the lodge, and he was meditating what to do then, whither to go and how to win over Yurand. He had moments of oppressive alarm, it is true, but, on the whole, the future seemed to him delightful. To love Danusia and split helmets with peacock-plumes on them was to be his life employment. Many a time the desire seized him to talk about this with the Cheh, whom he had taken now into his affection, but he remembered that Hlava, devoted with whole soul to Yagenka, would not be glad to talk about Danusia; bound moreover by a secret, he could not tell him all that had happened.

His health improved daily. A week before Christmas he mounted a horse for the first time, and, though he felt that he could not work yet in armor, he was comforted. He did not think that the need would come suddenly of putting on a breast-plate and a helmet, but he hoped in the worst event to have strength enough soon to do that were it needed. In

VOL. I. — 19

his room he tried to use his sword for pastime, and his success was not bad; the axe proved too heavy, still he thought that by using both hands he could wield it effectively.

At last, two days before Christmas eve, he gave command to make the sleighs ready and saddle the horses, informing the Cheh at the same time that they would go to Tsehanov. The trusty attendant was concerned somewhat, especially as there was a splitting frost, but Zbyshko said to him, —

" Not thy head commands here. There is nothing for us to do in this hunting-lodge, and even should I fall ill, there will be no lack of nursing in Tsehanov. Moreover, I shall not go on horseback, but on runners, up to my neck in hay, and under furs; only at the edge of Tsehanov itself shall I be on horseback."

Thus was it managed. The Cheh had learned already to know his young master, and understood that it would be ill for him to oppose, and still worse not to carry out a command quickly; so they started one hour later. At the moment of parting Zbyshko, seeing Sanderus enter a sleigh with his caskets, said to him, —

" But thou, why fasten to me like some burr to a sheep's fleece? Hast thou not said that thou wert going to Prussia? "

" I said that I wished to go to Prussia, but how could I go there alone in such snow ? The wolves would devour me before the first stars came out, and here I have nothing to work at. For me it is more agreeable to edify people in a town by my piety, offer sacred wares, and save men from Satan's snares, as I swore in Rome to the father -of all Christendom that I would do. Besides, I have conceived a wonderful affection for your Grace, and will not leave you till I set out for Rome, since it may happen me to render you a service."

" He is always ready, lord, to eat and drink for your sake," said Hlava, " and is most delighted to render such service. But if a great cloud of wolves fall on us in Prasnysh forest, we will throw him out to them at parting, for never will he be better fitted for another thing."

" But look to it that a sinful word does not freeze to your lips," retorted Sanderus; "for such icicles could be thawed only in hell."

" Oh, pshaw ! " answered Hlava, reaching with his gloved hand to his mustaches, which had hardly begun to be frosty.

" I shall see first to heating some beer for the journey, but I shall not give thee any."

" The commandment is to give drink to the thirsty. A new sin on your side!"

1 ' Then I will give thee a measure of water, but for the moment, this is what I have ready —"

Thus speaking, he gathered as much snow as he could take in his gloved hands, and threw it at Sanderus' beard, who dodged, and said, —

"You have nothing to show in Tsehanov, for there is a tame bear in that place which shovels snow."

Thus they abused and chaffed each other mutually. Zbyshko did not prevent Sanderus from going with him, for this strange man amused him, and seemed also to be attached to his person. They left the hunting-lodge on a bright morning in a frost so great that it was necessary to blanket the horses. The entire country was covered with deep snow. The tops of the houses were barely indicated under it; in places the smoke seemed to come straight up from white drifts and go to the sky arrow-like, rosy from the morning sunlight, and spread at the top in the form of a bush, like plumes on a knight's helmet.

Zbyshko rode in a sleigh, first to spare his strength, and second because of the great cold, against which he could defend himself more easily in an equipage filled with hay and fur. He commanded the Cheh to sit with him and to have the crossbows at hand for defence against wolves: meanwhile he chatted with him pleasantly.

" In Prasnysh," said he, " we shall only feed our horses, warm ourselves, and move on then immediately."

" To Tsehanov ? "

" First to Tsehanov, to salute the prince and princess and go to church."

"And then?"

Zbyshko smiled and answered, —

" Then who knows that we may not go to Bogdanets?"

The Cheh looked at him with astonishment. The idea flashed into his head that the young man might have given up Yurand's daughter, and it seemed to him the more likely since she had left the princess, and the report had come to his ears in the hunting-lodge that the lord of Spyhov was opposed to Zbyshko. Hence the honest fellow was rejoiced, though he loved Yagenka; still he looked at her as a star in the sky, and would have been delighted to purchase for her

happiness, even with his own blood. He loved Zbyshko, too, and desired from his whole soul to serve both to the death.

"Then your Grace will live at home," said he, with delight.

" How am I to live at home, when I have challenged those Kuights of the Cross, and still earlier Lichtenstein ? De Lorche said that very likely the Grand Master would invite the king to Torun. I may attach myself to the royal retinue, and I think that Zavisha of Garbov or Povala of Tachev will obtain from our lord permission for me to meet those monks of the Order. Surely they will fight in company with their attendants; so thou wilt have to fight also."

" I would do so even if I had to become a monk," answered Hlava.

Zbyshko looked at him with satisfaction.

"Well, it will not be pleasant for the man who comes under thy metal. The Lord Jesus has given thee tremendous strength, but thou wouldst do badly wert thou to plume thyself over-much on it, for modesty is the ornament of a genuine attendant."

The Cheh nodded in sign that he would not boast of his strength, but also that he would not spare it on the Germans. Zbyshko smiled, not at the attendant, but at his own thoughts.

"The old man will be glad when we return," said Hlava after a moment, " and there will be gladness at Zyh's house."

Zbyshko saw Yagenka as clearly as if she had been at his side in the sleigh. It happened always that when he chanced to think of Yagenka he saw her with wonderful definiteness.

" No! " said he to himself, " she will not be glad, for if I go to Bogdanets, it will be with Danusia — and let her take another." Then Vilk and young Stan flashed before his eyes, and the thought was bitter to him that the girl might go into the hands of one of those two. "Better far the first man she meets," thought he; "they are beer guzzlers and dice throwers, while the girl is honest." He thought also that in every case it would be disagreeable for his uncle to learn what had happened, but he comforted himself with this, that Matsko's first thought had always been turned to wealth and descent, so as to raise the distinction of his family. Yagenka, it is true, was nearer, for she was at the boundary of their land, but as a recompense Yurand was a greater heir than Zyh; hence it was easy to foresee that Matsko would not be angry very long over such a connection, all the more since he knew

of his nephew's love, and knew how much that nephew was under obligations to Danusia. He would scold, and then be glad and love Danusia as if she were his own child.

And suddenly Zbyshko's heart moved with affection and yearning for that uncle, who was a firm man, and who, more* over, loved him as the sight of his eyes. In battles that uncle had guarded him more than his own life; he had taken booty for him; he had worked to gain property for him. There were two lone men of them in the world. They had no relatives even, unless distant ones, like the Abbot of Tulcha; hence, when it came to parting, neither knew what to do without the other, especially the old man, who had no desires for himself any longer.

"Hei! he will be glad; he will be glad!" thought Zbyshko, "and I could only wish Yurand to receive me as he will."

And he tried to imagine what Yurand would say and do when he learned of the marriage. In this thought there was some dread, but not over-much, especially since the latch had fallen. It was not fitting that Yurand should challenge him to battle, for were he to oppose too much, Zbyshko might answer: " Consent while I beg you, for your right to Danusia is human, while mine is a divine one; she is not yours now, but mine." He had heard in his time from a cleric wise in Scriptures that a woman must leave father and mother and follow her husband; hence he felt that on his side was greater authority. Moreover, he hoped that between him and Yurand it would not come to stubborn disagreement and anger, for he considered that the prayers of Danusia would effect much, and also much, if not more, the mediation of the prince, of whom Yurand was a subject, and the princess, whom Yurand loved as the foster-mother of his daughter.

People advised them to pass the night in Prasnysh, and warned them against wolves, which, because of the cold, had gathered in such packs that they fell upon wayfarers even in large parties. But Zbyshko would not consider this; for it happened that in the inn he met a number of Mazovian knights, with their escorts, who were going to the prince at Tsehanov, and a number of armed merchants from Tsehanov itself, who were bringing laden sleighs from Prussia. In such large companies there was no danger; hence they set out for an all-night journey, though toward evening a sudden wind rose which brought clouds, and a fog set in. They

travelled on, keeping closely together, but so slowly that Zbyshko began to think that they would not reach Tsehanov even on Christmas eve.

In some places it was necessary to clear the drifts, for horses could not wade through them. Fortunately, the forest road was definite. Still it was dusk in the world when they saw Tsehanov.

It may be even that they would have gone around the place in the snow-storm and the whistling of the wind without knowing that they were right there, had it not been for fires which were burning on the height where the new castle was standing. No one knew certainly whether those fires had been lighted on that eve of the Divine Birth to serve guests, or because of some ancient custom, but neither did any one of those accompanying Zbyshko care at that moment, for all wished to find a refuge at the earliest.

The tempest increased every instant. The cutting and freezing wind swept along immense clouds of snow. It broke trees, roared, went mad, tore away entire drifts, carried them into the air, twisted them, shot them apart, covered horses and wagons with them, cut the faces of travellers with them as if with sharpened sand, stopped with them the breath and speech of people. The sound of bells fastened to sleigh tongues was not heard in the least, but in the howling and the whistling of the whirlwind sounded complaining voices, as if voices of wolves, as if distant neighing of horses, and sometimes as if the cries of people filled with fear and calling for assistance. Exhausted horses, leaning each with its side against the other, advanced more and more slowly.

"Hei! this is a snow tempest, indeed it is!" said the Cheh, with a panting voice. "It is lucky enough that we are near the town, and that those fires are burning, otherwise it would go hard with us."

"It is death to be out now," said Zbyshko; " but I do not see even the blaze there."

"Because there is such a mist that the light of the fire cannot pass through it. Besides that, the fire and the wood may have been blown away."

On other sleighs merchants and knights were also saying that whoever was caught by the storm at a distance from human dwellings would hear no church bell on the morrow. But Zbyshko was disquieted all on a sudden, and said, —

4 ' May God not grant that Yurand be out on the road somewhere! "

The Cheh, though occupied altogether with looking toward the fires, turned his head on hearing Zbyshko's words, and asked,—

"Then was the master of Spyhov to come?"

"He was."

" With the young lady?"

" But really the fire is hidden," remarked Zbyshko.

The flame had died out, in fact, but on the road right there near the sleighs appeared a number of horsemen.

"Why ride onto us?" cried the watchful Cheh, grasping his crossbow. " Who are ye? "

" People of the prince, sent to help wayfarers."

" Jesus Christ be praised! "

"For the ages of ages."

" Conduct us to the town! " called out Zbyshko.

" Has none of you dropped behind? "

"None."

" Whence come ye? "

" From Prasnysh."

" And saw ye no other travellers on the way? "

"We did not. But perhaps there are others on other roads."

" Men are looking for them on all the roads. Come with us. Ye have lost the road ! Turn to the right! "

They turned their horses. For some time nothing was heard save the roar of the tempest.

" Are there many guests in the old castle ? " asked Zbyshko, after a while.

The nearest horseman, who had not heard distinctly, bent toward him and asked, —

" What did you say ? "

" I asked if there were many guests with the prince and princess."

" As usual, a good number of them ! "

" But the lord of Spyhov, is he there?"

" He is not, but they expect him. People have gone out to meet him also."

"With torches?"

" How go with torches in this wind?"

They were unable to converse longer, for the noise of the snow-tempest increased.

" A real devil's wedding! " said the Cheh.

Zbyshko commanded him to be silent, and not mention foul names.

" Dost thou know," said he, " that on such holidays hellish power grows benumbed and devils hide themselves in holes ? Fishermen found one of those devils once in a pond near Sandomir the day before Christmas eve. He had a pike in his snout, but when the sound of church bells reached him, he lost strength right away, and they beat him with sticks until evening. This storm is a stiff one, but it is by permission of the Lord Jesus, who wishes the morrow to be filled all the more with rejoicing."

" True enough! If we were only at the castle; but had it not been for these men, we might have ridden till midnight, for we had got off the road," answered Hlava.

He said this, for the fire had gone down.

They had now really entered the town. Drifts of still deeper snow were lying on the streets there; so great were these drifts that in many places they almost hid the windows. For this reason people passing outside the town could not see lights. But the storm seemed less violent. On the streets none were celebrating the Christmas festival; citizens were sitting already at supper. Before some houses boys, with a crib and a goat, were singing in spite of the snowstorm. On the square were men wrapped in pea-straw, and acting as bears, but in general the place was empty. The merchants who accompanied Zbyshko, and other nobles on the road, remained in the town. Zbyshko and the nobles went to the old castle, in which the prince dwelt, and which had, even at that time, glass windows, which, in spite of the storm, shone brightly in front of the wayfarers when they drew near.

The drawbridge on the moat had been let down, for the old time of Lithuanian attacks had passed, and the Knights of the Cross, foreseeing war with the King of Poland, sought the friendship of the Prince of Mazovia. One of the prince's men blew a horn, and the gate was open directly. There were between ten and twenty bowmen there, but on the walls not a living soul, for the prince had given leave to go down. Old Mrokota, who had arrived two days earlier, met the guests, greeted them in the prince's name, and conducted them to rooms in which they could array themselves properly for the table.

Zbyshko fell at once to asking him about Yurand of Spyhov, and he answered that Yurand was not there, but that they expected him, since he had promised to come, and if his health had grown worse he would have informed them.

THE KNIGHTS OF THE CEOSS. 297

Stifl they had sent out a number of horsemen to meet him, because the oldest men could not remember such a storm.

" Then perhaps he will be here soon."

" Surely before long. The princess has commanded to set plates for them on her table."

Zbyshko, though he had always feared Yurand, rejoiced in heart, and said to himseLf: "Though I know not what he has done, he cannot undo this, that it is my wife who will come, my dearest Danusia! " And when he repeated that to himself, he was hardly able to believe his own happiness. Then he thought that perhaps she had told Turand all; that perhaps she had won him over, and persuaded him to give her at once. " In truth, what better has he to do? Yurand is a wise man, and knows that though he might forbid me, though he might refuse her to me, I would take her in every case, for my right is the strongest."

While dressing, Zbyshko talked with Mrokota ; asked him about the health of the prince, and especially the princess, whom from the time of his visit in Cracow he had loved as a mother. He was glad also when he learned that all in the castle were well and gladsome, though the princess grieved much at the absence of her dear little singer.

"Now Yagenka, whom the princess likes well, plays on the lute to her, but not in any way as the other."

"What Yagenka? " asked Zbyshko, with wonder.

"Yagenka of Velgolas, the granddaughter of an old man from Velgolas, — a nice girl, with whom that man from Lorraine has fallen in love."

" Then is Pan de Lorche here? '*

" Where should he be? He came from the hunting-lodge, and he remains here because it is pleasant for him. There is never a lack of guests in our prince's castle."

"I shall look on the Knight of Lorraine with pleasure; he is a man whom no one can reproach in any way."

"He, too, esteems you. But let us go; for the prince and princess will take their places at table directly."

They went out. In two chimneys of the dining hall great fires were burning, which were cared for by youths, and there was a multitude of guests and courtiers. The prince entered first in the company of a voevoda and a number of attendants. Zbyshko bent down to his knees, and then kissed his hand.

In return, the prince pressed his head, and, going a little aside with him, said, —

" I know of everything. I was angry at first that you did that without my permission, but in truth there was no time, for I was then in Warsaw, where I intended to pass the holidays. Finally, it is known that if a woman undertakes a thing, better not oppose her; for thou wilt effect nothing. The princess wishes as well to you as if she were your mother, and I prefer always to please rather than oppose her; for I wish to spare her tears and sadness."

Zbyshko bent a second time to the knees of the prince.

" God grant me to serve your princely Grace sufficiently."

" Praise to His name that thou art well. Tell the princess how kindly I have received thee. She will be gladdened. As God lives, her pleasure is my pleasure! And to Yurand I will say a good word in thy favor, and I think that he will give his permission; for he too loves the princess."

" Even should he be unwilling to give it, my right is the first."

"Thy right is the first, and he must agree; but he may withhold his blessing. No man can wrest that by force from him ; and without a parent's blessing there is no blessing from God."

Zbyshko grew sad when he heard these words; for up to that time he had not thought of this. At that moment, however, the princess came in with Yagenka of Velgolas and other damsels; so he sprang forward to pay homage to the lady. She greeted him still more graciously than had the prince, and began at once to tell him of the expected arrival of Yurand. " Here are plates set for them, and men are sent to bring them out of the storm. It is not according to decorum to delay the Christmas eve supper, for 'the lord' does not like that; but they will come surely before the end of supper."

"As to Yurand," said the princess, "it will be as God inspires. Either I shall tell him everything to-day or tomorrow after mass, and the prince has promised to add his word also. Yurand is self-willed, but not toward those whom he loves, and to whom he is under obligation."

Then she told Zbyshko how he was to bear himself toward his father-in-law, not to offend him — God forbid that! — and not to lead him to stubbornness. In general, she was of good hope ; but a person knowing the world better and looking at it more quickly than Zbyshko, would have noted a certain alarm in her speech. Perhaps it was there because the lord of Spyhov was in general not an easy man, and

perhaps, too, the princess began to be alarmed somewhat because they were so long in appearing. The storm was becoming more cruel out of doors, and all said that the man found in the open field by it might remain there. Another supposition also occurred to the princess, namely, that Danusia had confessed to her father that she had been married to Zbyshko, and Yuraud, being offended, had resolved not to come to Tsehanov at all. She did not wish, however, to confide these thoughts to Zbyshko, and there was not even time for it, since the young men in waiting had begun to bring in the food and place it on the table. But Zbyshko hastened to fall at her feet again, and ask, —

"But if they come, gracious lady, how will it be? Pan Mrokota has told me that there is a separate division for Yurand, where there will be hay beds for the attendants. But how will it be?"

The princess laughed, and striking him lightly on the face with her gloves, said, —
' k Be quiet! Wait till you see him! "

And she went to the prince, for whom the armor-bearers had already arrayed his chair, so that he might take his seat. Before doing that, however, one of them gave him a flat dish filled with thin strips of cake and bits of meat to be divided by the prince among guests, courtiers, and servants. Another similar one was held for the princess by a beautiful youth, the son of the Castellan of Sohachev. At the opposite side of the table stood Father Vyshonek, who was to bless the supper set out upon sweetly smelling hay.

In the door at this moment appeared a man covered with snow, who called aloud, —
" Gracious lord! "

"What?" asked the prince, not glad that the ceremony was interrupted.

" On the Radzanov road are travellers covered up in the snow. We must send more people to dig them out."

All were frightened when they heard this. The prince was alarmed, and turning to the Castellan, cried, —

" Horsemen with shovels, quickly ! "

Then he turned to the man who had brought the news.

" Are many snowed in? "

" We could not discover. There is a terrible darkness in the air. There are sleighs and horses, a considerable escort."

" Do ye not know whose they are? "

"People say that it is the heir of Spyhov."

CHAPTEK XXIH.

"WHEN Zbyshko heard the unfortunate tidings, •without even asking permission of the prince, he rushed to the stables, and commanded to saddle his horse. The Cheh, who, as a nobly born attendant, was with him in the supper hall, had barely time to go to their room and bring a warm fur robe; but he did not try to detain his young master; for having by nature strong sense, he knew that any endeavor to restrain him was useless, and that delay might be fatal. Mounting a second horse, he seized at the gate, from the keeper, a number of torches, and directly they were moving with the prince's people, whom the old Castellan led forward hastily. Beyond the gate darkness impenetrable surrounded them, but the storm seemed to have weakened. They might, perhaps, have gone astray immediately outside the town, had it not been for the man who had brought information, and who was leading them the more quickly and surely that he had with him a dog which knew the road.

On the open field the storm began to strike sharply in their faces, partly because they were going speedily. The highway was drifted in; in places there was so much snow that they were forced to go slowly; for the horses were in snow to their bellies. The prince's men lighted torches and lamps, and rode on amid the smoke and flame of torches which the wind blew as fiercely as if it wished to sweep those flames away from the pitchy sticks and carry them off into the fields and forests.

The road was a long one. They passed the villages nearer to Tsehanov and Nedzborz, then they turned toward Radzanov. Beyond Nedzborz, however, the storm subsided sensibly and grew weaker; the gusts of wind became fainter, and no longer carried whole clouds of snow with them. The sky became clearer. Some snow fell yet, but soon that stopped. Next a star glittered in a rift of the clouds. The horses snorted; the riders breathed more freely. The stars increased in number each moment, and the frost bit. After the expiration of a few " Our Fathers," the storm had ceased altogether.

De Lorche, who rode near Zbyshko, comforted him, saying that surely Yurand, in the moment of danger, had thought first of all of his daughter, and, though they should dig out all the others dead, they would find her alive surely, and sleeping under furs, perhaps. But Zbyshko understood little of what he said, and at last had not even time to listen; for after a while the guide going in advance turned from the road.

The young knight pushed forward and asked, —

" Why do we turn aside? "

" Because they were not snowed in on the highway, but off there ! Do you see the alder grove ? "

He pointed to a grove, which looked dark in the distance, and which could be seen on the white plain of snow when the clouds uncovered the shield of the moon and things became visible.

It was evident that they had left the highway.

" The travellers lost the highway, and rode in a curved line along a river. In time of storm and snow fog it is easy to do so. They went on and on until their horses failed."

" How did you find them? "

"The dog led us."

" Are there no houses near by? "

" There are, but on the other side of the river. The Vkra is right here."

" Hurry on ! " cried Zbyshko.

But it was easier to give a command than to execute it; for although th frost was sharp, there lay on the field snow yet unfrozen, drifts freshly collected and deep, in which the horses waded above their knees ; so they were forced to push forward slowly. All at once the barking of a dog reached them. Straight in front appeared the large and bent trunk of a willow, on which, in the light of the moon, gleamed a crown of leafless branches.

" They are farther on," said the leader, " near the alder grove; but here too must be something."

" There is a drift under the willow. Light up for us !'

A number of the prince's men dismounted and lighted the place with their torches ; then some one cried on a sudden, —

"Here is a man under the snow! "We can see his head right here! "

" There is a horse too ! " cried another immediately.

"Dig him out!"

Shovels began to sink in the snow and throw it on both sides.

After a while they saw sitting under the tree a man with head inclined on his breast and his cap pulled deeply over his face. With one hand he was holding the reins of a horse lying at his side with nostrils buried in the snow. Evidently the man had ridden away from the company, perhaps to reach human dwellings more quickly and obtain help, but when his horse fell he took refuge under the willow on the side opposite the wind, and there he was chilled.

" Bring a light!" called Zbyshko.

An attendant pushed up a torch to the face of the frozen man ; it was difficult to recognize him at once. But when another attendant turned the face upward, one cry was wrested from the breasts of all present, —

4 'The Lord of Spyhov!"

Zbyshko commanded two men to carry him to the nearest cottage and care for him; he himself, without losing time, galloped on with the rest of the servants and the guide to rescue the remainder of the party. On the way he thought that he should find Danusia there, his wife, perhaps not alive, and he urged the last breath out of his horse which struggled breast-deep in snow. Fortunately it was not very far, at the most a few furlongs. In the darkness voices were heard, *' Come this way! " — voices from the prince's men who had remained near the people snowed in. Zbyshko rushed up and sprang from his horse.

" To the shovels!"

Two sleighs had been dug out already by those left on guard. The horses and the men in the sleigh were frozen beyond recover\'7d 7 . "Where the others were might be known by hills of snow, though not all sleighs were entirely covered. At some were visible horses with their bellies pressed against drifts, as if while exerting themselves in running they had grown stiff in a supreme effort. In front of one pair stood a man sunk to his waist, and as immovable as a column ; at more distant sleighs the men had died near the horses while holding their bridles. Evidently death had caught them while trying to free the beasts from snowdrifts. One sleigh at the very end of the line was free altogether. The driver was on the seat with his hands over his ears; behind lay two people ; the long lines of snow blown across their breasts were united with a bank at the side and covered them like a blanket, so that they seemed sleeping

calmly and peacefully. Others, however, had perished while struggling to the last with the storm, for they were frozen in postures full of effort. Some sleighs were overturned; in some the tongues were broken. Time after time the shovels uncovered backs of horses bent like bows, or heads with teeth driven into the snow; men were in the sleighs and around the sleighs, but they found no women. At moments Zbyshko worked with the shovel till the sweat flowed from his forehead; at moments he looked with throbbing heart into the eyes of corpses, thinking whether he would see among them a beloved face — all in vain! The light shone only on the stern moustached visages of warriors from Spy-hov; neither Danusia nor any other woman was present.

' ' How is this 'i " asked the young knight of himself, with astonishment.

And he called to those who were working farther away, asking if they had not found anything; but they found only men. At last the work was done. The attendants attached their own horses to the sleighs, and sitting on the seats moved with the bodies toward Neclzborz, to see if they could not in the heat there restore to life any of the bodies. Zbyshko remained with the Cheh and two others. It came to his mind that Danusia's sleigh might have separated from the party if drawn, as was proper to suppose, by the best horses. Yurand might have ordered to drive it ahead or might have left it somewhere on the roadside at a cottage. Zbyshko knew not what to do; in every case he wanted to search the near drifts, the alder grove, and then turn back and search along the highway.

In the drifts they found nothing. In the alder grove wolf eyes gleamed at them repeatedly, but they found no trace of people or horses. The plain between the alder grove and the highway was glittering then in moon rays, and on the white sad expanse were seen here and there at a distance, a number of dark spots, but those too were wolves which at the approach of men vanished speedily.

" Your Grace," said Hlava at last, " we are riding and searching here uselessly, for the young lady of Spyhov was not in the retinue."

" On the highway! " answered Zbyshko.

"We shall not find her on the highway; I looked with care to discover if there were not boxes in the sleighs, and things pertaining to women. There was nothing. The young lady has remained in Spyhov."

The correctness of this remark struck Zbyshko, so he answered: —

"God grant it to be as thou sayest."

The Cheh went deeper still into his own head for wisdom.

1 ' If she had been in a sleigh the old lord would not have left it, or if he left the sleigh he would have taken her on the horse in front of him, and we should have found them together."

" Let us go there once more," said Zbyshko, in a voice of alarm, for it occurred to him that it might be as Hlava had said. In that case they had not searched with sufficient diligence. Yurand, then, had taken Danusia before him on the horse, and when the beast fell Danusia went away from her father to find some assistance. In that event she might be near by somewhere under the snow.

But Hlava, as if divining these thoughts, said, —

" In that case we should have found her things in the sleigh, for she would not go to the court with only the dress that she was wearing."

In spite of this just conclusion they went again to the willow, but neither under it nor for a furlong around the tree did they find anything. The prince's men had taken Yurand to Nedzborz, and round about all was deserted. Hlava made the remark, still, that the dog which had run with the guide and which had found Yurand, would have found the young lady also. Thereupon Zbyshko was relieved, for he became almost certain that Danusia had remained at Spyhov. He was able even to explain how it had happened. Evidently Danusia had confessed all to her father;

he, not agreeing to the marriage, had left her at home purposely, and was coming himself to lay the affair before the prince and ask his intervention with the bishop. At this thought Zbyshko could not resist the feeling of a certain solace, and even delight, for he understood that with the death of Yurand all obstacles had vanished.

"Yurand did not wish, but the Lord Jesus has wished," said the young knight to himself, " and the will of God is always the stronger."

Now he needed only to go to Spyhov, take Danusia as his own, and then accomplish his vow, which was easier on the boundary than in distant Bogdanets. "God's will! God's will!" repeated he in his soul. But he was ashamed of his hurried delight the next moment, and said, turning to Hlava, —

" I am sorry for him, and I will say so to every one."

" People declare," answered the attendant, " that the Germans feared him as death." Then after a moment he asked: "Shall we return to the castle now?"

" By way of Nedzborz," answered Zbyshko.

So they went to Nedzborz, and stopped before a residence in which an old noble, named Jeleh, received them. Yurand they did not find, but the old man gave good news.

"We rubbed him with snow to the bones almost," said he, " and poured wine into his mouth; then we steamed him in a bath, where he regained breathing."

"Is he alive? " inquired Zbyshko, with delight; for at this news he forgot his own affairs.

"He is alive, but God knows if he will recover; for the soul is not glad to turn back when it has made half the journey."

" Why was he taken from here?"

"He was taken because men from the prince came. We covered him with all the feather "beds in the house, and they took him."

" Did he not mention his daughter?"

" He had barely begun to breathe; he had not recovered speech."

"But the others?"

"Are now behind God's stove. Poor people; they will not be at mass unless at that one which the Lord Jesus Himself will celebrate in heaven."

" Did none revive ? "

" None. Enter, instead of talking at the porch. If you wish to see them, they are lying near the fire in the servants' hall. Come in."

But they did not go, though the old man pressed them; for he was glad to detain people and "chat" with them. They had a long piece of road yet from Nedzborz to Tsehanov; besides, Zbyshko was burning to see Yurand at the earliest, and learn something.

They rode, therefore, as rapidly as possible along the drifted highway. When they arrived it was past midnight, and the mass was just finishing in the castle chapel. To Zbyshko's ears came the lowing of cattle and the bleating of goats, which pious voices imitated according to ancient custom, in memory of the Lord's birth in a stable. After mass the princess came to Zbyshko with a face full of fear and anxiety.

" But where is Danusia?" asked she. VOL. i. —20

" She has not come. Has not Yurand told? — for I hear that he is alive."

" Merciful Jesus! This is a punishment from God, and woe to us! Yurand has not spoken, and he is lying like a block of wood."

" Have no fear, gracious lady. Danusia remained in Spyhov."

" How dost thou know? "

" I know, because in no sleigh was there a trace of a change of clothing for her. She would not have come in one cloak."

" True, as God is dear to me! "

And quickly her eyes began to sparkle with pleasure.

" Hei, dear Jesus, Thou who wert born this night, it is evident that not Thy anger, but Thy blessing is upon us."

Still the arrival of Yurand without Danusia surprised her; so she inquired further, —

" What could have kept her at home? "

Zbyshko explained his surmises. They seemed correct, but did not cause her excessive alarm.

"Yurand will owe his life to us now," said she; "and to tell the truth, it is to thee that he owes it; for thou didst go to dig him out of the snow. He would, indeed, have a stone in his breast were he to resist any longer! There is in this a warning of God, for him not to resist the holy Sacrament. The moment that he recovers and speaks, I will tell him so."

"He must recover first; for it is unknown why Danusia has not come. But if she is ill? "

"Do not talk foolishness. As it is, I am sorry that she is not here. If she had been ill he would not have left her."

"True!"

And they went to Yurand. It was as hot in the room as in a bath, and perfectly lighted; for immense logs of pine were burning in the chimney. Father Vyshonek was watching the sick man, who was lying on a couch under bearskins; his face was pale, his hair damp from perspiration, his eyes closed. His mouth was open, and his breast moved with labor, but so violently that the skins with which he was covered rose and fell from the breathing.

" How is he?" asked the princess.

" We have poured a mug of heated wine into his mouth," answered the priest, " am? he is perspiring."

"Is he sleeping?"

"It may be that he is not sleeping; for his breast moves tremendously."

" Have you tried to speak with him?"

" I have tried, but he gives no answer, and I think that he will not speak before daylight."

"We will wait for daylight," said the princess.

The priest insisted that she should go to rest, but she would not listen to him. It was with her a question always and in everything to equal in Christian virtues, and, therefore, in nursing the sick, the late queen, Yadviga, and redeem her father's soul by her merits; hence, in a country which had been Christian for centuries she missed no opportunity to show herself more zealous than others, and thus efface the remembrance that she had been born in pagan error. Moreover, the wish was burning her to learn something from Yurand touching Danusia; for she was not altogether at rest concerning her. So, sitting down at the side of his couch, she began to repeat the rosary, and then to doze. Zbyshko, who was not entirely well yet, and who in addition had labored immensely in the riding of the night, soon followed her example, and after an hour they had both fallen asleep so soundly that they would have slept till a late hour, perhaps, had not the bell of the castle chapel roused them at daybreak.

It roused Yurand also, who opened his eyes, sat erect on the couch quickly, and looked around with blinking eyes.

4 ' Praised be Jesus Christ! How is it with you ? " asked the princess.

But apparently he had not regained consciousness; for he looked at the princess as though he knew her not.

" Come this way! come this way to dig the drift! " called he after a moment.

"In God's name! You are in Tsehanov! " cried the lady.

Yurand wrinkled his forehead like a man who is collecting his thoughts with difficulty, and answered, —

"In Tsehanov? My child is waiting for me — and the prince and princess — Danusia! Dauusia! "

Then closing his eyes, he dropped again to the pillow. Zbyshko and the princess were terrified lest he had died; but at that very instant his breast moved with deep breath, as in the case of a man seized by heavy sleep.

Father Vyshonek placed a finger on his own lips and made a sign not to rouse the man; then he whispered, —

" He may sleep all day in this manner."

" True; but what did he say ? " asked the princess.

" He said that his child was waiting for him in Tsehanov," answered Zbyshko.

" He said that because he has not regained consciousness," explained the priest.

CHAPTER XXIV.

THE priest even feared that at a second awakening dizziness might seize the sick man and deprive him of his mind for a long time. But he promised the princess and Zbyshko that when Yurand spoke he would inform them. They left the chamber, and he went to sleep himself.

Yurand woke on the second day just before noon, but this time in perfect consciousness. The princess and Zbyshko were with him. He sat up on the couch, looked at the princess, recognized her, and said, —

" Gracious lady— as God lives, am I in Tsehanov, then?"

" Yes, and you have slept over Christmas."

"The snow covered me. Who saved me?"

"This knight, Zbyshko of Bogdanets. You remember, you saw him in Cracow."

Yurand looked a while with his sound eye at the young man, then said, —

" I remember. But where is Danusia?"

" Did she come with you? " asked the princess, with alarm.

"How could she come with me when I was going to her?"

Zbyshko and the princess looked at each other, thinking that fever was speaking through Yurand's mouth yet.

"Come to thyself," said the lady, "by the dear God! Was not the girl with you?"

"The girl! With me? " asked Yurand, with amazement.

"All your attendants perished, but she was not found among them. Why did you leave her in Spyhov?"

Yurand repeated once more, but now with alarm in his voice, —

" In Spyhov? Why, gracious lady, she is living with you, not with me."

"But you sent people and a letter for her to the hunting-lodge."

"In the name of the Father and the Son!" answered Yurand. " I have not sent for her at all."

That moment the princess grew pale.

" What is this? " asked she. " Are you sure that you are in your right mind ? "

«« By the mercy of God! where is my child ? " cried Yurand, springing up.

" Listen. An armed escort came for Danusia to the hunting-lodge, bringing a letter from you. In the letter it was \vntten°that during a fire beams had crushed you; that you were half blind, and wished to see your daughter. Then they took Danusia and drove away."

" Woe! " cried Yurand. " As God is in heaven, there was no fire in Spyhov, and I did not send for her."

Now the priest returned with a letter, which he gave to Yurand, and asked, —

" Is this the writing of your priest? "

" I do not know."

"But the seal?"

" The seal is mine. What is in the letter? "

Father Vyshonek read the letter; Yurand listened, grasping his own hair.

" The letter is false," said he; " the seal imitated ! Woe to my soul! They have seized my child, and will destroy her."

"Who?"

" The Knights of the Cross! "

" God's wounds! We must inform the prince. Let him send messengers to the Grand Master! " cried the lady. " Merciful Jesus, rescue her, aid her! "

Saying this, she hurried out of the room with a cry. Yurand sprang from his bed, and began feverishly to draw the clothing onto his immense back. Zbyshko sat as if petrified, but after a while his set teeth gritted ominously.

" How do you know that the Knights of the Cross took her? " asked the pi'iest.

" I will swear on the Passion of Christ! "

"Wait! It is possible. They went to the hunting-lodge to complain against you. They wanted vengeance."

" They carried her away! " cried Zbyshko on a sudden.

He rushed out of the room, and running to the stables commanded to make sleighs and saddle horses ready, without knowing clearly himself why he did so. He understood only this, that they must rescue Danusia, and go at once, —even to Prussia, — and there snatch her from enemies' hands or perish.

He returned then to tell Yurand that arms and horses would be ready immediately. He was sure that Yurand also would go with him. In his heart anger was boiling, and

pain and sorrow, but he did not lose hope; for it seemed to him that he and the terrible Knight, could do anything, and that they might attack even all the power of the Order.

In the room, besides Yurand, the priest, and the princess, he found Prince Yanush, De Lorche, and Pan Mikolai, whom the prince, when he had learned of the affair, sum-moned»also to counsel; and he did so because of the old man's sound sense and perfect knowledge of the Knights, among whom he had passed long years in captivity.

"We should begin prudently; avoid mistakes caused through anger, and not ruin the girl," said Pan Mikolai. " We should complain at once to the Grand Master, and if your Princely Grace gives me a letter, I will deliver it."

" I will give the letter, and you will go with it," answered the prince. " We will not let the girl perish, so help me God and the holy cross! The Grand Master fears war with the King of Poland, and for him it is important to win over my brother and me. You may be sure that she was not carried off at his command — and he will order that she be delivered to us."

" But if it was at his command? " asked the priest.

" Though he is a Knight of the Cross, there is more honor in him than in others," answered the prince, " and as I have said to you, he would prefer at present to please rather than anger me. Oh, they put tallow into our skins as long as they were able, but now they understand that if we Mazovians help Yagello, it will go ill with them."

" True," said Pan Mikolai. " The Knights of the Cross do nothing without a reason; so I conclude that if they have carried off the girl, they have done so only to knock the sword from Yurand s hand, or get a ransom, or exchange her."

Here he turned to the lord of Spyhov.

" Whom have you among prisoners? "

" De Bergov," answered Yurand.

" Is he a considerable person? "

"Evidently a man of distinction."

De Lorche hearing the question inquired about him, and when he learned what the question was, said, —

" He is a relative of the Count of Guelders, a great benefactor of the Order, and of a family which has served it."

" That is true," said Pan Mikolai, after he had interpreted

De Lorche's words to those present. " Men of his family have held high office in the Order."

" Danveld and De Lowe mentioned him very emphatically," said the prince. " Whenever one of them opened his mouth he said that De Bergov must be liberated. As God is in heaven, they carried off the girl beyond doubt to liberate him."

" Then they will yield her up," said the priest.

"But it is better to learn where she is," said Pan Mikolai. " For suppose that the Grand Master asks, ' Whom shall I command to yield her up ?' what answer shall we give ? "

" Where is she! " asked Yurand, in a dull voice. "They are not keeping her surely on the boundary, out of fear that I might capture her, but they have taken her somewhere to a distant island of the sea, or the Vistula."

" We will find her and rescue her,' said Zbyshko.

But the prince broke out suddenly with suppressed anger:

"The dog brothers! they have seized her from my house, and insulted me; while I live I shall not forgive them. I have had enough of their treasons! enough of their attacks ! Better for any one to have wolf men for neighbors! But now the Grand Master must punish those comturs, return the girl, and send envoys to me with excuses. Otherwise I will summon a levy! "

Here he struck the table with his fist, and added, —

"Oh, indeed! My brother of Plotsk will go with me, and Vitold, and the power of Yagello the king. There is an end of moderation! A saint would snort patience out of himself through the nostrils. I have had enough of it! "

All grew silent, waiting with their counsel till the prince's anger should be calmed. The princess rejoiced that he took the affair of Danusia to heart so much, for she knew that he was patient, but resolute, and that once he had undertaken a thing he would not leave it until he had won victory.

Then Father Vyshonek began, —

" Once there was obedience in the Order, and no comtur dared begin anything without permission of the Chapter and the Grand Master. For this reason God gave into their hands countries so considerable that He raised them almost above every other temporal power. But now there is among them neither obedience, justice, faith, nor honesty. Nothing but greed and such rage as if they were wolves and not men. How are they to obey the commands of the Grand

Master or the Chapter when they do not obey those of God? Each
in his own castle is like a ruling prince, and each helps the other in wickedness. If we complain to the Master they will deny. The Master will command them to yield up the girl, but they will not do so, or they will even say: ' She is not with us; we did not carry her away.' If he commands them to take an oath, they will take one. What are we to do then?"

" What are we to do ? " said PanMikolai. " Let Yurand go to Spyhov; if they carried her away, either they will give her for a ransom or exchange her for De Bergov; they must inform some one, and they will inform no one else but Yurand."

" The men who came to the hunting-lodge took her," said Father Vyshonek.

" Then the Grand Master will summon them to account, or command them to meet Yurand in the field."

"They must meet me!" exclaimed Zbyshko, "for I sent the first challenge."

Yurand took his hands from his face, and inquired, —

" Who were at the hunting-lodge? "

" Dan veld, old De Lowe, and the two brothers, Gottfried and Rotgier," answered the priest. " They complained and wished the prince to command you to free De Bergov from captivity. But the prince, learning from De Fourcy that the Germans attacked first, reproached them and sent them away unsatisfied."

" Go to Spyhov," said Prince Yanush, " for they will make announcement there. They have not done so yet, because the armor-bearer of this young knight here crushed Danveld's arm when he carried the challenge. Go to Spyhov, and when they make announcement let me know. They will send you your child in place of De Bergov, but still I shall not omit revenge, for they have offended me by taking her from my house."

Here anger seized him anew, for really the Knights of the Cross had exhausted his patience, and after a while he added, —

"Hei! they have blown and blown the fire, but at last they will burn their own snouts in it."

" They will deny 5 " repeated the priest.

" As soon as they notify Yurand that they have the girl, they will not be able to deny," answered Pan Mikolai, somewhat impatiently. " I believe that they are not keeping her on the boundary, and that, as Yurand has justly remarked,
either they took her to some distant castle or to some island near the coast, but when there is proof that they did it they will not deny before the Master."

But Yurand began to repeat in a kind of strange and terrible voice,—

" Danveld, De Lowe, Gottfried, Rotgier! "

Pan Mikolai recommended besides to send experienced and very adroit men to Prussia to inquire in Schytno and Insbork about Danusia, — was she there, and if not whither had they taken her. The prince seized his staff and went out to give needful orders ; the princess turned to Yurand, wishing to strengthen him with a kind word.

"• How do you feel?.." asked she.

He made no answer for a while, just as if he had not heard the question, but later he said on a sudden, —

" As if some one had struck me in an old wound."

" Have faith in God's mercy, — Danusia will return; only give them De Bergov."

" I would not begrudge them even blood."

The princess hesitated whether or not to mention the marriage to him, but when she had thought a little she did not like to add a new pain to Yurand's misfortunes, which were already grievous, and moreover a certain fear seized her. " He and Zbyshko together will search for her; let Zbyshko tell him at an opportunity," thought she ; " but now it might disturb his brain altogether." So she preferred to talk of something else.

" Do not blame us," said she. " Men came in your colors with a letter bearing your seal, and announcing that you were sick; that sight was leaving you; that you wished to see your child once more. How could we oppose, and fail to carry out the order of a father ? "

Yurand fell at her feet.

" I blame no one, gracious lady."

" And know this, that God will restore her to you; for His eye is above her. He will send her rescue, as he sent it at the last hunt when the wild bull attacked us, and the Lord Jesus inspired Zbyshko to defend Danusia and me, for which reason the prince gave him spurs and a belt. You see ! the hand of God is above her. Of course you grieve for your daughter, and I myself am filled with sorrow. I thought that she would come with you; that I should see my dearest, but meanwhile —

Her voice trembled and tears came to her eyes, but in

Yurand despair, which up to that moment had been restrained, burst forth; for a while it was as sudden and terrible as a whirlwind. He seized his long hair with his hands and fell to beating the timbers of the wall with his head, groaning and repeating in a hoarse voice, —

"O Jesus! O Jesus! O Jesus!"

Zbyshko sprang to him, and shaking him by the arms with all his might, cried, —

" To the road with us! To Spyhov!"

CHAPTER XXV.

" WHOSE escort is this ? " asked Yurand beyond Radzanov, starting up from meditation as if from a dream.

" Mine," answered Zbyshko.

"But did all my men perish?"

"I saw them dead in Nedzborz."

" The old warriors are gone! "

Zbyshko made no answer, and they rode on in silence, but quickly; for they wished to be in Spyhov at the earliest, hoping to find there messengers from the Knights of the Cross. Fortunately for them, frosts had come, and the roads were beaten, hence they could hurry. Toward evening Yurand spoke again, and inquired about those monks of the Order who had been at the hunting-lodge. Zbyshko explained everything, and told also of their complaints and their departure; of the death of De Fourcy, and the action of his own armor-bearer, who had crushed Danveld's arm in such terrible fashion. During this narrative one circumstance struck him, the presence at the lodge of that woman who had brought the healing balsam from Danveld. At the stopping-place he fell to inquiring of Hlava and Sanderus touching this person, but neither of them knew exactly what had become of her. It seemed to them that she had gone away either with the men who had come for Danusia or soon after. It occurred then to Zbyshko that she might have been sent to warn those men in case Yurand had been present at the hunting-lodge. In that event, they would not have presented themselves as people from Spyhov; they could have some other letter prepared to give the princess, instead of the false one attributed to Yurand. All this was planned with hellish acuteness, and Zbyshko, who till then had known the Knights of the Cross in the open field only, thought for the first time that hands were not sufficient to oppose them, but that a man had to conquer them with his head also. To him this thought was bitter; for his immense pain and sorrow turned first of all to desire for blood and struggle. To him even the rescue of Danusia presented itself as a series of battles, either alone or in company; meanwhile he

saw that it might be needful to chain down desire of revenge and head-breaking as he would a bear, and seek new ways entirely of finding and saving Danusia. While thinking of this, he regretted that Matsko was not with him. Matsko was as adroit as he was valiant. Still he resolved to send Sanderus from Spyhov to Schytno to find that woman, and endeavor to learn from her what had become of Danusia. He said to himself that though Sanderus might wish to betray him, he could not injure the cause much, and if he were true he might render considerable service; for his occupation gave him access to all places.

Wishing to take counsel first with Yurand, he deferred this matter till they reached Spyhov, all the more as night had fallen, and it seemed to him that Yurand, as he sat on his lofty saddle of a knight, had fallen asleep from his toils, his suffering, and grievous sorrow. But Yurand was riding with hanging head only for the reason that misfortune had bent him. And it was evident that he was thinking of it continually ; for his heart was full of cruel fears, since he said at last, —

" Would that I had frozen to death at Nedzborz. Was it thou who dug me out of the snow ? "

"I, with others."

*' And at that hunt it was thou who saved my child? "

*' What was it my duty to do ? "

" And now wilt thou help me? "

But in Zbyshko love for Danusia burst forth, and hatred against the Knights of the Cross so great that he rose in his saddle and spoke through his set teeth as if with difficulty, —

" Listen to what I say: Though I had to gnaw Prussian castles with my teeth, I would gnaw them down and get her."

A moment of silence followed. The vengeful and unrestrained nature of Yurand responded evidently with all its force under the influence of these words; for he gritted his teeth in the darkness, and after a while repeated the names, —

" Danveld, Lowe, Rotgier, Gottfried."

In his soul he thought that if they wished him to release De Bergov he would release him; if they demanded pay in addition, he would pay, though he were to add all Spyhov. But woe later on to those who had raised hands on his only child.

All that night sleep did not close the eyes of those two

men for one moment. Toward morning they could hardly recognize each other, so much had their faces changed in that single night. At last Zbyshko's suffering and resolve astonished Yurand ; so he said, —

" She covered thee with a veil and wrested thee from death — I know that. But dost thou love her besides ? "

Zbyshko looked him straight in the eyes with a face almost insolent, and answered, —

" She is my wife."

At this Yuraud stopped his horse, and gazed at Zbyshko, blinking from amazement.

" What hast thou said? " inquired he.

" I say that she is my wife, and that I am her husband."

The Knight of Spyhov covered his eyes with his glove, as if his sight had been dazzled by a lightning flash, but he said nothing. After a while he rode on, and pushing to the head of the escort advanced in silence.

CHAPTEE XXVI.

ZBTSHKO, riding behind, was unable to restrain himself long, and said in his soul, " I would rather see him burst out in anger than become stubborn."

So he rode up and said, touching Yurand's stirrup with his own, —

" Listen and hear how it was. You know what Danusia did for me in Cracow, but you do not know that in Bogdanets they wished me to marry Yagenka, the daughter of Zyh of Zgorzelitse. My uncle, Matsko, and her father wished the marriage, and the Abbot of Tulcha, our relative, a rich man, wished it also. But why talk long of this? She is an honest maiden, beautiful as a deer, and has a proper dowry. But it could not take place. I wanted Yagenka, but I wanted Danusia more, and I went to her in Mazovia; for I tell you sincerely I could not live longer without her. You remember how you yourself loved — remember that! and you will not wonder at me."

Here Zbyshko stopped while waiting for some word from Yurand, but, as he remained silent, the young man continued, —

" At the hunting-lodge God granted me to save the princess and Danusia from a wild bull, and the princess said immediately after: ' Now Yurand will not be opposed; for how could he refuse reward for such a deed ?' But even then I had not thought of taking her without your parental permission. Besides, I had no chance of doing so; for the savage beast had so crushed me that he almost squeezed out my soul. But afterward, you know, those people came for Danusia, as if to take her to Spyhov, and I had not risen from my bed yet. I thought that I should never see her again; I thought that you would take her to Spyhov and give her to some other man. In Cracow you were opposed to me, you know. I thought that I should die. Hei, mighty God, what a night that was ! Nothing but suffering; nothing but sorrow! I thought when she went away from me that even the sun would not rise again. You understand people's love and their sorrow."

For a moment tears quivered in Zbyshko's voice, but he had a brave heart, so he mastered himself, and continued, —

" Men came for her in the evening, and wanted to take her immediately, but the princess commanded them to wait till morning. Now, the Lord Jesus inspired me to implore the princess and beg of her Danusia. I thought that if I were to die I should have even that consolation. Remember that the girl was to go, and I was to remain there sick, almost dying. There was no time to beg for your permission. The prince was not at the hunting-lodge, so the princess hesitated; she had no one with whom to advise: At last she and Father Vyshonek took pity on me, and Father Vyshonek married us. God's might, God's justice."

"• God's punishment," added Yurand, in a deep voice.

"Why punishment?" asked Zbyshko. "Only notice, they sent for her before the marriage, and whether it took place or not they would have carried her away."

Yurand said nothing, and rode on shut up in himself, gloomy and with such a stony face that Zbyshko, though he felt immediately that consolation which the confession of a long-hidden secret always produces, was frightened at last, and said to himself with increasing alarm, that the old knight had grown stubborn in his anger, and that thenceforth they would be as strangers to each other and enemies.

And a moment of great affliction came on him. Never had he been in such a plight since the day of leaving Bogdanets. It seemed to him that there was no hope of reconciling Yurand, and, what was worse, no hope of saving Danusia; it seemed that all was useless; that in future there would fall on him only increasing misfortune and increasing misery. But this oppression was brief, or rather, in accordance with his nature, it turned quickly into anger and a desire for quarrel and battle.

" He wants no agreement," thought Zbyshko, in reference to Yurand; "let there be disagreement, let come what may! " And he was ready to spring at the eyes of Yurand himself, lie was seized with a desire for battle with some one about some question ; he wished to do something if he could give escape to his regret, his bitterness and anger; if he could find some relief.

Meanwhile, they halted on the cross-road at an inn called Svetlik, where Yurand, when on journeys from the prince's castle to Spyhov, usually gave rest to his men and horses. He stopped now unconsciously. After a time Yurand and

Zbyshko found themselves in a room apart. On a sudden Yurand halted before the young knight, and fixing a glance on him inquired,—

" And hast thou wandered in here for her? "

Zbyshko answered almost rudely, —

" Do you think that I shall hesitate to answer? "

And he looked straight into Yurand's eyes, ready to burst out with anger against anger. But in the old warrior's face there was no stubbornness; there was only sadness almost without limit.

" And didst thou save my child? " asked he after a while, " and dig me out of the snow? "

Zbyshko looked at him with wonder and fear lest his brain might have become unsettled; for Yurand repeated exactly the same questions which he had asked already.

" Sit down," said he; " for it seems to me that you are weak yet."

But Yurand raised his hands, placed them on Zbyshko's shoulders, and all at once he drew him with what strength he had to his heart. Zbyshko, when he recovered from momentary astonishment, seized him around the waist, and they held each other long; for common suffering and misfortune had bound them together.

"When they let go of each other, Zbyshko grasped the old knight's knees, and then kissed his hand, with tears in his eyes.

" Then you will not be offended with me? " asked he.

To which Yurand answered, —

" I was opposed to you; for in my soul I had devoted her to God."

" Y"ou devoted her to God, and God to me. It is His will."

" His will! " repeated Yurand; " but now we need mercy."

" Whom should God aid if not a father looking for his child, or a husband seeking his wife? He will not assist bandits, be sure."

" Still they carried her away," answered Yurand.

"Then give them De Bergov for her."

"I will give them everything they ask."

But at thoughts of the Knights of the Cross old hatred was roused in him at once, and embraced him like a flame; for after a while he added through his set teeth, — " And I will give that which they do not want." "I, too, have made a vow," said Zbyshko; "but now we must be off to Spyhov! "

VOL. I. —21

And he urged the saddling of the horses. In fact, when the horses had eaten oats and the people had warmed themselves in the rooms somewhat, they moved on, though it had grown dark out of doors. Since the road before them was long, and there were severe frosts at night,

Yurand and Zbyshko, who had not regained all their strength yet, rode in a sleigh. Zbyshko told of his uncle, Matsko, for whom he was yearning in spirit. He grieved, too, that that uncle was not present; for his cunning might be of equal use with his valor, cunning which against such enemies was even more needed than valor. At last he turned to Yurand, and asked,—

" But are you cunning ? For I am not able in any way to succeed in that."

"Neither am I," answered Yurand. "It was not with cunning that I warred against them, but with this hand and with the grief that is in me."

"Ah, that I can understand," said the young knight. " I understand because I love Danusia, and they carried her away. If they should — but God preserve — "

And he did not finish; for at the very thought he felt in his breast, not his own, but a wolfs heart. For some time they went forward in silence over the white road filled with moonlight, and then Yurand said as it were to himself, —

" Had they reason for revenge, I should not say anything. But, by the dear God, they have none. I fought with them in the field when I was going on an embassy from our prince to Vitold, but here I lived with them as neighbor with neighbor. Bartosh Nalench seized forty knights who were going to Malborg; he put them in chains and confined them underground in Kozmiu. The Knights of the Cross had to pay half a wagon-load of money for them. As to me, when a German guest happened along who was going to the Knights of the Cross, I entertained him as one knight another, and gave him presents. More than once Knights of the Cross came across the swamp to me. I was not harsh to them in those days, and still they did to me that which even to-day I would not do to my greatest enemy."

And terrible recollections rent him with increasing force; the voice died in his breast for a time, then he continued, half groaning, —

" I had one dear lamb, the same to me as the single heart in my breast; they bound her with a rope as they might bind

a dog, and she grew pale and died on that rope of theirs. Xow they have taken my child — Jesus! O Jesus!"

Again there was silence. Zbyshko raised toward the moon his youthful face, in which was depicted amazement; then he looked at Yurand.

" Father," said he, " it would be better for the Knights to win the love of men and not their vengeance. Why do they work so much harm on all people and all nations?'"

Yurand spread out his arms as if in despair, and said in a dull voice, —

"I know not."

Zbyshko meditated a time over his own question, but after a while his mind turned to Yurand, —

" People say that you have wreaked on them a praiseworthy vengeance."

Yurand choked down his pain, recovered, and said, —

" Yes, for I vowed it to them—and I vowed to God that if He would let me wreak that vengeance I would devote to Him the child which was left to me. For this reason I was opposed to thee. But now I know not if that was done by His will or if thou hast roused His anger by thy act."

" No," said Zbyshko. " Just now I have told you that if the marriage had not taken place, the dog brothers would have seized her anyhow. God accepted your wish, but Danusia He gave to me: for without His will we should not have done anything."

" Every sin is against the will of God."

" A sin is, but not a sacrament. A sacrament is a thing of God."

" For this reason there is no cure in thy case."

"Glory to God that there is not! Complain not, moreover; for no man could help you against these bandits as I shall. Look here ! I will pay them for Danusia in my own way, but if there is even one of those alive who carried off your dead one, give him to me, and you will see 1"

Yurand shook his head.

"No," answered he gloomily. " Of those, not a man is alive."

For some time nothing was audible but the snorting of horses and the dull tread of hoofs as they struck the beaten snow.

" Once, one night," continued Yurand, " I heard some voice, as if coming out of the wall, and it said to me, ' Ven-

geance enough!' but I did not obey; for that was not her voice."

"And what voice might it have been?" inquired Zbyshko, with alarm.

" I know not. Often in Spyhov some one speaks in the wall to me, and groans sometimes; for many of them have died in chains in the cellar."

" But what does the priest say?"

" The priest blessed the castle, and told me to stop taking vengeance; but that cannot be. I became too grievous to the Germans, and then they set out to take vengeance themselves. They formed ambushes and challenged me to the field. That was the case lately. Meinegger and De Bergov challenged me first."

" Have you ever taken ransom ? "

" No. Of those whom I seized captive, De Bergov will be the first to go out alive."

The conversation stopped; for they turned from the broad highway to a narrow road, along which they advanced slowly; for it was steep, and in places changed into forest hollows full of snow-drifts difficult to cross. In spring or summer, in time of rains, this road must have been almost impassable.

" Are we near Spyhov now?" inquired Zbyshko.

" Yes," answered Yurand. " There is a large strip of pine wood yet, and then a swamp; in the midst of that swamp is my castle. Beyond are meadows and dry fields, but to the castle it is impossible to go except by a dam. More than once the Germans wanted to reach me, but they could not, and of their bones a great many are decaying along the forest edges."

"Then it is not easy to go there," said Zbyshko. "If the knights send people with letters, how will they find the way to you ? "

" They send often; they have people who know the way."

" God grant us to meet them in Spyhov."

The wish was to be realized earlier than the young knight imagined; for when they had driven out of the wood to an open plain, on which stood Spyhov in the midst of a swamp, they saw two men on horseback, and a low sleigh, in which were sitting three dark figures. The night was very clear, so that on the white cover of snow they could see the whole company distinctly. The hearts of Yurand and Zbyshko beat more quickly at sight of it; for who

would go to Spyhov at night except messengers from the Order ?

Zbyshko directed the driver to go with more speed, and soon they approached so considerably that the people heard them, and the two horsemen, who were watching evidently over the safety of the sleigh, turned toward them, and raising crossbows from their shoulders, cried, —

" Wer da (who is there)?"

" Germans," whispered Yurand to Zbyshko.

" Then he raised his voice, and said, —

" It is my right to inquire, thine to answer. Who are ye? *"

"Wayfarers."

" What kind of wayfarers? *

"Pilgrims."

"Whence?"

"From Schytno."

" They are the persons!" whispered Yurand again.

The sleighs were now near each other, and at the same time in front of both appeared six horsemen. These were guards from Spyhov, who night and day watched the dam leading to the castle. In front of the horses ran dogs, dangerous and large, quite like wolves.

The guards, on recognizing Yurand, called out in his honor, but in the calls was heard wonder that the heir was returning so soon and unexpectedly ; but he, occupied entirely with the messengers, turned to them a second time.

" Whither are ye going? " asked he.

"To Spyhov."

" What do ye wish? "

" We can only tell that to the master himself."

The words, " I am the master of Spyhov," were on Yurand's lips, but he restrained himself, understanding that the conversation could not take place before people. He gave command to go almost as fast as the horses could gallop.

Zbyshko was so impatient also for news from Danusia that he could turn attention to no other thing. He was all impatience when the guards stopped his way twice on the dam, impatient when they let down the bridge beyond which was an enormous palisade on the wall, and though formerly a desire had seized him often to see what sort of a look that castle of ominous repute had, at sight of which Germans made the sign of the cross on themselves, he saw nothing now save those messengers of the Order, from whom he might

learn where Danusia was and when freedom would be restored to her. But he did not foresee that grievous disappointment was waiting for him in a moment.

Besides the horsemen given for defence and the driver, the embassy from Schytno was composed of two persons, one of whom was that same woman who had brought the healing balsam to the hunting-lodge; the other a young pilgrim. Zbyshko did not know the woman, for he had not seen her; the pilgrim seemed at once to him a disguised attendant. Yurand conducted both to the corner chamber. He stood before them, immense in size and almost terrible in the light which fell on him from the fire blazing in the chimney.

'' Where is my child ? " asked he.

They were frightened when they stood eye to eye with the terrible Yurand. The pilgrim, though his face was insolent, simply trembled like a leaf, and the woman shook in every limb. Her glance passed from Yurand's face to Zbyshko, then to the shining, bald head of Father Kaleb, and again returned to Yurand, as if with the question, What are those two doing here?

" Lord," said she at last, " we know not what your question means; but we are sent here to you on important business. He who sent commanded us expressly to talk to you without witnesses."

"I have no secrets before them," said Yurand.

" If you command them to remain, we shall pray you for nothing save permission to leave here to-morrow."

On the face of Yurand, who was unaccustomed to resistance, anger was evident. For a time his yellow moustache moved ominously, but he remembered that Danusia was in peril, and restrained himself. Zbyshko, for whom the first question was that the conversation should take place at the earliest, and who was certain that Yurand would repeat it to him, said, —

" Since it is to be so, remain alone."

And he went out with Father Kaleb, but he had hardly found himself in the main chamber, the walls of which were covered with shields and armor won by Yurand, when the Cheh approached him.

" Lord," said he, " this is the same woman."

" What woman ? "

" From the Knights of the Cross, who brought the Her-cynian balsam; I recognized her right away, and so did

Sanderus. She has come evidently to spy, and she knows surely where the young lady is."

** And we shah 1 know," said Zbyshko. " Dost thou recognize the pilgrim too? "

" No," replied Sanderus. " But buy no indulgences from that man; for he is a false pilgrim. If he were put to torture, one might learn much from him."

" Wait," answered Zbyshko.

"Barely had the door of the corner room closed behind Zbyshko and the priest, when the woman pushed up quickly to Yurand, and whispered, —

" Bandits carried off your daughter."

" Bandits with crosses on their mantles? "

"No. But God blessed the pious brothers; so they rescued her, and now she is in their possession."

" Where is she ? " I ask.

" She is under the protection of the pious brother, Schaum-berg," answered the woman, crossing her hands on her breast and bowing with humility.

Yurand, when he heard the terrible name of the executioner of Vitold's children, grew as pale as linen. After a while he sat,on a bench, closed his eyes, and began to wipe away the cold sweat which was in drops on his forehead.

Seeing this, the pilgrim, though unable just before to restrain his terror, put his hand on his hip, threw himself on a bench, stretched out his feet, and looked at Yurand with eyes full of pride and contempt. A long silence followed.

" Brother Markwart helps Brother Schaumberg to care for her," said the woman. "It is a diligent attention, and no harm will happen to the young lady."

" What am I to do to induce them to give her up to me ?" asked Yurand.

" To become humble before the Order," answered the pilgrim, with pride.

Hearing this, Yurand rose, went to the man, and, bending over him, said, with a restrained and terrible voice, —

" Silence! "

The pilgrim was frightened again. He knew that he might threaten and might say something which would restrain and break Yurand, but heVas afraid that before he could utter the word something terrible might happen him; so he was as silent, and turned on the terrible face of the master of

Spyhov eyes as round as if petrified from fear, and sat motionless, but his chin began to quiver.

Yurand turned to the sister of the Order.

" Have you a letter? "

" I have no letter. "What we have to convey, we must, by command, convey through word of mouth."

"Then speak!"

She repeated once more, as if wishing that Yurand should beat it well into his memory,

—

" Brothers Schaumberg and Markwart are guarding the young lady; therefore restrain your anger; for, though you have wronged the Order during many years, the brothers wish to pay you with good for evil, if you will satisfy their just wishes."

"What do they wish?"

" That you free Pan de Bergov."

Yurand drew a deep breath of relief.

" I will give them De Bergov."

" And other prisoners which you have in Spyhov?"

" There are two attendants of Meinegger and De Bergov, besides their servants."

" You must free them, and reward them for their captivity."

" May God not permit me to haggle over the freedom of my daughter."

" The pious Knights of the Cross expected this," said the woman; " but this is not all that they commanded me to say to you. People of some sort, undoubtedly bandits, stole away your daughter. They did so of course to receive a rich ransom. God permitted the brothers to rescue her for you, and now they ask nothing but that you render up their guest and comrade. But the brothers know, and you know, what a hatred there is toward them in this country, and how unjustly all suspect their most pious acts even. For this cause they are sure that if people here should learn that your daughter is among them, they would suspect that it was they who stole her, and in this way, in return for their virtue, they would receive nothing but complaints and slander. Oh, what I say is true! evil and malicious people of this country have paid them often in that way, by which the fame of the pious Order has suffered greatly, fame which the brothers must protect; and, therefore, they lay down one more condition, that you inform the prince of this country and all the stern knighthood how the truth is; that not the

Knights of the Cross, but bandits, carried off your daughter, and that you had to ransom her from robbers."

" It is true," said Yurand, " that robbers stole my child, and that I must ransom her from robbers."

" And you must not speak otherwise to any one; for if even one man should learn that you had negotiations with the brothers, if even one living soul, or even one complaint should go to the Master or the Chapter, serious difficulties would follow."

Alarm appeared on Yurand's face. At the very first it had seemed to him quite natural that the comturs wished secrecy because they feared responsibility and ill repute; now the suspicion rose in him that there might be some other cause; but since he was unable to understand this cause, such fear seized him as seizes the most daring men when danger threatens, not themselves, but those who are near and dear to them. He resolved, however, to learn something further from the woman.

" The comturs wish secrecy," said he, " but what secret is there to keep when I release De Bergov and those others in ransom for my daughter? "

" You will say that you took a ransom for De Bergov so as to have something with which to pay the bandits."

" People will not believe; for I have never taken ransom," answered Yurand, gloomily.

"Well, it has never been a question of your child," hissed back the woman.

Again came silence, after which the pilgrim, who had summoned boldness now, and judged that Yurand needed still more curbing, said, —

"Such is the will of Brothers Schaumbergand Markwart."

" You will say that this pilgrim, who has come with me, brought you a ransom," continued the woman. "We will go from here with the noble De Bergov and the other captives."

"How is that?" asked Yurand, frowning. "Do you suppose that I will yield up captives before you return me my daughter?"

" Then choose another way. You can go to Schytno for your daughter; the brothers will take her there to meet you."

"I? ToSchytno?"

" Yes; for should bandits seize her on the road again, your suspicion and that of people here would fall upon the

pious knights a second time; therefore they prefer to give your child into your own hands."

" But who will guarantee me a return after I have crawled into the wolf's throat ? "

" The virtue of the brothers, their piety and justice."

Yurand walked up and down in the room; he began to foresee treason, and he feared it, but he felt at the same time that the Knights of the Cross had power to impose such conditions as pleased them, and that in presence of them he was powerless.

But evidently some plan came to his head; for stopping before the pilgrim on a sudden, he examined him quickly; then he turned to the woman, and said, —

" Well, I will go to Schytno. You and this man, who has on him the dress of a pilgrim, will await my return, after that you will go from here with De Bergov and the captives."

kt You do not wish, lord, to believe the knights," replied the pilgrim ; " how, then, are they to believe that when you return you will release us with De Bergov and the others ? "

Yurand's face grew pale from indignation, and a terrible moment came, in which it seemed that he was just ready to seize the pilgrim by the breast and put him under his knees, but he throttled the anger in his bosom, drew a deep breath, and spoke slowly with emphasis, —

' ' Whoever thou be, bend not my patience over much lest it break."

But the pilgrim turned to the sister.

" Tell what is commanded thee."

" Lord," said she, " we would not dare to doubt your oath on the sword and the honor of a knight, but it would not be proper for you to take an oath before people of common position, and we were not sent here for your oath."

" For what did they send you? "

" The brothers told us that you are not to mention to any one that you must be in Schytno with De Bergov and the captives."

At this Yurand's arms began to push backward and his fingers to spread out like the talons of a bird of prey; standing before the woman, he bent, as if he wished to speak into her ear.

" Did they not tell you that I would give command to break you and De Bergov on the wheel in Spyhov ? "

" Your daughter is in the power of the knights, and in the

care of Schaumberg and Markwart," replied the sister, with emphasis.

" Bandits, poisoners, hangmen! " burst out Yurand.

" Who will be able to avenge us, and who told us at parting : ' If all our commands are not complied with, it would be better that the girl died as did the children of Vitold.' Take your choice ! "

" And remember that you are in the power of the comturs," added the pilgrim. "They have no wish to wrong you, and the starosta of Schytno sends word by us that you will be free to go from his castle; but they wish you to come to bow down before the mantle of the knights, and beg the favor of the conquerors in return for what you have done to them. They wish to forgive you, but they wish first to bend your proud neck. You have denounced them as traitors and oath-breakers, so they wish you to give yourself up on faith in them. They will return freedom to you and your daughter, but you must beg for it. You have trampled them; you must swear that your hand will never rise again in hostility to the white mantle."

" So wish the comturs," added the woman, " and with them Schaumberg and Markwart."

A moment of deathlike silence followed. It seemed only that somewhere among the beams of the ceiling some muffled echo repeated, as if in terror: "Schaumberg, Markwart." From outside the window came also the cries of Yurand's archers watching on the bastions of the wall.

The pilgrim and the sister of the Order looked for a long time, now at each other, now at Yurand, who sat leaning against the wall motionless, and with face sunk in the shadow falling on it from a bundle of skins hung at the side of the window. In his head there remained one thought alone, that if he would not do the knights' will, they would strangle his daughter; if he should do their will, even then, perhaps, he would not save either himself or Danusia. And he saw no help, no escape. He felt above him a merciless superiority of power which was crushing him. He saw in spirit already the iron hands of the knights on the neck of Danusia; for, knowing them, he doubted not for an instant that they would kill her, cover her up in the ditch of the castle, and then deny, swear themselves out of it. Who would be able then to prove that they had kidnapped her? Yurand had, it is true, the messengers in his hands; he might take them to the prince to obtain a confession through torture, but the knights had

Danusia, and on their part might spare no torture on her. And for a time it seemed to him that his child was stretching her hands to him from a distance and imploring rescue. If even '.he knew certainly that she was in Schytno, he might move that same night to the boundary, fall upon the Germans who expected no attack, seize the castle, cut down the garrison, and free his child; but she, perhaps, was not in the castle, and surely not in the village of Schytno. Again it flashed through his head like lightning that if he should seize the woman and the pilgrim and take them straight to the Grand Master, perhaps the master would obtain from them a confession, and command the release of Danusia; but that lightning flash was quenched as quickly as it shone. Moreover, these people might say to the Master that they went to Spyhov to ransom De Bergov; that they had no knowledge of any girl. No! that road led to nothing — but what road led to anything? For he thought that if he should go to Schytno, they would put him in chains and thrust him into a dungeon; but Danusia they would not release anyhow, even for this reason, lest it be discovered that they had kidnapped her. Meanwhile death was above his only child; death was above the last life that was dear to him. And, finally, his thoughts grew confused, and his pain became so great that it strained itself and passed into numbness. He sat motionless, because his body had grown dead, as dead as if cut out of stone. Had he wished to stand up at that moment, he would not have been able to do so.

Meanwhile the others had grown tired of long waiting; so the woman rose and said, —

" Dawn is not distant, so, lord, permit us to withdraw; for we need rest."

" And refreshment after the long road," added the pilgrim.

Both bowed then to Yurand, and went out. But he continued sitting motionless, as if seized by sleep, or death. After a while, however, the door opened, and in it appeared Zbyshko^behind him the priest.

" Well, where are the messengers? What do they want? " inquired the young knight, approaching Yurand.

Yuraud quivered, but did not answer immediately; he merely blinked greatly, like a man roused from sleep.

" Are you not sick, lord?" asked the priest, who, knowing Yurand more intimately, saw that something unusual was happening within him.

"No," answered Yurand.

"But Danusia," continued Zbyshko, — "where is she, and what did they tell you? What did they bring?"

" A ran-som," answered Yurand, slowly.

" A ransom for Bergov ? "

" For Bergov."

" How for Bergov? "What has happened to you? "

" Nothing."

But there was in his voice something so strange and, as it were, imbecile, that both men were seized with sudden fear, especially since Yurand spoke of a ransom, and not of the exchange of De Bergov for Danusia.

" By the dear God!" exclaimed Zbyshko, " where is Danusia ? "

" She is not with the Knights of the Cross," answered Yurand, with a sleepy voice.

And he fell from the bench to the floor like a dead man.

CHAPTER XXVII.

THE messengers had a meeting with Yurand on the following day about noon; an hour later they drove away, taking with them de Bergov, two attendants, and a number of other captives. After that, Yurand summoned Father Kaleb, to whom he dictated a letter to Prince Yanush, with information that the Knights of the Cross had not stolen away Danusia, but that he had succeeded in discovering where she was hidden, and hoped in the course of a few days to find her. He repeated the same to Zbyshko, who since the night before had been wild from amazement and fear. The old knight would answer no question, but told him to wait patiently and undertake nothing toward freeing Danusia, because it would be superfluous. Toward evening he shut himself in with the priest, whom he commanded first of all to write his last will; then he confessed, and, after receiving communion, summoned Zbyshko and the old, ever-silent Tolima, who had been his companion in all expeditions and battles, and who in time of peace managed the lands in Spyhov.

" Here is," said he, turning to the old warrior and raising his voice as if speaking to a man hard of hearing, " the husband of my daughter, whom he married at the court of Prince Yanush, and for which he has received my consent. After my death he is to be therefore the owner and inheritor of this castle, the lands, the forests, the meadows, the people, and all kinds of property existing in Spyhov."

When he heard this, Tolima was greatly astonished, and turned his square head now toward Zbyshko, now toward Yurand; he said nothing, however, for he rarely said anything; he merely inclined before Zbyshko and clasped his knees lightly.

But Yurand spoke on, —

" Which will of mine Father Kaleb has written, and at the end of the writing my seal is placed in wax; thou art to testify that thou hast heard this from my lips, and that I have commanded thee to give the same obedience to this young knight as to me. Therefore, whatever plunder and money there is in the treasury thou wilt show him, — and thou wilt be faithful to him in peace and in war until death. Hast thou heard me ? "

Tolima raised his hands to his ears and bowed his head; afterward, at a sign from Yurand, he bowed and withdrew. The knight turned to Zbyshko then, and said with emphasis:

"There is enough in the treasury to tempt the greatest greediness, and ransom not merely one, but a hundred captives. Remember this."

But why dost thou give me Spyhov ? " inquired Zbyshko

"I give thee more than Spyhov, for I give thee my child.'

" And the hour of death is unknown," said the priest.

" Indeed, it is unknown," repeated Yurand, as if with sadness. " For instance, not long ago the snow covered me, and, though God saved me, I have not my former strength."

"By the dear God! " cried Zbyshko, " what has changed in you since yesterday ? — and you are more willing to mention death than Danusia! By the dear God! "

" Danusia will return," answered Yurand. " God's care is above her. But hear what I say; when she returns, take her to Bogdanets, and leave Spyhov in care of Tolima. He is a trusty man, and this is a difficult neighborhood. There they will not seize her on a rope from thee, — there it is safe."

" Hei! " cried Zbyshko, " but you are talking now as it were from the other world. What does this mean ? "

" I have been more than half in the other world, and now it seems to me that some kind of sickness has laid hold of me. But my child is the question for me, for she is all that I have. Though I know that thou lovest her — "

Here he stopped, and drawing from its sheath a short sword of the kind called misericordia, he turned the hilt of it toward Zbyshko.

" Swear to me on this cross," said he, " that thou wilt never do her a wrong, and wilt love her always."

Zbyshko, with tears in his eyes, threw himself on his knees in a moment, and putting his finger on the hilt, exclaimed, —

" By the Holy Passion, I will do her no wrong, and I will love her always."

" Amen ! " said the priest.

Yurand put the misericordia into its sheath and opened his arms to Zbyshko.

" Now thou art my child too! "

After that they separated, for deep night had come, and for some days they had had no good rest. Zbyshko, however, rose next morning at dawn, for the evening before he had been afraid that some sickness was coming on Yurand,

and he wished to learn how the old man had passed the night.

Before the door of Yurand's room he stumbled on Tolima, who had that moment come out of it.

" How is your master? Is he well? " inquired he.

Tolima bowed, and then surrounding his ear with his palm, asked, —

" What does your Grace command ? "

" I ask how is your master," repeated Zbyshko, in a ' louder voice.

" He has gone away."

" Whither?" know not. He was in armor."

CHAPTER XXVIII.

DAYLIGHT had just begun to whiten the trees, the bushes, and the large blocks of limestone scattered here and there on the field, when a hired guide walking at the side of Yurand's horse stopped, and said, —

" Permit me to rest, lord knight, for I am out of breath. There is dampness and fog, but it is not far now."

" Lead me to the road, and return," said Yurand.

"The road is to the right beyond the pine wood, and from the hill you will see the castle directly."

The peasant fell now to slapping his hands crosswise under his arm-pits, for he was chilled from the morning dampness; then he sat on a stone, for he was still more out of breath after this exercise.

" And knowest thou if the comtur is in the castle?" asked Yurand.

"Where should he be, since he is sick?"

" What is the matter with him? "

" People say that the Polish knights gave him a dressing," answered the old peasant. And in his voice could be felt a certain satisfaction. He was a subject of the Order, but his Mazovian heart was delighted at the superiority of Polish knights. Indeed, he added after a while, —

" Hei! our lords are strong, though they have hard we rk with the others. But he glanced quickly at the knight, as if to be sure that nothing evil would meet him for his words, which had shot out incautiously.

" You speak in our way, lord," said he; "you are not a German? "

" No," answered Yurand; " but lead on."

The peasant rose, and walked again near the horse. Along the road he thrust his hand from time to time into his pouch, took out a handful of unground wheat, and turned it into his mouth. When he had appeased his first hunger in this way, he explained why grain was unground, though Yurand, occupied with his own misfortune and his own thoughts, had not noticed what he was doing.

" Glory to God even for this? " said he. "A grievous life under our German lords. They have put such taxes on grind-

VOL. i. — 22

ing that a poor man must chew unskinned grain, like a beast; for if they find a mill in the house they punish the man, take away his cattle, and, more than that, do not spare even women or children. They fear neither God nor priest, as they did not when they carried off the parish priest of Velbor in chains because he blamed them. Oh, it is hard to live under the Germans! Whatever grain a man grinds between two stones he keeps the handful of flour from it for Easter week, and even on Friday people eat grain as birds do. But glory to God even for grain, because two months before harvest we have no grain. It is not permitted to fish or to kill wild beasts — not as in Mazovia."

Thus did the peasant subject of the knights complain, speaking partly to himself, partly to Yuraud; meanwhile they had passed the open space, which was covered with fragments of limestone sheltered under the snow, and entered the forest, which in the early light seemed gray, and from which came a damp, severe cold. It had dawned completely, otherwise it would have been difficult for Yurand to pass along the forest road, which was rather steep, and so narrow that in places his immense war-horse was barely able to push past between the tree-trunks. But the wood ended soon, and a few " Our Fathers" later they found themselves on the summit of White Hill, through the middle of which passed a beaten highway.

" This is the road," said the peasant; " you will be able to go on alone now."

" I shall be able," answered Yurand. " Go back to thy house, man."

And reaching to a leather bag which was fastened to the front of his saddle, he drew out a silver coin and gave it to the guide.

The man, more accustomed to blows than to gifts from Knights of the Cross in that district, was almost unwilling to believe his own eyes, and, seizing the money, he dropped his head toward Yurand's stirrup, and embraced it.

" O Jesus and Mary! " cried he; " God reward your great mightiness."

"« Be with God."

" May the might of God conduct you. Schytno is before you."

He inclined once more toward the stirrup and vanished. Yurand remained alone on the hill, and looked in the direc-

tion indicated by the villager; he looked at the gray, damp barrier of mist which screened the world before him. Behind the mist was concealed the castle, that evil enemy toward which ill fate and superior force were impelling him. It was near now, near! hence, what had to happen and be accomplished would happen and be accomplished soon. At thought of this, in addition to his fear and anxiety about Danusia, in addition to his readiness to ransom her, even with his blood, from the hands of the enemy, an unheard-of bitter feeling of humiliation was born in his heart, a feeling never felt by him up to that moment. He (Yurand), at the remembrance of whom the comturs of the boundary had trembled, was going now at their command with a penitent head. He, who had overcome and trampled so many of them, felt conquered and trampled at that moment. They had conquered him, not in the field, it is true, not with courage and knightly strength, but still he felt conquered. And for him, that was something so unheard-of that the whole order of the world seemed to him inverted. He was going to humiliate himself before the Knights of the Cross, — he, who, had it not been for Danusia, would have preferred to meet all the power of the Order single-handed. Had it. not happened that a single knight, having the choice between shame and death, had struck on whole armies? But he felt that shame might meet him also, and at that thought his heart howled from pain, as a wolf howls when he feels the shaft in his body.

But this was a man who had not only a body, but also a soul of iron. He was able to break others; he was able to break himself also.

"I will not move," said he, " till I have chained this angel which might ruin my child instead of saving her."

And immediately he seized, as it were by the shoulder, his proud heart, with its stubbornness and desire for battle. Whoso might have seen on that hill the man in armor motionless, on that immense horse, would have thought him some giant cast out of iron, and would not have suspected that that motionless knight there was fighting at that moment the hardest battle that ever he had fought in his life. But he wrestled with himself till he conquered and till he felt that his will would not fail him.

Meanwhile the mist grew thin, and, though it had not vanished entirely, there appeared dimly at the end of it something of deeper color. Yurand divined that that was the walls of the castle of Schytno. At sight of this he did not move from his place, but he began to pray as ardently and fervently as a man prays for whom there is nothing left in this world but God's mercy.

And when he moved forward at last, he felt that solace of some kind was entering his heart. He was ready now to endure everything that might meet him. He called to mind that Saint George, a descendant of the greatest family in Cappadocia, had endured various humiliating tortures, and still he not only did not lose his honor, but is seated on the right hand of God, and is named patron of all earthly knighthood. Yurand had heard frequent narratives of his adventures from pilgrims who had come from distant lands, and with the remembrance of them he strengthened his heart at that moment.

Gradually even hope itself was roused in him. The Knights of the Cross had, it is true, been noted for vengeful-ness ; hence, he doubted not that they would work revenge on him for all the defeats which he had inflicted, for the shame which had fallen on them at every meeting, and for the terror in which they had lived so many years.

But it was this very thing which gave him courage. He thought that they had carried off Danusia only to get him; so when they had him what would they care for her? That was it! They would put him in chains, beyond doubt, and, not wishing to keep him in the neighborhood of Mazovia, would send him to some remote castle, where he would groan to the end of his life in a dungeon, but Danusia they would free. Even should it appear that they had taken him by deceit and were tormenting him, the Grand Master would not take it very ill of them, nor would the Chapter; for he (Yurand) had been really grievous to the Germans, and had squeezed more blood out of them than any other knight then alive. But that same Grand Master would punish them, perhaps, for imprisoning an innocent maiden, and, moreover, a. ward of the prince of Mazovia, whose good-will he was trying diligently to win, in view of the threatening war with the King of Poland.

And hope was taking possession of Yurand with increasing force. At moments it seemed to him almost certain that Danusia would return to Spyhov under Zbyshko's strong protection. "He is a firm fellow," thought Yurand ; "he" will not let any man harm her." And he recalled with a certain emotion all that he knew of Zbyshko. " He had

fought with the Germans at Vilno; he had met them in duels; the Frisians he and his uncle challenged to a battle of four, and he attacked Lichtenstein, also; he saved my child from the wild bull, and surely he will not spare those four Germans whom he challenged." Here Yurand raised his eyes, and said, —

" I give her to Thee, O God, and do Thou give her to Zbyshko! "

And he became still fresher, for he judged that if God gave her to the young man, he would not permit the Germans to trifle with him, and would wrest her from their hands, even though the whole power of the Order were detaining her. Then he thought of Zbyshko again: " Indeed, he is not only a firm fellow, but he is as true as gold. He will guard her, he will love her, and grant the child, O Jesus, what Thou mayest of the best. But it seems to me that with him she will regret neither the prince's court nor her father's love." At this thought Yurand's lids became moist on a sudden, and in his heart there sprang up immense yearning. He would like, of course, to see his child in life again, and sometime or another to die in Spyhov near them, and not in the dark dungeons of the Order. But God's will! Schytno was visible now. The walls were outlined with increasing clearness in the mist; the hour of sacrifice was near, hence he strengthened himself more, and said to himself, —

" Surely it is the will of God! The evening of life is near. A few years more, a few less, will come out all the same. Hei! I should like to look at the two children again, but in justice I have lived my time. What I had to experience I have experienced, what I had to avenge I have avenged. And now what? Rather to God than to the world, but since there is need to suffer, I must suffer. Danusia and Zbyshko, though in the greatest enjoyment, will not forget me. Surely, they will mention me more than once, and take counsel: " Where is he? Is he alive, or is he with God in the heavenly host?" They will inquire everywhere and learn where I am. The Knights are eager for vengeance, but they are eager also for ransom. And Zbyshko would not spare anything to ransom even my bones. And for a mass Danusia and Zbyshko will surely give money many a time. Both have honest and loving hearts, for which do Thou, O God, and Thou, O most Holy Mother, bless them."

The highroad not only increased in width, but numbers of people appeared on it. Peasants were drawing loads of

wood and straw toward the town. Herdsmen were driving cattle. Men were drawing on sleighs frozen fish from the lakes. In one place four bowmen were leading a chained peasant to judgment, evidently for an offence, since his hands were bound behind his back and on his feet were fetters, which, dragging on the snow, hardly let him move forward. From his distended nostrils and open mouth the breath came forth as rolls of steam, but the bowmen sang as they urged him. When they saw Yurand they looked at him curiously, evidently amazed at the size of the knight and his horse, but at sight of his golden spurs and girdle they lowered their crossbows in sign of salutation and honor. In the town there were more people still, and it was noisier; they gave way to an armed man, however, hurriedly. He passed the main street and turned toward the castle, which, sheltered in the fog, seemed to be sleeping.

But not all were asleep round about; at least crows and rooks were not sleeping; whole flocks of them were whirling above the elevation which formed the approach to the castle, flapping their wings and cawing. When Yurand had ridden up nearer, he understood why those birds were circling there. At the side of the road leading to the castle gate stood a large gibbet; on it were hanging four bodies of Mazovian peasants, subjects of the Knights of the Cross. There was not the least breeze, so that the bodies, the faces of which seemed to be looking at the feet, did not swing, except when the dark birds perched on their shoulders and on their heads, quarrelling with each other, pulling at the ropes, and pecking the drooping heads. Some of the four must have hung for a long time, for their skulls were entirely bare, and their legs had stretched out beyond proportion. At the approach of Yurand the flock flew away with great noise, but soon made a turn in the air and alighted again on the crossbeam of the gibbet. Yurand passing by made the sign of the cross, approached the moat, and stopping in the place where the drawbridge was raised near the gate, blew the horn.

Then he sounded a second, a third, and a fourth time. There was not a living soul on the walls, and from inside the gate came no voice. But after a while a heavy slide, inside the grating evident!\'7d 7 , was raised with a gritting sound in a loophole near the gate.

" Wer da (who is there) ? " inquired a harsh voice.

" Yurand of Spyhov! " answered the knight.

After these words the slide was dropped again, and deep silence followed.

Time passed. Inside the gate not a movement was audible, but from the direction of the gibbet came the croaking of birds.

Yurand stood a long while yet before he raised the horn and blew in it a second series of times.

But he was answered by silence again.

He understood now that they were detaining him before the gate through the pride of the Knights, which knew no bounds in presence of the conquered. They desired to humiliate him, as if he had been a beggar. He understood, too, that he would have to wait perhaps till evening, or even longer. At the first moment the blood boiled in Yurand; the desire seized him all at once to come down from his horse, raise one of the large stones that lay before the moat, and hurl it against the gate. He would have acted thus at another time, and every other Mazovian or Polish knight also, and let them rush out afterward from behind the gate and fight with him. But recollecting why he had come, he recovered his mind and restrained himself.

" Have I not offered myself for my child ? " said he in his soul.

And he waited.

Meanwhile something began to grow dark on the wall. Fur-covered heads showed themselves, dark cowls, and even iron helmets, from under which curious eyes gazed at the master of Spyhov. These figures increased in number every mo ment, for the terrible Yurand was waiting alone at the gate, —* this for the garrison was an uncommon spectacle. Those who before that had seen him in front of them saw their own death, but now it was possible to look at him safely. Heads rose higher and higher till at last all the battlement near the gate was covered with serving-men. Yurand thought that surely those higher in rank must be looking at him through the grating of windows in the gate-tower, and he raised his glance upward, but the windows there were cut in deep walls, and through them one could see only distant objects. But the crowd on the battlement, which had looked first at him in silence, began to call out. This and that man repeated his name, here and there was heard laughter, hoarse voices called to him as to a wolf, more and more loudly, more and more insolently; and when evidently no one from inside forbade, they began at last to hurl lumps of snow at the knight without motion.

He, as if unconsciously, moved forward with his horse, then in one instant the lumps of snow ceased to fly, the voices stopped, and even some heads disappeared behind the wall. Terrible indeed must have been Yurand's name. But even the most cowardly recollected that a moat and a wall divided them from the terrible Mazovian, so the rude soldiery began again to hurl not only balls of snow, but ice, rubbish, and small stones, which rebounded with a noise from his armor and the horse-trappings.

" I have sacrificed myself for my child," repeated Yuraud to himself.

And he waited. Then noon came ; the walls were deserted; the soldiers were summoned to dinner. Not many were those whose duty it was to stand guard, but they ate on the wall, and after eating amused themselves again by throwing bare bones at the hungry knight. They began also to talk among themselves, and inquire one of the other who would undertake to go down and give the knight a blow on the neck with a fist or the shaft of a lance. Others, after returning from dinner, called to him, saying that if disgusted with waiting, he might hang himself; for there was one unoccupied hook on the gibbet and a rope with it. Amid such ridicule, cries, outbursts of laughter, and curses, the afternoon hours passed away. The short winter day inclined to its close gradually, but the bridge was ever in the air, and the gate remained fastened.

Toward evening the wind rose, blew away the fog, cleared the sky, and disclosed the brightness of evening. The snow became blue, and afterward violet. There was no frost, but the night promised clear skies. The people went down from the walls again, except the guards; the crows and rooks flew away from the gibbet to the forest. At last the sky became dark, and complete silence followed.

" They will not open the gate till sometime about night," thought Yurand. And for a while it passed through his head to return to the town, but immediately he rejected the idea. " They want me here," said he. " If I turn back they will not let me go to a house, but will surround me, seize me, and then say that they are not bound to me in anything; for they took me by force; and, though I should ride through them, I should have to return."

That immense power of Polish knights in enduring cold, hunger, and toil, admired by foreign chroniclers, allowed them frequently to perform deeds which more effeminate

people in the West could not accomplish. Yurand possessed this endurance in a greater degree than others; so, though hunger had begun to twist him internally, and the cold of evening penetrated his coat covered with armor, he resolved to stay, though be were to die at that gate.

But suddenly, before night had set in completely, he heard steps behind him on the snow.

He looked around; six men were coming from the side of the town. They were armed with spears and halberds. In the middle of them went a seventh, supporting himself with a sword.

" Perhaps the gate will be opened, and I shall enter with them," thought Yurand. " They will not try to take me by force or kill me; for they are too few; but were they to strike me, that would be a sign that they do not wish to keep faith, and then — woe to them ! "

Thus thinking, he raised the steel axe hanging at his saddle, an axe so large that it was even too heavy for both hands of a common man; and moved with his horse toward them.

But they had no thought of attacking him. On the contrary, the soldiers planted the ends of their spear-shafts and halberds in the snow, and, since the night was not dark altogether yet, Yurand noticed that the shafts trembled in their hands somewhat.

The seventh man, who seemed to be an officer, stretched forward his left arm hurriedly, and turning his fingers upward, inquired,—

Are you the knight Yurand of Spyhov ? " I am."

Do you wish to hear why I have been sent here ? " I am listening."

The mighty and pious comtur Danveld commands me to declare that till you dismount the gate will not be opened to you."

Yurand remained a while motionless; then he came down from his horse, onto which one of the spearmen sprang immediately.

" And your arms are to be delivered to us," said the man with the sword.

The lord of Spyhov hesitated. " Will they fall on me while unarmed and thrust me through, like a wild beast? Will they seize me and throw me into a dungeon? " But then he thought that if that had been their intention, a greater number of men would have been sent. For were they to rush

at him, they would not be able to pierce his armor at once, while he might wrest a weapon from the nearest German and destroy them all before help could come. Moreover, they knew what manner of man he was.

" And even," said he to himself, " if they wish to let my blood out, I have not come here for another purpose."

With this thought, he threw down his axe, then his sword; next his misericordia, and waited.

They seized all these; then that man who had spoken to him withdrew a few tens of paces, halted, and said in a voice loud and insolent, —

" For all the wrongs which thou hast done the Order, thou art, at command of the comtur, to put on thyself this hempen bag which I leave thee, tie to thy neck on a rope the scabbard of thy sword, and wait humbly at the gate till the grace of the comtur gives command to open it."

And after a little Yurand was alone in darkness and silence. On the snow lay black before him the penitential bag and the rope, but he stood there long, feeling that something in his soul was unhinging, something breaking, something coming to an end, something dying, and that soon he would be no longer a knight, no longer Yurand of Spyhov, but a wretch, a slave without name, without fame, without honor.

So much time passed before he approached the penitential bag, and said, —

" How can I act differently? Thou, O Christ, knowest that they will kill my innocent child unless I do what they command. And thou knowest also that I would not do this to save my own life. Shame is a bitter thing! Oh, bitter! but before Thy death men put shame on Thee. Well, then, in the name of the Father and the Son."

He stooped down, put on the bag, in which there were holes for his head and arms, then on the rope around his neck he hung the sheath of his sword, and dragged himself to the gate. •

He did not find it open, but it was all one to him at that moment whether they opened it earlier or later. The castle sank into the silence of night; the guards called to each other now and then at the corners. There was light in one little window high up in the gate tower; the others were in darkness.

The night hours passed one after another; on the sky rose the sickle of the moon and lighted the castle walls gloomily.

There was such silence that Yurand might have heard the beating of his own heart, but he had grown benumbed and altogether stony, just as if the soul had been taken out of him, and he gave no account to himself of anything. Only one idea remained to the man, that he had ceased to be Yurand of Spyhov, but what he had become he knew not. At moments something quivered before him, it seemed, in the night; that Death was coming to him stealthily over the snow from those corpses on the gibbet which he had seen in the morning.

All at once he quivered and recovered completely.

" O merciful Christ, what is that? "

Out of the lofty little window in the gate tower came certain sounds of a lute, at first barely audible. Yurand, when going to Schytno, felt sure that Danusia was not in the castle, but those sounds of a lute in the night roused his heart. In one instant it seemed to him that he knew them, and that no one else was playing but his child, his love. So he fell on his knees, joined his hands in prayer, and listened, while trembling as in a fever.

With that a half-childish and immensely sad voice began:

" Oh, had I wings like a wild goose, I would fly after Yasek; I would fly after him to Silesia! "

Yurand wanted to answer, to cry out the dear name, but the words stuck in his throat as if an iron hoop had squeezed them down. A sudden wave of pain, tears, sadness, misfortune rose in his breast; he threw himself on his face in the snow, and began with ecstasy to cry to heaven in his soul, as if in a thanksgiving prayer, — " O Jesus! I hear my child yet! O Jesus! " And sobbing rent his gigantic body. Above him the yearning voice sang on in the undisturbed silence of night:

" I would sit on a fence in Silesia; Look at me, Yasek dear, Look at the poor little orphan."

Next morning a bearded, burly man at arms kicked the side of the knight who was lying before the gate.

"To thy feet, dog! The gate is open, and the comtur commands thee to stand before his face."

Yurand woke as if from sleep. He did not seize the man by the throat; he did not crush him in his iron hand;

Yurand's face was calm and almost submissive. He rose, and without saying one word followed the German through the gate.

He had barely passed it when he heard behind him the bite of chains; the drawbridge rose, and in the gateway itself dropped the heavy iron grating.

CHAPTER XXIX.

WHEN Yurand found himself in the courtyard of the castle he knew not whither to go, for the servitor, who had conducted him through the gateway, left him and went toward the stables. At the wall stood men at arms, it is true, some singly, some in small groups, but their faces were so insolent and their glances so jeering that the knight could divine easily that they would not show him the way, and that were they to answer his question they would do so contemptuously or with rudeness. Some laughed and pointed their fingers at him, others began to throw snow, as on the day previous. But he, noting a door larger than others, over which Christ on the Cross was carved in stone, made toward it, thinking that if the comtur and officers were in another part of the castle, or in other chambers, some one would in every case have to turn him from the mistaken way.

And that was what happened. At the moment when Yurand was approaching the door the two halves of it opened suddenly, and a youth stood before him tonsured like a cleric, but wearing the dress of a layman.

" Are you Pan Yurand of Spyhov? " inquired he.

"I am."

" The pious comtur has commanded me to conduct you. Follow me."

And he led on through a great arched entrance-chamber toward a stairway. At the steps, however, he halted, and casting his eyes on Yurand inquired, —

"Have you weapons on your person? They have ordered me to search you."

Yurand raised both arms so that the guide might see his whole body clearly, and answered, —

" Yesterday I surrendered all."

Thereupon the guide lowered his voice and said almost in a whisper, —

" Guard against breaking into anger, for you are under power, and power which is superior."

" But I am under the will of God too," answered Yurand.

Then he looked at his guide more attentively, and finding in his face something in the nature of compassion and pity, he said, —

" Honesty is looking out of thy eyes, boy. Wilt thou answer me truly touching that which I ask ? "

" Hurry, lord," answered the guide.

" Will they give me my child?"

The youth raised his brows in astonishment.

" Is that your child who is here? "

" My daughter."

" That damsel in the tower at the gate? "

" Yes. They promised to send her home if I would give myself up to them."

The guide made a motion in sign that he knew not, but his face expressed doubt and fear.

Yurand added another question, however, —

" Is it true that Schaumberg and Markward are guarding her? "

" Those brothers are not at this castle. But take your daughter away before Danveld, the starosta, recovers."

Yurand trembled on hearing this, but there was no time to make further inquiry, for they had come to a hall on the story where Yurand was to stand before the starosta of Schytno. The youth opened the door and withdrew to the stairway.

The knight of Spyhov entered, and found himself in a large chamber which was very dark, for the glass panes, fitted into leaden sash, admitted light scantily, and moreover the day was wintry and cloudy. In a great chimney at the farther end of the room a fire was burning, it is true, but the wood, being imperfectly seasoned, gave out little flame. Only after a time, when Yurand's eyes had grown accustomed to the gloom, did he see in the distance a table with knights sitting near it, and beyond their shoulders a whole company of armed attendants, also men at arms, among whom was the castle jester, who held a tame bear by a chain.

Yuraud had fought with Danveld on a time, later he had seen him twice at the court of Prince Yauush in the character of envoy, but since those times some years had passed ; still, in spite of the darkness he recognised him at once, by his corpulence, by his face, and finally by this, that he was sitting at a table, in the centre of the room, in an easy-chair, with his arm bound in splints and resting on the side of the

chair. At his right sat old Siegfried de Lowe of Insburg, an implacable enemy of Poles in general, and Yurand of Spyhov in particular; at his left were the younger brothers Gottfried, and Rotgier. Danveld had invited them purposely to behold his triumph over the terrible enemy, and also to enjoy the fruits of that treachery which they had thought out together, and in the execution of which the other three had assisted him. So they sat comfortably arrayed in garments of dark material, with small swords at their sides — joyful, self-confident, looking at Yurand with pride and with that boundless contempt which they felt at all times for the weaker and the conquered.

Silence continued long, for they wished to sate themselves with looking at the man before whom they had simply been terrified, and who stood now with drooping head before them, arrayed in the hempen bag of a penitent, with a rope around his neck from which depended his scabbard.

They wished also, as was evident, the greatest number of people to witness the humiliation of Yurand. for through side doors leading to other chambers every one who wished had the entry, and the hall was almost half filled with armed spectators. All gazed with measureless curiosity on the captive; they spoke loudly and made remarks which referred to him. But while looking at them he only gained consolation, for he thought in his soul: " If Danveld had not wished to keep his promise he would not have summoned such a number of witnesses."

Danveld raised his hand and conversation ceased; thereupon he gave a sign to one of the shield-bearers, who approached Yurand and, seizing the rope which encircled his neck, drew him a number of steps toward the table. Danveld looked then in triumph on the spectators and said, —

" See how the power of the Order overcomes pride and malice! "

" God grant that it be thus at all times! " answered those present.

Now came a moment of silence, after which Danveld turned to the prisoner, —

"Like a mad dog thou hast bitten the Order, and God has brought thee to stand like a dog before us, with a rope around thy neck, waiting for pardon and favor."

" Compare me not to a dog, comtur," answered Yurand, " for thou art belittling the honor of those who have met me, and fallen by my hand."

352 THE KNIGHTS OF THE CROSS.

At these words a murmur rose among the armed Germans; it is not known whether the daring of the answer roused their anger, or the truth of it struck them. The comtur was not rejoiced at such a turn of speech, so he added, —

" See, he spits into our eyes again by his pride and haughtiness."

But Yurand raised his hands like a man calling heaven to witness, and said,, nodding his head, —

" God sees that my haughtiness has remained outside the gates of this castle. God sees, and will judge whether by insulting my knightly dignity you have not insulted yourselves. The honor of knighthood is one in all places. Every belted man is bound in duty to respect it."

Danveld frowned, but that moment the castle-jester rattled the chain on which he held the young bear, and called, —

"A sermon! a sermon! A preacher has come from Ma-zovia! Listen ! A sermon! "

Then he turned to Danveld.

"Lord," said he, "Count Rosenheim, whenever the sexton roused him to a sermon too early by bell-ringing, commanded the man to eat the bell-rope from one knot to another; this preacher has a rope around his neck, command him to eat it before he reaches the end of his sermon."

After these words he looked with some fear at the comtur, for he was not sure whether Danveld would laugh, or give the order to flog him for untimely speech. But the Knights of the Cross, smooth, pliant, and even submissive when they did not feel themselves in power, knew no measure in presence of the conquered; hence Danveld not only nodded at the jester in sign that he permitted the indignity, but burst forth in rudeness so unheard of that astonishment was depicted on the faces of some of the younger armor-bearers.

"Complain not that thou art disgraced," said he ; "even were I to make tliee an under dog-keeper, a dog-keeper of the Knights of the Cross is superior to a knight of thy people! "

"Bring a comb," cried the buffoon, now emboldened, " and comb the bear; he will comb out thy shaggy locks with his paw!"

Laughter broke forth here and there, while a certain voice called from behind the brotherhood, —

" In summer thou wilt cut reeds on the lake ! "

"And catch crawfish with thy carrion ! " cried another.

" But begin now to scare away crows from the gallows!" added a third. "Thou wilt have no lack of work here."

Thus did they jeer at Yurand, who on a time was their terror. Joyousness seized the assembly gradually. Some, coming from behind the table, approached the prisoner to examine him from nearby, and to say: " Then this is the wild boar of Spyhov whose tusks are knocked out by our comtur; of course he has foam on his snout; he would gladly bite some one, but he cannot! " Danveld and other brothers of the Order, who wished at first to give a certain solemn semblance of judgment to the hearing, on seeing that the affair had taken a new turn, rose also from the benches and mingled with those who were approaching Yurand.

Old Siegfried of Insburg was not rejoiced at this, but the comtur said to him : ' ' Smooth your wrinkles; our amusement will be all the greater." And they also fell to examining Yurand. That was a rare opportunity, for up to that day those of the knighthood, or men at arms who had seen him in such proximity, closed their eyes forever after. Hence some said: "His shoulders are immense, even if he has a skin coat under the bag; one might wrap pea straw around his body and exhibit him in market-places;" others called for beer, so that the day might be still more joyous.

In fact a moment later the sound of tankards was heard, and the dark hall was filled with the odor of foam falling from under covers. The comtur grew merry and said: " Thus precisely is it proper, he need not think that an insult to him is important." So they approached Yurand again, and said, punching him under the chin with their tankards: "Thou wouldst be glad to moisten thy Mazo-vian snout!" And some, pouring beer on their palms, plashed it into his eye ; but he stood among them, howled at, insulted, till at last he moved toward old Siegfried, and feeling evidently that he could not restrain himself long, cried in a voice loud enough to drown the noise which prevailed in the hall, —

"By the passion of the Saviour, and your own soul's salvation, give my child to me as you promised!"

And he wished to seize the right hand of the old comtur, but Siegfried started back suddenly and said, —

" Away, slave ! What art thou doing? "

" I have liberated Bergov, and come hither alone, because in return for this you promised to give back my child to me; she is here." VOL. i. — 23

"Who promised? " inquired Dan veld.

"Thou, comtur, in faith and in conscience."

"Thou wilt not find witnesses, but no witness is needed in a question of word and honor."

"On thy honor! on the honor of the Order!" cried Yurand.

" In that case thy daughter will be given thee!" answered I) an veld.

Then he turned to those present and continued, —

"All that has happened him in this place is innocent play, not reaching the measure of his crimes and offences. But since we promised to return his daughter, should he come here and humiliate himself before us, know that the word of a Knight of the Cross must be like the word of God, sacred, and that girl whom we rescued from bandits we will present now with freedom, and after exemplary penance for his sins against the Order, Yurand may go home also."

This speech astonished some, for, knowing Danveld and his former feelings of offence against Yurand, they did not expect the like honesty. So old Siegfried and also Rotgier, with Brother Gottfried, looked at the man, raising their brows in amazement, and wrinkling their foreheads; he, however, feigned not to see their inquiring glances, and said, —

" I will send thy daughter away under escort, but thou wilt stay here till our escort returns safely, and till thou hast paid the ransom."

Yurand himself was somewhat astonished, for he had lost hope that even the sacrifice of his own life could serve Danu-sia; hence he looked at Danveld almost with gratitude, and answered, —

" God reward thee, comtur! "

" Recognize in me a Knight of Christ! " replied Danveld.

" All mercy comes from Him," answered Yurand. " But as it is long since I have seen my child, let me look at her, and give her my blessing."

"Yes, but in presence of us all, so that there should be witnesses of our good faith and favor."

Then he commanded an attendant youth to bring in Danusia, and moved himself up to Siegfried, Rotgier, and Gottfried, who, surrounding him, began to speak with animation and quickly.

" I oppose not, though thou hadst a different intention," said old Siegfried.

" How," asked the passionate Rotgier, who was noted for

cruelty and bravery, — " thou wilt free, not only the girl, but this hell hound to bite again ?"

" He will not bite as before!" exclaimed Gottfried.

" Oh, he will pay the ransom," answered Dan veld, carelessly.

"Though he were to give us all he has he would strip twice as much in one year from our people!"

" As to the girl I make no opposition," repeated Siegfried, " but the lambs of the Order will cry more than once because of that wolf."

" But our word? " inquired Danveld, with a laugh.

" Thou hast spoken differently on that point."

Danveld shrugged his shoulders.

" Have ye had too little amusement? " asked he. " Do ye want more ? " Yuraud was surrounded now by others, who. conscious of the glory which had come to all the brotherhood because of Danveld's act of honor, fell to boasting before the prisoner, —

" Well, bone-breaker! " said the captain of the archers to Yurand, " thy pagan brothers would not act thus with our Christian Knighthood!"

" Thou didst drink our blood."

" We give thee bread in return for a stone."

Yurand paid no heed to the pride or contempt in their words; his heart was full and his eyelids moist. He was thinking that in a moment he should see Danusia, and see her through their favor, hence he looked on the speakers almost with compunction, and finally he answered, —

"True, true! I have been stern against you—but not false."

Meanwhile at the other end of the hall a voice shouted: " They are leading in the girl! " and immediately there was silence. The men at arms stood apart on both sides. Though no man had seen Yurand's daughter, and the greater number, because of the mystery with which Danveld surrounded his acts, did not even know of her presence in the castle; those who did know hurried to whisper to others of her marvellous beauty. Every eye therefore turned with exceeding curiosity to the doorway through which she was to enter.

Now came the youth ; after him the serving woman of the Order, who was known to all, she who had gone to the hunting-lodge; behind her entered a girl dressed in white, with hair let clown at full length and then fastened above the forehead with a ribbon.

356 THE KNIGHTS OF THE CROSS.

All at once an immense burst of thunder-like laughter was heard through the hall. Yurand, who at the first moment was ready to spring toward his daughter, drew back on a sudden and stood as pale as linen, gazing with astonishment at the pointed head, blue lips, and expressionless eyes of an idiot whom they were giving him as Danusia.

" That is not my daughter!" said he, with a voice of alarm.

"Not thy daughter? " cried Dan veld. " By Saint Liborius of Paderborn! Then either we did not rescue thy daughter from the bandits, or some wizard has transformed her, for there is no other in Schytno."

Old Siegfried, Rotgier, and Gottfried exchanged swift glances filled with supreme admiration for the keenness of Danveld, but no man of them had time to speak, for Yurand cried in a terrible voice, —

" She is here ! my daughter is in Schytno, I heard her sing! I heard the voice of Danusia."

Thereupon Danveld turned to the assembly and said, coolly and with emphasis, —

"I take all here present to witness, but especially thee, / Siegfried of Insburg, and you pious brothers Rotgier and Gottfried, that, in accord with my word and pledged promise, I yield up this maiden whom bandits, vanquished by us, declared to be the daughter of Yurand of Spyhov. If she is not his daughter there is no fault of ours in this, but the will of God, who has given Yurand into our hands."

Siegfried and the two younger brothers inclined their heads in sign that they heard and would testify when needed. Then they exchanged swift glances a second time, for Dan-veld's work was more than they had been able to hope for: to seize Yurand, and not yield up his daughter, and still to keep promise apparently, — who else could have done that!

But Yurand cast himself on his knees and adjured Danveld by all the relics in Malborg, by the dust and the heads of his ancestors, to give him his daughter, and not to act as a trickster and a traitor who breaks oaths and promises. There was such sincerity and desperation in his voice that some began to divine the deceit ; to others it occurred that a wizard misrht have changed the girl really.

"God is looking at thy treason!" cried Yurand. "By the wounds of the Saviour! by the hour of thy death, give my child to me 1"

And rising from his knees he advanced, bent down double, toward Danveld, as if wishing to embrace his knees; his eye was gleaming with something like genuine madness, and his voice was breaking with pain, fear, desperation, and menace. Danveld, reproached in the presence of all with treachery and trickery, began to snort; at last anger broke forth on" his face like a flame, so, wishing to trample the ill-fated prisoner to the lowest, he pushed up to him, and bending to his ear hissed through set teeth, —

" If I give her to thee, it will be with my bastard! "

That instant Yurand roared like a wild bull; he seized Danveld with both hands and raised him above his head. In the hall was heard one piercing cry: " Spare!! " then the body of the comtur struck the stone floor with such terrible impetus that the brains of his broken skull were spattered on Siegfried and Rotgier who were standing right there.

Yurand sprang to the side wall on which were weapons, and, seizing a great double-handed sword, rushed like a storm at the Germans, who were petrified with terror.

Those men were accustomed to battles, blood, and slaughter, still their hearts sank to that degree that even when their stupor had passed they began to withdraw and flee as sheep from a wolf which kills with one snap of his teeth. The hall was filled with screams of terror, with trampling of feet, with the crash of overturned vessels, with cries of attendants, with despairing calls for weapons, shields, swords, and crossbows, and with the howls of the bear which broke away from the jester and climbed to a lofty window. At last weapons gleamed, and the points of some tens of them were directed at Yurand, but he heeded nothing; half insane he sprang toward them himself, and a wild, unheard-of battle began, — a battle more like a slaughter than a conflict with weapons. The youthful and passionate Brother Gottfried was the first to bar the way to Yurand; but Yurand with the lightning swiftness of his sword edge hurled off his head, and with it an arm and shoulder; after him fell the captain of the archers and the steward of the castle, Von Bracht, and an Englishman who, though he did not understand well what the question was, took pity on Yurand and his suffering and drew his sword only after the slaying of Danveld. Others, beholding the terrible strength and rage of the man, gathered into a crowd to resist in company ; but that method brought still more deplorable defeat, for Yuraud, with his hair on end, with wild eye, bespattered

with gore and breathing blood, enraged, out of his mind, broke, tore, and slashed that dense crowd with dreadful blows of his broadsword, hurling men to the floor with his reeking blade, as a tempest hurls limbs and trees to the earth. And again came a moment of ghastly terror, in which it seemed that the awful Mazovian would cut down and slay every one, and that they, like a pack of howling dogs, could not finish the maddened wild boar unless men with muskets assisted them; and in such degree were those armed Germans inferior in strength and rage to Yurand that a battle with him was simply death and destruction.

"Scatter! Surround him! Strike from behind!" cried old Siegfried.

So they scattered through the hall like a flock of starlings in a field when a crooked-beaked falcon swoops down from the sky on them; but those men could not surround him, for in his rage of battle, instead of seeking a place from which to defend himself, he hunted them around the walls, and the man whom he reached died as by a lightning stroke. Humiliation, despair, deceived hope turned into the single desire for blood seemed to intensify his savage strength tenfold. That sword, for which the strongest warriors of the Order needed both hands, he wielded like a feather with one. He was not seeking freedom or victory, he was not seeking to save his life ; he was seeking vengeance; and like a conflagration, or like a river which has swept away obstructions and is destroying blindly everything that stands before its current, he, the awful, the blinded destroyer, rends, smashes, tramples, murders, extinguishes.

They could not strike him from behind, for they could not overtake him ; besides, common warriors feared to approach the man, even from behind, knowing that if he turned no human power could save them. Others were seized by perfect terror at the thought that no unaided mortal could have made such slaughter, and that they had to do with one to whom superhuman power gives assistance.

But Siegfried and Rotgier rushed to a gallery which projected above the great windows of the hall, and called on others to follow and save themselves. They did so in haste, so that men crowded one another on the narrow staircase, wishing to be there at the earliest, and thence strike the giant with whom every hand-to-hand struggle had proved impossible. Finally the last man slammed the door leading to the gallery, and Yurand was alone on the ground floor.

Shouts of delight and triumph were heard in the gallery; heavy oaken tables, benches, iron sockets of torches began to fly now at Yurand. One of the missiles struck him above the brow and covered his face with blood. That moment the door of the main entrance was burst open, and in rushed a crowd of soldiers, summoned through the upper windows; they were armed with darts, halberds, axes, crossbows, pointed stakes, hooks, ropes, or whatever weapon each one had seized in a hurry.

1 But with his left hand the raging Yurand wiped the blood from his face so that it might not darken his eyesight, collected himself, and rushed at the multitude. Again were heard in the hall groans, the clank of iron, the gritting of teeth, and the terrified voices of men in the midst of slaughter.

CHAPTER XXX.

IN that same hall, in the evening, at a table sat old Siegfried, who after Dauveld's demise had taken temporary charge of Schytno ; near him sat Brother Rotgier, the knight de Bergov, Yurand's recent captive, and two noble youths, novices, who were soon to assume the white mantle. A winter whirlwind was howling outside the windows; it shook the leaden sashes, and caused the torches burning in iron sockets to quiver, and blew from time to time rolls of smoke down the chimney, and through the hall. Silence reigned among the brothers, though they had assembled to take counsel. They were waiting for Siegfried's words, but he, with elbows on the table and his palms against his drooping gray head, sat gloomy, with his face in the shadow, and grim thoughts in his soul.

" On what are we to take counsel ? " asked Brother Rotgier, at last.

Siegfried raised his head, gazed at the speaker, and said, rousing himself from meditation, —

" On the misfortune and on this : What will the Grand Master and the Chapter say? Besides, we are to see that no harm come to the Order from our actions."

Then he was silent again, but after a time he looked around and moved his nostrils.

" There is still an odor of blood here."

" No," answered Rotgier, " I gave command to wash the floor, and smoke the place with sulphur. The smell is of sulphur."

Siegfried cast a strange glance on those present and said, —

" Have mercy, O God, on the soul of Brother Dan veld and on the soul of Brother Gottfried! "

But they understood that he implored the mercy of God on those souls because the thought of hell had occurred to him at the mention of sulphur; hence a shiver ran through their bones, and all answered in chorus, —

"Amen, amen, amen!"

For a time the howling of the wind was heard and the shaking of the window-panes.

" Where are the bodies of the comtur and Brother Gottfried?" asked the old man.

" In the chapel; the priests there are singing a litany over them."

" Are they in the coffins already?"

" In the coffins, but the comtur's head is covered, for hia face and skull are broken."

" Where are the other bodies ? — and the wounded ? "

" The bodies are on the snow, so as to stiffen before the coffins are finished. The wounded are cared for in the hospital."

Siegfried joined his hands above his head a second time.

"And one man did all this! O God, have the Order in Thy care when it comes to a general war with this wolfish race! "

At these words Rotgier cast a glance upward as if recalling something, and said, —

" At Vilno I heard the Voit of Sambia say to his brother the Grand Master: ' Unless thou raise a great war and destroy them so that their name be not left — woe to us and our people.'"

" God give such a war and grant a meeting with them! " said one of the noble novices.

Siegfried looked at him fixedly, as if wishing to say: "Thou couldst have met one to-day," but seeing the slender and youthful figure of the novice, and remembering, perhaps, that he himself, though renowned for courage, would not court sure destruction, he omitted to reproach him, and only asked, —

" Has any of you seen Yurand ? "

" I have," answered De Bergov.

"Is he alive?"

" Alive, but lying in the net in which they entangled him. When he regained consciousness the soldiers wished to finish him, but the chaplain would not permit."

" It is not permissible to kill him. He is a man of consideration among his own people, and there would be a terrible outcry," answered Siegfried. " It will be impossible too to conceal what has happened, for there were too many spectators."

"What are we to say then, and what must we do?" inquired Rotgier.

Siegfried meditated a while.

"You, noble Count de Bergov," said he at last, "go to the Grand Master at Malborg. You have groaned as a captive in Yurand's castle, and are a guest of the Order; being a guest, hence not obliged absolutely to speak in favor of the brothers, men will believe you all the more. Tell what you have seen. Say that Danveld captured a certain maiden from bandits on the boundary, and thinking her the daughter of Yurand, informed Yurand, who came to Schytno, and — what happened later you yourself know."

"Consider, pious comtur," said De Bergov, "I have suffered sore captivity at Spyhov, and as your guest I should be glad to testify at all times in your favor; but tell me, to satisfy my conscience, was not Yurand's daughter really in Schytuo, and did not Danveld's treachery bring her dreadful father to that madness ? "

Siegfried halted with the answer. In his nature lay profound hatred of the Poles, and also cruelty, in which he exceeded even Danveld, and rapacity whenever the Order was in question; and in it were pride and also greed, but falsehood was not there. Hence the great bitterness of his life and its deepest sorrow was this, that in recent times all interests of the Order had arranged themselves in such fashion, through self-will, disobedience, and debauchery, that falsehood had become a common weapon, and one of the most effective in the business of the Order. Therefore De Bergov's question touched the most painful side in his soul, and only after a long period of silence did he answer, —

" Danveld is standing before God, and God is judging him. If they ask you for opinions, tell what you please; if they ask what your eyes have seen, tell them that before we entangled the raging man in a net you saw nine corpses on the floor, besides the wounded, and among them those of Danveld, Brother Gottfried. Von Bracht, an Englishman, and two noble youths — God grant eternal rest to them. Amen!"

" Amen! Amen! " said the novices.

" And say also," added Siegfried, " that, though Danveld desired to quell the enemy of the Order, no one here drew the sword first on Yurand."

" I will only tell what my eyes have seen," replied De Bergov.

" Before midnight you will be in the chapel, where we also shall be, to pray for the souls of the departed," said

Siegfried. And he stretched forth his hand as a sign of thanks and dismissal, for till further consultation he desired to be alone with Brother Rotgier, whom he loved and in whom he had great confidence. In fact, after the departure of De Bergov he dismissed the two novices under pretext of hastening work on the coffins of the common soldiers slain by Yurand, but when the door closed behind them he turned to Rotgier quickly and said, —

" Listen to what I tell thee. There is only one salvation, — concealment; no living soul must ever know that Yurand's real daughter was with us."

" That will not be difficult," answered Rotgier; " no one knew that she was here except Danveld, Gottfried, us two, and that serving woman of the Order who has care of her. Dauveld gave command to intoxicate the men who brought her hither from the hunting-lodge, and then he hanged them. There were persons in the garrison who suspected something, but they were confused through that idiotic maiden, and now they know not whether we mistook the girl, or some wizard really metamorphosed Yurand's daughter."

" That is well."

" I have thought, noble comtur, of this: Should we not throw all the blame on Danveld, since he is not alive?"

" And acknowledge before the whole world that we in time of peace and while negotiating with Prince Yanush of Mazovia bore off from his court a foster daughter of the princess, her favorite damsel ? No, as God lives, that cannot be! People have seen us at the court with Danveld, and Danveld's relative, the Grand Hospitaller, knows that he and we undertook everything in company. If we accuse Danveld the Hospitaller will try to avenge his memory."

" Let us consider tin's point," said Rotgier.

"We must consider it well, or woe to us. If Yurand's daughter is set free she will say that we did not rescue her from bandits, but that the men who took her carried her to Schytno directly."

" That is true! "

" And God is witness that I am thinking not of responsibility alone; the prince will complain to the King of Poland, and their ambassadors will not fail to cry out at all courts against our violence, our crime, our treachery. God alone knows how much harm may result to the Order from this matter. If the Grand Master himself knew the truth he would be bound in duty to secrete that maiden."

" If that be true, when she disappears they will not complain of us, will they? " asked Rotgier.

" No ! Brother Danveld was very adroit. Dost thou remember that he laid this down as a condition to Yurand, that he was not only to present himself at Schytno, but before coming to declare, and to inform the prince by letter, that he was going to ransom his daughter from bandits, and knew that she was not in our possession?"

" True, but how justify that which has happened at Schytno?"

" We will say that as we knew Yurand to be searching for his daughter, and as we had rescued from bandits a girl who could not tell who she was, we notified Yurand, thinking that this might be his daughter ; but when he came he fell into a rage at sight of the girl, and, possessed by the evil one, shed so much innocent blood that frequently more is not shed in a battle."

" Indeed," answered Rotgier, " reason and the experience of age speak through you. Dan veld's evil deeds, even should we accuse him, would be laid on the Order, therefore on us all, on the Chapter, and the Grand Master himself; but when our innocence is evident all blame will fall upon Yurand, to the detriment of the Poles and their alliance with Satan."

"And after that let any one judge us who pleases: the Pope, or the Roman Caesar!"

"Yes!"

A moment of silence followed, after which Rotgier inquired, —

" What shall we do with Yurand's daughter? "

" Let us think over this."

" Give her to me."

Siegfried looked at him and answered, —

"No! Listen, young brother! In a question of the Order spare neither man nor woman, but spare not thyself either. The hand of God touched Danveld, for he wished not only to avenge wrongs done the Order, but to gratify his own desires."

" You judge me wrongly! " said Rotgier.

"Indulge not yourselves,"interrupted old Siegfried, " for ye will make both body and soul effeminate, and one day the knees of that stalwart race will press your breasts and ye will never rise afterward."

And for the third time he rested his gloomy head on his

hand, and evidently he was conversing with his conscience, and was thinking of himself solely, for he said after a while, —

" On me also much human blood is weighing, much pain, many tears — I, too, when it was a question of the Order and when I saw that I could not succeed through strength alone, had no hesitation in seeking other methods; but when I stand before the Lord I shall say to Him: ' I did that for the Order, but in my own case my choice was this.'"

And when he had spoken he opened the dark garment covering his bosom, under that garment a haircloth appeared.

Then he seized his temples with his two hands, turned his face and eyes upward, and cried, —

" Renounce luxury and dissoluteness, strengthen your hearts and bodies, for up there I see white eagle plumes in the air, and eagle talons with the blood of Knights of the Cross on them."

Further words were interrupted by a sweep of the tempest, which was so terrible that a window above the gallery opened with a crash, and the entire hall was filled with the howling and whistling of wind, bearing snowflakes.

"In the name of the Father, Son, and Holy Ghost! This is an evil night," said the old man.

" A night when foul spirits have power," answered Rotgier.

""But are there priests with Danveld's body?"

"There are."

" He left the world without absolution — O God, be merciful to him! "

And both were silent. Then Rotgier called attendants and commanded them to close the window and trim the torches. When they had gone he inquired again,—

"What will you do with Yurand's daughter? Will you take her to Insburg ? "

" I will take her to Insburg, and dispose of her as the good of the Order demands."

"Well, what am I to do? "

" Hast thou courage in thy soul ? "

" What have I done to cause you doubt on that point? "

" I doubt not, for I know thee and I love thee as a son because of thy manfulness. Go then to the court of the Mazovian prince and relate to him all that has happened here, just as we have described it between us."

"I may expose myself to certain destruction."

" Should thy destruction be to the glory of the Cross and the Order thou art bound to go. But no! Destruction is not awaiting thee. They will not harm a guest unless some one may wish perhaps to challenge thee, as did that young knight who challenged all of us — He, or some other may challenge, but of course that is not terrible."

" God grant it to come! But they may seize me and cast me into a dungeon."

"They will not. Remember that Yurand wrote a letter to the prince, and moi*eover thou wilt go to complain against Yuraud. Thou wilt tell truly what he did in Schytno, and they must believe thee. The case is this: we informed him first that there was a girl in our possession, we begged him to come and look at her; he came, he went mad, killed the comtur, slaughtered our people. Thus wilt thou speak,—but what can they say to thee in answer ? The death of Dan veld will be heralded throughout all Mazovia. In the face of that they will cease complaints. Evidently they will search for Yurand's daughter, but since Yurand himself wrote that she was not in our hands suspicion will not fall on us. We must be brave and shut their jaws, for they will think, if we do so, that were we guilty no man of us would dare go to them."

"That is true. After Danveld's funeral I will take the road immediately."

"May God bless thee, my son! If we do all that is proper, not only will they not detain thee, but they will perforce reject Yurand lest we say, ' See how they treat us!'"

" And we must complain thus at all foreign courts."

" The Grand Hospitaller will see to that for the good of the Order, and as a relative of Danveld."

" Yes, but if that Spyhov devil should recover and regain liberty?"

Siegfried glanced forward gloomily, then he answered slowly and with emphasis, —

" Even should he be free again he will not utter one word of complaint against the Order."

After that he began again to instruct Rotgier what to say and what to demand at the court of Mazovia.

CHAPTER XXXI.

Bur news of what had happened in Schytno preceded Brother Rotgier and roused astonishment and alarm in Tsehanov. Neither the prince himself nor any one of his court could understand what had happened. A little while earlier, just as Mikolai of Dlugolyas was starting for Mal-borg with a letter from the prince complaining bitterly that Danusia had been stolen by disorderly cornturs of the boundary, and asking with a threat almost to send her back straightway, a letter came from the master of Spyhov, announcing that his daughter had not been taken by Knights of the Cross, but by ordinary bandits of the border, and that soon she would be freed for a ransom. The envoy did not start, for it did not occur to any one that Knights of the Cross had forced such a letter from Yurand under threat of killing his daughter. It was difficult to understand what had happened if one believed the letter, for marauders of the boundary, as subjects of the prince and the Order, attacked one another in summer, not in winter, when snow would show their traces. Usually they fell upon merchants, or robbed throughout villages, seizing people, and driving their herds away; but to attack the prince himself and bear off his foster child, the daughter of a powerful knight who roused terror everywhere, was a deed which seemed simply beyond human credence. But to that, as to other doubts, the answer was Yurand's letter with his seal, and brought this time by a man whom they knew to have started from Spyhov. In view of these facts no suspicion was possible, but the prince fell into such rage as no one had seen for a long time, and commanded his men to hunt down bandits along every border, inviting also the Prince of Plotsk to do likewise, and spare no punishment on the turbulent.

Just at this juncture came news of what had happened in Schytno.

And passing from mouth to mouth it arrived with tenfold increase. Yurand, it was said, had gone with five others to Schytno; he had rushed in through the open gate and com-mitted such slaughter that few of the garrison were left among the living. It was said that they had to send for aid to neighboring castles, and summon the best of the knights and armed bodies of footmen, who only after a siege of two days had suceeeded in bursting into the fortress and cutting down Yurand, together with his comrades. It was said too that very likely these troops would cross the boundary, and a great war come undoubtedly.

The prince, who knew how very anxious the Grand Master was that in case of war with the Polish king the forces of the two Mazovian principalities should be neutral, did not believe these reports, for to him it was no secret that if the Knights of the Cross began war against the Prince of Plotsk, or against him, no human power could restrain Poland; hence the Grand Master feared war. He knew that war must come, but being of peaceful nature he wished delay, and moreover he knew that to measure himself with the power of Yagello he needed forces such as the Order had never put forth up to that time; he needed besides to assure himself of aid from the princes and knighthood, not only of Germany, but of all Western Europe.

The prince had no fear of war, therefore, but he wished to know what had happened, what he was to think really of the event in Schytno, of the disappearance of Dauusia, and of all those tidings brought in from the boundary; hence, though he could not endure the Order, he was glad when one evening the captain of the archers announced that a Knight of the Cross had come and requested an audience.

He received him haughtily, and, though he knew at once that the man was one of those brothers who had been at the hunting-lodge, he feigned not to remember him, and inquired who he was, whence he had come, and why he had visited Tsehanov.

"I am Brother Rotgier," answered he, "and had the honor not long since to bow down to the knees of your Princely Grace."

" Since you are a brother, why have you not the insignia of the Order on your person ? "

The Knight explained that he had not put on a white mantle because had he done so he would have been captured or slain beyond doubt by the knights of Mazovia. "In all the world elsewhere," said he. " in all other principalities and kingdoms, the cross on a mantle wins good-will and hos-

THE KNIGHTS OF THE CROSS. 369

pitality from people, in Mazovia alone does the cross expose to certain destruction him who bears it — "

" Not the cross exposes you," broke in the prince, angrily, " for we also kiss the cross, but your own criminality. And if somewhere else men receive you better than we do, it is because you are less known to them."

Then seeing that the knight was greatly offended by these words, he inquired, —

"Hast thou been in Schytno, or knowst thou what has happened there? "

" I have been in Schytno, and I know what has happened there," answered Rotgier, " and I have come hither not as the envoy of any one, but for this reason only, that the experienced and pious comtur of Insburg said to me: ' Our Grand Master loves the pious prince and confides in his honesty, hence while I hasten to Malborg do thou go to Mazovia and explain to him the wrongs and insults inflicted upon us, — explain our misfortune. Be sure that that just ruler will not favor the disturber of peace, the savage attacker who shed as much Christian blood as if he were serving not the Saviour, but Satan.'"

And now he narrated how everything had happened in Schytno. How Yurand, invited by the brothers to see if the girl taken from the bandits was his daughter, instead of showing gratitude, had fallen upon them madly; killed Danveld, Brother Gottfried, the Englishman Hugo, Von Bracht, and two noble youths, not counting soldiers; how the brothers, remembering God's commands, and not wishing to kill any one, were forced at last to entangle in a net the raging maniac, who then turned his weapons on himself and wounded his own body dreadfully; finally how, not only in the castle, but in the town, there were people who in the midst of the winter storm heard on that night after the battle laughter and hideous voices crying out in the air: "Our Yurand! The enemy of the Cross! the spiller of innocent blood ! Our Yurjnd! "

The whole narrative, but especially the last words of it, made a deep impression on all. Terror simply seized them. Has Yurand, thought they, really summoned unclean powers? — and deep silence fell on them. The princess, who was present, and who, loving Danusia, bore in her heart an incurable sorrow, turned to Rotgier with this sudden query, —

" You say, Knight, that when you had rescued the idiot VOL. i. — 24

you thought her Yurand's daughter, and therefore invited him to Schytno."

" True, Gracious Lady," answered Rotgier.

"But how could you think so, since you had seen Yurand's real daughter with me in the hunting-lodge ? "

At this Rotgier was confused, for he was not prepared for the question. The prince rose and fixed a stern glance on him; Mikolai of Dlugolyas, Mrokota, Yasko, and other Mazovian knights sprang at once toward him, asking one after another in threatening voices, —

" How could you think so? Say, German! How was that possible?"

But Rotgier rallied.

" We brothers of the Order," said he, "do not raise our eyes on women. At the lodge there were damsels not a few in attendance on the Gracious Princess, but who among them was Yurand's daughter no man of us knew."

" Dan veld knew her," said Mikolai. " He conversed with her even, at the hunt."

" Dan veld is standing in the presence of God," answered Rotgier, " and I will say only this of him, that on the morning after his death blooming roses were found on his coffin. As the season is winter no human hand could have put them there."

Again silence followed.

" How did ye know that Yurand's daughter was stolen?" inquired the prince.

" The very godlessness and insolence of the deed caused it to be bruited about in all places. Hence on hearing of it we had a mass celebrated in thanksgiving that it was only an ordinary damsel and not one of your Grace's children that was stolen from the hunting-lodge."

" But it is a wonder to me that ye could consider an idiot girl to be the daughter of Yurand."

To this Brother Rotgier answered, —

" Danveld said, ' Satan often betrays his servants, so perhaps he transformed Yurand's daughter." 1

" But the bandits could not, as they are ignorant people, forge a letter from Father Kaleb and put Yurand's seal on it. Who could have done that? "

"The evil spirit."

Again no one was able to find an answer. Rotgier looked carefully into the eyes of the prince, and said, —

" In truth these questions are as swords in my breast, for suspicion and doubt is contained in them. But confident in the justice of God and the power of truth, I ask your Princely Grace: Did Yurand himself suspect us of this deed, and if he suspected us why did he, before we invited him to Schytuo, search the whole boundary for bandits so as to ransom his daughter from them ? "

" Well," said the prince, "as to truth, though thou hide it from people, thou wilt not hide it from God. Yurand held you guilty at first, but afterward — afterward he had another idea."

" See how the brightness of truth conquers darkness," said Rotgier. And he looked around the hall with the glance of a victor, for he thought that in the heads of the Knights of the Cross there was more wit and keenness than in Polish heads, and that the Polish race would serve always as plunder and nourishment for the Order, just as a fly must be plunder and nourishment for a spider. So, casting aside his former pliancy, he approached the prince, and demanded in a voice which was haughty and insistent, —

"Reward us, Lord, for our losses, for the injustice inflicted on us, for our tears and our blood! This son of hell was thy subject, hence in the name of God, from whom comes the power of kings and princes, in the name of justice and the Cross, repay us for our wrongs and our blood! "

The prince looked at him with amazement.

" By the dear God," said he, " what dost thou wish? If Yurand shed blood in his rage, must I answer for his rage ?"

" He was thy subject, in thy principality are his lands, his villages, and his castle in which he imprisoned servants of the Order; hence let those lands at least and that godless castle become henceforth the property of the Order. Of course this will be no fitting return for the noble blood shed by him, of course it will not raise the dead to life, but it may even in part still God's anger and wipe away the infamy which otherwise will fall on this whole principality. O Lord! Everywhere the Order possesses lands and castles with which the favor and piety of Christian princes have endowed it, but it has not a hand's-breadth in your dominions. Let the injustice done us, which calls to God for vengeance, be redeemed even in this way, so that we may say that here too live people who have in their hearts the fear of God."

The prince was astonished still more on hearing this, and only after long silence did he answer, —

" By the wounds of God! But if this Order of yours is seated here, by whose favor is it here if not by the favor of my ancestors? Have ye not enough yet of those towns, lands, and regions which belonged to our people formerly and which to-day are yours? Besides, Yuraud's daughter is living yet, for no one has informed you of her death. Do ye wish then to seize an orphan's dowry and right with an orphan's bread some wrong done you?"

" Lord, thou recognizest the wrong," said Rotgier, " then give satisfaction as thy princely conscience and thy just soul dictates."

And again he was glad in heart, for he thought: "Now not merely will they not complain, they will take counsel how to wash their hands of the affair and squeeze out of it. No one will reproach us with anything, and our fame will be like the white mantle of the Order, stainless."

Meanwhile the voice of old Mikolai was heard unex> pectedly, —

" They accuse thee of greed, and God knows with justice, for in this case thou carest more for profit than the honor of the Order."

" That is true! " answered the Mazovian knights in a chorus.

Rotgier advanced a number of steps, raised his head haughtily, and said, measuring them with a lofty glance, —

" I have not come here as an envoy, but as a witness in a cause, and as a Knight of the Cross, ready to defend the honor of the Order with my own blood to the last breath of life. "\Vhoso dares then in the face of what Yurand himself has said to accuse the Order of taking part in the seizure of his daughter, let him take up this knightly challenge, and stand here before the judgment of God! "

Then he cast down before him his gauntlet of a knight, which fell on the floor. They stood in deep silence, for though more than one man would have been delighted to dint a sword on the shoulder of the German, they feared the judgment of God. It was a secret to no one that Yurand had testified explicitly that the Knights of the Order had not stolen his daughter, hence every man thought in his soul that truth, and therefore victory, would be on the side of Rotgier.

The knight grew more and more haughty, and, resting his hand on his hip, he inquired, —

" Is there a man who will take up this gauntlet? "

That moment some knight whom no one had seen enter,

and who at the door had been listening to the conversation, stepped into the middle of the room, took up the gauntlet, and said, —

"I am here! "

When he had spoken thus he cast his own gauntlet straight into Rotgier's face, and began in a voice which in the universal silence spread through the hall like thunder, —

" In the presence of God, in the presence of the worthy prince, and in presence of all the honorable knighthood of this land, I tell thee, Knight of the Cross, that thou liest like a dog against truth and justice — and I challenge thee into the lists to do battle on foot, or on horseback, with lances, with axes, with short swords or long ones — and not to loss of freedom, but to the last breath of life, to the death!"

In that hall one might have heard a fly on the wing. All eyes were turned to Rotgier, and to the challenging knight whom no one knew, for he had a helmet on his head, without a visor, it is true, but with round side pieces which went below his ears, covering the upper part of his face altogether and shading the lower part deeply. The Knight of the Cross was not less astonished than others. Confusion, pallor, and wild anger flashed across his face in succession, like lightning across a night sky. He seized the glove, which, slipping from his face, had caught on a link of his shoulder-piece, and inquired —

" Who art thou who callest on the justice of God?"

The other man unfastened the buckle under his chin, raised his helmet, from under which appeared a bright, youthful face, and said, —

"Zbyshko of Bogdanets, the husband of Yurand's daughter."

All were astounded, and Rotgier with the rest, for no one save the prince and princess, with Father Vyshonek and De Lorche, knew of Danusia's marriage. The Knights of the Cross felt certain that except her father, Danusia had no natural defender, but at that moment Pan de Lorche came forward and said, —

" On my knightly honor I testify to the truth of his words; whoso dares to doubt it to him I say: here is my gauntlet"

Rotgier was a stranger to fear, and in his heart anger was storming at that moment; he would perhaps have raised that gauntlet also, but remembering that the man who had cast it down was himself a great lord, and a relative of the Count of

Guelders, he restrained his anger; he did this all the more since the prince rose and said with a frown, —

" It is not permitted to raise the gauntlet, for I too testify that this knight has spoken truly."

When Rotgier heard this he bowed, and then said to Zbyshko, —

"If it be thy choice, then on foot, in closed barriers, with axes."

" I challenged thee the first time in that way," replied Zbyshko.

"God grant victory to justice!" cried the knights of Mazovia.

CHAPTEE XXXII.

IN the whole court, as well among the knighthood as the women, there was alarm because of Zbyshko, for he was loved universally. In view of Yurand's letter no one doubted that right was on the side of the German. They knew besides that Rotgier was one of the most renowned brothers of the Order. The armor-bearer Van Krist narrated, perhaps purposely, among the Mazovian nobles that his lord, before becoming an armed monk, had sat at the table of honor given by the Knights of the Cross, to which table were admitted only knights famed throughout Christendom, men who had made a pilgrimage to the Holy Land, or who had battled victoriously against dragons, giants, or mighty sorcerers. When the Mazovians heard these narratives of Van Krist, and also the assurances that his lord had fought frequently single-handed against five, having a misericordia in one hand and an axe or a sword in the other, they were frightened, and some said, —

" Oh, if Yurand were here he could manage two of them, no German ever escaped him; but woe to the youth! for that knight exceeds him in strength, years, and training." Others lamented that they had not taken up the gauntlet, declaring tli at had it not been for the tidings from Yurand they would have done so without fail—"but the fear of God's judgment." They mentioned also, when they could, and for mutual consolation, the names of Mazovian, or in general of Polish knights, who, either in court tournaments or in meetings with lances, had gained numerous victories over knights of the West. First of all, they mentioned Zavisha of Garbov, whom no knight in Christendom had equalled. But some were of good hope concerning Zbyshko also. " He is no decked-out knight," said they, " and as ye have heard he has hurled down German heads on trampled earth worthily." But their hearts were strengthened specially by Zbyshko's armor-bearer, Hlava, who., on the eve of the duel, when he heard Van Krist exalting the unheard-of victories of Rotgier, being an excitable young man, seized Van Krist bj

the chin, pushed back his head, and said: "If thou art not ashamed to lie before people look up, because God too hears thee! " And he held him in that way as long a time as would be needed to say one " Our Father; " the other, when he was freed at last, inquired about Hlava's family, and learning that he came of nobles challenged him straightway to axes.

The Mazovians were pleased at this, and again more than one of them said: " Such men will not limp on the field of combat, and if truth and God are on their side the brothers of the Order will not bear away sound bones from this struggle." But Rotgier had cast sand in the eyes of all so successfully that many were alarmed touching this point: on which side is truth, and the prince himself shared the alarm with others. Hence on the evening before the combat he summoned Zbyshko to an interview, and inquired of him, —

"Art thou sure that God will be with thee? Whence knowest thou that they seized Danusia? Did Yurand tell thee anything? For, seest thou, here is Yurand's letter, written by Father Kaleb, and upon it is his seal. In this letter Yurand declares that to his knowledge the Knights did not carry off Danusia. What did he say to thee ? "

" He said that it was not the Knights of the Cross."

" How canst thou risk life then and appear before the judgment of God ? "

Zbyshko was silent; but after some time his jaws quivered and tears gathered in his eyes. " I know nothing, Gracious Lord," said he. " We went away from here with Yurand, and on the road I told him of the marriage. He began to complain that that might be an offence against Heaven, but when I told him that it was God's will he grew pacified, and forgave me. Along the whole road he said that no one had carried off Danusia but Knights of the Order, and after that I know not myself what happened. To Spyhov came that woman who brought some medicine for my use to the hunting-lodge, and with her one messenger. They shut themselves in with Yurand and counselled. What they said I know not, only after that conversation Yurand's own servants could not recognize him, for he was as if saved from a coffin then. He said to us: " Not the Knights of the Cross," but he let out of the dungeon Bergov and all the captives whom he had taken, God knows why; he went away himself without attendant or servant. He said that he was

going to the bandits to ransom Danusia, and he commanded me to wait for him. Well, I waited till news came from Schytuo that Yurand had murdered Germans and had himself fallen. O, Gracious Lord! the land of -Spyhov was burning beneath me, and I came near running mad. I put men on horseback to avenge Yurand's death, but Father Kaleb said: ' Thou canst not take the castle, and do not begin war. Go to the prince; they may know something there of Danusia.' So I came, and happened in here just as that dog was barking about the wrong done the Order and the madness of Yurand. I took up his gauntlet because I had challenged him earlier, and though I know nothing, I know this one thing exactly, that they are hellish liars, without shame, faith, or honor. See, Gracious Prince, they stabbed De Fourcy and tried to cast the blame of that deed on my attendant. As God lives! they slaughtered De Fourcy like a bullock, and then came to thee, lord, for restitution and vengeance. Who will swear that they did not lie to Yurand, and have not lied now to thee ? I know not where Danusia is, but I have challenged this man; for though I should have to lose my life, death is sweeter to me than is life without her who in all the world is my dearest."

When he had said this he forgot himself; he tore the net from his head and the hair fell over his shoulders; he seized it and sobbed grievously. Anna Danuta, afflicted to the depth of her soul by the loss of Danusia, placed her hand on his head in compassion for his sufferings, and said, —

"God will aid, bless, and comfort thee! "

CHAPTER XXXIII.

THE prince did not oppose the duel, for, according to the custom of the time, he had no authority to do so. He simply caused Rotgier to write to the Grand Master and to Siegfried de Lowe, stating that he had cast down the gauntlet first before the Mazovian knights, that because of this he was to meet in combat Yurand's son-in-law, who moreover had challenged him on an earlier occasion. Rotgier explained to the Grand Master that if he fought without permission he did so because the honor of the Knights was in question, and he had to avert foul suspicion which might bring shame to the Order, which he, Rotgier, was ready at all times to vindicate with his life-blood. This letter was sent straightway to the boundary by an attendant of the brother ; beyond that it was to go to Malborg by post, which the Knights had invented many years before others, and introduced into the lands of the Order.

Meanwhile the snow in the courtyard of the castle was trampled and sprinkled with ashes, so that the feet of the combatants might not slip over its surface or sink in it. An uncommon movement reigned within the castle. Emotion had so seized the knights and damsels that no one slept the night before the combat. They said that a combat with lances on horseback, or even with swords, ended frequently with wounds, but on foot, and especially with the terrible axes, it was ever mortal. All hearts were on Zbyshko's side, and the greater the friendship for him or Danusia the greater the fear caused by reports of the skill and fame of the German. Many women passed that night in the church, where, after confessing to Father Vyshonek, Zbyshko himself performed penance. So women, when they saw his face, almost boyish, said to one another: " Why, he is a child yet! How can he expose his young head to the axe of the German?" And the more earnestly did they implore aid for him. But when he rose at dawn and went through the chapel to put on his armor their courage increased somewhat, for though Zbyshko's head and face were really boy-like, his body was

bulky and stalwart beyond measure, so that he seemed to them a chosen man, who could fight his own battle even against the strongest.

The combat was to take place in the courtyard of the castle, which was surrounded by a portico. When day had dawned completely, the prince and princess with their children came and sat down in a central place between the pillars, whence they could see the whole courtyard in the best manner. At both sides of them were the foremost courtiers, noble ladies, and the knighthood. These filled all corners of the portico. The servants fixed themselves beyond an embankment formed of snow which had been swept from the courtyard. Some had mounted on window-sills, and even on the roof. On these places the common people muttered: "God grant our man not to falter!"

The day was damp and cold, but clear. The air was full of daws, which had settled on the roofs and bastion points, but, disturbed by unusual movements, they circled above the castle with great fluttering. In spite of the cold, people were sweating from emotion, and when the first trumpet sound announced the arrival of the combatants, all hearts beat like hammers.

The two men entered from opposite sides of the barriers and halted at the ends of them. Breath stopped in the breasts of all spectators. Each thought: Two souls will soon fly to the judgment threshold of God, and two corpses will be left on the snow! The lips and cheeks of women grew blue and pallid at thought of that; the eyes of men were fixed on the opponents as on a rainbow; each wished to predict in his mind from their forms and weapons the side to which victory would fall.

Rotgier was arrayed in a blue enamelled breastplate, with a similar armor for the thighs, and wore a helmet of the same material with raised visor, and lordly peacock plumes on the top of it. Zbyshko's breast, sides, and back were covered by that splendid Milan armor which he bad won from the Frisians. On his head was a helmet not fastened under the chin, and without plumes; on his legs were raw bull-hides. On their left shoulders the men carried shields with their escutcheons : on the German's was a chessboard above, and below three lions rampant; on Zbyshko's, the "dull horseshoe." In their right hands they carried the broad, terrible axes with oaken handles, which had grown dark and were longer than the arm of a man full-grown. They were

accompanied by their armor-bearers, Hlava and Van Krist, both in dark iron-plate mail, both with shields and axes. On his escutcheon Van Krist had a sprig of broom. The escutcheon of the Cheh was the bullhead, with this difference, that on the head, instead of an axe, a short sword was sunk in the eye half-way.

The trumpets sounded a second time; after the third the combatants were to begin, according to agreement. They were separated from each other by only a small space, over which gray ashes were sprinkled. Above that space death was hovering like a bird of ill-omen. But before the third signal was given Rotgier, approaching the pillars between which the prince and the princess were sitting, raised his steel-incased head, and called with a voice so resonant that it was heard in all corners, —

"I take to witness God, thee, worthy lord, and all the knighthood of this land, that I am guiltless of the blood which will be shed here."

At these words hearts were straitened again, because the German felt so sure of himself and of victory. But Zbyshko, who had an honest soul, turned to Hlava and said, —

"That boasting is foul in my nostrils; it would have meaning after my death, but not while I am living. That boaster has a peacock plume on his helmet, and I at the very first made a vow to get three such, and later, I vowed to get as many as I have fingers on my hands. God will give success! "

"My master," said Hlava, bending down and gathering some ashes from the snow, so that the axe handle might not slip along his palms, "perhaps Christ will grant me to finish quickly with this Prussian; will it be permitted me then, if not to touch the German, at least to put an axe handle between his legs and bring him to the earth with it ? "

" God guard thee from doing that !" cried Zbyshko with vehemence; " thou wouldst cover thyself and me with dishonor."

With that the sound of the trumpet was heard for the third time. The attendants sprang forward quickly and with passion, but the knights approached each other more slowly and carefully, as their dignity and distinction demanded, till the first blows were given.

Few turned to the attendants, but those among men of experience and the servants who looked at them understood

straightway that Hlava had on his side a tremendous advantage. Van Krist's axe moved slowly in his hand, and the motions of his shield were more labored. The legs seen beneath his shield were longer, but slender and less springy than the powerful limbs covered by the close-fitting dress of Hlava, who pressed on so passionately that Van Krist had to retreat almost from the first moment. People understood this immediately: one of those opponents rushes on the other like a storm, he pushes, presses, strikes like a thunderbolt, while the other, in the feeling that death is above him, defends himself only to defer the dread moment to the utmost. Such was the case in reality. That boaster, who in general went to combat only when he could not do otherwise, saw that insolence and thoughtless words had brought him to that struggle with a man of great strength, whom he should have avoided as he would destruction; hence, when he felt that each of those blows might have brought down a bullock, the heart fell in him utterly. He forgot almost that it was not enough to catch blows on a shield, but that he must return them. He saw above him gleams of an axe, and thought that each gleam was the last one. When holding his shield up he shut his eyes in terror, doubting whether he would open them another time. He gave a blow rarely, and hopeless of reaching his opponent, he merely raised his shield higher and higher above his head to protect it.

At last he was tortured, but Hlava struck on with increasing vigor. As from a great pine-tree immense chips fly uncler °the axe of a peasant, so under the blows of the Cheh plates began to break and fall from the mail of the German attendant. The upper edge of his shield bent and broke, the shoulder-piece fell from his right shoulder, and with it the bloody, severed armor strap. The hair stood on Van Krist's head and mortal terror seized him. He struck still once and a second time with all the vigor of his arm against Hlava's buckler. Seeing at last that, in view of the terrible strength of his opponent, there was no rescue, and that nothing could save him except some uncommon exertion, he hurled himself suddenly at Hlava's legs with all the weight of his body and his armor.

Both fell to the earth and wrestled, turning in the snow and rolling. But the Cheh was soon the superior. He restrained for a time the desperate struggles of his opponent, till at last he pressed with his knee the iron network covering Van Krist's stomach, and drew from his own sword-belt a short, triple-edged misericordia.

" Spare! " whispered the German, raising his eyes to the eyes of Hlava.

But the latter, instead of an answer, stretched above him so as to reach with his hands more easily, and when he had cut the leather helmet strap under the chin of his enemy he stabbed the hapless man twice in the throat, directing the point downward toward the middle of his bosom.

Van Krist's eyes sank in his skull, his hands and feet rubbed the snow as if to clear it of ashes, but after a while he stretched and lay motionless, merely pouting his lips, covered now with red foam, and bleeding with uncommon profuseness.

The Cheh rose, wiped his misericordia on the clothing of the German, then raising his axe and leaning on the handle gazed at the more difficult and stubborn battle between Zbyshko and Brother Rotgier.

The knights of western Europe were in those days accustomed to luxury and comfort, while the "heirs" in Great and Little Poland, as well as in Mazovia, were severe in their lives and self-denying. Because of this they roused admiration even in enemies and strangers by their strength of body and endurance.

It turned out on this occasion that Rotgier was excelled by Zbyshko in strength of arms and legs no less than his attendant was excelled by Hlava, but it turned out also that Zbyshko being young was surpassed in knightly training by the German.

It favored Zbyshko in some degree that he had chosen to fight with axes, for parrying with that kind of weapon was impossible. With long or short swords a man had to know blows and thrusts and be skilled to p'arry them; in such combat the German would have had a notable advantage. As it was, both Zbyshko himself and the spectators knew by the movements and handling of his shield that they had before them in Rotgier a man of experience, and dangerous, who, as they saw, was not engaged for the first time in that sort of combat. To every blow given by Zbyshko the German presented his shield, and as the blow fell he withdrew it a little; by this move the blow, though most violent, lost some effect, and could not cut or even crack the smooth surface. At moments he withdrew, at moments he pushed forward, though so swiftly that the eye could barely take note of his movements. The prince feared for Zbyshko, and men's faces grew gloomy, since it seemed to them that the German

was playing with his opponent as if purposely. More than once he did not even present his shield, but at the instant when Zbyshko delivered the blow he made a half turn to one side, and thus Zbyshko's axe cut vacant air. That was for Zbyshko most perilous, as he might lose his balance and fall, in which case his ruin would be inevitable. Seeing this, Hlava, who stood over the slaughtered Van Krist, was alarmed also, and said in spirit:

" As God is dear to me, should my lord fall I will give the German a blow between the shoulders and let him tumble also."

But Zbyshko did not fall; he had immense strength in his legs, and, spreading them widely, was able to sustain on each one the whole weight of his blow and his body.

Rotgier noticed this straightway, and the spectators were mistaken in thinking that he despised his opponent. On the contrary, after the first blow, when in spite of all skill in withdrawing his shield his arm was benumbed almost, he understood that a sore struggle with that youth was awaiting him, and that if ho could not fell him luckily, the battle might be protracted and dangerous. He had calculated that after Zbyshko's blow in the air he would fall on the snow, and when that did not happen he grew alarmed immediately. From under his visor Rotgier beheld the fixed nostrils and lips of his opponent, and his gleaming eyes also, at instants, and thought that his ardor would bear him away, that he would forget himself, lose his head, and in blindness think more of giving blows than defending his person. But in this too he was mistaken. Zbyshko had not skill to dodge blows by half turns, but he minded his shield, and when raising his axe did not expose himself more than was needful. His attention was evidently redoubled, and noting the accuracy and experience of Rotgier, not only did he not forget, but he collected himself, grew more cautious, and in his blows there was a calculation to which not heated, but cool resolution, may bring a man.

Rotgier, who had been in many wars and had fought battles not a few, both single-handed and in company, knew from experience that some men, like birds of prey, are created for combat, and gifted specially by nature, — men who, as it were, divine what others acquire by whole years of experience, — and straightway he saw that with one of these he was now doing battle. This youth had that certain something which is in the falcon, which considers an opponent as

mere prey, and thinks of naught else save to grasp that prey in its talons. In spite of all his strength he noticed that in strength too he was no match for Zb\ T shko, and that if he became exhausted before he could give the settling blow, the combat with that terrible though less prepared youth would be fatal. Considering this, he resolved to fight with the least labor possible: he drew the shield toward his body; he did not advance too much, he did not withdraw too much; he limited his motions; he collected his M-hole strength of mind and arm for one decisive blow, and watched for the moment.

The fierce battle was protracted beyond usual duration. A deathlike silence had settled down on the portico. Nothing was heard save blows on the shields from the edges and backs of the axes, now dull, and now piercing. To the prince, princess, knights, and damsels such sights were not novel; still a feeling akin to terror pressed all hearts as with vices. They knew that there was no question then of showing strength, skill, or bravery, but that there was a greater rage in that combat, a deeper despair, a harder, a keener resolve, and a deadlier vengeance. On one side was a feeling of dreadful injustice endured, and with it love and grief beyond limit; on the other, the honor of a whole Order and with it concentrated hate. These two had met on that place of conflict to receive God's decision.

Meanwhile the pale winter morning had brightened, the gray obstruction of mist had been broken, and a sun-ray now lighted Rotgier's blue armor and the silvery Milan mail worn by Zbyshko. In the chapel the bell rang for the mid-forenoon prayer, and at sound of it flocks of daws flew again from the peaks of the castle, flapping their wings and croaking noisily, as if from delight at the spectacle of bloodshed and that corpse lying motionless there on the snow. Rotgier had cast his eyes at it more than once in the course of the battle, and felt now a great loneliness all on a sudden. Every eye which looked at him was the eye of an enemy. Every prayer, wish, and silent vow made by women were in favor of Zbyshko. Besides, though the brother of the Order felt perfectly sure that Hlava would not rush from the rear and fall on him treacherously, the presence and proximity of that terrible figure filled him with that kind of fear which people feel at sight of a bear, wolf, or buffalo from which they are not separated by a grating. And he could not ward off that feeling, all the more since Hlava, while follow-

Ing the course of the battle, moved and changed places, approaching the combatants, now from behind, now from the front, now from one side, inclining his head meanwhile and looking at the German with ominous gaze through the opening in the iron visor of his helmet, and raising somewhat at moments the bloody point of his sword, as though not noting that he did so.

Weariness began at last to seize Rotgier. He gave two short but fierce blows in succession, directing them against the right arm of Zbyshko. Zbyshko, however, repulsed them so forcibly with his shield that the axe turned in Rotgier's hand and he had to push back suddenly to escape falling, and thenceforth he pushed back continually. At last not only his strength but his patience and coolness of blood were exhausted. From the breasts of the spectators, at sight of his withdrawal, a number of shouts were rent, as if in triumph. These shouts roused in him desperation and anger. The blows of the axes grew more and more frequent. Sweat flowed from the foreheads of both combatants ; from between the parted teeth of both the hoarse breath of their breasts escaped. The spectators had ceased to bear themselves calmly, and from moment to moment were heard cries, at one time of men, at another of women: " Strike! " "At him!" " The judgment of God! " " The punishment of God!" "God aid thee!" The prince raised his hand a number of times to enforce silence, but he could not. The noise became louder, children began to cry here and there on the portico, and at last, right at the side of the princess, some young, sobbing voice of a woman called,—

" For Danusia, Zbyshko! "

Zbyshko knew without this reminder that he was there doing battle for Danusia. He was sure that that Knight of the Cross had assisted in stealing her, and that in fighting with him he was fighting to redress the wrong done her. But, as he was young and eager for struggle, in the moment of combat he thought only of combat. All at once that cry. brought before him his loss and her suffering. Love, sorrow, and vengeance put fire in his veins. The heart whined in him from suddenly roused pain, and the rage of battle seized him directly. Rotgier could not catch now the terrible blows which were* like those of a tempest, nor could he avoid them. Zbyshko struck his shield against the shield of the German with such force that the German's arm was benumbed that in-VOL. i. — 25

slant, and dropped without control. He retreated in terror and bent back, but the glitter of an axe flashed in his eyes, and its edge fell on his right shoulder like a thunderbolt. To the ears of the spectators came the single piercing shriek: " Jesus! " Rotgier withdrew one step more and fell backward to the centre.

Immediately there was an uproar, a movement on the balcony, as in a hive where bees, warmed by sun-rays, buzz and move. Knights ran down the steps in crowds, serving-men sprang over the wall of snow to look at the bodies. Everywhere were heard shouts of: "Here is the judgment of God! " " Yurand has an heir I" " Glory and thanks to him!" "He is a man for the axe! " Others cried: " Look at him and wonder! " "Yurand himself could not have cut better! " In fact a crowd of curious people formed around the body of Rotgier. He lay on his back with a face white as snow, his mouth widely open, and his bloody shoulder divided from the neck to the armpit so terribly that it held by some filaments only. Then a few men remarked: "He was alive a little while ago and walked over the earth proudly, but he moves no finger now! " And thus speaking, some wondered at his stature, for he occupied a great space on the field of combat, and seemed larger after death than before; others fixed the price of his peacock plumes as they changed colors marvelously on the snow, and a third group his armor, which was held to be worth a good village. But Hlava had just come up with two of Zbyshko's attendants to strip that armor from the dead man, and the curious surrounded Zbyshko, praising him to the skies and extolling him, for it seemed to them proper that his glory should fall on the whole knighthood of Mazovia and Poland. Meanwhile they removed his shield and axe to relieve him, and Mrokota unbuckled his helmet and covered his sweat-moistened hair with a cap of scarlet. Zbyshko, as if in a maze, stood, breathing heavily, with the fire in his eyes still unquenched, with face pale from resolve and exertion, trembling somewhat from excitement and struggle. They took him now by the arm and led him to the prince and princess, who were waiting, in a heated room, near the chimney. The young knight knelt before them and, when Father Yyshonek had blessed him and repeated eternal rest for the souls departed, the prince embraced Zbyshko.

" The Most'High God has judged between him and thee," said he, " and guided thy hand, for which praised be His name

— Amen! " Then turning to De Lorche and others, he added, " Thee, as a knight, and all of you here present, I take to witness that which I myself testify, that they fought according to rule and custom, in the way that the judgments of God are sought for in all places; hence this man has acted in knightly fashion and in obedience to God."

The warriors shouted in a chorus of agreement, and when the prince's words were interpreted to De Lorche he rose and announced that not only did he testify that all had been done in accordance with the law of knighthood and of God, but also that if any one from Malborg or the court of any prince should dare to call that in question, he, De Lorche, would challenge him straightway to meet within barriers on foot or on horseback, not only if he were an ordinary knight, but even a giant, or some sorcerer surpassing Merlin himself in magic.

Now Princess Anna Danuta, when Zbyshko was embracing her feet, asked, bending toward him, —

" Why art thou not glad? Rejoice and thank God, for if the Lord in His mercy has freed thee from this net He will not desert thee hereafter, and will bring thee to happiness."

"How can I rejoice, gracious lady?" answered Zbyshko. " God has given victory and avenged me on this brother of the Order, but Danusia, as she has not been found, is not recovered yet, and I am no nearer her now than I was before the battle."

" Her most inveterate enemies, Danveld, Gottfried, and Rotgier, are no longer alive," replied the princess, "and as to Siegfried, they say that he is juster than the others, though more cruel. Praise God's mercy then for even this. De Lorche has promised also that if the Knight of the Cross fell he would take the corpse to Schytno, and go immediately to Malborg and defend Danusia before the Grand Master of the Order. They will not dare, be assured of that, to disregard the Grand Master."

" God give health to Pan de Lorche," said Zbyshko, " and I will go with him to Malborg."

But the princess was as much frightened at these words as if Zbyshko had said that he would go unarmed among wolves, which gather in packs during winter in the great pine forests of Mazovia.

" Why! " exclaimed she. " To certain destruction ? Immediately after the duel neither De Lorche can assist thee,

nor the letters which Rotgier wrote before the combat. Thou wilt not save any one, and wilt destroy thyself."

" So help me God," said Zbyshko, rising and crossing his palms, " I will go to Malborg, and if need be beyond the *sea. So bless me, O Christ, as I shall seek her with the last breath in my nostrils, I will not stop unless I perish. It is easier for me to beat Germans and fight in armor, than for the orphan to groan in a dungeon. Oi, easier ! easier! "

And he spoke, as indeed he did whenever he mentioned Danusia, with such excitement and in such pain that at moments the words were wrested from him, as if some one were grasping his throat. The princess saw that it would be vain to seek to dissuade him, and that to hold the man back one would have to thrust him manacled into a dungeon.

But Zbyshko could not set out immediately. Knights of that period disregarded all obstacles, but they were not permitted to break knightly custom, which commanded every victor in a duel to pass the day of his triumph on the field of combat and stay there till the following midnight. This was done to prove that he was master of the field, and to show that he was ready for combat in case a relative or friend of the vanquished wished to challenge. This custom was observed by whole armies, who thus lost frequently the advantage which promptness after victory might have brought them. Zbyshko did not even try to escape this unbending ordinance, and, after strengthening himself to some degree and putting on his armor, he remained beneath a gloomy winter sky within the courtyard of the castle till midnight, waiting for an enemy who could not come from any side whatever.

Only at midnight, when the heralds announced by sound of trumpet his victory decisively, did Mikolai summon him to supper, and immediately after to a consultation with Prince Yanush.

CHAPTER XXXIV.

THE prince opened the consultation.

"It is unfortunate," said he, " that we have no letter or testimony against the comturs; our suspicion seems just, it is true, and I myself believe that they and no one else seized Yuraud's daughter, — but what of that? They will deny. And when the Grand Master demands proof what shall we show him ? Nay, more! Yurand's letter is proof in their favor." Here he turned to

Zbyshko. "Thou sayst that they extorted the letter from Yurand by threats. Perhaps that is really true, for if justice were on their side God would not have aided thee against Rotgier. But since they extorted one letter perhaps they extorted two. They may have a testimony from Yurand that they are innocent of seizing the unfortunate maiden. In that case they will show it to the Grand Master — what will happen then ? "

" But they themselves stated that they rescued Danusia from bandits, and that they have her."

"I know. But now they will say that they were mistaken and that it was another girl, the best proof of which is that Yurand himself rejected her."

" He did, for they showed him a different person; through this they enraged him."

" That is true indeed, but they can say that this is merely guess work on our part."

" Their lies," said Mikolai, " are like a forest. Something may be seen from the edge of a forest, but the farther a man goes the denser it becomes, till he gets astray and loses himself altogether."

Then he repeated in German his words to De Lorche, who said, —

" The Grand Master is better than they, and better than his brother; though insolent in spirit he is sensitive to knightly honor."

"True," answered Mikolai. "The Grand Master is humane, but has not power to restrain comturs or the

Chapter, and he cannot help this, that everything in the Order is built on injustice; but he does not rejoice in the injustice. Go, go, Knight de Lorche, and tell him what has happened here. Those monks fear foreigners more than us, they fear lest people should tell at foreign courts of their treasons and dishonest deeds, but if the Grand Master asks you for proofs say this : ' To know the truth is God's work, to seek for it is man's. If thou wish proofs, lord, search for them; give command to stir up the castles, examine people; let us seek, for it is folly and a fable to say that bandits of the forest seized the orphan."

"Folly and a fable," repeated De Lorche.

" Bandits would not have raised their hands against the prince's court, nor against Yurand's daughter. And even had they taken her it would have been to get a ransom; and they themselves would have declared that they had her."

" I will tell all this," said the man of Lorraine, " and I will find De Bergov also. We are from the same country, and, though I do not know him, people say that he is a relative of the Count of Guelders. He has been in Schytno; let him tell the Grand Master what he has seen."

Zbyshko understood something of these words, and Mikolai interpreted what he did not understand. Then Zbyshko seized De Lorche by the body and pressed him to his bosom with such vigor that the knight was forced to groan.

"But dost thou wish to go in every case?" asked the prince of Zbyshko.

" I do, Gracious Lord. What else am I to do? I wished to take Schytno, even if I had to gnaw the walls through, but how can I begin war without permission ? "

" The man who should begin war without permission would repent under the sword of an executioner," said Prince Yanush.

" Of course law is law," answered Zbyshko. " I wanted to challenge all who were at Schytno, but people said that Yurand had slaughtered them like bullocks; I could not tell who were living and who were dead. So help me God and the Holy Cross, I will not desert Yurand till my last breath."

"Thou speakesthonorably and pleasestme," said Mikolai. " But as thou didst not fly alone to Schytno it is clear that thou hast wit, for even a dull man would guess that they have not kept there either Yurand or his daughter, but taken both to other castles. God has given thee Rotgier because thou earnest hither."

"Yes!" said the prince, "as we have learned from Rotgier, of those four only old Siegfrie4 is alive; God has punished the others already, either with thy hand or Yurand's. As to Siegfried, he is less a scoundrel than the others, but is perhaps more cruel. It is unfortunate that Yurand and Danusia are in his power; there is need of swift rescue in their case. But lest an evil fate befall thee I will give a letter to the Grand Master. Only listen well, and understand that thou art not going as an envoy, but a confidant, and I will write to the Grand Master as follows: Since on a time they attacked us, the descendants of their benefactors, it is likely that they seized Yurand's daughter for the reason specially that they were angry at Yurand. I will ask the Grand Master to command a diligent search for her, and if he desires my friendship to deliver her into thy hands immediately."

On hearing this Zbyshko cast himself at the feet of the prince, embraced his knees, and said, —

" But Yuraud, Gracious Lord, what of Yurand? Take his part too! If he be wounded mortally, let him die in his own house at least, and near his children."

" There is something touching Yurand also," replied the prince with kindliness. " The Grand Master is to send two judges and I two, who will judge the comtur's acts and those of Yurand according to the rules of knightly honor. And those four will choose a fifth to be their head, and as all decide so will it be."

The consultation ended there. Zbyshko took farewell now of the prince, for they were to start upon the road immediately. But before parting Mikolai, who was experienced and knew the Knights of the Cross, took Zbyshko aside and asked, —

" But that young man, the Cheh, wilt thou take him with thee among the Germans? "

"It is sure that he will not leave me. But why the question ? "

"I am sorry for him. He is a splendid fellow, and do thou note what I say: thou wilt bring away a sound head from Malborg unless thou meet a better man in a duel, but Hlava's death is certain."

"Why?"

u Because the dog brothers complained that he stabbed De Fourcy. They must have written of his death to the Grand Master, and to a certainty they wrote that the Cheh shed his blood. The Knights at Malborg will not forgive that. Judgment and vengeance await him, for how wilt thou convince the Grand Master of Hlava's innocence? Moreover he crushed Danveld's arm, and Dan veld was a relative of the Grand Hospitaller. I am sorry for Hlava, and I repeat that if he goes he will go to his death."

" He will not go to his death, for I shall leave him in Spyhov."

But it did not happen thus, for other causes intervened and prevented the Cheh from remaining in Spyhov.

Zbyshko and De Lorche set out on the morrow with their escorts. De Lorche, whom Father Vyshonek freed from his vow touching Ulrika de Elner, was happy and devoted altogether to remembering the charms of Yagenka of Dlu-golyas; hence he travelled in silence. Zbyshko, unable to talk with him of Danusia, for the men did not understand each other well, talked with Hlava, who so far knew nothing of the intended expedition to the realms of the Order.

"I am going to Malborg," said Zbyshko, " but the time of my return is in the power of

God. Perhaps it will be soon, perhaps in the spring, perhaps a year hence, perhaps never. Dost understand ?"

" I understand. Your Grace is going surely to challenge the Knights there. And glory to God, for every knight of them has an attendant."

" No, I am not going there to challenge unless the challenge comes of itself. Thou wilt not go at all, but remain at home, at Spyhov."

On hearing this Hlava was terribly mortified, he fell to complaining piteously, and implored his young master not to desert him.

" I have sworn not to abandon your Grace. I have sworn on the Cross and my honor. Should any misfortune befall you how could I appear before my lady in Zgorzelitse ? I have taken an oath, therefore spare me so that I may not disgrace myself in her eyes."

" Hast thou not given her a vow to obey me? "

"Of course! In all things, but not to leave you. If your Grace sends me away I shall follow at a distance and be at hand when needed."

I have not dismissed thee," answered Zbyshko, "and I shall not; but it would be slavery for me if I could not send thee whithersoever I pleased, even over the longest road, and if I could not relieve myself of thy presence even for a day.

Thou wilt not stand above me, of course, like a headsman above an innocent person! And as to fighting, how art thou to assist me ? I will not say in war, for in war people fight together, but in a duel thou wilt not fight for me. If Rotgier had been the stronger his armor would not be on our wagon, but mine on his. And know besides that it will be worse for me there with thy company; thou mayst put me in danger."

" How so, your Grace? "

Zbyshko told how he had heard from Mikolai that the comturs, unable to acknowledge the murder of De Fourcy, had accused Hlava, and would pursue him vindictively.

"If they seize thee," said Zbyshko at last, "I shall of course not leave thee to them as to dogs, and for this cause I may lay down my own head."

The Cheh became gloomy on hearing these words, for he recognized truth in them; still he tried further to turn the affair according to his wishes.

" Those men who saw me are no longer in this world, for people say that the old master of Spyhov killed some, and your grace has slain Rotgier."

"Thou wert seen by attendants who dragged on at some distance in front, and Siegfried, that old Knight of the Cross, is still living and is surely in Malborg; or if he is not there he will go there, for the Grand Master will certainly summon him."

There was no answer to this, so they rode on in silence as far as Spyhov. They found perfect readiness for war in the castle, since old Tolima expected that either the Knights of the Cross would make an attack, or that Zbyshko would summon them forth to save the old master. The guards watched everywhere at passages through the swamp; they watched in the castle also. The people were armed; and, as war was nothing new to them, they waited for the Germans with willingness, promising themselves famous booty. Father Kaleb received Zbyshko and De Lorche, and immediately after supper showed them the parchment with Yurand's seal, on which parchment he himself had written the last will of the master of Spyhov.

" He dictated it to me," said the priest, " that night when he started for Schytno. Well — he did not expect to return."

" "Why did you say nothing? "

4 ' I said nothing because he declared under the secret of confession what he intended to

do. The Lord grant him endless rest, and let eternal light shine on him."

" Say no Our Father for him. He is living yet. I know that from Rotgier, with whom I fought in the courtyard of the prince's castle. The judgment of God was between us, and I killed him."

"All the more for that reason will Yurand not return — unless by the power of God."

" I will go with this knight here to wrest him from their hands."

"Then thou knowest not their hands, that is clear. I know them, for before Yurand received me into Spyhov I was a priest fifteen years in their country. God alone can save Yurand."

" And He can help us too."

"Amen!"

Then the priest unrolled the parchment and read it. Yurand had bequeathed all his land and property to Danusia and her descendants, and in case of her death without posterity to her husband, Zbyshko of Bogdanets. To conclude he confided this his testament to the care of the prince, "so that should there be anything not in accordance with law, the favor of the prince would make law of it." This conclusion was added since Father Kaleb knew only canon law, and Yurand himself, occupied exclusively with war, knew only the law of knighthood. After reading the document to Zbyshko the priest read it to the older men of the garrison ; these acknowledged the young knight at once as heir and promised obedience. They thought besides that Zbyshko would lead them straightway to rescue the old master, and they rejoiced, because stern hearts eager for battle were beating in their bosoms, hearts attached to Yurand; therefore great gloominess seized them on learning that they must remain at home, and that their lord with a small retinue was going to Malborg not to offer battle, but to make complaint. The Cheh shared their gloom, though on the other hand he rejoiced at the notable increase of Zbyshko's property.

" Ei," said he, "who will rejoice if not the old lord of Bogdanets? He would know how to manage in this place! What is Bogdanets if compared to an inheritance like Spyhov1 "

But Zbyshko was seized at that moment by a sudden yearning for his uncle, such a yearning as seized him often, especially in grievous and difficult junctures; so turning to the attendant he said without hesitation, —

" What hast thou to do sitting here in idleness? Go to Bogdanets; thou wilt take a letter."

" If I am not to be with your Grace I should prefer to be there," answered he, delighted.

" Call Father Kaleb to me; let him write, as is proper, of all that has happened; the priest of Kresno will read the letter to uncle, or the abbot will read it if he is in Zgorzelitse."

But the next moment he struck his palm on his youthful mustaches, and added, speaking to himself, —

"Oh! the abbot!"

And Yagenka passed before his vision blue-eyed, dark-haired, shapely as a deer, and with tears on her eyelids. He felt awkward, and for a time rubbed his forehead.

"Indeed the girl will feel sad, but not sadder than I," said he.

Meanwhile Father Kaleb appeared and sat down to write. Zbyshko dictated to him minutely all that had happened from the time of his coming to the hunting-lodge. He kept back nothing, for he knew that old Matsko when he looked into those matters carefully would be glad at last. Indeed it was not possible to compare Bogdanets with Spyhov, which was a broad and rich property, and Zbyshko knew that Matsko valued such things immensely.

When, after long effort, the letter was finished and closed with a seal, Zbyshko called his attendant a second time and delivered it, saying, —

" Perhaps thou wilt return with uncle; if so I shall rejoice greatly."

But Hlava's face was full of evident anxiety; he hesitated, stood on one foot, then on the other, and did not start till the young knight spoke, —

" If thou hast more to say, say it."

" I should wish to know this. If people ask how shall I answer? "

"What people?"

" Not those in Bogdanets, but in the neighborhood, — for certainly they will wish to know."

At this Zbyshko, who had determined to make no concealment of anything, looked at Hlava quickly, and answered, —

"With thee it is not a question of people, but only of Yagenka."

Hlava blushed, then he grew somewhat pale and said, —

'* Of her, lord."

" But how dost thou know that she has not been given in marriage to Stan of Rogov or Vilk of Brozova ? "

" The young lady has not married any one," said Hlava, with emphasis.

" The abbot may have commanded her."

" The abbot obeys the young lady, not she the abbot."

" What dost thou wish then ? Tell the truth to her, as to others."

Hlava bowed and went away somewhat angry.

" God grant," said he to himself, thinking of Zbyshko. "God grant her to forget thee. God grant her a better man. Thou art married but wifeless, and mayest thou be a widower before the marriage is finished."

Hlava had grown attached to Zbyshko, he had compassion on Danusia, but Yagenka he loved beyond everything, and from the time that he had heard of Zbyshko's marriage before the last battle at Tsehanov he carried pain in his heart, and bitterness.

" God grant that thou be a widower before thy marriage is real!"

But later other thoughts, evidently sweeter, came to his head, for coming to his horses he said, —

" God be praised for even this, that I shall embrace her feet."

Meanwhile Zbyshko was impatient for the journey, and a fever tormented him. Since he could not occupy himself with other matters he endured real torture, thinking always of Danusia and Yurand. But he had to remain in Spyhov one night at least, for Pan de Lorche, and for the preparations which such a long journey demanded. Besides he was wearied beyond every measure by the battle, by watching, by the journey, by lack of sleep, by grief. That night, very late, he cast himself on Yurand's hard bed in the hope that even a short slumber would visit him. But before he fell asleep Sanderus knocked at the door and entered.

" Lord, you saved me from death," said he, bowing down; " with you I have lived more pleasantly than I have lived for a long time. God has given you a great estate; you are richer than ever, and the treasury of Spyhov is not empty. Give me a purse of some sort; I will go from castle to castle in Prussia, and though it is not very safe for me there, perhaps I may serve you."

Zbyshko, who at the first moment wished to push him out of the room, stopped at these words, and after a while drew

from a traveling-bag at the bedside a large purse, threw it to him, and said, —

" Take this; go! If thou art a rogue thou wilt deceive, if honest thou wilt serve me."

" I will deceive cunningly," said Sanderus, " but not you; you I will serve truthfully."

CHAPTER XXXV.

SIEGFRIED DE LOWE was just ready to start for Malborg when the post-boy brought him unexpectedly a letter from Rotgier with news from the court of Mazovia. This news moved the old Knight of the Cross to the quick. First of all it was evident from the letter that Rotgier had presented and managed the case against Yurand with excellent skill before Prince Yanush. Siegfried smiled while reading how Rotgier had made a further demand that the prince should give Spyhov in feudal tenure as satisfaction for wrongs done the Order. But the second part of the letter contained unexpected and less desirable tidings. Rotgier wrote in addition that, to show more convincingly that the Order was innocent of seizing Yuraud's daughter, he had thrown down his gauntlet before the knights of Mazovia, challenging every doubter to the judgment of God; that is to a combat before the whole court. " No one took up the gauntlet," continued Rotgier, " for all knew that Yuraud's own letter testified in our favor, hence they feared the justice of God, but just then appeared a young man whom we saw at the hunting-lodge; he took up the gauntlet. Therefore be not astonished, wise and pious brother, that I delay in returning, for, since I gave the challenge myself, I must accept combat. And, since I did this for the glory of the Order, I hope that the Grand Master will not take the act ill of me, and that you will not, — you whom I honor and love as with the heart of a son. My opponent is a mere stripling, and combat to me, as you know, is no novelty, hence I shall shed this blood easily to the glory of the Order, and especially with the aid of Christ the Lord, who is surely more concerned for those who bear his cross than for some Yuraud, or for the wrongs of one paltry wench from Mazovia."

The news that Yurand's daughter was married astonished old Siegfried most of all. At the thought that a new enemy, terrible and vengeful, might settle in Spyhov, a certain alarm seized even that aged comtur. "It is clear," said the old man to himself, " that he will not forego revenge; all the

more will he not if he finds bis wife and she tells him that we took her away from the hunting-lodge. It would appear at once that we invited Yurand just to destroy him, and that no one had a thought of restoring the daughter to her father." Here it occurred to Siegfried that in answer to the prince's letters the Grand Master would probably order a search in Schytno, even to clear himself before that same prince of Mazovia. It was important to him and the Chapter, in case of war with the powerful King of Poland, that the princes should be neutral. Omitting those princes' troops, which were not among the fewest, it was proper, in view of the number of Mazovian nobles and their valor, not to despise Prince Yanush and his brother; peace with them secured the boundary along great spaces, and permitted the Order to concentrate its forces better. They had mentioned this frequently in Malborg before Siegfried, and comforted themselves with the hope that after conquering the King they would find later on some pretext against Mazovia, and then no power could snatch that land from the grasp of the Order. That was a great and certain reckoning, hence it was positive in that juncture that the Grand Master would do everything to avoid irritating Prince Yanush, who, married to Keistut's daughter, was more difficult to please than Ziemowit of Plotsk, whose wife, for undiscovered reasons, was thoroughly devoted to the Order.

In view of these thoughts old Siegfried, with all his readi-iness for every treachery, crime, and cruelty, and though he loved the Order, and its glory began to reckon with his conscience. " Would it not be better to liberate Yurand and his dauo-hter? Treason and foulness weighed down the name of Danveld, but he was not living. And even," thought he, "if the Grand Master should punish me and Rotgier severely, since we were in every case participants, will not that be better for the Order ? " But here his vengeful, cruel heart be^an to storm within him at the thought of l urand. Liberate him, that oppressor and executioner of people of the Order, a victor in so many conflicts, the author of so many defeats and so much shame, the conqueror, and later the murderer, of Danveld, the captor of De Bergov, the slaver of Meinegger, Gottfried, and Hugo, of him, who in Schvtno itself shed more German blood than is shed in a good engagement in time of warfare. " I cannot, I cannot;! repeated Siegfried in spirit. And at the very thought the grasping fingers of the old man contracted in a cramp, and

hia dried-up breast caught its breath with effort. " And still, if that were for the greater profit and glory of the Order ? If the punishment, which in that case would fall on those authors of the crime who are still living, should win Prince Yanush, hostile thus far, and facilitate a treaty, or even a truce, with him? They are passionate," continued the old comtur with himself, " but if one shows them a little kindness they forget their wrongs easily. The prince, for instance, was seized on his own territory, and still he takes no active vengeance."

Here the old man began to walk through the hall in great internal conflict, and finally he stopped before the crucifix, which opposite the entrance door occupied almost the height of the wall between both windows, and kneeling at the foot of it he began: "Enlighten me, O Lord, teach me, for I know not what to do ! If I liberate Yurand and his daughter our deeds will be discovered in all their nakedness. People will not say: ' Danveld did this,' or ' Siegfried did this;' they will say, ' the Knights of the Cross did this,' and infamy may fall on the whole Order, and hatred in that prince's heart will become still greater. If I do not liberate them, but hide or kill them, suspicion will remain on the Order, and I must defile my lips with lying in the presence of the Grand Master. What shall I do, O Lord ? Teach me and enlighten! If vengeance is urging me on, then judge me according to Thy justice; but teach me now, enlighten me, for it is a question of Thy Order, and whatever Thou commandest I will do, even though I were to wait for death and liberation in a dungeon and manacled."

And. resting his forehead on the wood of the Cross, he prayed a long time, for it did not flash through his head for an instant that that prayer of his was blasphemous and crooked. Then he rose more at peace, believing that favor from the tree of the Cross had sent him a simpler and a clearer thought, and that something from above said: " Rise and await the return of Rotgier." " Yes! it was necessary to wait. Rotgier would slay that youth without fail, and then he would have either to secrete or liberate Yurand and his daughter. In the first case the prince would not forget them, it is true, but having no proof as to who seized the girl, he would search for her, he would send letters to the Grand Master, not with a complaint, but inquiring — and the case would go on in unending deferment. In the second case, delight at the return of Yurand's daughter would be

greater than desire of vengeance for having carried her away. And besides, we can always say that we found her after Yurand inflicted the slaughter." This last thought pacified Siegfried thoroughly. As to Yurand, Siegfried had long since, in company with Rotgier, invented a method through which, if they should liberate him, he would have no power for complaint or vengeance. Siegfried rejoiced now in his savage soul as he remembered that method. He rejoiced also at thought of the judgment of God which was to take place at the castle of Tsehanov. As to the outcome of that mortal struggle no alarm troubled him. He called to mind a certain tournament in Krolevets where Rotgier had finished two knights of renown, who in their native Anjou were held to be invincible. He remembered also a battle at Vilno with a certain Polish knight, a follower of Spytko of Melstyn; this knight was slain by Rotgier. His face brightened and his heart swelled with pride, for though Rotgier was a renowned knight already, he, Siegfried, was the first to lead him in expeditions to reduce Lithuania and to teach him the best methods of warfare against the people of that country; hence he loved him as a son, with that deep love of which only those men are capable who have been forced to confine in the heart for a long time the desire of love and the power of it. And now this dear son will shed once again that hated Polish blood and will return clothed in glory. That is the judgment of God, and the Order will be cleansed of suspicion at the same time. " The judgment of God ! " For one twinkle of an eye the old man's heart was straitened with a feeling like fear. Rotgier had to stand up in mortal struggle to defend the innocence of the Knights of the Order — but they were guilty; he will fight for a lie then. But if a misfortune should happen ? After a moment, however, that seemed to Siegfried impossible. " Yes! Rotgier writes truly. Surely Christ will care more for the men who bear his cross than for Yurand and the wrongs of one paltry wench from Mazovia. Yes, in three days Rotgier will return — and return a victor."

When he had pacified himself in this way the old knight meditated longer: " Would it not be better meanwhile to send away Danusia to a more remote castle, which in no case would yield to an attack by Mazovians?" But after meditating a moment he dropped even this thought: Only the husband of Yurand's daughter could plan an attack and stand at the head of it; but he was about to perish at the hand of VOL. i. — 26

Rotgier. After that there would be on the part of the prince and the princess merely correspondence, questions, efforts, complaints, but just through these the affair would be blurred and effaced, not to mention delays well-nigh endless. " Before they reach a result," added Siegfried, "I shall be dead, and perhaps Yurand's daughter herself will grow old in the prisons of the Order."

But he gave command to have everything ready for defence in the castle and also for the road, since he knew not precisely what might result from his conference with Rotgier; and he waited.

Two days, then three and four, passed beyond the date at which Rotgier had promised at first to return; still no retinue appeared before the gate of Schytno. Only on the fifth day, just before dark, was heard the sound of a horn before the bastion of the gatekeeper. Siegfried, who had just finished his evening prayers, sent a boy at once to learn who had come.

The boy returned after a while with confused face, but Siegfried could not note the change, since the fire in the room burned in a deep chimney and lighted the gloom only a little.

" Have they come? " asked the old knight.

" Yes," answered the boy. But in his voice there was something which alarmed Siegfried immediately, so he said, —

" But Brother Rotgier?"

" They have brought Brother Rotgier."

At this Siegfried rose from his armchair. For a long time he held the arm with his hand as if fearing to fall, then he said in a suppressed voice, —

" Give me my mantle."

The boy placed the mantle on his shoulders. He had regained his strength evidently, for he drew the cowl over his head and walked out of the chamber.

He soon found himself in the courtyard of the castle, where it had grown dark completely. He walked over the squeaking snow with slow step toward the retinue, which had halted near the gate after passing it. A dense crowd of people had gathered already, and a number of torches held by soldiers of the garrison were gleaming there. At sight of the old brother of the Order the soldiers stood apart from one another. By the light of the torches alarmed faces were visible, and in the darkness low voices were whispering, —

" Brother Rotgier — "

" Brother Rotgier is slain."

Siegfried pushed up to the sleigh in which on straw lay a body covered with a mantle, and raised the mantle.

" Bring a light," said he, pushing his cowl aside.

One of the soldiers brought forward a torch, by the light of which Siegfried saw Rotgier's face pale as snow, frozen, surrounded by a dark kerchief with which they had bound his chin, so that his mouth might not open. The whole face was contracted, and thereby so changed that one might think him some other person. The eyes were covered with their lids, blue spots were around the eyes and on the temples. The cheeks were glazed with frost.

Siegfried gazed for a long time amid unbroken silence. Others looked at him, for they knew that he was as a father to the dead man, and that he loved him. But no tear flowed from his eyes; on his face there was merely a sterner expression than usual, and a certain icy calm.

" They sent him hither in that form!" said he at last.

But the next moment he turned to the castle steward and said, —

" Have a coffin made before midnight, and place the body in the chapel."

" There is one coffin left of those made for the men slain by Yurand; I will have it covered with cloth."

"And have a mantle placed over it," said Siegfried, covering Rotgier's face; " not one like this, but a mantle of the Order."

After a moment he added, —

" Do not close the lid."

The people approached the sleigh, Siegfried pulled the cowl over his head again, but called to mind something before going, for he asked, —

" Where is Van Krist ? "

" Slain also," answered one of the men, " but they buried him in Tsehanov, for he had begun to decay."

"That is well."

Then he walked away slowly, and returning to the chamber sat down in the same armchair in which the news had found him ; and he sat motionless, with a stony face, and sat so long that the boy grew alarmed and pushed his head in through the door more and more frequently. Hour followed hour; the usual noise ceased in the castle; only from the direction of the chapel came the dull, undefined blows of the hammer, and then nothing disturbed the silence save the calling of sentries. It was near midnight when the old knight woke as if from sleep and called the boy, —

" Where is Brother Rotgier? " asked he.

The boy, startled by the silence, the events, and sleeplessness, did not understand evidently, for he looked at him with alarm, and answered with a quivering voice, —

" I do not know, lord."

The old man smiled as if heart-broken and said mildly, —

" I asked, child, if he is in the chapel."

"He is, lord."

"That is well. Tell Diedrich to be here with a lantern and wait till I come. Let him have also a kettle with coals. Is there a light now in the chapel? "

" There are candles burning at the side of the coffin."

When Siegfried entered he surveyed the chapel from the door to see if any one was present, then he closed the door carefully, approached the bier, put aside two candles from the six which were burning in great brass candlesticks, and knelt at the coffin. His lips made no movement whatever, hence he was not praying. For some time he looked only at the stiffened but still comely face of Rotgier, as if wishing to find traces of life in it. Then amid the quiet of the chapel he called in low tones, —

"O son! O son!"

He was silent again. It seemed that he was waiting for an answer.

Then he stretched forth his hands, thrust his dried talon-like fingers under the mantle which covered Rotgier's bosom, and began to feel beneath it. He sought everywhere, at the middle, at the sides, below the ribs and along the shoulder-blades ; at last he felt through the cloth the cleft which extended from the top of the right shoulder to a point below the armpit; he pressed in his fingers, pushed them along the whole length of the wound, and again he spoke with a voice in which complaint seemed to tremble, —

" Oo — what a merciless blow! But thou didst say that he was just a stripling! The entire shoulder! The whole arm ! How often thou didst raise that arm against Pagans in defending the Order! And now a Polish axe has hewn it from thee, — and this is thy end ! This is the close of thy career! Christ did not bless thee, for it is evident that He cares more for one wrong done to man than for our

whole Order. In the name of the Father, and the Son, and the Spirit: thou hast defended the wrong, thou hast died for injustice, without absolution — and maybe thy soul "

The words broke in his mouth, his lips began to quiver, and in the chapel deep silence set in a second time.

"O son! O son!"

In Siegfried's words there was entreaty now, and at the same time he called in a still lower voice, as do people who are making inquiry touching some awful and terrible secret, —

" O merciful Christ! If thou art not damned, my son, give a sign, move thy hand, or open thy eyes for one instant, the heart is whining within my old bosom. Give a sign; I loved thee — speak! "

And resting his hands on the edge of the coffin he fixed his vulture-like eyes on Rotgier's closed lids.

" Oh, how couldst thou speak ! " said he finally; " cold and the odor of death issues forth from thee. But since thou art silent I will tell thee something, and let thy soul fly hither between the burning candles and listen."

Then he bent to the face of the corpse.

"Thou rememberest how the chaplain would not let us kill Yurand, and how we gave an oath to him. That is well; I will keep the oath, but I will comfort thee wherever thou art, though I be damned myself for it."

Then he withdrew from the coffin, put back the candlesticks which he had set aside, covered the body and the face with the mantle, and went forth from the chapel.

At the door of his chamber the wearied boy slept a deep sleep. Diedrich was waiting according to Siegfried's command. He was a short, strong man with bow-legs, and a square face which was partly concealed by a dark, jagged cowl which dropped to his shoulders. He wore a kaftan made from untanned hide of buffalo; above his hips was a belt of the same hide; behind this a bunch of keys and a short knife were thrust. In his right hand he held an iron lantern with membrane; in his left hand was a small brass kettle and a taper.

" Art ready? " inquired Siegfried.

Diedrich inclined in silence.

" I commanded thee to have coals in the kettle."

A second time the strong man made no answer; he merely pointed to sticks blazing in the chimney, took an iron shovel which was standing at the side of the chimney, and

began to take from under the sticks coals for the kettle, then he lighted the lantern and waited.

il Listen to me now, thon dog," said Siegfried. " Once thou didst babble out what Corntur Danveld commanded thee to do, and the comtur had thy tongue cut out. But since thou art able to show the chaplain on thy fingers whatever pleasest thee, I declare that if thou show with a single movement what thou doest at my order I will command to hang thee."

Diedrich bowed again in silence, but his face was distorted ominously by a terrible recollection, because the tongue had been torn from him for a reason entirely different from that given by Siegfried.

" Move ahead now, and lead to Yurand's dungeon."

The executioner seized the bale of the kettle with his gigantic hand ; he raised the lantern, and they left the room. Outside the door they passed the sleeping boy, and descending the steps went, not to the main door, but to the rear of the steps, behind which was a narrow corridor which extended along the whole width of the building, and ended at a heavy gate hidden in a niche of the wall. Diedrich pushed in the gate, and they found themselves beneath the open sky in a small courtyard, which was surrounded on four sides by stone storehouses, in which grain was kept for use in the castle during sieges. Under one of these storehouses on the right were subterranean dungeons for prisoners. There was no guard there, for should a prisoner be even able to break out of the dungeon he would find himself in the court out of which the only issue was through that gate.

"Wait," said Siegfried.

And resting his hand against the wall he halted, for he felt that something of no good import was happening to him, and that breath was failing him, as if his breast had been confined in armor that was too narrow. In simple fact, that through which he had passed was beyond his failing strength. He felt also that his forehead under the cowl was covered with sweat-drops, and he halted to regain the breath that was failing him.

After a gloomy day the night had grown unusually bright. The moon was shining in the sky, and the whole yard was filled with clear light, in which the snow appeared green. Siegfried drew the fresh and somewhat frosty air into Lis lungs greedily. But he recalled at the same time that on such a clear night precisely Rotgier went to Tsehanov, whence he was now brought back a corpse.

" But now thou art lying in the chapel," muttered he in a whisper.

Diedrich, thinking that the comtur was speaking to him, raised the lantern and lighted his face, which was terribly pale, almost corpse-like, and also resembling the head of an aged vulture.

" Lead on! " said Siegfried.

The yellow circle of light from the lantern trembled again on the snow, and they went farther. In the thick wall of the storehouse was a recess where a few steps led to a great iron door. Diedrich opened the door and began to descend along steps into the depth of a black passage, raising the lantern with effort to light the way for the comtur. At the foot of the steps was a passage; on the right and left sides of it were the exceedingly low doors of cells for prisoners.

"To Yurand," said Siegfried.

After a while the bolts squeaked and they entered. It was perfectly dark in that hole, therefore Siegfried, not seeing clearly by the dim light of the lantern, commanded to light the torch, and soon in the strong gleam of its flame he saw Yurand lying on straw. The prisoner had fetters on his feet, and on his arms a chain, which was long enough to let him reach food to his mouth. He was dressed in the same penitential bag in which he had stood before the comturs, but it was covered now with dark traces of blood; for on that day in which an end had been put to his fight, when mad from rage and pain they had entangled the knight in a net, the soldiers, wishing to kill the man, had stabbed him a number of times with their halberds. The local chaplain of Schytno had prevented the killing; the halberd thrusts had not proved mortal, but so much blood had left Yurand that he was taken half-dead to the prison. It was thought by all at the castle that he might die any hour, but his great strength had conquered death, and he lived though his wounds were not dressed, and he was thrust into that dreadful dungeon, where moisture dropped for whole days from the ceiling, and where in time of frost the walls were covered with a thick, snow-like coating and with ice-crystals.

He lay enchained on the straw, powerless, but so immense that, especially when prostrate, he produced the impression of a piece of a cliff cut into human form. Siegfried gave command to turn the light straight to his face, and for some time the old man gazed on it in silence, then, turning to Diedrich, he said, —

Thou seest that he has sight in one eye only; burn that one out of him."

There was in the old comtur's voice a certain weakness and decrepitude, but precisely because of that the dreadful order seemed still more dreadful. The torch trembled somewhat in the hand of the executioner, but he inclined it, and soou great flaming drops of pitch began to fall on the eye of the captive, and finally they covered it completely from his brow to his prominent cheek-bone.

Yurand's face writhed, his yellow mustaches turned upward and disclosed his set teeth, but he uttered no word, and whether it was through exhaustion, or the innate force of will in his tremendous nature, he groaned not.

"They promised to let thee go forth free," said Siegfried, " and thou wilt go, but thou wilt not be able to blame the Order, for the tongue with which thou hast blasphemed against it will be taken from thee."

Again he made a sign to Diedrich, who gave forth a strange guttural sound and indicated by winks that he needed both hands and wished the comtur to hold the light for him.

The old man took the torch and held it with outstretched, trembling hand, but when Diedrich pressed Yurand's bosom with his knees, Siegfried turned his face away and looked at the wall, which was lined with hoar-frost that night.

For a while the clatter of chains was heard, next the panting breaths of human breasts, after that something like a deep, dull groan, and then silence followed.

At last the voice of Siegfried was heard again, —

" Yurand, thy punishment had to meet thee in this way, but besides the punishment already suffered, I have promised Brother Rotgier, now slain by thy daughter's husband, to lay thy right hand in his coffin."

Diedrich, who had raised himself, when he heard these words bent anew over Yurand.

After a certain time the old comtur and Diedrich found themselves again in that yard which was filled with moonlight. While advancing through the corridor Siegfried took the lantern from the executioner, and also a dark object with a rag round it.

" Now back to the chapel," said he to himself aloud, " and then to the watch-tower."

Diedrich looked at him quickly, but the comtur commanded him to sleep, and, swinging the lantern, dragged on himself

toward the space lighted by the chapel windows. Along the road he pondered over what had happened. He felt a certain conviction that his end was now approaching, that these were his last deeds on earth, that for them he would have to answer before God alone; still his soul of a Knight of the Cross, though less false by nature than cruel, had, under the influence of implacable necessity, become so accustomed to the evasions of cheating, and to shielding the bloody deeds of the Order, that even now he thought involuntarily of casting the infamy of the torture and the responsibility for it both from himself and from the Order. Diedrich was dumb, he could make no confession, and though he could explain to the chaplain he would not do so from very terror. Then what? Then who could learn that Yurand had not received all those wounds in battle? He might easily have lost his tongue from a spear thrust between the teeth; a sword or an axe might have cut his right hand off; and he had only one eye, hence what wonder that that eye was knocked out when he hurled himself in madness on the whole garrison of Schytno? Ah, Yurand! The last delight of his life shook up for a moment the heart of old Siegfried. " Yes, Yurand, should he recover, must be freed! " Here Siegfried recalled how he had counselled with Rotgier touching this, and how the young brother said, with a smile, " Let him go then whithersover his eyes lead, and if he cannot find Spyhov let him inquire the way to it." For what had happened had been partly determined between him and Rotgier. But now, when Siegfried entered the chapel a second time, and, kneeling down at the coffin, laid Yurand's bloody hand at the feet of Rotgier, the joy which had quivered in him a moment earlier was reflected on his face for the last time.

" Seest thou," said he, " I have done more than we decided, for King Yan of Luxemburg, though blind, appeared in battle, and died with glory, but Yurand will not rise again; he will perish like a dog near some fence."

Here again he felt the lack of breath, just as before, when he was going to Yurand's prison, and on his head the weight as it were of an iron helmet; this lasted, however, but one twinkle of an eye. He breathed deeply, and continued, —

" Ei, and now comes my time. I had only thee, now I have no one. But if it is destined me to live longer, I vow to thee, my son, that on thy grave I will place the hand which Blew thee, or die myself. Thy slayer is living yet — "

Here his teeth gritted; such a mighty spasm seized him that the words stopped in his mouth, and only after some time did he begin anew to speak, with broken voice, —

" Yes, thy slayer is living yet, but I will reach him — and before I reach him I will inflict on him another torture worse than death itself."

And he was silent.

After a moment he rose, and approaching the coffin said in a calm voice, —

" Now I will bid thee farewell; I will look on thy face for the last time; I shall know, perhaps, if thou rejoice at my vow. This is the last time! "

And he uncovered Rotgier's face, but drew back on a sudden.

" Thou art smiling," said he, "but thy smile is terrible."

The body had thawed in fact under the cloak, and perhaps from the warmth of the candles ; as a result of this it had begun to decay with uncommon rapidity, and the face of the young comtur had become indeed terrible. His swollen, immense, blackened ears had in them something monstrous, and his blue puffed-out lips were twisted as if smiling.

Siegfried covered that ghastly human mask in all haste. Then taking the lantern he went out. On the road breath failed him a third time, so returning to his chamber he threw himself on his hard couch and lay for a while motionless. He had thought to fall asleep, but suddenly a strange feeling seized him. It seemed to the aged knight that sleep would never come again to him, but that if he remained in that chamber death would come directly.

Siegfried had no fear of death. In his measureless torture and without hope of sleep he saw in it a kind of boundless rest, but he had no wish to yield to death on that night.

" Give me time till morning," said he, rising on the couch.

With that he heard clearly a certain voice whispering in his ear, —

" Go forth from this chamber. To-morrow will be too late, and thou wilt not accomplish that which thou hast promised. Go forth from this chamber! "

The comtur, raising himself with effort, went forth. The sentries were calling on the battlements at the corners. Near the chapel a yellow gleam fell on the snow through the windows. In the middle of the square, near the stone well.

two black dogs were playing, pulling some cloth from each other; except them the court was empty and silent.

" Then to-night absolutely," said Siegfried. " I am wearied beyond measure, but I will go — all are sleeping. Yurand conquered by torture sleeps also, perhaps, but I shall not sleep. I will go, I will go, for death is in my chamber, and I have promised thee — let death come after that, since sleep is not to come. Thou art smiling there ; but strength fails me. Thou art smiling; it is evident then that thou art pleased. But thou seest my fingers have grown numb, strength has left my hand, I cannot finish that alone — the servant woman who sleeps with her will finish it — "

While speaking thus he went on with heavy step toward the tower which stood at the gate. Meanwhile the dogs which were playing at the stone well ran up and began to fawn around him. In one of them Siegfried recognized the mastiff which was an inseparable comrade of Diedrich; people said in the castle that the dog served the man at night for a pillow.

After greeting the comtur, the mastiff gave a low bark once or twice, then bounded toward the gate as if divining Siegfried's thought.

Soon the comtur found himself before the narrow door of the tower, which at night was bolted from the outside. Pushing back the bolt he felt for the stairway railing, which began right there inside the door, and ascended. He had forgotten his lantern through mental distraction ; he felt his way, stepping carefully, and searched for the steps with his feet.

On a sudden, after some advance, he halted, for higher up, but straight above, he heard something like the panting of a man, or a beast.

" Who is there?"

No answer was given, but the panting grew more rapid.

Siegfried was fearless; he had no dread of death, but his courage and self-command were exhausted to the last on that night of terror. Through his brain flashed the thought that Rotgier, or perhaps the evil spirit, was barring the way to him. The hair rose on his head, and his forehead was covered with cold perspiration. He withdrew almost to the very entrance.

" Who is there? " inquired he, with a choked voice.

But that moment something struck hini in the breast with such terrible force that he fell backward through the open door without uttering a syllable.

Silence followed. Then a dark figure pushed from out the tower and moved stealthily toward the stable which stood next to the arsenal on the left side of the courtyard. Diedrich's mastiff rushed after it in silence. The second dog sprang after that one and vanished in the shadow of the wall, but soon appeared with head toward the earth, coming back slowly and as it were sniffing the tracks of the man. In this manner it approached Siegfried, who was lying motionless; sniffed him carefully, then sat near his head, raised its jaws, and began to howl.

The howling was heard for a long time, filling that doleful night as it were with new sadness and terror. At last a door hidden in the niche of the great gate squeaked and the gatekeeper stood in the court with a halberd.

"A plague on the dog! I will teach thee to howl at night," said he.

And thrusting out the halberd point he wished to pierce the beast with it, but that moment he saw some one lying near the open door of the tower.

" Herr Jesus! what is this? "

Bending forward he looked into the face of the prostrate person and cried, —
Hither! Hither! Rescue! "
Then he sprang to the gate and pulled the bell-rope with all his might.


THE END VOL.I

THE

# KNIGHTS OF THE CROSS.

BY

HENRYK SIENKIEWICZ,

AUTHOR OF "QUO VADIS," "WITH FIRE AND SWORD,"
"CHILDREN OF THE SOIL," ETC.

*AUTHORIZED AND UNABRIDGED TRANSLATION FROM
THE POLISH BY*

JEREMIAH CURTIN.

SECOND HALF.

BOSTON:
LITTLE, BROWN, AND COMPANY.
1901.

MAP OF POLAND
AND THE
TERRITORY OF THE ORDER
BEFORE THE BATTLE OF
GRUNWALO

MAP SHOWING
CHANGES RESULTING FROM THE BATTLE OF

# KNIGHTS OF THE CROSS.

CHAPTER XXXVI.

THOUGH Hlava was hastening to Zgorzelitse he could not move so quickly as he wanted, for the road had grown immensely difficult. After a sharp winter and hard frosts, after snows so abundant that whole villages were hidden beneath them, great thaws came. February, in spite of its name Luty (Savage), did not turn out in the least degree savage. First rose dense and impenetrable fogs, then rains came which were almost downpours, rains from which the white drifts thawed before the eye. During intervals between downpours winds blew such as were usual in March, hence fitful and sudden, — winds which broke up and blew away swollen clouds in the sky ; on the earth they whined through thickets, roared through forests, and devoured that snow under which just before limbs and branches were dreaming in the calm sleep of winter. On the fields the widely spread water wrinkled its surface, rivers and streams rose. Fish alone were delighted with such abundance of the fluid element ; all other creatures, held as it were on a halter, hid iu huts and houses. In many places the passage from village to village was possible in boats only. There was no lack, it is true, in swamps and forests of roads or dams made of beams and round logs, but the dams had grown soft, and the logs in low places had sunk in quagmires, so that passage, over them was dangerous or quite impossible. Especially difficult for Hlava was the advance through Great Poland, which was full of lakes where the overflows were greater than in other parts, and travelling, particularly for horses, more difficult. He had to halt often, and wait entire weeks, either in small towns, or in villages with nobles who received him and his people hospitably, according to custom, glad to hear him tell of the Knights of the Cross, and to pay with bread and salt for the news which he gave them. Therefore spring had announced itself in the world

VOL. II. — 1

distinctly and March had passed in greater part before he found himself near Zgorzelitse and Bogdanets.

Hlava's heart throbbed when he thought that he would soon see his lady, for though he knew that he would never win her, just as he would never win stars from the sky, he extolled and loved her with all the soul that was in him.

But he determined to go directly to Matsko, first because he was sent to him, and second because he was taking men who were to remain at Bogdanets. After Zbyshko had slain Rotgier he took his retinue, composed, according to the regulations of the Order, of ten horses and as many men. Two had gone to Schytno with the fallen knight's body, but Zbyshko, knowing the eagerness of old Matsko in seeking for settlers, sent the rest with Hlava as a gift to his uncle.

The Cheh, on reaching Bogdauets, did not find Matsko. The old man had gone, as the servants informed him, with crossbow and dogs to the forest, but he returned during daylight, and, on learning that a considerable retinue had halted at his mansion, he hurried his steps so as to meet the newcomers, and offer entertainment; he was tremendously astonished at first, and, throwing his crossbow and cap on the ground, cried out, —

"As God lives! they have killed him! Tell what thou knoweat! "

He is not killed," answered Hlava; " he is well."

When Matsko heard this he was confused somewhat and fell to panting; at last he drew a deep breath.

" Praise to Christ the Lord ! " said he. "Where is the man ?" ' He went to Malborg and sent me hither with tidings." ' But why did he go to Malborg? " ' For his wife."

Ah ! fear the wounds of Christ, boy. What wife? "  The daughter of Yurand. There will be something to talk about, even the whole night through, but permit me, respected lord, to draw breath, for I am dreadfully road-weary, and since midnight I have lashed my beast forward."

Matsko stopped inquiries for a while, though mainly because astonishment had taken speech from him. When he had recovered somewhat he shouted to the boy to throw wood on the fire and bring food, then he walked through the room, waved his hands, and talked in soliloquy,  cannot believe my own ears — Yurand's daughter — Zbyshko married — "

"He is married and not married," said Hlava, who now

told slowly what had happened, and how it had happened. The old man listened eagerly, interrupting with questions at times, for not everything was clear in the narrative. Hlava did not know, for example, exactly when Zbyshko had married, for there had been no wedding, but he declared positively that there had been a ceremony performed at the instance of Anna Danuta, the princess, though it was announced publicly only after the arrival of Rotgier, with whom Zbyshko, after challenging him to the judgment of God, had fought in presence of the court of Mazovia.

" Ah! Has he fought? " cried Matsko, with flashing eyes, and immense curiosity. " Well, and what? "

" He cut the German in two; and God gave me luck also in fighting with Rotgier's attendant."

Matsko panted again, this time with satisfaction.

"Well, he is not to be laughed at. The last of the Grady, but, as God be my aid, not the least of them. Yes! and that time against the Frisians — a mere stripling in those days."

Then he looked once and a second time at the Cheh more attentively.

" But thou also dost please me. It is clear that thou art not lying. I know a liar even through a plank. That attendant I do not esteem overmuch; thou hadst no great work with him, as thou sayst, but thou didst wrench the arm of that dog-brother, Danveld, and earlier thou didst kill the wild bull, — those are praiseworthy deeds. But the plunder," asked Matsko on a sudden, — "was it considerable?"

"We took arms, horses, ten men, eight of whom the young lord has sent to you — "

" What did he do with the otjjer two? "

" He sent them away with the body."

" Could not the prince send his own men ? Those two will never come back to us."

Hlava smiled at such greed, which for that matter Matsko showed frequently, and he answered, —

" Spyhov is a great property."

" Great! But what of that? It is not his yet."

"Whose is it?"

Matsko rose up.

" Tell me! But Yurand ? "

" Yurand is in a dungeon with the Knights of the Cross, and death is hanging over him. God knows whether he will

recover; if he does, whether he will return. Even should he recover and return, Father Kaleb has read his will, and he has declared to all that the young lord is his heir."

This news produced, it was clear, an immense impression on Matsko, for it was so favorable and unfavorable that he could not grasp it, nor bring into order the feelings which shook him one after another. The news that Zbyshko had married pricked him painfully at the first moment, for he loved Yageuka as if he had been her father, and wished with all his soul to unite her and Zbyshko. But on the other hand he had grown accustomed to look on the matter as lost, and again Yurand's daughter brought that which Yagenka could not bring, the favor of Prince Yanush, and a dowry which, she being an only child, was much greater. Matsko saw Zbyshko in his mind as the prince's comes, lord in Bogdauets and Spyhov; nay more, a castellan in the future. The thing was not improbable, for people said also in those days of a poor noble: "He had twelve sons; six fell in battle, and six became castellans." Both nation and family were on the highroad to greatness. Considerable property could only help Zbyshko on that road; hence Matsko's greed and his family pride had something in which to find comfort. Still the old man had no lack of reasons for fear. He had gone once himself to the Knights of the Cross to save Zbyshko, and had brought back iron between his ribs from that journey, and now Zbyshko had gone to Malborg, as if into the throat of the wolf. " Will he wait for his wife, or for death there? They will not look on him kindly," thought Matsko, — "he who has just killed a famed knight, and before that rushed against Lichtenstein. They, the dog bloods, love vengeance." At this thought the old knight was concerned greatly. It occurred to him also that as Zbyshko was choleric he would not escape without a battle against some German. But touching this he felt less fear. Matsko's greatest dread was that they might seize him. "They had seized Yurand and his daughter, they had not hesitated on a time to seize the prince himself in Zlotorya; why should they spare Zbyshko ? "

Here this question occurred to him, " What would happen if the young fellow, though he should escape from the hands of the knights, were not to find his wife anywhere?" For an instant Matsko comforted himself with the thought that Zbyshko would inherit Spyhov after her, but that was brief comfort. The old man was concerned greatly

about property, but he was concerned no less about hi8 race, about Zbyshko's children. " If Danusia should disappear like a stone under water, and no one know whether she were dead or living, Zbyshko would not be able to marry another — and then there would be no Grady of Bogdanets in existence. Hei! with Yagenka it would be otherwise! A hen could not cover Mochycloly with her wings, nor a dog with his tail, and she would give a birth -every year without missing, just like that apple-tree out in the orchard." So Matsko's sorrow surpassed his delight at the new inheritance, and from this sorrow and alarm he fell again to inquiring of Hlava how and when the marriage had been solemnized.

"I have said, respected lord," answered Hlava, "that I know not; and I will not swear to my own guesswork."

" What is thy guesswork? "

"I did not leave the young lord during his sickness, I slept in the same room with him; but one evening he commanded me to go away, and later I saw how the Gracious Lady went to him, and with her the young lady, Pan de Lorche, and Father Vyshonek. I even wondered, for the young lady had a garland on her head, but I thought that they were to give my young lord the sacrament. Maybe it was at that time. I remember that he commanded me to array him beautifully, as for a wedding, but I thought then that it was to receive the Lord's body."

" And how was it afterwards? Were they alone?"

" Ei, they were not, and even if they had been he had not strength at that time to give himself food. And people had come who announced themselves as sent by Yurand, and she went away with those people in the morning."

"Has Zbyshko seen her since then?"

" Human eye has not seen her since that day."

Silence followed.

" What dost thou think ? " inquired Matsko after a while ; " will the Knights of the Cross give her up?"

Hlava shook his head and waved his hand. " To my thinking she is lost forever," said he, slowly.

"• Why so? " inquired Matsko, almost with fear.

" For this reason : If they were to say that they have her there would be hope; it would be possible to make a complaint, or pay a ransom, or take her by force. But they say: ' We intercepted a girl and informed Yurand. He would not own her as his daughter, and in return for our

kindness he slew so many of our men that a good battle would not have slain more of them.'"

" Then they did show Yurand some girl ? "

" The report is that they did, God alone knows. Perhaps this is not true, and perhaps they showed him another girl. That the master of Spyhov killed people is true, and the Knights are ready to take oath that they never carried off his daughter. Oh, -this is a terribly difficult matter. Even if the Grand Master should give an order they will say that they have never had the girl. Who can convict them ? The case is all the more difficult since the courtiers at Tsehanov speak of a letter from Yurand in which he states that his daughter is not with the Knights of the Cross."

" But maybe she is not."

" I beg your Grace! If bandits carried her away it was only to get a ransom. Besides, bandits could not have written the letter, nor imitated Yurand's seal, nor sent an honest-looking escort."

" True, but what did the Knights of the Cross want of her?"

" Revenge on Yurand. They prefer revenge to mead and wine, and as to cause, they have cause enough. The master of Spyhov was a terror to the Order, and that which he has done just now has enraged them to the utmost. My lord too, as I hear, raised hands on Lichtenstein, and he has killed Rotgier. God aided me in wrenching the arm of that dog brother, Danveld. Ei! just think of it, there were four of them, cursed be their mothers! Now only one is alive, and he is old. Your Grace, we can bite also."

Again came a moment of silence.

" Thou art clever," said Matsko at last. "To thy thinking what will they do with her? "

"Prince Vitold was a mighty prince; they say that the German Caesar bowed as low as his girdle to him, and how did the Knights treat Vitold's children? Are their castles few ? Are their dungeons few ? Are their walls few ? Are their ropes and halters few?"

" By the living God! " exclaimed Matsko.

" God stop them from hiding away my young master, even if he has a letter from Prince Yanush, and goes with Pan de Lorche, who is a powerful person and related to princes. Indeed I had no wish to come hither, for there it would be easier to fight, but he commanded me. I heard him talking once to the old master of Spyhov. 'Art thou cunning?'

asked he, 4 for I lack cunning; but with them cunning is needed. Oi,' said he, ' my uncle Matsko.is the man for this place!' And that is why he sent me to Bogdanets. But even you could not find Yurand's daughter, for she is in the other world perhaps by this time, and against death the greatest cunning is powerless."

Matsko fell into meditation, and only after long silence did he say, —

"Ah, there is no help then; cunning cannot fight against death. But if I should go there and discover even this, that they destroyed the girl, Spyhov would remain even in that case to Zbyshko, and he could come back alone and take another wife."

At this Matsko drew a deep breath, as if he had cast some weight from his heart, and Hlava inquired with a low, timid voice, —

" The young lady of Zgorzelitse ? "

"Yes," answered Matsko, "all the more that she is an orphan, and Stan of Rogov with Vilk of Brozova are attacking her more and more."

Hlava sprang to his feet.

" The young lady an orphan? Where is her father? "

" Then thou knowest nothing? "

"By the dear God, what has happened?"

" Indeed, how couldst thou know? Thou hast come here directly, and we have talked only of Zbyshko. She is an orphan. True Zyh never warmed a place in the house unless he had guests there. When he had no guests it was straightway unpleasant at home for him. The abbot wrote to Zyh some time ago that he was going to visit Prince Premko of Osvetsim and begged the knight to go with him. That was a delight for Zyh, so well was he acquainted with the prince, and more than once they had had gladsome times together. Zyh came to me. ' I am going to Osvetsim,' said he, ' and afterwards to Glevitse, but will you keep an eye on my house? ' Something struck me then, and I said to him, ' Do not go, take care of your land and Yagenka, for I know that Stan and Vilk are thinking up something evil.' And thou shoulclst know that the abbot, out of anger at Zbyshko, wanted Vilk or Stan for the girl; but later on, when he knew the fellows better, he had them beaten and thrown out of Zgorzelitse. This was well, but not very well, for they became desperately angry. There is a little peace just now, for they have had a duel and are in bed, but before that

there was not a moment of security. Everything is on my head, defence with, guardianship. And now Zbyshko wants me to go to him, — how will it be here with Yagenka ? I know not, but I will tell thee of Zyh. He paid no heed to my words; he went. Well, they feasted, they rejoiced. From Glevitse they went to visit old Nosak, Prince Premko's father.

"But Yasko, prince of Ratibor, out of hatred for Prince Premko, sent bandits against them under lead of a Cheh named Hrau. Premko fell, and with him Zyh, struck by an arrow in the windpipe. The abbot they so stunned with an iron flail that his head trembles yet from it; he knows nothing of this world, and has lost speech, perhaps forever. But old Prince Nosak bought Hran from the lord of Zampah and gave him such torture that the oldest men have not heard of like suffering; but mind thee, that torture did not soften Nosak's grief for his son, nor did it resurrect Zyh, nor dry the tears of Yagenka. There is their amusement for them! Six weeks ago Zyh was brought home and buried."

" Such a strong man! " said Hlava, with sorrow. " I was no broken bit of a warrior at Boleslavets, but he did not spend the time of one Our Father in taking me captive. That captivity, however, was such that I would not have changed it for freedom. A good, honest man! God grant him light eternal. Ah, I am sorry, sorry, but most of all for the young lady, the poor thing!"

" Yes, indeed, the poor thing. Many a girl does not love her mother as she did her father. And besides, it is dangerous for her to be in her own house alone. After the funeral the snow had not fallen on Zyh's grave when Stan and Vilk attacked Zgorzelitse. Luckily my people heard of their intention, so I took men and galloped over to help her. God granted us to beat Stan and Vilk grandly. After the battle the girl seized me by the knees. ' I cannot be Zbyshko's,' said she; ' I will not be any one's; only save me from these traitors, for,' said she, ' I would rather have death than either one of them.' I tell thee that thou wouldst not know Zgorzelitse, for it is a real castle. They attacked twice after that, but, believe me, they could do nothing. There is peace, since, as I say, they have cut each other up in such fashion that neither is able to move hand or foot for the moment."

Hlava was silent, but while listening to the tale of Stan and Vilk he gritted his teeth, which sounded as if some one

were opening and closing a squeaky door, and then rubbed his strong hands along his powerful thighs, on which evidently he felt an itching. At last from his mouth came with difficulty the single word, —

"Reprobates!"

At that moment voices were heard in the entrance, the door opened suddenly, and in rushed Yagenka with her elder brother, the fourteen-year-old Yasko, who resembled her as much as if he and she had been twins.

Yagenka, hearing from peasants of Zgorzelitse, who on the road had seen an escort, that certain people led by Hlava were going to Bogdanets, was frightened in just the same way as Matsko, and when she heard still further that they had not seen Zbyshko, she was almost certain that something evil had happened, hence she flew with one breath to Bogdanets to learn the truth of the matter.

".What has happened? By the dear God!" cried she from the threshold.

"What could happen? " answered Matsko. " Zbyshko is alive and well."

Hlava sprang toward his lady, and dropping on one knee, kissed the hem of her garment; she took no note of this whatever, for when she heard the answer of the old knight she turned her head from the fire to the shadow, and only after a while, as if recalling that she ought to give greeting, she said, —

" May Christ Jesus be praised!"

" For the ages of ages," answered Matsko.

But now, noticing Hlava at her knees, she bent toward him, and said, —

"I rejoice from my soul, Hlava, to see thee, but why hast thouleft thy lord?"

" He sent me hither, gracious lady."

" What did he command? "

" He commanded me to come to Bogdanets."

" To Bogdanets, — and what more ? "

" He sent me for help, with a greeting and a bow — "

" To Bogdanets, and nothing more? Then it is well. But where is he himself ? "

" He has gone to Malborg, to the Knights of the Cross."

Alarm was evident on Yagenka's face.

" Is life then not dear to him? Why did he go? "

" To seek, gracious lady, that which he will not find."

"I believe he will not find it! " added Matsko. "As tnou

canst not drive a nail without a hammer, so thou canst not force human will unless God's will be with thee."

" What do you mean? " inquired Yagenka.

Matsko answered her question with the question, —

"Has Zbyshko spoken to thee of Yurand's daughter? — for I have heard that he did speak."

Yageuka did not answer immediately; only after a time did she say, suppressing a sigh,
—

"Oh, he did. And why should he not speak?"

"That is well, for since he spoke it is easier for me to talk," said the old man.

And he told her what he had heard from Hlava, wondering himself that at times the narrative came to him in disorder and with difficulty. But as he was really crafty, and the question with him was in every case not to mislead Yagenka, he insisted greatly on this, and moreover he believed it, that Zbyshko might never be the husband of Danusia,. for Danusia was lost forever. From time to time Hlava supported him, repeating at one moment "As God lives," at another, " That is as true as life!" or, "It is thus, not otherwise."

The girl listened with eyelashes drooping toward her cheeks, making no inquiry, and so silent that the silence troubled Matsko.

"Well, and what dost thou say?" asked he, finishing the narrative.

She made no answer, but two tears glistened under her drooping lashes and rolled down her cheeks. After a while she approached Matsko, and kissing his hand said, —

" May He be praised! "

"For the ages of ages," answered the old man. "Then art thou hastening home? Stay with us."

But she would not stay, explaining that at home she had not given out supper. Matsko, though he knew that the noble woman Setsehova, who was at Zgorzelitse, might take her place, did not urge her overmuch to stay, understanding that sorrow is unwilling to show its tears, and that a man or woman is like a fish, which when it feels the hook within its body hides as deeply as possible under water. So he only stroked the girl's head, and conducted her in company with Hlava to the courtyard. But Hlava led forth his horse from the stable, mounted, and rode away after the lady.

Matsko, when he returned to the house, sighed, shook his head, aud muttered, —

"There is a fool for thee, Zbyshko! That girl leaves her odor in the room! "

And the old man was sorry. He thought that if Zbyshko had taken her after their return home there would have been delight and pleasure there up to that moment. But now what? "Whenever she thinks of him the teardrops from her eye, and the fellow is wandering through the world, and will knock his head somewhere against Malborg fences till he breaks it; and the house here is empty, only weapons staring from the walls. No good from management, industry is profitless, Spyhov and Bogdanets useless, since there will be no one to whom it will be possible to leave them."

Grief began to storm then in Matsko's soul. " Wait, thou vagabond," said he aloud; "I will not go for thee, and do thou do what may please thee! "

But at the same moment a terrible yearning for Zbyshko came on him as if in spite. ik No, I will not go," thought he, " but shall I sit here? This is the punishment of God! That I should not see that rascal even once again in life — this cannot be in any case! Again he has cut up a dog brother — and taken plunder. Another would have grown gray before winning a belt, but him the prince has belted already, and justly, though there are many splendid men among nobles; another like Zbyshko there is not, as I think." And growing altogether tender he examined the armor, the swords, and the axes which were growing dark in the smoke, as if considering which to take with him and which to leave behind. Then he went out of the room, first because he could not stay in it, and second to have the wagons tarred and a double portion of oats given the horses.

In the courtyard, where it was dark now, he remembered Yagenka, who a while before had mounted her horse, and again he grew sad on a sudden.

" If I go, then go," said he to himself, " but who will defend the girl here from Vilk and Stan ? Would to God that a thunderbolt might split them! "

Meanwhile Yagenka was riding with little Yasko along the forest road homeward, and Hlava was dragging on in silence behind them, his heart filled with love and with sorrow. He had seen the girl's tears; now he was looking at her dark form, barely visible in the gloom, and he divined her pain and sorrow. It seemed to him also that at any moment the robber hands of Stan or Vilk might reach out after her from

the forest darkness and density, and at this thought a wild desire for conflict seized him. This desire became at moments so great that the impulse came to grasp his axe or sword and slash even some pine-tree at the roadside. He felt that if he should give a good blow it would relieve him. Finally he would have been glad even to urge his horse into a rush, but they were riding on in front slowly, foot after foot, saying almost nothing; for little Yasko, though talkative usually, seeing after some attempts that his sister had no wish to speak, sank also into silence.

But when he was near Zgorzelitse sorrow rose in Hlava's heart and anger against Stan and Vilk. " I would not spare even blood," said he to himself, " if I could only comfort thee ; but what can I do, I, poor unfortunate, unless to say that Zbyshko gave command to bow down to thee, and God grant that that give thee comfort! "

So after meditation he urged his horse up to Yagenka's.

"Gracious lady."

" Art thou riding with us? " asked the girl, starting up as if from a dream. " But hast thou something to tell me?"

" I have, for I forgot to say that my lord, when we were parting at Spyhov, called me, and said: ' Fall at the feet of the young lady of Zgorzelitse, since in good or evil fortune I shall never see her; for that,' said he, * which she has done for uncle and for me may God reward her and preserve her in health.' "

"God reward him for the kind word," answered Yagenka. Then she added in a certain strange voice, so that Hlava's heart melted completely: "And thee, too, Hlava."

The conversation stopped for a time, but Hlava was pleased with himself, and with what she had answered, for he said in his mind: "At least let her not think that he has paid her with ingratitude." He began at once then to search in his honest head for something more to tell her of like sort, and after a while he began, —

" Young lady." '

"What is it?"

" This — I wish to say — what I said to the old lord in Bogdanets, that that woman is lost for the ages, and he will never find her, even if the Grand Master himself were to help him."

" She is his wife," answered Yagenka.

The Cheh began to torture his head. " She is such a wife as — "

THE KNIGHTS OF THE CROSS. 13

Yagenka did not answer, but at home, after supper, when Yasko and her younger "brother had gone to sleep, she commanded to bring a pitcher of mead, and turning to Hlava inquired, —

" Perhaps you would rather sleep; I hope not, for I should like to talk a little."

Hlava, though road-weary, was ready to talk even till daylight; hence he began to converse, or rather he related again minutely all the adventures of Zbyshko, Yurand, Danusia, and himself.

14 THE KNIGHTS OF THE CROSS.

CHAPTER XXXVII.

MATSKO was preparing for his journey, and Yagenka did not show herself in Bogdanets for two days; this time she spent in counselling with Hlava. The old man met her on the third day while going to church. She was on the way to Kresnia with her brother and a considerable number of armed attendants, for she was not sure that Vilk and Stan kept the bed yet and might not make an attack on her.

"I wanted to call at Bogdanets after mass," said she, greeting Matsko, " for with you I have urgent business, but we can talk of it now."

Then she rode out in front of the retinue, not wishing evidently that the young men should hear their words.

"Then are you going surely?" asked she, when Matsko was near her.

"Yes. To-morrow, with God's help, not later."

"And toMalborg?"

" To Malborg, or no, whithersoever it happens."

"Then listen to me. I have thought long over what I should do, and now I wish to ask advice of you. Formerly, you know, when father was living, and tfre abbot had strength in him, it was different. Besides, Stan and Vilk thought that I would choose one of them, and they restrained each other. But now I shall be defenceless; I shall be in Zgorzelitse as behind a palisade, as in a prison, for surely I shall suffer wrong from those two. Say yourself, is this true or not? "

" It is true ; I also have thought of it."

"And what have you thought out? "

"Nothing; but I must say that this is a Polish country, and punishments of the law for violence to a maiden are terrible."

" That seems well, but 'tis not difficult to spring over the boundary. I know too that Silesia is a Polish country; still the princes quarrel and attack one another. Were it not for that my dear father would be living. The Germans have

THE KNIGHTS OF THE CROSS. 15

got In there; they rouse disturbance and commit wrongs, so that he who wants to hide among them hides. Surely I should not give up easily to either Vilk or Stan, but I am anxious also for my brothers. If I am not here-there will be peace, but if I stay God knows what will happen. There will be attacks and battles. Yasko is fourteen years old, and no power, not to mention mine, can restrain him. The last time, when you hurried to help us, he rushed to the front. Stan struck into the crowd with his club, and barely missed Yasko's head. Yasko told the servants that he would challenge both those fellows to trampled earth. I tell you there will not be a day's peace, and something evil may happen Yasko and the other."

"Oh, Stan and Vilk are dog brothers," said Matsko with vehemence, " but they will not raise hands on children. Tfu! only Knights of the Cross would do that."

" They will not raise hands on children, but in an uproar, or, God preserve, at a fire, accidents are easy. What is the use of talking! Old Setsehova loves ray brothers as if they were her own children, so care and guardianship will not be lacking them; but without me it would be safer far than with my presence."

" Perhaps so," said Matsko. Then he looked quickly at the girl. " What dost thou wish ? "

" Take me with you," answered Yagenka with a lowered voice.

At this Matsko, though it was not difficult for him before to divine the end of the conversation, was astonished greatly; he stopped his horse, and cried, —

" Fear God ! Yagenka."

She dropped her head, and said as if with timidity, and sadness, —

"Well, I choose to speak sincerely rather than hide my thoughts. Both you and Hlava say that Zbyshko will never find that other one, and Hlava expects still worse. God is my witness that I wish her no evil. May the Mother of God preserve and guard her, the poor thing. She was dearer than I to Zbyshko, but there is no help for that! Such is my fate. But you see until Zbyshko finds her, or if, as you think, he never finds her, then — then — "

"Then what? " inquired Matsko, seeing that the girl was becoming more and more confused and halting.

"Then I do not wish to be Stan's or Vilk's, or any one's."

"I thought that thou hadst seen the man already," said Matsko, drawing breath with satisfaction.

Ei," answered she, still more sadly-

"Then what dost thou wish? How could I take thee among the Knights of the Cross? "

Not necessarily among the Knights of the Cross. I should like to go now to the abbot, who is cast down with sickness in Sieradz. He has no loving soul there near him, but he is my godfather and benefactor. Were he well I should seek his protection, for people fear him."

" I shall not oppose that," said Matsko, who at the root of the matter was rejoiced at Yagenka's decision, for knowing the Knights of the Cross he believed profoundly that Dauusia would not escape their hands alive. " I will only say this to thee, that there is terrible trouble with a girl on the road."

44 There might be with another, but not with me. I have never fought yet, but it is no new thing for me to handle a crossbow, and endure toils in hunting. Whenever there is need of doing a thing I shall do it, never fear. I will take Yasko's clothes, put my hair in a net, strap a sword at my side, and ride away. Yasko, though younger, is not a hair smaller, and he is so like me in the face that when we disguised ourselves at the carnival my dead father could not tell which was Yasko and which I. The abbot will not know, you will see, nor will another."

"Will not Zbyshko?"

"If I meet him — "

Matsko meditated a while, then he laughed unexpectedly, and said, —

" But Vilk and Stan will go wild! "

" Let them go wild! The worst is that they may follow us."

"Have no fear. I am old, but they would better not crawl under my fist. They have tried Zbyshko already."

Thus conversing they reached Kresnia. In the church was old Vilk, who from time to time cast gloomy looks at Matsko, but the latter paid no heed to him, and returned home light-hearted with Yagenka after mass. But when they had taken farewell at the crossroads, and when he found himself alone in Bogdanets, less joyful thoughts entered his head. He understood that neither Zgorzelitse nor Yagenka's family were really threatened by anything in case she went on a journey. "They are striving for the girl," thought he, 44 that is another thing; but against the orphans or their

property Vilk and Stan will not raise a finger, for they would cover themselves with dreadful infamy, and every living man would hunt them down as real wolves. But Bogdanets will be defenceless. They will fill up the moats, drive off the cattle, entice away tenants! When I return, God knows if I shall be able to recover anything; I shall- have to summon them to judgment, for not the fist alone, but law rules with us. Shall I return, though, and when? With me they are terribly angry because I have stood between them and Yagenka; but if she goes with me they will be angrier."

Sorrow and regret seized the old man, for he had begun to manage Bogdanets in proper fashion, and now he felt certain that should he return he would find desolation there and ruin.

" Well, we must find a cure," thought he.

So after dinner he had a horse saddled. He mounted and rode directly to Brozova, where he arrived about nightfall. Old Vilk was sitting in his front chamber at a cup of mead; the younger Vilk, who had been slashed by Stan, lay on a bench which was covered with skins; he was drinking also. Matsko went in unobserved and stood near the threshold, stern-faced, tall, bony, unarmed, but with a strong sword at his girdle. They recognized him immediately, for the bright light of the fire struck his face, and at the first moment both father and son sprang to their feet with the speed of lightning, and rushing to the wall each seized whatever weapon was nearest.

But the experienced Matsko, knowing men and their methods through and through, was not alarmed in any way ; he did not reach for his sword; he merely put his hand on his hip and asked with a calm voice in which there was a certain tone of banter,

"What do I see? Is this the noble hospitality, of Brozova? "

Their hands dropped at these words, and after a little the old man's sword fell to the floor with a clatter. Young Vilk let his lance go, and they stood with necks stretched toward Matsko ; their faces ominous, but astonished, and with shame on them.

Matsko smiled.

" Praised be Jesus Christ! " said he.

" For the ages of ages," answered Vilk with his son.

u And Saint George! "

" We serve him."

VOL. II. — 2

18 THE KNIGHTS OF THE CROSS.

" I have come to neighbors in good-will."

" And in good-will do we greet thee. A guest is a sacred person."

Old and young Vilk hurried toward Matsko; both pressed his right hand, then gave him the seat of honor at the table. In a moment wood was in the chimney, the table was covered with a mat on which were placed plates full of meat, a pitcher of beer with a flagon of mead, and they set about eating and drinking. From time to time young Vilk cast at Matsko peculiar glances, in which houor for the guest was struggling to overcome hatred for the visitor; but still he served the guest so diligently that he grew pale from exertion, for he was wounded, and deprived of his usual vigor. Curiosity was burning both father and son to know why Matsko had come to them, though neither inquired touching anything, but waited till he should begin of himself to speak.

He, as a polite person, praised food, drink, and hospitality, and only when he had satisfied himself well did he say with a dignified air, —

"It happens more than once that people quarrel, yes, and fight, but peace between neighbors is above everything."

"There is nothing more precious than peace," replied Vilk, with equal dignity. >

" When a man must prepare for a long journey it happens also," continued Matsko, "that although he has lived in unfriendliness with some one, he is sorry to leave that man, and will not go without taking farewell of him."

" God reward for the kind word."

" Not word alone, but deed also, for I have come hither."

" We are glad from our souls to see thee. Come every day even."

" Let me honor you in Bogdanets as befits people who know knightly honor, but I must go soon on a journey."

" To war, or to some holy place? "

" I should prefer to go to one or the other of these two, but I am to make a worse visit, for I am going to the Knights of the Cross."

"To the Knights of the Cross?" cried father and son at the same moment.

" Yes," answered Matsko. " But whoso goes among them without being their friend would better make peace with God as well as man, lest he lose not merely life, but eternal salvation."

"This is wonderful," said old Vilk. "I have not seen any man thus far who met them without suffering injustice and oppression."

l> Yes, it is the same with our whole kingdom!" added Matsko. " Neither Lithuania before it received holy baptism nor the Tartars were more grievous than those devilish monks are."

"The solid truth; but do you know this too: they have been gathering and gathering, until they have gathered in all, and now would be the time to finish them in this style! "

Then the old man spat lightly in both hands, and the young one added, —

" It cannot be otherwise."

" And surely it will be that way, but when? Not our head answers for that, but the king's. Maybe it will be soon, maybe not soon — God knows. Meanwhile I must go to them."

" And is it with a ransom for Zbyshko? "

At the mention of Zbyshko by his father, young Vilk's face grew pallid from hatred in an instant, and became threatening.

But Matsko answered calmly: " Perhaps with a ransom, but not for Zbyshko."

These words increased still more the curiosity of father and son, and the old man,unable to restrain himself longer, said,—

" You are free to answer or not. Why are you going there ? "

" I will tell, 1 will tell," said Matsko, nodding, " but first I will say something else. Now consider: after I go Bog-danets will remain under the sole care of God. At first, when Zbyshko went to war under Prince Vitold, the abbot looked after our property, yes, and Zyh also a little; but now neither the one nor the other will care for it. It is terribly painful for a man to think that he has been laboring and running for nothing. But you know how these things go. They will entice people away from me, will plow over the boundary; each will steal what he can of my cattle, and though the Lord Jesus permit my return in safety, I shall return to empty places. There is but one cure for this, one salvation: a good neighbor. Therefore I have come to beg you in neighbor fashion to take Bogdanets under your care, and let no one rob me."

When old Vilk heard this request he looked at young Vilk, and young Vilk looked at old Vilk, and both were astonished beyond measure. A moment of silence followed,

for neither one found an answer immediately. Matsko raised the goblet of mead to his lips, drank it, then talked on as calmly and comfortably as if both had been his most intimate well-wishers, —

"Now I will tell you sincerely from whom I expect the greatest damage. From no one except Stan of Rogov. Of you, though we separated in unfriendliness, I should have no fear, because you are knightly people, who will stand up before the eyes of an enemy but will take no unseemly revenge behind his back. Oh, with you it is something different. A knight is a knight ! — but Stan is a clown, and from a clown a man may expect anything; all the more since, as you know, he is terribly angry at me because I stood between him and Yagenka."

" Whom you are saving for your nephew!" burst out young Vilk.

Matsko looked at the youth, and for a while held him under his cool glance ; after that he turned to the old man, and said calmly, —

" You know my nephew has married a young heiress of Hazovia, and has received a worthy dowry."

Again followed a silence which was still deeper ; the father and son looked for some time at Matsko with open mouths. At last the old man said, —

"Hei, how is that? For people said— 'Will you tell about it?"

"It is just on that business," continued Matsko, as if paying no heed to the question, " that I must go, and therefore I beg you to look in from time to time at Bogdanets, and let no one do any harm there, and do you, as worthy and honest neighbors, protect me, especially from.. Stan's attacks."

By this time young Vilk, whose mind was sufficiently nimble, considered at once that if Zbyshko had married it was better for him to have Matsko's friendship, since Yagenka had confidence in the old man, and was ready to follow his advice in all things. Entirely new horizons opened at once before the eyes of the young water-burner. " I must do more than keep from opposing Matsko, I must have his favor," said he to himself. And, though somewhat in liquor, he stretched his hand under the table quickly, caught his father's knee, and pressed it as a sign not to say anything improper.

" Have no fear of Stan ! " said he to Matsko. " Oho, lei

him just try ! He has cut me a little, it is true, but I have slashed his woolly face for him so that his own mother would not know him. Fear nothing, go on your journey in peace. Not a crow will be lost in Bogdanets."

" That is the right thing. I see that you are honorable people. Do you promise?"

" We promise! " cried both.

"And on your escutcheon?"

" On our escutcheon ! More than that, on the Cross J So help us God! "

Matsko smiled to himself with pleasure, then said, —

" Well, this is what I expected. And since you act as you do I will say more. Zyh, as you know, gave me guardianship over his children; therefore I stood before Stan, and thee, young man, when you wanted to break into Zgorzelitse. But when I shall be in Malborg, or God knows where, poor guardianship will mine be. It is true that God stands above orphans, and that the man who wrongs them not only has his head cut off with an axe, but is declared infamous; still I am sorry to go, terribly sorry. Promise me then that not only will you not wrong Zyh's orphans, but that you will let no one else wrong them."

" We swear, we swear! "

" On your knightly honor and escutcheon?"

" On our knightly honor and escutcheon! "

" And on the Cross? "

" And on the Cross."

"God has heard. Amen," concluded Matsko; and he drew a deep breath of relief, for he knew that they would keep such an oath even though each one of them had to gnaw his fist from vexation and anger. And he began to take farewell immediately, but they detained him almost by violence. He had to drink more, and he became a gossip to old Vilk. Young Yilk, though he sought quarrels usually when in liquor, merely threatened Stan savagely, and attended Matsko as zealously as if he were to get Yagenka from him on the day following. But before midnight he grew faint from exertion, and when restored fell asleep like a stone. His father followed this example soon after, so that Matsko left both as if dead at the table. Having himself a head enduring beyond measure, he was not intoxicated, only somewhat rejoiced, so, while returning home, he thought almost with delight of what he had accomplished.

"Well," said he to himself, " Bogdanets is safe, and Zgorzelitse is safe. They will be enraged because Yagenka is going, but they will guard my property and hers, for they must do so. The Lord Jesus has given man cleverness. When a thing cannot be got by the fist we must get it by clear wit. If I come back I shall not escape the old man's challenge to the field, but never mind. God grant me to trap the Knights of the Cross in like manner. But with them it will be harder. Though a dog brother may be found among our people sometimes, if he swears on his knightly honor and escutcheon he will keep his oath; but for Knights of the Cross an oath is as spittle in the river. But maybe the Mother of God will support me, so that I ma\'7d- be of some use to Zbyshko, as I have been now to Zyh's children and to Bogdanets."

Then it occurred to him that really the girl need not go, for old and young Vilk would guard her as the sight of their eyes. After a while, however, he rejected that thought. " They will guard her, but Stan will attack all the more. Gods knows who will conquer, and it is sure that there will be battles and attacks in which Zgorzelitse will suffer,—Zyh's sons, and Yagenka herself even. It will be easier for old Vilk and his son to take care of Bogdanets, and better for the girl in every case to be far away from those two quar-rellers, and near the rich abbot."

Matsko did not believe that Daunsia could escape alive from the Knights of the Cross, so he did not abandon the hope that when Zbyshko returned a widower he would surely feel the will of God toward Yagenka.

"O mighty God!" thought he, "if having Spyhov he should marry Yagenka with Mochydoly, and with what the abbot will leave her, I should not begrudge a stone of wax for candles."

In such meditation the road passed quickly. But he came to Bogdanets late at night, and was astonished when he saw the membrane windows lighted brightly. The waiting-men were not asleep, for he had barely ridden into the yard when the stable-boy ran out to him.

" Are there guests?" asked Matsko, dismounting.

" Yes. the young lord from Zgorzelitse, with the Cheh."

Matsko wondered at this visit. Yagenka had promised to come before daylight in the morning, and they were to start immediately. Why had Yasko come, and so late? The old knight thought that something had happened in

Zgorzelitse and entered the house with some fear. In the large front chamber in a baked clay chimney, which in that house was used instead of the fireplace common in the middle of apartments, pitch-pine sticks were burning cheerily and brightly, and above the table were blazing in iron sockets two torches, by the light of which Matsko saw Yasko, Hlava, and another youth with a face as ruddy as an apple.

" What is the matter, Yasko? What is the matter with Yagenka? " asked the old noble.

" Yagenka gave command to tell thee," said the youth, kissing Matsko's hand, "that she has changed her mind and will stay at home."

Fear God, but what is this? How? What has shot into her head there?"

The youth raised his blue eyes to the old man and laughed.

'' Why art thou giggling ? "

At that moment Hlava and the other youth burst out also into joyous laughter.

"Well," cried the supposed Yasko, "who will know me since you do not? "

Only then did Matsko look closely at the charming figure, and cry, —

" In the name of the Father and Son! A regular carnival! But why art thou here, thou imp?"

"Why? Whoso has a journey to make must be on the road."

" But thou wert to come here to-morrow at daylight."

"What an idea! To-morrow at daylight, so that all might see me! To-morrow they will think in Zgorzelitse that I am here, and will not look around till the day after. The housekeeper and Yasko know that I am going, but Yasko has promised on his knightly honor to tell only when people are alarmed. But you did not know me, did you?"

Matsko laughed now in his turn.

" Let me look again at thee. Hei! a wonderfully handsome lad thou art! — and peculiar. From such one might expect a new race — I tell the truth. Oh, if I were not old— well! But I tell thee, girl, take care of seeing me too often, take care!"

And laughing, he threatened with his finger, but he looked at her with great satisfaction, for he had never seen such a youth. She had a net of red silk on her head, she wore a coat of green cloth, trousers wide at the hips and close-fitting lower down; one leg of the trousers was the color of the

head net, the other was in perpendicular stripes. With a handsome sword at her side, her face as bright as the dawn, it was impossible to take one's eyes from her, such was the girl's beauty.

"Upon my word," said the rejoiced Matsko, "art thou some wonderful youug lord, or a flower, or what? "

Then he turned to the other youth and asked: "But who is this here — some traitor of course ? "

"This is only Auulka," said Yagenka. "I should feel awkward among you if I were alone; how could I go? So I took Anulka; it is pleasanter with company than alone, besides I need help and service. No one will know her either."

" Well, granny, here is a weddiug for thee! One was not enough; we must have two."

" Do not tease."

" I will not tease, but in the daytime every one will know her and thee."

" Why should they?"

" Thy knees turn in — and hers also."

" Oh, give us peace! "

" I will, for my time is past; but will Stan and Vilk give it? God knows. Dost know, thou gadfly, whence I come? From old Vilk's house."

" By the dear God! What do you tell me? "

"The truth, as this is truth, that old and young Vilk will defend Bogdanets and Zgorzelitse against Stan. Well, to challenge enemies, to fight with them is easy, but to make enemies guard one's property, no drone can do that."

Here Matsko told of his visit at Vilk's house, how he had snared the men and hung them both on a hook. Yagenka listened with great astonishment, and when he had finished she said, —

" The Lord Jesus has not spared cunning in your case, and I see that everything will be as you wish."

l> Ah, girl, if everything were as I wish thou wouldst have been mistress of Bogdanets this long time."

At this Yagenka looked at him for a while with her blue eyes, and then approaching kissed his hand.

" Why dost thou kiss me?" asked the old man.

" Oh, nothing ! I merely say good-night to you, for it is late, and we must start before daybreak."

And taking Anulka with her she went out, and Matsko conducted Hlava to his room, where, after they had lain down on buffalo skins, both fell into deep, strengthening sleep.

CHAPTER XXXVIII.

THOUGH after the destruction, fire, and slaughter inflicted on Sieradz in 1331 by the Knights of the Cross, Kazimir the Great had rebuilt the place which had been levelled with the ground, it was not over-brilliant, and could not compare with other cities of the kingdom. But Yagenka, whose life had been passed till then between Zgorzelitse and Kresnia, could not contain herself from astonishment and wonder at sight of the walls, the towers, the town hall, and especially the churches, of which the wooden church at Kresno could not give the least idea. At the first moment she lost her usual resolution to such a degree that she did not dare to speak aloud, and inquired only in whispers of Matsko touching all those wonders which dazzled her eyesight. But when the old knight assured her that Sieradz was to Cracow as a common torch to the sun, she could not believe, for it seemed to her impossible that there could be another city on earth of such splendor.

They were received at the cloister by the same decrepit friar who remembered from years of childhood the slaughter inflicted by the Knights of the Cross, and who on a former occasion had received Zbyshko. News of the abbot caused them sorrow and anxiety. He had remained a long time in the cloister, but had gone two weeks before to his friend, the Bishop of Plotsk. He was ailing continually. He had his wits in the morning, but in the evening his mind wandered. He tried to spring up, commanded the attendants to put on his armor, and challenged Prince Yan of Ratibor to battle. His wandering clerics had to hold him in bed by force, — a thing which was not done without great difficulty, and even danger. Two weeks before, he had regained his mind completely, and, though he had grown weaker, he commanded to take him to Plotsk immediately.

" He declared that he had not such confidence in any man as in the Bishop of Plotsk," said the prior, " and that he wished to receive from his hands the Sacrament, and place his will in them. We opposed this journey as much as we

were able, for he was very weak, and we feared that he would not reach Plotsk alive. But it was not easy to oppose him, so his playmen prepared his carriage, and went away with him, God grant successfully."

" If he had died anywhere near Sieradz you would have heard of it," said Matsko.

We should, so I think that he did not die, or at least that he did not breathe his last this side of Lenchytsa ; but what may have happened beyond I know not. If you follow him you will learn on the road."

Matsko was afflicted by the news and went to consult with Yagenka, who had heard already from Hlava of the abbot's departure.

" What will be done? " asked he, " and what wilt thou do with thyself?"

" You will go to Plotsk, and I with you," answered Yagenka, mildly.

" To Plotsk? " repeated Anulka with her thin voice.

" See how they arrange matters ! They will go right away to Plotsk as straight as the cast of a sickle."

" But how could I go back atone with Anulka? Unless I go farther it would have been better not to leave home at all. Do you not think that there they will be more stubborn and angrier than ever? "

" Old and young Vilk will defend thee against Stan."

" I fear Vilk's defence quite as much as Stan's attack. I see that you are opposing just to oppose, not in earnest."

Of course Matsko did not oppose sincerely. On the contrary he preferred that Yagenka should go with him, so when he heard her words he laughed, and said, —

" She has put off her petticoats and wants to have wit."

" Wit is in the head only," said Yagenka.

" But Plotsk is out of my way."

Hlava says that it is not out of the way, that by the road through Plotsk it is shorter to Malborg.

" Then have ye been advising already with Hlava? "

" Of course ; and he said besides, ' If the young lord has fallen into any misfortune in Malborg much can be done through Princess Alexandra of Plotsk, for she is a relative of the King, and she is besides a special friend of the Knights of the Cross and enjoys great consideration among them.'"

" True, as God is dear to me! " cried Matsko. " All know that, and if she would give a letter to the Grand Master we could travel most safely through all lauds of the Order.

THE KNIGHTS OF THE CROSS. 27

They like her, for she likes them. That is good advice; that Hlava is not a dull fellow."

"Of course he is not!" cried Auulka, with enthusiasm, raising her blue eyes.

Matsko turned to her suddenly.

" But what hast thou to do in this case ? "

The girl was terribly confused, and drooping her long lashes grew as red as a rose.

Matsko saw that there was no other way but to take the two girls farther, and he was willing in secret to do so; hence he continued his journey next morning after taking farewell of the prior. Because of the melting snow and the increase of water, he advanced with greater toil than ever. On the way he inquired about the abbot at many noble residences and priest's houses, or, where these failed, at inns where he halted. It was easy to follow the abbot's traces, for he had given alms, he bad paid for masses, he had given for bells, and contributed to decaying churches, so that more than one poor grandfather who was travelling "to ask," more than one sexton, nay, more than one priest, remembered him with gratitude. People said generally that he " travelled like an angel," and they were praying for his health, though here and there fear was expressed that he was nearer eternal salvation than temporal recovery. In some places he had halted two or three days because of exceeding weakness; therefore it seemed probable to Matsko that they would overtake him.

But he failed in his reckoning, for the swollen waters of the Ner and the Bzura detained them. Before reaching Lenchytsa they were forced to halt four days in an empty inn which the innkeeper had deserted apparently through fear of high water. The road from the inn to the city, though covered with tree-trunks, had sunk, and for some considerable distance was changed to a mud-pit. Vit, Matsko's attendant, a native of that region, had heard something of a way through the forest, but was unwilling to serve as guide, for he knew that in the mud of Lenchytsa unclean powers had their residence, and especially the mighty Boruta, who was glad to entice people into bottomless places and rescue them only at the price of their souls' salvation. The inn itself was ill-famed, and though travellers in those days carried with them provisions and had no fear of hunger, a stay in such a house caused alarm even to Matsko.

At night they heard fighting on the roof; at times some

one knocked at the door. Yagenka and Anulka, who slept in a little room near the front chamber, heard also the pattering of small feet on the floor and ceiling, and even along the walls. This did not frighten them overmuch, for in Zgorze-litse they had been accustomed to imps which were fed by Zyh in his time, and which, by the general opinion of those days, were not malicious if one did not spare broken food on them. But one night a deep, ominous roar was given out in a neighboring thicket; next morning they found in the mud immense hoof tracks, which might be those of a wild ox or buffalo, but Vit said that they were tracks of Boruta, who though in the form of a man, and even of a nobleman, has hoofs instead of feet, and the boots in which he shows himself among people he takes off in the mud to spare them.

Matsko, on hearing that one might reconcile Boruta by drink, meditated all day over this: would it be sinful to show friendly feeling to an evil Spirit? — and he consulted with Yagenka.

" I might hang an ox-bladder of wine or mead on the fence at night," said he; "if it is drunk in the night, we shall know that Tie is about here."

"If the heavenly powers are not offended," replied Yagenka; "we must not offend, for we need a blessing to rescue Zbyshko."

"I am afraid of that too, but I think this way: mead is not the soul. I will not give my soul; but what do the heavenly powers care for one ox-bladder of mead?" Then he lowered his voice and added: " For a noble to entertain a noble, though the most worthless, is a common occurrence, and people say that he is a noble."

" Who ? " inquired Yagenka.

" I have no wish to mention the name of the unclean one."

But Matsko hung out on the fence with his own hands that evening a large ox-bladder in which drinks were carried usually, and next morning the bladder was empty to the bottom. It is true that Hlava, when they spoke of it, smiled somewhat strangely, but no one noticed him. Matsko was glad, for he hoped that when they crossed the swamp no unexpected hindrance or happening would meet them.

" Unless it is said untruly that he knows honor," thought Matsko.

The first need of all was to inquire if there was really a way through the forest. There might be, for wherever the

ground is kept solid by plants and tree-roots the earth does not soften from rain easily. Vit, who as a man of the place might carry out that work best, cried at the mere mention of it: "I will not go, though you kill me! " Vainly did they explain to him that in the daytime unclean power cannot act. Matsko wished to go himself, but they settled on this, that Hlava, who was a daring fellow and glad to exhibit his dai-ing before people, and especially before women, put an axe inside his girdle, took a staff in his hand, and started.

He set out before daylight, and they looked for his return about midday, but when they did not see him they began to fear. In vain did the servants listen near the edge of the forest. Vit merely waved his hand and said : ' ' He will not come back; if he does woe to us, for God knows whether it will not be with a wolf snout and changed into a wolf man." When they heard this all were afraid; Matsko was not himself ; Yagenka, turning toward the forest, made signs of the cross ; Anulka from moment to moment sought in vain for an apron on knees which were now covered with leggings, and not finding anything with which to shade her eyes, she shaded them with her fingers, which soon became wet from tears falling one after the other.

But about the time of evening milking, just at sunset, Hlava returned, not alone, but with some human figure which he drove on a rope before him. All ran out at once toward him with shouts, and were delighted, but they grew silent at sight of the figure, which was small, had bent hands, long hair, was black, and dressed in wolf skins.

" In the name of the Father and the Son, what kind of an imp art thou bringing us ? "cried Matsko.

"What do I care," answered Hlava; "he says that he is a man and a tar-burner, but what he is really I know not."

" Oh, that is no man ! " exclaimed Vit.

Matsko commanded silence, then he examined the prisoner carefully, and said on a sudden, —

Make the sign of the cross ! make the sign of the cross for me this minute ! "

Praised be Jesus Christ! " said the prisoner, and, making the sign as quickly as possible, he drew a long breath, looked with more confidence on the assembly, and said, —

"Praised be Jesus Christ! for I could not tell whether I was in the hands of devils or of Christians. O Jesus! "

"Have no fear. Thou art among Christians who are glad to hear holy mass. Who art thou? "

" A tar-burner, lord, and a watchman. There are seven of us in watch-houses with our wives and children."

" How far are ye from here? "

" Not quite ten furlongs."

" How do ye go to the city? "

" We have our way behind Charts! Vandol (Devil's Valley)."

" Chartsi Vandol? Make the sign of the cross again! "

" In the name of the Father, and the Son, and the Holy Ghost. Amen."

" That is well. Can a wagon pass by that road? "

" There is mud now everywhere, though not so much as on the high-road, for wind blows in the Vandol and dries the mud. But to Budy it is terrible ; though whoso knows the forest well can take a man to Budy slowly."

" Wilt thou show the passage for a skoitsa? Well, let it be for two ! "

The tar-burner undertook willingly to show the way, stipulating yet for half a loaf of bread; for though not dying of hunger in the forest those people had not seen bread for a long time. It was arranged to start on the following morning, since it was "bad" to start toward evening.

" Boruta," said the tar-burner, " storms dreadfully at times through the forest, but he does no harm to common people. He is only chasing other devils because he is jealous of the princes of Lenchytsa. Still it is bad for any man to meet him at night, especially if the man has been drinking. In the daytime and when sober, no one need fear."

" But thou wert afraid," said Matsko.

" Because that knight caught me without my knowing it, and with such strength that I thought he was not a man."

Yageuka laughed because they had all thought the tar-burner some foul being, and the tar-burner had thought them foul. Anulka laughed with her, till Matsko said, -

" Thy eyes are not dried yet from crying after Hlava, and now thou art grinning."

Hlava looked at her rosy face, and seeing that her eyelashes were still moist inquired, —

" Were you crying for me?"

" Oh, no," answered the girl, " I was afraid — that is all."

" You are noble; a noble person should be ashamed of

fear. Your mistress is not so timid. "What harm could meet thee here iii the daytime and among people? "

" Me? Nothing, but you."

" You say that you were not crying for me."

" Yes, because I was not."

" But why, then? "

" From fear."

" And now you are not afraid? "

" No."

"But why not?"

" Because you have come back."

Hlava looked at her with gratitude, smiled, and said, —

"In this way we might talk till morning. You are very cunning."

" Do not laugh at me," answered Anulka in an undertone.

Indeed, she might have been censured for anything rather • than cunning, and Hlava, who was himself a sharp fellow, understood that quite well. He understood also that the girl was drawing closer to him daily. He loved Yagenka, but loved her as a subject loves a king, hence with the greatest honor and without any hope. Meanwhile, the journey brought him nearer to Anulka. In time of travelling old Matsko rode in front, usually with Yagenka, and Hlava rode with Anulka; but since he was as powerful as a bison, and his blood was just boiling when on the journey he looked at her clear eyes, at the yellow tresses which would not stay beneath the net, at her whole form shapely and beautiful, and especially at her legs, wonderful as if sculptured, which embraced the black horse, shivers passed from head to foot through him. Hence he could not restrain himself from glancing more and more at those perfections, and thought involuntarily that if the devil were to change himself to such a youth he might tempt him easily. At the same time that youth was as sweet as honey, and so obedient that he merely looked into Hlava's eyes, and was as joyous as a sparrow on a roof. At times strange thoughts came to Hlava's head, and once, when he and Anulka were somewhat in the rear, near the pack-horses, he turned to her suddenly, and said, —

" Do you know, I am here near you like a wolf near a lamb."

" Would you like to eat me ? " asked she; and her white teeth just gleamed from sincere laughter.

" Yes, with all your bones! "

And he gazed at her with such a look that she blushed

under it; then silence fell between them, but their hearts beat powerfully, his with desire, hers with a certain sweet, intoxicating fear.

At first desire was uppermost in the Cheh, and when he said that he looked at Anulka as a wolf at a lamb, he told the truth. But that evening, when he saw her cheeks and eye-lashes moist with tears, the heart softened in him. She seemed good and in some way near to him, his as it were, and having an honest nature, which was also knightly, he did not become proud, and was not haughty at sight of those tears, but grew more hesitating, and considered her more. His former heedless speech left him, and though he trifled a little at supper with the timid girl, it was different, and at the same time he served her as the attendant of a knight was bound to serve a noble woman. Matsko, though consider-'ing mainly the journey of the morrow, noticed this, but merely praised him for his lofty manners, which, as the old man said, he must have acquired at the Mazovian court with Zbyshko. Then turning to Yagenka, he added, —

" Hei ! Zbyshko—he would find his place even with a king!'

After that service at supper, when they had to part for the night, Hlava, after kissing Yagenka's hand, raised in turn to his lips Anulka' s, wherewith he said, —

" Not only have no fear of me, but when near me fear nothing, for I will not yield thee to any one."

Then the men disposed themselves in the front room; Yagenka and Anulka in a side chamber on the same plank bed, which was broad and well-covered. Neither of them was able to fall asleep soon, for some reason, but especially Anulka, who turned every moment on her coarse blanket. So after a time Yagenka pushed her head up, and whispered, —

"Anulka!"

"What?"

" It seems to me that thou art terribly fond of the Cheh. How is it?"

The question remained without an answer, so Yagenka whispered again, —

" Well, I understand that; so tell me."

Anulka gave no answer; she merely pressed her lips to the cheek of her lady and kissed it repeatedly. But sighs raised the maiden breast of poor Yagenka time after time.

" Oi, I understand, I understand ! " whispered she so quietly that Anulka's ear barely caught the words.

THE KNIGHTS OF THE CROSS. 33

CHAPTER XXXIX.

Ox the morrow, after a mild, hazy night, came a day which was at times bright, at times gloomy, because of clouds which, driven by the wind, sped on in flocks through the sky. Matsko commanded to break camp just at the gray of dawn. The tar-burner, who had undertaken to guide them to Budy, declared that horses could pass everywhere, but in places men would have to take the wagons apart and carry them over in pieces just like packs, provisions, and clothing. This could not take place without delay and effort, but the people, hardened and accustomed to toil, preferred the greatest labor to slothful rest at the empty inn; therefore they took the road willingly. Even the timid Vit, emboldened by the words and presence of the tar-burner, showed no fear.

Immediately beyond the inn they entered a forest of lofty trees, without underbrush, in which with skilful driving it was possible to advance among the branches without taking the wagons to pieces. At times the wind ceased, at times it burst forth with unheard-of violence, striking the limbs of the pine-trees with giant wings, bending them, twisting them, turning them around as if they had been arms of windmills, and breaking them; the pine forest bent under the wild breath, and even during intervals between one attack and another it did not cease to roar and thunder, as if in anger at that attack and superior force. Now and then clouds hid the daylight completely, rain mixed with snow-flakes cut men's faces, and the air grew as dark as at evening twilight. At such times Vit lost his courage, and cried: "The evil one is angry and will harm us;" but no one paid heed to him. Even the timid Anulka did not take his words to heart, especially since Hlava was so near that she could strike his stirrup with hers, and he looked ahead as bravely as if he wished to challenge the very devil to combat.

Beyond the tall forest began one with an undergrowth, and therefore a thicket through which they could not go

with vehicles. They had to take the wagons apart; but that was done adroitly and in a twinkle. Wheels, poles, and axles, as well as packs and provisions, were borne by strong men on their shoulders. There were three furlongs of that bad road, and the party arrived at Budy late in the evening, where the tar-burners received them hospitably, and declared that they could reach the town through Chartsi Vandol, or, more correctly, by passing along the side of it. Those people, inured to life in the wilderness, saw bread and flour rarely, but they did not suffer from hunger, since they were wading in dried food of every sort, especially eels, with which all the swampy places were swarming. They gave these, therefore, bountifully, stretching out grasping hands to receive cakes in return for them. Among these people were women and children, all black from tar-smoke. One man more than a hundred years old remembered the massacre of Lenchytsa, and the utter destruction of that town by the Knights of the Cross in 1331. Matsko, Hlava, and the two young women, though they had heard almost the same narrative from the prior at Sieradz, listened with curiosity to the old man, who, sitting by the fire, and poking it, seemed to poke out the dreadful memories of his youth. So in Lenchytsa, as well as in Sieradz, they spared neither churches nor priests, and the blood of old men, women, and children flowed down the knife-blades of the conquerors. The Knights of the Cross, always the Knights of the Cross! Matsko's thoughts and Yagenka's flew continually toward Zbyshko, who was just then in the jaws of the wolf, as it were, among a hostile race, knowing neither pity nor guest rights. Anulka's heart grew faint ; she was not even sure that they would not have to go among those terrible people in their chase after the abbot.

But the old man began to tell of that battle of Plovtsi, which put an end to the invasion of the Order. He had fought with an iron flail in his hands at that battle, as an attendant in the infantry furnished by a commune of land-tillers. In this battle perished the Grady save one, hence Matsko knew all its details completely; still he listened as if it were new to that narrative of the dreadful defeat of the Germans, when they fell under the swords of Polish knights and the power of King Lokietek.

" Ha! I remember it well, be sure of that," said the old man. "They came into this land, they burnt towns and castles. Why ! they slaughtered children in the cradle; but

the black end came to them. Hei! that was a worthy battle. When I shut my eyes now I see the field there before me."

And closing his lids he was silent, merely moving the coals lightly in the ashes, till Yagenka, impatient for the narrative, asked,

"How was it?"

"How was it?" repeated the old man. "I remember the place as if I were looking at it this moment. There was brush, and on the right a swamp, and a strip of rye, a little field of it. But after the battle there was neither brush, nor swamp, nor rye ; nothing but iron on all sides, swords, axes, spears, beautiful armor, one piece on the top of another, as if some ope had covered the whole sacred earth with them. Never have I seen so many slain people together, never have I seen so much human blood flowing."

Matsko's heart was strengthened again by this remembrance, so he cried, —

"It is true! The Lord Jesus is merciful! They seized hold of the kingdom at that time, like a fire or a pestilence. They destroyed not only Lenchytsa and Sieradz, but many other towns also. And what? Our nation is tremendously vigorous, and has inexhaustible strength in it. Even if thou, O dog brother of a German, seize a Pole by the throat thou'lt not choke him, he will knock out thy teeth for thee. For just look! King Kazimir has built up Lenchytsa and Sieradz in such beauty that they are better than ever, and meetings take place as of old in them, and the Knights of the Cross who were trampled at Plovtsi are lying there and rotting. God grant such an end to them always! "

The old man, hearing these words, began at first to nod his head in agreement, but at last he said, —

" They are not lying there, and perhaps they are not rotting; the king commanded foot soldiers to dig ditches after the battle, and men from the neighborhood came to help in the work, till their backs were all breaking. We put away the Germans in ditches and covered them in good order, so that disease might not hatch from them, but they did not stay there."

" How, not stay? What happened? "

" I did not see this myself, but I tell what people said later After the battle an awful wind came, which lasted twelve weeks, but only in the night-time. In the day the sun shone as is proper, but at night the wind almost tore

the hair from men's heads and faces. That was devils; whole crowds of them were roaring in the night wind, each with a pitchfork, and when a devil came up he thrust his fork into the ground, raised out a Knight of the Cross, and flew off to Hell with him. The people in Plovtsi heard a noise like that of dogs howling in packs, but they could not tell whether the Germans were howling from terror, or the devils were howling from gladness. It was that way till a priest blessed the ditches, and the ground froze so hard at the New Year that no fork could go into it."

Here he was silent, but added after a while, —

" God grant, lord knight, such an end as you say, though I shall not see the time ; youths like these two will live to it, but they will not see what my eyes have seen."

Then he began to look at Anulka and Yagenka, to wonder at their beautiful faces, and shake his head.

" The poppy in the wheat field is no man's," said he, " and I have never seen any one like these two lads."

In this way they talked through a part of the night, then they lay down to sleep in the cabin on moss soft as down, and were covered with warm skins. When deep sleep had strengthened their limbs they moved on faster next morning, after clear daylight.

The road along Charts! Vandol was not very easy, but it was also not difficult; hence before sunset they saw the castle of Lenchytsa. The town had been raised again from its ashes. It was of red brick, and even partly of stone. It had lofty walls, defended by towers, and the churches were richer than the churches of Sieradz. From the Dominicans they got news of the abbot easily. He was better, they said, and rejoiced in the hope of recovery, and some days before he had gone on his journey. Matsko did not wish greatly to overtake him on the road, for he had determined already to take the two girls to Plotsk, whither the abbot would have taken them; but as he was in a hurry to find Zbyshko he was terribly distressed by news that after the abbot's departure the rivers had swollen so that it was quite impossible to go farther. The Dominicans, seeing a knight with a considerable escort, and going, as he said, to Prince Ziemovit's, received and entertained him hospitably, and even gave him a tablet of olive-wood, on which was written in Latin a prayer to the angel Raphael, the patron of travellers.

His forced stay at Lenchytsa lasted two weeks- during which time the young shield-bearer of the castle starosta dis-

covered that the passing knight's attendants were maidens, and fell in love madly with Yagenka; Hlava wished to challenge him to trampled earth straightway, but as this happened on the eve of their departure Matsko advised him against that action.

When they started on the journey to Plotsk the wind had dried the roads somewhat, for though frequent rains fell, as is usual in spring-time, they were brief in duration. The heat also was great, for spring had come at last. In the fields bright strips of water were shining in the furrows. From the plowed land came a strong odor of damp earth in the wind, the swamps were covered with buttercups; in the forest the wolf's foot had blossomed, and thrushes were raising a joyful twitter among branches. In the hearts of the travellers new hope and desire had risen, especially as they were travelling easily, and after sixteen days' journey they halted before Plotsk, but they arrived in the night-time. The gates were closed, hence they had to lodge outside the walls at a weaver's house. The girls, going to bed late, slept like stones, after the toil and hardships of a long journey. Matsko, whom no toil could conquer, did not wish to rouse them, but just as the gates were opened he went alone to the city, where he found the cathedral easily, and the bishop's house, where the first news which he heard was that the abbot had passed away six days earlier.

He was dead a week; but according to the custom of that age masses were celebrated over the coffin, and the funeral feasts continued six days. The burial was to take place that day, and after it services, and the final feast in honor of the departed.

Matsko from great distress could not look at the city, which moreover he knew somewhat from the time when he had travelled .taking a letter from Princess Alexandra to the Grand Master. He returned as quickly as possible to the weaver's house outside the wall, and on the way said to himself, —

" Well, he is dead; eternal rest to him! There is no help against death in this world ; but what am I to do now with those two girls ? "

And he began to hesitate over this, and to think whether it would be better to leave them with Princess Alexandra, or Princess Anna Danuta, or take them to Spyhov. More than once on the road it had occurred to him that were Danusia no longer alive there would be no harm were Yageuka near

Zbyshko. He had no doubt that Zbyshko would mourn long for Danusia, whom he loved beyond all people, and would weep long after her; but he had no doubt either that if a girl like Yagenka were there at his side she would have her own effect. He remembered the 3 r oung man, though his heart was tearing away beyond the pine woods of Mazovia, was taken by shivers when close to Yagenka. For these reasons, and believing also profoundly that Danusia had perished, he had thought more than once that in case the abbot died he would not send away Yagenka. But since he was somewhat greedy of earthly goods, he was concerned about property left by the abbot. The abbot had been angry at them, it is true, and had said that he would will them nothing; but might not compunction have come before death to him ? That he had left something to Yagenka was certain, for more than once he had mentioned that fact in Zgorzelitse ; through Yagenka it might also not miss Zbyshko. So at times a desire seized JSIatsko to tarry in Plotsk to learn the how and what, and occupy himself with that business; but he soon put an end to these thoughts. "I shall be here," said he, "bothering about property, and my boy may be stretching his hands from some dungeon of the Order, and awaiting salvation from his uncle."

True, there was one escape: to leave Yageuka under the guardianship of the princess and the bishop, with the entreaty not to let her be wronged in case the abbot had willed her some property. But that idea did not please Matsko in any way. "As it is, the girl has a good fortune," said he to himself; " if she inherits from the abbot, some Mazovian will take her, as God is in heaven, and she will not hold out long either, for even Zyh said that she was as if walking on live coals of fire." And the old knight was frightened at this idea, for he thought that in that way Danusia and Yagenka both might miss Zbyshko. and for aught on earth he would not have that come to pass.

" Let him have the one God has predestined, but one of these two he must take."

He determined first of all to save Zbyshko, and if he had to part with Yagenka he would leave her in Spyhov, or with Princess Danuta, not in Plotsk, where the court was incomparably more brilliant, and where there were handsome knights in good number.

Burdened with these thoughts he went with brisk steps toward the weaver's to announce to Yagenka the death of the abbot, but he promised in soul not to tell her itnmedi-

ately, for unexpected bad news might stop her breath and make the girl barren.

When Matsko reached the house he found both maidens dressed, even ornamented, and joyous as thrushes ; so sitting down on a bench he called the weaver's servant to bring a mug of heated beer, and then put frowns on a face which was stern enough without them.

"Dost hear," asked he, "how the bells of the town are ringing ? Guess why they are ringing, for it is not Sunday, and thou hast slept over early mass. Wouldst thou like to see the abbot ? "

" Of course I should like to see him," answered Yagenka

" Well, thou wilt see him, as King Nail."

" Has he gone farther?"

" He has gone farther indeed! But dost thou not hear that they are ringing bells?"

"Has he died?"

"Say eternal rest."

So all three knelt down and repeated eternal rest with voices resonant as a bell. Then tears flowed in streams along Yagenka's face, for she loved the abbot greatly. Though quick-tempered with people, he had wronged no one, and had done good with both hands, and her, his godchild, he loved as if she had been his own daughter. Matsko, remembering that the abbot was his kinsman and Zbyshko's, was moved also, and cried some; only when a part of his sorrow had vanished in tears did he take Hlava and the two girls to the church for the funeral.

The funeral was splendid. Bishop Yakob of Kurdvanov led the procession himself. All the priests and monks of Plotsk were there, all the bells were rung; discourses were delivered which no one understood save the clergy, for they were in Latin. Then clergy and laity returned to a feast at the bishop's.

Matsko went there taking the two youths, for he had every right as a relative of the dead man. The bishop too received him, as a kinsman of the abbot, with good-will and honor, but immediately after greeting he said, —

" There are some forests left you, the Grady of Bogdanets; but whatever remains and does not go to cloisters and abbeys is to belong to his goddaughter, a certain Yagenka of Zgorzelitse."

Matsko, who had not expected much, was glad of the forests, but the bishop did not see that one attendant of the old knight raised moist eyes, as blue as star thistles, and said, —

" God reward him, but I would rather he were living."

Matsko turned to her and said : "Be quiet, for thou wilt make shame for thyself."

But he stopped suddenly; astonishment gleamed in his eyes; then his face grew stern and wolf-like, for at a distance, near the side of the door through which Princess Alexandra was entering at that moment, he saw Kuno Lichtenstein, bent in courtly client fashion, that same man through whom Zbyshko came near his death in Cracow.

Yagenka in her life had never seen such a Matsko ; his face wrinkled like the jaw of an angry mastiff, and under his mustaches the teeth glittered. In one moment he tightened the belt around his waist, and moved toward the hated Knight of the Order. But half-way he restrained himself, and drew his broad hand along his hair. He remembered in season that perhaps Lichtenstein was at the court of Plotsk as a guest, or more likely an envoy, and that if he wished without making inquiry to fight with him, he would act just as Zbyshko had acted on the road from Tynets.

So, having more reason and experience than Zbyshko, he restrained himself, loosened his belt, made his face affable, and when the princess, after greeting Lichtenstein, spoke with the bishop, he approached her, bent low, reminded her who he was, and said that he considered her his benefactress because of the letter with which on a time she had furnished him.

The princess barely remembered his face, but she recalled the letter easily and the whole affair connected with it. She knew besides what had happened at the neighboring Mazovian court: she had heard of Yurand, and the kidnapping of his daughter, the marriage of Zbyshko and his deadly duel with Rotgier. Her curiosity was roused greatly by all these details, just as it would have been by a narrative of knighthood, or by one of those ballads which were sung by minstrels among the Germans, or by choristers in Mazovia. It is true that the Knights of the Cross were not so hateful to her as to Anna Danuta, the wife of Prince Yanush, especially since they, wishing to win her to their side, surpassed one another in flattery and homage, and showered gifts on the lady richly; but this time her heart was on the side of the lovers. She was ready to aid them; and moreover it pleased her to have

in her presence a man who could relate the whole course of events most minutely.

And Matsko, who had determined earlier to win the protection and aid of the powerful princess by every means possible, seeing with what attention she listened, told her willingly of the sad fate of Zbyshko and Danusia, and almost moved her to tears, and this the more quickly since he himself felt more keenly than any one the misfortune of his nephew, and grieved with his whole soul over it.

u I have heard nothing more touching in my life," said the princess at last, " and the greatest pity seizes me for this cause, that, having married the girl, she was his ; still he knew no happiness with her. But do you know surely that he did not ? "

" Ei, mighty God!" answered Matsko, "would that he had; but he married her at night, when he was tied to his bed with grievous illness, and at daybreak they took her."

" Do you think that Knights of the Cross took her ? For here they talk about robbers who deceived the Knights of the Cross by giving them another girl. They speak also of a letter from Yurand — "

" Not the judgment of people has decided this now, but the judgment of God. They say that that Rotgier was a great knight, who brought down the doughtiest, and still he fell at the hand of a stripling."

" Yes, such a stripling," said the princess, smiling, " that it would be very safe for any man not to creep into his way. An injustice was done, it is true, and you complain with reason ; but still of those four three are no longer living, and that old man who remains barely escaped death, as I hear."

"But Danusia, where is she? and where is Yurand ?" asked Matsko; " where are they ? God knows, too, whether some evil may not have befallen Zbyshko, who went to Malborg."

" I know, but really the Knights are not such scoundrels as you deem them. In Malborg, near the Grand Master and his brother Ulrich, who is a knightly person, nothing evil can have happened to your nephew; he has a safe-conduct and letters from Prince Yanush. Unless he challenged some knight there and fell, for in Malborg there is always a number of the most renowned knights from all countries."

" Ei, I do not fear that greatly," answered the old man. " If they do not shut him up in a dungeon, or slay him treacherously, and he has some iron in his grasp, I am not

much afraid. Only once was there found a" man stronger who put him back in the barriers, and that was the Prince of Mazovia, Henryk, he who was bishop here, and who was in love with the comely Ryngalla. Though Zbyshko was a mere boy in those days, he was as ready to challenge a certain man as to say amen to Our Father, — the man whom I, too, have promised to challenge and who is here."

And he indicated with his eyes Lichtenstein, who was conversing with the Voevoda of Plotsk.

But the princess frowned, and said with that severe and dry tone which she used always when anger was beginning to seize her, —

"Whether you have made a vow or not, remember this, that he is on a visit; whoso wishes to be our guest must observe politeness."

" I know, gracious lady," answered Matsko. "I had already tightened my belt, and was going toward him, but ] restrained myself, thinking that perhaps he was an envoy."

" Yes, he is an envoy. And the man is distinguished among his own people ; the Grand Master himself values his counsel, and does not refuse him anything. God perhaps granted that he was not in Malborg when your nephew was there. As to Lichtenstein, though of honorable family, people say that he is stubborn and vengeful. Did he recognize you ? "

" He could not have done so, for he has seen me little. We were in helmets on the Tynets road, and afterwards I visited him only once on Zbyshko's business, but that was in the evening when he was busy. I noticed now that he looked at me, but he did so only because I talked rather long with you, gracious lady, for he turned his eyes after that very quietly in another direction. He would have known Zbyshko, but he overlooked me, and has never heard of my vow, perhaps, having something better to think of."

" How better ? "

" Yes, better, for vows touching him have been made by Zavisha of Garbov, Povala of Tachev, Martsin of Vrotsi-movitse, Pashko Zlodye, and Lis of Targovisko. Each one of these, gracious lady, could manage ten like him, and what must it be when he has all of them against him? Better for him that he had never been born than to have one such sword above his head. As to me, not only shall I not remind him of my vow, but I shall try to enter into intimacy with him."

"For what purpose? "

Matsko's face took on a cunning expression immediately, and looked like the face of an old fox.

" For this purpose, that he should give me a letter of such kind that I may travel safely through the country of the Order, and, in case of need, rescue Zbyshko."

" Is that worthy of knightly honor ? " asked the princess, with a smile.

" It is," answered Matsko in tones of decision. " Were I, for example, to fall on him from behind, without calling on the man to turn, I should disgrace myself; but to trick an enemy in time of peace by quick wit is no disgrace to any one."

"Then I will make you acquainted," said the princess.

So she beckoned to Lichtenstein, and presented Matsko; thinking that even were Lichtenstein to recognize him, no great harm would come of that.

But Lichtenstein did not recognize Matsko, for really he had seen him in a helmet on the Tynets road, and afterward had spoken with him only once, and that in the evening when Matsko came to him to beg pardon for Zbyshko's offence.

Still he bowed rather haughtily; but when he saw behind the knight two splendid, richly dressed attendants, he thought that no ordinary noble could have such, and his face brightened somewhat, though he did not cease to curve his lips haughtily, as he did always when not dealing with ruling persons.

" This knight is going to Malborg," said the princess. " I myself will recommend him to the favor of the Grand Master; but he, hearing of the authority which you enjoy in the Order, would like to have a letter from you also." > Then she turned to the bishop. Lichtenstein fixed his cold, steel eyes on Matsko and asked, —

"What motive inclines you, sir, to visit our pious and modest capital ? "

" A pious and an honest motive," answered Matsko, raising his glance; " were it otherwise, the gracious lady would not have vouched for me. But, in addition to sacred vows, I should like also to become acquainted with your Grand Master, who makes peace on earth, and is most renowned in the world of knighthood."

" He for whom the gracious princess, your lady and benefactress, gives guarantee will not complain of our modest entertainment; but as to the Master, it will be difficult to

see him, for he went to Dantzig a month ago, whence he intended to go to Krolevets, and farther toward the boundary ; for though a lover of peace, he is forced to defend the inheritance of the Order against the treacherous attacks of Vitold."

When he heard this Matsko was vexed so evidently that Lichtenstein, before whose eyes no one could hide anything, remarked, —

" I see that your desire to know the Grand Master is equal to your wish to perform religious vows."

Yes, yes, of course," answered Matsko, promptly. "Then is war with Vitold certain? "

"Vitold has begun it himself by giving aid to insurgents in spite of his oath."

A moment of silence followed.

"Well, God grant that success to the Order which it merits," said Matsko at last. "I cannot make the acquaintance of the Grand Master, but in every case I will accomplish my vows."

But despite these words he did not know what he was to do, and with a feeling of immense vexation he put to himself this question, —

"Where am I to seek Zbyshko now, and where shall I find him?"

It was easy to foresee that if the Master had left Malborg and gone to war there was no reason to look for Zbyshko in Malborg, but in every case it was necessary to obtain more accurate information regarding him. Old Matsko was greatly vexed, but as he was a man of ready resources, he resolved to lose no time, but to continue his journey without delay on the morrow. It was easy for him to get a letter from Lichtenstein with the aid of Princess Alexandra, in whom the comtur had boundless confidence. He received, therefore, a recommendation to the Starosta of Brodnitsa and to the Grand Hospitaller in Malborg, but in return for these letters he presented Lich-teustein with a large silver goblet engraved beautifully in Vrotslav, such a goblet as the Knights were accustomed to place, filled with wine, near their beds at night, so as to have at hand, in case of insomnia, a remedy bringing sleep and consolation. This liberality of Matsko astonished Hlava, who knew that the old man was not overinclined to loading any one with presents, above all a German ; but Matsko said, —

"I did this because I have made a vow touching that Knight, and I must fight with him. I could not in any way attack the life of a man who rendered me a service. It is not our custom to strike a benefactor."

"But it is a pity to lose the beautiful goblet," answered Hlava a little rebelliously.

"I do nothing without calculation, have no fear. If the merciful Lord Jesus permits me to bring down that German I shall win back the goblet, and capture a multitude of other costly things with it."

Then the two men, and with them Yagenka, began to counsel as to what they should do. It came to Matsko's mind to leave Yagenka and Anulka in Plotsk with Princess Alexandra, and to do so because of the abbot's will, which .was deposited with the bishop; but the girl opposed this with all her unbending decision. It is true that it would have been easier to travel without her, for there would be no need of finding separate rooms, or thinking of ceremony, or danger, or various other things of similar import. However, they had not left Zgorzelitse to stay in Plotsk. The will in the bishop's hands would not be lost, and should it appear that the maidens must stay on the road somewhere, they would be safer in the care of Princess Anna than Alexandra, for at her court the people cared less for the Knights of the Cross, and were more inclined to Zbyshko. It is true that Matsko said, touching this, that wit does not belong to woman, and that it is not proper to argue with a girl, as if she had real reason; he did not oppose decisively, however, and soon yielded, for Yagenka drew him aside and said, with tearful eyes, —

"You know — God is looking at my heart — that I pray morning and evening for Danusia, yes, and for Zbyshko's happiness. God in heaven knows best of all the truth of this! But Hlava, and you too, declare that she is lost, that she will not escape from the hands of the Knights alive. If this be so, then I —"

Here she hesitated somewhat, the tears collected, flowed slowly down her cheeks, and she ended in a whisper, —

"Then I wish to be near Zbyshko — "

Those tears and words touched Matsko; still he answered,—

"If she perishes, Zbyshko will be so grieved that he will not look at thee."

"I do not want him to look at me, but I want to be near him."

"Thou knowest that I want what thou dost, but in his first grief he will be ready even to use harsh words against thee."

"Let him use harsh words," answered she, with a sad smile. "But he will not, for he will not know me."

"He will know thee."

"He will not know me. You did not know me. Tell him it is not I, but Yasko, and Yasko is like me to the very lips. Tell him that Yasko has grown, and it will not come to his head that it is I, and not Yasko."

The old knight said something now about knees bending inward, but as boys' knees also bend in sometimes, that could not be a hindrance, especially as Yasko's face was almost the same, and his hair, since the last cutting, had grown long again, and he wore it in a net like other noble youths, and knights also. For these reasons Matsko yielded, and now they fell to discussing the journey. They were to start on the morrow. Matsko decided to enter the lands of the Order, go to Brodnitsa, find an informant there, and if the Grand Master, in spite of the suppositions of Lichtenstein, was in Malborg yet, to go to Malborg; in the opposite case to cross the boundary of the Order in the direction of Spyhov, inquiring on the road for the young Polish knight and his retinue.

The old knight thought that he might learn something more easily of Zbyshko in Spyhov, or at the Warsaw court of Prince Yanush, than in any other place.

In fact they set out on the following morning. Spring had begun completely, hence there were overflows of water, and those of the Skrva and the Drventsa stopped the road, so that only on the tenth day after leaving Plotsk did they cross the boundary and find themselves in Brodnitsa. The town was clean and well-ordered, but immediately on entering one might recognize rigorous German rule, for immense walled gallows l had been built outside the town at the side of the Gorchenitsa road and decorated with bodies of hanged people, of whom one was a woman. On the watch-tower and on the castle waved a flag which had a red hand on a white field. But the travellers did not find the comtur himself in the place, for he had gone with a part of the garrison, and at the head of the neighboring nobility, to Malborg. This information was given to Matsko by an

The ruins of the gallows remained till the year 1818.

old Knight of the Order blind of both eyes, who on a time had been comtur of Brodnitsa, and growing attached to the town and the castle, was passing the last of his life there. When the local priest read to him the letter from Lichtenstein, he received Matsko hospitably, and since he was living in the midst of a Polish folk he knew Polish speech excellently, so that it was easy to converse with him. It had happened to him also to be summoned to Malborg six weeks before, whither he had been called to a military council as a knight of experience; hence he knew what was happening at the capital.

When they asked him about the young knight, he said that he did not remember his name, but that he had heard of some knight who had roused wonder first of all by this, that he was belted notwithstanding his youthful years, and then by his success at the tournament which the Grand Master had arranged for foreign guests before he set out on his expedition. Gradually he recalled even this, that Ulrichr von Jungingen, the noble-minded though quick-tempered brother of the Grand Master, had conceived a liking for that knight, had taken him under his care, and given him special letters, which the young man took with him and went away toward the eastern boundary.

Matsko was comforted immensely by these tidings, for he had not the least doubt that that knight was Zbyshko. In view of this there was no reason to go to Malborg, for though the Grand Hospitaller, or other dignitaries, and Knights of the Order who remained there might give more minute information, they could in no case tell where Zbyshko was at the moment. Moreover, Matsko himself knew best of all where to find him. It was not difficult to divine that he was circling about Schytno, or, if he had not found Danusia in that place, he was searching for her in the remoter Eastern castles or towns of the comturs.

So, without losing much time, he moved through the territory of the Order toward the east, and Schytno. He passed the road quickly, for the numerous towns and villages were joined by highways which the Knights of the Cross, or rather merchants in the towns, had made, and maintained in good condition, — highways scarcely inferior to those which had appeared in Poland under the managing and active care of King Kazimir's government. Moreover, the weather was marvellous; the nights starry, the days serene, and at the hour of afternoon milking a warm, dry

breeze blew, which filled people's bosoms with health and good feeling. Wheat was green in the fields, the meadows were covered richly with flowers, and pine woods gave out the odor of resin. Over the whole road to Lidzbark, and thence to Dzialdovo, and farther to Niedzbov, the travellers saw not a single cloud on the sky. In Niedzbov at night came the earliest shower, with thunder, heard then for the first time that spring. The shower was a short one, and next morning the dawn appeared clear, rosy, golden, and so filled with light that as far as the eye could see everything glittered like strings of pearls and diamonds; the whole earth seemed to smile at the sky and to rejoice in the wealth of existence.

On that morning they went out of Niedzbov toward Schytno. The Mazovian boundary was not distant, and they could have turned to Spyhov easily. There was a moment even when Matsko thought of doing so, but after weighing everything carefully, he chose to push on directly to that terrible nest of the Order in which a part of Zbyshko's fate had been decided so gloomily. He took a peasant guide, therefore, and commanded him to lead the escort to Schytno, though a guide was not absolutely needed, for a straight road led on from Niedzbov, and on this road German miles were marked with white stones at the wayside.

The guide went some tens of steps in advance ; after him came Matsko and Yagenka on horseback ; then, rather far behind them, was Hlava with the fair Anulka; and still farther were wagons surrounded by armed attendants. It was early in the morning. The rosy color had not left the eastern side of the sky yet, though the sun was shining well, changing to opals the drops of dew on the grass and the trees.

"Art thou not afraid to go to Schytno?" asked Matsko.

"I am not," answered Yagenka. "The Lord God is above me, for I am an orphan."

"Thou hast cause to fear, for they keep no faith in that place. Indeed Danveld was the worst of dogs; Yurand rubbed out him and Gottfried — so Hlava says. The second after Danveld was Rotgier, who fell under Zbyshko's axe, but the old man too is unpitying, sold to the devil. People know nothing clearly, but I think that if Danusia has perished it is at his hands. They say that some misfortune met him as well as the others, but in Plotsk the

princess told me that he had squeezed out of it. He is the man whom we are to meet in Schytno. It is well that we have a letter from Lichtenstein, for likely the dog brothers fear him more than even the Grand Master. They say that he has weight, that he is cruel and very strict, and moreover vengeful. He does not forgive the slightest injury. I should not go to Schytno so confidently without this letter."

"And what is the name of that old man?"

"Siegfried de Lowe."

"God grant us to defend ourselves against him."

"God grant!"

Here Matsko laughed, and after a time continued, —

"The princess in Plotsk said to me, ' The wrong you commit is that of lambs against wolves, but in this case of the wolves three are no longer living, for the innocent lambs have slaughtered them.' And she is right if the truth be told."

"But Danusia and her father?"

"I asked the same question of the princess. But I am glad in soul that it seems very dangerous to wrong us; we understand, seest thou, how to grasp an axe and use it worthily. As to Danusia and Yurand, I think, as Hlava does, that they are no longer in this world, but really no one knows exactly. I am sorry indeed for Yurand, since during life he was consumed with grief for his daughter, and if dead he has died an awful death."

"When any one mentions him in my presence, I think immediately of papa, who is no longer in this life," answered Yagenka.

And she raised her moist eyes. Matsko nodded, and said, —

"He is in God's assembly and surely in endless light, for a better man than he there was not in our whole kingdom."

"Oi, there was not, there was not!" sighed Yagenka.

Further conversation was interrupted by the peasant guide, who reined in his colt all at once, then turning, flew toward Matsko at a gallop, and cried in a strange and terrified voice, —

"Oh, for God's sake! Look, lord knight, some one is coming toward us down the hillside!"

" Who ? Where ? " inquired Matsko.

"Orer there! It must be a giant, or something."

VOL. II. 4

Matsko and Yagenka, reining in their pacers, looked in the direction indicated by the guide, and in fact they saw on the hill, half a furlong or more away, a form which seemed to exceed the usual dimensions of man considerably.

"The fellow says truly that he is large," muttered Matsko.

Then the old man spat toward one side on a sudden and said,—

"A charm on the dog!"

"Why do you adjure?" inquired Yagenka.

"Because I remember how on the same kind of morning Zbyshko and I saw on the road between Tynets and Cracow a giant of such size. The people said then that it was Valger the Charming. Well, it turned out to be the lord of Tachev; but nothing good came of the matter. A charm on the dog! "

"This is not a knight, for he is on foot," said Yagenka, looking more sharply. "I see even that he has no weapons, he has nothing but a stick in his left hand."

"And feels the way out in front, as if the time were night," added Matsko.

"And be barely moves. It is sure that he is blind, or something."

"He is blind, he is blind ! as I live! "

They spurred on, and soon halted in front of the old man, who, descending the hill very slowly, was searching for the road with a stick. He was indeed immense, though seen from near by he did not appear to them a giant. They discovered that he was entirely blind. Instead of eyes, he had two red depressions in his face. His right hand also was lacking; in place of it he carried a knot formed of a dirty rag. His white hair fell to his shoulders and his beard reached his girdle.

"The poor man has neither boy nor dog, and finds the road for himself by groping," said Yageuka. "In God's name I cannot leave him without help ! I do not know whether he can understand me, but I will speak to him in our speech."

She sprang from her horse quickly, and standing in front of the old man looked for money in the leather pouch which depended from her girdle.

The old man, when he heard the tramp of horses, and the noise, stretched his stick foward, and raised his head in the manner of blind people.

"Praised be Jesus Christ! 1 ' said Yagenka. "Do you understand Christian speech, grandfather ? "

But he, hearing her sweet voice, trembled, a wonderful ray shot across his face as it were of emotion and tenderness, he covered with his eyelids the empty pits of his eyes, and dropping the stick, fell before her on his knees with his arms stretched upward.

"Rise! I will help you. What is your suffering?" asked Yagenka with astonishment.

He made no answer, save that two tears rolled along his cheeks, and from his mouth came a sound something like a groan.

"Aa ! a!"

"By the pity of God are you dumb, or what?"

"Aa! a!"

When he had uttered this he raised his hand, made a sign of the cross with it first, then passed it across his lips.

Yagenka, not understanding, looked at Matsko, who said, —

"It must be that he is showing how they cut his tongue out."

"Did they cut your tongue out ? " asked the girl.

"Aa! a! a! a ! " repeated the old man a number of times, nodding his head therewith.

Then he pointed at his eyes with his fingers, thrust forth his right arm without a hand, and made a motion with his left like giving a blow.

Now both understood him.

"Who did this to you? " asked Yagenka.

The old man made a number of signs of the cross in the air.

"The Knights of the Cross! " cried out Matsko.

The old man dropped his head toward his breast in sign of affirmation. A moment of silence followed. Matsko and Yagenka looked at each other with fear, for they had before them a clear proof of that lack of mercy and absence of measure in punishment for which the Knights of the Cross were distinguished.

"Savage measures !" said Matsko at last; "grievously have they punished him, and God knows whether justly. But we shall not discover that. If only we knew where to take him, for he must be a man of these parts. He understands our speech, for the people here are the same as in Mazovia."

"Do you understand what we say ? " asked Yagenka. He confirmed with his head. ' Are you from this place ? " 'No," answered the old man with signs. 'Then you may be from Mazovia? " 'Yes.""

'From the dominions of Prince Yanush?" 'Yes."

'And what were you doing with the Knights of the Cross?"

The old man could not answer, but his face assumed in one moment an expression of such immense pain that the compassionate heart of Yagenka quivered with the greater sympathy, and even Matsko, though no small thing could move him, said, —

"Surely the dog brothers have done him evil, and perhaps without fault on his part."

Yagenka pressed into the palm of the poor man some small money.

"Listen," said she, "I will not leave you. You will go with us to Mazovia, and in every village we will ask if that is not your place. Maybe we shall talk the way to it somehow. And stand up now, for we are not saints."

But he did not rise; on the contrary he inclined and embraced her feet, as if giving himself into her protection, and returning thanks ; but at the same time a certain astonishment, and even, as it were, disappointment, shot over his face. Perhaps it was that while taking note .of her voice he had thought himself standing before a young girl, while now his hand touched rough leggings such as knights and attendants wore while on journeys. But she said, —

"This is what we will do. Our wagons will come soon; you can rest and gain strength. But you will not go at once to Mazovia, for we must go first to Schytno."

At this word the old man sprang to his feet. Dread and astonishment were expressed on his face. He opened his arms as if to bar the way, and from his mouth came wild sounds, as if he were filled with terror.

"What is the matter?" cried Yagenka, with alarm. But Hlava, who had now come up with Anulka, and who for some time had been looking fixedly at the old man, turned quickly to Matsko with a changed face, and said in a voice full of astonishment, —

"By God's wounds! let me speak to him, lord, for you do not think who he is ! "

Then, without waiting for permission, he sprang to the old man. placed his hands on his shoulders, and inquired, —

"Are you coming from Schytno?"

The old man, as if struck by the sound of his voice, grew calm, and nodded in affirmation.

"And were you not looking for your child there?"

A dull groan was the only answer to that question.

Hlava grew somewhat pale, looked a moment longer with his wild-cat glance at the features of the old man, then said slowly and with emphasis, —

"You are Yurand of Spyhov! "

"Yurand!!" screamed Matsko.

But Yurand tottered at that moment and fainted. The tortures which he had passed through, the lack of food, the toils of the journey had thrown him off his feet. That was the tenth day on which he was going along feeling his way, wandering, and searching for the road in front of him with a stick, in hunger, in struggling, uncertain whither he was going. Unable to ask for the road in the daytime, he directed himself only by the heat of the sunrays; the nights he passed in ditches by the wayside. When he passed through a hamlet or a village, or when he met people going in the opposite direction, he begged alms with his one palm and the voice that was left him; but rarely did a compassionate hand give him aid, for generally he was looked on as a criminal whom the punishment of law and of justice had overtaken. For two days he had kept himself alive with the bark of trees and with leaves, and he was in doubt whether he should be able ever to reach Mazovia — when on a sudden compassionate, kindred hearts had encircled him, and kindred voices, one of which reminded him of the sweet voice of his daughter — and when at last even his own name was mentioned, the measure of emotions overflowed, the heart was straitened in his breast, thoughts went around in his head like a whirlwind, and he would have fallen with his face in the dust of the road if the strong arms of Hlava had not caught him.

Matsko sprang from his horse, then both took Yurand, carried him to the wagons and placed him on some hay in one of them. Thei'e Yagenka and Anulka revived the man, gave him food, gave him wine to drink, and Yagenka, seeing that he could not grasp the cup, held the drink herself to

his lips. Immediately an invincible sleep seized the man, from which he was to wake on the third day only.

Meanwhile they held a prompt and decisive council.

"I will say at once," called out Yagenka, "that it is not for us to go now to Schytno, but to Spyhov, so as to leave him in a safe place among his own people, and leave him surrounded by every care."

"Look, how thou art ordering this," answered Matsko. "It is necessary to send him to

Spyhov, but not indispensable that we all go; one wagon can go with him."

"I do not order, but I think that we might learn much from him about Zbyshko and Danusia."

"In what language wilt thou talk with him, since his tongue is gone?"

"But who has shown you that he has no tongue, except himself? You see that without talking we have learned everything that was needed, and how will it be when we are accustomed to the indications of his head and hands? Ask him, for example, whether Zbyshko has returned from Mal-borg to Schytno, then be sure he will either affirm with his head, or deny; and it will be the same with other things."

"True!" said Hlava.

"I do not deny that this is true," said Matsko, "and I had the same thought myself; but with me judgment is first, and talk afterward."

Then he gave orders to turn the wagons toward the Mazovian boundary. On the way Yagenka approached time after time the wagon in which Yurand lay, fearing that he might have died while sleeping.

"I did not recognize him," said Matsko, "but that is no wonder. He was as strong as a wild bull ! the Mazo-vians said that he was the only man among them who was able to meet Zavisha of Garbov — but now he is a real skeleton."

"There were reports," said Hlava, "that they were killing him with torture, but some people could not believe that Christians would act so with a belted knight, one having, moreover, Saint George for his patron."

"It was God's will that Zbyshko avenged him even in part. But see the difference between us and them. It is true that of four dog brothers three have fallen; but they fell in battle, and no man has cut the tongue out of one of them in captivity, or taken his eye out."

"God will punish them," said Yagenka.

But Matsko turned to Hlava, —

'•'How didst thou know him? "

'I did not know him at once, though I saw him later thi» i you did. But something was going through my head, and the more I looked at him the more it kept going. He had no beard or white hairs before; he was a great lord, and a rich one; how was it possible to recognize him in such a beggar! But when the young lady said that we were going to Schytno and he began to howl, my eyes were opened that instant."

"It would be well to take him from Spyhov to the Prince, who cannot permit such a wrong done a man of importance to go unpunished."

"They will deny. lord. They carried off his child by deceit, and they denied; they will say of the master of Spyhov that he lost his tongue and his hand in battle, and his eye also."

"True!" answered Matsko. "Indeed they carried off the Prince himself on a time. He cannot war with them, for he cannot overcome them unless the king helps him. People talk of a great war, but here there is not even a small war."

"Yes, there is, with Prince Vitold."

"Praise be to God that he is a man who cares nothing for the Order. Hei, Prince Vitold is the prince for me! And in cunning they cannot beat him, for he alone is more cunning than all of them together. It used to happen that they, the dog bloods, would press on him till destruction, like a sword, was above his head, but he would slip away, like a snake, and bite them right there. Look out for him when he strikes, but look out still more when he coaxes."

"Is he that way with all? "

"Not with all, only with Knights of the Cross; with others he is kind and bountiful."

Here Matsko meditated, as if wishing to bring Vitold to mind better.

"He is a man entirely different from the princes in these parts," said he at last. "It was Zbyshko's duty to go to him, for under him and through him it is possible to do most against the Order."

After a moment he added, —

"Who knows that we may not find them both there yet, that is the place for most proper vengeance."

Then he spoke again of Yurand, of his evil fate, and the unutterable wrongs which he had suffered from the Knights of the Order, who first of all had murdered his beloved wife without cause, and then, paying vengeance with vengeance, had carried off his daughter, and tormented him with such cruel tortures that even Tartars would not have been able to invent anything to surpass them. Matsko and Hlava gritted their teeth when they thought that even the liberation of Yurand was a new and calculated cruelty. The old knight promised himself therefore in soul that he would try to find out accurately how that all was, and then pay for it with interest.

In such conversation and thoughts the journey to Spyhov passed. After a clear day came a calm, starry night, so they did not halt for a night rest; three times, however, they fed the horses plentifully. They crossed the boundary while it was still dark, and at dawn, under the direction of a hired guide, they were on the land of Spyhov. Old Tolima held everything under an iron hand there, evidently, for barely had they entered the forest when two armed men came out toward them; but these, seeing that there were no troops, merely a small escort, not only let them pass without question, but conducted them through flooded places and swamps impassable for persons unacquainted with the district.

At the castle, Tolima and Father Kaleb received the guests. The tidings that their lord had come, brought back by pious people, flew like lightning through the castle. But when they saw how he had come from the hands of the Knights of the Cross, such a storm of threats and rage burst forth that if there had been a knight in the dungeons of Spyhov no human power could have saved him from an awful death.

Horsemen wished to mount immediately, gallop to the boundary, seize what Germans they could find, and cast their heads at the feet of Yurand; but Matsko curbed this wish of theirs, for he knew that Germans lived in towns and castles, while the village people were of the same blood as he and Yurand's men, though living under the constraint of foreigners. But neither shouts, nor uproar, nor the squeak of well-sweeps could rouse Yurand, whom they carried from the wagon to his room on a bearskin, and placed on a bed there. At his side remained Father Kaleb, his friend from years of youth, and his foster-brother,

who loved him as if he had been his own brother. . He began an imploring prayer that the Saviour of the world would restore to the unfortunate Yurand his eyes, his tongue, and his hand.

The road-weary travellers lay down to sleep after morning refreshment. Matsko woke when it was well on in the afternoon and gave command to call Tolima.

Knowing already from Hlava that Yurand, before his departure, had enjoined on all obedience to Zbyshko, and that he had given to him the inheritance of Spyhov through the mouth of Father Kaleb, he said to the old man in the voice of a superior, —

"I am the uncle of your young master, and until he returns my orders will be in force here."

Tolima inclined his gray head, which resembled the head of a wolf somewhat, and surrounding his ear with his hand, inquired, —

"Then are you the noble knight of Bogdanets?"

"I am," replied Matsko. " Whence do you know of me?"

"The young lord, Zbyshko, expected you here, and asked about you."

When he heard this, Matsko sprang to his feet, and forgetting his dignity cried, —

"Zbyshko in Spyhov?"

"He was here, lord; he went away two days ago."

"By the dear God! Whence did he come, and whither did he go?"

"He came from Malborg and stopped at Schytno on the way; whither he was going he did not tell us."

"Did he not tell you?"

"He may have told Father Kaleb."

"Ei, mighty God! Then we passed each other," said Matsko, slapping his thighs with his hands.

Tolima put his hand around his other ear, —

"What do you ask, lord? "

"Where is Father Kaleb?"

"He is with the old master, at his bedside."

"Bring him here! — But no — I will go myself to him."

"I will call him! " said the old man.

And he went out. But before he brought the priest Yagenka came in.

"Come hither! Dost thou know what? Zbyshko was here two days ago."

Yagenka's face changed in one moment, her legs, enclosed in tight leggings, could be seen trembling under her.

"Was he here, and has he gone?" asked she with a throbbing heart. "Whither?"

"Two days ago, but whither perhaps the priest knows."

"We must see the priest!" said she with a voice of decision.

After a while Father Kaleb came in. Thinking that Matsko was calling for him to inquire about Yurand, he said, anticipating the question, —

"He is sleeping yet."

"I have heard that Zbyshko was here!" exclaimed Matsko.

"He was; he went away two days ago."

"Whither?"

"He did not know himself whither. He went to search, — to the boundary of Jmud, where there is war now."

"By the dear God, tell me, father, what you know of Zybshko."

"I know only what he told me. He was in Malborg and gained powerful protection there; that of the brother of the Grand Master, who is the first knight among them. At his command Zbyshko has permission to search all the castles."

"For Yurand and Danusia?"

"Yes, but he was not searching for Yurand, since they told him that Yurand was not living."

"Tell from the beginning."

"Immediately; but I will draw breath and come to myself, for I am returning from the other world."

"How from the other world? "

"From that world to which a man does not go on horseback, but on prayer, and from the feet of the Lord Jesus, from whom I have begged for mercy on Yurand."

"You have asked for a miracle? Have you such power? *' asked Matsko with great curiosity.

"I have no power whatever, but the Saviour has. If he wishes, he will return to Yurand eye, tongue, and hand."

"He can if he wishes," answered Matsko. "Still you have asked for no small thing."

Father Kaleb made no reply, perhaps he had not heard, for his eyes did not yet indicate full presence of mind, and it was evident that he had forgotten himself altogether in

prayer. So now he covered his face with his hands and sat some time in silence; at last he shook himself, rubbed his eyelids, and then said, —

"Now inquire."

"How did Zbyshko win over to his side the Voyt of Samba?"

"He is not Voyt of Samba now."

"No matter. Take note of what I ask, and tell what you know."

"He won him at the tournament. Ulrich Von Jungingen is fond of encounters within barriers, so he met Zbyshko; for there was a multitude of knightly guests in Malborg and the Grand Master had arranged tournaments. The saddle girth burst on Ulrich's horse, and Zbyshko might have brought him down easily, but he, seeing that, struck his spear against the ground, and besides supported the tottering man."

"Hei! Well, seest thou?" cried Matsko, turning to Yagenka. " Ulrich fell to loving him for that?"

"Yes, for that. He would not meet him with sharp lances, or dull ones, and became his friend, Zbyshko, on his part, told him his sufferings, and he, because he cares for knightly honor, was inflamed with dreadful rage, and sent Zbyshko with a complaint to his brother. God grant him salvation for that, since there are not many among the Knights who love justice. Zbyshko told me too that Pan de Lorche assisted him much because they respect him there for his wealth and great family, and he gave testimony for Zbyshko in everything."

"But what came of the complaint, and the testimony?"

"This, that the Grand Master commanded severely the comtur of Schytno to send to Malborg at once all captives and prisoners in Schytno, not excepting Yurand himself. As to Yurand, the comtur answered that he had died of his wounds and was buried near the church there. Other prisoners he sent to Malborg, among them the idiot girl, but our Danusia was not among them."

"I know from Hlava," said Matsko, "that Rotgier, he who was slain by Zbyshko, mentioned such a girl. He said at the court of Prince Yanush that they had mistaken her for Yurand's daughter; and when the princess answered that they had seen and knew the real daughter of Yurand, who was not an idiot, he said, ' You are right, but we thought that the Evil One had changed her." ;

"The comtur wrote the same to the Grand Master: that that girl was not in prison, but under guard; that they had taken her from robbers, who swore that she was Yurand's daughter, who had been transformed."

"And did the Master believe that?"

"He did not know himself whether he was to believe or not, but Ulrich flashed up with still greater anger, and obtained from his brother this, — that he should send an official of the Order with Zbyshko to Schytno, which happened. When they arrived at Schytno they did not find the old comtur, Siegfried, for he had gone to the war against Vitold, toward the eastern castles. They found an assistant voyt, who commanded to open all the cellars and dungeons. They searched and searched, but found nothing. They took people also to testify. One told Zbyshko that much might be learned from the chaplain, for he could understand the dumb executioner; but the old comtur had taken the executioner with him, and the chaplain had gone to Krolevets to some church congress. They meet there often, and send complaints against the Knights of the Cross to the Pope, for a hard life have the poor priests in the lands of the Order."

"But it is a wonder to me that they did not find Yurand," remarked Matsko.

"It is evident that the old comtur liberated him earlier. There was more malice in this liberation than if they had simply taken life from him; they wanted that he should suffer before death as much, nay more, than a man of his position could go through, blind, speechless, and without his right hand. Fear God! Neither able to go home, nor to ask about the road, nor to beg for bread. They supposed that he would die under a fence, sometime, from hunger, or that he would be drowned in water. — What did they leave to him ? Nothing but the memory of what he had been, and the experience of wretchedness. And besides, it was torture upon torture! He might have been sitting somewhere near a church, or at the roadside, and Zbyshko might have passed by and not recognized him. Perhaps even he heard Zbyshko's voice and could not call to him. Hei! I cannot talk from tears! God performed a miracle that you met him, therefore I think that He will perform one still greater, though my unworthy and sinful lips are those which beg for it."

"And what more did Zbyshko say? Whither did he go? "

"He said this: 'I know that Danusia was in Schytno, but they have either killed her or removed her. Old Siegfried, ' s^id he, ' did that, and as God be my aid I shall not rest henceforth till I put hand on him."

"Did he say that? Then it is certain that he has gone to the eastern boundaries, but there is war there at present."

"He knew that there was war, and therefore he went to Prince Vitold. He said that he should be able to accomplish something against the Knights of the Cross through Vitold more quickly than through the king even."

"To Prince Vitold! " cried Matsko, springing up.

Then he turned to Yagenka, —

"Seest thou what sense? Did I not say the same? I foretold as true as life that we should have to go to Vitold."

"Zbyshko had the hope," said Father Kaleb, "that Vitold would burst into Prussia and capture the castles there."

"If they give him time he will not fail," answered Matsko. "Well! praise God, we know at least where to look for Zbyshko."

"Then we must go at once," said Yagenka.

"Be quiet!" cried Matsko. "It is not proper for attendants to give counsel."

And he looked at her significantly, as if reminding her that she was an attendant, so she recollected herself, and was silent.

Matsko thought for a while, and then said, —

"We shall find Zbyshko certainly, for he is nowhere else, except at the side of Prince Vitold; but it will be necessary to know whether he has anything else to seek in the world besides those heads of the Knights of the Cross which he has vowed to get."

"And how can that be known? " asked Father Kaleb.

"If I knew that that priest of Schytno had returned from the council I should like to see him. I have letters from Lichtenstein and can go with perfect safety."

"That was no council, it was only a meeting," said Father Kaleb, "and the priest must have returned long ago."

"That is well. Leave the rest to my head; I will take Hlava, two attendants with war horses, and go."

"And then to Zbyshko?" inquired Yagenka.

"And then to Zbyshko; but meanwhile thou wilt wait

here till I return from Schytno. I think that I shall not be gone longer than three or four days. The bones in me are strong, and toil is nothing new to me. But first I will beg you, Father Kaleb, for a letter to the chaplain of Schytno. He will believe me the more easily if I show him your letter, since priests have always more confidence in one another than in laymen."

"People speak well of that priest," answered Father Kaleb, "and if any one knows anything it is he."

Towards evening the letter was ready, and next morning before sunrise old Matsko was no longer in Spyhov.

CHAPTER XL.

YURAND woke from his long sleep in presence of Father Kaleb, and having forgotten in his sleep what had happened to him, and not knowing where he was, he began to feel of the bed and the wall near which the bed stood. But Father Kaleb seized him in his arms, and weeping from tenderness said,—

"It is I! Thou art in Spyhov! Brother Yurand! God has visited thee, but thou art among thy own. Pious people have brought thee home. Oh, brother Yurand! My brother! "

And pressing him to his breast, he kissed his forehead, his empty eyes, and, pressing him to his breast, again he kissed him. Yurand at first was as if stunned, and seemed to understand nothing, but at last he passed his left hand over his forehead and head, as if wishiflg to push back and scatter the heavy clouds of sleep and stupor.

"Dost thou hear and understand me?" asked Father Kaleb.

Yurand gave a sign with his head that he heard, then he reached with his hand for the silver crucifix captured by him once from a rich German knight; this he took from the wall, pressed it to his lips, to his breast, and returned it to Father Kaleb.

"I understand thee, brother. He remains to thee, and as He has brought thee out of the land of captivity, so He can return everything that was taken from thee."

Yurand pointed upward in sign that everything of his would be turned thitherward, wherewith his eyepits were filled with tears, and immense pain was depicted on his suffering face.

Father Kaleb, seeing this movement and' pain, felt convinced that Danusia was no longer alive, so he knelt at the bedside, and said, "O Lord, give her endless rest, and may eternal light shine on her; may she be in endless peace. Amen."

At this the blind man rose, and sitting on the bed, began to move his head and motion with his hand, as if to forbid Father Kaleb, and restrain him; but they were unable to

64 THE KNIGHTS OF THE CROSS.

understand each other, for at that moment old Tolima entered, and behind him the garrison of the castle, tried men, the foremost and oldest of the land tillers of Spyhov, foresters, and fishermen ; they came because tidings of the return of the master of Spyhov had spread over all the place. They embraced his knees, they kissed his hand, and burst into plaintive weeping at sight of that maimed old man, who in nothing reminded them of the former terrible Yurand, the crusher of the Knights of the Order, the victor in every encounter. But some of them, namely, those who had followed him in expeditions, were swept away by a whirlwind of anger, hence their faces grew pale and became stubborn. After a while they collected in a group and whispered, pushing one another with their elbows, and shoving, until finally one of the garrison of the castle, who at the same time was the blacksmith of Spyhov, stood forth, a certain Suhar; he approached Yurand, seized his feet, and said, —

"As soon as they brought you hither, lord, we wanted to move on Schytno, but that knight who brought you forbade us. Do you, lord, give permission, for we cannot remain as we are without vengeance. Let it be as it was aforetime. They have insulted us, but they will not go unpunished, they will not. We went against them at your command, we will go now under Tolirna, or without him. We must capture Schytno and make dog blood flow out of it, so help us God!"

"So help us God! " repeated other voices.

"To Schytno!"

"We must have blood! "

And immediately a flame seized their passionate Mazovian hearts. Foreheads were frowning, eyes flashing, here and there was heard the gritting of teeth. But after a while voices and gritting of teeth ceased, and the eyes of all were intent on Yurand.

His cheeks flushed at once, as if the former resolution had sprung up in him and the former ardor of battle. He rose and began to search along the wall with his hand. It seemed to the men that he was feeling for his sword, but this time his fingers met the cross which Father Kaleb had hung in its old place. He took it from the wall a second time, then his face became pallid, he turned to the men, raised his empty eyepits, and extended the crucifix in front of him.

Silence followed. It was evening in the world outside. Through the windows came the twittering of birds, which were settling for rest at the gables of the castle and in the linden-trees growing in the courtyard. The last ruddy sun-rays fell as they penetrated the chamber on the upraised cross and on the white hair of Yurand.

Suhar, the blacksmith, looked at Yurand, he looked around at his comrades, he looked at Yurand a second time, then he made the sign of the cross and left the room on tiptoe. After hini went the others in like silence, and only when they had stopped in the courtyard did they begin to whisper to one another.

"Well, and what?"

"Shall we not go, or how?"

"He did not permit."

"He leaves vengeance to God. It is clear that the soul has changed in him."

And so it had in reality.

Meanwhile in the chamber with Yurand remained only Father Kaleb, old Tolima, and with them Yagenka and Anulka, who, having seen a group of armed men passing through the court, came to see what was happening.

Yageuka, bolder and more certain of herself than was Anulka, approached Yurand now.

"God give you His aid, Knight Yurand," said she. "It is we who brought you hither from Prussia."

His face brightened at the sound of that youthful voice. Evidently he recalled in more detail everything that had happened on the Schytno road, for he began to give thanks, nodding his head, and placing his hand on his heart repeatedly. She told him how they had met him, how Hlava had recognized him, Hlava, Zbyshko's attendant, and finally how they had brought him to Spyhov. She said also of herself that she with her comrade carried the sword, the helmet, and the shield for the knight Matsko of Bog-danets, the uncle of Zbyshko, who had set out from Bog-danets to seek his nephew and had gone to Schytno, but in three or four days would return again to Spyhov.

At mention of Schytno Yurand did not fall, it is true, into such excitement as on the road the first time, but great alarm was expressed on his face. Yagenka assured him, however, that Matsko was as cunning as he was resolute, that he would let no man trick him; moreover he had letters from Lichtenstein; with these he could go everywhere

VOL. II. — 5

safely. These words calmed Yurand notably. It was clear too that he wished to ask about many other things, and being unable to do so, he suffered in soul; seeing this the quick girl said, —

"When we talk oftener we shall be able to say everything."

At this he smiled, stretched his hand toward her, and placing it on her head by feeling, he held it there a long time, as if blessing her. He was very grateful to her indeed; but besides, her youth pleased his heart, and that short, quick talk of hers, which reminded him of the twittering of birds.

From that time, whenever he was not praying, — and he prayed for whole days almost, — or when he was not sunk in slumber, he sought for her near by; and if she was not present he yearned for her voice, and in every way endeavored to let Father- Kaleb and Tolima know that he would like to have that charming youth near him.

And she came, for her honest heart took sincere compassion on him; and besides, the time passed more quickly in his company, while she was waiting for Matsko, whose stay in Schytno was prolonged in some way strangely. He was to return in three days; meanwhile the fourth and fifth day had passed. The sixth day, toward evening, the alarmed girl was just going to beg Tolima to send men out to inquire, when information was sent from the watch oak that horsemen were approaching Spyhov.

After a while hoofs clattered on the drawbridge and Hlava rode into the courtyard with another attendant. Yagenka, who had already hurried down from the upper chamber, and was waiting, ran to him before he could spring from the saddle.

"Where is Matsko?" asked she, with throbbing heart.

"He has gone to Prince Vitold, and commands you to stay here," answered the attendant

CHAPTER XLI.

YAGENKA, when she learned that she was to stay at Matsko's command in Spyhov, was unable to utter a word for a while from astonishment, sorrow, and anger; she merely looked with widely opened eyes at Hlava, who, understood well how disagreeable the news was which he had brought her.

"I should like," said he, "to give you sL report of what we have heard in Schytno, for we heard much that is new and important."

"And is it about Zbyshko?"

"No; but there is Schytno news —you know — "

"I understand. Let the boy unsaddle the horses, and you come with me."

And commanding the boy, she took Hlava upstairs with her.

"Why did Matsko leave us? why must we stay in Spyhov? and why did you return? " asked she in one breath.

"I returned," said Hlava, "because the knight Matsko commanded. I wanted to go to the war, but a command is a command. ' Thou wilt return/ said the knight; ' thou wilt take care of the lady of Zgorzelitse, and thou wilt wait for news from me. It may be,' said he, 'that thou wilt have to conduct her home, for, of course, she cannot go alone there."

"By the dear God! what has happened? Have they found Yurand's daughter? Did Matsko go not to Zbyshko, but only to find Danusia? Hast thou seen her? Hast thou spoken to her? Why didst thou not bring her, and where is she at present?"

When Hlava heard this avalanche of questions, he bent down to the knees of the lady and said, —

"Let it not cause anger to your grace that I do not answer all questions at once, for I cannot; but I will answer in turn one after another, if there be no hindrance."

"Well! Have they found her, or not?"

"No. But still there is certain news that she was in Schytno, and that they have taken her somewhere, perhaps to eastern castles."

"And we, why are we to stay in Spyhov? "

"Should she be found, as your grace sees, there would indeed be no reason to stay here."

Yagenka was silent, but her cheeks flushed.

"I thought, and I think now," said Hlava, "that we shall not snatch her alive from those dog brothers, but everything is in the Lord's hand. I must tell from the beginning. We went to Schytno. The knight Matsko showed Lichtenstein's letter to the under-voyt, and the under-voyt. since he had carried a sword behind Lichtenstein in his youth, kissed the seal before our eyes, received us hospitably, and suspected nothing. If we bad had some men near by we might have taken the castle, so far did he trust in us. There was no hindrance either in seeing the priest, we talked two nights through, and learned wonderful things, which the priest knew from the executioner."

"The executioner is dumb."

"Dumb, but he knows how to tell the priest everything by signs, and the priest understands the man as if he were speaking with the living word to him. Wonderful is that which has happened ; the finger of God must have been in it. That executioner cut off Yurand's hand, plucked the tongue from him, and burnt out his eye. He is of such sort that when a man is in question he shudders at no punishment; even were they to command him to tear a man to pieces with his teeth, he would do so. But he will not raise a finger on any girl, and should they command him to do so, no punishment would move him. He is in this state of mind for the reason that once he himself had an only daughter whom he loved wonderfully, and whom the Knights of the Cross — "

Here Hlava hesitated and did not know how to continue ; seeing which Yagenka said, —
"What do I care about an executioner's daughter?"

"It touches the affair," answered Hlava. "After our young lord cut up the knight Rotgier the old comtur Siegfried became almost insane. In Schytno they say that Rotgier was his son, but the priest denies that; though he confirms this, that never has a father loved a son more, and to gain revenge, he has sold his soul to the devil, as the executioner has witnessed. He talked to the dead man, as I to you; the corpse smiled at him from the coffin, gritted its teeth, and licked its lips with its black tongue when the old comtur promised the head of Pan Zbyshko.

But, since he could not get Pan Zbyshko then, he gave command to torture Yurand, and put Yurand's tongue and his hand into Rotgier's coffin. The corpse began to eat them raw — "

"Oh, terrible to hear such things! In the name of the Father, the Son, and the Holy Ghost!" said Yagenka, and rising, she threw a billet of wood on the fire, for it had grown dusk then.

"That is how it was," continued Hlava. "I do not know how it will be settled at the last judgment, for what belonged to Yurand must be returned to him. But how that will be done is beyond human reason. The executioner saw all this. So when the old corntur had sated the vampire with human flesh he went to offer him Yurand's daughter, for the dead man had whispered to him, as it seems, that he wanted to wash down his food with the blood of that innocent. But the executioner, who, as I have said, would do anything except to endure wrong done a girl, hid on the staircase. The priest says that he is not in his full mind, and is really a beast; but he understands that one thing, and when there is need, no man can equal him in cunning. He sat then on the stairs and waited for the comtur. The old comtur heard the breathing of the executioner, saw his gleaming eyes, and was frightened, for he thought it was the devil. Then the executioner gave the comtur a blow of his fist on the neck, thinking that would shock his spine so that there would be no sign left of violence; still he did not kill him. But Siegfried fainted and was sick from fright, and when he recovered, he feared to attack Yurand's daughter."

"But he took her away?"

"He took her away, and with her the executioner also. The old comtur did not know that it was he who had defended Danusia; he thought that it was some unknown power, good or evil. But he did not choose to leave the executioner in Schytno. He feared his testimony, or something, — he is dumb, it is true, but in case of a trial he might tell through the priest what he knows. So the priest said at last to the knight Matsko: ' Old Siegfried will not destroy Yurand's daughter now, for he is afraid; and though he should command another to do so, while the executioner is alive he will not desert her, all the more that he has defended her already."

"Did the priest know whither they had taken her?"

"He did not know exactly, but he heard that they said something about Ragneta, which castle is not far from the Lithuanian, or Jmud boundary."

"But what did Matsko say to this?"

"When he heard this he said to me next morning: * If this is true maybe we shall find her; but I must go with all my breath to Zbyshko, so that they should not bring him to a hook, as they brought Yurand. If they tell him that they will give her up if he comes himself for her, he will go, and then old Siegfried will wreak on him such vengeance for the sake of Rotgier as human eye has never witnessed."

"That is true! that is true!" cried Yagenka with fear. "Since that is why he hurried off he did well."

After a while, turning to Hlava again, she said, —

"But he was mistaken in sending you back. Why guard us here in Spyhov? Old Tolima can guard, and there you would be useful to Zbyshko, for you are strong and clever."

"But in case of need, who will take you, young lady, to Zgorzelitse ? "

"In case of need you will come here before them. They must send news through some one; let them send it through you — and you will take us then to Zgorzelitse."

Hlava kissed her hand and asked with emotion, —

"You will stay here meanwhile?"

"God is above the orphan! We will stay here."

"And it will not be dreary for you. What will you do here?"

"Beg the Lord Jesus to return happiness to Zbyshko, and to preserve you all in health."

When she had said this she wept heartily, and he bent to her knees again.

"You are just like an angel in heaven," said he.

CHAPTEE XLII.

BUT she wiped away her tears and told the attendant to follow her and declare the news to Yurand. She found him in a large chamber, sitting with Father Kaleb, Anulka, and old Tolima; a tame she-wolf was at his feet. The sexton, who was also a chorister, was playing on a lute, and singing of some old battle which Yurand had fought against the "foul knights," and they, with heads leaning on their hands, were listening in deep thought and sadness. It was bright in the room from moonlight. After a day almost sultry had come a calm evening which was warm. The windows were open, and in the moonlight one could see bugs, which were flying about in the linden-trees growing in the courtyard. ' In the chimney a few bits of brands were smouldering yet, at which an attendant was heating mead mixed with sweet herbs and strengthening wine.

The chorister, or rather the sexton and servant of Father Kaleb, had just begun a new song about the "victorious meeting." "Yurand is advancing, under him is his chestnut steed," when Yagenka came in and said, —

"May Jesus Christ be praised! "

"For the ages of ages! " answered Father Kaleb.

Yurand was sitting on a bench with arms, his elbows leaning on the arms; but when he heard Yagenka's voice he turned at once toward her and greeted her with his head, which was milk white.

"Zbyshko's attendant has come from Schytno," said the girl, "and has brought news from the priest. Matsko will not return, for he has gone to Prince Vitold."

"How not return? " inquired Father Kaleb.

Then she told everything which she had heard from Hlava concerning Siegfried; how he had taken vengeance for the death of Rotgier, concerning Danusia, how the old comtur wished to sacrifice her to Rotgier, so that he might drink her innocent blood, and how the executioner had defended her unexpectedly. She did not conceal even this, that Matsko had hope now that he and Zbyshko would find Danusia, free her, and bring her to Spyhov. For this reason precisely he had gone straight to Zbyshko, and commanded them to remain at Spyhov.

Her voice trembled at last as if with sorrow, or sadness, and when she had finished a moment of silence followed. But from the lindens was heard the singing of nightingales, which seemed to beat in through the open window in the manner of a rain shower and fill *he room. The eyes of all were turned to Yurand, who, with closed lids and head thrown back, did not give the least sign of life.

"Do you hear?" asked Father Kaleb at last.

He bent his head back still more, raised his left arm, and pointed to the sky.

The light of the moon fell straight on his face, on his white hair, on his eyepits, and there was in his countenance such suffering, and at the same time such a boundless surrender to the will of God, that it seemed to all that they were looking at a soul freed from bodily bonds, a soul which had separated once and forever from earthly life, expected nothing in it, and looked for nothing.

Again followed silence, and again no sound was heard save the trilling of nightingale voices filling the yard and the chamber. But great compassion seized Yagenka on a sudden, and childlike love, as it were, for that hapless old man; so, following her first impulse, she sprang to him, and grasping his hand, fell to kissing it and covering it with .tears at the same time.

"I too am an orphan," cried she from the depth of her swollen heart—"I am no young man, I am Yagenka of Zgorzelitse. Matsko took me to keep me from wicked people, but now I will stay with you till God gives you back Danusia."

Yurand did not exhibit the least astonishment, just as if he had known before that she was a girl, but.he gathered her in toward him and inclined her to his bosom; while she, continuing to kiss his hand, spoke on in broken and sobbing accents, —

"I will stay with you now, and Danusia will come back. After that I will go to Zgorzelitse. God is above orphans. The Germans killed my father too, but your love will live and come back to you. God the Merciful grant this; grant it also the Most Holy Mother, the Compassionate! "

Then Father Kaleb knelt on a sudden, and called in a solemn voice, —

"Kyrie eleison!"

" Chryste eleison!" responded Hlava and Tolima together.

All knelt down, for they understood that to be a litany repeated not only in time of death, but for the rescue from mortal peril of persons near and dear to us. Yagenka knelt, Yurand dropped from the bench to his knees, and they continued in a chorus, —

"Kyrie eleison! Chryste eleison! — O Father in Heaven, O God, have mercy on us! O Thou Son, the Redeemer., Lord of the world, have mercy on us! "

The voices of people and the imploring words: "Have mercy on us! " were mingled with the trilling of the nightingales.

All at once the tame she-wolf rose from the bearskin lying near Yurand's bench, approached the open window, rested her forepaws on it, and raising her triangular face toward the moon, began to howl in a low, plaintive voice.

CHAPTEK XLIII.

THOUGH Hlava adored Yagenka, and his heart was growing more and more toward the beautiful Anulka, his young and brave soul was rushing forth to war first of all. It is true that he turned back to Spyhov at Matsko's order because he was commanded; still he found a certain consolation in the idea that he would be to both ladies a guard and protector. But when Yagenka herself said, which moreover was true, that nothing threatened them in Spyhov, and that his duty was at the side of Zbyshko, he accepted the statement with gladness. Matsko was not his immediate superior, hence he could easily excuse himself before the old knight by saying that he had not remained in Spyhov because his rightful lady had commanded him to go to Zbyshko.

Yagenka thought that a man of Hlava's strength and skill could always be of service to Zbyshko, and might rescue him from more than one strait. He had for that matter given evidence of this during the prince's hunt, where Zbyshko had almost lost his life by the wild bull. All the more might he be of service in war, especially a war like that on the Lithuanian boundary. Hlava was in such a hurry to the field, that while returning with Yagenka from visiting Yurand, he implored her. and said, —

"I wish to bow down before your grace to beg a kind word for the journey."

"How is that?" inquired Yagenka; "do you wish to go to-day even ? "

"To-morrow morning before daylight, so that the horses may rest the night through. Jmud is terribly distant!"

"Then go, for thou wilt overtake the knight Matsko more easily."

"It would be difficult to do so. The old man is very strong in every labor, and he is a number of days in advance of me. Besides, he will go through Prussia to shorten the road, while I must go through forests. He has letters from Lichtenstein which he can show on the way; I have nothing to show but this to open a free passage before me."

And he placed his hand on the sword hilt at his side, seeing which Yagenka exclaimed, —

"Ah, but be careful! Since thou art going it is needful to reach the end of thy journey, and not stop in some dungeon of the Order. And in forests have a care for thyself, for there many wicked demons are living whom people honored before they turned to Christ. I remember how the knights Matsko and Zbyshko spoke of those things at my father's house."

"I remember, but I have no fear; for those are poor things without power, they have no influence. I will take care of those demons and the Germans also, should I meet any, if war only breaks out in earnest."

"But has it not broken out? Tell me, what hast thou heard among the Germans of war? "

At this the prudent fellow knitted his brows, was silent a moment, and said, —

"It has, and it has not. We inquired carefully about everything, and especially did the knight Matsko inquire, for he is cunning and can circumvent any German. He asks, as it were, about something else, or pretends friendship, but he never betrays himself in any way; and he hits the quick every time, and from each man draws out news as a fish is drawn out with a hook. Should your grace wish to listen patiently, I will tell. Prince Vitold, some years ago, having plans against the Tartars and wishing peace on the German side, yielded Jmud to the Order. There was great accord and friendship. He permitted the Knights to build castles; he even helped them. He and the Grand Master met on an island, they drank, they ate, they declared mutual friendship. Even hunting in those forests was not forbidden the Knights of the Cross, and when the poor Jmud men rose against the dominion of the Order, Prince Vitold helped the Germans, and sent his forces to aid them, whereupon people murmured throughout all Lithuania because he was attacking his own blood. The under-voyt of Schytno told us all this and praised the rule of the Knights in Jmud, saying that they sent to the people of that region priests who were to baptize them, and in time of hunger sent wheat to feed them also. Perhaps they sent wheat, for the Grand Master, who has more fear of God than others, ordered it, but the Knights carried off the children to Prussia, and insulted the women before the eyes of their brothers and husbands. If any man opposed they hanged him, and for that reason, young lady, there is war now."

"But Prince Vitold?"

"The Prince closed his eyes for a good while to the wrongs of this people and loved the Knights of the Order. Not long since the princess, his wife, went to Prussia, to Mal-borg itself, on a visit. They received her there as if she had been Queen of Poland. And this was not long ago, just lately! They covered her with gifts, and what feasts, tournaments, and various wonders there were no man could reckon. People thought that love would last forever between the Knights and Prince Vitold, till all on a sudden the heart changed in him."

"I think, from what my late father and Matsko said about Vitold that his heart changes often."

"Toward honest men never, but toward the Knights of the Cross often through this cause, that they themselves never keep faith in anything. Just now they wished Vitold to render up fugitives, and he answered that people of low estate he would give, but a free man he did not think of giving, since a free man has the right to live where it pleases him. Therefore the Knights and Vitold began to dispute, they wrote letters with complaints, they threatened each other. When the Jmud men heard of this they rose straightway and fell on the Germans. They cut down garrisons, they stormed castles, and now they are attacking even Prussia. Vitold not only is not restraining them, but he smiles at German vexation and sends aid to the Jmud men in secret."

"I understand," said Yagenka. "But if the aid is secret, there is no war yet."

"There is war with the Jmud men openly, and with Vitold in fact. The Germans are going from all sides to defend their outlying castles, and they would be glad to make a great raid on Jmud; but they must wait for this yet a long time, that is till winter, for the country is swampy and the Knights cannot fight there. Where a Jmud man goes safely, a German will stick fast; for that reason winter is the friend of the Germans. When frost comes the whole force of the Order will move, and Prince Vitold will go to strengthen the Jmud men — and he will go with permission of the King of Poland, for the king is his liege lord and is above the Grand Prince and all Lithuania."

"Then perhaps there will be a war with the King of Poland?"

"People say so; both there among Germans and here among us. For this reason the Knights are begging aid at all courts, and the cowls are burning their foreheads, as is usual with scoundrels, for of course the strength of the King is no jest, and Polish knights, should any one mention the Knights of the Cross, would spit on the palms of their hands that same instant."

Yagenka sighed on hearing this, and said, —

"A man has always a pleasanter life in this world than a woman, for, to take an example, thou wilt go to the war, just as Zbyshko and Matsko will, but we shall stay here in the house at Spyhov."

"How can it be otherwise, young lady? You will be here, but in all safety. Terrible even to-day is the name of Yurand to the Germans; I myself saw in Schytno how dread seized them straightway when they learned that Yurand is now in Spyhov."

"They will not come here, we know that, for the swamp defends us, and old Tolima, but it is grievous to stay here and have no tidings."

"When anything happens I will inform you. I knew before our visit to Schytno that two good fellows were preparing to go to the war of their own will from this place. Tolima cannot prevent them, for they are nobles from Lenkavitsa. Now they will go with me, and in case of need, I will hurry one of them hither immediately."

"God reward thee. I have known always that thou hast strong sense in every position, but

I shall be grateful till death for thy kind heart and for thy good-will toward me."

"Not wrong of any sort, but benefactions, have I received from you. The knight, your father, took me captive and gave me freedom without ransom, but to serve you was dearer to me than freedom. God grant me, my lady, to shed my blood for you."

"God conduct thee, and go with thee!" answered Yagenka, extending her hand to him.

But he preferred to bend down and kiss her feet, thus giving her greater honor; that done, he lifted his head, and without rising from his knees, said with timidity and submission, —

"I am a simple man, but a noble, and I am your faithful servant — so give me some keepsake for my journey.

Do not refuse this! You may be sure that the hour of battle harvest is approaching, and Saint George is my witness that I shall be at the front, and not in the rear ranks of it."

"For what keepsake do you ask?" inquired Yagenka, somewhat astonished.

"Provide me with any little scrap for the road, so that should it happen me to die, it would be easier for me to die beneath your ensign."

Again he bowed to her feet, and a second time he joined his hands and entreated, looking into her eyes; but on Yagenka's face sad distress appeared, and after a moment she answered, as with an outburst of involuntary sorrow, —

"But, my dear, do not ask me for that, for nothing could come of a gift from me. Whoever is happy, let her give a gift to thee, for that person might bring thee happiness. But to speak truth, what is there in me? — nothing but sadness! And what is there before me? — nothing save misery! Oi! I cannot get happiness for thee, or for any one, since I do not possess it myself, and I cannot bestow it. Oh, my poor Hlava! it is evil in the world at this time, it is, it is —"

She stopped suddenly, feeling that if she were to say one word more she would burst into weeping; and, as it was, something like a cloud passed before her eyesight. Hlava was moved immensely, for he understood that it was bitter for her to go home to the neighborhood of the attacking Stan and Vilk, and also bitter to remain in Spyhov, to which place earlier or later Zbyshko might return with Danusia. Hlava understood perfectly what was passing in the heart of the maiden, but he saw no help for her misfortune, hence he only embraced her feet again, repeating, —

"Hei! if I could die for you! If I could die for you! "

But she said, —

"Rise! Let Anulka gird thee for battle, or give thee some other remembrance, for she looks on thee gladly this long time."

And she called her. Anulka came out soon from the adjoining chamber, for, listening near the door, she had failed to show herself merely through timidity, since the wish of taking farewell of the shapely attendant was seething in the maiden. Hence she came out confused, frightened, with throbbing heart, with eyes in which there were

both tears and a dreamy expression, and dropping her lids, she stood before him bright as an apple blossom, and speechless.

For Yagenka, Hlava felt, besides the profoundest attachment, both reverence and honor, but he dared not rise to her in thought; as to Anulka, since he felt hot blood in his veins, he could not escape her enchantment. Now her beauty seized him by the heart, and especially her tears and confusion, through which love appeared, as the golden bed of a river appears through clear water. So he turned to her.

"You know that I am going to the war," said he; "perhaps I shall fall in it. Do you grieve for me?"

"I grieve! " answered she, in a thin, girlish voice. And that instant she began to shed tears, for she had them always in readiness. Hlava was moved to the uttermost and fell to kissing her hands, repressing, in presence of Yagenka, the desire for still more intimate kisses.

"Gird him, or give him a remembrance for the journey so that he may fight under your ensign," said Yagenka.

But it was not easy for Anulka to give him anything, for she was wearing a man's dress. She began to search; neither a ribbon nor a knot of any kind. The dresses of the two women were still in bark boxes, unopened since they had left Zgorzelitse; she fell therefore into no small anxiety, from which Yagenka relieved her by advising to give him her head net.

"In God's name! let it be the net!" said Hlava, rejoiced somewhat. "I will put it on my helmet — and unhappy will the mother of that German be who tries to remove it! "

Anulka raised both hands to her head, and after a little, bright streams of hair were scattered over her neck and shoulders; when Hlava looked at her thus, dishevelled and charming, his face changed. His cheeks flushed, and then he grew pale; he took the net, kissed it, and put it in his bosom, embraced still again the knees of Yagenka, and then Anulka with greater energy than was needed.

"Let it be that way! " said he, and went out of the room without uttering another syllable.

Though he was road-weary and unrefreshed, he did not lie down to sleep; he drank to kill that night, with the two nobles from Lenkavitsa, who were going to Jmud with him. But he did not lose his head; at the first dawn he was in the courtyard, where horses were waiting, ready saddled.

In the rear wall a membrane window was pushed aside slightly, and through the opening blue eyes looked into the courtyard. Hlava saw this, and wished to move toward them to show the net fixed to his helmet, and to take one more farewell, but Father Kaleb and old Tolima hindered him. They had come down to give counsel for the journey.

"Go to the court of Prince Yanush," said Father Kaleb. "Maybe the knight Matsko has stopped there. In every case thou wilt find sure tidings, since for thee there is no lack of acquaintances in that place. The roads from there to Lithuania are known, and it is easy to find a guide through the forests. If thou wish surely to go to Pan Zbyshko, go not to Jmud directly, for a Prussian force is there, but take the road through Lithuania. Look to this too: the Jmud men might kill thee before thou couldst say who thou art, but the case is different if thou come from Prince Vitold. For the rest, God bless thee, and the two other knights. May ye return in health and bring back the maiden, for which intention I shall lie in cross form each day after vespers till the first stars appear."

"I thank you, father, for the blessing," said Hlava. "To rescue that victim from those devilish hands is not easy; still, all things are in the hands of the Lord Jesus, and it is better to be cheerful than downcast."

"Of course it is; therefore I do not lose hope. Yes — hope strengthens us, though the heart's warnings are not useless. The worst is that Yurand himself, if her name is but mentioned, points toward the sky, as if he were showing her there."

"Indeed, he may see her there, after he lost his eyes."

And the priest began to speak partly to Hlava and partly to himself, —

"It does happen this way: when a man loses his earthly eyes, just then he sees that which no one else can see. It happens this way, it happens! But it does seem impossible that God should permit wrong to such an innocent. For what harm had she done to the Knights of the Cross? None! And, mind thee, she was as innocent as a lily of the Lord, and so good to people, and she was like a bird of the field, which is singing its song! God loves children and has pity for human suffering. Nay, if they have killed her He might resurrect her, as be did Piotrovin, who, after he had risen from the grave, lived for years.

Go in health, and may the hand of God guard you all and guard her."

Then he returned to the chapel to say morning mass. Hlava mounted his horse, bowed still again before the closed window, and rode away, for day had come entirely.

voi-. ii. — 6

CHAPTER XLIV

PRINCE YANUSH of Mazovia and the princess had gone with a part of their court to the fishing of the spring season in Chersk, for they loved the sight greatly and considered it their foremost pleasure. Hlava learned from Mikolai of Dlugolyas many important things touching private affairs as well as questions of war. He learned, first of all, that the knight Matsko had evidently given up his intention of going to Jmud directly across the "Prussian hindrance," for he had been in Warsaw some days before, where he had found Prince Yanush and the princess. Concerning war, old Mikolai confirmed the reports which Hlava had heard in Schytno. All Jmud had risen as one man against the Germans, and Prince Vitold not only did not* assist the Knights of the Cross, but, without declaring war yet, and while deluding them with discussions, he strengthened Jmud with money, with men, with horses and wheat. Meanwhile both he and the Order were sending envoys to the Pope, to the Emperor, to all Christian rulers. They accused each other of faith-breaking, deceit, and treachery. From Prince Vitold went, with letters declaring these things, the wise Mikolai of Reniev, who understood how to unravel the threads twisted into each other by German cunning. He did this by showing accurately the measureless wrongs inflicted on the lands of Jmud and Lithuania.

At the same time, since at the Diet of Vilno the bonds between Lithuania and Poland had been strengthened, the hearts of the Knights of the Cross were growing timid, because it was easy to foresee that Yagello, as the overlord of all lands which were under the ruling of Vitold, would stand during war on his side. Count Yan Sayn, the comtur of Grudziansk, and Count Schwartzberg, of Dant-zig, went at command of the Grand Master to. Yagello to inquire what they were to expect of him. The king gave no answer, though they brought gifts to him, — precious vessels and hunting-hawks. Therefore they threatened war, but insincerely, since they knew well that the Grand Master and the Chapter were in their souls afraid of the terrible

THE KNIGHTS OF THE CROSS. 83

power of Yagello, and wished to defer the day of defeat and vengeance.

Hence all discussions broke like a spiderweb, especially those that were carried on with Vitold. In the evening, after Hlava's arrival at Warsaw, came fresh news to the castle: Bronish of Tsiasnota came, an attendant of Prince Yanush, whom he had sent somewhat earlier to Lithuania for tidings, and with him came two considerable princes of Lithuania with letters from Vitold, and from the Jmud men. The tidings were threatening. The Knights were preparing for war. They had strengthened castles, they had made powder, they had made stone cannon-balls, they had brought to the boundary camp-followers and knighthood, while divisions of lighter cavalry and infantry had already crossed the boundaries of Jmud and Lithuania from the direction of Ragneta, Gotteswerder, and other boundary castles. In forest depths, in fields, in villages, shouts of war were heard, and every evening, above the dark sea of forests, flames were blazing already. Vitold had taken Jmud under his evident protection at last; he had sent his managers, and had appointed as leader of the armed people Skirvoillo, famed for bravery. Skirvoillo attacked Prussia, he burnt, destroyed, ravaged. Prince Vitold himself hurried off troops toward Jmud;

some castles he provisioned, others, as, for instance, Kovno, he destroyed, lest it might become a stronghold for the Order; and it was no longer a secret to any man that when winter came and frost bound the swamps and wet places, or even earlier should the summer prove a dry one, a mighty war would begin, which would cover Jmud, Lithuania, and Prussian regions; for if the king aided Vitold, the day must come in which the German wave would either cover half a world, or be hurled back for long centuries into the bed occupied by it earlier.

But this was not to happen straightway. Meanwhile the groan of the Jmnd people was heard throughout the world, — their despairing complaints of wrong and their calls for justice. That letter of the unfortunate people had been read in Cracow, in Prague, at the court of the Pope, and in other capitals of western Europe. To Prince Yanush open letters had been brought by those people who had come with Bronish. Hence not a few in Mazovia put hands to their . sword-hilts involuntarily, considering in spirit whether they would not better place themselves under Vitold's banner of their own wish. They knew that Vitold,

the Grand Prince, liked the experienced Polish nobility, who were as stubborn in battle as the Lithuanians and Jmud men, and besides, better armed and better disciplined. Some were urged on by hatred for the ancient foes of the Polish race, and still others by compassion. "Listen to us, listen!" cried the Jmud people to kings, princes, and all nations. "We have been free and are people of good blood, but the Order wants to turn us into captives! They are not working for our souls, but for our land and our property. Our misery is such that we must beg or become robbers! How can they wash us in the water of baptism when their own hands are foul? We desire baptism, but not in blood and with the sword; we want religion, but we want it of the kind which is taught by honorable rulers like Yagello and Vitold. Hear us and save us, for we are perishing! The Knights of the Cross withhold baptism so as to oppress the more easily. Not priests are they sending, but hangmen; they have taken bees, cattle, all the fruits of the earth from us; now we are not permitted to fish, or to kill a wild beast in the forest. We are imploring ! Listen to us! for look, they have bent our once free necks to night work at their castles; they have borne away our children as hostages; they dishonor our wives and daughters before the eyes of their husbands and fathers. It would be more fitting for us to groan than to speak! Our families they have burned with fire; they have taken off to Prussia men of high standing, great persons,— the Korkutsie, Vassygin, Svolek, and Sangayla; they murder us, and are gulping our blood as if they were wolves. Oh, listen to us! We are in every case human beings, not wild beasts. Why is it that we turn to implore the Holy Father to command that we be christened by Polish bishops ? Because with our whole spirit we are thirsting for Christian baptism, but baptism in the water of love, not in the warm blood of extermination." Thus and similarly did the Jmud people complain; hence, when their complaints were heard at the court of Mazovia straightway a number of tens of knights and nobles decided to go and assist them, understanding that there was no need to ask Prince Yanush for permission, even for this reason that his wife was Vitold's sister. Universal rage of heart boiled up when they learned from Bronish and the others that many noble youths who were hostages in Prussia, unable to endure the insults and cruelties inflicted on them by the Knights, had committed suicide.

Hlava was rejoiced at the willingness of the Mazovian knighthood, for he thought that the more men went from Poland to Prince Vitold, the hotter would the war grow, and the more surely would they effect something against the Knights of the Order. He was comforted by this also, that he would see Zbyshko, to whom he had grown attached, and the old knight Matsko, of whom he had this thought, that he was worth looking at in action. And with these men he would see new wild regions, fresh cities, new knighthoods and armies, and finally Prince Vitold himself, whose glory was thundering widely through the world at that time.

So he resolved to go with "great and hurried marches," stopping in no place longer than was needed to rest horses. Those attendants who had come with Bronish and other Lithuanians to the court of Prince Yanush, and knew the roads and every passage, were to conduct him and all Mazovian volunteers from village to village, from city to city, and through wild and vast forests, with which Mazovia, Lithuania, and Jmud were covered for the most part.

CHAPTER XLV.

IN a forest about five miles west of Kovno, which Vitold himself had destroyed, were assembled the main forces of Skirvoillo, who, in case of need, moved them from place to place with the speed of a thunderbolt, and made swift attacks either across the Prussian boundaries or on large aud small castles still in the hands of the Order, thus rousing the flame of war throughout the whole country. It was in that forest that his faithful attendant found Zbyshko, and in his company Matsko, who had arrived only two days before. After the greeting with Zbyshko, Hlava slept the whole night like a dead man, and only next day, in the evening, did he go forth to greet the old knight, who, being tired and out of humor, received him in anger, and inquired why, according to orders given, he had not remained in Spyhov; and Matsko was pacified in some degree only when Hlava, finding a favorable moment while Zbyshko was not in the hut, justified himself by quoting the express command of Yagenka. He said also that in addition to her command and his inborn inclination for warfare, he was led to those regions by the wish to send in case of need a herald with information to Spyhov. "The lady," said he, "whose soul is like that of an angel, prays for Yuraud's daughter, though she prays against her own interest. But there must be an end to everything. If Yurand's daughter is no longer alive, may God give eternal light to her, for she was as innocent as a lamb; but should she be found, the need would come to let the lady know this at the earliest, so that she might go from Spyhov before, and not after the return of Yurand's daughter, so as not to seem pushed out with shame and without honor."

Matsko listened unwillingly, repeating from moment to moment: "That is not thy affair." But Hlava, having resolved to speak plainly, paid no heed, and at last he said,—

"Better the lady had remained at home; to her this journey has been of no service. We have persuaded the poor girl that Yurand's daughter is not living, but it may turn out the opposite."

"And who said that she was not living, unless thee?" inquired Matsko with auger. "Thou shouldst have .held thy tongue behind thy teeth. I brought her away, for she was afraid of Stan and Vilk."

"That was a mere excuse," answered Hlava. "She might have remained at home without danger, for they would have hindered each other. But you were afraid, lord, that in case of the death of Yurand's daughter niy lady might be lost to Pan Zbyshko, and that is why you "brought her."

"How hast thou grown so insolent? Art thou a belted knight, or a servant? "

"A servant, but her servant; for I am watching that no harm should come to my lady."

Matsko grew gloomily thoughtful, for he was not rejoiced at his own course. More than once he had blamed himself for taking Yagenka from home, for he felt that in taking the maiden to Zbyshko some kind of injury had been done her, and, in case Danusia were found, much more than injury. He felt also that there was truth in the bold speech of Hlava, and that he had taken the girl mainly to keep her, if need be, for Zbyshko.

"That had not come to my head!" but he said this to befog both himself and Hlava; "she herself insisted on coming."

"She insisted, for we persuaded her that the other was no longer in this world, and that her brothers would be safer without her than with her. That is why she left home."

"Thou didst tell her! " cried Matsko.

"I — and it was my fault. But now we must show her how things are. We must do something, lord. If not, better we perished."

"What wilt thou do here?" asked Matsko, impatiently, "in a war with such an army? If anything better comes it will be in July, for here there are two seasons of war for Germans, — the winter, and a dry summer. But seest thou, there is no fire yet, there is only smouldering. Very likely Prince Vitold has gone to Cracow to inform the king, and gain from him permission and assistance."

"But there are castles of the Order near by. If we could take about two of them, perhapa we might find Yurand's daughter, or learn of her death."

"Or that she is not dead."

"In every case Siegfried took her in this direction. They told us that in Schytno, and we ourselves always thought so."

"But hast thou seen the army here? Come out behind the tent and look. Some have only clubs, and some have bronze swords inherited from their great-grandfathers."

"Yes. I have heard, though, that they are splendid men in battle."

"But they cannot capture castles with their naked breasts, especially castles of the Order."

Further conversation was interrupted by the arrival of Zbyshko and Skirvoillo, the leader of the Jmud forces, — a man of small stature, about as tall as an armor-bearer, but strong in body and broad-shouldered. He had a breast so projecting that it seemed almost a hump, and disproportionately long arms, which extended well-nigh to his knees. In general, he reminded one of Zyndram, the famed knight with whom Matsko and Zbyshko had become acquainted in Cracow; he had an immense head, therefore, and was somewhat bow-legged. It was said of him, too, that he understood war well. His life had been spent in the field, hence against Tartars, with whom he had fought many years in Russia, and against Germans, whom he hated as he did pestilence. In those wars he had learned Russian, and later, at the court of Vitold, he learned something of Polish; he knew German, or at least repeated three words in it, — fire, blood, death. His immense bead was always full of plans, and war stratagems, which the Knights of the Cross were unable either to foresee or to baffle; hence they feared him in the neighboring provinces.

"We have been talking of an attack, uncle," said Zbyshko, with unusual animation, "and have come so that you might give your experienced opinion."

Matsko seated Skirvoillo on a pine log which was covered with a bearskin; then he ordered the servant to bring a small keg filled with mead, which the knights began to draw into tankards and drink, for it strengthened them properly; then Matsko inquired, —

"Do ye wish to go on an expedition?"

"To burn German castles."

"Which? Ragneta, or New Kovno? "

"Ragneta," answered Zbyshko. "Three days ago we were at New Kovno and they beat us."

"They did indeed," said Skirvoillo.

"How did they doit?"

"They did it well."

"Wait," said Matsko, "for I know not this country. Where is New Kovno, and where is Ragneta ? "

"From here to Old Kovno is not quite five miles," said Zbyshko, "and from Old to New Kovno the same distance. The castle is on an island. We wanted to go over to it, but they beat us at the passage. They followed us half a day, till we hid in this forest, and our men were so scattered that some of them only turned up this morning."

"But Ragneta?"

Skirvoillo stretched forth his arm, as long as a tree branch, toward the north, and said, —

"Far! far!"

"Just because it is far should we go," added Zbyshko. "There is peace there, because all the armed men in that region have joined us. The Germans in Ragneta expect no attack, hence we shall strike on men off their guard."

"That is true," said Skirvoillo.

"Do you think that we can take the castle?" asked Matsko.

Skirvoillo shook his head in sign of denial.

"The castle is strong," added Zbyshko, "by chance alone could we take it. But we shall ravage the country, burn towns and villages, destroy storehouses, and, above all, take captives, among whom may be considerable people, and such the Knights of the Cross ransom willingly, or else exchange for them." Here he turned to Skirvoillo: "You have acknowledged, prince, that I speak justly; and now consider: New Kovno is on an island. There we shall not destroy villages, drive away cattle, or take captives. And besides, they have just beaten us. Ei! let us go to a place where they are not expecting us at this moment."

"The victor is the last man to think of surprise," muttered Skirvoillo.

Here Matsko began, and began by supporting Zbyshko's opinion, for he understood that the young man had greater hope of learning something at Ragneta than at Old Kovno, and that at Ragneta he could more easily capture some considerable person whom he might exchange. He thought, too, that in every case it was better to go farther, and slip into a country less guarded, than to rush onto an island which was defended by nature, and guarded besides by a strong castle and a victorious garrison. As a man expe-

rienced in war, he spoke clearly and gave reasons so convincing that they might have satisfied any man. Both listened carefully. Skirvoillo moved his brows from time to time, as if in sign of agreement, and muttered: "He speaks justly." At last he pushed in his immense head between his broad shoulders, so that he seemed altogether a humpback, and fell to thinking deeply.

After a certain time he rose, and, without saying more, began to take leave.

"But, prince, how is it to be?" inquired Matsko. ""Whither are we to go? "

"To New Kovno," answered Skirvoillo, briefly.

And he passed out of the hut.

Matsko and Hlava looked for some time at Zbyshko in astonishment, then the old knight struck his palms on his thighs and cried, —

"Tfu! Just like a log! That is as if a man were to listen and listen and never hear anything but his own thought. It is too bad to wear one's lips out on — "

"I have heard that he is that kind of man," said Zbyshko, "and to tell the truth, all people here are stubborn as few are. They listen to another man's opinions and then act as if he had blown against the wind."

"But why did he consult us? "

"We are belted knights, and he did it to consider the two sides. But he is not stupid."

"At New Kovno perhaps they expect us less than at any place," remarked Hlava, "for this very reason, that just now they have beaten you. In this he is right."

"Let us go, then, to look at those men I lead," said Zbyshko, who felt stifled in the tent; "I must tell them to be ready."

And they went out. Night had fallen, a night dark and cloudy, lighted only by camp fires, at which Jmud men were sitting.

CHAPTER XLVI.

FOR Matsko and Zbyshko, who had served formerly under Vitold, and had seen warriors enough from Jmud and Lithuania, this camp had no new sight; but Hlava looked at it curiously, as he considered what might be expected of those men in battle, and compared them with the knighthood of Germany and Poland.

The camp stood on a plain surrounded by swamps and a pine forest, hence defended from attack perfectly, since no other army could wade through those treacherous morasses. The plain itself on which the huts stood was muddy and sticky, but they had covered it with fir and pine branches crosswise, and so thickly that men rested on them as firmly as on dry earth. For Prince Skirvoillo they had built hurriedly "numi," or Lithuanian huts of round logs and earth; for the more considerable people a number of huts had been made of branches; common men, warriors, were sitting around fires beneath the open sky, having as defence against changes of weather and rain only sheepskins and hides which they wore on their naked bodies. In the camp no one was sleeping yet, for the men, having no work to do since the last defeat, had slept in the daytime. Some were sitting or lying around bright fires, fed by dry wood and the branches of briars; others were digging in the half-dead and ash-covered embers, from which came the odor of the usual food of Lithuanians, roasted turnips, and also the odor of partly cooked flesh. Between the fires were seen piles of arms, placed conveniently, so that in case of need it would be easy for each man to grasp his own weapon. Hlava looked curiously at spears with long, narrow heads forged of tempered metal; at clubs of young oak-trees, into which spikes or flints had been driven, at short-handled axes, like those of Poland, which mounted knights used, and axes with handles almost as long as those of a halberd, with which men on foot fought. There were also bronze weapons handed down from old times when iron was little used in those remote regions. Some swords were of bronze also, but most were of good steel brought from Novgorod. Hlava took in his hands spears,

swords, axes, pitchy bows which had been scorched; by the light of the camp-fires he tested their quality. There were not many horses near the fires, for they were feeding at a distance in the forest and on fields under guard of watchful herdsmen; but as the most distinguished boyars wished to have their steeds near by, there were in the camp some tens of them fed from the hands of slaves. Hlava wondered at the shape of those animals, small beyond comparison, with strong necks, and in general so strange that Western knights considered them a distinct beast of the forest, more like unicorns than genuine horses.

"Bulky war steeds are of no use here," said the experienced Matsko, thinking of his old campaigns with Vitold, "for a big horse will mire at once in soft places, but one of these little nags will go through any place, almost as a man would."

"But on the field," said Hlava, "these beasts cannot overtake the great German horses."

"They can indeed. And besides, the German will not escape his Jmud enemy, nor will he overtake him, for the Jmud horse is as swift, if not swifter, than the Tartar."

"Still to me this is wonderful; the Tartar captives whom I saw brought in by the knight Zyh were not large, and any horse might bear one of them, but these are sturdy fellows."

The men were in truth well-bodied. By the fires were evident, under skins and coats of sheepskin, broad breasts and strong shoulders. Man for man they were rather thin, but tall and bony; in general they surpassed in size the inhabitants of other parts of Lithuania, for they lived on richer and better lands, where famines, which tortured that region at one time and another, put themselves in evidence more rarely. The Grand Prince's castle was in Vilno; to Vilno went princes from the East and the West; embassies went there, foreign merchants went; so the citizens of the place and the inhabitants of the region about grew acquainted with foreigners somewhat. In Jmud the foreigner appeared only under the form of a Knight of the Cross, or a Knight of the Sword, who brought into remote forest villages conflagration, captivity, baptism in blood; hence each man there was sterner, ruder, and closer to the old time, more unbending toward every new thing, more a defender of old customs, old ways of warfare, and the ancient religion, because the religion of the Cross waa

taught, not by a mild herald of the gospel, with an apostle's love, but by an iron-clad German monk, having in him the soul of an executioner.

Skirvoillo, and the more important princes and boyars, had become Christian already, since they had followed the example of Yagello and Vitold. Others, even the rudest and wildest warriors, carried in their bosoms a dim feeling that the end and the death of their old world and old faith was coming; and were ready to bend their heads before the Cross, should it only be a cross not raised by Germans, not raised by hands that were detested. "We implore baptism," cried they to all princes and peoples; "but remember that we are human, that we are not wild beasts to be given away, bought and sold." Meanwhile, since the old faith was dying, as a fire dies when no one casts a fresh stick on it, and since hearts were turned from the new faith which German preponderance represented, in their souls a vacuum was created, and fear with dreadful sorrow for the past, and deep sadness. Hlava, who from childhood had grown up in the jo\'7d T ous bustle of soldiers' life, with songs and sounding music, saw for the first time a camp so mournful and so silent. Scarcely here and there, near the fires of Skirvoillo's remotest huts, were heard the sounds of a pipe or a whistle, or the words of a low song hummed by a "burtinikas." The warriors were listening with bowed heads and eyes fixed on the light. Some were squatted in groups around the fires, with their elbows resting on their knees and their faces hidden by their hands, and covered with skins, like ravening beasts of the forest. But when they raised their heads toward the passing knights, a gleam of light from the fire showed blue eyes and mild faces, not at all fierce or robber-like, but resembling much more the faces of wronged and sad children. At the outskirts of the camping-ground, on mosses, lay those wounded warriors whom they had been able to bring in from the last battle. Soothsayers, or so-called "labdarysi" and "seitons," were muttering incantations above them and dressing their wounds, to which they applied healing herbs as the men lay there patiently in silence, enduring pain and torment. From among distant trees, from the direction of fields and meadows came the whistling of horseherds; at intervals wind rose, whirling the smoke of the camp around and filling with its voice the dark forest. As night advanced the fires became dimmer and died out;

94 THE KNIGHTS OF THE CROSS.

silence came down and intensified that picture of gloom and of mental depression.

Zbyshko gave out orders to the men whom he had brought, and with whom he could speak easily, for among them was a small number of Plotsk people; then he turned to his attendant, Hlava, and said,—

"Thou hast seen enough; it is time to sleep now."

"Of course I have seen enough," answered Hlava, "but I do not rejoice much at what I have seen, for it is evident in a moment that the people are beaten."

"Twice; four days ago at the castle, and the next day at the crossing. And now Skirvoillo wants to go for the third time, to pass through the third defeat."

"How is it that he does not understand that with such troops he cannot succeed against Germans? Pan Matsko told me, and now I myself see, that they must be poor men for combat."

"In this thou art mistaken, for they are warlike as few men on earth are. But they fight in a crowd, while the Germans fight in ranks. If you break the German line, a Jmud man will put down a German quicker than a German can put down a Jmud man. The Germans know this, close in, and stand like a stone wall."

"As to taking castles, of course there is no word to be said of that," remarked Hlava.

"Well, there are no materials for doing so," answered Zbyshko. "Prince Vitold has the materials, and till he comes we shall not get any castle, unless by chance or through treason."

Thus conversing, they reached the tent, before which a large fire was kept up by servants, and in it smoked meat prepared by them. It was damp in the tent and cold, so that both knights, and with them Hlava, sat down before the fire on rawhides. After they had refreshed themselves they tried to sleep, but sleep they could not. Matsko turned from side to side, and saw that Zbyshko, sitting near > the fire, had embraced both knees with his arms.

"Listen! " said he. "Why didst thou advise to go far away to Ragneta, and not near by to this Gotteswerder ? Why didst thou propose that? "

"Because something told my soul that Danusia is in Ragneta — and there they are less on guard than here."

"There was no time to talk long, for I myself was weary, and after the defeat thou wert collecting men through the

forest. But now tell me truly: Dost thou wish to search for that ghi?"

"That is no girl; she is my wife."

Then silence came, for Matsko knew well that there was no reply to that answer. If Danusia had been only Yurand's daughter he would, beyond doubt, have asked Zbyshko to think no more of her; but in view of the sacred-ness of marriage, it was simply a duty to search for her, and Matsko would not have put such a question had it not been that he had seen neither the betrothal nor the wedding, and thought always of Yurand's- daughter as a maiden.

"Ah!" said he, after a while, "all that I could inquire of thee for two days past I have inquired, and thou hast said that thou knowest nothing."

"I have said so because I know nothing, save this, that God's anger is on me."

Hlava, straightening up from the bearskin, rose, and turning his ear, began to listen carefully and with curiosity.

"While sleep does not take sense from me," said Matsko, "talk on. What hast thou seen, what hast thou done, what hast thou accomplished in Malborg?"

Zbyshko put back the hair which, uncut in front for a long time, reached down over his brow, sat a while in silence, and then began, —

"Ah, if God would only let me know as much of my Danusia as I know of Malborg! You ask what I saw there ? I saw the measureless strength of the Order, supported by all kings and all nations, and which is such that I know not whether anything on earth has power to conquer it. I saw a castle which no one save perhaps the Roman Caesar can equal. I saw treasures beyond calculation, I saw arms, I saw armored monks, knights, and soldiers as numerous as ant-swarms, and relics as many as the Holy Father in Rome has. I tell you that the soul just grew benumbed in me, for I thought thus: how is any one to attack them; who can overcome them; who can stand against them; who are the people who will not be broken by the strength of those Knights of the Order? "

"We! perdition take their mother! " cried Hlava, unable to restrain himself.

Zbyshko's words seemed strange also to Matsko, and though he wished to learn all about the adventures of his nephew, he interrupted him.

"But hast thou forgotten Vilno?" asked he. "And are the times few that we have fought shield to shield, face to face with them ? And hast thou forgotten what ill-success they had in meeting us — and how they complained of our stubbornness, saying that it was not enough to sweat horses and break lances, that they had to take our lives, or give their own up? There were men from foreign lands also who challenged us — but all went away in disgrace. Why hast thou grown there thus softened ? "

"I have not grown softened, for I fought in Malborg where men met with sharp lances. But you do not know all the strength of those people."

The old man grew angry.

"But dost thou know all the Polish strength? Hast thou seen our banners assembled ? Thou hast not. But the German strength rests on injustice to man, and on treachery; for there is not a finger's length of land where they are that belongs to them. Our princes took them in as a beggar is taken to a house — where gifts are given him; but they, when they had grown in strength, bit the hand that fed them, as a shameless mad dog might do. They gathered in lands, they took cities by treachery, that is where their strength lies! But though all the kings on earth went to aid them, the day of judgment and vengeance is approaching them."

"You asked me to tell what I saw, and now you are angry. Better let me be silent," said Zbyshko.

Matsko muttered for a time as if angry, but after a while calmed himself, and continued, —

"Well, the case is like this: A pine-tree, immense, as a tower, stands in the forest before a man; he thinks: 'That will stand for the ages of ages;' but let him give a good blow with the back of an axe, the tree will sound hollow, aud the dust of decay will drop from it. Such is the might of the Order. I asked thee to tell what thou hast done there, what thou hast accomplished. Hast thou met a man at sharp lances? — tell that to me."

"I have. With insolence and impoliteness did they receive me in the first days, for it was known to them that I had met Rotgier. Perhaps something ill would have happened me had I not gone with a letter from Prince Yanush; besides, De Lorche, whom they reverence, guarded me from their malice. But later came feasts and tournaments, during which the Lord Jesus blessed me. You have heard that Ulrich, the Grand Master's brother, took me into

his affection and gave a written command from the Master himself to deliver Danusia into my hands."

"People told us," replied Matsko, "that his saddle-girth burst, and seeing this thou didst refuse to strike him."

"I raised my lance point, and from that moment he loved me. Ei, dear God! but he gave me strong letters, with which I might go from castle to castle and search. I thought that the end of my torment and trouble had come — but now I am helpless here, sitting in a wild region, suffering in loneliness; day after day I am sadder and more tormented."

Here he was silent for a while, then he hurled a piece of wood into the fire with all his might, so that sparks shot up, and a burning brand with them.

"Yes," said he, "if that poor girl is groaning here somewhere in a castle, and thinks that I have forgotten her, may sudden death not escape me! "

And so much was there burning in him of evident impatience and pain that again he threw wood into the fire, as if carried away by a blind sudden pang, and all were astonished greatly, for they had not supposed that he loved Danusia to that extent.

"Restrain thyself!" exclaimed Matsko. "How was it with that letter? Did the comturs wish to disobey the Grand Master?"

"Command yourself, lord," said Hlava. "God will comfort you — perhaps quickly."

Tears glittered in Zbyshko's eyes, but he composed himself somewhat.

"The traitors opened castles and prisons," said he. "I went to all places. I searched till the war broke out — then, in Gerdavy Von Heideck, the voyt told me that military law changed everything, that letters of safe-conduct given in peace time were meaningless. I challenged him right there, but he would not meet me, and gave command to put me out of the castle."

"And in others?" inquired Matsko.

"From all the same answer. In Krolevets the comtur, who is Von Heideck's chief, was unwilling even to read the Master's letter; he declared that war was war, and told me to be off while I had a sound head on my shoulders. I asked for information in other parts — the same story everywhere."

VOL. II. — 7

"I know now," said the old knight. "It is clear that thou wilt effect nothing; thou hast chosen to come here, where at least revenge may succeed with thee."

"True. I thought also that I might take captives and seize some castles, but these men cannot take castles."

"Hei! wait till Prince Vitold himself comes; then it will be otherwise."

"God grant him to us."

"He will come. I heard at the Mazovian court that he will come, and perhaps the king will come too, and bring all the strength that is in Poland."

Further speech between them was interrupted by Skirvoillo, who came out of the shade unexpectedly and said, —

"We are marching to the conflict! "

When they heard this the knights stood up quickly. Skirvoillo approached his immense head to their faces and said in a low voice, —

"We have news: reinforcements are marching to New Kovno. Two Knights of the Cross are leading on soldiers with cattle and provisions. Let us stop them! "

"Then shall we cross the Niemen?" inquired Zbyshko.

"Yes. We know the ford."

"And do they know in the castle of those reinforcements?"

"They know, and will go out to meet them; on those who go out you will strike."

Then he explained where they were to lie in ambush, and in such wise as to hit unexpectedly on those who sallied forth from the castle. His plan was that two battles should take place at the same time, to avenge the defeats suffered recently; this might be carried out with the greater ease, since the enemy felt entirely safe after victory. Hence he designated the time of action and the places to which they must hurry ; the rest he left to their bravery and foresight. They were delighted in heart, for they saw at once that he spoke to them as an accurate and experienced warrior. When he had finished he commanded to follow him and returned to his cabin, in which princes and boyar captains were waiting. There he repeated his orders, issued new ones, and raising to his lips a tube of carved wolf-bone, gave a shrill and far-sounding whistle, which was heard from one end of the camp to the other.

At that moment something boiled up along the dying fire places; here and there sparks glittered, then small flames

appeared which rose and increased every instant, and in the light of them were seen forms of wild warriors assembling around the fires with their weapons. The forest shook and roused itself. Soon from the depth began to come the calling of horseherds as they drove in their beasts to the camp ground.

## CHAPTEE XLVH.

THEY reached the Nievaja in the morning and crossed; one on horseback, another holding to a horse's tail, another on a bundle of grape-vines. This passed so quickly that Matsko, Zbyshko, Hlava, and those Mazovians who had come as volunteers, were amazed at the skill of that people, and they understood then for the first time why neither pinewoods nor swamps nor rivers could stop Lithuanian onsets. When they had come out of the water no man put off his clothing, no man threw off a sheepskin or wolf-hide; each warrior dried himself standing with his back to the sun till steam rose from him as from a tarpit; and after a short rest they moved swiftly northward. At dusk they reached the river Niemen. There the crossing was not easy, since it was over a great river swollen with the waters of springtime. The ford, known to Skirvoillo, had changed in places into deep spots, so that horses had to swim more than a quarter of a furlong. Two men were swept away from Zbyshko's and Hlava's side; these they tried to save, but in vain; because of darkness and deep water they lost sight of them quickly. The drowning men dared not call for aid, since their leader had commanded earlier that the crossing should be made in the deepest silence. All the rest reached the other shore successfully and remained there till morning.

At daybreak the whole army was divided into two parts. With one Skirvoillo went to meet those knights who were bringing reinforcements to Gotteswerder, the other Zbyshko led straight toward the island, to intercept those castle people sallying forth to meet the reinforcements. The day had grown bright overhead, and calm, but the forest, the meadows, and bushes were veiled with a thick whitish mist, which hid them completely. This was for Zbyshko and his men a favorable condition, because the Germans marching from the castle could not see them and withdraw in time from an encounter. The young knight was delighted greatly for this reason, and said to Matsko, who was riding near him, —

"In a fog like this we shall strike before they can see us; God grant that it grow not thin till even mid-day! "

That moment he rushed forward to give commands to captains in advance, but he returned quickly.

"Soon we shall come," said he, "to a road going from the ford opposite the island toward the heart of the country. There we shall place ourselves in the forest and wait for them."

"How didst thou learn of the road?" inquired Matsko.

"From men of the place. I have some tens of them among my people; they lead us everywhere."

"But how far from the castle and the island wilt thou attack?"

"Five miles."

"That is well, for were it nearer soldiers from the castle might hurry up with assistance; as it is, not only will they be unable to do that, but no shouts will be heard."

"You see, I have given thought to this."

"Thou hast thought over one thing, think now of another. If thy men of that place are faithful, send two or three of them to see when the Germans sally forth, and then hurry back and report to us."

"That is done already."

"Then I will tell thee something else: Command a hundred or two hundred men as follows: take no part in the battle, but the moment it commences hurry awa\'7d- and cut off the road to the island."

"That is the first thing to do," answered Zbyshko, "and that order has been given already. The Germans will fall into a swamp, as it were, or a trap."

When Matsko heard this he looked at his nephew with pleased eye, for he was glad that Zbyshko, in spite of his early years, understood warfare so keenly; hence he smiled and muttered, —

"Ours is the right blood! "

But the attendant, Hlava, rejoiced more in soul than even Matsko, for to him there was nothing so delightful as battle.

"I know not," said he, "how our men will fight, but they are advancing quietly, in order, and in them a tremendous willingness is evident. If that Skirvoillo has thought out all his work well, not a living leg should escape that belongs to an enemy."

"God grant that few get away," said Zbyshko. "But I
have issued orders to take as many prisoners as possible, and should there happen among them a knight or a brother of the Order, not to kill him."

"But why is that, lord?" asked Hlava.

"Look thou sharply too that this order be earned out. A knight, if from foreign parts, goes about in cities, or in castles; he sees a world of people and hears a world of news, and if he is a knight of the Order he hears more than others. This, as God lives, is true: I have come here to capture some one of the more important men, and exchange him. That dear girl is all that remains to me — in case she is living yet."

When he had said this he put spurs to his horse and pushed out to the head of the division to give final orders and escape from sad thoughts, for which there was then no time, since the place of the ambush was not distant.

"Why does my young lord think that his wife is still living, and that she is in these regions?" asked Hlava.

"He thinks so because Siegfried did not kill her at the first impulse in Schytno; this being so, we may hope that she is still living. If he had killed her the Schytno priest would not have given us the account he did give, an account which Zbyshko himself heard. It is hard for the greatest brute, even, to raise hands on a defenceless woman. What, defenceless woman? — on an innocent little girl! "

"Hard, but not for a knight of the Order. Have you forgotten Prince Vitold's children?"

"It is true that they have wolf hearts, still it is true also that they did not kill her in Schytno, and that Siegfried himself came to these parts; hence he may have-hidden her in some castle."

*'Ei! in that case, if we could only surprise this island and this castle! "

"But look at those men," said Matsko.

"True! true! but I have an idea to give my young master — "

"If thou hadst ten ideas thou couldst not throw stone walls down with pikes! "

And Matsko pointed to the line of pikes with which the greater part of the warriors were provided; then he asked,—

"Hast thou ever seen such an army? "

Hlava had indeed never seen such an army. Before him advanced a dense legion of warriors, and they advanced

without order, for in that pine wood and among bushes it would have been difficult to preserve order. Besides, men on foot were mingled with men on horseback, and to keep up with the horses they held to the manes, tails, and saddles of the animals. The shoulders of the warriors were covered with skins of wolves, bears, and panthers, and from their heads were thrust out wild-boar tusks, stag horns, and shaggy wild-beast ears; so that had it not been for their weapons standing upward, and the bows which they carried, and the quivers behind their shoulders, any onlooker might have thought, especially in the morning mist, all that to be the host of forest wild beasts issuing from their native lairs, driven on by desire of blood and by hunger. There was in it something terrible, and also as unexampled as that wonder called the "gomon," during which, as simple people think, wild beasts rush forward in a throng, and with them stones and trees, even.

At this sight one of those nobles of Lenkavitsa who had come with Hlava approached him, made the sign of the cross, and said, —

"In the name of the Father and the Son! We are going with a legion of wolves, and not people."

Hlava, though he beheld such a host for the first time, said, like a man of experience, who knows everything, and is astonished at no sight, —

"Wolves run in packs during winter, but the beast blood of the Order tastes well even in springtime."

And in truth it was springtime — it was May. Leshchyna, which was encircled with pine trees, was covered with tender green. From the velvety, soft mosses, over which the steps of the warriors passed without noise, appeared the white and tender blue of the sasanka, the young berry, and the fern leaf with its tooth-edged border. The trees, moistened with abundant rain, had the odor of damp bark, and from the earth surface of the forest came a strong odor of fallen pine leaves and decaying timber. The sun played with rainbow light on the water-drops hanging from the forest leaves, and the bird world announced itself joyously.

They advanced with increasing swiftness, for Zbyshko urged them forward. After a while he turned again to the rear of the division, where Matsko and Hlava were with the volunteers from Mazovia. The hope of a good battle had roused him greatly, as could be seen, for on his face

the usual anxiety was no longer evident, and his eyes gleamed as in the old time.

"Well! " cried he. "We are to be in front now, not in the rear! " And he took them to the head of the division.

"Listen," added he; "we may strike the Germans unexpectedly, but if they see us and are able to form in line, then we must be the first of our people to fall on them, for our armor is the surest, and our swords are the best in this division."

"That is what we shall do! " said Alatsko.

Other men sat back with more weight in their saddles, as if they were going to make a charge straightway. This one and that drew breath into his breast and tried whether his sword would come easily from its scabbard.

Zbyshko repeated once more that if nobles or brothers in white mantles were found among men on foot they were not to be slain, but taken prisoners; then he sprang again to the guides, and after a moment stopped the division. They had come to the road which led from the landing-place opposite the island into the interior of the country. In fact there was no real road, but rather a trail made not long before through the forest, and levelled out only as much as was needed for warriors or wagons to escape from disaster. On both sides stood a lofty pine forest, and on both sides lay the great trunks of old pines cut down to open the roadway. The undergrowth of hazel was in places so dense that it hid altogether the depth of the forest. Zbyshko chose this place at a turn so that those approaching might not see him from a distance and have time to withdraw or to form in line of battle. He took both sides of the trail and gave command to await the enemy.

The Jmud men, accustomed to forest life, and to war in the wilderness, dropped down behind tree trunks, earth clumps, hazel bushes, and bunches of young fir as quickly as if the earth had swallowed them. Not a man gave out a sound, not a horse a snort. From time to time near the hiding people a little beast would pass, and then a big beast, which, when it saw that it had almost touched a man, roared and rushed terrified into the distance. At moments a breeze rose and filled the forest with a sound that was earnest and majestic, then there was stillness; after that naught was heard save the distant call of the cuckoo and the near hammering of woodpeckers.

The Jrnud men listened to those sounds with immense

delight, for the woodpecker .was to them the special herald of good tidings. Besides, the forest was full of those birds, and their hammering came in from all sides, strongly, insistently, like the labor of mankind. One might have said that all those birds had their forge in that forest, and since early morning had been hurrying thither to perform earnest labor. To Matsko and the men of Mazovia it seemed that they were listening to adzes fashioning rafters for a new house, and it called to their minds native regions.

But time passed, and still there was nothing to be heard save the voices of birds and the sounds of the forest. The mist lying near the ground was growing thinner, the sun had risen notably and had begun to give warmth, but the men were lying low all that interval. Finally Hlava, to whom waiting and silence had grown irksome, turned to Zbyshko's ear and whispered, —•

"My lord, if God grant that not one of the dog brothers go with his life, might we not advance in the night-time, oross the river, surprise the castle and take it?"

"Dost think that boats are not on guard there, and that the men in them have not a password? "

"They are on guard; but prisoners if under the knife will give that word, nay more, will call it out to them in German. If we reach the island the castle itself will — "

Here he stopped, since Zbyshko put his hand over his lips suddenly, for from the road came the croaking of a raven.

"Be silent," said he, "that is a signal."

Something like two "Our Fathers" later, on the road appeared a Jmud man on a small, shaggy horse, whose hoofs were bound in sheepskin, so as not to make noise or leave traces. ,

The rider looked quickly on both sides and, hearing on a sudden an answer to the croaking, darted into the forest, and in one moment was with Zbyshko.

"They are coming!" said he.

CHAPTER XLVIIL

ZBYSHKO asked hurriedly how they were moving, how many cavalry there were, how many men on foot, and above all, how far away they were. From the answer of the Jmud man he learned that the detachment was not greater than one hundred and fifty warriors; of these, fifty were horsemen not under the lead of a Knight of the Cross, but of some knight who was a layman and a foreigner; that they were advancing in rank, bringing behind them wagons on which was a supply of wheels; that in front of the division, at a distance of two shots of an arrow, was a guard formed of eight men, who left the road frequently to examine trees and bushes, and finally that they were about a mile and a quarter distant.

Zbyshko was not very glad that they were advancing in rank. He knew from experience how difficult it was to break united Germans, and how such a "union" could defend itself while retreating and fight like a wild boar surrounded by hunting-dogs. On the other hand he was pleased at the intelligence that they were not farther away than a mile and a quarter, for he inferred from this that the detachment which he had sent forward had gained the rear and that in case of German defeat this detachment would let no living soul escape. For the advance guard he did not care much; thinking beforehand that they would come, he had ordered the Jmud warriors either to let them pass without notice, or, if some tried to examine the forest, t» snatch them up to the last man in silence.

This command proved superfluous. The guard appeared quickly. Hidden by mounds near the road, the Jmud men saw those soldiers perfectly, and saw how, halting at the turns, they talked with one another. The leader, a sturdy, red-bearded German, imposing silence by a nod, began to listen. In a moment it was clear that he hesitated as to this: should he search the forest? At last, when he heard nothing but the hammering of woodpeckers, it was evident that to his thinking the birds would not work with that freedom were any one concealed near them; hence he waved his hand and led on the avant-guard.

Zbyshko waited till they vanished beyond the next turn; then he went to the edge of the road quietly at the head of the heavy-armored men, among whom were Matsko, Hlava, the two noblee from Lenkavitsa, three young knights from Tsehauov, and some tens of the weightiest and best-armed nobles among the Jmud men. Further concealment was not greatly needed; hence Zbyshko intended, the moment that Germans appeared, to spring into the middle of the roadway, strike on them, and break their circle. Should that succeed and the general battle be turned into a series of duels, he might be sure that the Jmud men would master the Germans.

Again followed a moment of silence, interrupted only by the usual forest whisper. But soon there came to the ear of the warriors, from the eastern part of the roadway, the voices of people. Confused and rather distant, it changed by degrees into something more expressive and nearer.

Zbyshko at that moment led his detachment to the middle of the roadway and placed it there in wedge form. He stood himself at the head of it, having immediately behind him both Matsko and Hlava. In the next rank were three men, beyond them four others. They were all armed properly; lacking, it is true, the strong "wood" or lances of the knighthood, — those lances were a great hindrance in forest fighting, — but they held in their hands the short and for the first onset the easiest weapon, the Jmud spear, and had swords and axes at their saddles for battling in a throng of warriors.

Hlava put forward his ear anxiously, listened, and then whispered to Matsko, —

"Perdition take their mother! they are singing."

"But it is a wonder to me that the pine wood is closed before us and that we cannot see them from this place," replied Matsko.

To this, Zbyshko, who considered further concealment or even quiet talking as needless, turned and said, —

"That is because the road goes along the river and turns frequently. "We shall see them all on a sudden; that will be better."

" Some one is singing a pleasant song! " put in Hlava.

In fact the Germans were singing a song far from religious; this was easy to discern from its note. After listening to it one discovered also that only a few tens of men were singing; and only one phrase was re-

peated by all, but this phrase went through the forest like thunder.

And so they came on to death, gladsome and full of rejoicing.

"We shall soon see them," said Matsko.

That instant his face became dark and was wolf-like, in some sort, for the soul in him had grown merciless and unforgiving; besides, he had not paid yet for that wound from a crossbow which he received when journeying to save Zbyshko, bearing with him a letter from Vitold's sister to the Grand Master. Hence his heart sprang up and the desire for vengeance flowed around it as if it had been in boiling water.

"It will not be well for the man who meets him first," thought Hlava, as he cast his eye on the old knight.

Meanwhile the breeze brought up clearly the phrase which all were repeating in their chorus: "Tandaradei! tandaradei! " and right away Hlava heard the words of a song known to him: —

" Bi den r6sen er wol mac, Tdndaradei I Merken wa mir'z houlet lac."

Now the song stopped, for on both sides of the road was given forth a multitude of croaks as loud and resonant as if a congress of ravens had been opened in that corner of the forest.

The Germans were astonished at this. Whence could so many of those birds have flown in, and why did all their voices come from the ground, and not from the treetops ?

The first rank of soldiers just showed itself on the turn and stopped, as if planted, at sight of unknown horsemen out there in front of them.

That instant Zbyshko bent toward his saddle bow, spurred his horse and rushed forward, —

"At them!"

After him shot on the others. From both sides of the forest rose the dreadful cry of Jmud warriors. About two hundred paces divided Zbyshko's men from the Germans, who in one twinkle lowered a forest of spears against the onriders; at the same instant the farther German ranks faced the two sides of the forest with equal swiftness, to defend themselves against two flank attacks. The Polish knights would have admired that accuracy had there been

time for admiration, and had not their horses swept them with the highest speed against the levelled, gleaming lances.

Through a chance, which for Zbyshko was fortunate, the German cavalry found itself in the rear of the detachment, near the wagons. They moved, it is true, at once toward the infantry, but could neither pass through nor ride around it, and consequently could not defend it from the first onset. Meanwhile crowds of Jmud warriors attacked the mounted Germans, rushing out of the thicket like a swarm of stinging wasps whose nest has been hit by the foot of a heedless traveller. Zbyshko struck with his men on the infantry. But his blow had no effect. The Germans put the ends of their heavy lances and halberds on the ground and held them with such firmness and so evenly that the light-horse of the Jmud men had not force to break that wall. Matsko's horse, struck by a halberd in the shank, reared on its hind-legs and then dug the earth with its nostrils. For a moment death was hanging over the old knight, but, experienced in all struggles and every adventure, he drew his foot out of the stirrups and grasped with his strong hand the sharp German spear, which, instead of entering his bosom, was used to support him; next he sprang out among the horses, and drawing his sword, struck right and left at spears and halberds, just as a keen falcon dashes savagely at a flock of long-billed storks. Zbyshko's horse was stopped in its speed and almost stood on its hind-legs. Zbyshko leaned on his spear for support and broke it, so he too took his sword. Hlava, who believed in the axe above all weapons, hurled his at the Germans, and was for a moment defenceless. One of the nobles from Lenka-. vitsa perished; at sight of this, rage so seized the other that he howled like a wolf, and, reining back his bloody horse till it reared, drove the beast toward the midst of the enemy at random. The boyars of Jmud hewed with their blades against the large and small spears, from behind which gazed the faces of soldiers, transfixed as it were with amazement, and also contracted by stubbornness and resolution. But the line did not break. The Jmud men, who struck at the flanks, sprang back at once from the Germans as from porcupines. They returned, it is true, but could effect nothing.

Some climbed in a twinkle into the trees at the roadside and began to shoot from bows into the midst of the soldiers.

whose leaders, seeing this, gave command to withdraw toward the cavalry. The German crossbows now gave answer, and from moment to moment a Jmud man hidden among branches fell to the earth like a ripe pine cone, and dying, tore with his hands the moss of the forest, or squirmed like a fish when 't is swept out of water. Surrounded on all sides, the Germans could not indeed count on victory; seeing, however, the seriousness of their own defence, they thought that even a handful might push out of those straits and escape to the riverside.

The thought came to no man to yield himself, for never having spared prisoners themselves, the\'7d' knew that they could not count on the pity of a people brought to despair and to uprising. Hence they retreated in silence, man at the side of man, shoulder to shoulder, now raising, now lowering their lances and halberds, cutting, thrusting, or shooting from crossbows in so far as the confusion of battle permitted, approaching always their cavalry, which was fighting a life and death battle with other legions of the enemy.

Then something unlooked-for took place, something which settled the fate of the desperate struggle. That noble o£ Lenkavitsa, whom frenzy had seized at the death of his brother, bent forward, without dismounting, and raised the corpse from the earth, wishing evidently to secure it and put it somewhere in safety, so as to find it more easily when the battle was over. But that same moment a new wave of frenzy rushed to his head and deprived him entirely of reason; for, instead of leaving the road, he struck straight on the Germans and hurled the corpse onto their lance points, which, fastened now in its breast, sides, and bowels, went down beneath the burden. Before the soldiers could pull out their lances, the madman had rushed through the gap in their ranks unresisted, overturning men in his course like a tempest.

In a twinkle tens of hands were stretched toward him, tens of spears pierced the flanks of his horse; but meanwhile the ranks were broken, and before they could close again, one of the Jmud men, the one happening nearest, rushed in, after him Zbyshko, after him Hlava; and the awful struggle grew and increased every instant. Other nobles grasped also dead bodies and whirled them on to the German lance points. Jmud men attacked again from the two flanks. The whole detachment, up to that time well-

ordered, shook like a house in which the walls are bursting, opened like a log when a wedge is driven into it, and finally dropped apart.

The battle was changed in one moment into slaughter. The long German lances and halberds were useless in the onrush. On the other hand, the swords of the horsemen bit the skulls and the necks of the German footmen. The horses reared in the crowds of people, overturning and trampling the unfortunate soldiers. For horsemen it was easy to strike from above, so they cut without halting or resting. From the sides of the road rushed forth crowd after crowd of wild warriors in wolfskins, and with a Avolf's thirst for blood in their bosoms. Their howls drowned voices imploring for pity, and drowned also the groans of the dying. The conquered threw away their weapons; some tried to escape to the forest; some, (feigning death, fell on the earth there; some stood erect, with faces as pale as snow and with blinking eyes; others prayed; one, whose mind seemed lost from terror, began to play on a whistle, then raising his eyes up, he laughed till Jmud swords laid his skull open. The pine woods ceased to sound, as if terrified at the slaughter.

At last the handful of men of the Order melted. But for a time was heard in the brushwood the sound of brief fights, or the sharp cry of terror. Zbyshko and Matsko, and behind them all the light-horse, rushed now at the German cavalry, which, defending itself yet, had formed in a circle, for in that way the Germans always defended themselves when the enemy succeeded in meeting them with greater forces. The cavalry, sitting on good horses and in better armor than the footmen, fought bravely and with persistence which deserved admiration. There was no white mantle among them; they were mainly of the middle and smaller nobles of Prussia, whose duty it was to stand in line at command of the Order. Their horses were for the greater part armored, some with breast armor, and all in iron frontlets with a steel horn from the middle of the forehead. Leadership over them was held by a tall, slender man, in dark-blue armor and a helmet of the same shade with closed visor.

From the forest depth a shower of arrows was falling on them, but these shafts dropped harmless from their visors, hard shoulder-pieces, and breastplates. A wave of Jmud men on foot and on horseback had surrounded them closely,

but they defended themselves, cutting and thrusting with their long sword-blades so stubbornly that before their horses' hoofs lay a garland of corpses. The foremost attacking ranks wished to withdraw, but, pushed from behind, were unable. Round about came a crush and a trample. Eyes were dazed by the glitter of .spears and the shining of sword-blades. Horses whined, bit, and stood on their hind-legs. The boyars of Jmud rushed in with Zbyshko, Hlava, and the Mazoviaus. Under their heavy blows the "circle" bent and swayed, like a forest in a strong wind, while they, like woodmen chopping where trees are thick, pushed forward slowly in the heat and the hard work.

Matsko gave command now to collect on the battle-field the long German halberds, and arming with these, about thirty warriors broke a way with them through the crowd to the Germans. "Strike the legs of the horses!" cried he, and a ghastly result ensued. The German knights could not reach these men with their swords, while the halberds cut the horses' legs terribly. The blue knight saw that the end of the battle was coming, and that nothing was left but to break through that crowd which cut off the road to retreat; if not, he and his party must perish.

He chose the first; at his command and in one twinkle a line of knights turned front to the side from which they had started. The Jmud men were at once on their backs, till the Germans, putting their shields on their shoulders, cut in front and at both sides, broke the ring which surrounded them, spurred on their beasts, and rushed like a hurricane eastward. Just then they were met by that detachment which was coming up toward the battle, but crushed by superior arms and horses, it fell flat before the Germans, like wheat beneath a wind storm. The road to the castle was open, but rescue was uncertain and distant, for the Jmud horses were swifter than those of the Germans. The blue knight understood this to perfection.

"Woe!" said he to himself; "not a man will escape, though I buy his life with my own blood !"

Thus thinking, he ordered those nearest to hold in their horses, and without noting whether any obeyed, he turned face to the enemy.

Zbyshko raced up first; the German struck at him and hit the side-piece of the helmet which covered bis cheek, but did not crack it, and did not injure his face any. Zbyshko,

instead of answering with a blow, seized the knight by the middle, and wishing to take him alive at all costs, strove to drag the man from his saddle; but his own stirrup broke from excessive weight, and both combatants went to the earth. For a while they struggled, fighting with hands and feet; but soon the stronger and younger man mastered his opponent, and, pressing his bowels with his knees, held him there, as a wolf holds a dog which has dared to thrust a face up before him in the thicket. And he held him beyond need, for the German fainted. Meanwhile Matsko and Hlava ran up; when he saw them, Zbyshko shouted, —

"Come and bind him! He is some knight— and belted! "

Hlava sprang from his horse, but seeing how helpless the knight was, did not bind him, but opened his armor, took off his girdle with a misericordia which hung from it, cut the strap binding his helmet, and came finally to the screw which held the visor. But barely had he looked on the face of the knight when he sprang up.

"Oh, my lord! but just look! " cried he.

"De Lorche! " called out Zbyshko.

But De Lorche lay there pale, with sweating face and closed eyes, corpselike and motionless.

VOL. II. —3

CHAPTER XLIX.

ZBYSHKO commanded to put him on one of the captured wagons, which was laden with new wheels and axles for that expedition which was advancing to the aid of the castle. He himself mounted another horse and moved on with Matsko in further pursuit of the fleeing Germans. That pursuit was not over-difficult, for German horses were bad for escape, above all on a road softened by spring rains considerably. Matsko especially, having under him a swift and lightly-built mare, which came to him from the dead noble of Lenkavitsa, passed after a few furlongs almost all the Jmud men, and soon overtook the nearest German. He hailed him, it is true, according to knightly custom, intending that he should either surrender as a captive, or turn back to give battle; but when the other, feigning deafness, threw away his shield to relieve his horse, and bending forward put spurs to the animal, the old knight struck him cruelly with his broad axe between the shoulders and hurled him from the saddle.

Thus did he avenge himself on the fugitives for that traitorous arrow which he had received, and they fled before him like a herd of deer, in which each bears in its heart fright unendurable, but in that heart no wish for defence or battle, no wish but that of escape from the terrible pursuer. Some ran into the forest; but one mired near a brook, and him the Jmud men choked with a halter. Whole crowds rushed into the thicket after the fugitives, and then began a wild hunt full of shouts, exclamations, and outcries. For a good while the secret places among trees resounded with yells, till the last man was taken. Then the old knight from Bogdanets, Zbyshko, and Hlava returned to the first field, on which the slain German soldiers were lying. The bodies had been stripped, and some of them mutilated cruelly by the vengeful hands of Jmud warriors.

The victory was considerable, and the men were roused by delight at it. After the recent defeat of Skirvoillo dissatisfaction had begun to seize Jmud hearts, especially as the reinforcements promised by Vjtold had not come with such

speed as had been expected; but now hope and enthusiasm flashed up again, like a fire when fresh wood is thrown on its embers.

Too many had fallen on both sides for burial, but Zbyshko commanded to dig with spears graves for the two nobles of Lenkavitsa, who had been the main cause of victory, and to bury them under two pine-trees, on the bark of which he cut crosses with his sword-point. Next he intrusted Hlava with guarding De Lorche, who was still unconscious; then he moved his men on, and marched hurriedly by that same road toward Skirvoillo, so as to give effective aid, if needed. He marched long before he struck upon the battlefield, but the action was over; it was covered, like the first field, with bodies of Jmud men and Germans. Zbyshko understood easily that the terrible Skirvoillo must have won also a notable victory; for if he had been beaten, they would have met Germans marching toward the castle. The victory must have been bloody, however, since farther on, beyond the real field of battle, the bodies of slain men were lying closely together. The experienced Matsko concluded from this that a part of the Germans had been able to retreat from the disaster. Whether Skirvoillo had overtaken them or not was difficult to determine, since the trails were deceptive and effaced one by another. Still, Matsko inferred that the battle had taken place there much earlier, — earlier, perhaps, than Zbyshko's battle, for the bodies were blackened and swollen, and some were gnawed by wolves, which fled to the thicket when armed men approached them.

In view of this, Zbyshko resolved not to wait for Skirvoillo, but to go back to the last and safe camping-place. Reaching there late in the evening, he found the Jmud leader, who had arrived somewhat earlier. His face, usually gloomy, was lighted up now with an ominous pleasure. He inquired immediately about Zbyshko's battle, and learning of the victory, said, with a voice like the croaking of a raven, —

"I am pleased with thee and pleased with myself. Reinforcements will not come soon; but if the Grand Prince comes, he too will be pleased, for the castle will belong to us."

"Whom have they taken as prisoners? " asked Zbyshko.

"Only roaches; no pike. There was one, there were two, but they got away. Pikes with sharp teeth! they bit through our men and vanished."

"God gave me one," said Zbyshko. "A rich knight, and distinguished, though a layman — he is a foreigner."

The terrible commander put his hands at both sides of his neck, then made a gesture, as if pointing upward, and indicated a rope going from his neck in that direction.

"It will be thus for him," said he, "as well as for the others — this way! "

Zbyshko frowned.

"Hear me, Skirvoillo," said he. "It will not be that way for him, or any way like that; he is my friend and captive. Prince Yanush belted us at the same time, and I will not let thee lay a finger on him."

"Thou wilt not?"

"I will not."

And they looked each into the eyes of the other, frowning, wherewith Skirvoillo's face contracted and resembled the head of a bird of prey. It seemed that both might burst out in passion; but Zbyshko, unwilling to quarrel with the old leader, whose virtue he knew, and whom he respected, and having moreover a heart that was quivering from the events of the day, seized him by the shoulders suddenly, pressed him to his bosom, and asked, —

"Can it be possible that thou wouldst take him from me, and with him my last hope? Why do me an injustice?"

Skirvoillo did not ward off the embrace, and at last, sticking his head forth from between Zbyshko's arms, he looked at him from under his eyebrows, and panted.

"AVell," said he, after a moment of silence, "to-morrow I shall give command to hang my captives, but if thou need one, I will give him."

Then they embraced a second time and parted in good feeling, to the great delight of Matsko, who said,—

"It is evident that with him thou canst effect nothing through harshness, but by kindness thou mayst mould him as wax."

"That is the nature of the people," answered Zbyshko; "but the Germans do not know it."

Then he gave command to bring to the fire De Lorche, who was resting in the hut; Hlava soon brought him, without his weapons, without his helmet, but in a skin coat, on which his armor had left traces, and with a red cap on his head. De Lorche had learned from Hlava whose prisoner he was; but for that very reason he came cold, haughty,

THE KNIGHTS OF THE CROSS. 117

with a face on -which, by the light of the fire, one could read contempt and decision.

"I thank God," said Zbyshko to him, "that He gave thee into my hands, for from me nothing threatens thee."

And he stretched his hand toward him with friendliness, but De Lorche did not move even.

"I will not give a hand to knights who have disgraced knightly honor, and who are fighting at the side of Saracens against Christians."

One of the Mazovians present interpreted these words, the meaning of which Zbyshko himself divined; so that at the first moment the blood boiled up in him as water in a caldron.

"Idiot!" shouted he, grasping, in spite of himself, the hilt of his misericordia.

But De Lorche reared his head.

"Kill me!" said he, "for I know that ye spare no prisoners."

"But do ye spare them?" exclaimed the Mazovian, unable to endure such words quietly. " Were ye not the men who hanged on the shore of the island all those whom ye captured in the battle before this ? In return, Skirvoillo hangs your men."

"They were hanged," replied De Lorche, "but they were Pagans."

One might detect a certain shame in his answer, and it was not difficult to divine that in his soul he had no praise for such an action.

Meanwhile Zbyshko recovered himself, and said with calm dignity, —

"De Lorche, we received belts and spurs from the same hand; thou knowest me, therefore, and knowest that the honor of knighthood is dearer to me than life and happiness; so listen to what I will say under an oath on Saint George: Many of the people hanged were baptized long before yesterday, and those who are not Christians yet are stretching their hands to the Cross as to redemption; but knowest thou who hinder them, who keep them from redemption and baptism?"

The Mazovian interpreted Zbyshko's words in a minute, so De Lorche looked with inquiring glance at Zbyshko's face.

"The Germans."

"Impossible! " cried the Knight of Lorraine.

"By the lance and the spurs of Saint George, it is the Germans! for if the Cross should prevail here they would lose the excuse for invasions, and for lording it over this land and oppressing the unfortunate people. Moreover, thou hast learned them, De Lorche, and knowest better if their acts are caused by justice."

"I thought that it destroys sin to fight with Pagans, and bend them to baptism."

"But the Germans baptize them with a sword and with blood, not with the water of salvation. Read this letter, and thou wilt know straightway if thou art not serving those men of injustice, those robbers and elders of hell, against the faith and the love of the Saviour."

And he handed De Lorche the letter of the Jmud men to kings and princes, which letter had been sent around everywhere. De Lorche took the letter and began to run his eyes over it near the firelight.

He read it quickly, for reading was no strange trick to him ; he was astonished beyond measure.

"Is all this true?" asked he.

"It is, so help me, and thee, God! who knows best that I am serving, not my own cause alone, but the cause also of justice."

De Lorche was silent for a time, and then said, —

"I am your prisoner."

"Give thy hand," replied Zbyshko. "Thou art my brother, not my prisoner."

So they gave their right hands to each other and sat down to a common supper, which Hlava had commanded the attendants to make ready. During the meal De Lorche learned with no less astonishment that Zbyshko, in spite of the letters, had not discovered Danusia, and that the com-turs had denied the validity of his safe-conduct because of the outbreak of war.

"Now I understand why thou art here," said he, "and I thank God that He gave me to thee as a prisoner, for I think that the Knights of the Cross will exchange for me the one for whom thou art looking; otherwise there would be a great outcry in the West, for I come from a great family."

Here he struck his hand on his cap suddenly, and said, —

"By all the relics in Aix La Chapelle! At the head of the reinforcements which were moving toward Gotteswerder were Arnold von Baden and old Siegfried de Lowe. We know this from letters which have come to the castle. Are they not taken prisoners ? "

"No!" answered Zbyshko, springing up. "None of the more important were taken. But, as God lives, thou givest me great tidings. As God lives! there are other prisoners, from whom I shall know before they hang them whether Siegfried was not bringing some woman."

He summoned the attendants to bring torches and ran to the place where Skirvoillo's captives were; De Lorche, Matsko, and Hlava ran with him.

"Listen to me," said De Lorche on the way. "Let me out on my word; I myself will search all Prussia through for her, and if I find her I will return to thee, and then thou canst exchange me for her."

"If she is living! if she is living! " said Zbyshko.

By this time they had run to where Skirvoillo's captives were. Some of them were lying on their backs, others were near the trees, lashed to them cruelly with bark ropes. The torch gleamed brightly over Zbyshko's head, so that the eyes of all those unfortunates were turned toward him.

Then from the depth came a shrill voice full of terror, —

"Oh, my lord and defender! save me! "

Zbyshko snatched from the hands of the attendant a couple of flaming torches, sprang to the tree from beneath which the voice came, and raising the torches cried, —

"Sanderus! "

"Sanderus! " exclaimed Hlava, astounded.

But Sanderus, unable to move his stiffened arms, stretched his neck up, and again cried, —

"Mercy! I know where the daughter of Yurand is! Save me!"

CHAPTER L.

THE attendants unbound him immediately, but since his limbs were benumbed, he fell to the earth; and when they raised him, he fainted time after time, for he had been terribly frightened. They took him to the fire at command of Zbyshko, gave him food and drink, rubbed him with tallow, and covered him warmly with skins. Sanderus did not regain consciousness, but fell into a sleep so profound that Hlava was barely able to rouse him at noon the day following.

Zbyshko. whom impatience was burning as with fire, came to him straightway. But at first he was unable to learn from him anything; for, either through terror after dreadful experiences, or through the helplessness which possesses weak souls when the threatening danger has passed them, such an irresistible weeping seized Sanderus that he struggled vainly to answer the questions put to him. Sobs closed his throat, his lips quivered, and tears flowed from his eyes as abundantly as if his life were going out with them.

At last, recovering a little, and strengthened by mare's-milk, which the Lithuanians had learned to use from the Tartars, he fell to complaining that those "sons of Belial" had fastened him to a crab-tree with lances, that they had taken his horse, on which he was carrying relics of exceptional virtues and value, and to finish all, after they had lashed him to the tree, ants so bit his legs and body that certain death was awaiting him, if not that day, then the morrow.

At last Zbyshko became angry, sprang up, and said, —

"Answer, vagabond, the questions which I put, and see to it that something worse does not strike thee! "

"My lord," said Hlava, "close by is a hill of red ants; give command to put him on that hill and he will find a tongue between his lips very quickly."

Hlava did not say this in earnest, and he smiled even, for in his heart he had good-will for Sanderus; but Sanderus was terrified.

"Mercy! Oh, mercy!" cried he. "Give me a little more of that Pagan strong drink, and I will tell everything; what I have seen and what I have not seen! "

"If thou tell one lie I will drive a wedge between thy teeth! " replied Hlava.

But he brought a skin of mare's-milk a second time. Sanderus seized it, fastened his lips to it greedily, like a child to the breast of its mother, and began to sob, opening and closing his eyes in succession, till he had drained off two quarts, or perhaps more, then he shook himself, put the skin on his knee, and said, as if yielding to necessity, —

"This is foulness! " Then he turned to Zbyshko: "Now inquire, my deliverer! "

"Was my wife in that detachment in which thou wert? "

On Sanderus' face appeared a certain astonishment. He had heard, it is true, that Danusia was Zbyshko's wife, but that the marriage was secret, and that she had been carried off immediately; so he thought of her always as the daughter of Yurand. Still, he answered in a hurry, —

"Yes, Voevoda! she was, but Siegfried de Lowe and Arnold von Baden broke through the enemy."

"Didst thou see her?" asked the young man, with throbbing heart.

" I did not see her face, lord, but between two horses I saw a basket cradle, entirely closed; they were carrying some one in the cradle, and that same lizard was looking after it, that same serving-woman of the Order who came from Danveld to the hunting-lodge. And I heard sad singing also, and it came from the cradle."

Zbyshko grew pale from emotion; he sat on a tree trunk, and for a time did not know what more to ask. Matsko and Hlava were also moved immensely, for they heard great and important news. Hlava thought, perhaps, at the same time of his own beloved lady, who had remained in Spyhov, and for whom this news would be the sentence of misfortune.

Silence followed.

At last the cunning Matsko, who did not know Sanderus and had barely heard of the man previously, looked at him with suspicion and asked, —

"What sort of person art thou, and what wert thou doing among the Knights of the Order ? "

"What sort of man am I, great, mighty knight," answered the vagrant, "let these present answer, — this valiant prince (he indicated Zbyshko), and this brave count here from Bohemia, who know me this long time."

It was evident that the mare's-milk had begun to help him, for he grew lively, and turning to Zbyshko said in a clear voice, in which there was no sign of his previous faintness, —

"My lord, you have saved my life twice. Without you the wolves would have eaten my body, or the punishment of bishops would have struck me; they, led into error by my enemies — oh, how unthankful this world is! — gave command to prosecute me for selling relics which they suspected of being unauthentic. But you, lord, took me in your train. Thanks to you the wolves did not eat me, and prosecution did not strike me, for I was considered as one of your people. Never have I lacked food or drink in your following — better than this mare's-milk here, which is dis-gusting, but which I drink to show that a poor, pious pilgrim draws back from no trial."

"Buffoon, tell at once what thou knowest, and jest no further! " cried Matsko.

Sanderus raised the skin to his lips and emptied it; then, as if not listening to Matsko's words, he turned a second time to Zbyshko.

"I love you, lord, because you protected me. The saints, as the Scriptures say, sinned nine times each day, so it happens to Sanderus also to sin sometimes; but Sanderus has not been, and will never be ungrateful. Hence, when misfortune came to you, you remember, lord, that I said to you: I will go from castle to castle, and, while edifying people along the highway, I will seek for what you have lost. Of whom have I not made inquiry! Where have I not been! It would need a long time to tell; it is enough that I found her; and from that moment a burr does not stick to a coatflap as I stuck to old Siegfried. I made myself his servant, and from castle to castle, from the place of one comtur to that of another, from city to city, I went with him unceasingly up to this last battle."

Emotion now mastered Zbsyhko and he said, —

"I am thankful to thee, and reward will not miss thee. But tell now what I ask: Wilt thou swear on thy soul's salvation that she is living? "

"I will swear on my soul's salvation!" answered Sanderus, seriously .

"Why did Siegfried leave Schytno?"

"I know not, lord, but I imagine why. He was never starosta in Schytno, and he left it fearing, perhaps, the command of the Grand Master, who, as men say, wrote to him to give up the captive girl to the Princess of Mazovia. Maybe he fled in view of this letter, for the soul in him was roasting from pain and desire of vengeance for Rotgier. They say now that Rotgier was his own son; I know not how that is, but I do know that something has turned in his head from rage, and that while he is living he will never let Yurand's daughter— I intended to say the young lady — go out of his possession."

"This all seems strange to me," interrupted Matsko on a sudden; "for if that old dog is so vindictive against the whole blood of Yurand he would have killed Danusia."

"He wanted to kill her," retorted Sanderus, "but something happened of such sort that he was very sick afterward, and just missed giving out his last breath. His servants whisper much concerning this. Some say that while going at night to the watch-tower to kill the young lady he met the Evil Spirit; others say that it was an angel. But in every case, they found him on the snow in front of the tower, and no breath in him. Now, when he remembers this, the hair stands on his head, and he dares not raise hands on the lady, and fears to order others to kill her. He takes with him the dumb executioner of Schytno, but it is unknown why he does so, for the executioner is afraid as well as others to kill her."

These words made a great impression. Zbyshko, Matsko, and Hlava drew up to Sanderus, who made the sign of the cross, and continued, —

"It is not pleasant to be there among them. More than once have I heard and seen things which make the hair rise on a man's body. I have told your graces that the old comtur is wrong in the head somehow. Nay, there must be something more, since spirits from the other world visit him. Whenever he is alone something pants near him, exactly as when breath is beginning to fail a man. But this is that Danveld, who was slain by the terrible master of Spyhov. And Siegfried says to him: ' What dost thou want here? Masses cannot help thee; why dost thou come to me? ' The other grits his teeth, and again pants. But still oftener comes Rotgier, after whom there is also a smell of sulphur in the chamber, and he talks still more with the comtur. 'I cannot!' answers Siegfried to him, 'I cannot! When I am alone I will do it, but not this time!' I heard also how he asked: ' Would this ease thee, my son?'

" And it always happens that for two or three days after such a visit he says no word to any man, and on his face dreadful suffering is evident. He guards the cradle carefully, both he and that serving-woman of the Order, so that no person at any time can see the young lady."

"But do they not torture her? " asked Zbyshko, in a dull voice.

"In clear truth I will tell your lordship that blows or cries I have not heard, but I have heard sad singing, and sometimes it was as if a bird piped complainingly."

"Woe! " cried out Zbyshko.

But Matsko interrupted further inquiry.

"Enough of this!" said he. "Tell now of the battle. Didst thou see it? How did they escape, and what happened to them ? "

"I saw," answered Sanderus, "and I will tell everything. They fought at first savagely, but when they knew that they were surrounded on all sides, they began to think how to burst through. The knight Arnold, who is a real giant, was the first to break the ring and open such a road that he made a way for the old comtur, and also some people, with the cradle borne by two horses."

"And was there no pursuit? How did it happen that no one caught up with them ? "

"There was pursuit, but it could do nothing, for when it came near the knight Arnold faced around and engaged it. May God not grant any man to meet him, for he has strength so dreadful that it is nothing for him to fight alone with a hundred. Three times did he turn, and three times tvas pursuit stopped. The men who were with him perished — all of them. He was alone at last, wounded, it seems to me, and his horse wounded also, but he survived, and gave time to the old comtur for safe escape."

Matsko, listening to this narrative, could not help thinking that Sanderus was speaking truly, for he remembered that, beginning with the place where Skirvoillo had fought, the road in its further continuation was covered with bodies of Jmud men, slashed as dreadfully as if the hand of a giant had slain them.

"But how couldst thou have seen all this?" inquired he.

"I saw it," answered the vagrant, "because I slipped in behind the tail of one of the horses which was carrying the cradle, and I fled with those beasts till a hoof struck rny

stomach; then I fainted and fell into the hands of your mightiness."

"This may have happened," said Hlava, "but see that thou lie not; if thou do thou'lt come out badl\'7d 7 ."

"The mark is on me yet," said Sanderus; "whoso wishes may examine; still it is better to believe my word than be damned for incredulity."

"Though thou mightst tell the truth sometimes without wishing it, thou wilt howl for dealing falsely in sacred wares," added Hlava.

And they began to chaff, as they had formerly, but the conversation was interrupted by Zbyshko, —

"Thou hast passed through this country, hence thou knowest it. What castles are there near here, and where, as it seems to thee, might Arnold and Siegfried secrete themselves? "

"Castles near by there are none, for everything here is a forest, through which this road was cut a short time ago. Settlements and villages there are not, since those which existed the Germans have burnt, for the reason that when this war broke out the people off there, who are of the same race as those here, rose up also against the dominion of the Order. I think, lord, that Arnold and Siegfried are wandering now through the forest and will go back to the place whence they came, or go secretly to that fortress to which we were marching before this unfortunate battle."

"Surely this is true," said Zbyshko.

And he thought deeply. From his wrinkled brows and concentrated expression it was easy to see with what effort he was thinking, but this did not last long. After a while , he raised his head and said, —

"Hlava, let horses and men be ready, for we will take the road straightway."

The attendant, who had the habit of never inquiring for the reason of orders, rose, and, without answering, ran to the horses; but Matsko fixed his eyes on his nephew, and asked with astonishment, —

"Ah! Zbyshko? Hei! But whither art thou going? What? How?"

But Zbyshko answered with a question: "What do you think, ought I not do this? "

The old knight was silent. The astonishment quenched on his face gradually, he moved his head once and a second

time, then breathed from his full breast, and said, as if in answer to himself, —

"Well! let it be so — there is no help! "

And he went himself toward the horses. Zbyshko turned toward De Lorche, and through a Mazovian, who knew German, said to him, —

"I cannot ask thee to help me against people with whom thou art serving under one banner; hence thou art free, go whithersoever it please thee."

"I cannot help thee now with the sword against my knightly honor," answered De Lorche, "but as to freedom, I will not take it. I will remain thy captive on word of honor, and present myself at summons wherever thou mayest indicate. But do thou in case of need remember that for me the Order will exchange any captive, for not only do I come of a powerful family, but from one that has served the Order."

And they began to take farewell, placing, as the custom was, their hands on each other's shoulders, and kissing each other's cheeks, during which De Lorche said, —

"I will go to Malborg, or to Mazovia, to the court, so that thou mayest know where to find me; if not here, I shall be there. Let thy envoy just say two words to me: Lorraine Guelders."

"Very well," answered Zbyshko. "I will go now to Skirvoillo to get the sign which every Jmud man will reverence."

He went then to Skirvoillo. The old leader gave the sign, and made no difficulty as to departure, for he knew what the question was; he loved Zbyshko, he was grateful for the last battle, and besides, he had no right to stop a knight who was of another people, and who had come through personal desire alone. So thanking Zbyshko for the notable service which he had rendered, he gave him provisions which might be of use in that ravaged country, and took farewell, with the wish that they might meet in life again during some great and decisive conflict with the Order.

Zbyshko was impatient, for "something like a fever was consuming him. When he came to his escort he found everything ready, and among the people his uncle on horseback, in chain mail, and on his head a helmet. So, approaching him, he asked,—

"Are you, also, going with me?"

"But what am I to do?" inquired Matsko, somewhat testily.

To this Zbyshko said nothing; he merely kissed the mailed right hand of his uncle, then mounted his horse, and rode forward.

Sauderus rode with them. Zbyshko and his uncle knew the road well to the field of battle, but farther Sanderus was to be the guide. They counted also on this, — that they would meet somewhere in the forest local peasants, men hating their lords of the Order; these would help them in tracking the old comtur and Arnold von Baden, of whose unearthly strength and bravery Sanderus had told so much.

CHAPTEE LI.

To the battlefield on which Skirvoillo had cut down the Germans the road was easy, because it was known; they reached it, therefore, quickly, but rode on in haste because of the unendurable odor given out from unburied corpses. The passing knights dispersed wolves, immense flocks of crows, daws, and ravens. Soon after, they began to search for tracks along the way. Though a whole detachment had passed that road earlier, the experienced Matsko found on the trodden earth gigantic hoof-prints going in a direction opposite to that by which the expedition had come, and explained as follows to the young men less acquainted with military questions, —

"It is lucky that there has been no rain since the battle. Just look! Arnold's horse, as carrying a man bulky beyond others, must have been immense also, and it is easy to note that galloping in escape, he struck the earth more forcibly with his feet than if he had been going slowly, and so he dug deeper holes in it. Look, whoever of you has eyes, how the horseshoes have left their marks in damp places! With God's help we will track on the dog brothers worthily, unless they have found refuge behind walls by this time."

"Sanderus said," answered Zbyshko, "that there are no castles in the neighborhood; and this is true, for the country has been occupied freshly by the Knights of the Order, and they have not been able to build themselves up in it. Where are they to hide? The common men, who live here, are in the camp with Skirvoillo, for they are the same people as the Jmud men. The villages, as Sanderus has told us, have been burnt by the Germans, the women and children are hidden in secret parts of the forest. We shall overtake unless we spare our horses."

"We need to spare them, for even if we should overtake those men our salvation is in the horses afterward," said Matsko.

"Knight Arnold," put in Sanderus, "was struck during the battle on his shoulders with a club. He paid no attention at first to this; he fought on; but afterward it must

have affected him, for it is always so; at first such a wound is not much, but it pains later on. For this reason he cannot flee quickly, and may be forced to take rest."

"But the people, hast thou said that with the knight Arnold and the old comtur there are no people?" inquired Matsko.

"There are two men with the cradle, which is borne between two saddles: There was a good sized party of others, but those the Jmud men overtook and cut to pieces."

"It must be this way," said Zbyshko; "the men at the cradle will be tied by our attendants, you, uncle, seize Siegfried, and I will strike on Arnold."

"Indeed," answered Matsko, "I am able to handle Siegfried, for through the love of the Lord Jesus there is strength in my bones yet. But do not trust overmuch in thyself, for that man must be a giant."

"Oh, we shall see," answered Zbyshko.

"Thou art strong, I do not deny that, but there are stronger. Hast 'thou forgotten those knights of ours whom we saw in Cracow? Couldst thou manage Povala of Tachev, or Pashko Zlodye, or still more, Zavisha Charny? Do not vaunt too much, think of the issue."

"Rotgier was no piece of a man," muttered Zbyshko.

"But will there be no work for me?" inquired Hlava.

He received no answer, for Matsko's mind was occupied with another thing.

"If God bless us," said he, "we must reach Mazovian forests somehow. There we shall be safest, and finish everything at one blow."

But after a while he sighed, thinking surely that even then not everything would be finished, for they would have to do something for Yagenka.

"Hei!" muttered he, "wonderful are God's dispensations! I think often of this: why did it not happen thee to marry quietly, and me to sit near thee in peace? For that is the way it happens oftenest among nobles in our kingdom; we alone are dragging our way along through various lands and pathless places, instead of keeping house at home in Christian fashion."

"Well, that is true, but God's will!" answered Zbyshko.

And they rode on for a time in silence; then the old knight turned again to his nephew.

"Dost thou believe in that vagabond? What sort of man is he?".

VOL. II. — 9

"He is frivolous and a rogue, perhaps, but to me he is very well-wishing, and I fear no treachery on his part."

"In that case let him ride ahead, for if he overtakes them they will not be frightened. He will say that he has fled from captivity, which they will believe easily. It will be better so; for if they see us from a distance, they will be able either to hide somewhere or make ready to defend themselves."

"At night he will not advance alone, for he is timid," answered Zbyshko; "but in the daytime it would be better as you say. I will tell him to halt three times in the day and wait for us; if we do not find him at the halting-place it will mean that he is with them, then we can follow on his trail and strike unexpectedly."

"But will he not forewarn them?"

"No. He is more well-wishing to me than to them. I will tell him, too, that when we attack we will bind him also, so that he need not fear their revenge afterward. Let him not know us at all."

"Then dost thou think to leave them among the living? "

"Well, how is it to be?" answered Zbyshko, with vexation. "If this were in Mazovia, or somewhere in our country, we could challenge them, as I challenged Rotgier, and fight to the death with them; but here in their land this cannot be. Here it is a question of Danusia, and of speed. Here we must act in a breath and quietly, so as not to call peril on our heads by inquiring; after that, as you have said, we are to rush with what breath is in our horses to Mazovia. If we strike unexpectedly, we may find them without weapons, nay, without swords even! How kill them then ? It would be a shame. We are both belted knights, and so are they."

"That is true," answered Matsko. "But it may not come to fighting."

Zbyshko wrinkled his brows and on his face was expressed deep resolution, evidently innate in all men from Bogdanets; at that moment he had become, especially in his looks, as much like Matsko as if he had been his uncle's own son.

"How I should like," said he, in a deep voice, "to throw that blood y cur Siegfried under Yurand's feet! God grant me to do so ! "

"Oh, may He grant it! " repeated Matsko, immediately.

Thus conversing, they rode over a good piece of road.

Night had fallen, — a pleasant night, indeed, but without moonlight. They had to Tialt to rest the horses and strengthen the men with food and sleep. Before resting, however, Zbyshko told Sanderus that he was to go ahead, and alone, on "the morrow. To this he agreed willingly, stipulating only, that in case of peril from wild beasts, or people of the country, he should have the right to return to them. He begged also that he might stop, not three, but four times in the day, for some alarm always seized him in a lonely country, even where there were provisions; but what must it be in a forest as wild and ugly as that in which they found themselves! .

The night camp was pitched, and having strengthened their bodies, they lay down on skins before a small fire made at a bend and distant from the road about half a furlong. The attendants took turns in watching the horses, which, when unsaddled, dozed after they had eaten oats, one putting its head on the neck of another. But barely had dawn silvered the treetops when Zbyshko sprang up, roused the others, and they moved on their further journey at daylight. The tracks left by the immense hoofs of Arnold's stallion were found again without difficulty, for stamped in the low, muddy earth, common there, they remained without drying. Sanderus went ahead and vanished from sight, but half-way between sunrise and mid-day they found him at the resting-place, and he told them that he had not seen a living thing except a bison, before which he had not fled, however, for the beast stepped out of the road first. At mid-day, at the first meal, he declared that he had seen a bee-keeper with a ladder; that he did not stop him, simply out of fear that in the forest depth there might be others like him. He asked the man about this and that, but they could not understand each other.

During the next march Zbyshko began to be alarmed. What would happen should they come to more elevated and drier places, where on a hard road tracks would fail? Also if pursuit should continue too long and bring them to a more inhabited country, where, among people accustomed from of old to obey the Order, an attack and the rescue of Danusia would be almost impossible; where Siegfried and Arnold, though unprotected by the walls of any castle, would be safe, for the local people would take their part surely.

But luckily those fears proved vain, for at the next halt

they did not find Sanderus at the time appointed, but discovered on a pine-tree, standing at the roadside, a large cut in the form of a cross, made freshly as was evident. Then they looked at each other, their faces grew serious and their hearts beat more quickly. Matsko and Zbyshko sprang from their saddles to examine the tracks, and sought carefully, but not long, for the same thing was evident to both men.

Sanderus had left the road for the forest, following the tracks of the great horse, not so deeply made as on the road, but with sufficient clearness; for the ground was turfy, and the great beast pressed down at every step the needle-like pine leaves, on which were left dark depressions at the edges of the hoof-prints.

Before the quick eyes of Zbyshko were not hidden other tracks; hence he mounted his horse, Matsko mounted his also, and they counselled with Hlava in voices which were as low as if the enemy had been right there before them.

Hlava advised to advance on foot at once, but they were unwilling to do so, for they knew not how far they might have to go through that forest. Foot attendants, however, were to go before, and send back word if they saw anything.

They moved into the forest soon. The next cut on a pine-tree assured them that they had not lost the traces of Sanderus. Soon, too, they discovered that they were on a road, or at least on a forest trail over which people must have gone more than one time. So now they felt sure that they would find some settlement, and in it those for whom they were searching.

The sun had sunk already toward its setting and was shining with golden light among the pine-trees. The evening promised to be clear. The forest was quiet, for birds and animals were inclining toward their night rest. Only here and there among branches still in sunlight jumped squirrels all red from evening sunshine. Zbyshko, Matsko, Hlava, and the attendants rode one behind another, in goose Hue. Knowing that the foot attendants were in advance considerably, and would forewarn in season, the old knight was speaking to his nephew and did not restrain his voice excessively.

"Let us count with the sun," said he. "From the last resting-place to the point where the cross was cut we passed a big piece of road. On the clock of Cracow it would be

about three. That being the case, Sanderus is a good while among them, and has had time enough to tell his adventures. If only he .does not betray us."

"He will not betray us."

"And if they believe him," said Matsko; "for if they do not believe him it will go ill with us."

"But why should they not believe him? Or do they know us ? But him they know. It happens frequently that prisoners escape."

"This is important: if he tells them that he is escaping from captivity, perhaps they will fear pursuit of him, and move on immediately."

" No. He will be able to explain that. And they will understand that such a pursuit could not happen."

For a while they were silent; then it seemed to Matsko as if Zbyshko were whispering something to him, so he turned and asked,—

"What dost thou say?"

But Zbyshko had his eyes raised and was not whispering to Matsko; he was committing to God Danusia and his bold undertaking.

Matsko himself was beginning to make the sign of the cross, but he had hardly made the first move in it when one of the attendants in front turned back suddenly from the depth of the forest.

"A tarpit! " said he. "They are there! "

"Stop! " whispered Zbyshko, and that instant he sprang from his horse.

After him Matsko, Hlava, and the attendants, three of whom received the command to hold themselves with their horses in readiness, and see, God defend, that none of the horses neighed. To the five others Matsko said, —

"There are two horseboys there and Sanderus; these you will bind in one flash for me, and if any one who is armed tries to defend himself, strike his head."

And they moved forward immediately. On the road Zbyshko whispered yet to his uncle, —

"You take old Siegfried, and I will take Arnold."

"Only be careful," answered the old man.

And then he beckoned to Hlava, letting him know that at every instant he must be ready to give aid to his master.

Hlava nodded, meaning that he would; then he drew breath into his breast, and felt to find if the sword would

leave its scabbard easily. But Zbyshko saw that and said, —

"No! To thee I give command to rush to the cradle straightway, and not leave it for the space of a hand's breadth during battle."

They went on quickly and in silence, always amidst dense hazel-brush; but they had not gone far, at the most two furlongs, when the brush ceased on a sudden and formed the border of a small plain, on which were evident the extinguished remnants of a tarpit, and two earthen huts, or "numis," in which, beyond doubt, had dwelt tarburners till war expelled them. The rays of the setting sun lighted with immense gleam the plain, the pit, and the two huts standing at some distance from each other. On a log before one of them two knighls were sitting; before the other a broad-shouldered, red-haired man, and Sanderus. These two were occupied with cleaning armor with cloth, but at Sanderus' feet were lying in addition two swords which he had the intention of cleaning later.

"Look," said Matsko, pressing Zbyshko's arm with all his force, so as to restrain him. "He has taken their swords and armor from them purposely. Well done! He with the gray head must be — "

"Forward! " cried Zbyshko, suddenly.

And they shot out to that plain like a whirlwind. Men there sprang up also, but befor.e they could run to Sanderus the terrible Matsko had seized Siegfried by the breast, bent him onto his back in one instant and was above him. Zbyshko and Arnold closed like two falcons, wound their arms around each other, and began to wrestle desperately. The broad-shouldered German, who before that had been sitting near Sanderus, rushed with his sword, it is true; but before he could wield it, Matsko's man, Vit, had struck him with the back of an axe on his red head and stretched him. They hurried then, at command of the old man, to bind Sandeuus. He, though knowing that the thing was agreed on, roared from fright, as a year-old calf does when a man is cutting its throat.

But Zbyshko, though so strong that he had pressed sap from the limb of a young tree, felt that he had come, as it were, not into the arms of a man, but a bear. He felt this, too, that were it not for the armor, which he wore, not knowing but he might meet with sword points, the gigantic German would crush his ribs or break the backbone in him.

It is true that the young man raised Arnold from the ground somewhat, but the German then raised him still higher, and summoning all his strength, strove to strike the earth once with him in such fashion that he would never rise from it.

But Zbyshko also pressed him with such fierce effort that the German's eyes were bloodshot; then he drove his leg between Arnold's knees, struck him behind one knee-joint and whirled him to the earth.

More correctly, both fell, and Zbyshko fell under; but that moment the observant Matsko, throwing the half-crushed Siegfried into the hands of his attendants, rushed himself to his prostrate nephew, and in one twinkle bound Arnold's legs with his belt; then he sprang up and sat on him, as on a slaughtered wild boar, and put the point of his misericordia to the man's throat.

The German screamed piercingly, his arms dropped without strength at both sides of Zbyshko, and he groaned, not alone from the prick of the weapon, but because he felt pain inexpressible from the blow on his shoulders received in the battle with Skirvoillo.

Matsko grasped him by the neck with both hands and dragged him off Zbyshko; Zbyshko rose from the earth into a sitting posture, then tried to rise to his feet, but had not the strength for it; he sat down again and for a long time was motionless, his face pale and sweat-covered, his eyes bloody, his lips blue, and he gazed forward fixedly, as if not completely conscious.

"What is this?" inquired Matsko, frightened.

"Nothing; but I am terribly wearied. Help me to stand on my feet again."

Matsko put his hands under Zbyshko's armpits and raised him.

"Canst thou stand now? "

"I can stand."

"Art in pain? "

"I am not, but breath fails me."

Meanwhile Hlava, who noticed that evidently on the open place everything was over, appeared before the hut, holding by her shoulder the serving-woman of the Order. At sight of her Zbyshko forgot his struggle; his strength returned to him, and he sprang to the hut in one instant as though he had never fought with the dreadful Arnold.

"Danusia! Danusia! " cried he.

But to that cry there was no answer.

"Danusia! Danusia! " repeated Zbyshko.

And he was silent. It was dark in the hut, so at the first moment he could see nothing. But from beyond the stones, which were piled around the fireplace, a quick and loud breathing came, which was like that of a beast driven into a corner.

"Danusia! by the living God! It is I! I am Zbyshko!"

And then he saw her eyes in the gloom; they were opened widely, filled with dread, and no gleam of mind in them.

So he sprang to her and caught her in his arms; but she did not know him, and tearing herself from his grasp, she repeated in a panting whisper,—

"I 'm afraid! I 'm afraid! I 'm afraid! "

CHAPTEE LIT.

NEITHER mild words nor fondling nor imploring availed; Danusia recognized no person, and did not regain her senses. The one feeling which had mastered her whole being was a trembling terror, like that which birds show when captured. She would eat nothing in presence of any one, though, when food was brought, from the greedy looks which she cast at it hunger was evident, perhaps even hunger of long standing. When left alone she rushed to eat with the greed of a wild beast; but when Zbyshko entered the hut she sprang away and hid behind a bundle of dry hops in one corner. Vainly did her husband open his arms, vainly did he stretch his hands toward her, vainly did he implore, while repressing his tears. She would not leave that hiding-place even when the fire was stirred, and when by its light she could recognize Zbyshko. Memory seemed to have left her together with her reason. But he gazed at her and at her thin face, which had on it an expression of terror grown rigid; he gazed at her sunken eyes, at the torn rags of clothing which covered her, and the heart whined in the man from pain and rage at the thought of what kind of hands she had been in, and how they had treated her. At last such fierce and mad anger mastered him that he grasped his sword, rushed at Siegfried, and would have slain him surely had Matsko not seized his arm.

Uncle and nephew wrestled then almost as enemies, but the young man was so weakened by recent struggling with Arnold that the old knight overcame him and held his hand twisted.

" Art mad?" asked he.

"Let me go!" answered Zbyshko, gritting his teeth, "or the soul will tear apart in me."

"Let it tear apart! I will not free thee! Better break thy head on a tree-trunk than disgrace thyself and our family."

And pressing Zbyshko's hand as in an iron vice, he said, threateningly, —

"Look here! Revenge will not escape thee, and thou art a belted knight. How is this ? Wilt thou slaughter a bound captive? Thou wilt not help Danusia by doing so, and what wilt thou gain? Nothing save infamy. Wilt thou say that kings and princes have slain captives? They may have done so, but not in our land. And what the world forgives them it would not forgive thee. They had kingdoms, cities, castles, but what hast thou? Knightly honor. The man who would not blame them would spit in thy eyes. Master thyself, in God's name ! "

A moment of silence followed.

" Unhand me ! " repeated Zbyshko, gloomily; " I will not kill him."

" Go to the fire ; we will take counsel."

Matsko led him to a fire which the attendants had made near the tarpits. When he was seated the old knight thought a while, and said, —

" Remember, too, that thou hast promised to deliver this old hound to Yurand. Yurand will avenge the tortures which he has passed through, and also Danusia's sufferings. He will repay Siegfried, have no fear ! And it is thy duty to yield to Yurand in this case. It belongs to him. Besides, what is not permitted thee is free to Yurand. He did not take the prisoner, but he will get him as a gift from thee. Without disgrace, nay, without blame, he may skin him alive if he wishes. Dost understand?"

" I understand. Thou speakest with reason."

" It is evident that reason is coming back to thee. Should the devil tempt a second time, remember this among other things: thou hast vowed to fight Lichtenstein and other knights; shouldst thou slay a captive, and the deed be bruited about by attendants, no knight would meet thee, and he would be right not to do so. God preserve thee from such a plight! There is no lack of trouble in any case, but whatever happens let no disgrace come. Let us talk now rather of what we are to do, and how we are to manage."

"Talk on," said Zbyshko.

"I would counsel this way: that serpent who is attending Danusia might be killed, but it would not beseem knights to stain themselves with woman's blood, so we will deliver her to Prince Yanush. She was plotting treason even in the hunting-lodge, in presence of the prince and princess; let Mazoviau courts judge her, then, and if they

fail to break her on the wheel, they will offend God's justice. Till we find another woman to attend Danusia, she will be needed; after that she may be tied to the tail of a horse. Now we must go hence to the Mazovian wilderness at the quickest."

" Not this moment, of course, for it is night. Perhaps also God will give more memory to Danusia to-morrow. Let the horses rest well. We will move at daybreak."

Further conversation was interrupted by Arnold von Baden, who, lying on his back at some distance, and bound with his own sword behind his knees, had begun to cry out something in German. Old Matsko rose and went to him, but unable to understand his speech well he looked around for Hlava.

Hlava was unable to come at once, for he was occupied. When the two men had begun their talk at the fire, he went to the serving-woman of the Order, put his hand on her neck, and shaking her like a pear-tree, said, —

"Listen! Thou wilt go to the hut and spread a bed of skins for the lady; but first thou wilt put on her thy own good clothing, and take for thyself the rags in which ye have forced her to travel. Thy mother is in hell!"

And he, also unable to restrain his sudden anger, shook her with such force that the eyes were creeping out of her head. He might have broken her neck, perhaps, but as she seemed to him of use yet, he let her go at last, saying, —

" We will choose out a limb later on for thee."

She seized his knee in terror, but when in answer he kicked her, she ran into the hut, and threw herself at Danusia's feet.

" Defend me! " screamed she. " Do not give me up! "

Danusia merely closed her eyes, and from her lips came the usual panting whisper, —

" I 'm afraid! I 'm afraid ! I 'm afraid ! "

And then she grew rigid altogether, for every approach of that woman had caused this result always. She let herself be unclothed and dressed in the new garments. The serving-woman spread the bed, and laid Danusia on it as she might a figure of wax or wood; then she sat by the fire, not daring to leave the hut.

But Hlava came in after a while and, turning to Danusia, said, —

" You are among friends, my lady ; sleep quietly, in the name of the Father, the Son, and the Spirit." He made

the sign of the cross, then, without raising his voice, lest he might frighten Danusia, he said to the woman of the Order, —

" Thou wilt lie bound outside the door; but if thou make an outcry and frighten her I will break thy neck the next minute. Stand up, and go! "

Leading her out of the hut he bound her, as he had promised, strongly, then he went to Zbyshko.

" I gave command to dress the lady in the clothing which that lizard herself wore," said he. " The bed is spread and the lady is sleeping. Better not go in, lest she be frightened. God grant that she regain her mind to-morrow after sleep ; and think now of food for yourself, and rest."

" I will lie at the threshold of the hut," answered Zbyshko.

" In that case I will take the woman aside to that corpse with the red hair ; but you must eat, for there is a long road and no small toil before you."

So saying he went to bring dried meat and dried turnips, which they had taken in Skirvoillo's camp for the road, but barely had he put a supply before Zbyshko when Matsko sent him to Arnold.

"Find out carefully," said he, "what that mountain roller wants, for though I know some of their words I cannot understand this fellow."

"I will bring him to the fire; then, lord, you may talk with him."

And ungirding himself Hlava put his belt under Arnold's arms and drew him onto his back. He bent greatly under the weight of the giant, but being a strong fellow he bore him to the fire and threw him down like a bag of peas near Matsko.

" Take the bonds from me," said the knight.

" I may do so," answered Matsko, " through Hlava, if thou wilt swear by thy knightly honor to hold thyself a prisoner. And even without that I will command to take the sword from beneath thy knees and unbind thy arms so thou mayest sit near us, but 1 will not take the bonds from thy feet till we have bargained."

And he beckoned to Hlava, who cut the ropes on the German's arms, and then helped him to sit upright. Arnold looked haughtily at Matsko and Zbyshko, and inquired, —

" What sort of people are ye? "

"How clarest thou inquire? What is that to thee? Discover for thyself."

THE KNIGHTS OF THE CROSS. 141

" It is this to me, that I can swear on knightly honor only to knights."

"Then look! "

And Matsko, pushing aside his coat, showed the belt of a knight above his hips.

At this Arnold was greatly astonished, and inquired only after a while, —

" How is this? And still ye plunder people through the forest, and help pagans against Christians."

" Thou liest! " exclaimed Matsko.

And the conversation began thus, unfriendly, haughty, at moments like fighting. But when Matsko shouted angrily that it was the Order alone which prevented the baptism of Lithuania, and when he brought forward all the arguments, Arnold was astonished again, and stopped talking, for the truth became so evident that it was impossible not to see it, or to deny it. The German was struck specially by these words from Matsko, who made the sign of the cross as he uttered them, —

"Who knows whom ye serve really, —if not all, then some of you ? " and he was struck because there was in the Order itself a suspicion that certain comturs rendered honor to Satan. No action was brought against them, lest infamy might result to all, but Arnold knew well that those reports were whispered among the Brothers, and that stories of that kind were current. Meanwhile Matsko, knowing Siegfried's strange deeds from what Sanderus had told, alarmed the simple-minded giant Arnold thoroughly.

" And that Siegfried with whom thou wert marching to the war," said he. " Is he serving God and Christ? Hast thou never heard how he talks with evil spirits, how he whispers to them and laughs or gnashes his teeth in their company ? "

" It is true ! " muttered Arnold.

But Zbyshko, to whose heart sorrow and anger flowed in a new current, shouted suddenly, —

"And thou art talking of knightly honor! Shame on thee, for thou hast helped a hangman and a hell-dweller! Shame on thee, for thou hast looked calmly at the torture of an unprotected woman, a knight's daughter, and perhaps thou hast tortured her thyself. Shame on thee! "

Arnold stared and said, making the sign of the cross, —

"In the name of the Father, the Son, and the Spirit! How is this ? Do you speak of that possessed girl in whose head twenty-seven devils are living ? I — ? "

" Woe! woe! " broke in Zbyshko with a hoarse voice. And seising the hilt of his misericordia he looked again with a wild glance toward Siegfried, who was lying in the dark at some distance.

Matsko put his hand on his nephew's arm quietly and squeezed it with all his might to restore thought to the young man, and turning toward Arnold, he said, —

"That woman is the daughter of Yurand of Spyhov, and is the wife of this knight. Thou canst understand now why we tracked thee and thy company, and why thou hast become our prisoner."

"In God's name!" said Arnold. "Whence? How? Her mind is disturbed ! "

"For the Knights of the Cross stole her away as they might steal an innocent lamb, and brought her by torture to that state."

At the words "innocent lamb" Zbyshko brought his fist to his lips and pressed his knuckles against his teeth, while from his eyes great tears of irresistible pain dropped one after another. Arnold sat thoughtfully. Hlava told him in a few words of Danveld's treachery, the seizure of Danusia, the torture of Yurand, and the duel with Rotgier. When he had finished there was a silence unbroken save by the sound of the forest and the crackling of sparks in the camp-fire.

They sat thus for some time, till at last Arnold raised his head.

"I swear," said he, "not only on knightly honor, but on the cross of Christ, that I have hardly seen that woman, that I knew not who she was, and that I have moved no hand to torture her in any way, at any time."

" Swear now that thou wilt go with us of thy own will, without trying to escape, and I will command to unbind thee altogether," said Matsko.

" Let it be as thou sayest; I swear! Whither wilt thou take me? "

" To Mazovia, to Yurand of Spyhov."

Thus speaking, Matsko himself cut the ropes on Arnold's legs and pointed to the meat and the turnips. After a ^|hile Zbyshko rose and went to lie at the threshold of the hut, where he did not find the serving-woman of the Order, for the attendants had taken her to their place among the horses. Zbyshko lay on a skin which Hlava brought him, and resolved to wait without sleep, hoping that daylight would bring a happy change to Danusia.

Hlava returned to the fire, for something was weighing on his soul, which he wished to tell the old knight from Bog-danets. He found him sunk also in thought, paying no heed to the snoring of Arnold, who after his toil had eaten of meat and turnips immensely and was sleeping as soundly as a stone.

" But are you awake ? " inquired Hlava.

"Sleep flies from my lids," answered Matsko. "God grant a good morrow." Then he looked toward the stars. " The Great Bear is in the sky, and I am thinking how all this will turn out."

"I too have no thought of sleep, for the lady of Zgorzelitse is in my head."

" Hei, true, a new trouble! She is in Spyhov, that is true."

"Yes, in Spyhov. We took her from her home. Why did we take her ? "

" She herself wished to go," was the impatient answer of Matsko, who talked of this matter reluctantly, for in his soul he felt guilty.

"True, but what now? "

" Ah, what? I will take her home, and let the will of God be done; " but after a while he added: " Very well, let the will of God be done; if only Danusia were in health and like other people we should know at least what to do. But now, the devil knows! If she does not recover — and if she does not die — May the Lord Jesus incline either to this or to that side — "

But Hlava at that moment was thinking of Yagenka.

"You see, your Grace," said he, "when I left Spyhov and took farewell of the lady, she said: ' In case something happens, come hither thou before Zbyshko and Matsko ; they must send some one with news, let them send thee, and thou wilt take me to Zgorzelitse.' "

" Oh! it is true," answered Matsko, "that when Danusia comes it would be awkward for Yagenka in Spyhov. It i"s sure that she would need to go home immediately. I am sorry for the orphan, I am sorry, but, since the will of God did not favor, the position is difficult! How arrange this ? Wait — thou sayest that she commanded thee to return before us with the news, and take her home?"

" She commanded as I have told thee faithfully."

" Well, then, thou mayest go before us. There is need also to tell Yurand that his daughter is found, so as not to kill

the man with sudden joy. As God is dear to me there is nothing better to be done. Return; say that we have recovered Danusia and will come soon with her, and do thou take that poor girl and conduct her home."

The old knight sighed. In truth he was sorry for Yagenka, and those plans which he had cherished in his soul. After a while he said, —

" Thou art a man of wit, and thou art stalwart I know that, but wilt thou be able to guard her against wrong or accident ? On the road the one or the other may happen."

" I shall be able, even were I to lay down my head. I can take a number of good men whom the master of Spyhov will not begrudge me, and conduct her safely to the end of the earth were it needed."

" Do not trust over much in thyself. Remember too that thou must have an eye on Vilk and Stan in Zgorzelitse — but I am not speaking to the point; we had need to watch them while there was another man in view, but as she has no hope now of Zbyshko she must marry some one."

" Still I shall guard the lady even from those two knights, for Pan Zbyshko's wife, the poor thing, is barely breathing — she is just as if dead! "

"True, as God is dear to me, the poor thing is barely living, she is as if dead."

' c "We must leave that to the Lord God ; and now let us think only of the lady."

" In justice," said Matsko, " I ought to conduct her to her father's house. But the position is difficult. For various great reasons I cannot leave Zbyshko. Thou sawest how he gritted his teeth and rushed at that old comtur to stab him, as one would a wild boar. Should that girl die on the road, as thou sayest, I am not sure that even I could restrain him. Should I be absent nothing could hold him back, and infamy would fall on him and our whole family forever. God avert this, amen ! "

"There is a simple method," said Hlava. "Give me Siegfried. I will not lose him, and only in Spyhov will I shake him out of the bag before Pan Yurand."

" God give thee health ! Oh thou hast wit ! " cried Matsko, delighted. "A simple thing! a simple thing! Take him, and if thou deliver him alive at Spyhov, do with him as thou choosest."

" Give me also that Schytno bitch. If she does not resist on the road, I will take her also to Spyhov; should she resist I will hang her on a limb."

" Terror might leave Danusia sooner, and she might come to her mind more quickly were she freed from the sight of those two. But if thou take her what are we to do without the help of a woman?"

"You will surely meet people in the forest, or find fugitives with women. Take the first woman you come upon; any will be better than that wretch. Meanwhile Pan Zbyshko's care will suffice."

"To-day thou art speaking with more wit than common. That too is true. She may come to herself more quickly when she sees Zbyshko always near her. He can be to her a father and a mother. Let it be so. When wilt thou start?"

" I shall not wait for the dawn, but lie down now. It is not midnight yet, I think."

" The Great Bear is still shining, but the triangle has not appeared."

" Praise be to God that we have settled on something, for I was cruelly saddened."

Hlava stretched then before the dying fire, covered himself with a shaggy skin, and was asleep in a moment. But the sky had not whitened in the least, and it was deep night when he woke, crawled forth from under the skin, looked at the stars, stretched his limbs, which were somewhat stiffened, and roused Matsko.

" For me it is time to be off," said he.

"But whither?" asked Matsko, half asleep, rubbing his eyes with his fists.

"To Spyhov."

"Oh, true? Who is this snoring beside us? He would wake a dead man."

" Knight Arnold. I will throw limbs on the fire and go to the attendants."

He went, but returned with a hurried step and called in a low voice from some distance,

—

" I have news, lord, — and bad news! "

"What has happened?" cried Matsko, springing up.

"The serving-woman has fled. The attendants took her to their place among the horses— may the thunderbolts split them ! — when they fell asleep she slipped out, like a snake, from among them, and fled. Come, lord."

Matsko was alarmed and moved quickly with Hlava toward the horses, but they found only one attendant; the others had rushed off in search of the fugitive. But that search was a stupid one, through darkness and among thickets; in fact, they returned soon with their heads down. Matsko belabored them with his.lists, but without words; then he went back to the fire, for there was nothing else to do.

Zbyshko came soon from his post of sentry at the hut door. Sleepless he had heard the tramping and wished to learn what the trouble was. Matsko told him of the arrangement with Hlava, then of the escape of the serving-woman.

"That is no great misfortune," said he. "She will die of hunger in the forest, or be.found by people who will beat her, unless wolves find her earlier. The one pity is that punishment in Spyhov has missed her."

Zbyshko was sorry that punishment had missed her, but otherwise he received the news calmly. He did not oppose the departure of Hlava with Siegfried, for everything which did not touch Danusia directly was to him indifferent. He began at once to speak of her, —

"I will take her to-morrow on the horse, in front of me, and we shall travel on in that way."

"Is she sleeping?" inquired Matsko.

" Sometimes she whines a little, but I cannot tell whether she is awake or asleep. I am afraid to go in, lest I frighten her."

Further conversation was interrupted by Hlava, who, seeing Zbyshko, said, —

"Oh, your Grace is up also? Well, it is time for me to go. The horses are ready, and the old devil is tied to the saddle. It will be dawn soon, for the nights are short at this season. God be with you, your Graces."

" Go with God, and be well!"

But Hlava drew Matsko aside, and said, —

" I wished to make an earnest request of you. If some-tiling happens, some misfortune, or — what shall we call it? — hurry a man off directly to Spyhov, and if we have gone from there let him overtake us."

"Very good," said Matsko, "I forgot to tell thee to take Yagenka to Plotsk. Go to the bishop there, tell him who she is, say that she is the goddaughter of the abbot, that he, the bishop, holds a will in her favor, and

mention the guardianship over her, for that is in the will also."

• k But if the bishop commands us to remain in Plotsk? "

"• Obey him in all things, and do what he advises."

" Thus will it be, lord. With God! "

"With God!"

CHAPTEE LIII.

THE knight Arnold, on hearing next morning of the flight of the serving-woman, smiled, but said the same as Matsko, that either the wolves would devour her or the Lithuanians would kill the wretch. In fact this was likely, for villagers of Lithuanian origin hated the Order and all who had relations with it. The peasants had fled in part to Skirvoillo, in part they had revolted, here and there they had slain Germans and then concealed themselves quickly, with their families and cattle, in deep inaccessible forests. Matsko and Zbyshko sent out to search for the serving-woman next day, but without result, for the search was not over earnest, since the two men had their heads filled with other things, and had not given orders with sufficient sternness. They were in haste to set out for Mazovia, and wished to move at once after sunrise, but could not do so, for Danusia had fallen into deep slumber before daylight, and Zbyshko would not permit any one to rouse her. He had heard her " whining" in the night, and thought that she was not sleeping, so now he expected much good from this sleep. Twice he stole up to the hut, and twice, by the sunlight coming in between the logs, he saw her closed eyes and open mouth, as well as the deep flush on her face, such as children have when sleeping soundly. The heart melted in him from emotion. "God give thee health and rest, dearest flower!" said he. And then he said again: "Thy misfortune is over, thy weeping is ended, and the merciful Lord Jesus will grant thy happiness to be as the waters of a river which have not flowed past yet." As he had a simple soul and was generous, he raised it to God and asked himself, " With what am I to give thanks; with what can I repay; what can I offer to some church, from my possessions, my grain, my herds, wax, or other things of like nature precious to Divine Power? " He would have promised even then and mentioned exactly what he was offering, but he preferred to •wait, since he knew not in what health Danusia would wake, or whether she would wake in her senses; he was not sure yet that he would have anything for which to be thankful.

Matsko, though knowing that they would be perfectly safe only in the territories of Prince Yanush, thought that it was not proper to disturb Danusia's rest, as it might be her salvation; so he kept the attendants ready and also the pack-horses, but he waited.

Still, when midday had passed and she slept on, they grew frightened. Zbyshko, who looked through the cracks and the door unceasingly, entered the hut for the third time and sat on the log which the serving-woman had drawn to the bedside, and on which she had changed her clothes for Danusia's.

He sat there and looked at her; she had not opened her eyes yet, but after as much time had passed as would have been needed to say without haste one " Our Father" and "Hail, Mary," her lips quivered a little and she whispered, as if she beheld him through her closed eyelids, —

"Zbyshko!"

In an instant he threw himself on his knees before her, seized her thin hands, and kissed them with ecstasy.

"Thanks to God! " said he, in a broken voice; " Danusia, thou hast recognized me."

His voice roused her; she sat up on the bed and with eyes now open repeated, —

"Zbyshko!"

Then she muttered and stared around as if in wonder.

"Thou art not in captivity," said he ; "I have torn thee away from them, and we are going to Spyhov."

But she drew her hand away from his grasp, and said, —

" All this happened because father's leave was not given. Where is the princess ? "

" Wake, oh, my berry! The princess is far from here, but we have taken thee from the Germans."

" They have taken my lute too and broken it against a wall," continued she, as if talking to herself without hearing him.

" By the dear God ! " exclaimed Zbyshko.

Now he noted for the first time that her eyes were gleaming and vacant, her cheeks on fire. At that moment the idea flashed through his head that perhaps she was grievously ill and mentioned his name twice only because it occurred to her in the fever; his heart quivered from dread, and cold sweat came out on his forehead.

" Danusia! " said he, " dost thou see me and understand ? " But she answered in a voice of humble entreaty: " Water — Drink !"

" Merciful Jesus! "

He sprang out of the hut, and at the door struck against Matsko; he threw at him the one word " Water," and rushed toward the brook which was flowing near by through forest moss and a thicket.

He returned soon with water, which he gave to Danusia, who drank eagerly. Matsko had entered the hut, for he had come to learn how things were, and was looking with a frown at the sick woman.

" She is in a fever," said he.

" Yes," groaned Zbyshko.

" Does she understand what thou sayest?"

"No."

The old man frowned again, then raised his hand and rubbed the back of his head and his neck with it.

"What is to be done?"

" I know not."

" There is only one thing," said Matsko.

But Dauusia interrupted him at that moment When she had finished drinking she fixed on him eyes widely open from fever, and said, —

" I have not offended thee; forgive."

" I forgive, child; I wish only thy good," answered the old knight, with some emotion.

" Listen," said he to Zbyshko. " There is no reason why she should stay here. When the wind blows around her, and the sun warms her, she may feel better. Do not lose thy head, boy, but put her into that same cradle in which they carried her,"or on thy saddle, and to the road! Dost understand?"

After these words he started to leave the hut and give final orders, but barely had he looked out when he stood as if fixed to the earth. A strong detachment of infantry, armed with spears and halberds, had surrounded on four sides, as with a wall, the hut, the field, and the tarpits.

" Germans! " thought Matsko.

His soul was filled with a shudder, but he grasped his sword-hilt, gritted his teeth, and stood like a wild beast which, brought to bay by dogs on a sudden, is preparing to defend itself desperately. Meanwhile the giant Arnold with some other knight approached from the tarpits, and when he had come up be said, —

"The wheel of fortune changes; I was your prisoner, but now you are ours." He looked then with pride at the

old knight, as at some creature beneath him. He was not a bad man at all, nor over-cruel, but he had the defect common to Knights of the Order, who, affable in misfortune, and even yielding, could never restrain their contempt for the conquered, or their limitless pride when they felt superior power behind them. " You are prisoners," repeated he, loftily.

The old knight looked around gloomily. In his breast beat a heart that was not timid, it was even bold to excess. Had he been in armor on his war-horse, had Zbyshko been at his side, if both had held in their hands swords, axes, or those terrible " trees" which the Polish knights of that period wielded so skilfully, he might have tried, perhaps, to break through that wall of spears and halberds. It was not without reason that foreign knights called to the Poles at Vilno, " Ye despise death too much," thus reproaching them. But Matsko was on foot before Arnold, alone, without armor; so when he saw that the attendants had laid down their weapons, and remembered that Zbyshko was in the hut with Danusia and unarmed, he understood, as a man of experience and greatly accustomed to warfare, that he was helpless; so he drew his sword from its sheath slowly and cast it at the feet of the knight who was standing near Arnold. That knight spoke with no less pride than Arnold, but in good Polish and affably: —

" What is your name, sir? I shall not command to bind you if you give your word, since you, as I see, are a belted knight, and have treated my brother humanely."

" I give my word," answered Matsko. And when he had told who he was, he inquired if he might go to the hut and warn his nephew against any unwise act. On receiving permission he vanished in the door, and after a while appeared again bearing in his hand a misericordia.

" My nephew," said he, " has not even a sword with him, and begs to remain with his wife till you start from here."

" Let him stay," said Arnold's brother. " I will send food and drink to him, for we shall not start immediately; the men are tired, and we need food and rest ourselves. I beg you to join us."

They turned then and went toward that same fire at which Matsko had spent the night previous, but whether through rudeness or pride, — the former was common enough among Germans, — they went in advance, letting Matsko follow. But he, having seen very much, and understanding what manners were proper on every occasion, inquired, —

" Gentlemen, do you invite me as a guest or as a prisoner ? "

Arnold's brother was ashamed, for he halted and said, —

" Pass on, sir."

The old knight went ahead, but not wishing to wound the vanity of a man who to him might be greatly important, he said, —

"It is evident, sir, that you know not only various languages, but polite intercourse."

Arnold understood only a few words. ""Wolfgang," asked he, "what is the question? What is he saying?"

"He talks sensibly," answered Wolfgang, who was flattered by Matsko's words, evidently.

They sat at the fire, to which food and drink were brought. The lesson given the Germans by Matsko was not lost, for Wolfgang ordered to serve him first. In conversation the old knight learned how he and his nephew had been caught: Wolfgang, a younger brother of Arnold, was leading the Chluhov infantry to Gotteswerder, also against the insurgent Jmud men. As they came from a distant province they had failed to come up with the cavalry. Arnold had no need to wait for them, knowing that on the road he would meet other mounted divisions from towns and castles near the Lithuanian boundary ; for this reason the younger brother came somewhat later, and was on the road in the neighborhood of the tarpits when the serving-woman who had fled in the night-time, informed him of the mishap which had met his elder brother. Arnold, listening to that narrative, which was repeated to him in German, laughed with satisfaction, and declared at last that he had hoped things would turn out so; but the experienced Matsko, who in every strait tried to find some relief, thought it useful to win those two Germans; so he said, —

"It is always grievous to fall into captivity, but I am grateful that God has not given me into other hands, for, by my faith, you are real knights who observe honor."

At this Wolfgang closed his eyes and nodded, rather stiffly, it is true, but with evident satisfaction.

" And you know our speech so well," continued Matsko. "God, I see, has given you a mind for everything."

"I know your language, for in Chluhov the people talk Polish. My brother and I have served seven years there under the comtur."

"And you will receive his office after him; it cannot be
otherwise. But your brother does not speak our language as you do."

"He understands some, but does not speak. My brother has more strength than I, though I am not a piece of a man, but his wit is duller."

" Oh, he is not dull, as it seems to me," said Matsko.

" Wolfgang, what does he say?" inquired Arnold again.

" He praises thee."

"Of course I do," added Matsko, "for he is a true knight, and that is the main thing. I tell you sincerely that I intended to free him to-day on his word, and let him go whithersoever he wished, if he would return in a year even. That is as it should be among belted knights; " and he looked into Wolfgang's face carefully.

Wolfgang frowned and said: "I would let you go on your word perhaps, if you had not helped pagan dogs against our people."

" We have not," answered Matsko.

And now rose the same kind of sharp dispute as on the day previous with Arnold. Though truth was on the old knight's side, he had more trouble now, for Wolfgang was keener than his brother. But from the discussion came this good, that the younger brother too heard of all the crimes of Schytno, its false oaths and treacheries, and also of the fate of the unfortunate Danusia. Touching this and the crimes which Matsko brought before him, he had nothing to answer. He was forced to confess that their revenge was just, and that the Polish knights had the right to act as they had acted.

"By the sacred bones of Liborius, I shall not pity Dan-veld. They say that he practised the black art, but God's power and justice are greater than the black art. As for Siegfried, I have no means of knowing if he served the devil also, but I shall make no pursuit to save him ; for, first, I have not the cavalry, and, second, if he tortured that girl, let him not peep even once out of hell." Here he stretched himself and added : " God aid me now and at my death hour."

" But with that unfortunate martyr, how will it be?" inquired Matsko. " Will you not give permission to take her home? Is she to die in your dungeons? Think of God's anger."

"I have no affair with the woman," answered Wolfgang, abruptly. "Let one of you take her to her father if ho will come back, but I will not let off the other."

" Not if I were to swear on my honor, and the spear of Saint George?"

Wolfgang hesitated somewhat, for the oath was a great one, but at that moment Arnold asked him the third time, " What does he say?" And on learning what the question was he opposed passionately and rudely the liberation of both on their word. In this he found his own reckoning. He had been beaten by Skirvoillo in the greater battle, and in single combat by those Polish knights. As a soldier he knew too that his brother's infantry must return to Mal-borg, for if they wished to go on to Gotteswerder they would go after the destruction of the previous detachments, as if to be slaughtered. He knew, therefore, that he would have to stand before the Master and the marshal, and he understood that his disgrace would be decreased could he show even one considerable captive. One living knight whom he could present to the eye would mean more than a story stating that he had captured two.

Matsko, hearing the hoarse outburst and curses of Arnold, understood straightway that he ought to accept what they gave since he would gain nothing more, and he said, turning to Wolfgang, —

"Now I ask you for another thing; I am sure that my nephew will himself understand that he is to be with his wife, and I with you ; but in every case permit me to inform him that there is no parleying in this matter, for such is your will."

"Very good; it is all one to me," answered Wolfgang; "but let us talk of the ransom which your nephew is to bring for himself and for you, since on this depends all."

"Of the ransom?" inquired Matsko, who would have deferred this conversation till another day. " Have we not time enough before us? When one has to do with a belted knight a word is the same as ready money ; and as to the amount, we may leave that to conscience. Before Gotteswerder we took captive a considerable knight of yours, a certain Pan de Lorche, and my nephew, he it was who took him, let the knight go on his word, making no mention at all of the amount of the ransom."

" Did you capture De Lorche?" asked Wolfgang, quickly. " I know him ; he is a wealthy knight. But why have we not met him on the road ? "

•'Because, as is evident, he went not to Malborg, but to Gotteswerder or Ragueta," answered Matsko.

'* Oh, he is wealthy and of noted family," said Wolfgang. " You have made a rich capture; it is well that you mentioned this, I will not free you now for a trifle."

Matsko bit his moustache, but raised his head proudly, and said,—

" We know our worth without that."

" So much the better," answered the younger Von Baden; but immediately he added, " so much the better, but not for us, —we are humble monks who have vowed poverty, —but better for the Order, which will use your money to the glory of God."

Matsko made no answer to this, but he looked at Wolfgang as if to say, " Tell that to some other man," and after a while they began to arrange the terms. This for the old knight was disagreeable and difficult, for on the one hand he was very sensitive to losses,, and on the other, he understood that it became neither him nor Zbyshko to put on themselves too small a value. He -squirmed therefore like an eel, all the more since Wolfgang, though of smooth and pleasant speech, proved to be immensely greedy, and as hard as stone. The only comfort for Matsko was the thought that De Lorche would pay for all, but he regretted the lost hope of gain. He did not count on the ransom of Siegfried, for he thought that Yurand, and even Zbyshko, would not renounce the old comtur's head for any sum. After long talk he agreed as to the amount of money and the interval, and, having stipulated the number of attendants and horses which Zbyshko was to take, he went to tell him. At the same time he advised his nephew to set out immediately. Evidently he did this through fear lest some new thought might strike the Germans.

" Such is the knightly condition," said he, sighing; " yesterday thou hadst them by the head, to-day they have thee. Yes, it is difficult; God grant that our turn come another day. But lose no time; .by going quickly thou wilt overtake Hlava, and it will be safer for you both in company; but once out of the forest and in the inhabited part of Mazo-via ye will find entertainment, assistance, and care at the house of any noble or land-tiller. With us no one refuses these services to a stranger, much less to our own people; for this poor woman there will be perhaps salvation in the journey."

Thus speaking, he looked at Danusia, who, sunk in half lethargy, breathed loudly and quickly. Her transparent

hands lying on the dark bearskin trembled feverishly. Matsko made the sign of the cross on her, and said, —

" God change this, for she is spinning fine, as it seems to me."

" Do not say that," cried Zbyshko, with despairing emphasis.

" God is mighty. I will direct to bring the horses here, and do thou go."

Matsko went from the hut, and arranged everything for the journey. The Turks given by Zavisha brought the horses with the cradle, which was lined with moss and skins, and Vit, the attendant, brought Zbyshko's saddle-horse.

After a while Zbyshko bore Danusia out of the hut on one arm. There was something so touching in this that the brothers Von Baden, whose curiosity had led them to the hut, when they saw the half-childish form of Danusia, her face which resembled the faces of sacred virgins in church pictures, and her weakness so great that she could not move her head which had dropped heavily on Zbyshko's shoulder, looked at each other, and their hearts rose against the authors of such misery.

" Siegfried had the heart of an executioner, not of a knight," whispered Wolfgang to his brother; " and though she was the cause of freeing thee, I will have that serpent flogged with rods."

They were moved by this too, that Zbyshko was carrying Danusia on his arm as a mother would a child, and they understood his love, for both had the blood of youth in their veins yet.

Zbyshko hesitated a while whether to take the sick woman to the saddle, and hold her before him on the road, or put her in the cradle. He decided finally for the cradle, thinking that it would be easier for Danusia to travel lying down. Then approaching his uncle, he bent to kiss his hand in parting. Matsko, who loved him. as the apple of his eye, though he had no wish to show emotion before Germans, did not restrain himself, but embraced Zbyshko firmly, pressing his lips to his rich golden hair.

" God go with thee," said he ; " but think of the old man, for captivity is bitter in every case."

" I will not forget," answered Zbyshko.

" May the Most Holy Mother give thee solace! "

" God reward thee for those words, and for everything."

After a while Zbyshko was on his horse, but Matsko

thought of something, for he sprang to his nephew, and putting his hand on his knee, said,

—

" Listen! If thou overtake Hlava, be careful as to Siegfried that thou bring no disgrace on thyself and my gray hairs; Yurand may act, not thou. Swear to me on thy sword and on thy honor! "

" Until you are freed I will restrain Yurand also, so that the Germans should not avenge Siegfried on you," answered Zbyshko.

" Art thou so concerned about me ? "

"Thou knowest me, I think," replied Zbyshko, smiling sadly.

"To the road! Go in health! "

The horses started and soon the bright hazel thickets hid them. Ah 1 at once Matsko grew terribly sad and lonely; his soul was tearing away with all its force after that dear boy, in whom the whole hope of his race lay. But immediately he shook himself out of his sorrow, for he was a firm man, with self-mastery.

" Thank God that 1 am the captive, not Zbyshko," thought he; and turning to the Germans, he asked, —

" And, gentlemen, when will you start, and whither will you go?"

" We will start when it pleases us," answered Wolfgang, " and we shall go to Malborg, where first of all you will have to stand before the Grand Master."

" Hei, they are ready there to cut my head off for helping the Jmud men," thought Matsko. But he was comforted by this, that De Lorche was in reserve, and that the Von Badens themselves would defend his life if only to save the ransom.

" If they take my head, Zbyshko will not need to come himself, and decrease his property; " and this thought brought him a certain solace.

CHAPTER LTV.

ZBYSHKO could not overtake his attendant, for Hlava travelled night and day, resting only as much as was absolutely needed to save the horses from falling dead. These beasts, since they ate only grass, were weak and could not go so far through the forests in a day as in places where oats were found easily. Hlava spared not himself, and had no regard for the advanced age and weakness of Siegfried. The old Knight of the Cross suffered terribly, therefore, all the more since the strong Matsko had hurt his bones previously at the tarpit. But most grievous for the old man were the gnats swarming in the damp forests. He could not drive them away, for his hands were tied, and his feet bound under the horse's belly. Hlava did not, it is true, inflict any torture, but he had no pity on Siegfried, and freed his right hand only when they halted for eating. " Eat, wolf snout, so that I may bring thee alive to the master of Spyhov." Such were the words with which he encouraged him to refreshment. At the beginning of that journey the thought had come to Siegfried to kill himself by hunger ; but when he heard Hlava-say that he would open his teeth with a dagger, and put nourishment down his throat forcibly, he preferred to yield rather than permit insult to his honor as a knight, and his dignity as a member of the Order.

Hlava wished at all costs to reach Spyhov considerably earlier than Zbyshko, so as to save his lady from confusion. He, a petty noble, simple but clever and not deficient iu knightly feeling, understood clearly that there would be something of humiliation for Yagenka to be in Spyhov at the same time with Danusia. " We may tell the bishop in Plotsk," thought he, " that the old lord of Bogdanets, because of guardianship, had to take her with him ; and then, let it be only mentioned that she is under the protection of the bishop, and that she has at Zgorzelitse an inheritance from the abbot, even a voevoda's son will not be too much for her." This reckoning sweetened the toils of his journey, for he was troubled by the thought that the happy news which he was taking to Spyhov would be for his mistress a sentence of misery.

Anulka appeared before his eyes often as blushing as an apple. At those times he touched the sides of his horse with spurs, as much as the road permitted, such was his hurry to Spyhov.

They advanced by uncertain roads, or rather without roads, straight ahead as the cast of a sickle. Hlava knew only that going always a little to the west and always to the south they must reach Mazovia, and then all would be well. In the daytime he followed the sun, and when the journey stretched into the night he looked at the stars. The wilderness before him seemed to have neither bound nor limit. Days and nights flowed past in a night-like gloom. More than once Hlava thought that Zbyshko would not bring a woman alive through those terrible uninhabited regions, where there was no place to find provisions, where at night they had to guard their horses from bears and wolves, and leave the road in the daytime before bulls and bisons, where terrible wild boars sharpened their tusks against pine roots, and where frequently he who did not shoot from a crossbow, or pierce with a spear the spotted sides of a fawn or a young pig, had no food for days in succession.

"What will he do," thought Hlava, " travelling with a woman nearly tortured to death and almost breathing her last breath ? "

Time after time he had to go around broad morasses or deep ravines at the bottom of which torrents, swollen by spring rains, were roaring. There was no lack, in this wilderness, of lakes in which he saw at sunset herds of elk or deer swimming in ruddy, smooth waters. Sometimes he noticed smoke, announcing the presence of people; a number of times he approached such forest places, but wild men ran out to meet him; these wore skins of wild beasts on their naked bodies, they were armed with clubs and bows, and stared ominously from beneath matted locks. The attendants mistook them for wolf-men. Hlava had to make quick use of the first astonishment caused by the spectacle of a knight, and ride away as swiftly as possible. Twice arrows whistled behind him, and the shout " Vokili! " (Germans !) followed. But he chose rather to fly than explain who he was. At last after many days he began to suppose that he might have passed the boundary. He learned first

from banters speaking Polish that he was on Mazovian ground at last.

It was easier there, though eastern Mazovia was one rustling wilderness. Uninhabited places had not ended yet; still, wherever there was a house, the inhabitants were less morose, — perhaps because they had not met with continual hatred, and perhaps, too, because Hlava spoke a language understood by them. His only trouble was the immense curiosity of those people, who surrounded the horsemen in crowds and overwhelmed them with questions.

" Give him to us, we will take care of him ! " said they, on learning that the prisoner was a Knight of the Cross.

And they begged so persistently that Hlava was forced often to be angry, or to explain that the prisoner belonged to Prince Yanush. Then they yielded. Later on, in a region inhabited by nobles and land-tillers, it did not go easily either. Hatred was seething there against the Knights of the Order, for people remembered vividly in all places the treachery and wrong inflicted on the prince when in time of profound peace the Knights seized him in Zlotoria and held him prisoner. They did not wish, it is true, " to do justice " there to Siegfried, but this or that sturdy noble said: "Unbind him. I will give him a weapon and call him to death inside a barrier." Into the head of those, Hlava drove the idea as with a spade that the first right to vengeance belonged to the ill-fated master of Spyhov, and that they were not free to take that right from him.

In settled regions the journey was easy, for there were roads of some kind, and the horses were fed everywhere with oats and barley. Hlava drove quickly, therefore, halting in no place, and ten days before Corpus Christi he was at Spyhov.

He arrived in the evening, as he had when Matsko sent him back from Schytno with tidings of his departure for the Jmud land, and, just as on that day, Yagenka, seeing him from the window, ran down quickly. He fell at her feet, unable to utter a word for some time; but she raised him and took the man upstairs as quickly as possible, not wishing to ask questions before people.

" What news? " inquired she, quivering from impatience, and hardly able to catch her breath. "Are they alive? Are they well ? "

" They are alive! they are well."

" And she? — have they found her?"

" She is found. They have rescued her."

" Praised be Jesus Christ! "

But in spite of these words Yagenka's face became as if frozen, for all her hopes were scattered to dust in one moment. But strength did not leave her; she did not lose presence of mind; after a while she mastered herself perfectly, and asked,—

" When will they be here? "

"After some days. The road with a sick woman is difficult."

"Is she sick?"

" Tortured to death. Her mind is disturbed from suffering."

"Merciful Jesus!"

A brief silence followed, but Yagenka's lips grew pale, and moved as if in prayer.

" Did she not come to her mind in presence of Zbyshko?" asked she.

" Maybe she did, but I do not know, for I left there immediately to inform you, my lady, before they could reach Spyhov."

" God reward thee. Tell how it was."

Hlava narrated briefly how they had intercepted Danusia and captured both the giant Arnold and Siegfried. He declared too that he had brought Siegfried to Spyhov, since the young lord wished to deliver him to Yurand as a gift and for purposes of vengeance.

"I must go now to Yurand," said Yagenka when the narrative was finished.

And she went, but Hlava was not long alone, for Anulka ran out to him from a closet, and he, whether he was not entirely conscious from immense toil and weariness, or whether he was yearning for her and forgot himself the moment he saw the girl, he seized her by the waist, pressed her to his bosom, and kissed her cheeks, lips, and eyes in such a way as if long before he had told her all that is told young girls usually before such an action.

And perhaps really he had told her in spirit during his journey, for he kissed and kissed without stopping; he drew her to him with such vigor that the breath was almost stopped in her. She did not defend herself, at first because she was astonished, and then because of faintness, which was so great that she would have fallen to the floor perhaps if less powerful arms had held her. Fortunately this did not

VOL. II. 11

f<62 THE KNIGHTS OF THE CROSS.

last long, for steps were heard on the stairway, and Father Kaleb burst into the chamber.

They sprang away from each other, and the priest overwhelmed the Cheh with questions, which were hard for him to answer since he could not catch breath. The priest thought the man's trouble caused by toils of the journey, and when he had heard confirmation of the news that Danusia was found and recovered, and her torturer brought to Spy-hov, he fell on his knees to thank God. Meanwhile the blood quieted in Hlava's veins somewhat, and when the priest rose the Cheh told calmly how they had found and rescued Danusia.

"God did not restore her," said the priest on hearing everything, "to leave her mind and soul in darkness and in control of unclean powers. Yurand will place his holy hands on her, and bring back health and reason with one prayer."

" The knight Yurand?" asked Hlava, with astonishment "Has he power like that? Can he become a saint during earthly life?"

"Before God he is a saint while alive, and when he dies people will have in heaven, one more patron, a martyr."

" But you have said, reverend father, that he will place his hands on his daughter's head. Has his right hand grown out again ? — for I know that you begged the Lord Jesus to make it grow."

"I have said 'hands,' as is said usually," answered the priest; " but with divine grace even one hand suffices."

" Surely," answered Hlava.

But there was in his voice a certain disappointment, for he had hoped to witness an evident miracle. Further conversation was interrupted by the coming of Yagenka.

" I have told him the news carefully," said she, " so that sudden joy might not kill him. He dropped down at once in cross form and is praying."

" He lies whole nights thus, but now he will be sure not to rise till to-morrow," answered Father Kaleb.

That was in fact what happened. They looked in a number of times at him, and each time they found him lying, not asleep, but in prayer so earnest that it equalled mental oblivion. The guard, who from the tower of the castle overlooked the land and watched over Spyhov according to custom, declared later on that he saw during that night a certain unusual brightness in the chamber of the "old master."

Only next morning, considerably after matins, when Ya-genka looked in again, did he inform her that he wished to see Hlava and the captive. They brought Siegfried in from the dungeon then. His hands were bound crosswise on his breast, and, in company with Tolima, all went to Yurand.

At the first moment Hlava could not see Yurand well, for the membrane windows admitted little light, while the day was dark because of clouds which had covered the sky completely, and announced a dreadful tempest. But when his keen eyes had grown used to the gloom, he barely recognized the old man, so thin had he grown, and so wretched. The giant had changed into an immense skeleton. His face was so white that it did not differ much from the milky color of his beard and hair, and when he bent toward the arm of the chair and closed his eyelids, he resembled a real corpse, as it seemed to Hlava.

Near the armchair stood a table; on the table was a crucifix, near it a pitcher of water and a loaf of black bread ; in the latter was thrust a misericordia, or that dreadful knife which knights used to despatch the wounded. Yurand had taken no nourishment save bread and water for a long time. A coarse hair shirt served him as clothing; this he wore on his naked body; the shirt was girded by a grass rope. Thus lived the wealthy and once terrible knight of Spyhov since his return from captivity in Schytno.

When he heard people enter he pushed away with his leg the tame she-wolf which kept his feet warm, next he straightened his body; then it was that he seemed to Hlava like a dead man. A moment of expectation followed, for those present thought that he would make a sign for some one to speak; but he sat motionless, white, calm, with lips somewhat open, as if he had sunk really into the endless repose of death.

"Hlava is here," said Yagenka, in her sweet voice, at last; "do you wish to hear him? "

He nodded in sign of assent; then Hlava began his narrative for the third time. He mentioned briefly the battles fought with the Germans near Gotteswerder, described the struggle with Arnold von Baden and the recovery of Danusia, but not wishing to add pain to those glad tidings brought the old martyr, and rouse new fear in him, he concealed the fact that Danusia's mind was disturbed by long days of cruel torture.

But since his heart was envenomed against the Knights of the Order, and he desired that Siegfried should be punished

unsparingly, he took pains not to hide that they had found her terrified, reduced to wretchedness, so sick that it could be seen how they had treated her in the fashion of hangmen, and that if she had remained longer in their dreadful hands she would have withered and died, just as flowers wither and perish when trampled. After this new narrative came the no less gloomy roar of the approaching tempest. Meanwhile bronze-colored cloud-packs rolled forward more and more mightily over Spyhov.

Yurand listened without a movement or a quiver, so that it might have seemed to those before him that he was sleeping But he heard every word and understood it, for when Hlava spoke of Danusia's misery, two great tears gathered in his empty eye-pits and flowed down his cheeks. Of all earthly feelings, there remained to him only this one: love for his daughter.

Then his bluish lips moved in prayer. Outside were heard still distant thunderpeals, and from moment to moment lightning illuminated the windows. Yurand prayed long, and tears fell to his white beard a second time. At last he ceased to weep, and a long silence followed, which continuing beyond measure grew irksome to those present, for they knew not what to do with themselves.

At last old Tolima, the right hand of Yurand, his comrade in all battles, and the main guardian of Spyhov, said, —

" Standing before you, lord, is that hell-dweller, that wolf-man of the Order who tortured your child and tortured you ; let me know by a sign what I am to do with him, and how I am to give him punishment."

At these words a sudden light passed over Yurand's face, aud he motioned to bring the prisoner near him.

In a twinkle two attendants seized Siegfried by the shoulders and brought him to the master of Spyhov. Yurand stretched out his hand and passed his palm over Siegfried's face, as if wishing to recall those features, or impress them on his memory for the last time, then he dropped his hand to the captive's breast, felt the arms lying on it crosswise, touched the cords, — and, closing his eyes, bent his head forward.

Those present supposed that he was meditating. But whatever he was doing, the act did not last long, for after a while he recovered and directed his hand toward the loaf into which was thrust the ominous misericordia.

Then Yagenka, Hlava, even old Tolima, and all the attendants held the breath in their breasts. The punishment was a hundred times deserved, the vengeance was just, but at the thought that the old man half alive there before them would grope his way to the slaughter of a bound captive, the hearts shuddered in their bosoms.

But he, taking the knife by the middle of the blade, stretched his index finger to the point, so that he might know what it touched, and then he began to cut the cords on the arms of Siegfried.

Wonder seized all, for they understood his wish now, and were unwilling to believe their eyesight. This deed, however, was too much for them. Hlava murmured first, after him Tolima, and then the attendants. But Father Kaleb inquired in a voice broken by irresistible weeping, —

"Brother Yurand, what is your desire? Is it to liberate the prisoner ? "

*' Yes," answered Yurand, with a motion of his head.

" Do you wish that he should go unpunished, free of vengeance? "

"Yes!"

The muttering of indignation and of anger increased, but Father Kaleb, not wishing that the unparalleled deed of mercy should be hindered, turned to the murmurers, and cried, —

" Who dares oppose a saint's will? To your knees! "

And kneeling himself, he began, —

" Our Father who art in heaven, hallowed be Thy name. Thy kingdom come — "

And he said the Lord's prayer to the end. At the words, " and forgive us our trespasses as we forgive those who trespass against us," his eyes turned involuntarily to Yurand, whose face was brightened really as with light from another world.

And this sight together with the words of the prayer conquered the hearts of all present, for old Tolima, with a soul hardened in endless battles, made the sign of the holy cross, and embraced Yurand's knees.

" If your will is to be accomplished, lord," said he, " it is necessary to conduct the prisoner to the boundary."

" Yes," nodded Yurand.

Lightning flashed oftener and oftener at the window ; the tempest drew nearer and nearer.

CHAPTER LV.

Two horsemen were riding toward the boundary of Spyhov in the wind, and in rain which at moments became a downpour. These two were Tolima and Siegfried. Tolima was conducting the German lest the peasant guards, or the servants at Spyhov, who were burning with terrible hatred and desire of revenge, might slay him on the road. Siegfried rode without weapons, but unbound. The rain driven by wind was already on them. Now and then when an unexpected thunderclap came, the horses rose on their haunches. The two men rode in silence along a deep valley ; often they were so near each other, because of the narrow road, that stirrup struck stirrup. Tolima, accustomed for years to guard captives, looked from moment to moment at Siegfried with watchful eye even then, as if for him it were a question that the captive should not rush away unexpectedly ; and each time a quiver passed through him, for it seemed to the old man that the knight's eyes were glittering in the darkness like the eyes of a vampire or an evil spirit. He even thought of making the sign of the cross on him, but remembering that under the sign of the cross he might howl with a voice that was not human, then change, and gnash his teeth, a still greater fear possessed him. The old warrior, who could strike alone on a whole crowd of Germans, as a falcon strikes partridges, was afraid of unclean powers, and had no wish to deal with them. He would have preferred simply to show the road to the German and return, but he was ashamed of himself for this thought, and conducted Siegfried to the boundary.

There, when they reached the edge of the Spyhov forest, an interval in the rain came, and the clouds were brightened by a certain strange yellow light. It grew clearer, and Siegfried's eyes lost their former unearthly gleam. But then another temptation attacked Tolima. "They commanded me," said he to himself, " to conduct to the boundary this mad dog in the greatest security; I have conducted him, but _is he to go away untouched by vengeance or punishment, this torturer of my lord and his child? Would it not

be a worthy deed and dear to God to destroy him ? Ei! I should like to challenge him to the death. We have no weapons, it is true, but five miles from here, in my lord's house at Vartsimov, they will give the wretch a sword, or an axe, and I will fight with him. God grant me victory and then I will cut him up, as is proper, and bury his head in a dung heap! " So spoke Tolima to himself, and, looking greedily at the German, he moved his nostrils, as if catching the odor of fresh blood. And he was forced to struggle with his desire grievously, to fight with himself sternly, till, remembering that Yurand had granted the prisoner life and freedom, not to the boundary merely, but beyond it, and that if he should slay him the holy act of his lord would be defeated, and the reward for it in heaven be decreased, he overcame himself at last, reined in his horse, and said, —

" Here is our boundary, and to yours it i£ not distant. Go in freedom; if remorse does not choke thee, and God's thunderbolts do not strike, nothing threatens thee from people!"

Then Tolima turned about, and Siegfried rode on with a certain wild petrifaction in his face, without answering a word, and as if not hearing that any one had spoken. He went on by a road now wider, and was as if sunk in a dream.

The cessation in the storm was brief, and the clearness of short duration. It grew so dark again that one might have thought that the gloom of night had fallen on the world. The clouds sank almost to the tops of the pine-trees. From above came an ominous growl, and as it were an impatient hiss and the quarrelling of thunders which the angel of the storm was restraining yet. But lightning illuminated from moment to moment with a blinding glitter the awful sky and the terrified earth, and then was to be seen a broad road lying between two black walls of forest; advancing along the middle of that road, was a lone man on horseback. Siegfried rode forward half conscious, devoured by fever. Despair was eating his soul from the time of Rotgier's death; the crimes which he had committed through revenge, the remorse, the terrifying visions, the tortures of his soul had dimmed his mind for a time to such a degree that only with the greatest effort did he defend himself from madness, and even at moments he gave way to it. Recently the toils of the journey, under the firm hand of Hlava, the night passed in the prison of Spyhov, and the

uncertainty of his fate, but above all that unheard-of act of favor and mercy which was almost superhuman, and which simply terrified him, — all these rent the old knight to the last degree. At times thought became torpid and dead in him, so that he lost power of seeing what was happening to him; but again fever roused him, and there rose in the man at once a certain dull feeling of despair, of loss, of ruin, — a feeling that all was now quenched, ended, gone, that a limit of some sort had been reached, that around him was naught but night and nothingness, and, as it were, a kind of ghastly pit filled with terror, to which he must go in every case.

" Go! go! " whispered suddenly some voice at his ear.

He looked around, and saw Death, in the form of a skeleton sitting on a skeleton horse, pushing along at his side there, and rattling his bones.

" Art thou here? " asked the Knight of the Cross.

"I am. Go on ! go on ! "

And at that moment Siegfried saw that he had a companion on the other side also ; stirrup to stirrup with him was riding some kind of thing with a body like that of a man, but with a face that was not human, for the thing had a beast's head with ears standing erect, long, pointed, and covered with black hair.

" Who art thou? " cried Siegfried.

But that thing, instead of an answer, showed its teeth, and growled deeply.

Siegfried closed his eyes, but immediately he heard a louder rattle of bones, and a voice speaking into his very ear.

" It is time ! it is time! hurry! go on! "

And he answered, "I go." But that answer came from his breast as if some one else had given it.

Then, as if pushed by some irresistible force from outside, he dismounted, and removed from his horse the high saddle of a knight, and then the bridle. His companions dismounted also, but did not leave him for the twinkle of an eye ; they led him from the middle of the road to the edge of the forest. There the black vampire bent down a limb and then helped him to fasten the reins of the bridle to it.

" Hurry! " whispered Death.

"Hurry!" whispered certain voices from the tree tops.

Siegfried, as it were sunk in sleep, drew the second rein through the buckle, made a halter, and standing on the

saddle, which he had placed under the tree, put the halter around his neck.

" Push away the saddle !— It is done! Aa! "

The saddle pushed by his foot rolled some steps away, and the body of the ill-fated knight hung heavily.

For a flash it seemed to him that he heard some hoarse, repressed roar, that the ghastly vampire rushed at him, shook him, and tore his breast with its teeth, so as to bite the heart in him. But afterward his quenching eyes saw something else : Death dissolved into a kind of white cloud there before him, pushed up to him slowly, embraced, surrounded, enveloped him, and finally covered everything with a ghastly, impenetrable curtain.

At that moment the storm grew wild with immeasurable fury. A thunderbolt struck with an awful explosion in the middle of the road, as if the earth had sunk in its foundations. The whole forest bent under a whirlwind. The roar, the whistle, the noise, the crashing of tree-trunks, and the crack of breaking limbs filled the depth of the forest. Torrents of rain, driven by wind, hid the light, and only during brief bloody lightning-flashes was the corpse of Siegfried visible, whirling wildly above the road.

Next morning a rather numerous escort advanced along that same road. At the head of it rode Yagenka with Anulka and Hlava; behind them were wagons conducted by four attendants armed with swords and crossbows. Each of the drivers had at his side also a spear and an axe, not counting forks and other weapons useful on journeys. These were needful both in defence against wild beasts and robber bands, which raged always along the boundaries of the Order. Against these it was that Yagello complained bitterly to the Grand Master, both in letters and personally in the meetings at Ratsiondzek. But having trained men and defensive weapons, one might be free of fear. The escort advanced, therefore, with self-confidence and boldly.

After the storm came a marvellous day, fresh, calm, and so clear that where there was no shade the eyes of the travellers blinked from excess of light. Not a leaf moved on the trees, and from each leaf hung great drops of rain which glittered with rainbow colors in the sun. Amid the needle-like leaves of the pine, these drops glistened like great diamonds. The downpour of rain had formed on the

road little streams which flowed toward lower places with a gladsome murmur, and formed shallow pools in depressions. The whole region was irrigated, wet, but smiling in the clearness of morning. On such mornings delight seizes man's heart, so the drivers and attendants sang to themselves in low voices, wondering at the silence which reigned among those who were riding before them.

They were silent, for sorrow had settled down in Yagen-ka's soul. In her life something had come to an end, something was broken; and the girl, though not greatly used to meditation, and unable to explain to herself clearly what was happenin. in her mind and what appeared to her, still felt that everything by which she had lived up to that time had failed her, and gone for nothing; that every hope in her had been dissipated, as the morning mist is blown apart on the fields, that she must renounce everything, abandon everything, forget everything, and begin life anew. She thought too that though by the will of God the future would not be altogether bad, still it could not be other than sad, and in no case so good as that might have been which had just ended.

And her heart was pressed by immense sorrow for that past which was now closed forever, and the sorrow rose in a stream of tears to her eyes. But she would not let those tears come, for, in addition to the whole burden which weighed down her soul, she felt shame. She would have preferred never to have left Zgorzelitse rather than return as she was returning then from Spyhov. She had not gone there merely to deprive Stan and Vilk of a reason for attacking Zgorzelitse; this she could not hide from herself. No! This was known also to Matsko, who had not taken her for that reason either, and it would be known surely to Zbyshko. At the latter thought her cheeks burned, bitterness filled her heart. " I was not haughty enough for thee," said she in spirit, " and now I have received what I worked for." And to anxiety, uncertainty of the morrow, regretful sadness and undying sorrow for the past, was joined humiliation.

But the further course of her grievous thoughts was interrupted by some man hurrying to meet them. Hlava, who kept a watchful eye on everything, spurred his horse toward the man, and from the crossbow on his shoulder, his badger-skin bag, and the feathers on his cap, recognized a forester.

" Hei, but who art thou? Halt! " cried he, to make sure.

The man approached quickly, his face full of emotion, as

men's faces are usually when they wish to announce something uncommon.

" There is a man," cried he, " hanging on the road before you!"

Hlava was alarmed lest that might be the work of robbers, and inquired quickly, —

"Is it far from here?"

" The shot of a crossbow — at the very road."

" Is no one with him?"

" No, no one; but I frightened away a wolf which was sniffing him."

The mention of a wolf pacified Hlava, for it showed that there were no people near by, nor any ambush. Meanwhile Yagenka said, —

" See what it is ! "

Hlava galloped forward and after a while returned still more quickly.

" Siegfried is hanged! " cried he, reining in his horse before Yagenka.

"In the name of the Father, the Son, and the Spirit! Siegfried? The Knight of the Cross?"

"The Knight of the Cross. He hanged himself with the bridle."

"Hanged himself?"

"It is evident that he did, for the saddle is lying near him. If robbers had done the deed they would have killed the man simply, and taken the saddle, for it is of value."

" How shall we pass? "

" Let us not go that way! let us not go! " cried Anulka, in fear. " Something will catch us."

Yagenka too was frightened a little, for she believed that foul spirits gathered in great crowds around bodies of suicides. But Hlava was daring and felt no fear.

"Oh," said he, "I was near him and even pushed him with a lance, and still I feel no devil on my shoulder."

" Do not blaspheme! " called Yagenka.

"I am not blaspheming," answered Hlava, "but I trust in the power of God. Still, if you are afraid we can go around through the forest."

Anulka begged them to go around, but Yagenka thought a while, and said, —

" Ei, it is not proper to leave a corpse unburied. Burial is a Christian act enjoined by the Lord Jesus. Siegfried was a man in every case."

"True; but a Knight of the Cross, an executioner who hanged himself! Let crows and wolves work at him."

" Do not say idle words. God will judge him for his sins, but let us do our part. No evil will attach to us if we carry out a pious command."

" Let it be as you wish," answered Hlava.

And he gave needful orders to the attendants, who obeyed with disgust and hesitation. But fearing Hlava, with whom dispute was dangerous, they took, in the absence of spades, forks and axes to make a hole in the earth, and went to work. Hlava went with them to give an example, and when he had made a sign of the cross he cut with his own hands the strap by which the corpse was hanging.

Siegfried's face had grown blue in the air and was ghastly, for his eyes were not closed and they had a terrified expression. His mouth was open as if to catch the last, breath.

They dug a depression there at his side quickly, and with fork-handles stuifed the body into it, face downward. After they had covered it the attendants sought stones, for the custom was from time immemorial to cover suicides with stones, otherwise they would rise at night and waylay travellers. There were stones enough on the road and among the mosses of the forest. So there soon rose above the Knight of the Cross a tomb, and then Hlava cut out with an axe, on the trunk of the pine-tree, a cross, — which he made, not for Siegfried, but to prevent evil spirits from assembling on that spot, — and then he returned to the company.

" His soul is in hell, but his body is in the earth," said he to Yagenka; " now we may go."

And they moved forward. But Yagenka when riding past broke a twig from the pine-tree and threw it on the stones. Following the example of their lady, all the others did in like manner, for custom comnlanded that also. They rode on a long time in thoughtfulness, thinking of that evil enemy the Knight of the Cross, and the punishment which had overtaken him, till at last Yagenka said, —

" The justice of God does not spare, and it is not proper to say even ' eternal rest,' for that man, since there is no rest for him."

" You have a compassionate heart, since you commanded to bury him," answered Hlava. And then he added with a certain hesitation: "People say — well not people perhaps,

only wizards and witches — that a rope, or a strap even, on which a man has hanged himself gives luck in all things; but I did not take the strap from Siegfried's neck because for you I expect happiness, not from enchantment, but from the power of the Lord Jesus."

Yagenka made no answer at the moment, and only after a while, when she had sighed a number of times, did she say, as if to herself, —

CHAPTEE LV1.

ONLY on the ninth day after Yagenka had gone did Zbyshko appear on the boundary of Spyhov, but Danusia was so near death then that he had lost every hope of bringing her alive to her father. Next day, when she answered disconnectedly, hfe saw at once that not merely was her mind shattered, but that her body was seized by sickness of some kind, against which there was no more strength in that child exhausted by captivity, confinement, torment, and continual terror. It may be that the noise of the desperate encounter between Zbyshko, Matsko, and the Germans had overfilled the measure of her fear, and that the sickness had come in that moment. It is enough that fever had not left her from that day till almost the end of the journey. This had been a favoring circumstance thus far, for Zbyshko had brought her like a dead person, without consciousness or knowledge, through the terrible wilderness by means of immense efforts.

After they had passed the wilderness and entered a grain country where there were land-tillers and nobles, toils and dangers were over. When people learned that he was bringing a child of their own race i*escued from the Knights of the Order, and moreover a daughter of the famed Yurand, of whom minstrels sang so many songs, in castles, houses, and cottages they outstripped one another in services and assistance. They furnished provisions and horses. All doors stood open. Zbyshko had no further need to carry her in the cradle between horses, for sturdy youths bore her in a litter from village to village with as much care and reverence as if they were bearing a sacred object. Women surrounded her with the tenderest attention. Men, while listening to the narrative of the wrongs wrought on her, gritted their teeth, and more than one of them put his iron armor on straightway and seized his sword, axe, or lance to set out with Zbyshko and avenge " with addition," for it did not seem enough to that stern generation to avenge one wrong by another evenly.

Zbyshko was not thinking at that moment of vengeance, but only of Danusia. He lived amid glimpses of hope when the sick woman seemed better for a moment, and in dull despair when her condition grew worse to appearance. As to the last, he could iiot deceive himself longer. At the beginning of the journey the superstitious thought flew through his head frequently, that perhaps somewhere in those long, roadless places through which they were passing, Death was following step by step after them, just lurking for the moment to rush at Danusia and suck the remnant of life from her. This vision, or rather this feeling, was so distinct, especially in dark nights, that the desperate wish seized him often to turn back, challenge that vision, as a knight may be challenged, and fight to the last breath with it. But at the end of the road the case was still worse, for he felt Death, not behind, but in the midst of the company; not visible, it is true, but so near that its freezing breath blew around them ; and he understood that against such an enemy bravery was of no avail, a strong hand of no use, a weapon of no use,— that he must surrender to that enemy the dearest life as booty, supinely, without a struggle.

And that feeling was of all the most dreadful, for with it was connected a sorrow as irresistible as a whirlwind, as deep as the sea. How was his soul not to groan in Zbyshko, how was it not to be rent with pain when, looking at his beloved, he said to her, as if with involuntary reproach : u Have I loved thee for this, have I sought thee for this, and fought thee free, just to cover thee with earth the day after, and never see thee a second time? " And while speaking thus he gazed at her cheeks blooming with fever, at her dull, wandering eyes, and again he asked: "Wilt thou leave me? Dost thou not grieve? Dost thou prefer to be away from me rather than with me ? " And then he thought that there might be disorder in his own head ; his breast rose with immensely great weeping, which rose but could not burst forth, since a certain rage was barring the way to it, and a certain anger at the merciless, cold, and blind power which had unfolded itself above that guiltless woman. Had that evil Knight of the Cross been present there then, Zbyshko would have torn him asunder in the manner of a wild beast.

When they reached the hunting-lodge he wished to halt there, but it was deserted during autumn. From the guards he learned, moreover, that Prince Yanush had gone to his

brother at Plotsk and taken the princess ; he abandoned his plan, therefore, of visiting Warsaw, where the court physician might save the sick woman. He must go to Spyhov, and to him this was terrible, for he thought that all was ending, and that he would take only a corpse home to Yurand.

But just a few hours of road before Spyhov a brighter ray of hope struck his heart again. Danusia's cheeks grew pale, her eyes became less dull, her breath, not so loud, was less hurried. Zbyshko saw this at once and soon commanded the last halt so that she might rest the more quietly. They were about five miles from Spyhov, far from human dwellings, on a narrow road between a field and a meadow. But a wild pear-tree standing near-by offered shelter from the sunrays; they halted, therefore, under its branches. The attendants dismounted and unbridled their horses, so that the beasts might eat grass more easily. Two women occupied in serving Danusia, and the youths who carried her, wearied by the road and by heat, lay down in the shade and fell asleep quickly. Zbyshko alone watched at the litter, and sitting on the roots of the pear-tree did not take his eyes from the sick woman.

She lay there in the afternoon silence, motionless, with closed eyelids. But to Zbyshko it seemed that she was not sleeping. Indeed, when at the other end of the broad meadow a man who was mowing stopped and began to sharpen his scythe with a whetstone, she quivered slightly, opened her eyes for an instant, and closed them; her breast rose as if with a deeper breathing, and from her lips came a barely audible whisper, —
" Sweet flowers."

Those were the first words not feverish and not wandering which she had uttered since the beginning of the journey; indeed from the meadow warmed by the sun the breeze brought a really strong perfume, in which were felt hay and honey with various fragrant plants. So

Zbyshko's heart trembled from delight at the thought that consciousness was returning to the sick woman.

In his first rapture he wished to cast himself at her feet, but fear that he might frighten her restrained him, and he only knelt at the litter, bent over her, and said quietly, —

"Danusia! Danusia!"

She opened her eyes, looked at him some time, then a smile brightened her features, and she said " Zbyshko," just as she had in the tarburners' hut, but with far greater con-

sciousness. And she tried to stretch her hands to him, but failed because of surpassing weakness; he put his arms around her with a heart as full as if he were thanking her for some immense favor.

" Thou hast come to thyself," said he. " Oh, praise to God — to God — "

Then his voice failed him, and for some time they looked at each other in silence. The silence of the field was broken only by the fragrant meadow-breeze which murmured among the leaves of the pear-tree, the chirping of crickets in the grass, and the distant, indistinct singing of the mower.

Dauusia gazed with growing consciousness and did not cease smiling, just like a child that in its sleep sees an angel. But in her eyes began now to appear a certain wonder.

"Where am I?" asked she.

Then a whole swarm of brief answers, interrupted through delight, broke from Zbyshko's lips, —

" Thou art with me! Near Spyhov. We are going to thy father. Thy misfortune is ended. Oi! my Danusia! Danusia! I sought thee and redeemed thee in battle. Thou art not in German power now. Have no fear of that! We shall soon be in Spyhov. Thou hast been ill, but the Lord Jesus had mercy. How much pain there was, how much weeping! Danusia! — Now it is well! — There is nothing before thee but happiness. Ei, how I have searched, how I have wandered ! — Ei, mighty God! — Ei! "

And he drew a deep breath, but almost with a groan, as if he had thrown the last weight of pain from his heart.

Danusia lay quietly, recalling to herself something, pondering something, till at last she asked, —

" Then thou didst not forget me? "

And two tears which had gathered in her eyes rolled down her face slowly to the pillow.

" I forget thee !" exclaimed Zbyshko.

There was in that restrained exclamation more force than in the greatest vows and declarations, for he had loved her with his whole soul at all times, and from the moment when he had found her she was dearer than the whole world to him.

Meanwhile silence came again; only, in the distance the mower stopped singing and began to whet his scythe a second time.

Danusia's lips moved again, but with a whisper so low that Zbyshko could not hear it; so, bending down, he inquired,—

" What dost thou say, berry? "

VOL. II. — 12

And she repeated,—

" Sweet flowers."

" We are at a meadow," answered he, " but soon we shall go to thy father, who is freed from captivity also. And thou wilt be mine till death. Dost hear me well, dost understand?"

With that, great alarm racked him, for he noted that her face was growing paler, and that small drops of sweat were coming out on it thickly.

" What is the matter ? " asked he, in desperate fear.

He felt the hair rising on his head, and cold passing through his bones.

" What troubles thee? Tell! " repeated he.

" Darkness ! " whispered she.

" Darkness? The sun is shining, and does it seem dark to thee? " asked he, with panting voice. "Just now thou wert speaking reasonably. In God's name, say one word even!"

She moved her lips again, but could not even whisper. Zbyshko divined only that she was uttering his name, that she was calling him. Immediately after that her emaciated hands began to tremble, and hop on the rug with which she was covered. That lasted a moment. There was no cause for mistake then — she was dying!

But terrified and in despair, Zbyshko fell to imploring her, as if a prayer could do anything, —

"Danusia! O merciful Jesus! — Wait even to Spyhov! Wait! wait! O Jesus! O Jesus! O Jesus!"

While he implored thus the women woke, and the attendants ran up; they had been at a distance near the horses in the meadow. But understanding with the first cast of the eye what was happening, they knelt and began to repeat aloud the Litany.

The breeze stopped, the leaves ceased to rustle on the pear-tree, and only words of prayer were heard amid the great silence of the meadow.

Dauusia, before the very end of the Litany, opened her eyes once more, as if wishing to look for the last time on Zbyshko and the world of the sun; next moment she dropped into the sleep of eternity.

The women closed her eyelids and then went to the meadow for flowers. The attendants followed; and they moved in sunshine, among abundant grass, like spirits of the field, bending down from moment to moment and weeping,

for in their hearts they had pity. Zbyshko knelt in the shadow at the litter, with his head on Danusia's knees, without a movement or a word; he was as if dead himself, but they circled about, now nearer, now more distant, plucking the yellow marigolds, the white pimpernel, the thickly growing rosy sorrel, and white flowers with the odor of honey. In damp depressions they found also lilies of the valley, and broom on the green ridge next the fallow land. When they had each an armful they surrounded the litter in a mournful circle and strewed flowers and plants on the remains of the dead woman, leaving exposed only her face, which amid the lilies looked white, calm, at rest in a sleep that could not be broken; the face was serene and simply angelic.

To Spyhov it was not quite five miles ; so after some time, when sadness and pain had passed with their tears, they raised the litter and moved toward the pine forest from which the lands of Spyhov began.

The attendants led the horses after the procession. Zbyshko himself helped to carry the litter in front, and the women, laden with bundles of plants and flowers, preceded, singing pious hymns; they advanced slowly between the green meadow and the level, gray, fallow land, like any procession of mourners.

On the blue sky there was not the slightest cloud, and the whole world was nestling in golden sunlight.

CHAPTER

THEY came at last with the remains of Danusia to the pine forests of Spyhov, at the edge of which Yurand's armed guards stood night and day watching. One of these hurried off with the news to old Tolima and Father Kaleb; others conducted the procession by what was at first a winding and sunken, but later a broad forest roadway, till they reached the place where trees ended, and open, wet lands began, and sticky morasses swarming with water-birds; beyond these quagmires on a dry elevation stood Yurand's fortress. They saw at once that the sad tidings concerning them had reached Spyhov, for barely had they emerged from the shade of the pine woods onto the bright open plain when to their ears came the sound of a bell from the fortress chapel. Soon after, they saw many people, men and women, coming toward them from a distance. When this company had approached to a point within two or three bow-shots Zbyshko could distinguish persons. At the head of the procession walked Yurand himself, supported by Tolima. and feeling with a staff out in front of his body. It was easy to distinguish the master of Spyhov by his immense stature, by the red pits in place of eyes, and by the white hair which fell to his shoulders. At his side in a white surplice, and holding a cross in his hand, walked Father Kaleb. Behind them was borne a banner with Yurand's ensign; with it moved the armed " warriors " of Spyhov, and behind them married women with veils on their heads, and young girls with hair hanging loose on their shoulders. In the rear of the procession was a wagon on which they were to place the remains of Danusia.

On seeing Yurand, Zbyshko commanded to put down the litter, — he himself was carrying the end next the head, — then he approached Yurand and cried in that terrible voice with which immense pain and despair express themselves, —

" I sought her till I found her and freed her, but she preferred God to Spyhov."

And pain broke him utterly, for he fell on Yurand's breast, embraced him, and groaned out, —

" O Jesus! O Jesus! O Jesus ! "

At this sight the hearts of the armed attendants were enraged, and they fell to beating their shields with their spears, not knowing how to express in another way their pain and their desire for vengeance. The women raised a lament, they wailed one louder than another, they put their aprons to their eyes, or covered their heads with them altogether, and called in heaven-piercing voices: " Ei! misfortune ! misfortune! For thee there is gladness, for us only weeping. Ei! misfortune ! Death has cut thee down ! The Skeleton has seized thee! Oi! oi! " — while some of them, bending their heads backward and closing their eyes, cried: " Was it evil for thee with us, 0 dearest flower; was it evil? Thy father is left in great mourning, while thou art there in God's chambers ! Oi! oi! " Others again told the dead woman that she had not pitied her father or her husband in their tears and loneliness. And this wail of theirs and this weeping were expressed in a half chant, for those people could not express their pain otherwise.

At last Yurand, withdrawing from Zbyshko's arms, reached out his staff in sign that he wished to go to Danusia. That moment Tolima and Zbyshko caught him by the arms and led him to the litter; there he knelt by the body, passed his hand over it from the forehead to the hands of his dead daughter, which were crossed, and'he inclined his head repeatedly, as if to say that that was his Danusia and no other, that he knew his own child. Then he embraced her with one arm, and the other, which had no hand, he raised upward ; all present answered in the same way, and that dumb complaint before God was more eloquent than any words of sorrow. Zbyshko, whose face after the momentary outburst grew again perfectly rigid, knelt on the .other side, silent, resembling a stone statue ; round about it became so still that the chirping of the field crickets was heard and the buzz of each passing fly.

At last Father Kaleb sprinkled Danusia, Zbyshko, and Yurand with holy water, and began "Itequiem ceternam." After the hymn he prayed aloud a long time; during the prayer it seemed to the people that they heard the voice of a prophet, for he begged that the torture of that innocent woman might be the drop which would overflow the measure of injustice, and that the day of judgment, wrath, punishment, and terror would come.

Then they moved toward Spyhov; but they did not place Danusia on the wagon, they bore her in front of the procession on the litter strewn with flowers. The bell ceased not to toll, it seemed to summon and invite them; and they moved on across the broad plain singing in the immense golden light, as if the departed were conducting them really to endless glory and brightness. It was evening, and the flocks had returned from the fields when they arrived. The chapel, in which they laid the remains, was gleaming from torches and lighted tapers. At command of Father Kaleb seven young girls repeated in succession the litany over the body till daylight. Zbyshko did not leave Danusia till morning, and at matins he placed her in a coffin which skilled workmen had cut out of an oak-tree in the nighttime, and put a plate of gold-colored amber in the lid above her forehead.

Yurand was not present, for strange things had happened to him. Immediately after reaching home he lost power in his feet, and when they placed him on the bed he lost movement as well as consciousness of where he was and what was taking place there. In vain did Father Kaleb speak to him; in vain did he ask what his trouble was. Yurand heard not, he understood not; but lying on his back, he raised the lids of his empty eyepits and smiled with a face transfixed and happy, and at times he moved his lips, as if speaking with some person. The priest and Tolima thought that he was conversing with his rescued daughter, and smiling at her. They thought also that he was dying, and that with the sight of his soul he was gazing at his own eternal happiness, but in this they were mistaken, for, deprived of feeling and deaf to all things, he smiled whole weeks in the same way. Zbyshko, when he set out at last with the ransom for Matsko, left his father-in-law in life yet.

CHAPTER LVIII.

AFTER the burial of Danusia Zbysnko was not confined to his bed, but he lived in torpor. For a few days at first he was hot in such an evil condition : he walked about, he conversed with his dead bride, he visited Yurand and sat near him. He told the priest of Matsko's captivity, and they decided to send Tolima to Prussia and Malborg, to learn where the old knight was and ransom him, paying at the same time for Zbyshko the sum agreed on with Arnold von Baden and his brother. In the cellars of Spyhov there was no lack of silver, which Yurand in his time had received from his lands or had captured, so Father Kaleb supposed that the Knights if they received the money would liberate the old man without trouble, and would not require the young knight to appear in person.

"• Go to Plotsk," said the priest to Tolima at starting, " and take from the prince there a letter of safe conduct. Otherwise the first comtur on the way will rob and imprison thee."

" Oh! I know them myself," said Tolima. " They are able to rob even those who have letters."

And he went his way. But Father Kaleb was sorry, soon after, that he had not sent Zbyshko. He had feared, it is true, that in the first moments of suffering the young man would not be able to conduct himself in the way needed, or that he might burst out against the Knights of the Cross and expose himself to peril; he knew also that it would be difficult for him to leave immediately the tomb of the beloved with his recent loss and fresh sorrow, and just after such a terrible and painful journey as that which he had made from Gotteswerder to Spyhov. But later he was sorry that he had taken all this into consideration, for Zbyshko had grown duller day by day. He had lived till Danusia's death in dreadful effort, he had used all his strength desperately : he had ridden to the ends of the earth, he had fought, he had saved his wife, he had passed through wild forests;

and on a sudden all was ended as if some one had cut it off with a sword-stroke, and naught was left but the knowledge that what he had done had been done in vain, that his toils had been useless, — that in truth they had passed, but with them a part of his life had gone; hope had gone, good had gone, loving had perished, and nothing was left to him. Every man lives in the morrow, every man plans somewhat and lays aside one or another thing for use in the future, but for Zbyshko to-morrow had become valueless; as to the future, he had the same kind of feeling that Yagenka had had, while riding out of Spyhov, when she said, " My happiness is behind, not before me." But, besides, in his soul that feeling of helplessness, emptiness, misfortune, and evil fate had risen on the ground of great pain and of ever-increasing grief for Danusia. That grief penetrated him, mastered him, and at the same time was ever stiffening in him. So at last there was no place in Zbyshko's heart for another feeling. Hence he thought of it only ; he nursed it in himself and lived with it solely, insensible to everything else, shut up in himself, sunk, as it were, in a half dream, oblivious of all that was happening around him. All the powers of his soul and his body, his former activity and valor, dropped into quiescence. In his look and movements there appeared a kind of senile heaviness. Whole days and nights he sat, either in the vault with Danusia's coffin, or before the house, warming himself in sunlight during the hours after midday. At times he so forgot himself that he did not answer questions. Father Kaleb, who loved him, began to fear that pain might consume the man as rust consumes iron, and with sadness he thought that perhaps it would have been better to send him away, even to the Knights of the Cross, with a ransom.

" It is necessary," said he to the sexton, with whom in the absence of other men he spoke of his own troubles, " that some adventure should pull him, as a storm pulls a tree, otherwise he may perish utterly." And the sexton answered wisely by giving the comparison, that when a man is choking with a bone it is best to give him a good thump behind the shoulders.

No adventure came, but a few weeks later Pan de Lorche appeared unexpectedly. The sight of him roused Zbyshko, for it reminded him of the expedition among the Jmud men and the rescue of Danusia. De Lorche did not hesitate in the least to rouse these painful memories. On the contrary, when he learned of Zbyshko's loss he went at once to pray with him above Danusia's coffin, and spoke of her unceasingly. Being himself half a minstrel, he composed a hymn for her which he sang with a lute, a$ night, near the grating of the vault, so tenderly and with such sadness that Zbyshko, though he did not understand the words, was seized by great weeping which lasted till the daylight following.

Wearied by sorrow, by weeping and watching, he fell into a deep sleep; and when he woke it was clear that pain had flowed away with his tears, for he was brighter than on preceding days, and seemed more active. He was greatly pleased with Pan de Lorche, and thanked him for coming; afterward he inquired how he had learned of his misfortune.

De Lorche answered, through Father Kaleb, that he had received the first tidings of Danusia's death in Lubav, from old Tolima, whom he had seen there in the prison of the comtur, but that he would have come to Spyhov in every case to yield himself to Zbyshko.

News of Tolima's imprisonment made a great impression on the priest and on Zbyshko; they understood that the ransom was lost, for there was nothing nlore difficult on earth than to snatch from the Knights of the Cross money once seized by them. In view of this it was necessary to go with ransom a second time.

"Woe!" cried Zbyshko. "Now my poor uncle is waiting there and thinking that I have forgotten him. I must go with all speed to my uncle."

Then he turned to De Lorche, —

"Dost know how it has come out? Dost know that he is in the hands of the Knights of the Order?"

"• I know, for I saw him in Malborg, and that is why I have come hither."

Father Kaleb fell now to complaining, —

"We have acted badly, but no one had a head. I expected more wisdom from Tolima. Why did he not go to Plotsk, instead of rushing in without a letter among those robbers?"

At this De Lorche shrugged his shoulders, —

"What are letters to them ? Or are the wrongs few which the Prince of Plotsk, as well as your prince, has suffered? On the boundary attacks and battles never cease, for your men, too, are unforgiving. Every comtur then, what! every voit, does as he pleases, and in robbery one merely outstrips another."

"All the more should Tolima have gone to Plotsk."

"He wanted to do so, but they seized htm near the boundary on this side in the night-time. They would have killed him if he had not said that he was taking money to Lubav for the comtur. In this way he saved himself, but now the comtur will produce witnesses to show that Tolima made that declaration."

•' But Uncle Matsko, is he well? Are they threatening his life there ? " inquired Zbyshko.

"He is well," answered De Lorche. " Hatred against ' King' Vitold, and against those who helped the Jmud men, is great, and surely they would have slain the old knight were it not that they do not wish to lose the ransom. The brothers von Baden defended him for the same cause, and finally the Chapter are concerned about my head ; were they to sacrifice that, they would rouse the knighthood of Guel-ders, Burgundy, and Flanders. Ye know that I am kin to the Count of Guelders."

"But why are they concerned about thy head?" interrupted Zbyshko, in wonder.

"Because I was captured by thee. I said the following in Malborg: If ye take the life of the old knight of Bog-danets, his nephew will take my head."

"I will not take it ! so help me God !"

"I know that thou wilt not, but they are afraid that thou wilt, and Matsko will be safe therefore. They answered me that thoi> wert in captivity also, for the Von Badens let thee go on thy word of a knight, therefore that I had no need to go to thee. But I answered, that thou wert free when I was captured. — And I have come to thee! While I am in thy hands, they will do nothing to thee or Matsko. Do thou pay the Von Badens thy ransom, and for me demand twice or thrice as much. They must pay. I do not say this because I think that I am of more value than thou art, but to punish their greed, which is despicable. Once I had quite a different opinion, but now they and life among them have disgusted me completely. I will go to the Holy Land to seek adventures there, for I will not serve among the Knights of the Cross any longer."

"Oh, stay with us, lord," said Father Kaleb. "And I think that thou wilt, for it does not seem to me that they will ransom thee."

"If they will not pay, I will pay myself. I am here with a considerable escort. I have laden wagons, and that which is in them will sullice."

Father Kaleb repeated these words to Zbyshko. Matsko surely would not have been indifferent to them ; but Zbyshko was a young man and thought little of property.

"On my honor," said he, " it will not be as thou sayst. Thou hast been to me both friend and brother; for thee I will take no ransom."

Then they embraced each other, feeling that a new bond had been secured between them. De Lorche smiled, and said,—

a Let it be so. Only let not the Germans know of this, for they will tremble about Matsko. And they must pay, for they will fear that if they do not I shall declare at Western courts and among the knighthood that they are glad to see foreign guests, and as it were invite them and are pleased at their arrival; but when a guest falls into captivity they forget him. And the Order needs men greatly at this moment, for Vitold is to them a terror, and still more are the Poles and King Yagello."

" Then let it be in this way," said Zbyshko. " Thou wilt stay here or wherever thou wishest in Mazovia, and I will go to Malborg for my uncle, and will feign tremendous animosity against thee."

" Do so, by Saint George ! " answered De Lorche. " But first listen to what I tell thee. In Malborg they say that the King of Poland is to visit Plotsk and meet the Grand Master there or in some place upon the boundary. Knights of the Order desire this meeting greatly, for they wish to note whether the king will help Vitold, should he declare war against them openly for the Jmud land.

"Ah! they are as cunning as serpents, but in Vitold they have found their master. The Order is afraid of him, for never does it know what he is planning, or what he may work out. ' He gave Jmud to us,' say they in the Chapter, 4 but by this land he holds a sword above our heads, as it were, continually. Let him utter one word,' say they, ' and rebellion is ready.' In fact, that is the case. I must go to Vitold's court when I can. Maybe it will happen me to fight in the lists there, and besides, I have heard that women of that region are of angelic beauty sometimes."

" Thou hast spoken of the coming of the Polish king to Plotsk?" said Father Kaleb.

" I have. Let Zbyshko attach himself to the royal escort. The Grand Master wishes to win Yagello and will refuse him nothing. Ye know that when the need comes no men can be more humble than the Knights of the Cross are. Let Zbyshko be of the king's retinue, and let him claim his own ; let him complain as loudly as is possible against the evil doings of the Order. The Germans will listen differently in presence of the king, and in presence of Cracow knights, who are famous everywhere, and whose decisions are widely current in the world of knighthood."

" Excellent advice ! by the Cross of the Lord, it is excellent !" exclaimed Father Kaleb.

"It is!" confirmed De Lorche. "And opportunity will not be lacking. I heard in Malborg that there will be feasts and tournaments, for foreign knights will surely wish to meet the knights of Poland. As God is true ! Juan of Aragon is coming; he is the greatest knight of all in Christendom. Do ye not know that from Aragon he sent his gauntlet to your Zavisha, so that it should not be said in foreign courts that there is on earth another man who is his equal?"

The arrival of De Lorche, the sight of him, and conversation with the man so roused Zbyshko from that painful torpor in which he had been buried, that he listened to the news with curiosity. Of Juan of Aragon he knew, for it was the duty of every knight in that age to know and recollect the names of all who were most renowned as champions; the fame of the nobles of Aragon, especially of Juan, had passed through every Christian land. No knight had ever equalled him inside barriers ; the Moors fled at the very sight of his armor; and the opinion was universal that he was the greatest knight in Christendom.

At this news, therefore, the warlike, knightly soul of Zbyshko responded, and he asked very eagerly, —

" Did he challenge Zavisha Charny?"

"It is about a year since the gauntlet came and Zavisha sent his own to Aragon."

" Then will Juan come surely?"

"It is not known whether he will come, but there are reports that he will. The Knights of the Order have sent him an invitation long ago."

"God grant us to see such things."

"God grant!" said De Lorche. "And though Zavisha should be killed, as may happen easily, it is great glory for him that such a man as Juan of Aragon challenged him; nay, honor for thy whole people."

" We shall see! " answered Zbyshko. "I only say, ' God jirant us to see such things.' "

" And I add my voice."

But their wish was not to be accomplished then ; for the old chroniclers relate that the duel of Zavisha with the renowned Juan of Aragon took place only some years later in Perpignan, where in presence of the Emperor Sigismund, Pope Benedict XIII., the King of Aragon, and many princes and cardinals, Zavisha Charn\'7d- of Garbov hurled down from his horse with the first touch of his lance his opponent, and won a famous victory. Meanwhile both Zbyshko and De Lorche comforted their hearts, for they thought that even if Juan of Aragon could not appear at that time, they would see famous deeds of knighthood, for champions were not lacking in Poland who were little inferior to Zavisha, and among the guests of the Order it was possible at all times to find the foremost men in wielding weapons from France, England, Burgundy, and Italy, — men ready to struggle for the mastery with every comer.

" Hear me," said Zbyshko to Pan de Lorche. " It is irksome to me without my Uncle Matsko, I am in a hurry now to ransom him, so I will start for Plotsk to-morrow. But why shouldst thou stay here? If thou art my captive, come with me, and thou wilt see Yagello and the Polish court."

" I desired to ask this of thee," said De Lorche, " for I have long wished to see the Polish knights, and besides I have heard that the ladies of the royal court are more like angels than dwellers in this earthly vale."

" A little while ago thou didst say something like this of Vitold's court," remarked Zbyshko.

CHAPTEE LIX.

ZBYSHKO had said to himself in spirit reproachfully that while suffering he had forgotten his uncle. And since he was accustomed in every case to accomplish quickly whatever he had planned, he set out with De Lorche for Plotsk the next morning. Roads at the boundary even in time of greatest peace were full of peril because numerous ruffian bands were upheld there by the Knights of the Order, and attended by their fostering care. With this King Yagello reproached them keenly. In spite of complaints which were supported in Rome even, in spite of threats and stern measures of justice, the neighboring comturs often permitted their hirelings to join robber bands, disowning, it is true, those who had the ill fate to fall into Polish hands, but giving refuge to those who returned with booty and prisoners, not only in villages of the Order, but also in castles.

Into robber hands of just this kind did travellers fall frequently and also inhabitants near the border, and especially were children of wealthy parents snatched away for the sake of ransom. But the two young knights, having considerable retinues, composed each, besides wagoners, of a number of armed footmen and mounted attendants, did not fear attack, and reached Plotsk without adventure; there a pleasant surprise met them immediately on their arrival.

At the inn they found Tolima, who had come a day earlier. It had happened in this way: the starosta of the Order at Lubav, hearing that Tolima, when attacked near Brodnitsa, had succeeded in hiding a portion of the ransom, sent him back to that castle with an order to the comtur to force him to show where the money was hidden. Tolima made use of that circumstance and fled. When the knights wondered that he had succeeded so easily, he explained the affair to them as follows : "It was all through their greed. The comtur at Brodnitsa would not send a more numerous guard with me, for he did not wish to make a noise about the money. Perhaps he had agreed with the man of Lubav to divide, and

they thought if there was noise they would have to send a large part to Malborg, or give those Von Badens all thou didst remit to them. So he- seat only two guards to take me, — one a confidential man at arms, who had to row with me on the Drventsa, and some kind of scribe. Since they wished no one to see us, they sent us at nightfall, and ye know that the boundary is near by there. They gave me an oar of oak — well — and God's favor, for here 1 am in Plotsk."

"I know, but did not the others return?" called out Zbyshko.

A savage smile lighted Tolima's face.

"The Drventsa flows always into the Vistula," said he. " How could they return against the current? The Knights of the Cross will find them perhaps in Torun."

After a while he added, turning to Zbyshko, —

" The comtur of Lubav took from me a part of the money, but that which I hid when attacked I recovered, and have given it, lord, to thy attendant for keeping; he lives in the castle with the prince, and it is safer in his hands than with me in the inn here."

" Then is my attendant in Plotsk? What is he doing?" inquired Zbyshko, with wonder.

" He, after bringing Siegfried, went away with that young lady who was at Spyhov and is now in waiting on the princess here. As I told thee."

But Zbyshko, dazed by his grief for Danusia, had not inquired and knew nothing. Now he remembered that Hlava had been sent away in advance with Siegfried ; and while recalling this his heart was straitened with sorrow, and'with desire for vengeance.

" True," said he. " But where is that executioner? What has happened to him ? "

"Did not Father Kaleb tell? Siegfried hanged himself, and you have passed his grave in coming hither."

A moment of silence followed.

" Hlava said that he was going to you, and he would have gone long ago, but he was forced to guard the young lady, who fell ill here after coming from Spyhov."

u What young lady?" inquired Zbyshko, shaking himself out of painful remembrances, as if out of a dream.

" Why, that one, your sister or kinswoman who came with the knight Matsko to Spyhov in a man's dress, and found our lord groping along on the highway. Without her, neither the knight Matsko nor your attendant would have recog-

nized our lord Yurand. Our lord loved her greatly after that, for she took as much care of him as would a daughter, and she was the only one except Father Kaleb who understood him."

The young knight opened his eyes widely with astonishment.

" Father Kaleb told me nothing of a young lady, and I have no kinswoman."

" He did not tell, since you forgot everything through pain. You knew not God's world."

" And what is the name of that young lady ? "

" Yagenka."

It seemed to Zbyshko that he was dreaming. The idea that Yagenka could come from distant Zgorzelitse to Spyhov had not occurred to him. Why should she come? It was no secret that the girl was glad to see him and was attached to him in Zgorzelitse, but he had told her that he was to marry Danusia; in view of this he could not suppose in any case that Matsko would bring her to Spyhov with the intent to give her to him in marriage. Besides, neither Matsko nor Hlava had mentioned her. Hence all this seemed to him wonderful!\'7d* strange and beyond explanation, so he fell to overwhelming Tolima with questions like a man who cannot believe his own ears and desires that incredible news be repeated.

Tolima could not tell him more than he had told already, but he went to the castle to look for Hlava, and soon, before sunset, returned with him. The Cheh greeted his young master gladly but also with sorrow, for he had heard of everything which had happened in Spyhov. Zbyshko also was glad from his whole soul, feeling that Hlava had a faithful and friendly heart, one of those which a man needs most in misfortune. He grew tender and sorrowful in telling of Danusia's death, and Hlava shared his sorrow, pain, and tears, just as a brother might share them with a brother. All this lasted long, especially as at the prayer of Zbyshko Pan de Lorche repeated for them that morning hymn which he had composed about the dead woman, and sang it to the sound of a cithara at the open window, raising his eyes and his face toward the stars.

At last they were relieved considerably, and then spoke of affairs awaiting them in Plotsk.

" I have taken this road to Malborg,"said Zbyshko, "for thou knowest that my uncle is a captive, and I am going to him with ransom."

"I know," replied Hlava. "You have done well, lord; I wished myself to go to Spyhov to advise you to come hither. King Yagello will have a meeting in Ratsiondz with the Grand Master; near the king it will be easier to make a claim, because in presence of majesty the Knights of the Cross are not so haughty, and they feign Christian honesty."

" Tolima told me that thou hadst the wish to go to Spyhov, but the ill health of Yagenka, Zyh's daughter, detained thee. I hear that Uncle Matsko brought her to these regions, and that she was in Spyhov. I wonder greatly at this. Tell me, why did my uncle take her from Zgorzelitse ? "

" There were many reasons. The knight Matsko was afraid that if he left her without protection the knights Vilk and Stan would fall on Zgorzelitse, and injustice be inflicted on the younger children. Her absence, as you know, was better than her presence, for in Poland it happens that a noble takes a girl by force if he cannot get her otherwise, but no one would raise a hand on little orphans; the sword of an executioner prevents that, and infamy severer than a sword. But there was another reason: the abbot died and made the young lady heiress to his lands over which the bishop here has care. Therefore knight Matsko brought the lady here to Plotsk."

" But did he take her to Spyhov?"

"' He took her during the absence of the bishop and the prince and princess, for there was no one with whom to leave her. And it is well that he took her to Spyhov, for had the young lady not been with us, we should have passed the lord Yurand as a strange old beggar. It was only when the lady pitied him that we discovered who the old beggar was. The Lord God arranged this all through her pitying heart."

And he told how Yurand afterwards could not live without her, how he loved and blessed her; and though Zbyshko knew this already from Tolima, he listened to that narrative with emotion, and with gratefulness to Yagenka.

"God give her health!" said he at last. "But it is a wonder to me that ye did not mention her."

Hlava was a little troubled, and wished to gain time to think over the answer, and asked,

—

"Where, lord?"

"With Skirvoillo, off there in the Jmud land."

" Did we not say anything ? As I live! It seems to me

VOL. II. — 13

that we said something, but there were other thoughts in your head."

11 Ye said that Yurand had returned, but not a word of Yagenka."

"Ei! have you not forgotten? But God alone knows! Perhaps the knight Matsko thought that I spoke of her to you, and I thought that he spoke. To tell you anything at that time, lord, would have been the same as not to tell. And no wonder! Now it is different. Luckily the lady is in Plotsk; she will be of service to the knight Matsko."

"What can she do?"

"Just let her say one word to the princess, Alexandra, who loves her greatly! The Knights of the Cross refuse nothing to the princess, for, first, she is the king's own sister, and, second, she is a great friend of the Order. Now, as you have heard, perhaps, Prince Skirgello (the king's brother) has risen up against Vitold, and fled to the Knights of the Cross, who wish to assist him and put him in the place of Vitold. The king is very fond of the princess, and lends his ear to her gladly, as they say; so the Knights of the Order wish that she should incline the king to the side of Skirgello against Vifcold. They understand, their mother is in hell! that could they be free of Vitold, they would be at rest. Therefore the envoys of the Order are bowing down before the princess from morning until evening, and try to divine every wish of hers."

" Yagenka loves my uncle greatly, and will take his part," said Zbyshko.

"Be sure of that. She will not do otherwise. But go, lord, to the castle, and tell her how to act and what to say."

" I am going with Pan de Lorche to the castle, in any case. I came here for that purpose. We have only to curl our hair now, and dress befittingly."

After a while he added, —

"I intended to cut my hair in mourning, but forgot to do so."

" It is better as it is," said Hlava.

He stepped out to summon the attendants, and returned with them while the two young knights were arraying themselves properly for the evening banquet at the castle, then he narrated further what was happening at the courts of the king and the prince.

" The Knights of the Order," said he, "undermine Vitold with all their power; for while he is alive and rules a power-

ful country at commission of the king, they can know no peace. In fact, he is the only man they fear. Hei! they are digging and digging, like moles ! They have roused against him already the prince and princess here, and people say that even Prince Yauush bears anger against him because of Vizna."

"But have Prince Yanush and Princess Anna Danuta come also?" inquired Zbyshko. " There will be a multitude of people here whom I know ; I am not in Plotsk now for the first time."

" Yes," answered Hlava, "they are both here ; they have many affairs with the Knights of the Order, which they will bring up against the Grand Master in presence of the king."

"Well, and the king, on whose side is. he? Is he not angry at the Knights, and does he not shake his sword above them ? "

" The king does not like the Knights of the Order, and they say that he has been threatening them with war this long time. As to Vitold, the king prefers him to his own brother, Skirgello, who is a drunkard and a whirlwind. And therefore the knights who attend his Majesty say that the king will not declare against Vitold, and will not promise the Order not to help him. This may be true, for during some days past Princess Alexandra is very attentive to the king and seems in some way anxious."

"Has Zavisha Charny come?"

"He has not, but a man cannot take his eyes from those here already, and should there be war— Mighty God! chips and splinters will fly from the Germans! "

" It is not I who will pity them."

A few Our Fathers later, they were in splendid dress and on the way to the castle. The evening feast that day was to be, not at the prince's palace, but at the house of the city starosta, Andrei of Yasenets, whose spacious mansion stood within the castle walls at the Greater Bastion. Because of the wonderful night, which was almost too warm, the starosta, fearing lest the air might be too sultry in the chambers, commanded to set the tables in the court, where between the stone flags grew yew and service trees. Burning tar kegs illuminated the place with a clear yellow light, but clearer still were the rays of the moon, which on a cloudless sky, amid swarms of stars, shone like the silver shield of a champion. The crowned guests had not appeared yet, but there was a throng already

of the local knighthood, of clergy and of courtiers, both of the king and the princes. Zbyshko knew many of them, especially those of Prince Yanush, and of his former acquaintances of Cracow: he saw Kron of Koziglove, Lis of Targovisko, Martsin of Vrotsimovitse, Domarat of Koby-lany, and Stashko of Harbimovitse, and finally Povala of Tachev, the sight of whom pleased him specially, for he remembered the kindness which that famous knight had shown him formerly.

But he was unable to approach any man immediately, for the local knighthood of Mazovia had surrounded each of them in a close circle, inquiring of Cracow, of the court, of the amusements, of various warlike excellencies, gazing meanwhile at their brilliant dresses, their hair, the splendid curls of which were rubbed with the white of eggs to give consistency, taking from them models of manners and politeness in everything.

But Povala recognized Zbyshko, and, pushing aside the Mazovians, h'e approached him.

"I know thee, young man," said he, pressing his hand. " How art thou, and whence hast thou come? God bless me ! I see a belt and spurs on thee. Other men wait for these till gray hairs, but thou, it seems, art serving Saint George most worthily."

" God give you happiness, noble lord!" answered Zbyshko. "Had I hurled down from his horse the best German, I should not be so glad as I am to see you in health at this moment."

" I am glad to see thee. But where is thy father?"

" That was my uncle, not my father. He is a captive among the Knights of the Cross, and I am going with ransom to release him."

" And that maiden who put a veil on thee?"

Zbyshko made no answer, he only raised his eyes, which filled with tears in one moment, seeing which the lord of Tachev said, —

'• This is a vale of tears, a real vale of tears, nothing else. But let us go to a bench under the service-tree; there thou wilt tell thy sad adventures."

And he drew him to a corner of the courtyard. Zbyshko sat down at his side and told of Yurand's misfortunes, of the seizure of Danusia, how he had sought her, and how she had died after he had rescued her. Povala listened carefully, and on his face were seen in turn wrath, amazement,

compassion, and horror. At last, when Zbyshko had finished, he said, —

"I will tell this to our lord the king. He has in every case to make claim of the Master on behalf of little Yasko of Kretkov, and obtain the stern punishment of those who' seized the boy; and they seized him to get a rich ransom. For them it is nothing to raise hands on children."

Here he was thoughtful for a while, then he spoke on as if in soliloquy, —

"An insatiable race, worse than Turks and Tartars. In their souls they dread the king and us ; still they cannot hold back from robbery and murder. They attack villages, slaughter land-tillers, drown fishermen; they seize children as wolves might. What would they do did they not fear us? The Grand Master sends letters against our king to foreign courts, but fawns before his eyes like a dog, for he knows our strength better than others do. But at last he has overfilled the measure."

Again he was silent for a moment, then he laid his hand on Zbyshko's arm.

" I will tell the king," repeated he; " this long time wrath is boiling yi him, like water in a pot, and be sure of this, that dreadful punishment will not miss the authors of thy suffering."

" O lord,"replied Zbyshko, " not one of them is alive now."

Povala gazed at him with great well-wishing friendliness.

" God give thee aid ! It is clear that thou dost not forget injustice. Lichtenstein is the only man whom thou hast not repaid, for I know that thou hast not had the chance yet. We also made a vow against him in Cracow; but to fulfil this vow there must be war — God grant us to see it! — Lichtenstein could not fight a duel without the Grand Master's permission, and the Master needs Lichtenstein's wit, therefore he sends him continually to various courts; he will not give him permission easily."

" First, I must ransom my uncle."

" Yes, true; and I have inquired about Lichtenstein. He is not here, and will not be in Ratsiondz ; he has been sent to the King of England for archers. But let not thy head ache over thy uncle. If the king or the princes here say a word, the Grand Master will not permit evasion touching the ransom."

" All the more, as I have a considerable captive who is a rich man and famous among them. He would be glad surely

to bow down to you, lord, and become acquainted, for no one respects famous knights more than he does."

Then he nodded to De Lorche, who had come near; and he, having asked previously who the knight was with whom Zbysnko was conversing, approached hurriedly, for indeed he had flushed up with desire to know a man so famous aa Povala.

When Zbyshko had made them acquainted, the polished knight of Guelders bowed with the utmost elegance, and added, —

"There could be only one greater honor beyond pressing your hand, and that would be to meet you within barriers, or in battle."

At this the strong knight of Tachev smiled, for near the slender and small De Lorche he looked like a mountain.

"But I am glad," said he, "that we shall meet at full cups only; God grant never elsewhere ! "

De Lorche hesitated somewhat, and then answered as if with a certain timidity, —

"But shouldst thou assert, noble lord, that the damsel Yagenka of Dlugolyas is not the most beautiful and most virtuous lady on earth, it would be for me a great honor — to contradict, and — "

Here he stopped and looked into the eyes of Povala with respect, nay, even with homage, but quickly and with attention.

Povala, whether it was because he knew that he could crush De Lorche with two fingers, as he might a nut, or because he had a soul which was immensely kind and gladsome, laughed aloud and said, —

" On a time I made a vow to the Princess of Burgundy, and she in those days was ten years older than I; but if you, sir, wish to assert that my princess is not older than your damsel Yagenka, we shall have to take to horse straightway."

When he heard this, De Lorche looked in amazement for a while at the lord of Tachev, then his face began to quiver, and at last he burst into kindly laughter.

Povala bent forward, put one arm around De Lorche's body, then raised him from the ground and swayed him back and forth as easily as if the man had been an infant.

"Pax/ pax! as Bishop Kropidlo says!" exclaimed Povala. " You have pleased me, knight, and as God is true we will never fight for any lady."

Then embracing De Lorche, he placed him on the ground ; for just at the entrance the trumpets sounded suddenly, and the Prince of Plotsk entered with his consort.

" The prince and princess here precede the king and Prince Yanush," said Povala, " for though the feas| is given by the starosta, it is given in Plotsk, where they are rulers. Come with me to the princess, for thou knowest her since the feast at Cracow, when she took thy part before Yagello."

And seizing Zbyshko by the arm, he conducted him through the court. Behind the prince and princess came courtiers and damsels, all in grand array, and brilliant; since the king was to be there, so the whole space was as bright from them as if they had been flowers. Zbyshko, while approaching with Povala, examined faces from a distance, thinking to find among them some acquaintance, and all at once he halted from astonishment; for close behind the princess he saw, a figure and a face well known indeed to him, but so serious, beautiful, and queenlike that he thought his eyes must be deceiving him.

"Is that Yagenka — or perhaps the daughter of the Prince of Plotsk?"

But that was Yagenka, the daughter- of Zyh, for at the moment when their eyes met, she smiled at once with friendliness and compassion; then she grew pale a little, and, dropping her eyelids, stood with a golden circlet on her dark hair, and with the immense brilliancy of her beauty, tall and wonderful, resembling not merely a young princess but a ruling queen.

CHAPTER LX.

ZBYSHKO fell at the feet of Princess Alexandra of Plotsk and offered her his service. She did not recognize the young knight at first, for she had not seen him for a long time. Only when he told her his name did she say,—

" Indeed ! But I thought you some one from the king's court. Zbyshko of Bogdanets! Of course ! Your uncle was a guest here, the old knight of Bogdanets, and I remember how tears gushed in streams from me and my damsels when he told us thy story. And have you found your bride? Where is she at present?"

" She is dead, gracious lady."

" O dear Jesus! Do not say that, for I shall not restrain my weeping. She is in heaven surely, that is the one consolation, and thou art young. A weak creature is woman. But in heaven there is recompense for all things, and there thou wilt find her. But the old knight of Bogdanets, is he here with thee ? "

" He is not, for he is a captive with the Knights of the Cross, and I am going now to ransom him."

" Then he too has failed of luck! But he seemed a quick man, who knew every custom. ' But when he is ransomed, come here to us. We shall be glad to see you both, for I say sincerely that he is not lacking in wit, as thou art not lacking in comeliness."

" I will do so, gracious lady, all the more since I have come hither now purposely to beg of your Grace a favor for my uncle."

" Very well, come to-morrow before the hunt; I shall have time then."

Further conversation was interrupted by a new outburst of drums and trumpets announcing the arrival of Prince Yanush and his princess. As Zbyshko and the Princess of Plotsk stood near the entrance, Anna Danuta saw the young knight and approached him immediately without noticing the obeisance of their host, the starosta.

The young man's heart was rent again at sight of Princess Anna, so he knelt before her, and seizing her knees remained in silence. She bent over him and pressed his temples, dropping tear after tear on his bright head, exactly as a mother while weeping over a son's misfortunes.

And to the great astonishment of guests and courtiers she wept long, repeating, —

"O Jesus! O Jesus the Compassionate!" Then she raised Zbyshko and said: " I weep for my Danusia, and I weep over thee. But God has so disposed that thy toils were fruitless, and now our tears are fruitless also. But do thou tell me of her, and of her death, for though I were to listen till midnight I should not hear enough."

And she took him to one side, as the lord of Tachev had done previously. Those of the guests who did not know Zbyshko inquired concerning his adventures, and for some time all conversed only of him, and Danusia, and Yurand. The envoys of the Order asked also Friedrich von Wenden, the comtur of Torun, sent to meet the king, and Johann von Schonfeld, the comtur of Osterode. The latter, a German, but from Silesia, knowing Polish well, inquired easily what the question was, and when he had heard it from the lips of Yasko of Zabierz, an attendant of Prince Yanush, he said, —

" Danveld and De Lowe were accused before the Grand Master of practising the black art."

Then observing quickly that even the statement of such things might cast a shadow on the whole Order, like that which had fallen on the Templars, he added immediately, —

"That was a statement of gossips, but it was not true, for there are no men of that kind in our order." But Povala, who was standing near, answered, —

" They who prevented the baptism of Lithuania may oppose the Cross."

"We wear the Cross on our mantles," answered Schonfeld, haughtily.

" But men should wear it in their hearts," said Povala.

That moment the trumpets sounded still louder, and Yagello appeared with the archbishop of Gniezen, the bishop of Cracow, the bishop of Plotsk, the castellan of Cracow, and other dignitaries and courtiers, among whom were Zyndram and the young Prince Yamont, an attendant of Yagello. The king had changed little since Zbyshko had seen him first. He had the same quickly glancing eyes, on

his cheeks was the same pronounced ruddiness, he wore his hair long, as at Cracow, and put it behind his ears frequently. It seemed to Zbyshko, however, that he had more dignity of bearing and more majesty in his person, as if he felt surer on that throne which after the death of the queen he had desired to leave straightway, not knowing that he would be firm on it, and as if he were now more conscious of his great power and importance. The two Mazovian princes took their places at once at both sides of the sovereign; in front the German envoys greeted him with bows; and round about stood dignitaries and the foremost courtiers. The walls surrounding the court trembled from unceasing shouts, the sound of trumpets, and the thundering of drums.

When at last silence came, the envoy Von Wenden began to mention something touching the affairs of the Order; but the king, when he noted whither the conversation was tending, waved his hand impatiently and said in his deep, sonorous voice, —

" Better defer negotiation. We have come to this place for pleasure and are glad to see food and drink, not thy parchments."

Meanwhile he smiled affably, not wishing the Knight of the Cross to think that he was answering in anger, and added, —

" There will be time in Ratsiondz to speak of affairs with the Grand Master." Then he turned to the Prince of Plotsk, -

" But to-morrow to the wilderness to hunt — is it so?"

This question was a declaration at the same time that he did not wish to speak that evening of aught besides hunting, which he loved with all his soul, and for which he came to Mazovia gladly, since Little and Great Poland were less wooded and so populous in places that forests were lacking altogether.

The faces of guests then grew gladsome, for the\'7d' knew that the king, whenever he conversed of hunting, was joyous and indeed gracious also. The Prince of Plotsk began at once to tell whither they would go, and what game would be provided. Prince Yanush had sent one of his attendants to bring from the city his two "defenders" who had led wild bulls out of snares by the horns, and had broken the bones in bears, for he wished to show these two men to Yagello.

Zbyshko wished greatly to go and bow down to Prince Yanush, but he could not approach him. He saw from a dis-

tance, however, Prince Yamont, who had forgotten evidently the sharp answer which on a time the young knight had given him in Cracow, for he nodded in a friendly manner, telling him by winks to come whenever possible. At that moment some hand touched the young man's shoulder, and a sweet, sad voice was heard right at his side there, —

"Zbyshko!"

He turned quickly and saw Yagenka. Occupied earlier in greeting the Princess of Plotsk, and then in converse with Anna Danuta, he could not approach Yagenka; so she herself, making use of the confusion caused by Yagello's entrance, came to him.

" Zbyshko," repeated she, " may God and the Most Holy Lady comfort thee ! "

" God reward you," answered Zbyshko.

And he looked with gratitude into her blue eyes, which at that moment were as if covered with dew. They stood face to face there in silence. For though she had come to him like a kind and mourning sister, she seemed in her queenly bearing and brilliant court dress so different from the former Yagenka that at the first moment he dared not even say thou to her, as had been his wont at her father's house, and in Bogdanets. And it seemed to her that after those words which she had spoken there was no more to say to him. This continued till embarrassment was evident on their faces. But just at that moment it became less crowded in the court, for the king sat down to supper.

Princess Anna Danuta approached Zbyshko again, and said, —

"This will be a sad feast for us both, but serve me as before."

So the young man had to leave Yagenka; and when the guests were seated he stood behind the princess to change dishes and to pour out water and wine for her. While serving he looked involuntarily from time to time at Yagenka, who, being a damsel of the Princess of Plotsk, sat at her side, and he could not but admire her beauty. Yagenka, since he had seen her at home, had grown considerably; she was not changed so much by her stature, however, as by a dignity of which she had not had a trace before. Formerly, when in a sheep-skin coat and with leaves in her dishevelled hair she chased through forests and pine woods on horseback, she might have been taken really for a beautiful peasant; now, at the first cast of the eye, she seemed a maiden of

birth and high blood, such repose was there in her face. Zbyshko noted also that her former gladsomeness had vanished ; but he wondered less at this, for he had heard of her father's death. He was astonished still more by that peculiar dignity of hers, and at first it seemed to him that her garments gave this appearance. So he looked in turn at the golden circlet which surrounded her forehead white as snow, and her dark hair falling in two tresses to her shoulders, then on her blue, closely fitting robe embroidered with a purple strip, beneath which was indicated clearly her arrowy form and her maiden bosom. "A real princess." But he saw afterward that it was not her dress alone which had caused the change, and that though she were to put on a simple sheep-skin at that time, he could not consider her so lightly and bear himself with her so freely as in past time.

He noticed also that various young men, and even older knights, gazed at her eagerly and with attention ; and once, when he was changing the plate before the princess, he saw Pan de Lorche lost in gazing at her, and, as it were, rapt into Paradise. And at this sight he felt anger in his soul at him. The knight of Guelders did not escape the watchfulness of Princess Anna Danuta, who, recognizing him, said quickly, —

" See Pan de Lorche! He is falling in love again surely, for he is dazed altogether."

Then bending over the table somewhat, she glanced toward Yagenka side wise.

"By my faith," said she, " other lights will pale before this torch."

Zbyshko was drawn toward Yagenka, for she seemed to him like a beloved and loving kinswoman, and he felt that a safer confidant for his sorrow he could not find, nor could he find more compassion in any heart; but he had no chance to speak to her that evening, for first he was occupied with service, and, second, during the whole time of the feast the chorus sang songs, or the trumpets made such loud music that even those who sat side by side could hardly hear one another. The princesses and ladies left the feast earlier than the king, princes, and knights, whose custom it was to amuse themselves at goblets till late hours. Yagenka carried a cushion for the princess, so it was not possible to delay ; she, too, departed, but in going she smiled at Zbyshko a second time, and bowed to him.

It was almost daylight when the young knight, Pan de Lorche, and their two attendants went back to the inn. They walked on for a time, sunk in thought; but near the inn De Lorche said something to his attendant, a Pomorian who spoke Polish easily, and the man turned to Zbyshko, —

"My lord," said he, "would like to ask something of your Grace."

u Very well," replied Zbyshko.

De Lorche spoke to his attendant again awhile. The Pomorian, smiling slightly, said, —

" My lord would like to inquire if it is certain that that damsel with whom your Grace conversed before the feast is a mortal being, or if she is some saint or angel."

" Tell thy lord," answered Zbyshko, with a certain impatience, " that he has asked me that question already, so I wonder now to hear it a second time. In Spyhov he told me that he was going to Vitold's court to see the beauty of Lithuanian damsels, then for a similar cause he wished to visit this place, in Plotsk to-day he wished to challenge the knight Povala in behalf of Yagenka of Dlugolyas, and now again he is aiming at another. Is that his constancy ; is that his knightly faith?"

Pan de Lorche listened to this answer through the mouth of his attendant, sighed deeply, looked awhile at the sky, which was growing pale, and then answered, —

" Thou speakest justly. Neither constancy nor faith, for I am a sinful man and unworthy to wear the spurs of knighthood. As to Panna Yagenka of Dlugolyas, I have made a vow to her, it is true, and God grant that I shall keep it; but see how I shall move thee when I tell how cruelly she treated me at Chersk."

Here he sighed again, and looked at the sky, on the eastern rim of which a strip was growing clearer. When the Pomorian had interpreted his words De Lorche continued, —

" This is what she said to me : ' I have an enemy, a master of the black art: he dwells within a tower in the middle of a forest; he sends a dragon out every year against me; this dragon comes to Chersk in autumn, and watches to see if he can seize me.' When she told this I declared immediately that I would give battle to that dragon. Ah! consider my story further: when I reached the appointed place I saw a dreadful monster waiting for me; delight filled my soul, for I thought that either I should fall or rescue the maiden from his disgusting jaws, and win eternal glory. But when I went near and thrust a spear into the monster — Canst

thou think what I discovered ? An immense bag of straw on wooden wheels, and it had a tail all stuffed with straw! I won people's laughter instead of glory, and then I had to challenge two Mazovian knights; from both I suffered sad defeat inside barriers. Thus was I treated by the woman whom I had exalted beyond all others, and whom alone I wished to love."

The Pomorian, while interpreting these words, thrust his tongue into his cheek and bit it at moments, so as not to burst into laughter, and Zbyshko at another time would have laughed surely, but pain and unhappiness had destroyed gladness in him utterly, so he answered with a serious face,—

" She may have done this only through frivolity, and not in malice."

" I have forgiven her, and thou hast the best proof of that in this, that I wished to fight with the knight Povala in defence of her beauty and her virtue."

" Do not fight with him," said Zbyshko, more seriously.

" I know that it would be death, but I would rather fall than live in endless suffering and sadness."

" Povala has no such things in his head. Better go to him with me to-morrow, and conclude a league of friendship."

" I will do so, for he has pressed me to his heart; but to-morrow he is going with the king to hunt."

" Then we will go early. The king loves to hunt, but does not despise rest, and he has conversed long to-night."

And they did thus, but in vain; for Hlava, who had gone still earlier to the castle to see Yagenka, announced that Povala had slept, not in his own lodgings, but in the king's chambers. Their disappointment, however, was recompensed, for Prince Yanush met them, and commanded both men to join his escort. Thus they were able to be present at the hunt. While going to the forest Zbyshko found the chance of speaking to Prince Yamont, who gave him pleasant tidings.

"While undressing the king for sleep," said he, "I reminded him of thee, and of thy Cracow adventure. And the knight Povala, who was present, added immediately that thy uncle had been seized by the Knights of the Cross, and he begged the king to claim him. The king, who is dreadfully incensed at the knights for stealing little Yasko, and for other attacks, grew still more raging. ' Not with a pleasant word,' said he, ' should one meet them, but with a lance! with a lance! with a lance!' And Povala threw fuel on that fire purposely. This morning, when the envoys of the Order were waiting at the gate, the king did not even look at them, though they bowed to the earth before his Majesty. Hei! they will not get a promise now that the king will not assist Prince Vitold, and they will not know what first to lay their hands on. But be sure of one thing, the king will not fail to press the Master about thy uncle Matsko."

Thus. Prince Yamont delighted Zbyshko's heart, and still more did Yagenka delight it; for, accompanying Princess Alexandra to the forest, she strove to ride back side by side with Zbyshko. During hunts there was always great freedom ; people returned usually in couples. And since it was not important for one couple to be too near another, they could speak without restriction. Yagenka had heard earlier of Matsko's captivity from Hlava, and had lost no time in helping. At her request the princess had given a letter to the Grand Master and had gained, besides, this, that Von Wenden, the comtur of Torun, had mentioned the affair in a letter in which he gave an account of what was happening in Plotsk. He boasted before the princess that he had added, " Wishing to please the king, we should not raise difficulties in this case." And the Grand Master was concerned beyond measure at that moment to please the powerful sovereign as far as possible, and turn all his own forces with perfect safety on Vitold, whom thus far the Order had been quite unable to manage.

" I have done what I could, taking care to avoid delay," said Yagenka; "and since the king will not yield to his sister in great tilings, he will try to please her at least in the smallest, hence I have great hope."

" Were the affair not with such treacherous people," said Zbj-shko, " I would take the ransom straightway, and thus end the matter; with them, however, it may happen to a man as it happened with Tolima, — they will take the money, and not free the person who brought it unless power stands behind him."

"I understand," said Yagenka.

"You understand everything now," answered Zbyshko; " and while I live I shall be grateful to you."

"Why not say thou to me, as an acquaintance from childhood?" asked she, raising her sad and kind eyes to him.

" I know not," answered he, innocently. " Somehow it is

not easy for me ; and you are not the young girl of former days, but — as it were — something — entirely — "

And he could not find the comparison ; but she interrupted his efforts and said, — •

" Some time has been added to my age — and the Germans have killed my father in Silesia."

" True ! God grant eternal light to him! "

They rode on some time side by side in silence, and thoughtfully, as if listening to the low sound of the pine-trees, then she inquired, —

"But after ransoming Matsko wilt thou stay in these parts ? "

Zbyshko looked at her as if in wonder, for up to that moment he had been given so exclusively to mourning and sadness that it had not come to his head to think of what would happen later. So he raised his eyes as if in meditation, and after a while he said, —

I know not ! O merciful Christ ! how can I know ? I know that when I travel anywhere my fate will follow after me. Hei! a sad fate! I will ransom my uncle, and then go perhaps to Vitold to accomplish my vows against the Knights of the Cross; and perhaps I shall perish."

At this the girl's eyes grew misty, and bending toward the young man somewhat, she said in a low voice, as if entreating, —

" Do not perish ; do not perish ! "

And again they ceased to speak, till at the very walls of the place Zbyshko shook himself out of thoughts that were gnawing him.

" But you — but thou — wilt thou stay here at the court ? " asked he.

" No. It is dreary for me here without my brothers, and without Zgorzelitse. Stan and Vilk must be married before this, and even if they are not I do not fear them."

" God grant me to bring Uncle Matsko to Zgorzelitse. He is such a friend of thine that thou mightst depend on him always. But do thou remember him also."

"I promise sacredly to be, as it were, his own child t> him."

And after these words she wept in earnest, for in her heart there was gloom and trembling.

Next day Povala of Tachev appeared at Zbyshko's inn and said to him,—

" After communion the king will go to meet the Grand Master; thou art numbered with his knights and wilt go with us."

Zbyshko flushed from delight at these words, for not only did the fact of including him with the knights of the king protect him from the treachery and attacks of the Knights of the Cross, but conferred great renown on him also. Among those knights were Zavisha Charny and his brothers Farurey and Kruchek, Povala himself, and Kron and Pashko Zlodye, and Lis, with many other tremendous and glorious knights, famed at home and in foreign countries. Yagello took a small detachment, for some he had left at home, and some were seeking adventures in distant lands and in lands beyond the sea; but he knew that with them he might go even to Malborg without fearing the treachery of the Order, for in case of need they would crush walls with their mighty arms and open a road for him among Germans. Zbyshko's young heart might warm also with pride at the thought that he would have such companions.

At the first moment he forgot his own grief even, and pressing Povala's hand, he said with delight, —

" To you, and to no one else, am I indebted, —to you! to you! "

"Tome in part," answered Povala, " in part to the gracious princess here, but most to our gracious sovereign. Go at once and embrace his feet, so that he may not suspect thee of ingratitude."

"In so far as I am ready to die for him, so help me God ! " exclaimed Zbyshko.

V6L. II. —14

CHAPTER LXI.

THE meeting at Ratsioudz, on an island of the Vistula, to which the king went about Corpus Christi, took place with bad omens, and did not lead to such agreement and settlement of various questions as those which took place two years later, and at which the king recovered the land of Dobryn, and with Dobryn Bobrovniki, which had been mortgaged treacherously by Opolchik.

At his arrival Yagello was greatly irritated by the calumny against him spread by the Knights of the Cross at the courts of western Europe, and in Rome even, and he was indignant at the dishonesty of the Order. The Grand Master would not discuss the affair of Dobryn; he refrained purposely; and both he and other dignitaries repeated to the Poles daily : ' v We wish no war with you, nor with Lithuania, but the Jraud land is ours, for Vitold himself gave it. Promise not to help Vitold, and war with him will be ended sooner; there will be leisure then to speak of Dobryn, and we will make great concessions." But the king's counsellors, having quick wit with much experience, and knowing the deceit of the Order, did not let themselves be tricked. " When ye increase in power, your insolence will increase also," said they to the Grand Master. " Ye say that ye have no concern with Lithuania, but ye wish to seat Skirgello on the throne in Vilno. By the dear God! that is Yagello's inheritance; he alone can decide whom he wishes to make prince in ^Lithuania. Therefore restrain yourselves, lest our great 'king punish you."

To this the Master replied that if the king was the real lord of Lithuania, let him command Vitold to abandon war and give Jmud back to the Order, otherwise the Order must strike Vitold wherever it could reach and wound him. In this manner the disputes dragged on from morning until evening, like a road winding round in a circle. The king, not wishing to bind himself to anything, grew more and more impatient, and told the Master that if Jmud were happy under

the control of the Order, Vitold would not move a finger, for he would have neither excuse nor reason. The Grand Master, who was a man of peace, and knew Yagello's strength more clearly than did others, strove to pacify the king; and notwithstanding the muttering of some comturs who were proud and passionate, he spared no flattering words, and at moments showed humility. But since even in that humility veiled threats were heard frequently, all ended in failure. Discussions on important points were dropped quickly, and on the second day they spoke only of inferior questions. The king attacked the Order sharply for maintaining bands of ruffians and for attacks and robberies along the border, for the stealing of Yurand's daughter and of little Yasko, for murdering fishermen and land-tillers.

The Grand Master denied, evaded, swore that, that had been done without his knowledge, and in return he made reproaches, saying that not only Vitold, but Polish knights as well had assisted pagan Jmud men to war against the Order. To prove this he gave instance of Matsko of Bog-danets. Fortunately, the king knew through Povala what the knigbts of Bogdanets were seeking in the Jmud land, and was able to answer the reproach, all the more easily that in his retinue was Zbyshko, and in that of the Master the two Von Baclens, who had come with the hope of fighting with Poles inside barriers.

But there was no meeting of that sort. The Knights of the Cross had wished, in case discussions went smoothly, to invite King Yagello to Torun, and have feasts there and spectacles for many days to do him honor ; but as discussions had failed, producing only mutual dislike and anger, desire for amusements was lacking. Only privately, in the morning hours, knights tried one another a little in strength and dexterity, but as the gladsome Prince Yamont said, that went against the grain of the Knights of the Cross, for Povala proved stronger in the arm than Arnold von Baden, Dohek of Olesuitsa at the lance, and Lis of Targovisko in jumping over horses surpassed all men. On this occasion, Zbyshko arranged the ransom with Arnold. De Lorche, as a count and a man of great note, looked down on Arnold, opposed that arrangement, and affirmed that he took all on himself. But Zbyshko considered that knightly honor commanded him to pay the amount of ransom promised ; therefore, though Arnold was ready to reduce the sum, he would not accept the reduction, or Pan de Lorche's interference.

Arnold von Baden was a simple soldier whose highest merit was the giant strength of his arm; he was dull enough, not loving money, and wellnigh honest. There was no cunning of the Order in that man, hence he did not hide from Zbyshko why he was willing to decrease the ransom. " It will not come," said he, "to negotiations between the great king and the Master, but it will to exchange of prisoners, and then thou wilt take thy uncle for nothing. I prefer to get a part rather than nothing, for my purse is ever slender, and often can stand hardly three tankards of beer a day, while I suffer when I have less than five or six of them."

Zbyshko was angered by these words. " I pay," said he, "because I gave my knightly word; I will pay no less than what I promised, so thou mayst know that we have that much value." Thereupon Arnold embraced him, while the Polish knights and those of the Order gave praise, saying: "Justly dost thou wear a belt and spurs while so young, for thou knowest dignity and honor."

Meanwhile the king and the Grand Master arranged indeed for exchanging prisoners, whereupon strange things came to light which caused bishops and dignitaries of the kingdom to write letters afterward to the Pope and to various courts in Europe. In the hands of the Poles there were, it is true, many prisoners, but these were grown men in the bloom of life, captured with armed hand in battles and engagements on the boundary; while in the hands of the Knights of the Cross were found mainly women and children seized during night attacks and held for ransom. The Pope himself turned attention to this; and despite the acuteness of Johann von Felde, the procurator of the Order at the Holy See, he gave in public expression to his indignation and his anger.

There were difficulties as to Matsko. The Master did not make them seriously, but only in appearance, so as to add weight to each concession. He declared, therefore, that a Christian knight, who had fought side by side with the Jmud men, should in justice suffer death. In vain did the king's counsellors bring up anew all that was known to them of Yurand and his daughter, and the terrible wrong inflicted on them and on the knights of Bogdanets by the servants of the Order. Through a strange chance the Master in his answer used words employed- by the Princess

Alexandra when speaking to the old knight of Bogdanets, —

" Ye call yourselves lambs and our people wolves, but of

the four wolves who took part in carrying off Yurand's daughter not one is alive now, but the lambs are going safely through the world yet."

And this was true, but to this truth the lord of Tachev, who was present, answered with the following question, —

" True. But has any one of them been slain by treachery, or have those who fell not fallen sword in hand, every man of them?"

The Master had no answer to this ; and when he saw also that the king had begun to frown and his eyes to flash, he yielded, not wishing to bring the dread sovereign to an outburst. It was agreed then that each side should send envoys to receive the captives. On the Polish side were appointed Zyndram, who wished to look from near by at the power of the Order, and Povala, also Zbyshko.

Prince Yamont rendered this service to Zbyshko. He spoke to the king on his behalf, with the idea that the young knight would thus see his uncle sooner, and bring him away the more surely, since he would go for him as an envoy of Yagello. The king did not refuse the prayer of the prince, who, because of his joyful nature, kindness, and unusual beauty, was the favorite of his Majesty and all the court officials; withal he never asked for himself any favor. Zbyshko thanked him from his whole soul, for now he felt convinced that Matsko would escape from the Knights of the Order.

" No man envies thee," said Zbyshko to Yamont, " thy place near the king ; and thou art near him justly, since thy intimacy is used for the good of others, and a better heart than thine, I think, no one has."

u It is pleasant near the king," replied Yamont, "but I would rather be in the field against Knights of the Order, and this I envy thee, that thou hast fought against them."

After a while he added, —

"Von Wenden, the comtur of Torun, arrived here yesterday, and this evening ye will go to him for the night, with the Master and his retinue."

" And then to Malborg? "

" And then to Malborg."

Here Prince Yamont laughed,—

" That road is not long, but it will be unpleasant, since the Germans have won nothing from the king, with Vitold too they will have no pleasure. He has gathered all the power of Lithuania and is marching to the Jmud land."

214 THE KNIGHTS OF THE CROSS.

" If the king assists, there will be a great war."

" All our kuights are begging the Lord God for it. But even if the king, through regard for Christian blood, should not make a great war, he will help Vitold with grain and money; and it will not be without this, too, that Polish knights will go as volunteers to him."

" As I live they will go," answered Zbyshko. " And perhaps the Order will declare war against the king because of that."

" Oh, no! while the present Master lives there will be no war."

And he was right. Zbyshko had known the Master earlier; but now on the road to Malborg, being, with Zyn-dram and Povala, at his side nearly all the time, he could observe more closely and estimate the man more accurately. In fact, that journey only confirmed him in the conviction that the Grand Master, Conrad von Jungingen, was not depraved and wicked. He was forced often to act unjustly, for the whole Order was founded on injustice. He had to commit injustice, for the Order reposed on injustice to man. He had to utter calumny, for the practice of calumny had come to him, together with the insignia of his office, and from early years he had grown accustomed to consider calumny as diplomatic skill merely. But he was not a tyrant; he feared the judgment of God, and as far as he was able he restrained the pride and insolence of those dignitaries of the Order who were urging on to war against the power of Yagello. He was a weak man, however. The Order had been accustomed for generations to prey on the property of others, to plunder, to take adjoining lands by force or treachery ; since Conrad not only was unable to restrain that predatory hunger, but in spite of himself, by force of acquired impetus, he yielded to it and strove to satisfy this craving. Distant were the days of Winrich von Kniprode, days of iron discipline, with which the Order astonished the whole world of that time. Even during the rule of Conrad "NValleurod, the Master who preceded Jungingen, the Order grew intoxicated with its own might, which was always growing, and which temporary defeats could not diminish, it became intoxicated with glory, with success, with human blood, so that the bonds which held it in union and in strength were loosened. In so far as he was able the Master maintained right and justice ; in so far as he was able he lightened personally the iron hand of the Order, which weighed on peasants, on

citizens, and even on the clergy and on nobles living by feudal right on lands of the Order; hence near Malborg this or that citizen or land-tiller might be not only well-to-do, but wealthy; while in more remote places the tyranny, cruelty, and disorder of the comturs trampled justice, spread oppression and extortion, squeezed out the last copper by means of taxes imposed without warrant and even without pretext, pressed out tears, and often blood, so that in whole extensive regions there was one groan, universal wretchedness, and universal complaint. If even the good of the Order commanded greater mildness, as at times in Jmud, those commands came to naught in view of the disorder of the comturs and their native cruelty. So Conrad von Jungingen felt like a charioteer who is driving maddened horses and has dropped the reins from his hands, abandoning his chariot to the will of fate. Hence evil forebodings mastered his soul frequently, and frequently those prophetic words occurred to him : "I established them as bees of usefulness ; I settled them on the threshold of Christian lands ; but they have risen against me. They care not for the souls, and they have no compassion for the bodies, of the people who turned from error to the Catholic faith, and to me. They have made slaves of those people, and by neglecting to teach them the commands of God, and by depriving them of the holy sacraments, they expose them to greater torments of hell than if they had continued Pagans, They make wars to satisfy their own greed, hence the hour will come when their teeth will be broken, and the right hand will be cut from them, and their right leg shall be lame, so that they will confess their offences."

The Master knew that those reproaches, which the mysterious Voice uttered against the Order in the vision to Saint Bridget, were true. He understood that, that edifice, reared on the land of another, and on wrong done another,— that edifice, resting on calumny, treachery, and tyranny, could not endure. He feared that, undermined for whole years by blood and by tears, it would fall from one blow of the strong Polish hand ; he felt that the chariot drawn by raging horses would end in the abyss, so he strove that at least the hour of judgment, defeat, wrath, and suffering should come as late as possible. In spite of his weakness, he presented therefore in one thing an invincible opposition to his insolent and haughty counsellors: he would not permit a war with Poland. In vain did they reproach him with fear and incompetence; in

vain did the comturs of the border urge war with all their might. He, when the fire was just ready to burst forth, always withdrew at the last moment, and then gave thanks to God at Malborg that he had been able to arrest the sword raised above the Order.

But he knew that war must come. Hence that knowledge that the Order was built, not on the justice of God, but on injustice and calumny, and that feeling of an approaching day of destruction, made him one of the most unhappy men on earth. He would beyond doubt have given his life and blood could it have been otherwise, and were there time yet to turn to a way of justice ; but he felt that it was late then. To turn would mean to give to the rightful owners all those rich and fertile lands seized by the Order, God knows how long since, and with them a multitude of cities as rich as Dantzig. And that was not all ! It would mean to renounce the Jmud region; to renounce attacks on Lithuania; to put the sword in the scabbard; finally, to remove altogether from those regions in which there were no more people for the Order to Christianize, and settle in Palestine a second time, or on some of the Grecian islands, to de-feud the Cross there from real Saracens. But this was impossible, since it would have been equivalent to a sentence of destruction to the Order. Who would agree to that? What Grand Master would ask for it? The soul and life of Conrad were covered with a shadow, but if a man were to appear with an advice of this sort, the Master would be the first to condemn him to a dark chamber as one who had lost his senses. The Order had to go on and on till the day when God himself should fix the limit.

So Conrad advanced, but in gloonl and in suffocating sorrow. The hair on his chin and temples had grown silvery, and his e3 7 es, once quick, were half covered with their heavy drooping lids. Zbyshko did not note a smile even once on his countenance. The Master's face was not severe nor even overcast ; it was only tortured, as if by silent suffering. In his armor, with a cross on his breast, in the centre of which was a black eagle on a quadrangular field, and in a great white mantle also adorned with the Cross, he produced the impression of dignity, of majesty and sorrow. Conrad had been a joyous man, he had loved jests, and even at that time he was not av.erse to splendid feasts, spectacles, and tournaments, nay, he even 'took part in them ; but neither in the throng of brilliant knights, who came as guests to

Malborg, nor in a joyous outcry, amid the sounds of trumpets and the clatter of weapons, or amid goblets filled with Malvoisie, was he ever gladsome. When all around seemed full of strength, splendor, inexhaustible wealth, invincible power; when the envoys of the emperor and of kings of the west shouted with enthusiasm that the Order could stand by itself for all kingdoms, and the strength of the world, — he alone was not deceived, he alone remembered the ominous words in the vision of the saint: " The time will come when their teeth will be broken, and their right hand cut from them, when their right leg will be lame, so that they will confess their offences."

CHAPTER LXII.

THEY went by land through Helmno to Grudziondz, where they stopped for the night and passed the next day, for the Grand Master had to judge a question of fishing between the castle starosta of the Order and the neighboring nobility whose lands bordered on the Vistula. Thence they sailed on barges of the Order down the river to Malborg. Zyndram, Povala, and Zbyshko passed all the time at the side of the Master, who was curious to learn what impression would be made, especially on Zyndram, by the might of the Order when he looked from near by at it. This concerned Conrad, because Zyndram was not only a valiant and terrible knight in single combat, but an uncommonly skilful warrior. There was no other man in the kingdom who knew, as he did, how to lead large armies, muster regiments for battle, build castles as well as storm them, and throw bridges across broad rivers; no other man who understood "guns" so well,

— that is, arms of various nations, and all military tactics. The Master, knowing that much depended on the opinion of Zyndram in the counsel of the King, thought that if he could astonish him by the greatness of the Order's wealth, and by its army, war would be deferred for a long time. And, above all, the sight of Malborg might itself fill the heart of every Pole with dread, for no other fortress on earth could compare, even approximately, with that one, counting the High Castle, the Middle Castle, and the First Castle. 1 Already, from afar, in sailing down the Nogat, the knights saw the mighty bastions standing out against the sky. The day was bright and clear, so they could see them perfectly; and after some time, when the barges had approached, the points of the churcn gleamed still more on the lofty castle and the gigantic walls, towering some above others, partly in red brick, but mainly covered with that celebrated gray-white coating which only masons of the

1 Frederic II.. Kin? of Prussia, brought Malborg to complete ruin after the fall of the Polish Commonwealth.

Order had the skill to fabricate. The immensity of the walls surpassed every structure which the Polish knights had seen in their lives thus far. It might seem that edifice grew there on edifice, creating in that place, low by nature, as it were, a mountain, the summit of which was the High Castle, the sides the Middle and the First Castle. There radiated from that giant nest of armed monks such uncommon might and power that even the long and usually gloomy face of the Grand Master cleared somewhat as he gazed at it.

" Ex Into Marienburg. Marienburg 1 from the mud," said he, turning toward Zyndram; " but no human power can crush that mud."

Zyndram made no answer, and in silence he took in with his eyes all the bastions and the immensity of the walls strengthened by monstrous escarps.

" You gentlemen," added Conrad, after a moment of silence, "who understand fortresses, what do you say to this?"

" The fortress seems to me impregnable," replied the Polish knight, as if in meditation; "but —

" But what? What can you criticise in it?"

"But any fortress may change masters."

At this the Grand Master frowned.

" In what sense do you speak? "

" In this sense, that the judgments and decisions of God are hidden from the eyes of man."

And again he looked in meditation on the walls, while Zbyshko, to whom Povala had interpreted his answer correctly, looked at him admiringly and with gratitude. He was struck at that moment by the resemblance between Zyndram and the Jmud leader Skirvoillo. Both had immense heads of the same kind, driven in, as it were, between broad shoulders ; both had mighty breasts and the same form of bowed legs.

Meanwhile the Master, not wishing that the last word should remain with the Polish knight, began a second time:

" They say that our Marienburg is six times greater than Vavel, the castle of Cracow."

" In Cracow on the cliff there is not so much space as here on the plain," replied Zyndram; "but our heart in Vavel is greater."

Conrad raised his brows wonderingly, —

"I do not understand."

" But what is the heart in any fortress, if not the church? Our cathedral in Vavel is three times as large as that here."

While saying this, he indicated the fortress church, really not large, on which glittered a great mosaic figure of the Most Holy Lady on a golden background.

Again Conrad was not pleased with the turn of speech.

" You have ready but strange answers," said he.

Meanwhile they had arrived. The excellent police of the Order had evidently notified the town and the castle of the Grand Master's coming, for at the landing, in addition to a number of brothers, were trumpeters of the town, who greeted the Grand Master usually with their trumpets when he landed. Horses were waiting at the shore for him. When the party had mounted, they passed through the town and entering the Weaver's Gate at the side of the Sparrow Bastion, rode up to the First Castle. At the gate the Master was greeted by the Grand Comtur, Wilhelm von Helfenstein, — who bore only the title, since for some months his duties had been performed actually by Kuno Lichtenstein, then absent on a mission to England, — and, besides, by the Hospitaller Conrad Lichtenstein, a relative of Kuno, by the Grand Master of the Wardrobe, Rumpenheim, and the Grand Treasurer, Burghard von Wobecke, and finally by the Petty Comtur, the overseer of the workshops and the management of the castle. Besides these dignitaries there were some ordained brothers, who had charge of church affairs in .Prussia, and who oppressed other cloisters grievously, as well as parish priests, whom they forced to work on roads even, and at ice-breaking. With those ordained men stood a multitude of lay brothers, — that is, knights not bound to canonical observances. Their large and strong bodies (the Order accepted no weak men), their broad shoulders, curly beard, and stern faces made them resemble the greedy robber knights of Germany more than brothers. From their eyes stared flaring insolence and boundless pride. They did not like Conrad because he feared war with the might of Yagello; frequently at the Chapters they reproached him openly with cowardice, made pictures of him on the walls, and roused jesters to ridicule him to his eyes. But this time they inclined their heads with apparent humility, especially since the Master appeared in company with foreign knights; and they hurried quickly to hold his horse's bridle and the stirrups.

The Master alighted, and turned at once to Helfenstein.

'• Are there tidings from Werner von Tettingen? " asked he.

Tettingen, as Grand Marshal, or commander of the armed forces of the Order, was on an expedition then against the Jmud men and Vitold.

"There is nothing important," answered Helfenstein, •'but damage has been done. The rabble burnt villages near Ragneta and towns around other castles."

" In God is our hope, that one great battle will break T,heir rage and stubbornness, " replied the Master.

When he had spoken, he raised his eyes, and his lips moved a moment in a prayer for the success of the armies of the Order.

Then he turned toward the Polish knights and said, —

" These are envoys of the King of Poland : the knight of the Mashkovitse, the knight of Tachev, and the knight of Bogda-nets, who have come with us for the exchange of prisoners. Let the comtur of the castle show them guest-chambers, and entertain and treat them as is proper."

The Knights of the Order looked with curiosity at the envoys, but especially at Povala, whose name, as a renowned champion, was known to some of them. Those who had not heard of his deeds at the courts of Bohemia, Burgundy, and Poland were filled with wonder at his stature, and his battle stallion of such size that he reminded men who in youth had visited the Holy Land

and Egypt, of elephants and camels.

Some recognized Zbyshko, who had fought within barriers at Malborg; and those greeted him rather kindly, remembering that Ulrich, the strong brother of the Master, who enjoyed great favor in the Order, had shown him real esteem and friendship. Not less attention and wonder were roused by him who, in a future then not distant, was to be the most dreadful of all the scourgers of the Order, namely, Zyndram; for when he had dismounted he seemed, because of his uncommon strength and lofty shoulders, to be almost humpbacked. His arms of exceeding length and his bow-legs roused smiles on the faces of the younger brothers. One of them, known for his love of jesting, even approached him, wishing to say a word, but when he looked into the eyes of the lord of Mashkovitse, he lost desire somehow, and walked away in silence.

Meanwhile the comtur of the castle went with the guests, conducting them. They entered, first, a court of no great
width, in which, besides a school, an ancient storehouse, and a saddler's workshop, was the chapel of Saint Nicholas; then passing the Nicholas bridge they entered the First Castle proper. The comtur for some time conducted them amid strong walls, strengthened here and there by greater or smaller bastions. Zyndram looked with care at everything ; the comtur, even without inquiry, indicated various buildings willingly, as if he wished the guests to see all objects in the utmost detail.

" That great building which your Graces see before you on the left is," said he, "our stable. We are poor monks, but people say that elsewhere even knights are not lodged as horses are in this place."

" People do not reproach you with poverty," said Povala; " but there must be something here besides horse-stalls, since this building is so high, and you, of course, do not lead your horses up stairways."

"Above the stable, which is on the ground-floor and in which there are four hundred horses, are storehouses; these contain a stock of wheat to last ten years, I think. There will never be a siege here ; but even should there be, no enemy will conquer us by famine."

Then he turned to the right and again passed a bridge between the bastion of Saint Laurence and the Armor Bastion, and led them to another square, immense, lying in the very centre of the First Castle.

" Observe, your Graces," said the comtur, " that what you see to the north there, though by the power of God impregnable, is only the ' Vorburg,' and may not be compared in strength with the Middle Castle, to which I shall conduct you, still less with the High Castle."

In fact, a separate moat and a special drawbridge divided the Middle Castle from that square; and only in the castle gate, which stood considerably higher, could the knights, when they had turned, at the suggestion of the comtur, take in once more with their vision all that great quadrangle which was called the First Castle. Edifice rose there at the side of edifice, so that it seemed to Zyudram that he saw a whole city. There were inexhaustible supplies of wood laid away in piles as large as houses, heaps of stone cannon-balls standing up like pyramids, cemeteries, hospitals, and magazines. Somewhat aside, near a lake in the centre, were the mighty red walls of the " Temple; " that is, an immense storehouse, with an eating-hall for mercenaries and servants.

At the north wall were to be seen other stables for the horses of knights, and for choice steeds of the Master. At the opposite side of the quadrangle were dwellings for various managers and officials of the Order ; again storehouses, granaries, bakeries, rooms for clothing, foundries, a great arsenal, prisons, the old cannon foundry, — each building so strong and so fortified that in each it was possible to make a stand as in a separate fortress, and all were surrounded by a wall, and by a crowd of tremendous bastions; outside the wall was a moat; outside the moat a circle of great palisades ; beyond the palisades, on the west, rolled the yellow waves of the Nogat. On the north and west gleamed the surface of a broad lake, and on the south towered up the still more strongly fortified Middle and High Castles.

A most terrible nest, which had an expression of immense strength, and in which were joined the two greatest powers known to man in that century, — the power of the church and the power of the sword. Whoso resisted the first, was cut down by the second. Whoso lifted an arm against both, against him rose a shout through all Christendom, that he had raised that arm against the Cross of the Saviour. And straightway knights rushed together from all lands to give aid. That nest, therefore, was swarming at all times with armed men and artisans, and in it, at all times, activity buzzed as in a beehive. Before the great buildings, in the passages, at the gates, in the workshops, there was everywhere movement, as at a fair. Echo bore about the sound of hammers and chisels fashioning stone cannon-balls, the roar of wind-mills and tread-mills, the neighing of horses, the rattle of arms and of armor, the sound of trumpets and fifes, calls and commands. On those squares all languages were heard, and one might meet warriors from every nation; hence the unerring English archers, who pierced a pigeon tied to a pole a hundred yards distant, and whose arrows went through breastplates as easily as through woollen stuff, and the terrible Swiss infantry who fought with double-handed swords, and the Danes, valiant, though immoderate in food and drink, and the French knights, inclined equally to laughter and to quarrel, the silent and haughty Spanish nobles, the brilliant knights of Italy, the most skilful swordsmen of all, dressed in silk and satin, and during war in impenetrable armor forged in Venice, Florence, and Milan, the knights of Burgundy, Friesland, and finally Germans from every German country. The

" white mantles" circled about among all as superiors and masters. " A tower filled with gold," or, more accurately, a separate chamber, built in the High Castle next the dwelling of the Grand Master, really filled from top to bottom with coin and bars of precious metal, permitted the Order to entertain "guests" worthily, as well as to assemble mercenaries, who were sent on expeditions and to all castles to be at the disposition of voits, starostas, and comturs. So that to the power of the sword and the power of religion were joined here great wealth, and also iron discipline, which, though relaxed in recent times by excess of confidence, and intoxication over the strength of the Order, was still maintained by the force of ancient custom. Monarchs went there not only to fight against Pagans or to borrow money, but to learn the art of governing; knights went there to learn the art of war, for in all the world of that day no one knew how to govern and wage war as did the Order. When it settled in those regions, it owned not one span of earth save a small district and a few castles bestowed on it by a heedless Polish prince ; now it possessed a broad country, larger than many kingdoms, containing fertile lands, strong cities, and impregnable castles. It possessed and watched, as a spider possesses its extended web, every thread of which it holds beneath its body. From out that place, from out that High Castle, from the Grand Master, and from the "white mantles," went in every direction, by post messengers, commands to feudatory nobles, to city councils, to mayors, to voits and assistant voits, to captains of mercenary troops; and what there in that centre had been originated and determined by mind and will was executed far from there and quickly by hundreds and by thousands of fists in armor. Hither flowed in money from whole regions, wheat, all kinds of provisions, tribute from the secular clergy groaning under a grievous yoke, and also from other cloisters at which the Order looked with unfriendly eye. From out that place, finally, grasping hands were stretched against all surrounding lauds and nations.

The numerous Prussian people of Lithuanian speech had been swept from the earth at that period. Lithuania had felt till recently the iron foot of the Knight of the Cross weighing on her breast so cruelly that for every breath she gave, blood went from her heart with it. Poland, though victorious in the dreadful battle at Plovtse, had still lost in the time of Lokietek her possessions on the left bank of

the Vistula, together with Dantzig, Ghev, Gniev, and Sviet. The Order of Livonian Knights stretched out after Russian lands; and those two Orders moved forward, like the first gigantic wave of a German sea, which was covering Slav lands with an ever-widening deluge.

Suddenly the sun of the German Order was obscured behind a cloud. Lithuania had received the Cross from Poland, and Yagello had received the throne at Cracow with the hand of the marvellous Yadviga. The Order, it is true, had not lost a single land through this, or a single castle, but it felt that against its power a power was now arrayed, and it lost the reason of its existence in Prussia. After the baptism of Lithuania the Order had only to return to Palestine and guard pilgrims on their way to the Holy City. But to return would be to renounce.wealth, rule, power, dominion, cities, lands, and whole kingdoms. So the Order began to squirm in rage and terror, like a monstrous dragon in whose side the barbed shaft has sunk deeply. The Grand Master Conrad feared to risk all on one cast of the die, and trembled at the thought of war with Yagello, the ruler of Polish and Lithuanian lands and of those broad Russian regions which Olgierd had dragged from the throat of the Tartar; but the greater number of the Knights of the Cross urged on to war, feeling that they must light a life-and-death battle while their forces were intact and before the halo of the Order should grow pale, while the whole world was hastening to give aid to them, and before the thunders of the Papacy could fall upon that nest of theirs. It was a question of life and death then for the Order not to spread the Christian faith, but to uphold the heathen.

Meanwhile, among nations, and at the courts of Europe, they accused Yagello and Lithuania of having performed a baptism that was false and counterfeit, declaring it impossible that that could be done in a single year which the sword of the Knights had not done in generations. They incensed against Poland and its sovereign, kings and knights, as against guardians and defenders of Pagan institutions; and their complaints, which were disbelieved in Rome alone, went through the world in a broad wave, and brought to Malborg princes, counts, and knights from the west and south of Europe. The Order gained confidence and felt itself all-mighty. Marienburg, with its two tremendous castles and its First Castle, dazzled men through its strength more than ever. They were dazzled by its wealth and its seeming

TOL. II. — 15

discipline; and the whole Order appeared more commanding, more inexhaustible for coming ages, than it had been at any time; and no man among princes, no man among knightly guests, no man even among Knights of the Order, save the Grand Master Conrad, understood that from the hour when Lithuania had become Christian, something of such character had happened as if those currents of the Nogat, which defended on one side the formidable fortress, had begun to undermine its walls in silence and irresistibly. No man understood that, though power remained yet in that enormous body, the soul had flown from it; whoso came freshly and looked at that Marienburg reared ex luto, at those walls, bastions, black crosses on gates, mantle-rooms, and storehouses, thought, first of all, that even the gates of hell would not prevail against the Cross there, in its northern capital.

"With a similar thought did not only Povala and Zbyshko look at it, they who had been there previously, but also Zyndram, a man far keener of mind than they were. Even he, as he gazed at that armored swarming place of soldiers, embraced by the circle of bastions and by gigantic palisades, grew dark in the face, and to his mind came, in spite of him, the insolent words with which the Knights of the Cross had threatened Kazimir, the Polish king, —

"Our force is greater; if thou yield not, we will hunt thee to Cracow itself with our sword-blades."

Meanwhile the comtur of the castle conducted the knights farther on, to the Middle Castle, in the eastern flank of which were guest-chambers.

CHAPTEE LXIII.

MATSKO and Zbyshko held each other in a long embrace, for each had loved the other always, and during recent years adventures and mishaps met in common made that love still stronger. The old knight divined from the first glance at his nephew that Danusia was not in the world then, so he made no inquiry; he merely drew the young man to his bosom, wishing to show by the power of that pressure that Zbyshko was not altogether an orphan, that there was still a kindred soul which was ready to share a sad fate with him. At last, when sorrow and pain had flowed away with their tears considerably, Matsko asked, after a long silence, — "Did they seize her again, or did she die in thy arms?" " She died in my arms at the very edge of Spyhov," said Zbyshko.

And he told what had happened, and how it had happened, interrupting his narrative with sighs and weeping. Matsko listened attentively; he sighed also, and at last inquired, — "But is Yurand still living?"

" Yurand was living when I left Spyhov> but he has not long to abide in this world, and to a certainty I shall not see him again."

" It would have been better, perhaps, to remain at Spyhov." " But how was I to leave you in this place? " "A couple of weeks earlier or later would be the same." Zbyshko looked at his uncle carefully, and said, — " You must have been sick. You look like Piotrovin." * " Perhaps, for though the sun warms the world, it is always cold underground, and the dampness is terrible because there is water around all these castles. I thought that the mould here would kill me. There was no air to breathe, and my wound opened because of my suffering, — that wound, thou knowest, through which the arrow splinter came out after I had drunk bear's oil."

1 A man brought to life according to popular tradition by Saint Stanislav.

"I remember," said Zbyshko, "for Yagenka and I went for the bear. But did the dog brothers keep you underground here ? "

Matsko nodded his head, and answered, —

"To tell the truth, they were not glad to see me, and it was going ill with me. There is great hatred here against Vitold and the Jmud men, but still greater against those of our people who help them. It was useless for me to tell why we went to the Jmud land. They wished to cut my head off, and if they did not cut it off it is only because they did not wish to lose the ransom; for, as thou knowest, money has more charms for them than even vengeance, and besides they wish to have in hand a proof that King Yagello helps Pagans. That the Jmud people, the unfortunates, beg for baptism, if only it is not from German hands, is known to us who have been in their country; but the Knights pretend not to know this, and they calumniate those people at all courts, and with them our king, Yagello."

Here Matsko was seized by a panting fit, so he had to be silent for a time, and only after he had regained breath did he continue, —

" And I might have died underground, perhaps. It is true that'Arnold von Baden took my part; he wished to save the ransom. But Arnold has no weight here, and they call him a bear. Luckily De Lorche heard of me from Arnold, and he made a tremendous uproar immediately. He may not have told thee of this, for he hides his own good deeds willingly. They hold him in consideration here, for a De Lorche held high office once in the Order, and this man is rich and of renowned family. He told them that he was our captive, and that if they took my life, or if I died through dampness and hunger, thou wouldst behead him. He threatened even to tell throughout the courts of western Europe how the Knights of the Cross treat belted knights. They were frightened, and removed me to a hospital where there is better food and the air is purer."

" I will not take one copper from De Lorche, so help me God."

" It is pleasant to take ransom from an enemy, but it is a proper thing to forgive a friend," added Matsko; "still, since there is, as I hear, an agreement with the king about exchange of prisoners, thou wilt not have to ransom me."

"Well, but our knightly word?" inquired Zbyshko.

"The king's agreement is an agreement, still Arnold might accuse us of dishonor."

When he heard this Matsko was concerned; he thought a while and said, —

"But it might be possible to reduce the amount somewhat."

"We put our own estimate on ourselves. Are we of less value now ? "

Matsko was concerned still more, but there was an expression of wonder in his eyes, and, as it were, of still greater love for Zbyshko.

" He will guard his honor; he was born with that power," muttered the old man.

And he sighed. Zbyshko thought that it was from regret for the money which they had to pay Arnold, so he said, —

*'• You know that we have wealth enough now, if only our fate were not so grievous."

" God will change it for thee," said the old knight, with emotion. " I have not long to live in this world as I now am."

" Do not say that! You will be well, only let the wind blow around you."

"The wind? The wind bends a young tree,but breaks an old one."

" Nonsense! the bones are not decaying in you yet, and it is a long way from you to old age. Be not sad ! "

" Wert thou gladsome, I should laugh. But I have another cause for sadness, and to tell the truth, not only I, but all of us."

"What is it?"

" Dost remember how I reproached thee in Skirvoillo's camp because thou didst glorify the might of the Order? Our men are firm in the field, I know they are, but from near by, I see these dog brothers now for the first time."

Matsko lowered his voice, as if fearing lest some one might overhear him.

" And I see now that thou wert right; I was not. May the hand of God defend us ; what power, what strength! The hands of our knights are itching, and they wish to strike the Germans at the earliest; but they do not know that all nations and kings are helping the Order, that Knights of the Cross have more money, that they are better trained, that their castles are stronger and their battle weapons better.

May God's hand defend us! Both among us, and here, people say that it must come to a great war, and will come ; but when it comes may God have mercy on our kingdom and our people!"

Here he clasped his iron-gray head with his palms, rested his elbows on his knees, and was silent.

"Well," said Zbyshko, "you see, taken separately, many of our men are stronger than single champions on their side, but as to a great war you yourself have grown thoughtful."

" Oi! I have indeed! And God grant that those envoys of the king will grow thoughtful also, but especially Zyndram."

" I saw how gloomy he became. He is a great man in war, and they say that no one in the world is so skilful in battle."

" If this is true, perhaps there will be no war."

" If the Knights of the Cross see that they are stronger, then war will come surely. And I tell you sincerely, God grant us an end of some sort, for we cannot live longer ia this way."

In his turn Zbyshko, as if crushed by his own and the general misfortune, dropped his head.

" I grieve for our noble kingdom," said Matsko; "but I fear that God has punished us for great boasting. Thou re-memberest how, in front of the cathedral in Cracow before mass, at the time when thy head was to be cut off, and was not, the knighthood challenged Timur the Lame, the master of forty kingdoms, the man who made a mountain of human skulls, — the Knights of the Cross were not enough for them, they must challenge all opponents at once, — and in this was offence against God, perhaps."

Zbyshko at this reminder seized his golden hair, for great grief had come on him unexpectedly, and he cried, —

"But who saved me at that time from the headman, if not she ? O Jesus ! My Danusia! O Jesus ! "

And he tore his hair, and then began to gnaw his fist, with which he tried to stifle his sobbing, so did the spirit whine in the man from sudden pain.

" Keep God in thy heart, boy ! be quiet! " cried Matsko. "What wilt thou gain ? Restrain thyself ! Be calm ! "

But Zbyshko was unable for a long time to calm himself, and he came to his mind only when Matsko, who was really ill yet, grew so faint that he tottered on his feet, and fell to the bench quite unconscious. Then the young man placed

him on the bed, strengthened him with wine, which the comtur of the castle had sent, and watched over him till the old knight dropped asleep.

They woke late next morning fresher and rested.

" Well," said Matsko, "it must be that my time has not come yet; and I think that if the breeze of the field were blowing about me I could ride to the end of my journey."

" The envoys will remain here some days yet," answered Zbyshko, " for people are coming with requests about captives caught in Mazovia or Great Poland while robbing; but we may go whenever you wish, and when you feel strong enough."

At this moment Hlava came in.

" Dost know what the envoys are doing?" asked the old knight of him.

" They are visiting the church and the High Castle, —the comtur of the castle acts himself as their guide; afterward they will go to the chief refectory to a dinner to which the Grand Master is to invite your Graces."

" But what hast thou been doing since early morning?"

" Looking at German mercenaries, infantry, which captains are drilling, and I compared them with our Cheh men."

" Dost thou remember Cheh infantry?"

" I was a stripling when the knight Zyh captured me, but I remember well, for I was curious about such things from boyhood."

"Well, and what?"

" Oh, nothing! The infantry of the Order is strong and well trained, but the men are bullocks, while our Chehs are wolves. Should it come to action — but then your Graces know that bullocks do not eat wolves, and wolves like beef tremendously."

" That is true," said Matsko, who evidently knew something of this; " the man who rubs against your people jumps back from them as from a porcupine."

" In battle a mounted knight is as good as ten footmen," said Zbyshko.

" But only infantry can take Malborg," answered Hlava.

Remarks on infantry stopped there, for Matsko, following the course of his own thoughts, said, —

" Hear Hlava; to-day, when I get up and feel in strength, we will go."

"But whither?"

"Of course to Mazovia. To Spyhov," said Zbyshko.

" And shall we stay there?"

Here Matsko looked at his nephew inquiringly, for thus far they had not spoken of what they were to do in future. The young man had his decision ready, but evidently had no wish to grieve his uncle, so he replied indirectly, —

"First, you must be well."

"And then what?"

"And then? You will go back to Bogdanets. I know how you love Bogdanets."

"Butthou?"

" I love it too."

" I do not say that thou shouldst not go to Yurand," said Matsko, slowly, " for if he dies, we ought to bury him properly; but attend to what I say, for being young thou art not my equal in prudence. Spyhov is unfortunate in some way. Whatever good has met thee, has met thee elsewhere, but in Spyhov, only grievous suffering and anguish."

tk You speak the truth, but Danusia's body is in Spyhov."

"Be quiet!" exclaimed Matsko, fearing lest unexpected pain should seize Zbyshko, as it had the day previous.

But on the young man's face were reflected only tenderness and sorrow.

"There will be time for counsel," said he, after a while. " You must rest in Plotsk anyhow."

"Care will not fail your Grace in Plotsk," put in Hlava.

"True," added Zbyshko. "Do you know that Yagenka is there? She is a damsel of Princess Alexandra. But of course you know, for you brought her there. She was in Spyhov too. It was a wonder to me that you said nothing of her while we were with Skirvoillo."

" Not only was she in Spyhov, but had it not been for her, Yurand would be groping along a highway with his stick, or would have died somewhere at the roadside. I brought her to Plotsk for the Abbot's legacy, and I said nothing to thee about her ; if I had, thou wouldst not have heard it. Thou wert paying no attention to anything, poor fellow, at that time."

"She loves you greatly," said Zbyshko. "Praised be God that we needed no letters, but she got letters from the princess on your behalf, and through the princess from the envoys of the

Order."

" God bless the girl, for on earth there is not a better than she! " replied Matsko.

Further conversation was interrupted by the entrance of Zyndram and Povala, who, since they had heard of Matsko's fainting fit, had come to visit him.

"Praised be Jesus Christ! " said Zyndram, when he had crossed the threshold. " How is it with you to-day ? "

"God reward you! In a small way. Zbyshko says that if the wind were to blow around me I should be well immediately."

"Why should you not? You will be well! All will be well," put in Povala.

" Besides, I have rested thoroughly. Not like your Graces, who, as I hear, rose early."

" First people came to us to claim prisoners," said Zyndram, " and afterward we examined the management of the Order, — in the First Castle and the other castles."

" Firm management, and firm castles ! " muttered Matsko.

" Surely they are firm. In the church there are ornaments in the Arabic style; the Knights said that they had learned that style from the Saracens in Sicily, and in the castles are special rooms on pillars which stand al6ne, or in clusters. You will see yourselves the great refectory. The fortress is tremendous in all its parts, such a fortress as there is in no other place. Such walls a stone cannon-ball, though the greatest, could not bite in any way. By my faith,* there is pleasure in looking at it."

Zyudram said this so joyously that Matsko looked at him with astonishment, and asked,
—

" But their wealth and good order, and troops, and guests, have you looked at them ? "

"They showed us all, as if through friendliness, but really to make the hearts sink in us."

"Well, and what?"

" Well, God grant that when war comes we shall drive them from here, beyond the mountains and seas, — to the place whence they came."

Matsko, forgetting his sickness at that moment, sprang to his feet in astonishment.

" How is this, lord? " asked he. " Men say that you have a quick mind. As to me, I grew faint when I saw what their power is. In God's name, whence do you get your conviction ? "

Here he turned to his nephew.

" Zbyshko, command to bring wine, that which they sent us. Sit down, your Graces, and talk, since a better cure

for my sickness than your discourse no physician could think out."'

Zbyshko, also very curious, put the wine on the table himself, and with it goblets; all sat around the table then, and Zyndram spoke as follows, —

" This fortress is nothing; for what the hand of man has reared, the hand of man can pull down. Ye know what keeps brick together? Mortar! But do ye know what keeps people together? Love."

"By God's wounds! honey is flowing from your lips!" exclaimed Matsko.

Zyndram, rejoiced in his heart by that praise, continued, —

" Of the people in this region one has in bonds with us a brother, another a son, another a relative, another a son-in-law, or some one else. The comturs of the boundary command their men to go out and rob us ; hence many of them are slain, and many of them we capture. But since people here have learned already of the exchange of prisoners between the king and the Grand Master, they came to us from early morning to give the names of captives, which names our scribe entered down. First of all came a cooper, a rich citizen, a German, who has a house in

Malborg, when he said at last : ' If I could serve your king and kingdom in any way, I would give my life and not merely my property.' I sent him away, thinking the man a Judas. But after him came a parish priest from near Oliva, to ask about his brother, and he spoke as follows: ' Is it true, lord, that ye are going to war with our Prussian masters? If ye are, be it known to you that the whole people here when they say "Thy kingdom come," are thinking of your sovereign.' Afterward appeared two nobles for their sons: these nobles live near Shtum on feudal lands; there were merchants from Dantzig, there were artisans, there was a bell-founder from Kvidjyn, there was a crowd of various people, and they all said the same thing."

Here Zyndram stopped and looked around to see that no men were listening behind the doors; on returning he finished in a somewhat lower voice, —

" I inquired long about everything. Throughout all Prussia the Knights of the Cross are hated by priests, nobles, citizens, and land-tillers. And not only are they hated by people who use our speech, or the Prussian, but even by Germans. The man who is forced to serve, serves : but the

plague is more beloved than the Knights of the Cross are. That is the truth of the matter."

" Yes, but what has this to do with the power of the Order ? " asked Matsko, anxiously.

Zyndram smoothed his broad forehead with his hand, thought a while, as if seeking a comparison, then smiled, and inquired, —

" Have you ever fought within barriers? "

" I have, and fought frequently."

" Then what do you think — Will not a knight be thrown from his horse at the first onset, even though he be the mightiest, who has the saddle girths cut under him, and also his stirrup straps ? "

" As true as life! "

" Well, do you see? the Order is a knight like that."

" It is, as God is just! " shouted Zbyshko. " Even in a book thou 'lt find nothing to beat that! "

And Matsko was so excited that he said in a voice trembling somewhat, —

" God reward you. For your head, lord, the armorer must fashion a helmet purposely, as there is none ready made on earth to fit it."

CHAPTER LXIV.

MATSKO and Zbyshko promised themselves to leave Mal-borg straightway, but they did not depart during the day on which Zyndram had strengthened their spirits so mightily, for there was a dinner at the High Castle, and then a supper in honor of guests and envoys, to which Zbyshko was invited, and for Zbyshko's sake also Matsko. The dinner was given to a select company in the Grand Refectory, into which light came by ten windows, and the ceiling of which in pointed arches rested, through a rare architectural device, on one column. Of foreigners, besides Yagello's knights, there sat down to the table only one Suabian count, and one Burgundian, who, though a subject of rich lords, had come at their command to borrow money from the Order. Of local persons, besides the Grand Master, four dignitaries took part in the dinner, so-called pillars of the Order ; that is, the grand comtur, the almoner, the master of the wardrobe, and the treasurer. The fifth pillar, the marshal, was at that time on an expedition against Vitold.

Though the Order had vowed poverty, they ate on gold and silver and drank Malvoisie, for the Master wished to dazzle the Polish envoys. But despite a multitude of dishes and abundant cheer, that feast was somewhat irksome to the guests, because of difficulty in conversation and ceremonies which were to be observed on all sides. But supper was more gladsome, in the Grand Refectory (Convents Remter), for the Order met there, and all those guests who had not marched yet against Vitold with the army of the marshal. No dispute disturbed its joyousness, nor any quarrel. It is true that knights from other lands, foreseeing that they would have to meet the Poles sometime, looked at them with unfriendly eye, but the Knights of the Cross had informed them beforehand of the need to conduct themselves quietly, and had begged them most earnestly to do so, fearing lest they might offend the king and the entire kingdom in the persons of the envoys. But even then the ill-will of the Order was made manifest; they forewarned the guests

against Polish temper: " For every .word," said they, " sharper than common, the Poles will tear a man's beard out, or thrust a knife into his body." So the guests were astonished afterward at the courtesy of Povala and Zyndram, and the more quick-witted said that Polish manners were not rude, but that the tongues of the Knights of the Cross were malignant and venomous.

Some of them, accustomed to refined amusements at the polished courts of western Europe, took away ideas not entirely favorable concerning the manners of the Knights in Malborg; for at that feast there was an orchestra noisy beyond measure, there were rude songs of " playmen," rough jests of buffoons, and dances of barefooted maidens. And when guests wondered at the presence of women in the High Castle, it was said that the prohibition had been removed long before, and that the great Winrich Kniprode himself had danced in his day there with the beautiful Maria von Alfleben. The brothers explained that women not only lived in the Castle, but came to feast in the refectory, and that the past year Prince Vitold's wife, who lodged in the old armory of the First Castle, had appeared every day in the refectory to play draughts made of gold, which the Knights presented each time to her.

They played that evening also, not only draughts, but chess and dice; there was more of play than conversation, which was drowned by songs and by that too noisy orchestra. Still, amid the universal uproar quieter moments came, and, seizing one of these, Zyndram, as if knowing nothing, asked the Grand Master whether its subjects in all lands loved the Order.

To this Conrad gave the following answer, —

" Whoso loves the Cross is obliged to love the Order."

That answer pleased the Knights and the guests, hence they praised it. The Grand Master, pleased at this, continued, —

" Whoso is our friend is happy under us; but whoso is an enemy, against him we have two methods."

"What are they?" inquired Zyndram.

'. 4 Perhaps your Honor does not know that I come from my chambers to this refectory by small stairways in the wall, and near those stairways there is a certain vaulted chamber ; were I to conduct you hither you would know the first method."

"As true as life !" exclaimed the brothers.

Zyndram divined that the Master was speaking of that "tower" filled with gold, of which the Knights boasted, so he hesitated a while, and then said,—

"Once, oh, very long ago, a certain German Caesar showed an ambassador of ours, whose name was Skarbek, such a chamber, and said: ' I have something with which to overcome thy lord!' But Skarbek threw into it a costly ring, and added, ' Go thou gold to gold ; we Poles like iron better.' And you know what came after that, your Honor? After that came Hundsfeld." 1

" What is that Huudsfeld? " inquired a number of knights together.

"That," answered Zyndram, quietly, "was a field on which they were unable to bury all the Germans, and at last dogs finished the burial."

Knights of the Order and brothers when they heard this were greatly confused, and knew not what reply to make, while Zyndram said, as if in ending,—

" Thou wilt do nothing with gold against iron."

"Well," exclaimed the Master, "our second method is always iron. Your Honor saw at the First Castle armorers' workshops. Hammers are forging night and day there, and they forge swords and armor that have no equal elsewhere."

In answer Povala stretched out his hand to the middle of the table, and took a strip of iron used for cutting meat; in length it was an ell and in width more than half a span. This he wound into a roll easily, like parchment, and raised it high so that all might see the roll; after that he gave it to the Master.

" If the iron of your swords is of this sort, you will not do much with them."

And he smiled with satisfaction, while the spiritual and lay knights rose from their seats and hurried in a crowd to the Grand Master; then they passed the iron roll from one to another, but all were silent, having timid hearts in their breasts in view of this strength in Povala.

" By the head of Saint Liborius ! " exclaimed the Master at last, " you have iron hands, lord."

But the Burgundian count added, —

" And better iron than this. He folded the strip as if it were wax."

" He did not even flush, and his veins were not swollen," said one of the brothers.

1 Dogsfield (Psie Pole in Polish). This battle was fought in 1109 near Breslau.

"Yes," answered Povala; "our people are simple: they have not such wealth and comfort as 1 see in this place, but they are healthy."

And now Italian and French knights approached him and spoke to him in their resonant speech, of which Matsko said that it was as if some one were rattling tin plates. They wondered at his strength; then he touched goblets with them and answered, —

" Such things as this are done at feasts among us frequently, and it happens that even a girl will roll a smaller strip."

But the Germans, who liked to boast among strangers of their size and strength, were enraged and out of countenance, so old Helfenstein called across the table, —

"This is a shame for us! Brother Arnold von Baden, show that our bones, too, are not made of church tapers! Give Arnold a strip."

The servants brought a strip quickly and placed it before Arnold; but he, whether it was that the sight of so many spectators confused him, or that he had really less strength in his fingers than Povala, bent the strip halfway, but was unable to finish.

More than one of the foreign guests, to whom the Knights of the Cross had whispered previously, and more than one time, that war with the King of Poland would begin the next winter, fell to thinking deeply, and remembered that winter in those regions was terribly inclement, and that it would perhaps be better to return in time to a softer climate and their native castles.

There was this wonderful thing in the situation, that such thoughts came to their heads in July, — a time of hot days and splendid weather.

CHAPTER LXV.

AT Plotsk, Zbyshko and Matsko found no one at the court, for the prince and princess, with their eight children, had gone to Chersk, at the invitation of Princess Anna Dauuta. From the bishop they learned that Yagenka was to remain in Spyhov with Yurand till he died. This news was agreeable, for they themselves were on the way to Spyhov. Meanwhile Matsko praised greatly Yagenka's kindness, since she had remained with a dying man, who was not even kin to her, instead of going to Chersk, where dances and pleasures of every sort would surely not be lacking.

" Perhaps she did this not to miss us," said the old knight. " I have not seen her this long time, and should be glad to see her now, for I know that she likes me. The girl must have grown, and must still be handsome."

" She has changed wonderfully," said Zbyshko. " She was always a beauty. I remember her as a simple maiden, while now she might go to kings' chambers."

" Has she changed so? Well, hers is that old Yastrem-bets stock of Zgofzelitse which in time of battles called, 'To feasts!'"

A moment of silence followed, then the old knight said again, " It will be as I have told thee; she will wish to go to Zgorzelitse."

" I wonder that she left it."

"But the abbot's property? Besides, she feared Stan and Vilk; I told her myself that for her brothers it would be safer without her than with her."

" By my faith, they could not attack orphans, anyhow."

Matsko thought awhile.

" But will they not take vengeance on me because I took her away, and does there remain even one beam in Bogda-nets ? God knows! I know not, besides, whether I shall be able to defend myself when I go back. The fellows are young and strong, while I am old — "

"Ei! old ; say that to the man who does not know you," answered Zbyshko.

Matsko did not speak in perfect sincerity, for with him it was a question of something else, but immediately he waved his hand. .

" If I had not been sick in Malborg — well, that too," said he. " But we will talk of it in Spyhov."

And next day, after their night rest, they set out for Spyhov.

The days were clear, the road dry, easy, and besides safe; for because of the recent agreement the Knights of the Cross restrained robbery on the border. Moreover, the two knights were of that class of travellers whom it was better for a robber to bow to from afar than attack at close quarters, so the journey passed quickly, and the fifth day after leaving Plotsk they halted in the morning at Spyhov. Yagenka, who esteemed Matsko as her best friend on earth, greeted him almost as she would her father; while he, though no common thing could move him, was moved by that kindness of the girl whom he liked so much, and when later, Zbyshko, after he had inquired about Yurand, went to the tomb of his Danusia, the old knight sighed deeply.

"Well," said he, u God took the one He wished to take, and left the one He wished to leave; but I think that our troubles and wanderings in wildernesses and wild places are ended."

After a while he added, —

" Ei! where has the Lord Jesus not carried us during these recent years !"

" But the hand of God guarded you," said Yagenka.

" True, it guarded us, but indeed it is time to go home."

" We must stay here while Yurand lives."

"But how is he?"

" He looks up and smiles. It is clear that he sees Paradise, and in it Danusia."

" Dost thou look after him?"

" I do ; but Father Kaleb says that angels look after him. Yesterday the housekeeper saw two of them."

" They say," answered Matsko, " that it is most fitting for a noble to die in the field, but it is well, too, to die on a bed if one dies like Yurand."

" He eats nothing, he drinks nothing, but smiles con-tinually."

" Let us go to him ; Zbyshko must be there."

But Zbyshko remained only a short time with Yurand, who recognized no one ; he went then to Danusia's coffin in the

VOL. II. 16

vault. There he remained till old Tolima went to bring him to refreshment. When coming out he noticed by the light of the torch that the coffin was covered with garlands of star thistles and marigolds, while the space round about was swept clean and strewn with odorous plants. The young man's heart rose at sight of this, and he asked,—

" Who adorned the tomb in this way ? "

" The young lady from Zgorzelitse," answered Tolima.

Zbyshko said nothing then, but later, when he saw Ya-genka, he bowed down to her knees quickly, embraced them, and cried, —

" God reward thee for thy goodness and for those flowers placed above Danusia ! "

And when he said this he wept earnestly, while she embraced his head with her hands, like a sister who consoles a mourning brother.

"O my Zbyshko," said she, "would that I could comfort thee still more ! "

Then abundant tears fell from her eyes also.

CHAPTER LXV1.

SOME days later Yurand died. Father Kaleb celebrated masses a whole week above his body, which showed no decay, — in this all beheld a miracle, — and for a week guests came in crowds to Spyhov. Then followed a time of quiet, such as there is usually after a funeral. Zbyshko went to the vault, and sometimes he went to the forest with his crossbow, from which, however, he shot at no beast, but walked in forgetfulness; till at last one evening he returned to the chamber where the girls were sitting with Matsko and with Hlava.

" Listen to what I will say," said he, unexpectedly. " Sorrow profits no one; hence it is better for you to go to Zgorzelitse and Bogdanets than to sit here grieving."

Silence followed, for all divined that words of great import were coming, and only after a time did Matsko add, —

" Better for us and for thee as well."

But Zbyshko shook his bright head.

" No ! I will return, God grant, to Bogdanets, but now I must take another road."

"Ei! " cried Matsko; "I said that the end had come, but now there is no end! Fear God, Zbyshko! "

" But you know that I made a vow — "

" Is that a reason? Danusia is gone, and the vow is gone also. Death has released thee from the oath

" She would have released me, but I did not swear to her; I swore to God on my knightly honor. What do you wish? On knightly honor!"

Every word touching knightly honor had an influence on Matsko that seemed as it were magical. He guided himself in life by few commands except those of God and the Church, but he guided himself by those unswervingly.

" I do not tell thee not to keep thy oath," replied Matsko.

"But what?"

" This, that thou art young and hast time for everything. Come now with us; thou wilt rest — shake thyself free of

pain and sorrow — and then thou wilt go whithersoever thou wishest."

"I will tell you as truly as at confession," answered Zbyshko: " I am going, you see, whither I must go; I talk with you, I eat and drink, like every man, but I say truly that within me and within my soul I cannot help myself in any way. There is nothing in me but sadness, nothing but pain, nothing but those bitter tears which flow from my eyes whether I will or not."

" Among strangers it will be still worse."

" No; God sees that I should die in Bogdanets. "When I tell you that I cannot, it means that I cannot! I need war, for in the field one forgets more easily. I feel that when I accomplish my vow, when I am able to say to that saved soul, ' I have fulfilled everything that I promised,' only then will she release me. Earlier she will not. You could not hold me with a rope in Bogdauets."

After these words there was such silence in that chamber that flies were heard as they passed beneath the ceiling.

" If it would kill him to be in Bogdanets, better let him go," said Yagenka, finally.

Matsko put his two palms on his neck, as was his custom at moments of perplexity, sighed then deeply, and said, —

" Ei, mighty God! "

But Yagenka continued, —

"Zbyshko, but thou wilt swear, that if God preserves thee, thou wilt not remain off there, but return to us? "

"Why should I not return? I shall not avoid Spyhov, but I will not remain here."

" For," continued the girl, in a voice somewhat lower, "if thou art concerned for the coffin we will take it to Kresnia."

" Yagus !" 1 cried Zbyshko, with an outburst.

And he fell at her feet in the first moment of transport and gratitude.

CHAPTEE LXVII.

THE old knight wished absolutely to go with Zbyshko to the armies of Prince Vitold, but Zbyshko would not permit his uncle even to speak of this. He insisted on going alone, without retinue, without wagons, with only three mounted men, one of whom was to carry provisions, the other, arms and clothing, the third, bearskins on which to sleep. In vain did Yagenka and Matsko implore him to take even Hlava, as a man of tried strength and devotion. He resisted, and refused, saying that he must forget the pain which was gnawing him, while the presence of Hlava would remind him of all that had happened and was past.

But before he departed there were weighty discussions as to what should be done with Spyhov. Matsko's advice was to sell the estate. He called that land unfortunate; it had brought, he said, nothing save disaster and misfortune to any one. There was in Spyhov much wealth of every kind: money, arms, horses, clothing, sheepskin coats, precious furs, costly implements, herds of cattle. In Matsko's soul the question was to increase with that wealth Bogdanets, which was dearer to him than any other spot. They counselled long over this, but Zbyshko would not consent to sell Spyhov at any price.

"How am I," said he, "to sell Yurand's bones? Ami to repay in that way the benefactions with which he has covered me?"

"We have promised to take Danusia's coffin," answered Matsko; " we can take Yurand's body also."

" But he is here with his fathers, and without his fathers he would be wretched in Kresnia. If you take Danusia, he will be here far away from his daughter; if you take him with her, then the fathers will be here without both."

" Dost thou not remember that Yurand in Paradise sees all people daily ? and Father Kaleb says that he is in Paradise," answered the old knight.

But Father Kaleb, who was on Zbyshko's side, said, —

" His soul is in Paradise, but his body will be on earth till the day of judgment."

Matsko stopped a while, and following further his own thought, added,—

" Well, Yurand does not see a man who is not saved ; for that there is no remedy."

" What use in trying to get at God's judgments ?" said Zbyshko. " But may the Lord not permit a stranger to dwell above the sacred remains of Yurand! Better leave all here, but Spyhov I would not sell, though I got a principality in return for it."

Matsko knew after these words that there was no help; he knew his nephew's stubbornness, and did homage in the depth of his soul to it, as well as to everything that was in the young man ; so after a while he added, —

" It is true that the boy speaks against my grain, but there is truth in what he tells us."

Aud he was vexed, for in every case he knew not what to do. But Yagenka, who had been silent so far, appeared now with a new advice, —

" If an honest man could be found to manage Spyhov, or to rent it, that would be excellent Best would be to rent the place, for there would be no trouble, nothing but ready money. Might not Tolima? He is old and understands war better than land management; but if not he, then perhaps Father Kaleb ? "

" Dear young lady," answered the priest, "there is land ready for me and Tolima, but that which will cover us is not that on which we are walking."

Then he turned to Tolima.

"Is this true, old man?"

Tolima surrounded his pointed ear with his palm, and asked what the question was, and when they explained in a lower voice, he answered,—

" That is the holy truth. I am not for land management. I go deeper with an axe than a plough; before I die I should like to avenge my lord and his daughter."

And he stretched forth his lean but sinewy hands with fingers curved like the talons of a bird of prey, then turning his gray head, which resembled a wolf's head, toward Matsko and Zbyshko, he added, —

"Take me, your Grace, against the Germans ; that is my service! "

And he was right. He had added no little to Yurand's wealth, but it was by war and plunder, not by land-tilling.

So Yagenka, who during this conversation had been thinking what to say, spoke again, —

"A young man is needed- here, a man who fears no one, for the boundary of the Order is close by; a man who not only would not hide from the Germans, but would hunt them ; so, without hesitation, I think that Hlava is the man for this place."

" See how she will fix it! " cried Matsko, who, in spite of his love for Yagenka, was unwilling that a woman should have a voice in such matters, and moreover a woman who was unmarried.

But Hlava rose from the seat where he had been sitting, and said, —

" God sees that I should go to the war gladly with Pan Zbyshko, for he and I have shelled out German souls somewhat, and we might shell out more of them in the future. But if I am to stay, I will stay. Tolima is a friend of mine; he knows me. The boundary of the Order is near by. Well! that is just as is proper. We shall see which neighbor will be first to grow sick of the other. I fear them! No; let them fear me. May the Lord Jesus not permit me either to wrong your Graces and grasp everything. In this matter the lady can speak for me ; she knows that I would rather die a hundred times than show dishonest eyes to her. Of land management I know what I have learned in Zgor-zelitse; but I see that the axe and sword are more needed here than the plough in land management. And this all is greatly to my liking; but still, to stay here — "

"Well, what?" inquired Zbyshko. "Why dost thou hesitate? "

Hlava was confused greatly, and stammered as he said, —

"It is this, when the young lady goes away all will go with her; to make war is well, and to manage land is well also, but to do it here all alone — without assistance. It will be awfully dreary without the young lady — and without this — just as I wanted to say — and as the young lady is going away not without attendants — then as no one would help here — I do not know — "

" What is the man talking about?" inquired Matsko.

" You have a quick mind, but have not noticed anything," answered Yagenka.

"What is it?"

Instead of answering, she turned to Hlava, —

" But if Anulka were to stay with thee, couldst thou holdout?"

At this Hlava fell at her feet so suddenly that dust rose to the ceiling.

" With her I could hold out in hell! " cried he, embracing Yagenka's feet.

When Zbyshko heard this cry he looked at Hlava with astonishment, for he had not known anything previously and had not suspected. Matsko wondered also at how much woman means in man's affairs, and how through her everything may succeed or may fail altogether.

"God is gracious to me," muttered he, "because I am not curious about women."

However, Yagenka, turning again to Hlava, said, —

"Now we only need to ask if Anulka will hold out with thee."

She called Anulka, who entered, knowing or guessing evidently what the question was, for she came in with her arm across her eyes, and her head drooping so that they saw only the parting of her bright hair, which was much brighter from the sunlight which now fell on it. Anulka halted at the door; then, springing forward to Yagenka, dropped on her knees before her, and hid her face in the folds of the lady's skirt.

But Hlava knelt near her, and said to Yagenka, —

" Bless us, young lady! "

THE KNIGHTS OF THE CROSS. 249

CHAPTEK LXVIII.

NEXT day came the moment of Zbyshko's departure. He was sitting high on a large war-horse, and his friends had surrounded him. Yagenka, standing near the stirrup, raised her sad blue eyes to the young man in silence, as if wishing to look at him sufficiently before parting. Matsko and Father Kaleb were at the other stirrup, and near them stood Hlava and Anulka. Zbyshko turned his face first toward one side, then toward the other, exchanging such brief words as are said usually before a long journey: "Be well! " " May God conduct thee ! " " It is time ! " " Hei! it is time ! it is time ! "

He had taken farewell before of all, and of Yagenka, at whose feet he had fallen in giving thanks for her goodness. But now, as he looked at her from his lofty saddle, he wished to say some new heartfelt word, since her uplifted eyes and face said to him so expressively, " Come back! " that the heart rose in him with palpable gratitude. And as if responding to her unspoken eloquence he said, —

" Yagus, to thee as to my own sister— Thou knowest! I will say no more ! "

" I know. God reward thee."

" And remember uncle."

" And do thou remember — "

" I shall return, be sure of that, unless I perish."

" Do not perish."

Once already, in Plotsk, when he had mentioned this expedition, she said the same words to him, " Do not perish ; " but this time these words came from profounder depths of her spirit, and, perhaps to hide her tears, she bent the same moment, so that her forehead touched Zbyshko's knee for an instant.

Meanwhile the mounted attendants at the gate, who were holding pack-horses ready now for the road, began to sing :

" The ring will not be lost; the golden ring

Will not be lost.

A raven will bear it back from the field To the maiden."

"To the road! " called out Zbyshko.

"To the road."

" God conduct thee! The Most Holy Mother! "

Hoofs resounded on the wooden drawbridge, one of the horses gave a prolonged neigh, others snorted loudly, and the party moved on.

But Yagenka, Matsko, Father Kaleb, Tolima, and Hlava, with his wife and the servants who remained in Spyhov, went out on the bridge and looked after them as they departed. Father Kaleb continued making the sign of the cross after them for a long time, till at last they disappeared beyond an alder thicket.

" Under that banner no evil fate will strike them," said he.

" True, but it is of good omen also that their horses gave tremendous snorts," added Matsko.

But neither did he remain long at Spyhov. In a fortnight the old knight finished arrangements with Hlava, who took the estate as a tenant. Matsko, at the head of a long row of wagons surrounded by armed attendants, set out with Yagenka toward Bogdanets. Father Kaleb and old Tolima looked at those wagons without entire satisfaction, for in truth Matsko had stripped Spyhov to some extent, but since Zbyshko had left all things to his management no one dared oppose him. He would have taken still more had he not been restrained by Yagenka, with whom he disputed, it is true, being astonished at her " woman's reasons," but still he obeyed her in almost everything.

They did not take Danusia's coffin, however, for as Spyhov was not sold, Zbyshko preferred that she should remain there with her fathers. They took a large stock of money and wealth of various sorts, captured for the greatest part from Germans in battles fought by Yurand. So Matsko, as he looked at the laden wagons covered with matting, was delighted in soul at the thought of how he would strengthen and arrange Bogdanets. His delight was poisoned, however, by the fear that Zbyshko might fall, but knowing the knightly skill of the young man he did not lose hope that he would return in safety, and he thought of this with rapture.

" Perhaps God wished," said he to himself, " that Zbyshko should obtain Spyhov first, then Mochydoly, and all that remained after the abbot. Let him only come back, I will build him a worthy castle in Bogdanets ; and then we shall see!"

Here it occurred to him that Stan and Vilk would to a certainty not receive him with superfluous delight, and that perhaps he would have to fight them; but he had no fear of this, just as an old war-horse feels no fear when he must go to battle. His health had returned; he felt strength in his bones, and knew that he would manage easily those quar-rellers who were dangerous, it may be, but without knightly training. He said something different, it is true, a short time before, to Zbyshko, but he said it only to restrain that young man from going.

" Hei! I am a pike, and they are gudgeons," thought he; " they would better not come near me head foremost."

But something else alarmed him immediately: "God knows when Zbyshko will come back ; meanwhile he looks on Yagenka only as a sister. Now does not the girl look at him also as a brother, and will she wait for his uncertain return? "

So he looked at her and said, —

" Listen to me, Yagna: I will not talk of Stan and Vilk, for they are uncouth peasants, and not for thee. Thou art now a court lady! But as thy years — my late friend, Zyh, told me that the will of God was on thee then, and that was some time ago. For I know — they say, that when a girl feels the garland too tight on her head she seeks some one to remove it. It is to be understood that neither Stan nor Vilk — but what dost thou notice ? "

" Of what are you inquiring ? " asked Yagenka.

" Wouldst thou marry no man? "

" I ? I shall be a nun."

" Do not say anything frivolous ! But if Zbyshko comes back?"

She shook her head.

" I shall be a nun."

" But if he should love thee? If he should beg, and beg terribly ?"

The girl turned her blushing face toward the field ; but the wind, which was blowing from the field just then, brought to Matsko the low-voiced answer, —

" I would not be a nun."

CHAPTEE LXIX.

THEY remained a time in Plotsk on business of Yagenka'a inheritance and the abbot's will ; afterward, when provided with documents, they moved forward without resting much on their journey, which was easy and safe, for the heat had dried swamps and narrowed rivers, while the roads lay through a peaceful country inhabited by people who were of Polish race, and hospitable. From Sieradz, however, the careful Matsko despatched an attendant to Zgorzelitse, to announce his own coming and that of Yagenka ; because of this Yasko, Yagenka's brother, hurried out halfway to meet them and conducted them home at the head of armed attendants.

There was much rejoicing when they met, with many greetings and many outcries. Yasko and Yagenka had always resembled each other as much as two drops of water, but he had outgrown her. He was a splendid young fellow, daring, joyous, like his father, from whom he had inherited a love for singing, and he was as lively as a fire spark. He thought himself a person of years and strength; he considered that he was a mature man, for he managed his attendants as a genuine chief, and they carried out ever\'7d 7 command of his in a flash, fearing evidently his power and importance.

Matsko and Yagenka wondered at this; while Yasko looked with delight at the beauty and polish of his sister, whom he had not seen for a long time. He told them meanwhile that he had been preparing to visit her, and had they delayed a little in coming they would not have found him at home. He wished to see the world, he said, rub against men, get knightly training, and find a chance to fight in one and another place with knights on their wanderings.

" To learn the world and the manners of people is a good thing," said Matsko in answer, " for a man learns what he is to do and say in every juncture, and it strengthens the native wit in him. But as to fighting, it is better that I should say that thou art too young yet than that a strange knight should say so, and besides not fail to laugh at thee."

"He would cry after laughing," said Yasko; " if not he, then his wife and children would surely cry."

And the youth glanced around with tremendous daring, as if to say to all knights wandering through the world, "Prepare for death!" But the old man of Bogdanets inquired, —

" Well, Stan and Vilk, have they left thee in peace? I ask, for they were glad to look at Yagenka."

"They have indeed; Vilk was killed in Silesia. He at-.tacked a German castle there, and he took it; but they hurled down a beam of wood from the walls on him, and two days later he let his last breath out."

"A pity for him. His father went also in his day to Silesia against the Germans, who oppress our people — and plunder them. To take castles is the worst work of all, for neither armor nor knightly training assist a man. God grant that Prince Vitold will not try castles, but will crush the Knights of the Order in the field ! But Stan, what is he doing?"

Yasko began to laugh.

" Stan is married. He took the daughter of a free land-tiller in Wysoki Breg, a great beauty. Hei! not only a good-looking girl, but a manager: she does not give the man his will once, and slaps his hairy face for him; she leads Stan by the nose, as a bear-trainer leads his beast on a chain."

The old knight was immensely amused when he heard this.

"Look at her! All women are the same! Yageuka, thou too wilt be like the others ! Praise to God that there was no trouble with those two quarrellers; it is a real wonder to me that they did no harm to Bogdanets."

" Stan wanted to do something, but Vilk, who was wiser, gave him no chance. He came to us at Zgorzelitse, and inquired, 'What has become of Yagenka?' I told him that she had gone for an inheritance from the abbot. ' Why did not Matsko tell me ?' asked he. ' But is Yagenka thine, that he should tell thee? ' said I to him. So, after thinking a while he said, ' True, she is not mine.' And as he had a quick mind, he saw, of course, that he would win you and us to his side by defending Bogdanets from Stan. So they met on the Lavitsa near Piaski, cut each other up, and then drank to kill, as they always did."

" Lord light Vilk's soul! " added Matsko.

And he sighed deeply, glad that there were no damages in Bogdanets beyond those caused by his long absence.

In fact, he found none; on the contrary there was an increase of cattle, and from the small herd of mares there were colts, some from the Frisian war horses unusually large and powerful. There was a loss only in this, that some captives had fled, but not many, for they could flee only toward Silesia, and there the Germanized robber knights treated captives worse than did Polish nobles. But the enormous old house had inclined toward its fall considerably. The plaster had fallen; the walls and ceiling had grown crooked; and the larch beams, cut two hundred years or more before, had begun to rot. Throughout all the rooms, inhabited of old by the numerous Grady of Bogdanets, it leaked during the great summer rains. There were holes in the roof, which was covered by broad patches of green and reddish moss. The whole building had squatted and looked like an immense mouldering mushroom.

" With care it would last, for it began to decay only a little while ago," said the knight to old Kondrat, the head laborer, who in the absence of his lords looked after the property.

"I could live here till death," added Matsko after a time, " but Zbyshko needs a castle."

" For God's sake! A castle ? "

"Hei! But why not?"

It was the darling idea of the old man to build a castle for Zbyshko and his future children. He knew that a noble who dwelt, not in an ordinary mansion, but behind a moat and a palisade, and who besides had a watch-tower where a guard gazed on the surrounding regions, was considered as somebody right away by his neighbors, and such a man managed more easily. Matsko did not desire much for himself at that time, but for Zbyshko and Zbyshko's sons he would not stop at little, all the more since their property had increased now considerably.

" Let him take Yagenka, and with her Mochydoly and the abbot's inheritance : no one in these parts could equal us then. God grant such an outcome !"

All this depended on one thing: would Zbyshko come home? that was uncertain and dependent again on God's mercy. Matsko said then in his mind, that for him it was needful to be in the best favor with the Lord God and not merely offend Him in nothing, but win Him in every way possible. With this intent he spared on the church of Kresnia neither wax nor game; and a certain evening when visiting at Zijorzelitse, he said, —

" I will go to-morrow to the grave of Yadviga, our holy queen."

Yagenka sprang up from the bench in great fear, —

" Have you bad. tidings? "

" I have none of am" kind, for I could not at this time. But thou rememberest how, when I was sick from that splinter in my side,—that one, thou knowest, when ye went, thou and Zbyshko, for beavers, — I vowed that if God would return me health, I would go to her grave. All praised my desire then. And indeed! The Lord God has holy servants enough up there, but not every saint — and there are many — has such influence as our Lady, whom I fear to offend, because I am concerned about Zbyshko."

"True, as life!" said Yagenka. "But you have only just returned from a terrible journey."

" Never mind! I want to finish all, and then sit down at home quietly till Zbyshko comes back here. Only let our queen intercede for him before the Lord Jesus, and even ten Germans cannot beat him with his good armor. After the journey I shall build the castle with firmer hope."

" But you have strong bones."

"It is true that I am still active. I will say something else too. Let Yasko, who is impatient for a journey, go with me. I have experience, and shall be able to restrain him. And should any accident happen, — for the boy's hands are itching, — thou knowest that for me it is no new thing to fight on foot or on horseback, with sword or with axe."

" I know. No one could guard him better .than you."

" But I think that it will not happen to him to fight; while the queen was alive, Cracow was filled with foreign knights, who wished to look at her beauty, but now they prefer Malborg, since there is more Malvoisie to be found in the kegs there."

" Yes, but there is a new queen now."

Matsko made a wry face and waved his hand.

"I have seen her! And will say no more — dost understand ? "

After a while he added, —

" In three or four weeks we shall be back here."

In fact, that happened. The old knight commanded Yasko to swear on his kuightly honor and on the head of Saint George that he would not insist on a longer journey, and they rode away.

They reached Cracow without accident, for the country was at peace, and safe from all attacks of Germanized princes beyond the border, and from robber German knights by fear of the power of the kingdom and by the determined bravery of the knighthood. After performing their vows, the old knight and Yasko were presented at the royal court by Povala of Tachev and the little prince, Yamont. Matsko supposed that at the court and in offices they would ask him eagerly about the Knights of the Cross, since he had become well acquainted with the Order, and had looked at it closely. But after consulting with the chancellor and with the sword-bearer of Cracow, he saw with astonishment that their knowledge of the Knights of the Cross was not less than his, but still greater. They knew to the minutest detail all that was happening in Malborg itself and in other castles, even the remotest. They knew what detachments of troops there were, how many warriors there were, how many cannon, how much time was required to assemble the armies, what the plans were in case of hostilities. They knew even details concerning every comtur, — was he quick-tempered and abrupt, or was he thoughtful ; and they had recorded all points as carefully as if war had been appointed for the morrow.

The old knight was immensely delighted at this, for he understood that they were preparing for war far more deliberately, strenuously, and wisely than in Malborg.

"The Lord Jesus has given us as much, or greater bravery," said Matsko to himself, " and surely more mind and greater foresight."

And such was the case at that period. He learned also soon whence information came to them: it was given by inhabitants of Prussia, people of all ranks, Germans as well as Poles. The Order had succeeded in rousing such hatred against itself that all people in Prussia looked at Yagello's armies as salvation. Matsko remembered then what Zyndram had told him in Malborg, and said to himself in spirit, —

" That man has a head indeed ! — a pile of wisdom."

And he recalled every word of Zyndram's; and once he borrowed even from that wisdom, for when it happened that young Yasko inquired concerning the Knights of the Cross, he answered, —

" They are strong, the beasts; but what thinkest thou, will not a knight fly out of his seat, even though he be the

mightiest, if the saddle-girth and the stirrup-straps are cut under him?"

" He will fly out, as true as I stand here," said the youth.

"Ha! seest thou? " cried Matsko, with a thundering voice. " This is what I wanted to bring thee to!"

"Why so?"

" Because the Order is just such a knight."

And after a while he added, —

" Thou wilt not hear this from any common mouth — never fear."

And when Yasko could not understand clearly what the question was, he fell to explaining the affair to him, but forgot to add that he had not thought out the comparison himself, but that it had come word for word from the strong head of Zyndram.

CHAPTER LXX.

THEY did not remain long in Cracow, and would have remained there a shorter time had it not been for the prayer of Yasko, who wanted to look at the people and the city, for all seemed a marvellous dream to him. But the old knight was in an immense hurry to return to his domestic hearth and his fields, so even prayers did not avail much, and on Assumption Day both had returned, — one to Bogdanets, the other to Zgorzelitse.

And thenceforward life began to drag on for them rather monotonously, filled with the toil of land management and e very-day work in the country. In Zgorzelitse, which was low, and especially in Yagenka's Mochydoly, the harvest was excellent ; but in Bogdanets, because of the dry year, the crops turned out to be thin, and no great labor was needed to collect them. In general there was not much tilled land in Bogdanets, for the property was under forest, and because of the long absence of the owners even those plots which the abbot had fitted for ploughing by grubbing up roots were abandoned through lack of workmen. The old knight, though sensitive to every loss, did not take this to heart overmuch at that time, for he knew that with money it would be easy to introduce order and arrangement in all things, — if only there was some one for whom to work and labor. But just this uncertainty poisoned his days and his industry. He did not let his hands drop, however: he rose before day, he rode out to the herds, looked at the work in the field and the forest, he even selected a place for the castle and was choosing out timber for building ; but when after a warm clay the sun was dissolving in the golden and ruddy gleams of evening, a terrible yearning would seize the man, and, besides yearning, a fear such as he had never experienced till those days. " I am running about here, I am toiling," said he to himself; " while off there my poor boy is lying in some field, perhaps pierced by a spear, and wolves in packs are snapping their teeth at him." At this thought

his heart straitened with great love and great pain. He listened then carefully to hear the sound of horse hoofs which announced the daily coming of Yagenka, for through pretending in her presence that he had good hope, he gained it for himself and strengthened his suffering soul somewhat.

She appeared each day, usually toward evening, with a crossbow at her saddle, and with a spear, against attack when going home. It was not a thing at all possible that she should ever find Zbj'shko at Bogdanets unexpectedly, since Matsko did not dare to look for him before a year or a year and a half had passed; but evidently even that hope was hidden in the girl, for she did not appear as she had in the old time, in a skirt girded with a strip of tape, in a sheepskin coat wool outward, and with leaves in her dishevelled hair, but with a beautifully braided tress, and her bosom covered with colored cloth of Sieradz.

Matsko always went out to meet her, and his first question was ever the same as if some one had written it down for him. '• But what? " And her first answer was, " Well, nothing ! " He conducted her then to a large room, and they chatted, near the fire, about Zbyshko, Lithuania, the Knights of the Cross, the war, — talking always in a circle, always about the same things, — and never did these conversations annoy either one of them; on the contrary, they never had enough of those subjects.

And so it continued for months. It happened that Matsko rode to Zgorzelitse, but Yagenka went oftener to Bogdanets.

Sometimes, when there was disturbance in the neighborhood, or when old he-bears in a rage were inclined to attack, Matsko conducted the girl home. When well armed the old man, thanks to uncommon strength, feared no wild beasts, since he was more dangerous to them than they could be to him. At such times he rode stirrup to stirrup with Yagenka, and frequently the pine forest gave forth a threatening sound from the depth of it, but they, oblivious of everything which might happen, conversed only of Zbyshko: where was he? what was he doing? had he killed, or would he kill quickly, as many Knights of the Cross as he had promised Danusia and her mother? would he return soon? Yagenka put questions to Matsko which she had put hundreds of times to him, and he answered them with as much thought and attention as though he heard them then for the first time.

" Do you say," inquired she, "that a battle in the field is not so dangerous for a knight as the taking of castles ? "

*•* But look, what happened to Vilk ? Against a beam of wood thrown from a wall no armor can save a man; but on the field, if a knight has proper training, he may avoid surrender though ten be against him."

" But Zbyshko? Has he good armor? "

" He has a number of suits of good armor, but that taken from the Frisians is the best, because it was forged in Milan. A year ago it was a little large, but now it is just right for him."

" Then against armor like that no weapon prevails, does it?"

" What the hand of man has made may be destroyed by the hand of man also. Against Milan armor is the Milan sword, or the arrows of the English."

" The arrows of the English? " asked Yagenka, with alarm.

"But have I not told thee of them? There are no better archers on earth than the English, unless those of the Mazovian wilderness; but the Mazovians have not such good bows as the English. An English arrow will go through the best armor a hundred yards distant. I saw them at Vilno. And not a man of them missed, and there were some who could hit a falcon while flying."

" Oh, the sons of Pagans! How did you manage them?"

"There was no other way but to rush straight at them. They handle halberds well, the dog-ears, but hand to hand our man will take care of himself."

"Besides, the hand of God guarded yon, and now it will guard Zbyshko."

"I pray often in this way: 'O Lord God, thou hast created and settled us in Bogdanets, so guard us henceforth and let us not perish.' Ha ! it is God's business now to protect us. Indeed, it is no small affair to manage the whole world and miss nothing, but first we must bring ourselves into notice as best we can by being bountiful to the holy church, and, second, God's mind is not man's mind."

Thus did they converse frequently, giving consolation and hope to each other. Meanwhile days, weeks, and months flowed by. In the autumn Matsko had an affair with old Vilk. There had been from of old a boundary dispute between the Vilks and the abbot, about a forest clearing which the abbot, when he held the mortgage on Bogdanets, had seized and cleared of roots. In his day he had challenged

even the two Vilks to a duel with lances or long swords, but they had no wish to fight with a churchman, and before the court they could effect nothing. Old Vilk claimed that land now; and Matsko, who was not so eager for anything on earth as for land, following his own impulse, and roused also by the thought that barley would grow on that fresh soil to perfection, would not hear of surrender. They would have gone to law beyond doubt had they not met by chance at the priest's house in Kresnia. There, when old Vilk, after a harsh dispute, said at last on. a sudden, " I will rely on God rather than people; He will take revenge on your family for the injustice done me," the stubborn Matsko grew mild immediately; he became pale, was silent for a moment, and said then to his quarrelsome neighbor, —

" Listen, it was not I who began this affair, but the abbot. God knows which side is right; but if you intend to say evil words against Zbyshko, take the place, and may God so give health and happiness to Zbyshko as I from my heart give this land to you."

And he stretched his hand out to Vilk, who, knowing him from of old, was greatly astonished, for he did not even suspect what love for his nephew was hidden in that heart which seemed so hard to him. For a long time he could not utter a syllable, till at last, when the priest of Kresnia, pleased at such a turn of affairs, made the sign of the cross on them, Vilk said, —

" If that be the case, it is different! I am old and have no one to whom I could leave property. I was not thinking of profit, but of justice. If a man meets me with kindness, I will add to him even out of my own store. But may God bless your nephew, so that in old age you may not weep over him as I over my one son!"

They threw themselves into each other's arms then, and for a long time they disputed over this, who was to take the newly cleared land. But Matsko let himself be persuaded at last, since Vilk was alone in the world, and had really no one to whom he might leave the property.

Then Matsko invited his neighbor to Bogdanets, where he entertained him with food and drink generously, for he had in his own soul immense gladness. He was comforted by the hope that barley would come up on that new land most splendidly, and also by the thought that he had turned God's disfavor from Zbvshko.

"If he returns, he will have no lack of land and cattle," thought Matsko.

Yagenka was no less pleased with that settlement.

" Now then," said she, after hearing how all was ended, *' if the Lord Jesus wishes to show that concord is dearer to Him than quarrels, He must bring back Zbyshko unharmed to you."

At this Matsko's face grew as bright as if a sun-ray had fallen on it.

" So I think too!" said he. "The Lord Jesus is all-powerful, there is no doubt of that, and there are ways to win the heavenly powers, but a man must have prudence."

" You have never lacked that," said the girl, raising her eyes to him. And after a while, as if she had thought over something, she said, —

'' But you do love that Zbyshko of yours! You love him ! Hei ! you do love him."

Who would not love him ? " replied the old knight. '' And thou ? Dost thou hate him ? "

Yagenka did not answer directly ; but as she was sitting on a bench by Matsko's side, she moved up still nearer, and turning her head away punched him then slightly with her elbow.

" Give peace ! " said she ; " how have I offended you! "

CHAPTEE LXXI.

BUT the war about Jmud between the Knights of the Cross and Vitold had occupied people in the kingdom so greatly that they could not avoid inquiring as to its progress. Some felt sure that Yagello would give aid to his cousin, and that all would soon see a general expedition against the Order. The knighthood were impatient for action ; and in all settlements of nobles, men said to one another that a considerable number of the lords of Cracow, who were in the king's council, had inclined to war, considering that it was necessary to finish once for all that enemy who would never be satisfied with his own, and whose mind was intent on seizing what belonged to another even when fear before the power of his neighbor had seized him. But the prudent Matsko, who as a person of experience had seen and learned much, did not believe that war was impending, and he spoke of this matter often to Yasko and other neighbors whom he met at Kresnia. fc

" While the Grand Master Konrad lives, nothing will come of this, for he is wiser than others, and he knows that it would be no common war, but a slaughter: ' Thy death, or mine.' And he, knowing the power of the king, will not let matters go that far."

" Yes; but if the king should declare war first?" inquired the neighbors.

Matsko shook his head.

" You see, I have examined everything closely, and I have noted some points. If the king were of our ancient stock, if he were of kings Christian for generations, he might perhaps strike first on the Germans. But our Vladislav Yagello (I have no wish to diminish his fame, for he is an honorable lord, may God preserve him in health) was Grand Prince of Lithuania and a pagan before we chose him king; Christianity he received only some time ago, while the Germans calumniate his Majesty throughout the world and say that the soul in him is pagan. For this reason it would seem terribly unbecoming in him to declare war first, and spill the blood of Christians. For this cause he

will not move to help Vitokl, though his hands are itching, for I know this, that he hates the Knights of the Cross as he does leprosy."

By such speeches Matsko acquired for himself the reputation of being a keen man who could lay everything out, as it were, on the table. So in Kresnia people gathered around him in a circle after Mass every Sunday, and afterward it was customary for this or that neighbor, when he heard news, to turn in at Bogdanets, so that the old knight might explain to him what an ordinary noble head could not analyze. Matsko received all with welcome, and spoke to each of them willingly ; and when at last the guest, having said what he wanted, was departing, the host never forgot to take farewell of him in these words, —

" You may wonder at my reason, but when Zbyshko, with God's will, comes back here, you will begin to wonder really ! He might sit even in the king's council, such a wise and ingenious man is he."

And by persuading guests of Zbyshko's greatness he persuaded himself of it at last, and also Yagenka. Zbyshko seemed to them both from afar like the king's son in a fairy tale. When spring appeared they could hardly remain in the house. Swallows returned, storks returned, land-rails were playing in the meadows, quails were heard in the green growth of gtain; earlier than all, flocks of cranes and teal had come. Zbyshko alone did not return to them. But after the birds had flown back from the south, a winged wind from the north brought news of war. Men spoke of battles and numerous encounters in which the clever Vitold at one time was victor, at another the vanquished; they spoke of great disasters, which winter and diseases had wrought among the Germans. Till at last the joyful news thundered throughout the country, that Keistut's valiant son had taken New Kovno, or Gottes-werder; he had destroyed it, he had not left one stone on another, or one beam on another. When this news reached Matsko, he mounted his horse and flew off to Zgorzelitse without halting.

"Ha!" said he, "those places are known to me; for Zbyshko and I with Skirvoillo beat the Knights of the Cross there, — beat them mightily. There it was that we captured that honest De Lorche. Well, it was God's will to sprain the German foot this time, for that castle was hard to take."

Bat Yageuka had heard before Matsko came of the storm-ing of New Kovno, — she had even heard more; namely, that Vitold had begun negotiations. This last news concerned her more than the former,-for should peace be concluded Zbyshko would return home, of course, were he living.

Then she fell to inquiring of the old knight if that were credible; and he, when he had thought a while, answered, — " Every news is credible in Vitold's case, for he is a man different altogether from others, and surely the keenest of all lords in Christendom. When he needs to extend his dominion toward Russia, he makes peace with the Germans; and when he has done what he planned, he takes the Germans again by the forelock ! They cannot manage either him, or that suffering Jmud laud. One time he takes it away from them, another time he gives it, and not only gives it, but helps them to crush it. There are men among us, yes, in Lithuania also, who take this ill of him that he plays thus with the blood of that ill-fated people. And I, to speak truth, would consider it infamous on his part, if he were not Vitold. But I think to myself, ' Well, he is wiser than I, and he knows what he is doing.' I have indeed heard from Skirvoillo himself that Vitold has made of that land a boil always festering in the body of the Order, so that that body should never have health in it. Women in the Jmud land will always bear children, and it is no harm to spill blood unless it be spilt to no purpose." "I care only for this: will Zbyshko come back," said Yagenka.

" If God permit, he will come; but may the Lord grant, girl, that thou hast said these words at a lucky moment."

Still months passed. News came that peace had been really concluded, grain with its heavy ears had grown yellow, the fields sown with buckwheat were ruddy, but of Zbyshko no tidings.

At last when the first work was done, Matsko could endure no longer and declared that he would hurry to Spyhov, and as it was nearer to Lithuania get news there and inspect Hlava's management.

Yagenka insisted on going with him, but he would not take her, so they began disputes on this point, which held out a whole week if not longer. At length, on a certain evening when they were disputing in Zgorzelitse, a youth from Bogdanets rushed into the yard like a whirlwind, barefoot, without a cap on his yellow head, and cried to them before the porch on which they were then sitting, —

" The young lord has come home! "

Zbyshko had come home indeed, but he was strange in some way: not only had he grown thin and was tanned by the winds of the fields and seemed suffering, but he was also indifferent and of few words. Hlava, who, with his wife, had come also, spoke for Zbyshko and for himself. He said that the young knight's expedition had found success evidently, for he had placed on the tomb of Danusia and her mother in Spyhov a whole bundle of peacock and ostrich plumes from knights' helmets. He had brought back captured horses and suits of mail, two of which were of very great value, though terribly hacked with blows of swords and axes. Matsko was burning with curiosity to know everything in detail from the lips of his nephew, but the latter merely waved his hand and answered in single syllables, and the third day he fell ill and was forced to his bed. It appeared that his left side had been battered and that two of his ribs had been broken, these, being badly set, " hindered" him in walking and in breathing. The injuries received in his encounter with the bison were felt also, and to complete the breaking up of his strength the journey from Spyhov was added. All this of itself was not terrible, for the man was young, and as sound as an oak-tree; but at the same time he was possessed by immense weariness of some kind, as if all the toils which he had ever gone through had begun now to move through his bones for the first time. Matsko thought, to begin with, that after two or three days' rest in bed all would pass, but the opposite had happened. There was no help from rubbing with ointments, or smoking with herbs, which the local shepherd recommended, nor from the decoctions sent by

Yagenka and the priest of Kresnia: Zbyshko grew weaker and weaker, more and more wearied, more and more gloomy.

k ' What is the matter with thee? "Wouldst thou like something, perhaps? " inquired the old knight.

"I want nothing: all things are the same to me," replied Zbyshko.

In this way, day followed day. Yagenka, coming to the idea that this was perhaps something more than an ordinary cough, and that the young man must have some secret which was crushing him, fell to urging Matsko to try once more to discover what that could be.

Matsko consented without hesitation, but after thinking a while he said, —

" Well, but would he not tell it more easily to thee than to me ? For — as to liking — he likes thee, and I have seen this, that when thou art moving through the room his eyes follow thee."

" Have you seen that? " inquired Yagenka.

"If I have said that his eyes follow, they follow. And when thou art not here for a long while, he looks time after time toward the door. Ask him thou."

And it rested there. But it turned out that Yagenka did not know how, and did not dare to ask. When it came to something serious, she understood that it would be necessary to speak of Danusia and of Zbyshko's love for the dead woman, and those things could not squeeze through her lips.

"You are shrewder," said she to Matsko, " and you have more mind and experience : speak you; I am not able."

Matsko, willing or unwilling, set about the task; and one morning when Zbyshko seemed somewhat fresher than usual, the old man began a conversation of this sort.

" Hlava tells me that thou hast placed a good bundle of peacock plumes in the vault of Spyhov."

Zbyshko, without taking his eyes from the ceiling, at which as he lay face upward he was gazing, merely nodded his head in agreement.

" Well! The Lord Jesus has given thee luck; for in war it is easier to find camp followers than knights. A man may get as many common warriors as he pleases; but to find a knight one must look around very carefully sometimes. But did they come under thy sword of their own will?"

" Some I challenged a number of times to trampled earth, and once they surrounded me in battle," said the young man, lazily.

" And thou didst bring booty enough? "

" Something; Prince Vitold gave me a present."

"Is he so bountiful yet?"

Zbyshko nodded his head again, not having evidently the wish to speak further.

But Matsko did not yield up the victory, and determined to approach the real subject.

"Tell me sincerely," said he: "when the tombs were covered with those crests, thou must have been relieved immensely? A man is always glad when he accomplishes a vow. Wert thou glad?"

Zbyshko removed his sad eyes from the ceiling, turned them on Matsko, and answered as if with a certain astonishment, —

"No."

"No? Fear God! I thought that when thou shouldst satisfy those saved souls, there would be an end to thy trouble."

The young man closed his eyes for a moment, as if in thought, and answered at last, --

"It is clear that souls in paradise do not wish human blood."

A moment of silence followed.

" Then why didst thou go to that war?" inquired Matsko, at last.

"Why?" answered Zbyshko, with a certain animation; " I thought that it would ease me. I thought that I should please Danusia and myself. But when all was over I was astonished. I came out of the vault where the coffins are, and I was as much oppressed as before. So it is clear that to souls in paradise human blood has no value."

" Some one must have told thee that, for never wouldst thou have thought it out thyself."

" I remarked it myself just because the world did not seem more gladsome to me afterward than before. Only Father Kaleb said,—

" ' To kill an enemy in war is no sin, it is even praiseworthy,' and these were enemies of our race."

" I do not consider it a sin either, and I am not sorry for those Germans."

" But is thy grief always for Danusia? "

"Well, when I think of her I am sorry. But it is the will of God ! She is happier in the court of heaven, and — I am now accustomed to my present state."

" Then why not shake off these glooms ? What dost thou need?"

"If I knew what."

" Thou wilt not fail of rest, the cough will soon leave thee. Go to the bath, bathe well, drink a bottle of mead, perspire, and hots! "

"Well, and what next?"

" Thou wilt be glad right away."

"Whence shall I get gladness? I shall not find it in myself; and as to lending me gladness, no one will lend it."

li But thou art hiding something ! "

Zbyshko shrugged his shoulders.

" I have no gladness in me, but I have nothing to hide."

And he said this so sincerely that Matsko dropped his suspicions that moment, and began at once to smooth his gray forelock with his broad palm, as was his custom when thinking severely, and at last he said, —

" Well, I will tell it, something is lacking thee. One work is finished, but the other is not begun yet; dost understand?"

"Perhaps I do, but not clearly," answered the young man. And he stretched himself like one who is sleepy.

But Matsko was convinced that he had divined the true reason. He was greatly delighted, and his alarm ceased altogether. He gained also more confidence in his.own prudence, and said in spirit, "It is not to be wondered at that men ask advice of me ! "

And when after that conversation Yagenka came on the evening of that same day, before she could dismount he told her that he knew what troubled Zbyshko.

The girl slipped down from the saddle in one moment, and then for the inquiry, —

"Well, what is it? tell!

" It is just thou who hast the medicine for him."

"I? what?"

And he put his arm around her waist and whispered something into her ear, but not long, for in a moment she sprang back from him as if burned, and hiding her blushing face between the saddle-cloth and the high saddle, she cried, —

" Go away ! I cannot endure you! "

"As God is dear to me, I am telling truth," replied Matsko, laughing.

## CHAPTER LXXII.

OLD Matsko had divined the truth clearly, but only half of it. In fact one part of Zbyshko's life had ended completely. Whatever the young knight thought of Dan-usia, he grieved for her, but he said to himself that she must be happier in the court of heaven than she had been at the court of Prince Yanush. He had grown inured to the idea that she was no longer in the world; he had become familiar with it, and considered that the position could not be changed in any way. When in Cracow he had admired immensely the figures of sacred virgins outlined on glass aud framed in lead on church windows. These figures were colored and gleaming in the sunlight, and now he imagined Dauusia as being just like them. He saw her transparent, heavenly, turned toward him in profile, with palms placed together, and eyes uplifted, or he saw her playing on a lute among a host of celestial musicians, who in heaven play to the Holy Mother and the Divine Infant. There was nothing earthly in her now ; to his mind she had become a spirit so pure and disembodied that when at times he remembered how Danusia had served the princess at the hunting-lodge, how she had laughed and conversed, how she had sat down at the table with others, he was filled as it were with wonder that such things could be. During his expedition with Vitold, when questions of warfare and battles had swallowed his attention, he ceased to yearn for his celestial one as a man yearns for a woman, and thought of her only as a devotee thinks of his patron saint. In this way his love, by losing gradually earthly elements, changed more and more into what was only a remembrance, sweet and pure as the sky itself, and became simply religious reverence.

Had he been a man of frail body and deeper thought he would have become a monk, aud in the calm life of a cloister would have preserved that heavenly reminiscence as something sacred till the moment in which his soul could fly from the shackles of its body into endless space, just as a bird rushes forth from its cage. But the third decade of his years had begun not long before; he was able to squeeze with his fist the sap out of green chips and could so press the horse under him with his legs as to take the beast's breath away. He was like all nobles of that period. If they did not die in childhood or become priests, they knew neither bound nor limit in physical vehemence and vigor; they let themselves out into robbery, loose life, drunkenness, or they married in youth and went to war in mature age when summoned, taking with them twenty-four or more sons, all of whom had the robustness of wild boars.

But he knew not that he was a man of this kind, all the more since he had been sick. Gradually, however, his ribs, which had been set unskilfully, grew together, and showed merely a slight lump on one side which ' hindered him in no way, and which not only mail but ordinary clothing might conceal entirely.

His weariness had passed. His rich yellow hair, cut in sign of mourning for Danusia, had grown again to a point below his shoulders. His former extraordinary beauty had returned. When some years before he had walked forth to meet death at the hands of the executioner he looked like a youth of great family, but now he had become still more beautiful, a genuine king's son. In shoulders, in breast, in arms and loins he was like a giant, but in features he resembled a maiden. Strength and vigor were boiling in him, as liquid in a caldron; invigorated by continence and long rest, life was coursing through his bones like blazing fire. He, not knowing what this meant, thought himself sick yet, and continued to lie in bed, glad that Matsko and Yagenka nursed him, cared for him, and divined his wishes. At moments it seemed to Zbyshko that he was as happy as if in heaven ; at moments, especially when Yagenka was not there, existence appeared wretched, sad, unendurable ; fits of yawning and stretching, with feverishness, seized him at such moments, and he declared to Matsko that on recovering he would go again to the ends of the earth against the Germans, Tartars, or some other like savagery, to rid himself of life, which was weighing him down terribly. Matsko, instead of opposing, nodded and agreed; meanwhile he sent for Yagenka, after whose coming thoughts of new expeditions vanished from Zbyshko as snows melt when warmed by the sun of springtime.

Yagenka came promptly, both when summoned and of her own accord, for she loved Zbyshko with all the strength of her heart and soul. During her stay at the court of the

bishop and that of the prince in Plotsk she saw knights as fine and as famous for strength and bravery as Zbyshko, knights who knelt before her more than once and vowed faith for a lifetime; but this was her chosen one, she had loved him from early years with her first love, and the misfortunes through which he had passed only increased that love to the degree that he was dearer to her, and a hundredfold more precious, not only than all knights, but than all princes on earth. Now, when returning health each day made him more splendid, her love turned almost into madness and hid all the rest of the world from her.

But she did not confess this love to herself, even, and from Zbyshko she concealed it most carefully, fearing lest he might disregard her a second time. Even with Matsko she was now as secretive and silent as she had been aforetime outspoken. The care shown in nursing the young knight was all that could betray her, so she strove to give to it another pretext; hence on a certain day she said hurriedly to Zbyshko, —

" If I look after thee a little it is from good will toward Matsko, but didst thou think otherwise ? "

And, as if to arrange the hair on her forehead, she shaded her face with her hand, and looked at him carefully through her fingers. Attacked thus on a sudden by the question, he blushed like a young girl, and only after a while did he answer, —

" I did not think anything. Thou art now another person."

A moment of silence followed.

" Another person?" asked Yagenka at last, in a peculiar low and soft voice. • " Well, it is sure that I am different. But that I should not endure thee, may God not permit that! "

" God reward thee for even this word," replied Zbyshko.

And thenceforth it was pleasant for them in each other's company, though in some way uneasy and awkward. At times it might seem that they were speaking of something aside, or that their thoughts were elsewhere. Silence was frequent between them. Zbyshko never rose from the bed, and, as Matsko had stated, followed Yagenka with his eyes whithersoever she went, for she seemed to him, especially at moments, so wonderful that he could not look at her sufficiently. It happened too that their glances met unexpectedly, and then their faces flamed, the maiden's breast

moved with hurried breathing, and her heart beat as if she expected to hear something which would make the soul melt and flow apart in her. But Zbyshko was silent, for he had lost his former boldness completely; he feared to frighten her with some heedless word, and, in spite of what his eyes saw, he persuaded himself that she was showing him mere sisterly kindness out of friendship for Matsko.

He mentioned this once to his uncle; he tried to speak calmly, with indifference; he did not even note that his words became more and more like a complaint, half sad and half filled with reproaches.

Matsko listened patiently. At last he said the single word, " Simpleton ! " and walked out of the room.

But when, he was in the stable he rubbed his hands, and struck his thighs with great gleefulness.

"Ha!" said he, "when she came to thee for nothing thou would st not even look at her. Take thy fill of fright now, since thou art a simpleton. I will build the castle, and thou meanwhile, let thy mouth water. I will say nothing to thee; I will not take the cataract from thy eye, even wert thou to make more noise than all the horses in Bogdanets. When shavings are piled on a smouldering fire a blaze will burst up sooner or later in every case, but I will not blow, since there is no need, I think."

And not only did he not blow, but he even opposed Zbyshko and teased him like an old fox glad to trifle with youthful inexperience. So one day when Zbyshko said again that he would go to some distant war to rid himself of a life which was unendurable, the old man said to him,

—

"While the lip under thy nose was bare I directed thee, but now — thou hast thy own will! If thou wish at all risks to trust in thy own wit and go — go."

Zbyshko sprang up with astonishment and sat erect in bed.

" How is this? Thou dost not oppose? "

Why should I oppose ? I only grieve terribly for our family which inight perish with thee, but I may find a way to avoid this."

" How a way?" inquired Zbyshko, in alarm.

"How? Well, my years are considerable, no use in denying that — but there is no lack of strength in my bones. Seest thou, some younger man might chance to please Yagenka — but as I was a friend of her father—who knows but I —

" You were a friend of her father," answered Zbyshko,

VOL. II. 18

"but you never had any good feeling for me—never! never! "

And he stopped, for his chin began to quiver, and Matsko said, —

" Pshaw! since thou hast resolved to destroy thyself, what can I do?"

"Well! do what you like — but I will leave here this very day! "

"Simpleton!" repeated Matsko.

And he left the room to look at the laborers, both men from Bogdanets and those whom Yagenka had lent him from Zgorzelitse and Mochydoly to help dig the moat which was to surround the castle.

CHAPTER LXXIII.

ZBYSHKO did not carry out his threat, it is true, and did not leave Bogdanets, but after the course of another week his health had returned to him completely and he could not remain longer in bed. Matsko declared that it was their duty to visit Zgorzelitse and thank Yagenka for the care bestowed on him. So on a certain day, after he had steamed himself well in the bath, Zbyshko resolved to go straightway. With this object he commanded to take from the chest his beautiful garments so as to use them instead of the every-day clothes he was wearing, and then he occupied himself with curling his hair; but that was no small, easy task, and the difficulty lay not alone in the wealth of that hair which dropped down behind like a mane below his shoulders. Knights in every-day life wore their hair in a net shaped like a mushroom, which in time of expeditions had this good side, that the helmet chafed them perhaps less, but on various ceremonial occasions, such as a wedding, or visits to houses in which there were young ladies, they arranged it in beautifully twisted rolls, which frequently were rubbed with the white of an egg to give them consistency and gloss. Precisely in this way did Zbyshko wish to dress his hair. But the two women summoned from the servants' house were unused to such work and were unable to do it. His hair, all dry, standing out after the bath, could not be made to lie down, and was like a badly thatched roof of straw on a cottage. The combs, cut out of buffalo horn artistically and won from the Frisians, did not help, nor did a curry-comb for which one of the women went to the stable. Zbyshko began at last to be impatient and angry—when Matsko walked into the room with Yagenka, who had come unexpectedly.

" Praised be Jesus Christ! " said she.

" For the ages of ages! " answered Zbyshko, with a radiant face. " Well, this is wonderful! We were just making ready to go to thy house, and thou art here! "

His eyes gleamed with delight, for it was thus with him always; whenever he saw her it was as bright in his soul as if he were looking at the sunrise.

But when Yageuka saw the women, comb in hand, and troubled, when she saw the curry-comb lying on the bench at Zbyshko's side and his hair standing out in all directions, she fell to laughing.

"By my word, it is a bundle of straw, a bundle of straw! " cried she, showing the wonderful white teeth between her coral lips. " We might put thee in a hemp field or a cherry garden, to frighten the birds away! "

Zbyshko frowned.

*' We were making ready to visit Zgorzelitse," said he;. '•in Zgorzelitse thou wouldst not attack a guest, but here thou hast the privilege of making sport of me as much as may please thee, and upon my faith thou art always glad to make sport of me."

" I glad to make sport of thee!" exclaimed Yagenka. " Oh, mighty God ! Why, I have come to invite you both to supper ; and I am laughing not at thee, but at these women. If I were in their place I could arrange matters quickly."

" Thou couldst not."

" But who dresses Yasko's hair? "

" Yasko is thy brother," answered Zbyshko.

" Of course he is! "

Here the old and experienced Matsko resolved to assist them.

"In families," said he, "when a knightly youth's hair grows, after cutting, his sister dresses it; in mature age a man's wife dresses his hair for him; but it is the custom also that if a knight has no sister or wife, a noble maiden serves him, even though she be entirely unrelated."

"Is there really such a custom?" inquired Yagenka, dropping her eyes.

" Not only in mansions, but in castles. Yes! even at the king's court," answered Matsko.

Then he turned to the women.

" Since ye can do nothing, go to your own place!"

" Let them bring me warm water," added Yagenka.

Matsko went out with the women, as if to see that there was no delay in serving, and after a moment he had warm water brought in, and when it had been placed in the room the young people were left with each other. Yagenka having wet a towel moistened Zbyshko's hair well with it; when the hair had stopped flying up and had lain down with the weight of dampness, she took a comb and sat on the bench at the side of the young man to proceed with the work.

And they sat there side by side, both comely beyond

measure, both immensely in love with each other, but ill at ease and silent. Yagenka began at last to arrange his golden hair, and he felt the vicinity of her upraised arms, of her hands, and he shivered from head to foot, restraining himself with all his force of will lest he might seize her by the waist and press her with all his might to his bosom.

In the silence the hurried breath of both was audible.

"Perhaps thou art ill?" inquired the girl after awhile. "What troubles thee?"

" Nothing," answered the young knight.

"But somehow thou art panting."

" Thou art panting too — "

Again there was silence. Yagenka's cheeks were as red as roses, for she felt that Zbyshko did not take his eyes from her face for an instant; so, to talk away embarrassment, she asked,—

" Why dost thou look at me in that way? "

" Does it annoy thee?"

" It does not annoy, but I ask."

"Yagenka?"

"What — "

Zbyshko drew in a long breath, sighed, moved his lips as if for further conversation, but it was clear that he had not sufficient courage yet, since he merely repeated again, —

"Yagenka."

"What?"

"If I am afraid to tell something —

" Be not afraid. I am a simple girl, not a dragon."

" Of course not a dragon ! But Uncle Matsko says that he wants to take thee! "

" Yes he does, but not for himself."

And she stopped as if frightened at her own words.

" By the dear God ! My Yagus ! — but what answer hast thou to give, Yagus ? " cried Zbyshko.

But unexpectedly Yagenka's eyes filled with tears, her beautiful lips began to quiver, and her voice became so low that Zbyshko could hardly hear it when she said, —

" Papa and the abbot wished — while I — as thou knowest! — "

At these words delight burst forth in Zbyshko's heart like a sudden flame; so he caught the girl in his arms, lifted her up as he might a feather, and shouted wildly, —

" Yagus ! Yagus ! thou my gold ! my sun — hei! hei! "

And he shouted so that old Matsko, thinking that some strange thing had happened, rushed into the room. When he saw Yagenka raised aloft by his nephew, he was astonished that everything had passed with such unlooked-for rapidity, and he exclaimed, —

" In the name of the Father and the Son, restrain thyself, boy!"

Zbyshko rushed toward him, placed Yagenka on the floor, and both wished to kneel down, but before they could do so Matsko seized them in his bony arms and pressed them with all his strength to his breast.

Praised be He! " said the old man. "I knew that it would come to this, but still my delight! God bless you! It will be easier for me to die now. The girl is like the purest of pure gold. Before God and the world! In truth ! Let come now what may, since I have lived to this delight. God has visited, but He has comforted us. We must go right away and tell Yasko. Ei, if Zyh were alive now ! — and the abbot — But I will take the place of both, for in truth, I so love you that I am ashamed to tell it."

And though he had in his bosom a heart that was steeled, he was so filled with emotion that something pressed his throat; so he kissed Zbyshko again, and after that Yagenka on both cheeks, and coughing out, half in tears, " Honey, not a woman! " he went to the stables to have the horses saddled.

When he had gone from the room he stumbled with delight against sunflowers growing in front of the house, and began to look at their dark disks surrounded with yellow leaves; he was just like a drunken man.

" Well! There is many a seed there," said he, " but God grant that there will be a greater number of Grady in Bog-danets." Then going toward the stables he began again to mutter and to count, —

" Bogdanets, the abbot's property, Spyhov. Mochydoly

— God always knows whither He is taking things. Old Vilk's day will come, and it is worth while to buy Brozova

— fine meadows ! "

Meanwhile Yagenka and Zbyshko came out to the front of the house, joyous, happy, radiant as the sun.

" Uncle ! " called Zbyshko from afar.

The old man turned toward them, stretched out his arms, and cried out, as he might in the woods, —

" Hop! hop ! Come to me! "

CHAPTER LXXTV.

ZBTSHKO and Yagenka lived in Mochydoly while old Matsko was building a castle for them in Bogdanets. He built it with toil, for he wished that the foundations should be of stone laid in lime mortar, and the watchtower of brick, which was difficult to procure in that neighborhood. During the first year he dug the moat, which work was rather easy, for the eminence on which the castle was to stand had been entrenched on a time, perhaps in days which were still pagan; hence he needed only to clear those depressions of trees and hawthorn bushes with which they were overgrown, and then extend and deepen them sufficiently. While digging, the men reached an abundant spring, which in no long time filled the moat, so that Matsko had to provide an exit for the excess of water. Then on the rampart he reared a palisade and began to collect building timber for the walls of the castle, — oak beams, so thick that three men could not embrace one of them, and larch, which rots neither under clay plaster nor under a turf covering. He set about raising those walls only after a year, although he had the assistance of men from Zgorzelitse and Mochydoly. But he set about it all the more earnestly since Yagenka had given birth to twins. Heaven opened before the old knight then, since there was some one for whom he might la*bor and bustle, and he knew that the race of the Grady would not perish, that "The Dull Horseshoe" would be moistened yet more than once in the blood of the enemy. To the twins were given the names Matsko and Yasko.

"They are boys," said the old man, "to be praised, such boys that in the whole kingdom there are not two to equal them — and it is not evening yet."

He loved them immediately with a great love, and as to Yagenka, she hid the world from him. Whoso praised her before his eyes could get anything from the old man. People really envied Zbyshko for having such a wife, and glorified her not merely for the wealth which she had brought, since she was as brilliant in that region as the most beautiful flower in a field. She had given her husband a great dowry; but she had given more than a dowry,

for she had given immense love, and beauty which dazzled the eyes of men, and noble manners, and a vigor of such sort that many a knight could not boast of the like. It was nothing for her some days after childbirth to rise up to house management, and then go to hunt with her husband, or to hurry on horseback from Mochydoly to Bogdanets and return before midday to Yasko and Matsko. So her husband loved her as the sight of his eyes, old Matsko loved her, she was loved by the servants for whom she had a humane heart, and in Kresnia, when she entered the church on Sunday, she was greeted by murmurs of admiration and homage. Her former worshipper, the quarrelsome Stan of Rogov, had married the daughter of a free laud-tiller. Stan after mass used to visit the inn with old Yilk, and, having drunk somewhat, say to the old man: " Your son and I cut each other HP more than once because of her, and we wanted to marry the lady, but that was just like reaching for the moon in heaven." Others declared aloud that -one might look for another such woman only at the king's court in Cracow. In addition to her wealth, beauty, and refinement people honored also her incomparable health and vigor, and there was only one opinion on this point : " that she was the first woman who had ever planted a bear with a fork in the forest, and she had no need to crack nuts with her teeth; she put them on the table pressed them in her hand suddenly and cracked them as if they had been crushed with a stone." So she was praised in the parish of Kresnia and in the neighboring villages, and even in Sieradz, the chief town of the province.

But while envying Zbyshko of Bogdanets because he hifd won her, men did not wonder over much, for he too was illustrious by such military fame as no one else in that region. The younger possessors and nobles related to one another all the stories touching Germans whose souls Zbyshko had " shelled out" of them in battles under Prince Vitold, and on trampled earth in duels. They said that no man had ever escaped him, that in Malborg he had unhorsed twelve knights, among others Ulrich, the Grand Master's brother; finally, that he was able to meet even knights of Cracow, and that the invincible Zavisha Charny himself was a well-wishing friend of his. Some were unwilling to give faith to such uncommon stories; but even those men, when it was a question whom the neighborhood ought to choose, should it come to rivalry between Polish and foreign knights, said: "Of course, Zbyshko!" and only afterward did the hairy Stan of Rogov and other local strong men, who in knightly training were far behind the young heir of Bogdanets, come into consideration.

Great wealth equally with his fame had won for Zbyshko honor from his neighbors ; for he had received with Yagenka Mochydoly and the great property of the abbot. That was not his merit, but earlier he had Spyhov together with immense treasures accumulated by Yurand, and besides people whispered to one another that the booty alone won and taken by the knights of Bogdanets in arms, horses, clothing, and jewels, would suffice to buy three or four good villages. Men saw therefore in this a certain special favor of God toward the race of the Grady with the escutcheon " The Dull Horshshoe," which till recent times had been so reduced that besides empty Bogdanets it had nothing — now it had increased beyond all others in that region. "Moreover, there had remained in "Bogdanets after the fire only that poor, bent, decayed house," said old people, " and from lack of laboring hands the owners of the property had been forced to mortgage it to their relative — but now they are building a castle!" Astonishment was great, but since it was accompanied by the general instinctive feeling that the whole nation was advancing with irresistible impulse toward some immense acquisition, and since by the will of God such was to be the future order, there was no malicious envy; on the contrary, the region about boasted and was proud of those knights of Bogdanets. They served as a living proof of what a noble might do if he had a strong arm and a manful heart, with knightly eagerness for adventure. More than one man, therefore, at sight of them felt that for him the place was too narrow among his household goods, and within his native limits, and that beyond the boundary there was a hostile power, great wealth and broad lands, which he might win with immense gain to himself and the kingdom. That excess of strength, which was felt by families, extended over the whole nation, so that it was like a seething liquid which must boil over in a caldron. The wise lords at Cracow, and the king, who loved peace, might restrain that strength for a season, and defer war with the hereditary enemy, but no human power could extinguish it, or even restrain that impetus with which the general spirit of the people was advancing toward greatness.

LXXV.

MATSKO had lived to happy years in his life. He declared to his neighbors repeatedly that he had received raore than he himself had hoped for. Even old age had only whitened the hair on his head and in his beard; it had not taken from him health or strength. His heart was full of such great joyfulness as up to that time he had never experienced. His face, formerly severe, had become more and more kindly, and his eyes smiled at people with a friendly expression. In his soul he had the conviction that all evil had ended forever, that no care, no misfortune would dim the days of his life now flowing onward as quietly as a clear river. To war till old age, to manage in old age and increase wealth for his " grandchildren," — that at all times had been the highest wish of his heart; and now all this had come to pass perfectly. Land management went just as he desired. The forests had been felled in considerable part, the stumps rooted out, and the new land was green every spring with a fleece of various kinds of grain; herds increased, in the fields were forty mares with colts, which the old noble inspected daily. Flocks of sheep and herds of cattle pastured in groves and on fallow lands. Bogdanets had changed thoroughly; from a deserted settlement it had become a populous, a wealthy place, and the eyes of him who approached it from Zgorzelitse by the forest highway were dazzled by the watchtower seen from afar, and the walls of the castle still unblackened and glittering with gold in the sun and the purple evening twilight.

So old Matsko was rejoiced in heart by cattle, by management, by his fortunate fate, and he did not contradict when •people said that he had a lucky hand.

A yedr after the twins there came to the world another boy, whom Yagenka called Zyh in honor of her father.

Matsko received the new visitor with delight and was not troubled in the least by this, that were it to go farther in such wise the property accumulated with so much effort and toil would have to be divided. " For what had we?" asked he, speaking of this once to Zbyshko. " Nothing! still

i

God prospered us. Old Pakosh of Sulislavitse has one village and twenty-two sons, but they are not dying of hunger. Are the lands in the kingdom and Lithuania small in extent? Are the villages and castles in the hands of the dog brother Knights few in number? Hei! well, since the Lord Jesus has favored us so much, there will be a proper place (for them) since there are castles there, all of red brick, of which our gracious king may make places for castellans." And it was a thing worthy of note that though the Order had risen then, as it were, to the summit of its greatness, because in wealth, power, and the number of trained troops it surpassed all Western kingdoms, still this old knight thought of the castles of the Order as future residences for his grandsons ; and surely many in Yagello's kingdom had a like thought, not merely because those were old Polish lands on which the Order had settled, but because a feeling of mighty power was storming in the nation, and seeking an outlet on every side.

Only in the fourth year, counting from Zbyshko's marriage, was the castle finished, and even then with the assistance not only of local laborers and men from Zgorzelitse and Mochydoly, but also from the region about, especially from old Vilk of Brozova, who, left alone in the world after the death of his son, had become very friendly to Matsko, and afterward turned his heart toward Zbyshko and Yagenka.

Matsko adorned the chambers of the castle with booty which either he and Zbyshko had taken in war, or which had been inherited from Yurand of Spyhov ; added to these were effects left by the abbot and others which Yagenka had brought from her own home. He put in glass windows from Sieradz, and arranged a magnificent residence.

Zbyshko with his wife and children moved into the castle only on the fifth year, when the other buildings, such as stables, cowhouses, kitchens, and baths were finished, and also cellars, which old Matsko had made of stone and lime-mortar, so that they should have endless durability. But he did not move into the castle himself; he preferred to remain in the old bent house, and to every prayer of Zbyshko and Yagenka he answered in the negative, expressing his mind in the following manner. —

" I will die here where I was born. You see, during the time of the war of the Grymaliti and Nalentchi Bogdanets was burned to the ground, all the cottages, yes, even the

fences, but this old house remained. People said that it did not burn because of the abundance of moss on the roof, but I think that the favor of God and His will were in this occurrence, so that we should return here and increase again out of the old house. During the time of our campaigning I complained more than once that we had nothing to which we might return, but not altogether justly did I say that. By my faith, there was nothing to keep house here with, and as to putting something into one's mouth — but there was a place in which to take refuge. Well, for the young people it is quite different, but I think this, since that old house has not left us, it is not proper for me to leave it."

And he remained. But he liked to visit the castle, so as to look at its grandeur and greatness in comparison with the old dwelling, and at the same time to look at Zbyshko and

Yagenka, and at his " grandsons." All that he saw was in considerable part his own work; but it filled him with pride and admiration. Sometimes old Vilk visited him to "chat" at the fireside, or he visited Vilk in Brozova for the same purpose. So once he explained to him his ideas touching " the new order."

" You know," said he, " it is strange to me sometimes. Though in truth Zbyshko, even in Cracow, was at the king's castle — why! they came near cutting his head off there ! — and in Mazovia, and at Malborg, and with Prince Yanush. Yagenka was reared also in wealth, but they had not their own castle. Now, however, it is as if they had never lived in another way. They walk, I tell you, they walk in the chambers, walk, — and give commands to the servants, and when they are tired they sit down. A real castellan and his lady! They have also a chamber in which they dine with mayors, managers, and dependants, and in it there are higher seats for him and for her; others have lower seats and they wait till the master and mistress have been served properly. That is court usage, but I am to remember that they are not some great lords, but a nephew and a nephew's wife, who take me, their old pet, and seat me in the first place, and call me benefactor."

" For that reason the Lord Jesus blesses them," remarked old Vilk.

Then, nodding his head in sadness, he drank a little mead, stirred brands in the fire with an iron poker, and said, —

" But my boy is dead ! "

" God's will."

" Well ! His older brothers, of whom there were five, laid down their lives long ago. But you know that. The will of God, of course. But this last boy was the best of them all. A real Vilk; and if he had not fallen he too would be living now in his own castle."

" Better that Stan had fallen."

"What is Stan? He is as if carrying millstones on his shoulders. But how many times did my boy cut him up. My son had knightly training, while Stan's wife now raps him on the face, for, though he is a strong fellow, he is stupid."

" Hei! he is as dull as a horse's rump !" added Matsko.

And when there was an occasion he exalted to the skies not only Zbyshko's knightly training, but also his wit, saying that in Malborg he had met the foremost knights within barriers, " and that for him to converse with princes was the same as to crack nuts." He praised also his nephew's wisdom and skill in management, without which he would soon consume the castle and the property.

Not wishing, however, that old Vilk should suppose that anything similar could threaten Zbyshko, he finished in a lowered voice, —

"Well, with the favor of God there is rich property enough — more than people think; but do not repeat this to any one."

People divined, they knew and told one another to exaggeration, especially of the wealth which the lord and lady of Bogdanets had removed from Spyhov. It was said that they had brought money in salt kegs from Mazovia. Matsko had accommodated with a loan of between ten and twenty gryvens the wealthy heirs of Konietspole, and this confirmed the belief of the neighborhood absolutely in his " treasures." For that reason the significance of the lords of Bogdanets increased, the respect of people rose, and there was never a lack of guests at the castle ; which fact Matsko, though sparing, did not consider with an unwilling eye, for he knew that that too added to the fame of the family.

More especially splendid were the christenings, and once a year, after the Assumption of the Blessed Virgin, Zbyshko gave a great feast to the neighborhood, at which noble women were present to look at knightly exercises, hear stones, and dance with young knights by the light of pitch torches till morning. Then old Matsko rejoiced his eyes and delighted his heart in gazing at Zbyshko and Yagenka,

they looked so dignified and lordly. Zbyshko had become more manful in appearance; he had grown, and though with his powerful and tall figure his face seemed always too young, still when he fastened his abundant hair with a purple band, arrayed himself in splendid garments embroidered with silver and gold threads, not only Matsko, but many a noble said to himself in soul: "God be merciful! He is really a prince sitting in his own castle." But often knights who knew western customs knelt before Yagenka, and begged her to be the -lady of their thoughts. She was ra-diaut with such splendor of health, strength, and beauty. The old master of Konietspole, who had been voevoda of Sieradz, was astonished at sight of her, and compared her to the morning dawn, and also to the " dear sun," which gives brightness to the world, and puts enlivening heat even into old bones.

CHAPTEE LXXVI.

IN the fifth year, however, when uncommon order had been introduced into all the villages, when above the watch-tower a banner with " The Dull Horseshoe" had been waving for some months, and Yagenka had given birth to a fourth son, whom they called Yuraud, old Matsko said one day to Zbyshko, —

" Everything succeeds, and if the Lord Jesus would give one more thing I could die iu peace."

Zbyshko looked at his uncle inquiringly, and after a while asked,—

" Are you speaking of war with the Knights of the Cross? — for what else do you need?"

" I will say to thee what I have said before, that while the Grand Master Conrad lives there will be no war."

" But is he to live forever? "

" I cannot live forever either, and therefore I am thinking of something else."

"Of what?"

" Better not ask. Meanwhile I am setting out for Spyhov, and perhaps I shall visit the princes in Plotsk and in Chersk."

This answer did not astonish Zbyshko greatly, for in the course of recent years, old Matsko had gone to Spyhov a number of times; hence he only asked, —

'•Will you stay long?"

" Longer than usual, for I shall halt at Plotsk."

Something like a week later, Matsko started, taking with him a number of wagous, and good armor, " for the event of having to fight within barriers." When going he declared that he might remain longer than usual, and in fact he did remain during half a year, and there were no tidings of him. Zbyshko began to be alarmed, and at last sent a messenger purposely to Spyhov, but that man met Matsko beyond Sieradz and returned with him.

The old knight was rather gloomy at first, but after he had inquired of Zbyshko carefully touching everything which had happened during his absence, and was set at

rest because all had gone well, his face cleared somewhat, aiid he began first to speak of his expedition.

" Dost thou know that I have been in Malborg?" asked he.

"In Malborg?"

" But where else ? "

Zbyshko looked at his uncle for a while with astonished eyes, then he slapped his own thighs suddenly, and added, —

As God is true! But I had forgotten about death! "

" Thou art free to forget, for thou hast accomplished thy vows," said Matsko; "but God forbid that I should set aside my oath and honor. It is not our custom to neglect — and, so help me the holy cross, as long as there is breath in my nostrils I shall not neglect anything."

Now it grew dusky, and Matsko's face became threatening and resolute in such a way as Zbyshko had seen only in former years, when with Vitold and Skirvoillo they were going to battle with the Knights of the Cross.

'•' Well, and did you accomplish your vow? "

" No. I did not, for he would not meet me."

"Why so?"

" He has become grand comtur."

" Is Kuuo Lichtenstein grand comtur? "

" Yes. Perhaps they will choose him Grand Master. Who knows ? Even now he thinks himself the equal of princes. They say that he manages everything, and that all affairs of the Order are on his shoulders, while the Grand Master undertakes nothing without him. How was such a man to appear on trampled earth ? To ask him would be to rouse the laughter of people."

" Did they bring thee to ridicule?" asked Zbyshko, and his eyes flashed suddenly with anger.

"The Princess Alexandra of Plotsk laughed. ' Go,' said she, ' and challenge the Roman Caesar. To Lichtenstein,' said she, ' as we know challenges have been sent by Zavisha Charny, Povala of Tachev, and Pashko Zlodye, and even to those men he gave no answer, for he cannot. He is not lacking in courage, but he is a monk and he has an office so considerable and of such dignity that those things do not come to his head, — and he would lose more honor by accepting than by not paying attention to challenges.' That is what Princess Alexandra said."

" And what was your answer ? "

" I was terribly cast down, but I said that even in that

case I must go to Malborg, so that I might say to God and man that I did what was in my power. I begged the lady then to arm me with some message, and give me a tetter to Malborg, for I knew that otherwise I should not bring my head out of that wolf's-nest. In my soul I thought this way : ' He would not, it is true, grant a meeting to Zavisha, or Povala, or Pashko, but if, in presence of the Master himself, of all the cointurs and guests, I slap him on the face or pull his beard and mustache, he will meet me.' "

" God support you! " cried Zbyshko, with enthusiasm.

"Well," continued the old man. "There is a way for everything if a man has a head on his shoulders. But in this case the Lord Jesus withdrew his favor, for I did not find Lichtenstein in Malborg. They told me that he had gone to Vitold as an envoy. I knew not what to do then, whether to wait or to follow him. I was afraid of missing him on the road. And since I was acquainted from former times with the Grand Master and the grand keeper of the wardrobe, I explained to them, as a secret, why I had come; they shouted at me that that could not be."

"Why ?"

"For the very same reason which the princess in Plotsk had given. And the Grand Master said also: ' What wouldst tbou think of me should I fight a duel with every knight from Mazovia or Poland?' Well, he was right, for he would have been out of the world long ago. Then he and the keeper of the wardrobe were astounded, and told of this at the supper table in the evening.

Their story acted on the company as the blowing of a man would on a swarm of bees, especially on the guests; a crowd started up at once. 'Kuno,' cried they, ' may not fight, but we may.' I chose three then> wishing to fight with them in turn, but the Master, after great petitions, gave permission to fight with only one, whose name was Lichtenstein, and who was a relative of Kuno."

"Well, what?" cried Zbyshko.

" This — I have brought back his armor, but I am sorry for its condition; it is smashed so that no one would give a gryven for it."

" Fear God! then you have fulfilled your vow?"

" At first I was glad, for I thought myself that I had, but afterward I thought: ' No, that is not the same! ' And now I have no peace, for it is not the same."

Zbyshko fell to consoling him, —

VOL. II. — 19

" You know that in such matters I do not spare myself, or any one, but if things had happened to me as to you I should be satisfied. And I say now that the greatest knights in Cracow will support me. Zavisha Charny himself, who knows most of knightly honor, will surely say nothing different."

" Dost thou say that? " inquired Matsko.

"But just think: they are famous throughout the whole world, and they challenged him also, but none of them have done so much as you. They vowed death to Lichteustein, but you have slaughtered a Lichtenstein."

" That may be," said the old knight.

But Zbyshko, who was curious in knightly affairs, said,—

" Well ! tell me : was he young, or old, and how was the struggle ? on horseback, or on foot? "

" He was thirty-five years old, he had a beard to his girdle, and was on horseback. God assisted me so that I overcame him with the lance, but after that it came to swords. I tell thee the blood gushed from his mouth so that his whole beard was drenched with it."

" But have you not complained frequently that you are growing old ? "

"Yes, for when on horseback, or on the ground, I hold firmly, but I cannot spring into the saddle in full armor."

" But Kuno himself would not have escaped you."

The old man waved his hand contemptuously, in sign that with Kuuo it would have gone much easier, then they went to look at the captured "plates," which Matsko had taken only as proof of victory, for they were too much shattered, and therefore without value. But the hip piece and the leg armor were uninjured and of excellent workmanship.

"But I should prefer that these were Kuno's," said Matsko, gloomily.

" The Lord God knows what is best," answered Zbyshko. " You will not reach Kuno if he becomes Grand Master, unless in some great battle."

" I inclined my ears to what people said, " replied Matsko. " Some declared that after Conrad would come Kuno, while others mentioned Ulrich the brother of Conrad."

" I should prefer Ulrich," said Zbyshko.

' " I too, and kuowest why? Kuno has more mind and is more cunning, while Ulrich is passionate. He is a truthful knight who observes honor, but he just quivers for war with us. They say also that were he to be Grand Master there would coine such a tempest as has not been in the world. Fits of weakness fall frequently on Conrad. Once he fainted in my presence. Hei, perhaps we may live to it."

" God grant! But are there some new misunderstandings with the Kingdom ? "

" There are both old and new. A Knight of the Cross is always a Knight of the Cross. Though he knows that thou art stronger, and that it is evil to quarrel with thee, he will lie in wait since he cannot do otherwise."

"But they think that the Order is mightier than all kingdoms."

" Not all of the Knights think so, but many do, and among others Ulrich; for really their power is tremendous."

"But you remember what Zyndram said — "

" I remember. And every year it is worse among them down there. A brother does not receive a brother, as even Germans in Prussia received me when no Knight of the Cross was looking on. All the people have enough of the Knights."

" Then there is not long to wait? "

" Not long, or even long," answered Matsko. And after stopping a while he added : " But meanwhile it is necessai-y to labor and increase property, so as to appear in the field worthily."

CHAPTER LXXVII.

THE Grand Master Conrad died only a year later. Yasko of Zgorzelitse, Yagenka's brother, first heard the news in Sieradz, both of his death and of the election of Ulrich von Jungingen; he was the first also to bring it to Bogdanets, where, as well as in all noble houses, it shook souls and hearts to their depth. " Such times are come as have not been hitherto," said old Matsko, with solemnity, while Yagenkr. brought at the first moment all the children to Zbyshko, and began herself to take farewell of him, as if he had to set out next morning.

Matsko and Zbyshko knew, it is true, that war would not break out as suddenly as fire in a chimney, but nevertheless they believed that it would come to war, and they began to prepare. They chose horses, arms, exercised their attendants and servants in the military art, — the mayors of villages managing by German law, who were obliged to appear in expeditions on horseback, and the poorer nobles and possessors were glad to join themselves to the more wealthy. The same thing was done on all other estates. Everywhere hammers were beating in forges, everywhere men were cleaning old armor, rubbing bows and straps with tallow melted in kettles, wagons were ironed, supplies of provisions, both grits and dried meat, were prepared. In churches on Sundays and holidays people inquired for news; they were sad when tidings of peace came, for every man carried deep in his soul the conviction that there was absolute need to finish immediately with that dreadful enemy of the whole Polish race, and that the kingdom could not flourish in strength, peace, and labor till, according to the words of Saint Bridget, the teeth of the Order were broken and its right hand cut from it.

In Kresnia more especially did men gather around Matsko and Zbyshko as persons who knew the Order and knew what war with the Germans was. People not only asked news of them, but inquired about methods against the Germans. " How are we to fight best with them ? " asked they. " What is their style of warfare? In what are they superior to the

Poles, and in what inferior? When lances are broken, is it easier to smash the armor on them with an axe, or is a sword better?"

In truth Matsko and his nephew were expert in these things, so people listened to them with great attention, all the more since the conviction was universal that the war would not be easy, that the Poles would have to measure themselves with the foremost knights of all nations, and not be satisfied with crushing the enemy at this point or that, but crush thoroughly " to the foundation," or perish utterly. So nobles said then among one another and among landowners: " Since it is necessary, we must go through it, — their death or ours." And to that generation of men who bore in their souls a prophetic feeling of coming greatness this did not decrease willingness, — on the contrary, it increased that willingness every day and hour; but they approached the work without empty boasting and self-praise, or rather they approached it with a certain resolute concentration, with gravity, and prepared for death.

" Destruction is written down for them or for us."

But meanwhile time passed and extended, and there was no war. There were reports, it is true, of disagreements between King Vladislav Yagello and the Order, and also reports touching the land of Dobryn, which had been purchased years before, and touching boundary disputes and a certain Drezdeuko of which they heard then much for the first time, but concerning which both sides were disputing, as was said ; but there was no war. Some began to doubt if there would be, for there had always been disputes, but they ended usually in meetings, negotiations, and the despatch of envoys. In fact news went out that this time two certain envoys of the Order had come to Cracow, while Polish envoys had gone to Malborg. There were reports of mediation by the kings of Bohemia and Hungary, and even by the Pope himself. At a distance from Cracow people knew nothing in detail, hence various, though frequently strange and impossible, reports circulated through the country; but there was no war.

At last even Matsko, within whose memory not a few threats of war had been made and negotiations had taken place, did not know what to think of the whole situation, so he set out for Cracow to obtain more reliable data. He did not remain long in the city, for on the sixth week he returned, and returned with a face greatly brightened ; so when the nobility, curious for news, as usual surrounded him in Kresnia, he answered their numerous queries with the question, —

" Well, are your lances and spears and axes sharpened? "

"But what? Well now! By the wounds of God! what news ? Whom have you seen ? " called out people from all sides.

"Whom have I seen? Zyndram of Mashkovitse! But what news ? Such news that ye will have to saddle your horses at once, I think."

"As God is true ! How is that ? Tell."

" Have ye heard of Drezdenko? "

" Of course we have heard. But the little castle is like many a one, and there is no more land there than with you in Bogdanets, we think."

" That is a vain cause for war — is it not? "

" Of course it is a vain cause for war. There were greater, but afterward nothing came of them."

' • But do ye know what a saying Zyndram uttered because of Drezdenko? "

" Tell quickly, for the caps are burning our heads! "

" He said this to me: ' A blind man was going along the road and he fell over a stone. He fell because he was blind, still a stone was the cause of his fall.' This Drezdenko is such a stone."

" How is that? How ? But the Order is standing yet."

" Ye do not understand? Then I will tell you again in this way. If a vessel is too full one drop will make the liquid in it overflow."

Such great enthusiasm seized those knights that Matsko had to restrain it, for they wished to mount their horses and ride to Sieradz.

" Be ready," said he, "but wait patiently. They will not forget us, be sure."

So the people continued in readiness, but they waited long, so long indeed that some began to doubt a second time.

But Matsko did not doubt, for as the coming of birds announces spring, he, as a man of experience, knew how to infer from various signs that war was approaching, and a great war.

First of all, such immense hunts had been ordered in all forests and wildernesses of the crown as the oldest men could not remember.. Beaters were assembled in thousands to drive in game. In these hunts fell whole herds of buffaloes, bulls, deer, wild boar, and also smaller animals. The forests were

smoking for entire weeks; meat was dried, smoked, salted for future use and sent to the chief towns of provinces, and thence to be stored at Plotsk. It was evident that the question was one of supplies for great armies. Matsko knew well what to think of this, for Vitold had ordered the very same kind of hunts before each large expedition to Lithuania. But there were other signs also. For instance, peasants had begun to flee in crowd's from " under the German " to the kingdom and to Mazovia. To the district of Bogdanets mainly the subjects of German knights in Silesia had come, but people saw that everywhere the same movement was going on, but especially in Mazovia. Hlava, who was managing in Spyhov in Mazovia sent from there between ten and twenty Mazovians who had fled to him from Prussia. These men had begged permission to take part in the war " on foot," for they wished to avenge wrongs on the Knights whom they hated with all their souls. They said that some boundary villages in Prussia were almost wholly deserted, for the free land tillers had moved out of them with their wives and children to the Mazovian Principalities.

The Knights of the Cross hanged, it is true, all fugitives whom they caught, but nothing could restrain the unfortunate people, and many a one of them preferred to die rather than live under the terrible yoke of the Germans. Later "grandfathers" (minstrels) from Prussia swarmed through the whole kingdom. All went to Cracow. They came from Dantzig, from Malborg, from Torun, and even from distant Krolevets, from all Prussian towns and from all places where there were commandants. Among them were not only minstrels, but sextons, organists, various cloister servants, and even clerics and priests. It was thought that they would bring information touching everything carried out in Prussia, such as: military preparations, strengthening of castles, garrisons, mercenary troops, and foreign officers. In fact people whispered to one another that the voevodas in the chief towns of provinces, and, in Cracow, members of the city council, had shut themselves in with those visitors for whole hours, listening to them and writing down the facts which they gave. Some went back unobserved to Prussia and then returned anew to the kingdom. News came from Cracow that the king and the lords of the council knew through them of every step taken by the Knights of the Cross.

The opposite took place in Malborg. A certain spiritual

personage who had fled from that capital stopped at Koniets-pole and told the masters there that U Irich von Jungingeu and other Knights of the Order did not trouble themselves about news from Poland, feeling certain that with one blow they would conquer and overturn all the kingdom, " so that not a trace would be left of it." He repeated therewith the words of the Grand Master Ulrich uttered at a feast in Malborg: "The more there are of them the cheaper will sheepskin coats be in Prussia." Hence they prepared for war with delight and intoxication, confident in their own strength, and in the aid which all, even the most distant kingdoms, would send them ; but in spite of these signs of war preparations and efforts, the war did not come so quickly as people wished.

It was tedious at home for Zbyshko of Bogdanets also. All things had long since been made ready, the soul in him was rushing forth to battle and to glory, hence each day's delay annoyed him. and frequently he mentioned this to his uncle, just as if war or peace depended on Matsko.

" You see you promised to a certainty that it would come, and now there is nothing and nothing," said Zbyshko.

"Thou art wise, but not very!" answered Matsko. " Dost thou not see what is happening? " •

" But if the king at the last hour agrees? They say that he does not want war."

" They say so, for he does not. But who, if not he, shouted: ' I should not be a king were I to permit them to take Drezdenko!' but as the Germans took Drezdeuko they keep it to this hour. Of course the king does not wish to spill Christian blood, but the lords of the council who have quick wit, feeling the superior power of the Poles, are pushing the Germans to the wall — and I may say this to thee, that if Drezdenko were not in question, something else would be discovered."

" As I have heard, the Grand Master Conrad himself took Drezdenko, and he feared the king, surely."

" He feared him, for he knew Polish strength better than others, but even he was unable to restrain the greed of the Order. In Cracow they told me as follows: Old von Ost, the heir of Drezdenko, at the time when the Knights seized Nova Marchia, did homage as feudatory of the king, for that had been Polish land for ages, so he wished to belong to the kingdom. But the Knights of the Cross invited him to Malborg, made him drunk with wine, and enticed from him a document. Then the king's patience failed him at last."

'' By my faith it must have failed him ! " exclaimed Zbyshko.

"It is as Zyndram said," added Matsko. "Drezdenko is only a stone over which the blind man stumbled."

" If the Germans give up Drezdenko, what will happen? "

"Another stone will be discovered. But the Order will not give up that which it has once swallowed, unless we open its stomach, and God grant us soon to do that."

"No!" cried Zbyshko, strengthened in spirit, "Conrad might have surrendered it, Ulrich will not. He is a true knight on whom there is no stain, but he is terribly passionate."

So they conversed with each other, and meanwhile an event came like a stone which, pushed down a steep mountain-path by the foot of a traveller, rushes to the abyss with ever growing impetus. Suddenly the news thundered throughout the whole country that the Knights had attacked and plundered Santok, which had been mortgaged to the Yohanites. The new Grand Master, Ulrich, when the Polish envoys came to congratulate him on his election, left Malborg purposely. From the first moment of his government he commanded to use German instead of Latin in communications with the king and Poland, and thus showed at last what he was. The lords at Cracow, who were urging to war in secret, understood that he was urging to it publicly, and not only publicly, but blindly and with such insolence toward the Polish people as the Grand Masters had never shown, even when their power was really greater and the kingdom was less than at that time.

But dignitaries of the Order, less passionate and craftier than Ulrich, men who knew Vitold, strove to win him to their side by gifts, and used flattery which passed every measure so that one would have had to seek for its like in those times when temples and altars were reared to Roman Caesars while still living. "The Order has two benefactors." said the envoys of the Orfler as they bowed down before the viceroy of Yagello: " the first is God, the second Vitold, for this reason every wish and every word of Vitold is sacred for the Knights of the Ci'oss." And they implored Vitold to mediate in the affair of Drezdenko with this idea, that if, as a subject of the king, he would undertake to judge his superior, he would offend -him thereby, and

298 THE KNIGHTS OF THE CROSS.

the good relations between them would be broken, if not forever, at least for a long time. But since the lords who formed the council in Cracow knew of everything which was done and planned in Malborg, the king also chose Vitold as arbiter.

And the Order regretted the choice. The dignitaries of the Order to whom it seemed that they knew the Grand Prince, did not know him sufficiently, for Vitold not only adjudged Drezdenko to the Poles, but, knowing also, and divining how the affair must end, roused Jmud again and more fiercely, — showing a more and more threatening visage to the Order, he began to assist Jmud with men, with weapons, and with grain sent from fertile lands in Poland.

When this took place— all, throughout every land of the immense State, understood that the decisive hour had struck.

It had struck indeed.

Once in Bogdanets, when old Matsko, Zbyshko and Ya-genka were sitting in front of the castle gate, enjoying the warmth and the marvellous weather, an unknown man appeared suddenly on a foaming horse, he reined back his steed before the gate, threw at the feet of the Knights something that looked like a garland woven from the osier and the common willow. Then he shouted: "Vitsi! Vitsi!" (the summons, the summons) and shot away.

They sprang to their feet in great excitement. Matsko's face became threatening and solemn. Zbyshko stepped forward to urge the messenger to hasten on with his summons; then he turned with fire in his eyes, and shouted, —

" War! God has given it at last ! War ! "

" And not such a war as we have seen before, but a great one! " added Matsko, with solemnity.

Then he turned to the servants, who in one moment gathered around their master.

" Sound horns on the watehtower toward the four sides of the world ! " shouted he; " and let others run to the villages for the mayors! Bring out the horses and attach them to the wagons ! Do it in a breath ! ! "

His voice had not ceased to sound yet when the servants hurried in different directions to carry out his orders, which, moreover, were not difficult, since all had been ready long before : men, wagons, horses, armor, arms, provisions. The knights had nothing to do but take their seats and drive on.

But before starting Zbyshko asked Matsko, —

"Will you not remain at home?"

" I ? What is in thy head? "

" According to law you can stay, for you are a man of advanced years, and there should be some protector for Yagenka and the children."

" Well, listen to that! I have waited to white hairs for this hour."

It sufficed to look at his cold, resolute face to know that words were of no use in that case. Besides, notwithstanding his seventh cross, 1 the man was as sound as an oak, yet; his arms moved easily in their joints, and an axe wielded by them just whistled through the air. He could not, it is true, spring in full armor on to a horse without touching the stirrups, but there were many young men, especially knights of western Europe, who could not do that either; he had immense training, however, in knightly deeds, and in all that region there was not a warrior of more experience.

It was evident also that Yagenka had no fear of remaining alone, for on hearing her husband's words she rose, kissed his hand, and said, —

" Be not troubled about me, dear Zbyshko, for the castle is a good one; and know this, that I am not over timid; to me neither crossbow nor lance is a novelty. It is not the time now to think of wife and children, when there is need to save the country. God will be our guardian."

Her eyes filled quickly with tears, which rolled down in great drops on her beautiful lily-like face, and pointing to the group of children she spoke on with emotion, and a quivering voice, —

Hei! were it not for those little ones, I should lie at thy feet till I received permission to go to the war with thee."

" Yagus! " cried Zbyshko, seizing her in his arms.

She embraced his neck, nestling up to him with all her strength, and said, " Only come back to me, my golden, my only one. my dearest of all!"

" But thank God every day that he has given thee such a wife," added Matsko, in a deep voice.

An hour later they lowered the flag from the watchtower in sign that the master was absent.

Zbyshko and Matsko permitted Yagenka with the children to accompany them as far as Sieradz. One hour later all set out with men and a whole train of wagons. The day was clear and still. The forests were in a motionless quiet.

1 Seven X.'s — seventy years.

The herds on the fields and fallow lands enjoyed the midday rest, chewing their cuds slowly, as if in thought. Because of the dryness of the air there rose in one and another place along the roads rolls of yellow dust, and above those rolls gleamed, as it were, numberless little fires glittering in the sunlight; Zbyshko pointed them out to his wife and children, saying, —

" Do ye know what is glittering there above the dust? Those are spears, lances, and darts. It is clear that the summons has reached every one, and the people are marching against the Germans from all sides."

In fact such was the case. Not far beyond the boundary of Bogdanets they met Yageuka's brother, Yasko, who, as heir of Zgorzelitse, was quite wealthy; he marched with three lancers, and took with him twenty men. Soon after, at a crossroad, rose up toward them from beyond dust-clouds the face of Stan of Rogov, overgrown with hair; he was not, it is true, a friend of the lords of Bogdanets, but this time he called from a distance, —

"Bear down on the dog brothers!" He bowed toward them with good will, and galloped on farther in the grayish dust.

They met also old Vilk of Brozova. His head trembled a little from age, but he too was marching on, to avenge the death of his son, whom the Germans had slain in Silesia.

And as they approached Sieradz the clouds of dust on the road were more and more frequent, and when from afar the tower of the city was visible the whole road was swarming with knights and their wagons, with armed townspeople who were all marching to the place of muster. Seeing that numerous, healthy, stalwart people, stubborn in battle and enduring beyond all others in foul weather, in rains, in cold, and every kind of toil, old Matsko was strengthened in spirit.

And such a stream of well-equipped warriors were approaching towns not only in the kingdom, but throughout the whole immense extent of the lands ruled by Yagello and Vitold.

From the Carpathians and the Black Sea to the shores of the Baltic peoples were hurrying to restrain the German inundation, and put an end to the quarrel of ages with one giant effort.

CHAPTER LXXVIII.

AND war had burst forth at last. Not abounding in battles, and during the early moments not over favorable to the Poles. Before the 'Polish forces had come up the Knights of the Cross captured Bobrovniki, levelled Zlotoria with the ground, and invaded the unhappy land of Dobryn, won recently with so much effort. But Bohemian and Hungarian mediation allayed for a time the storm of war. A truce followed, during which Vatslav, King of Bohemia, was to arbitrate the dispute between Poland and the Order.

Neither side ceased, however, to assemble troops and concentrate them during the months of winter and spring. When the King of Bohemia, who was bribed, gave his decision in favor of the Order, war of necessity burst forth anew.

Meanwhile summer came, and with it arrived the " nations " under Vitold. After crossing the river at Cherveusk both armies united, and the regiments of the princes of Mazovia joined them. On the other side, in the camp at Sviet. were a hundred thousand Germans encased in iron. Yagello wished to cross the Drventsa and advance by the shortest road to Malborg, but when the crossing proved to be impossible, he turned from Kurentnik to Dzialdova, and after destroying Dombrovna, or Gilgenburg, a castle of the Order, he encamped there.

He, as well as the Polish and Lithuanian dignitaries, saw that a general battle must come soon, but no one supposed that it could come before a number of days had passed. They supposed that the Grand Master, having stopped the road before the king, would give rest to his legions, so that they might come to a life-and-death battle fresh and unwearied. With this expectation the armies of the king halted for the night at Dombrovna.

The capture of the fortress, though without orders, and even against the will of the military council, filled the hearts of the king and Vitold with pleasure; for the castle was strong,* surrounded by a lake, it had thick walls, and was held by a numerous garrison. Still the Polish knights took

it almost in the twinkle of an eye, and with such irresistible spirit that before the whole train had come up there remained of the town and the castle only ruins and burnt remnants, in the midst of which the wild warriors of Vitold, and the Tartars under Saladin, were cutting down the last of the German infantry, who defended themselves with desperation.

But the fire did not last long, for it was extinguished by a shower of short duration though tremendously violent.

The whole night of July 14 was marvellously changeable and showery. Whirlwinds brought tempest after tempest. At moments the heavens seemed to be ablaze from lightning, and thunders mingled in awful explosion from the east to the west. Frequent lightning filled the air with the odor of sulphur, then again the roar of rain outsounded all else. Again wind scattered clouds, and amid the tattered fragments of them stars and the great bright moon were visible. Only after midnight did it calm down somewhat so that men could at least kindle fires. In fact thousands and thousands of them blazed up then in the immense camp of the Poles and Lithuanians. The warriors dried their drenched garments and sang songs of battle.

The king was watching also, for in a house standing at the very edge of the camp, in which he had taken refuge from the storm, a council of war was in session to which account was rendered of the capture of Gilgenburg. Since the regiment of Sieradz had taken part in storming that castle, its leader, Yakob of Konietspole, was summoned with others to justify himself for storming the place without orders, and for not stopping the attack though the king had sent to restrain them his own usher and a number of confidential attendants.

For this reason the voevoda, uncertain whether blame would meet him, or even punishment itself, took with him a number of the foremost knights, and among others old Matsko and Zbyshko, as witnesses that the usher appeared only when they were on the walls of the castle and at the moment of most stubborn struggle with the garrison. As to this, that he had attacked the castle, " It is difficult," said he, " to inquire about everything when the troops are dispersed over a space of many miles. Sent out in advance, I understood that I was bound to crush obstacles before the army and to fight with the enemy wherever I met them."

On hearing these words the king, Prince Vitold, -and the lords, who in soul were delighted with what had happened,

not only did not censure the voevoda and the men of Sieradz, but praised their valor, saying that they had captured the castle and the brave garrison quickly. Matsko and Zbyshko were able then to gaze at the chiefs commanding in the kingdom, for, besides the king and the princes of Mazovia, were present the two leaders of all the legions: Vitold, who had brought up the troops of Lithuania, Jmud, Rus, Bessarabia, Wallachia, and the Tartars, and Zyndram of Mashkovitse, with his escutcheon "The same as the sun," the sword-bearer of Cracow, and supreme manager of the Polish forces, who surpassed all in his knowledge of military science. Besides him there were in that council many warriors and statesmen ; for instance : the castellan of Cracow, Krystin of Ostrov, the voevoda of Cracow, Yasko of Tarnov, the voevoda of Posnan, Sendzivoi of Ostorog and Sandomir, Mikolai Mihalovitse and the parish priest of Saint Florian, and the vice chancellor Mikolai Tromba, and the marshal of the kingdom, Zbigniev of Brezie, and Peter Shafranyets, the chamberlain of Cracow, and finally Ziemovit, son of the Prince of Plotsk, the only young man among them, but a man wonderfully " wise in war," and whose opinion the great king himself esteemed highly.

But in the adjoining roomy chamber the greatest knights were waiting so as to be at hand and in case of inquiry give aid with counsel. The fame of these men sounded widely throughout Poland and in foreign kingdoms. So Matsko and Zbyshko saw there Zavisha Charny and his brother Farurey, and Skarbek Abdank, and Dobko of Olesnitsa, who on a time had unhorsed twelve German knights in Torun in a tournament, and the gigantic Pashko Zlodye, and Povala of Tachev, who was their good friend, and Kron of Koziglove, and Martzin of Vrotsimovitse, who carried the grand banner of the kingdom, and Florian Yelitchik, and Lis of Targo-visko, who was terrible in hand-to-hand conflict, and Stashko of Harbimovitse. who in full armor could leap over two horses.

There were many other famous knights who marched before the banner from various lands, and from Mazovia, who were called " men before the banner " because they went in the front ranks to battle.

Their acquaintances and especially Povala greeted Matsko and Zbyshko with gladness, and began to converse of former times and events with them.

"Hei!" said Povala to Zbyshko. "Thou hast heavy reckonings indeed with the Knights of the Cross, but I think now thou wilt pay them for everything."

" I will pay them with blood even; indeed I will pay for everything!"

"But thou knowest that thy Kuno Lichtenstein is now grand comtur ? "

"I know, and my uncle knows also."

" God grant me to meet him," interrupted Matsko; " for I have a special account with that man."

"I know! but we too have challenged him," answered Povala. " He answered that his office did not permit him to meet us. Well! perhaps it will permit him now."

To this, Zavisha, who spoke always with great dignity, said, —

" He will be his to whom God predestines him."

But Zbyshko from pure curiosity laid his uncle's case before the judgment of Zavisha, and asked if Matsko had not accomplished his vow by this, that he had fought with a relative of Lichtenstein, who had offered himself as substitute, and which relative he had killed. All cried out that he had accomplished it. The stubborn Matsko alone, though he was comforted by the decision, said, —

" Yes, but I should feel surer of salvation if I could meet him."

And then they began to talk of the capture of Gilgenburg, and of the approaching great battle, which they expected soon, for there was nothing left the Grand Master but to bar the way before Yagello.

Just as they were breaking their heads over the question of how many days there would be before the encounter, a tall, thin knight approached them ; he was dressed in red cloth with a cap of similar material on his head, and spreading his arms he said in soft, almost feminine accents, —

A greeting to thee, Knight Zbyshko of Bogdanets! "

" De Lorche ! " exclaimed Zbyshko, " thou here! "

And he seized him in his embrace, for a pleasant memory of the man had remained with him, and when they had kissed each other, as if they were the nearest of friends, he inquired with delight, —

" Art thou here on our side?"

" There are many knights of Guelders perhaps on the other side," answered De Lorche. " but I owe service from Dlugolyas to my lord, Prince Yauush."

" Then thou art the heir of old Mikolai of Dlugolyas? "

"Yes. After the death of Mikolai, and of his son, who was killed at Bobrovniki, Dlugolyas came to the wonderful Yagenka, who for the last five years is iny wife and lady."

" In God's name ! " cried Zybshko, " tell how all this happened to thee! "

But De Lorche, greeting old Matsko, said, —

" Your former armor-bearer, Hlava, told ine that I should find you both here, and now he is waiting in my tent, and is watching over the supper. True, it is far from .here, since it is at the other end of the camp, but we will pass quickly on horseback — so come with me."

Then turning to Povala, with whom he had become acquainted formerly at Plotsk, he added, —

"And you, noble sir. It will be an honor and a happiness for me."

" Very well," answered Povala. " It is pleasant to converse with acquaintances; and besides, we shall look at the camp."

And they went out to mount their horses. But before mounting, De Lorche's servant put the cloak on his shoulders, which evidently he had brought on purpose. When this man approached Zbyshko, he kissed his hand, and said, —

"An obeisance and honor to you, lord. I am your servant of years ago, but you cannot recognize me in the dark. Do you not remember Sanderus ? "

" As God is dear to me ! " cried Zbyshko.

At that moment was renewed in him the remembrance of past pains and sorrows, and of former misfortunes, just as a couple of weeks before, when the troops of the king joined the regiments of the princes of Mazovia, and he met his former armor-bearer Hlava after a long interval. So he said, —

"Sanderus! Well, !_ remember those former times and thee! What hast thou done since those days, and where hast thou been? Art thou bearing relics about yet?"

" No, lord. Till last spring I was a sexton at the church in Dlugolyas, but as my late father occupied himself with the military art, when the war broke out brass on the church bell-towers became disgusting to me, and the desire for steel and iron was roused in me —

" What do I hear?" cried Zbyshko, who somehow could not imagine to himself Sanderus standing up to battle, with a sword, or a spear, or an axe in his hand.

But, while holding the stirrup for him, Sauderns said, —

" A year ago, at command of the Bishop of Plotsk, 1 went VOL. n. —20

306 THE KNIGHTS OF THE CROSS.

to Prussian regions, and thereby rendered considerable service, — but I will tell that later ; and now mount, your greatness, for that Bohemian count whom you call Hlava is waiting for us with supper at the tent of my lord."

Zbyshko sat on the horse, and approaching Pan de Lorche he rode at his side so as to speak with him freely, for he was curious to learn his story.

kt I am tremendously glad," said Zbyshko, " that thouart on our side, but I wonder, for thou hast served the Knights of the Cross."

" Those serve who take pay," replied De Lorche, " but I have never taken pay. No, — I went to the Knights of the Cross only to seek adventures and win the belt of a knight, which, as is known to thee, I received from the hands of a Polish prince. And while remaining long years in those countries I came to know on whose side was justice ; and when I also married here and settled down, how could I appear against you ? I am now a man of this country, and observe how I have learned your language. • I have even forgotten my own somewhat."

u But thy property in Guelders? For, as I have heard, thou art a relative of the ruling house there, and an heir to many castles and villages."

"I yielded my inheritance to my relative, Foulk de Lorche, who paid me for it. Five years ago I was in Guelders and brought back from there considerable wealth, with which I purchased property in Mazovia."

"But how did it happen thee to marry Yagenka of Dlugolyas?"

" Ah, who can understand a woman? She trifled with me always till the time came when I was tired of such action, and declared to her that from grief I would go to a war in Asia, and never return again. She began to cry unexpectedly, and said, ' Then I will be a nun.' I fell at her feet for those words and two weeks later the Bishop of Plotsk blessed us in church."

" Hast thou children ? " inquired Zbyshko.

" After the war Yagenka is going to the grave of Queen Yadviga to implore her," answered De Lorche, sighing.

" That is well. The\'7d' say that method is certain, — and that in such cases there is no better intercessor than our holy queen. Before long all will go to Cracow, for a decisive battle will take place in a few days, and then peace will come."

" Yes."

" But the Knights of the Cross of course consider thee as a traitor ? "

"No," answered De Lorche. " Thou knowest how I guard my knightly honor. Sanderus, at command of the Bishop of Plotsk went to Malborg, so I sent through him a letter to the Grand Master Ulrich, in which I notified him of the end of my service and explained to him the reasons why I am on your side."

"Ha! Sanderus!" cried Zbyshko. "He told me that brass in the church bells has become disgusting to him, and that a desire for steel is roused in him, which seems strange to me, for he had always the heart of a hare."

Pan de Lorche laughed.

"Sanderus," said he, "has only this much to do with steel that he shaves me and my armor-bearers."

"Is that it?" asked Zbyshko, amused.

They rode on sometime in silence, then De Lorche raised his eyes toward the sky, and said, —

" I have invited you to supper, but it will be breakfast before we reach my tent."

" The moon is shining yet. Let us go on ! "

So coming up with Matsko and Povala they rode four abreast through the broad street of the camp, which was traced out, at command of the leaders, between tents and fires, so that passage might be commodious.

Wishing to reach the tents of the Mazovian regiments which were at the other end of the camp, they had to pass the whole length of it.

"Since Poland is Poland," said Matsko, "no one has seen such armies, for nations have come in from all regions of the earth."

" No other king can bring out such armies," answered De Lorche, " for no king has such a mighty kingdom."

But the old knight turned to Povala, and asked, —

" How many regiments have come with Prince Vitold ? "

"Forty," answered Povala. "Our Polish and the Mazovian regiments number fifty, but they are not arranged in the same way as Vitold's men, for with him sometimes a number of thousands serve under one banner. Ha! We have heard that the Grand Master called them a rabble, better at spoons than at swords, but God grant that he said that in an evil hour for himself, since I think that the Lithuanian spears will be terribly reddened with the blood of the Order."

"But these whom we are passing now, who are they?" inqiiil-ed Pan de Lorche.

"Those are Tartars ; Vitold's feudatory, Saladin, brought them."

" Are they good in battle ? "

" Lithuania understands how to war with those Tartars, and has conquered a considerable part of them, for this reason they were forced to come to this war. It is difficult for knights of western Europe to meet them, for they are more terrible in retreat than attack."

"Let us look at them more nearly," said De Lorche.

And they rode toward the fires, which were surrounded by men whose arms were entirely naked. They were dressed, notwithstanding the summer season, in sheep-skin coats, the wool outside. They were sleeping for the greater part directly on the ground, or on straw which was steaming from heat, but many were sitting on their heels near the blazing fires; some were shortening the night hours by singing wild songs in nasal tones and striking in accompaniment one shin bone of a horse against another, which produced a strange and disagreeable clatter; some had small drums or were thrumming on stiffly drawn bow-strings; others were eating pieces of meat freshly snatched from the fire, still steaming and bloody, on which they blew through pouting, bluish lips. In general these people looked so wild and ill-omened that it was easier to take them for some terrible creatures of the forest than human beings.

The smoke of the fires gave out a sharp odor of the horseflesh and mutton which were roasting in them, and round about from burnt hair and heated sheep-skin coats the smell was unendurable, while from fresh hides and blood it was nauseating.

From beyond the street, where there were horses, came the smell of dung and sweat; those beasts, a number of hundreds of which were kept for scouting in the neighborhood, had gnawed the grass from beneath their own feet and were biting one another, squealing shrilly, and snorting. Horseboys quieted them with their voices and with rawhide whips.

It was unsafe to go alone among the Tartars, for those wild people were greedy to a degree unheard of. Directly behind them were a few companies of Bessarabians, a little less wild, with horns on their heads; and long-haired Wal-lachians, who instead of steel armor had wooden, painted

plates on their breasts and shoulders, and wore masks representing vampires, skeletons, or beasts ; and farther on, Serbs, whose camp, asleep at that hour, sounded in the daytime at halts, as if it were one immense lute ; so many flutes, balalaikas, moltaukas, and various other musical instruments were there in it.

The fires flashed, and from the sky, amid clouds which the strong wind blew apart, shone the great clear moon, and by those gleams our knights reviewed the camp. Beyond the Serbs were situated the unfortunate Jmud men. The Germans had drawn torrents of blood from those people, and still they sprang up to new battles at every summons from Vitold. And now, as if with a prescience that their evil fate would end soon and forever, they had marched to that camp under lead of Skirvoillo, whose name alone filled the Germans with rage and with, terror. The fires of the Jmud men touched directly on those of Lithuania, for they were the same people, they had the same customs, and almost the same language.

But at the entrance of the camp of Lithuania a gloomy picture struck the eyes of the knights. There on a gallows made of unhewn poles were hanging two bodies, which the wind swayed with such force that the gallows-frame squeaked complainingly. The horses snorted at sight of the bodies and rose on their haunches, while the knights made the sign of the cross with devotion, and when they had ridden farther Povala said, —

" Prince Vitold was with the king, and I was there when men brought in the criminals. Our bishops and lords had complained previously that Lithuanians are too savage in warfare, and do not even spare churches. So when these" were brought in (they were considerable people, but the unfortunates had, as it seems, desecrated the Holy Sacrament) the prince was so filled with anger that it was a terror to look at him, and he commanded the two men to hang themselves. One of them urged on the other: ' Well, hurry! thou wilt make the prince still more angry!' And terror fell on all, for the men did not fear death, but the anger of the prince, just as much, or more, than God's anger."

" Yes, I remember," said Zbyshko, "when in Cracow the king was enraged at me about Lichtenstein, Prince Yamont, who was an attendant of the king, advised me immediately to hang myself. And he gave that advice out of friendship, though I should have challenged him to trampled earth had

it not been, as is known to you, that they were to cut my head off."

"Prince Yamont has learned knightly customs since then," said Povala.

Thus conversing the\'7d' passed the great camp of Lithuania and the three splendid regiments of Rus, of which the largest was that of Smolensk, and went to the Polish campground. In that were fifty regiments, the kernel and also the forehead of all the forces. In that camp the armor was superior, the horses larger, and the knights better exercised, being second in nothing to those from the "West of Europe. In strength of body, in endurance of hunger, of cold, and of labor, those men from Great and Little Poland even surpassed the warriors of the West, who were softer and more intent on their own comfort. The Poles were simpler in manners, their armor was more rudely forged, but its temper was better, while their disdain for death and their immense persistence in battle astonished many a time those knights from afar, in those days, the French and English.

De Lorche, who knew Polish knights from of old spoke thus, —

" Here is the strength and the hope. I remember that in Malborg the knights complained more than once that in battle they were forced to purchase every hand-breadth of earth with streams of blood."

" Blood will flow in a river now also," said Matsko, " for the Order has never assembled such forces thus far."

"The Knight Korzbog, who went with letters from the king to the Grand Master," added Povala, " declared that the Knights of the Cross say that neither the Roman Caesar nor any king has such forces, and that the Order could conquer all kingdoms."

" Pshaw ! we are greater in number," said Zbyshko.

" That is true, but they think little of Vitold's forces, because made up, as they say, of men armed in any fashion, and because they are crushed at the first blow, like an earthen pot beneath a hammer. But whether that be true or untrue, I know not."

"It is true, and untrue," answered the prudent Matsko. 41 Zbyshko and I campaigned with them once. Their weapons are inferior, and their horses are small, hence it happens often that they flee before the onset of Knights of the Order ; but their hearts are as brave, or even braver than those of the Germans."

" That will be shown soon," said Povala. " Tears flow to the king's eyes continually at the thought that so much Christian blood will be shed, and at the very last moment he would be glad to conclude a just peace, but the pride of the Knights will not let matters end thus."

"• As true as life ! I know the Knights of the Order, and we all know them," added Matsko. " God has already arranged the scales on which he will place our blood and that of the enemies of our race."

They were not far now from the Mazovian regiments, among which stood the tent of Pan de Lorche, when the\ - saw in the middle of the " street " a large crowd of people close together and looking at the sky.

" Stand, there ! stand ! " cried a voice in the crowd.

" But who is speaking, and what are ye doing? " inquired Povala.

"I am the parish priest of Klobuko. But who are ye?"

"Povala of Tachev, the knights of Bogdanets, and Pan de Lorche."

"Oh, that is you, lords," said the priest in a mysterious voice, as he approached Povala's horse. "But look at the moon and see what is happening on it. This night is prophetic and wonderful! "

The knights raised their faces and looked at the moon, which had grown pale, and was near to its setting.

"I cannot distinguish anything," said Povala. "But what do you see ? "

" A monk in a cowl is fighting with a king who is wearing his crown. Look! Oh, there! In the name of the Father, the Son, and the Spirit ! Oh, how terribly they wrestle, — God be merciful to us sinners."

There was silence round about, for all held the breath in their breasts.

" Look ! look! " cried the priest.

" True, there is something there," said Matsko.

" True ! true ! " confirmed others.

"Ha! the king has thrown the monk!" cried the priest on a sudden. " He has put his foot on him ! Praised be Jesus Christ ! "

" For ages of ages ! "

At that moment a great black cloud covered the moon, and the night became dark, but the light of fires quivered in bloody stripes across the road.

The knights rode on, and when they had gone some distance Povala inquired, —

Did ye see anything? "

"At first, nothing," answered Matsko, "but afterward I saw distinctly both the king and the monk." • "Audi."

" And I."

" That is a sign from the Lord," said Povala. " Ah, in spite of the tears of our king, it is evident that there will be 110 peace."

"And the battle will be such as the world does not remember," said Matsko.

And they went farther in silence, with hearts overflowing and solemn.

But when they were not far from De Lorche's tent a whirlwind rose with such force that in the twinkle of an eye it scattered the fires of the Mazovians. Through the air went thousands of firebrands, blazing splinters, and sparks, while it was filled with clouds of smoke.

" Hei; it is blowing dreadfully!" said Zbyshko, pulling down his cloak which the wind had thrown over his head.

" And in the wind it is as if groans and the weeping of people were heard."

" Dawn is not distant, but who knows what the day will bring him?" added De Lorche.

CHAPTER LXXIX.

AT dawn the wind not only did not cease, but it rose to such a degree that men could not pitch that tent in which from the beginning of the expedition the king had heard three holy masses each day. At last Vitold ran up with entreaties and the prayer to defer service to a more fitting time in forest quiet, and not to delay the advance. His wish was in fact gratified, for it could not be otherwise. At sunrise the armies moved in a body, and behind them an endless train of wagons.

After they had marched an hour the wind went down somewhat, so that the flags were unfurled. And then the fields to an immense extent were covered, as it were, with flowers of a hundred colors. No eye could embrace the legions, or that forest of various banners under which the regiments moved forward. The land of Cracow advanced under a red banner with a white, crowned eagle; that was the grand banner of the kingdom, the chief standard of all the troops. It was borne by Martsin of Vrotsimovitse, a knight mighty and famous. Behind it marched the household regiment; one body had the double cross of Lithuania above it, the other a knight with a sword raised to strike. Under the banner of Saint George marched a powerful division of mercenaries and foreign volunteers, formed mainly of Moravians and Bohemians. Many of these had volunteered for that war, since the 49th regiment was made up of them exclusively. Those men were properly infantry, which marched behind the lancers ; they were wild, unruly, but so trained to battle, and so terrible in encounter, that all other infantry when they struck on these sprang away as quickly as possible, just as a dog starts back from a porcupine. Battle-axes, scythes, common axes, and especially iron flails formed their weapons, which they wielded in a manner that was simply terrible. They took service with any one who paid them, as their only element was war, plunder, and slaughter.

At the side of the Moravians and Bohemians marched under their own banner sixteen regiments of the Polish lands, among these one from Premysl, one from Lvov, one from Galicia, three from Podolia, and behind them infantry from

the same lands armed mainly with pikes and scythes. The princes of Mazovia, Yanush, and Ziemovit led the 21st, 22nd, and 23rd regiments. Next marched the bishops', and then the nobles' regiments to the number of twenty-two. Hence Yasko of Tarnov, Yendrek of Tenchyn, Spytko Leliva, Kron of Ostrovo, and Mikolai of Mihalov, and Zbigniev of Brezie, and Kuba of Konietspole, and Yasko of Ligenza, and the Kmitas, and the Zakliks, — and besides them the houses of Gryfits, and the Bobovskis, and Kozli Rogi, and others who assembled in battle under a common escutcheon and " watchword." And so the land bloomed beneath them, as fields bloom in spring. A sea of horses moved forward, and a sea of men, above them a forest of lances with colored streamers, like small flowers, and in the rear, in clouds of dust, the townspeople and the free earth-tillers' infantry. They knew that they were going to a dreadful battle, but they knew that it was " necessary," hence they advanced with willing hearts.

On the right wing moved the legions of Vitold, under banners of various colors, but with the same device, the Lithuanian knight with upraised sword. No eye could take in all the legions, for they marched through fields and forests for a width of almost five English miles.

Before midday the armies came near Logdau and Tannen-berg. and halted at the edge of a forest. The place seemed to be suited for rest and secure from sudden attack ; for on the left flank it was protected by the water of Lake Dom-brovna, on the right by Lake Luben; before the armies an expanse of field was open to the width of five miles.

In the centre of that expanse, rising gently toward the west, were the fields of Griiuwald, and a little to the right stood the gray straw roofs, and the empty melancholy fallow lands of Tannenberg. The enemy, who could descend toward the forest from the height, might be seen easily, but it was not supposed that they could come up sooner than the day following. So the armies halted there only to rest; but since Zyndram, skilled in matters of war, had preserved, even while marching, the order of battle, they took position so that they might be ready for action at any instant.

At command of the leader they sent forward immediately, on light and swift horses, scouts in the direction of Griin-wald and Tannenberg, and still farther to examine the region around. But meanwhile the chapel tent was pitched on the

lofty bank of Lake Luben, for the king was eager for divine service, so that he might hear his usual masses.

Yagello, Vitold, the Mazovian princes, and the military council betook themselves to the tent. Before it had assembled the foremost of the knights, both to commit themselves to God before the dreadful day and to look at the king. And they saw him as he went in coarse campaign clothing, with a serious countenance on which grievous care had settled visibly. Years had changed his form little, and had not covered his face with wrinkles or whitened his hair, which at that time he put behind his ears with the same quick movement as the first time when Zbyshko saw him in Cracow. But he walked as if bent beneath that tremendous responsibility which weighed on his shoulders, and as if he were sunk in great sorrow. In the army men said to one another that the king wept continually over the Christian blood which was to be shed, and it was so in reality. Yagello trembled in view of war, especially with men who bore the cross on their mantles and banners, and he desired peace with all his soul. In vain did the Polish lords, and even the Hungarian mediators Stsibor and Gara represent to him the haughtiness and confidence of the Order, with which the Grand Master Ulrich was filled. Ulrich was ready to challenge the whole world to battle. It was in vain that the king's own envoy, Peter Korzbog, swore on the cross of the Lord, and on his own escutcheon that the Order would not hear of peace, and that Count von Wende, the comtur of Gniev, was the only man inclined toward it; other knights of the Order covered Count Wende with ridicule and insults, and still the kin<$ had hope that the enemy would recognize the justice of his demands, spare human blood, and end the terrible dispute with a just treaty.

He went, therefore, to pray for this object in the chapel; his simple and kindly soul was tormented with immense fear. In former days Yagello had visited with fire and sword the lands of the Order; that he had done, however, when he was a pagan prince of Lithuania, but now, when as a Polish king and a Christian he saw burning villages, ruins, blood, and tears, he was seized with the fear of God's anger, especially since that was only the beginning of war. If it might stop even there! But to-day or to-morrow nations would exterminate each other, and the earth would be steeped in blood. That enemy is unjust indeed, but still he carries the cross on his mantle, and he is defended by such great

and holy relics that the mind draws back before them in terror. The whole army also thought of these relics with fear. Not spears, nor swords, nor axes did the Poles dread chiefly, but those holy relics. "How raise a hand on the Grand Master?" asked knights who knew no fear, "if on his armor he bears a reliquary, and in it the bones of saints and the wood of the cross of the Saviour."

Vitold was burning for war, it is true; he urged to it and he hurried to the battle, but the pious heart of the king became cowardly when he thought of those heavenly powers with which the Order had shielded its injustice.

CHAPTER LXXX.

FATHER BARTOSH of Klobuko had finished one mass, Yarosh, the parish priest of Kaliska, was soon to begin a second, and the king had gone out in front of the tent to straighten his knees wearied somewhat with kneeling, when a noble, Hanko Ostoichyk, rushed up on a foaming horse, like a whirlwind, and shouted before he sprang from the saddle, —

" Germans! Gracious lord ! — they are coming! "

At these words the knights started, the king's face changed; he was silent during the twinkle of an eye, and then exclaimed, —

"Praised be Jesus Christ! Where didst thou see them, and how many regiments ? "

" I saw one regiment at Griinwald," answered Hanko, with a panting voice; " but beyond the hill dust is moving, as if more were advancing."

" Praised be Jesus Christ," repeated the king.

Hereupon Vitold, to whose face the blood rushed at the first word from Hanko, and whose eyes began to burn like coals, turned to the courtiers, and cried, —

" Defer the second mass ! Bring a horse for me ! " 'The king placed his hand on Vitold's shoulder, and said: " Go thou, brother, but I will remain and hear the second mass."

Vitold and Zyndram sprang to their horses; but just at the moment when they turned toward the camp, Peter Oksha, a second scout, flew up shouting from a distance, —

" The Germans ! the Germans ! I saw two regiments ! "

" To horse !! " called voices among the courtiers and the knights.

But Peter had not ceased shouting, when again the clatter of horse-hoofs was heard, and a third scout rushed up, after him a fourth, a fifth, and a sixth. All had seen German regiments advancing in greater and greater numbers. There was no longer a doubt that the whole army of the Order would bar the road to the troops of Yagello.

The knights scattered in a twinkle; each rushed to his own regiment. With the king at the chapel tent remained

only a company of courtiers, priests, and attendants. At that moment a bell sounded, in sign that the parish priest of Kaliska was beginning the second mass, so Yagello, stretching out his arms, placed his hands together piously, and raising them toward heaven, entered the tent with deliberate step.

A Yhen, after the second mass, the king went out again in front of the tent, he could convince himself with his own eyes that the scouts had spoken truly., for on the edges of the broad sloping plain something seemed black, as if a pine wood had grown up suddenly on the empty fields, while above that pine wood, colors played and changed in the sunlight, a rainbow of banners. Still more distant, far off beyond Grilnwald and Tannenberg, a gigantic cloud of dust was rising toward the sky.

The king took in at a glance that whole tremendous horizon, then turning to the reverend vice-chancellor Mikolai, he inquired, —

"Who is the saint of to-day? "

" This is the day of the sending of the Apostles," answered the vice-chancellor.

The king sighed, and said in a sad, broken voice, —

" So the clay of the apostles will be the last in life, for the many thousands of Christians who will fall on this field."

And he indicated with his hand the broad, empty plain in the middle of which, about half-way to Tannenberg, stood a group of oaks centuries old.

Meanwhile, his horse was led up, and in the distance appeared sixty lancers whom Zyndram had sent to be the king's body-guard.

This guard was led by Alexander, the youngest son of the Prince of Plotsk, a brother of that Ziemovit who, gifted with exceptional "wisdom in war," had sat in the military council. Next to Alexander in command was Zygmunt Korybut, a Lithuanian, and nephew of the monarch, a. youth of great hopes and great destinies, but of restless spirit. Of the knights most famous were: Yasko Monjyk of Dombrova. a genuine giant, almost equal in bulk to Pashko, and in strength yielding but little to Zavisha Charny; Zolava, a Bohemian baron, small and slender, but of immense skill, famous at the courts of Bohemia and Hungary for duels, in which he had brought down between ten and twenty Austrian nobles ; and Sokol, another Bohemiau,

an archer above archers; Beniash Verush of Great Poland, and Peter of Milan, and the Lithuanian boyar Senko of Po-host, whose father, Peter, led a Smolensk regiment; and Prince Fedushko, a relative of the king ; Prince Yamont, and finally Polish knights '• chosen from thousands ; " these had all sworn to defend the king from every mishap of war, to the last drop of their blood. And immediately near the person of Yagello were the reverend vice-chancellor Mikolai, and the royal secretary Zbigniev of Olesnitsa, a young man of learning, skilled in letters and in writing, who at the same time surpassed in strength men of his years considerably. The king's weapons were cared for by three armor-bearers: Chaika of Novy Dvor, Mikolai of Moravitsa, and Danilko of Rus, who carried the king's bow and quiver. The suite was completed by some tens of attendants who, mounted on swift horses, were to rush to the armies with orders.

The armor-bearers arrayed their lord in brilliant, glittering mail, then they led up to him a chestnut steed, also " chosen from thousands," which snorted, as a good omen, beneath its steel head-piece, and, filling the air with a neigh, reared somewhat, like a bird about to fly. The king, when he felt the steed under him and a spear in his hand, changed in a flash. Sadness vanished from his face, his small dai'k eyes glittered, and on his cheeks appeared a flush; but that was only during an instant, for when the reverend vice-chancellor began to make the sign of the cross on him he grew serious again and bent humbly his head, which was covered with a silvery helmet.

Meanwhile the German army, descending gradually from the elevated plain, passed Grvinwald, passed Tannenberg and halted at the middle of the plain in complete battle array. From below, from the Polish camp, that tremendous line of gigantic knights and horses enclosed in mail, was perfectly visible. In so far as was permitted by the wind which moved the banners, quick eyes distinguished accurately various designs embroidered on them, such as crosses, eagles, griffins, swords, helmets, lambs, bison and bear heads.

Old Matsko and Zbyshko, who had warred previously with Knights of the Order and knew their troops and escutcheons, showed their Sieradz friends two regiments of the Master himself, in which served the very flower and choice of the knighthood, and the grand banner of the whole Order, which was carried by Friedrich von "Wallenrod, and the banner of Saint George with a red cross on a white

ground — and many other banners of the Order. But unknown to them were the standards of the various foreign guests, thousands of whom had come from every country in Europe: from Austria, Bavaria, Suabia, Switzerland, from Burgundy, famous for its knighthood, from rich Flanders, from sunny France,— whose knights, as Matsko had declared on a time, even if prostrate on the earth, would still utter words of bravery, — and from England beyond the sea, the birthplace of terrible archers whom Mazovian hunters alone could equal — and even from distant Spain, where amid ceaseless struggles with Saracens manhood and honor had flourished in a way to surpass all other countries. And the blood began to storm in the veins of those strong nobles from Sieradz, Konietspole, Kresnia, Bogdanets, Rogov, and Brozova, as well as from other Polish lands, at the thought that they would have soon to join battle with the Germans, and with all that brilliant knighthood of Europe. The faces of the older men grew stern and serious, for they knew how dreadful and merciless that work would be; while the hearts of the young men began to whine, just as hunting dogs whine when, held on a leash, they see the wild beast at a distance. So some of them, grasping more firmly in their hands lances, hilts of swords, and handles of axes, reined back their horses, as if to let them go at a dash; others breathed hurriedly, as if for them it had grown too narrow in their armor.

But the more experienced warriors calmed the younger men by saying: "It will not miss you; there will be plenty for each — God grant that there be not too much."

But the Knights of the Cross, looking from above at that forest plain, saw on the edge of the pine wood only a few Polish regiments, and they were not at all certain that the army with the king at the head of it was before them. It was true that on the left, at the lake, were visible also gray crowds of warriors, and in the bushes glittered something like lance-points, that is, light spears used by Lithuanians. That, however, might be only a considerable scouting party of Poles. Spies from captured Gilgenburg, a number of whom had been brought before the Master, were the first to declare that in front of him stood all the Polish-Lithuanian forces.

But in vain did they speak of the strength of those forces. The Grand Master would not believe them, for from the beu;inuino; of that war he believed only what was favorable

to him, and which augured inevitable victory. He sent out neither scouts nor spies, thinking that there must be a general battle in every case, and that the battle could end only in dreadful defeat for the enemy. Confident in a force such as no previous Grand Master had ever brought to the field he despised his opponent, and when the comtur of Gniev, who had made investigations himself, explained to him that Yagello's troops were more numerous than those of the Order, he answered: "What troops are they? With the Poles alone shall we have to struggle soteewhat but the rest, even if greater in number, are the last of men, better at a spoon than a weapon."

And, hastening with all his forces to the battle, he was flushed with great delight, for all at once he found himself face to face with the enemy. The purple of the grand banner of the kingdom, seen on the dark background of the forest, permitted no further doubt that before him the main army had its position.

It was impossible, however, for the Germans to attack the Poles standing near the pine wood and in it, for the Knights of the Order were formidable only on the open field; they did not like battle in dense forests, and knew not how to fight in them.

Therefore they assembled in brief council, at the side of the Grand Master, to determine how to entice the enemy out of the forest.

"By Saint George! " exclaimed the Grand Master. "We have ridden ten miles without resting; the heat is oppressive and our bodies are covered with sweat beneath our armor. We shall not wait here till it please the enemy to come forth to meet us! "

To this Count Wende, a man important through age and knowledge, replied, —

"My words have been ridiculed here already, and ridiculed by those who, as God knows, will flee from this field on which I shall fall " (here he looked at Werner von Tetlingen), "but I shall say what my conscience commands as well as my love for the Order. The Poles lack not courage, but, *as I know, the king is hoping till the last moment for messengers of peace."

Werner von Tetlingen made no reply; he merely snorted with contemptuous laughter.

Wende's words were not pleasing to the Grand Master, so he answered, — voi. n. — 21

"Is it a time now to think of peace? We have to counsel about another affair."

"There is time always for God's business," answered Von TVende.

But Heinrich, the fierce comtur of Chluhov, who had sworn that he would have two naked swords borne before him till he could plunge both in Polish blood, turned his thick, sweating face to the Master and exclaimed in great auger, —

"Death is dearer to me than infamy, and even were I alone, I should attack with these swords the whole Polish army!"

Ulrich frowned somewhat.

"Thou art speaking against discipline!" said he.

Then he said to the comturs, —

"Take counsel only as to how we shall entice the enemy out of the forest."

So different men gave different counsels, till finally Gers-dof's plan pleased both the comturs and the foremost guests, namely: to despatch two heralds to the king with the announcement that the Grand Master sends two swords to him, and challenges the Poles to mortal combat; and if they have not field enough, he will withdraw somewhat with his army so as to yield proper space to them.

The king was going just then from the edge of the lake to the left wing of the Polish regiments, where he had to belt a whole assembly of knights, when on a sudden he was informed that two heralds were coming from the army of the Order.

Vladislav Yagello's heart beat with hope.

"Now they are coming with a just peace! "

"God grant! " said the priests.

The king sent for Vitold, but he, occupied with marshalling his troops, could not go to Yagello. Meanwhile the heralds, without hurry, approached the camp. In the bright sunlight they were perfectly visible on immense war-horses covered with housings; one of the men had on his shield the black eagle of the Caesar on a golden ground, the other, who was a herald of the Prince of Stettin, had a griffin on a white ground. The ranks opened in front of them; they dismounted and stood for a while before the king, and then kneeling, but not to show honor, accomplished their mission.

"The Grand Master Ulrich," said the first herald, "challenges thy majesty, O lord, and Prince Vitold to mortal battle, and to rouse the bravery which evidently is lacking you, he sends these two naked swords."

When he had said this he placed the swdrds at the king's feet.

Yasko Monjyk of Dombrova interpreted these words, but barely had he finished, when the second herald pushed forth and spoke thus,—

"The Grand Master Ulrich has commanded to inform you also, lord, that if the field for battle is too narrow he will withdraw his troops somewhat so that you should not remain idle in the forest."

Yasko again interpreted his words, and silence followed. But in the king's suite the knights gritted their teeth in secret at such insolence and insults.

Yagello's last hopes were dissipated like smoke. He had waited for an embassy of peace and concord; an embassy of pride and war had come. He raised his tearful eyes, and answered,—

"We have swords in abundance, but I accept these as a presage of victory which God himself sends into my hands through you. And the field of battle will be determined also by Him, to whose justice I turn now and make complaint of the wrongs done my people, and of your pride and injustice."

Two great tears flowed down his sunburnt cheeks. Meanwhile the voices of the knights in the suite were heard saying,—

"The Germans are withdrawing. They are giving the field!"

The heralds rode away, and after a while they were seen again advancing up the hill on their immense horses, and seemed brilliant in the sunlight from silk which they wore above their armor.

The Polish armies advanced somewhat from the forest and thickets in regular order. In front marched the body which was called "the forehead," formed of the most formidable knights; behind them the "main body," and after the main body infantry and mercenaries. In that way was formed between the bodies two long streets through which Zyndram and Vitold were flying; the latter, without a helmet on his head, in splendid armor, was like a flame driven forward by the wind.

The knights took deep breaths into their breasts and fixed themselves firmly in their saddles. The battle was to begin right there.

The Grand Master was looking meanwhile at the king's army which had come out of the forest.

He looked long at the immensity of it, at the wings spread out like those of an enormous bird, at the banners moved by the wind, and suddenly the heart was pressed in him by some terrible, unknown feeling. It may be that he saw with the eyes of his soul piles of corpses and rivers of blood. He had no fear of man, but perhaps he feared God, who up there in the heights of heaven was holding the scales of victory. For the first time it came to his mind what a ghastly day that would be, and for the first time he felt the responsibility which he had taken on his shoulders.

His face grew pale, his lips quivered, and from his eyes came abundant tears. The comturs glanced at their leader with amazement.

"What is troubling tbee, lord?" inquired Count Wende.

"Indeed this is a fitting time for tears!" said the fierce Heinrich, comtur of Chluhov.

The grand comtur, Kuno Lichtenstein, pouted, and said,—

"I censure this openly, Master, for now it becomes, thee to rouse the hearts of the knights, and not weaken them. In truth we have never seen thee thus up to this moment."

But in spite of all efforts tears flowed to the Grand Master's black beard, as if some other person were weeping within him.

At last, however, he controlled himself somewhat, and turning stern eyes on the comturs he commanded, —

"To the regiments!"

They sprang each man to his own regiment, for the Master had uttered his words with great power; and stretching his hand to the armor-bearer, he said, —

"Give me the helmet! "

Men's hearts in both armies were beating like hammers, but the trumpets had not given the call yet for battle. A moment of expectation had come, which was more grievous perhaps than battle itself. On the field, between the Germans and the army of the king, there towered up, on the side toward Tannenberg, a group of oaks, centuries old, on to which peasants of the neighborhood had climbed, so

as to gaze at the struggle of those armies more gigantic than the world had seen within time to be remembered. But apart from this one group of trees the whole field was vacant, gray, ghastly, resembling a lifeless steppe. Nothing moved on it but the wind, while above it death was hovering in silence. The eyes of the knights turned in spite of them to that ominous and silent plain. Clouds which rushed over the sky hid the sun at intervals, and the gloom of death settled down in those moments.

A whirlwind rose up now. It roared through the forest tearing thousands of leaves away; it rushed into the field, seized dry grass-blades, whirled clouds of dust upward, and bore them into the eyes of the Knights of the Order.

At that very moment the air quivered from the shrill sound of horns, crooked trumpets, whistles; and the entire Lithuanian wing rose like a countless flock of birds when ready to fly.

They started, as was their custom, at a gallop. The horses, stretching their necks and dropping their ears, tore forward with all the strength that was in them; the riders flew on with a terrible shout, raising their swords and lances, against the left wing of the Knights of the Order.

The Grand Master was there just at that moment. His emotion had passed, and from his eyes sparks issued now instead of tears. Seeing the hurrying legions of Lithuania, he turned to Friedrich Wallenrod, who led the left wing of the Order, and said, —

"Vitold has attacked first. Begin you — in the name of God!"

And with a movement of his right hand he sent forward fourteen regiments of the Knights encased from head to foot in iron.

"Gott mit uns (God with us)! " cried Wallenrod.

The regiments, lowering their lances, began to advance at a walk. Then, precisely like a rock pushed from a mountain side which falls and gains ever increasing impetus, they from a walk passed to a trot, and then to a gallop, and rushed forward irresistible, like an avalanche which must rub out and crush everything in front of it.

The earth groaned and bent under them.

The battle might extend any moment and flame up along the whole line, hence the Polish regiments began to sing the ancient war hymn of Saint Voytseh. A hundred thousand heads covered with iron, and a hundred thousand pairs of

eyes were upraised, and from a hundred thousand breasts came forth one gigantic voice which was like the thunder of heaven,

" Mother of God, Virgin, Glorified of God, Mary! From Thy Son, our Lord, O Mother whom we implore, only Mother, Obtain for us — pardon of sins 1 Kyrie eleison!"

And there was such an immense, such a tremendous and conquering force in those voices and in that hymn, as if indeed the thunders of heaven had begun to tear themselves free. Spears quivered in the hands of the knights, banners and flags quivered, the air quivered, tree branches quivered in the forest, and the echoes roused in the pine wood began to answer in the depths, to call, and, as it were, to repeat to the lakes, to the fields, to the whole land in the length and the breadth of it, —

" Obtain for us — pardon of sins ! Kyrie eleison!! "

And they sang on, —

" This is the holy time Of Thy Son the Crucified. Hear Thou this prayer which we raise to Thee; Bear it to Him, we implore of Thee: ' Give, Lord, on earth worthy life to us; After life give us a dwelling in paradise,' Kyrie eleison — "

The echo repeated in answer, "Kyrie Eleiso-o-o-on! " Meanwhile, on the right wing a stubborn battle had commenced, and it moved more and more toward the centre.

The uproar, the squealing of horses, the terrible shouts of men were mingled with the hymn. But at moments the shouts ceased, as if breath failed the combatants, and during one of those intervals it was possible once more to distinguish those thundering voices, —

" Adam, thou God's assistant, Thou who art in Divine company, Place us, thy children, where Angels are reigning; Where there is gladness, Where there is love, Where angels see their Creator forever, Kyrie eleison — "

And again the echo "Kyrie eleiso-o-on! " rushed through the pine wood. The shouts on the right wing increased, but no one could see or distinguish what was taking place there, for the Grand Master Ulrich, looking from above at the battle, hurled on the Poles in that moment twenty regiments under the lead of Kuno Lichtenstein.

Zyndram rushed like a thunderbolt to the Polish head legion, in which the very foremost knights were, and pointing with his sword to the approaching host of Germans, he cried so piercingly that the horses in the first rank rose on their haunches, —

"At them! —Strike!"

Then the knights, bending forward over the shoulders of their horses, and pointing their spears out in front of them, started.

The Lithuanians bent beneath the terrible onrush of the Germans. The first ranks, formed of the best armed and richest boyars, fell to the ground as flat as a bridge. The following ones closed in rage with the Knights of the Order; but no bravery, no endurance, no human power could save them from defeat and destruction. And how could it be otherwise, since on one side fought a knighthood completely enclosed in armor, and on horses protected also with armor; on the other, large men, it is true, and strong, but on small horses, and protected themselves by skins only? In vain, therefore, did the stubborn Lithuanians seek to reach the skin of the Germans. Spears, sabres, lance-points, clubs set with flint or nails rebounded from the metallic "plates" as they would from a cliff, or the wall of a castle. The weight of the German warriors and horses crashed Vitold's unfortunate legions; they were cut by swords and axes, their bones were pierced and crushed by halberds, they were trampled by horse-hoofs. Prince Vitold hurled vainly into those jaws of death new legions; vain was persistence, useless was rage, fruitless contempt of death, and rivers of blood were unavailing!

The Tartars fled first, then the Bessarabians with Walla-chians; and soon the Lithuanian wall burst, and wild panic seized all the warriors.

^ The greater part of the Lithuanian troops fled in the direction of Lake Luben, and after them chased the main German forces, making such a terrible harvest that the whole shore was covered with corpses.

Meanwhile the second and smaller part, in which were three regiments of Smolensk, withdrew toward the Polish wing pressed by six German regiments, and later by those also who returned from pursuing. But the men of Smolensk, better armed, gave more effective resistance. The battle here turned into a slaughter. Every step, almost every hand's breadth of laud was bought with torrents of blood. One of the Smolensk regiments was almost cut to pieces, but two others defended themselves with desperation and rage, resembling that of a wild boar when attacked by a company of bears. Nothing, however, could stop the irrepressible Germans.

Some of their regiments were seized by the frenzy of battle. Single knights, spun-ing their rearing steeds, rushed on at random with upraised axe or sword into the densest throng of the enemy. The blows of their swords and axes were almost preterhuman; the whole body, thrusting, trampling, and crushing horses and riders of the Smolensk regiments, came at last to the flank of the main forehead, and main Polish legion, for two regiments during more than an hour had struggled with the Germans led by Kuno Lichtenstein.

The task was not so easy for the Knights of the Order in that spot, since there was equality of arms and horses, and similar knightly training. So the Polish "wood" even stopped the Germans and pushed them back, especially when three terrible regiments struck them: the Cracow, the light horse, under Yendrek of Brohotsitse, and the household regiment, which was led by Povala of Tachev.

But the battle raged with the greatest din when, after the spears had been broken, men took to swords and axes. Shield struck shield then, man struggled with man, horses fell, banners were hurled to the earth; under the blows of hummers and axes, helmets, shoulder-pieces and breastplates burst, iron was covered with blood, heroes dropped from their saddles as pines fall when their trunks are chopped through.

Those Knights of the Cross who at Vilno had been in battles with the Poles, knew how "unbending" and "persistent" a people they were, but new men and guests from abroad were seized at once with amazement akin to terror. Many a knight reined in his steed without thinking, looked ahead with doubt, and before he could decide what to do he had perished.

And just as hail falls unsparingly from bronze-colored clouds on to wheat fields, so thickly did merciless blows fall, swords struck, axes struck — they struck without halt, without pity; they sounded like iron plates in a forge; death extinguished lives as a whirlwind puts out tapers; groans were wrested from breasts, eyes were quenched, and the whitened faces of youth sank into endless night.

Upward flew sparks struck out by iron, fragments of lance-handles, shreds of flags, ostrich and peacock plumes. Horse-hoofs slipped on bloody armor lying on the ground, and on bodies of horses. Whoso fell wounded was mashed by horseshoes.

But of the foremost Polish knights no one had fallen thus far, and they advanced in a throng and an uproar, shouting the names of their patrons, or the war cry of their families. They went as fire sweeps along a parched steppe, fire which devours grass and bushes. The foremost,

Lis of Targovisko seized the conitur of Osterode, Gamrat, who, losing his shield, wound his white mantle around his arm and shielded himself from blows with it. But Lis cut through the mantle and the armor and crushed the German shoulder-blade with a thrust; he pierced the comtur's stomach, and his sword-point gritted against the man's spinal column. The people of Osterode screamed with fear on seeing the death of their leader, but Lis rushed in among them as an eagle among cranes, and when Stashko and Domarat hurried to help him, the three together shelled lives out dread-full\'7d", — just as bears shell pods after entering a field in which green peas are growing.

There Pashko killed a brother of the Order, Kune Adels-bach; Kune, when be saw the giant before him, grasping a gory axe on which were blood and matted hair, was terrified in heart and wished to yield himself captive; but to his destruction Pashko did not hear in the din, and rising in his stirrups split the man's head with its steel helmet as one might cut an apple. Immediately afterward he quenched Loch of Mexlenburg and Klingenstein, and the Swabian Helmsdorf of a great county family, and Limpach of May-ence, and Nachtervits also from Mayence, till at last the Germans began to retreat before him to the left and the right in terror; but he struck at them as at a tottering wall, and every moment it was seen how he rose in his saddle for a blow, then were visible the gleam of his axe and a German helmet going down between horses.

330 THE KKIGHTS OF THE CROSS.

There also was the powerful Yendrek of Brohotsitse, who, when he had broken his sword on the head of a Knight who had an owl's face on his shield, and a visor in the form of an owl's head, seized him by the arm, crushed him, and snatching the man's sword, took his life from him with it immediately. He also seized the young Knight Dunnheim, whom, seeing without a helmet, he had not the heart to kill; being almost a child, Dunnheim looked at him with the eyes of a child. Yendrek threw him, therefore, to his attendants, not thinking that he had taken a son-in-law, for that young knight afterward married his daughter and remained thenceforth in Poland.

Now the Germans pressed on with rage, wishing to rescue young Dilunheim, who came of a wealthy family of counts on the Rhine, but the knights before the banner, Sumik and two brothers from Plomykov, and Dobko Okwia, and Zyh Pykna, pushed them back, as a lion pushes back a bull, and pressed them toward the banner of Saint George, spreading destruction and ruin among them.

With the knightly guests fought the royal household regiment, which was led by Tsiolek of Zelihov. There Povala of Tachev overturned men and horses with his preterhuman strength, and crushed steel helmets as if they had been eggshells. He struck a whole crowd alone; and with him went Leshko of Goray, also another Povala, of Vyhuch, and Mstislav of Skrynev, and two Bohemians, Sokol and Zbis-lavek. Long did the struggle last here, for three German regiments fell on that single one; but when Yasko of Tarnov came with the 27th regiment to assist, the forces were more or less equal, and the Germans were driven back almost half the shot of a crossbow from the point where the first encounter had happened.

But they were hurled still farther by the great Cracow regiment, which Zyndram himself brought, and at the head of which among the men before the banner went the most formidable of all Poles, Zavisha Charny. At his side fought his brother Farurey, and Florian Yelitchyk, and Skarbek. Under the terrible hand of Zavisha valiant men perished, as if in that black armor death were advancing in person to meet them. He fought with frowning brow and distended nostrils, calm, attentive, as if performing some ordinary labor; at times he moved his shield slightly, warded off blows, but at each flash of his sword the terrible cry of a stricken man gave answer, while he did not even

look around, but advanced, toiling forward, like a black cloud out of which from moment to moment a lightning flash crashes. ,

The regiment of Poznan, having for its ensign a crown-less eagle, fought also for life and death, while the archbishop's regiment and the three Mazovian regiments advanced with it in rivalry. But all the others too surpassed one another in venom and in valor. In the Sieradz regiment Zbyshko of Bogdanets rushed like a raging wild boar into the thickest of the throng; at his side went old Matsko, terrible, fighting with judgment, as a wolf fights which bites to kill and not otherwise.

Matsko sought Kuno Lichtenstein with his eyes on all sides, but, unable to see him in the throng, he selected others, those who wore the richest armor, and he hewed persistently. Not far from the two knights of Bogdanets the ominous Stan of Rogov fought wildly. At the first encounter his helmet was broken; so he fought bareheaded, terrifying the Germans with his hairy and bloody face which seemed not human, but the face of some monster of the forest which they saw before them.

But hundreds and then thousands of knights, on both sides, covered the earth — till at last, under the blows of raging Poles, the battered German wall began to totter; then something happened capable of changing the fate of the whole battle in one moment.

Returning from the pursuit of the Lithuanians, heated and intoxicated with victory, the German regiments saw before them the flank of the Polish wing. Judging that all the king's armies were beaten and the battle won decisively, they were returning in great unordered crowds, with shouting and singing, when they beheld all at once in front of them a savage slaughter, and the Poles, almost victorious, surrounding the German legions.

So these Knights of the Order, lowering their heads, looked with astonishment through the openings of their visors at what was happening, and then where each one stood he thrust spurs into his horse's flanks and rushed into the whirl of battle.

And so thr6ng followed throng, till soon thousands hurled themselves at the Polish regiments now wearied with battle. The Germans shouted with delight when they saw approaching aid, and began to strike at the Poles with new ardor.

A desperate battle seethed up throughout the whole line -, torrents of blood flowed along the earth; the sky grew cloudy and dull thunder rolls were heard, as if God himself wished to interfere between the combatants.

But the victory was inclining toward the Germans. Disorder was just beginning in the Polish body; the legions of the Knights of the Order were growing frenzied, and had begun in one voice to sing the hymn of triumph, —

" Christ ist erstanden ! (Christ has arisen! )"

But just then something still more tremendous took place. One of the Knights of the Order while lying on the ground opened with a knife the belly of the horse ridden by Mart-sin of Vrotsimovitse, who bore the grand banner of Cracow, a crowned eagle, which was sacred for all the king's armies. Steed and rider went down on a sudden ; with them the banner tottered and fell.

In one moment hundreds of arms were stretched out to grasp the banner. From all German breasts a roar of delight burst forth. It seemed to them that the end had come, that terror and panic would seize the Poles straightway, that the hour of defeat, death, and slaughter was at hand, that they would have merely to hunt and cut down the fugitives.

But just there a bloody deception was in wait for them.

The Polish armies shouted as one man, in desperation at sight of the falling banner, but in that shout, 'and in that desperation there was no fear, only rage. One might have said that living fire had fallen on their armor; the most formidable men of both armies, not thinking of rank, without order, each from where he stood, rushed to one spot like raging lions. That was not a battle now around the banner, but a storm let loose. "Warriors and horses were packed into one monstrous whirl, and in that whirl men's arms moved like whips, swords clanked, axes bit, steel gritted against steel; there was a groaning, there were wild cries from men whom others were slaughtering. All these sounds were mingled in one ghastly roar which was as terrifying as if the damned had torn free on a sudden from the abyss of hell. Dust rose and out of it rushed, blinded from terror, riderless horses with bloodshot eyes and manes scattered wildly.

But this lasted only a brief time. Not one German came out of that tempest. After a while the rescued banner waved again over the Polish legions. The wind stirred it, unfurled it, and it bloomed forth'in splendor, like a gigantic flower, -

a sign of hope, a sign of God's wrath against Germans, — and of victory for the knights of Poland.

The whole army greeted the banner with a shout of triumph ; and they fell upon the Germans with such rage as if every regiment had come with double strength and twice as many warriors.

Now the Germans were attacked without mercy, without rest, without even such an interval as is needed to draw a single breath. They were pressed on all sides, cut unsparingly with blows of swords, scythes, axes, and maces; they began to totter — and withdraw.

Here and there were heard voices calling for quarter. Here or there fell out of action some foreign knight with face white from fear and astonishment, and he fled in frenzy whithersoever he was borne by his no less terrified steed. The majority of the white mantles, which brothers of the Order wore over their armor, were lying now on the field of battle.

Grievous alarm seized the hearts of the leaders of the Order, for they understood that their only salvation was in the Grand Master, who up to that time stood ready at the head of sixteen reserve regiments.

He, looking from above on the battle, understood also that the moment had come, and he moved his iron legions as a storm moves heavy waves, which bring ruin to ships on the sea.

But still earlier, on a raging steed appeared Zyndram before the third Polish line, which had not taken part yet in the conflict. Zyndram watched over everything and was mindful of the course of the battle. There, among the Polish infantry, were some companies of heavy Bohemian infantry. One of these had hesitated earlier before the engagement, but repentant in season it remained on the field, and, rejecting its leader, was flaming now with desire for battle, so as to redeem with its valor a moment of weakness. The main power, however, was made up of Polish regiments composed of cavalry, but unarmored, poor landholders, and of infantry from towns, and, more numerous than others, free land-tillers armed with pikes, heavy lances, and scythes point downward.

" Make ready ! Make ready !! " shouted Zyndram, in his tremendous voice, as he flew along the ranks with lightning swiftness.

" Make ready!! " repeated the inferior leaders.

Understanding that the hour had come to them these men rested the handles of their spears, flails, and scythes on the

ground, and making the sign of the holy cross they fell to spitting on their immense and toil-marked hands.

And that ominous spitting was heard through the whole line ; then each man seized his weapon, and drew breath. At that moment an attendant rushed up to Zyndram with a command from the king, and with panting voice whispered something in his ear. But Zyndram, turning to the infantry, waved his sword, and shouted, —

"Forward!"

" Forward! ! " was shouted by the leaders.

" Advance! On the dog brothers! At them ! !"

They moved. To go with even steps and not break ranks they all began to repeat at once, —

" Hail — Ma — ry — full — of — gra — ce — the Lord — is — with — thee! !"

And they advanced like an inundation. The mercenary regiments advanced, the town infantry, the free land-tillers from Little and Great Poland, and the Silesians who before the war had taken refuge in the kingdom, and the Mazovians who had fled from the Knights of the Order.

The whole field glittered and gleamed from their scythes, pikes, and lances.

At last they arrived.

" Strike! " shouted the leaders.

" Uch! " Each man grunted as a strong woodcutter grunts when he strikes the first blow with his axe, and they began with all the strength that they had, and all the breath that was in them.

The uproar and shouts reached the sky.

The king, who from a height had followed the whole battle, continued to send messengers in every direction. He had grown hoarse from giving orders, and, seeing at last that all the troops were engaged, he began himself to be eager for conflict.

His attendants would not permit this, out of fear for the sacred person of their sovereign. Polava seized the horse's bridle, and though the king struck him with a lance on the hand he did not let go. Others stopped the way, begging, imploring, and representing that he could not change the battle by taking part in it.

But all at once the greatest danger hung over the king and his whole retinue.

The Grand Master, following the example of those who

had returned after the dispersal of the Lithuanians, and wishing also to attack the Polish flank, advanced in the arc of a circle; in consequence of this his sixteen chosen regiments had to pass very near the eminence on which stood the king, Vladislav Yagello. The danger was noted, but there was no time to withdraw. They merely furled the royal banner, and at the same time the king's secretary, Zbigniev of Olesnitsa, rushed with all speed on horseback to a neighboring regiment which was just making ready for the oncoming enemy, and which was led by the knight Mikolai Kielbasa.

" The king is in danger! To the rescue! " cried Zbigniev.

But Kielbasa, having lost his helmet, pulled away from his head a piece of cloth wet with blood and sweat, and showing it to the messenger shouted in terrible anger, —

" Look if we are idle here! Madman ! Dost thou not see that that cloud is sweeping down on us, and we should merely lead it to the king were we to leave this place? Be off, or I shall put a sword through thee !"

And unmindful of the man with whom he was speaking, panting, borne away with anger, he aimed really at Zbigniev, who, seeing with whom he had to deal, and what was more, that the old warrior was right, raced back to the king and repeated what he had heard.

Hence the royal suite pushed forward in close rank to protect the sovereign with their breasts. This time, however, the king permitted no one to restrain him, he stood in the first rank. But barely had they taken their places when the German regiments were so near that the escutcheons on their shields could be distinguished perfectly. The sight of these regiments was indeed sufficient to fill the most daring hearts with a quiver, for that was the very flower and pick of the knighthood.

Arrayed in brilliant armor, on horses as immense as bisons, not wearied by battle, in which they had taken no part up to that hour, they advanced like a hurricane, with a thundering of horse-hoofs, with a roaring, with a rustling of flags and banners, and the Grand Master himself flew before them in a broad white mantle, which, spread out by the wind, looked like the giant wings of an eagle.

The Grand Master had passed the king's retinue and was rushing to the main battle, for what did a handful of knights standing at one side signify to his mind ? He did not suspect that the king was among them, and did not recognize him.

But from one of the regiments sprang forth a gigantic German, and whether it was that he recognized Yagello, or was enticed by silvery armor, or wished to show his knightly valor, he bent his head forward, levelled his spear, and rushed directly at Yagello.

The king put spurs to his horse and before his suite could detain him he had sprung toward the German. And they would have met without fail in mortal combat had it not been for that same Zbigniev, the youthful secretary of the king, who was skilled in the knightly calling as well as in Latin. He, having a piece of a lance in his hand, rode against the German from one side, and striking him on the head with it crushed his helmet and brought him to the earth. That moment the king struck the man with a sword on the naked forehead and killed him.

Thus perished a famous German knight, Dippold von Kockeritz. Prince Yamont seized the horse, and the German knight lay, mortally stricken, in his white mantle above his steel armor, and with a gilded girdle. The eyes turned in his head, but his feet dug the earth for some time yet, till death, the greatest pacifier of mankind, covered his head with night and put him to rest forever.

Knights from that same regiment of Helmno wished to avenge the. death 6f their comrade, but the Grand Master, shouting, " Herum ! herum ! " barred the way, and hurried them on to where the fate of that bloody day was to be decided, that is, to the main battle.

And again something wonderful happened. Mikolai Kielbasa, who was nearest the field, recognized the enemy, it is true, but in the dust, the other Polish regiments did not recognize them, and thinking them Lithuanians returning to the battle, did not hasten to meet them. Dobko of Olesnitsa was the first to spring out before the oncoming Grand Master, and recognized him by his mantle, his shield and the great gold reliquary, which he wore on his breast outside the armor. But the Polish knight dared not strike the reliquary with his lance, though he surpassed the Grand Master in strength immensely ; Ulrich, therefore, threw up the knight's spear-point, wounded his horse somewhat, then the two, passing each other, described a circle, and each went to his own people.

"Germans! The Grand Master himself!" shouted Dobko.

When they heard this the Polish regiments rushed with the greatest impetus toward the enemy. Mikolai Kielbasa was the first to strike them with his regiment, and again raged the battle.

But whether it was that the knights from the province of Helmno, among whom there were many of Polish blood, did not strike earnestly, or that nothing could restrain the rage of the Poles, it suffices that this new attack did not produce the effect which the Grand Master had looked for. It had seemed to him that his would be the finishing l>low to the power of Yagello; meanwhile he saw soon that it was the Poles who were pushing, advancing, beating down, cleaving, taking, as it were, in iron vices his legions, while his knights were rather defending themselves than advancing. In vain did he urge them with his voice, in vain did he push them with his sword to the battle. They defended themselves, it is true, and defended themselves mightily, but there was not in them either that sweep or that fire which victorious armies bear with them, and with which Polish hearts were inflamed. In battered armor, in blood, in wounds, with dinted weapons, their voices gone from their breasts, the Polish knights rushed on irresistibly to the densest throng of the Germans, as wolves rush at flocks of sheep; and the Germans began to restrain their horses, then to look around behind, as if wishing to learn whether those iron vices were not surrounding them more and more terribly, and they drew back slowly, but continually, as if desiring to withdraw unobserved from the murderous enclosure.

But now from the direction of the forest new shouts sounded suddenly. This was Zyndram, who had led out and sent the country people to battle. Soon was heard the biting of scythes on iron and the hammering of flails on armor; bodies began to fall more and more densely; blood flowed in a stream on the trampled earth; and the battle became like one immense flame, for the Germans, seeing salvation only in the sword, defended themselves desperately.

And both sides fought in that way, uncertain of success, till huge clouds of dust rose all at once on the right flank of the king's army.

" The Lithuanians are returning! " roared Polish voices hi gladness. VOL. ii. — 22

They had divined the truth. The Lithuanians, whom it was easier to disperse than to conquer, were returning, and, with an unearthly uproar, they rushed, like a whirlwind, on their swift horses to the conflict.

Then some comturs, and at the head of them Werner von Tetlingen, raced up to the Grand Master.

" Save thyself, lord! " cried the comtur of Elblang, with pallid lips. u Save thyself and the Order, before their circle encloses us! "

But the knightly Ulrich looked on him gloomily, and waving his hand toward heaven, he cried, —

" May God not permit me to leave this field on which so many brave men have fallen! May God not permit me! "

And, shouting to his men to follow, he hurled himself into the density of the battle. Meanwhile the Lithuanians had rushed up, and such a chaos and such a seething began that in it the eye of man could distinguish nothing.

The Grand Master was struck in the mouth by the point of a Lithuanian lance and twice wounded in the face. He warded off blows for a time with his failing right hand, but thrust finally with a spear in the neck he fell to the earth, like an oak tree.

A crowd of warriors dressed in skins covered him completely.

Werner von Tetlingen with some regiments fled from the field of battle, but an iron ring closed around all the remaining regiments, a ring formed of Yagello's warriors.

The battle turned into a slaughter, and the defeat of the Knights of the Cross was so exceptional in all human history that few have happened which we might compare with it. Never in Christian times, from the days that Romans struggled with Goths, or with Attila, and Charles Martel with the Arabs, did armies fight with each other so mightily. But now, like reaped grain, one of the two forces lay on the field for the greater part. Those regiments which the Grand Master had led last to the battle surrendered. The Helmno men planted their flags on the ground.

Other Knights sprang from their horses, in sign that they were willing to go into captivity, and knelt on the blood-covered earth. The entire regiment of Saint George, in which foreign guests served, surrendered also, with the Knight leading it.

But the battle continued yet, for many regiments of the Order chose to die rather than beg for captivity or quarter.

The Germans fought then, according to their military custom, in an immense ring and defended themselves as wild boars do when wolves have surrounded them. The Polish-Lithuanian circle enclosed that ring, as a serpent encloses the body of a bull, and became narrower and narrower, Again arms thrashed, flails thundered, scythes bit, swords cut, spears pierced, and axes hewed. The Germans were cut down as a forest is cut — and they died in silence, gloomy, immense, unterri-fied. Some raising their visors, took farewell of comrades, giving one to another the last kiss before death; some hurled themselves blindly into the seething battle, as if seized by insanity, others struggled as in a dream; in cases they killed each other, one thrusting his misericordia into the throat of another, or one opened his breast to a comrade with the prayer, "Stab!" The rage of the Poles soon broke the great circle into a number of smaller groups, and then again it was easier for single Knights to escape. But in general those separate groups fought with rage and despair. There were few at that stage who knelt down begging for quarter, and when the terrible onset of the Poles dispersed the smaller groups also, even single Knights would not yield themselves alive to the victors. That was for the Order and all Western knighthood, a day of the greatest disaster, but also of the greatest glory. Under the gigantic Arnold von Baden, who was surrounded by country infantry, a rampart of Polish bodies had been piled up, while he, mighty and invincible, stood above it, as stands a boundary pillar on an eminence. At last Zavisha Charny himself came to him; but seeing the knight without a horse, and not wishing to attack him from behind contrary to knightly usage, he sprang off his horse and called to him from a distance.

" Turn thy head, German, and surrender, or meet me."

Arnold turned and recognizing Zavisha by his black armor, and his shield, said in his gloomy soul, —

" Death is present, and my hour has come, for no one can escape that man alive. But if I could conquer him I should win immortal glory, and save my life perhaps."

Then he sprang toward him and they struggled like two tempests on that ground covered with corpses. But Zavisha surpassed all men in strength so tremendously that unfortunate were the parents to whose children it happened to meet him in battle. In fact Arnold's shield, forged in Malborg

burst, his steel helmet cracked like an eartlicn pot, and the giant fell with his head split in two.

Heinrich, the comtur of Chluhov, that most inveterate enemy of the Polish race, who had sworn that he would have two swords borne in front of him till he plunged both in Polish blood, was rushing from the field stealthily, as a fox slips away when surrounded by a legion of hunters, when Zbyshko of Bogdanets barred the road to him. "Erbarme dich meiner! (Have pity on me!)," cried the comtur, when he saw the sword above his head, and he clasped his hands in terror. The young knight, hearing this, was unable indeed, to withhold his hand and the blow, but he was able to turn his sword and strike only with the side of it, the fat and sweating face of the comtur. He pushed the man then to his attendant, who tied a rope around his neck and took him, like an ox, to the place whither they conducted all captive Knights of the Order.

Old Matsko searched the bloody field for Kuno Lichten-stein, and the fate of that day, for the Poles lucky in everything, gave the man into his hands finally.' A handful of Knights of the Cross, fleeing from the dreadful defeat, had secreted themselves in the forest. The sunlight reflected from their armor betrayed their presence to pursuers. All fell on their knees • and surrendered immediately, but Matsko, learning that the grand comtur of the Order was among the prisoners, commanded Lichtenstein to stand before him, and removing the helmet from his own head, he inquired, —

"Kuno Lichtenstein, dost thou know me?"

Wrinkling his brows, and fixing his eyes on the face of the old knight, he replied after a while, —

"I saw thee in Plotsk, at the court."

"Not there," answered Matsko; "thou didst see me before that! Thou didst see me in Cracow, when I begged thee for the life of my nephew, who, for an inconsiderate attack on thee was condemned to loss of life. At tbat time I made a vow to God, and swore on my knightly honor, that I would find thee and meet thee in mortal combat."

"I know," answered Lichtenstein, and he pouted his lips haughtily, though immediately afterward he grew very pale. "But now I am thy prisoner, and thou wouldst disgrace thyself wert thou to raise a sword on me."

At this, Matsko's face contracted ominously, and it became, as was usual on such occasions, exactly like a wolf's face.

"Kuno Lichtenstein," said he, "I will not raise a sword on a disarmed man, but I tell thee this: If thou refuse me battle, I will command to hang thee with a rope, like a dog."

"I have no choice. Come out! " cried the grand comtur.

"To the death, not to captivity," forewarned Matsko.

"To the death!"

And after a while, they fought in presence of the German and Polish knights. Kuno was younger and more adroit, but Matsko surpassed so much in strength of arms and legs his opponent that in the twinkle of an eye, he brought him to the ground, and pressed his breast with his knee.

The comtur's eyes turned in his head with terror.

"Spare!" groaned he, throwing out foam and saliva from his lips.

"No!" answered the implacable Matsko.

And putting the misericordia to the neck of his opponent, he thrust it in twice.

Kuno coughed dreadfully; a wave of blood burst through his lips, death quivers shook his body, then he stretched — and the great pacifier of knights put him to rest forever.

The battle became now a pursuit and a slaughter. TVhoso would not surrender perished. There were many battles and conflicts in the world during those centuries, but no man remembered a defeat so dreadful. Before the king had fallen, not only the Order of the Cross, but all the Germans who as the most brilliant knighthood assisted that "Teutonic vanguard," which was eating more and more deeply into the Slav body. Of about seven hundred "white mantles," who as leaders went before that Germanic deluge, there remained barely fifteen. More than forty thousand bodies (of the Knights of the Cross and guests) lay on that blood-stained field in endless sleep. The various banners which as late as midday waved over that immense army of the Order had all fallen into the bloody and victorious hands of the Poles, — not a single banner was saved; and now the Polish and Lithuanian knights threw them down at the feet of Yagello, who, raising his pious eyes heavenward, repeated with emotion, —

"O God! thou hast wished this! "

The foremost captives were presented to his Majesty. Abdank Skarbek brought in Prince Kazimir of Stetten; the Bohemian knight of Trotsnov 1 brought Conrad, prince in Olesnitsa; Predperko of Koplidov brought Gersdof, who was fainting, from wounds; he had led all the foreign knights under the banner of Saint George.

Twenty-two nations had taken part in that battle of the Order against the Poles, and now the king's secretaries were writing, and they recorded the prisoners who, kneeling before his Majesty, begged for pardon, and a return home when ransomed.

The entire army of the Order had ceased to exist.

The Polish pursuit captured the immense camp of the Knights of the Cross, and in it, besides those who had escaped, a great number of wagons laden with fetters for the Poles, and wine to be used at a great feast after victory.

The sun was near its setting. A brief, abundant shower had laid the dust. The king, Vitold, and Zyndram, were preparing to visit the field of battle, when men bore in before them bodies of fallen leaders. The Lithuanians brought the body of the Grand Master, Ulrich von Jun-gingen, pierced with spears, covered with dust and clotted blood, and placed it before Yagello. The king sighed with pity, and looking at the immense body lying on the ground, face upward, he said, —

"Here is the man who, this morning, thought himself superior to every potentate on earth —"

Then tears began to flow like pearls along his cheeks; after a while he said, —

"But he died the death of the valiant; so we will celebrate his manfulness, and honor him with a proper Christian burial."

And immediately, he issued an order to wash the body carefully in the lake, array it in splendid robes, and cover the coffin with a mantle of the Order.

Meanwhile, they brought in more and more bodies, which the captives recognized. They brought in Kuno Lichten-stein, his throat cut terribly with a misericordia, and Friedrich Wallenrod, the marshal of the Order; the grand keeper of the wardrobe, Count Albrecht von Schwartzberg, and the grand treasurer, Thomas Mercheim, and Count 1 Yan Zisca, afterward the famous leader of the Hussites.

Wende, who fell at the hand of Povala of Tachev, and more than six hundred bodies of famous comturs and brothers. The servants placed them one by the other, and they lay, like felled trees, with faces looking heavenward, and white as their mantles, with open, glassy eyes, in which rage, pride, the frenzy of battle, and terror had grown fixed. At their heads were planted the captured banners — all of them! The evening breeze now furled, now unfurled the colored banners, and they rustled above those men lying there as if in sleep. From afar, about twilight, were visible Lithuanian divisions bringing in captured cannon, which the Knights used for the first time in open battle, but which had not caused any harm to the conquerors.

Around the king on the eminence, had assembled the greatest Polish knights, and breathing with wearied breasts they looked at those flags, and at those corpses lying at their feet, just as reapers, wearied from heat, look at cut and bound sheaves. Grievous had the day been, and terrible the fruit of that harvest; but now the great, divine, gladsome evening had come.

Hence, immeasurable happiness brightened the faces of the conquerors, for all understood that that evening had put an end to the suffering and toils not only of that day, but of whole centuries.

The king, though conscious of the immensity of that defeat of the Order, looked still as if in amazement before him, and at last he inquired, —

"Is the whole Order lying here?"

To this the vice-chancellor, Mikolai, who knew the prophecies of Saint Bridget, said, —

"The time has come when their teeth are broken, and the right hand cut from them! "

Then he raised his hand, and began to make the sign of the cross, not only on those who lay near, but on the whole field between Griinwald and Tannenberg. In the air, which was bright from gleams after the setting sun, and purified by the rain, they could see distinctly the immense battlefield steaming and bloody, bristling with fragments of spears, lances, and scythes, with piles of bodies of horses and men, amid which were thrust upward dead hands and feet and hoofs; and that sad field of death extended, with its tens of thousands of bodies, farther than the eye could reach. Camp followers were moving about over that immense cemetery, collecting arms and removing armor from the dead bodies.

But above in the ruddy air were storming and circling flocks of eagles, crows, and ravens, screaming and croaking with delight at sight of the food before them.

And not only was the perfidious Order of the Knights lying there stretched at the feet of the king, but all the German might, which up to that battle had been flooding unfortunate Slav lands like a sea, had broken itself against Polish breasts on that great day, that day of purification and redemption.

So to thee, great festival of the past, and to thee, blood of sacrifice, be praise, honor, and glory through all ages.

CHAPTER LXXXI.

MATSKO and Zbyshko returned to Bogdanets. The old knight lived long after that, and Zbyshko waited in health and strength to see those memorable moments in which through one gate the Grand Master of the Order went forth out of Malborg with tears in his eyes, and through another gate entered, at the head of troops, the Polish voevoda to take possession, in the name of the king and the kingdom, of the city and the whole country as far as the blue waves of the Baltic.


THE END.
THE
KNIGHTS OF THE CROSS
By HENRYK SIENKIEWICZ